Journeys of the Catechist

Journeys of the Catechist

Carnivores of Light and Darkness
Into the Thinking Kingdoms
A Triumph of Souls

ALAN DEAN FOSTER

SCIENCE FICTION

CARNIVORES OF LIGHT AND DARKNESS
Copyright © 1998 by Thranx, Inc. Publishing history:
Warner Aspect hardcover, June 1998

INTO THE THINKING KINGDOMS   Copyright
© 1999 by Thranx, Inc. Publishing history: Warner
Aspect hardcover, April 1999

A TRIUMPH OF SOULS   Copyright © 2000 by
Thranx, Inc.   Publishing history: Warner Aspect
hardcover, March 2000

First SFBC printing: March 2000

Published by arrangement with
Warner Books, Inc.
1271 Avenue of the Americas
New York, New York 10020

Visit the SFBC online at http://www.sfbc.com

Visit Warner Books online at http://
www.warnerbooks.com

ISBN 0-7394-0792-9

PRINTED IN THE UNITED STATES OF AMERICA

CONTENTS

Carnivores
of
Light
and
Darkness

For Absalom. . .
Who burned to know how to read.

Cape Cross Station, Skeleton Coast, Namibia
November 1993

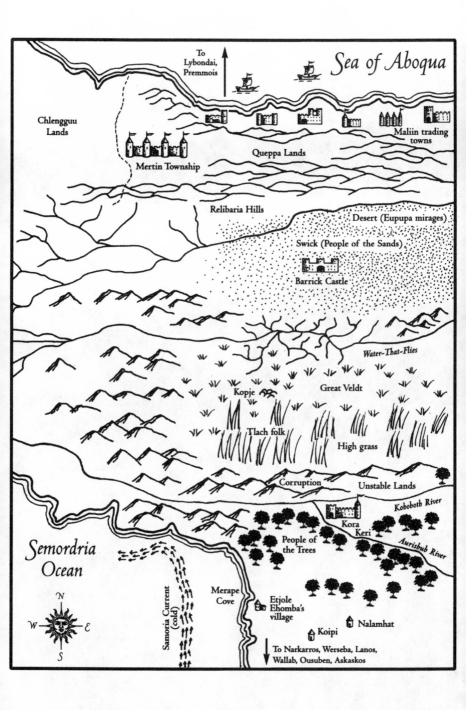

1

It was the morning after the sensuous second full moon of Telengarra, which heralds the coming of the spring rains, when little Colai came running into the village to cry that there were dead people washing up on the beach. And not just dead people, but people of unnatural aspect attired in strange clothes, whose pale faces were unmarked by ritual scars yet sometimes overgrown with hair.

Most of the village was not yet awake when the frantic boy came running and shrieking past the houses. At first his mother thought it was a trick. She caught him and shook him, angry that he should disturb everyone's morning for the sake of a joke. Then she saw something that, like a piece of grit, had become caught at the bottom of his eyes, and stopped shaking him. Together they hurried to the house of the chief.

Asab was just emerging as they arrived. He fumbled to adjust his fine musa-skin cloak with the impressive dark blue stripes and the phophilant headdress with its sweeping crest of intense red and yellow feathers. He was clearly upset at having been rousted from his sleep before normal cockcrow. Hastily donned, his headdress kept threatening to slip from his head.

"I saw them, I saw them!" In addition to Asab, a crowd had begun to gather around Colai and his mother as the boy declaimed breathlessly.

"Now, child," the chief intoned solemnly, "what is it you think you have seen?" Other men and a few of the women clustered close, rubbing sleep from their eyes while fighting back the sour morning taste of recent dreams.

"Dead people, Chief Asab! Many of them, very different from us."

The boy barely paused for air as he turned and pointed. "On the beach. Above where the mussels and the tyrex shells grow!"

Sleepy faces glistening with a reluctance to believe turned to the tall, lanky head of the village. Asab briefly considered the child's harangue before finally frowning down at the anxious, panting youth.

"We will go and see. And for your sake, boy, there had better be something on the sand besides shells and dried sea noodles!"

While barren of all vegetation save a little grass and a few hardy weeds, the beach was not devoid of wood. Gigantic logs cast ashore by the cold Samoria Current littered the sand and protruded from rocky outcroppings where they had been hurled by violent storms. Interspersed among the unbranched, well-traveled forest giants were the whitening bones of demised sea creatures large and small: whales and serpents, birds and batwings, fish and stoneaters. From such bountiful detritus did the villagers recycle useful materials for their homes and barns.

"There!" Colai pointed, but the gesture was unnecessary. Everyone saw the hungry dragonets circling over the spot.

There were a dozen or more of the little black scavengers. Wings folded, another four or five sat on the sand picking at irregular lumps that on closer inspection resolved themselves into perhaps a dozen human figures. Ululating and waving their spears as they approached, the villagers frightened the carrion-eaters away. Hissing their displeasure, the raven dragonets rose into the transparent air on noisome, membranous wings, content for now to circle slowly overhead. They would wait.

Truth to tell, if anything Colai had understated the matter. The bodies were more than passing strange. Just as he had claimed, several showed faces matted with hair, mostly black or brown but some as yellow as the gold that Morixis the Trader brought from the far southern mountains. The figures were clad in an excessive amount of clothing, all of it dyed overbright and some fashioned of cloth so fine it was soft as a little girl's tears.

On top of this barbaric display of color most also wore armor of heavy cured leather of a type unknown to Asab or any of the other village warriors. Scenes that showed men fighting with one another and strange animals and buildings were deeply embossed on breastplates and leggings. With so much weight to carry it was a wonder that any of them had been washed ashore.

Asab and two of his best warriors knelt beside one man. With one exception, all the bodies on the beach were shorter and stockier than the average villager. They were also exclusively male.

"See." Tucarak ran a finger along the dead man's exposed cheek. It was cold with the damp of the sea and infused with death. "How smooth the skin is. How untouched." With his other hand he traced the curving scar, a sign of manhood, that decorated his own cheek.

"And how pale," added a disapproving Houlamu as he rose. "Who are these men, and where do they come from?" Raising his gaze, he squinted out to sea. Nothing was to be seen save the dark, chill water, not even a lingering cloud. There were only the endlessly rolling waves and the amazingly homogeneous deep blue of the morning sky.

"Well, they are dead, and I am sure they would not want their dying to be wasted." With that Asab ceremoniously began the salvaging of the deceaseds' belongings, beginning with their curious apparel and assiduously examining every bulge and pocket for anything, however foreign and exotic, that might prove useful to the village.

"Can we safely eat them, do you suppose?" Tucarak held a blood-and-salt-water-soaked shirt up to the sun. "They look like men. So they should taste like men."

"Ho-yah," agreed Asab. "We will let old Fhastal try a bit of leg. She will eat anything." The chief chuckled softly. "If it does not kill her, we will know it is safe for the rest of us."

Houlamu contemplated the proposed dismemberment with distaste. "You can eat them if you wish. I only eat what I know. Or who I know." He nudged another of the limp bodies roughly with the butt of his spear.

"These are plumper folk than the Koipi or the Nalamhat." As he spoke, Tucarak was tugging hard on the corpse's unusual footgear. It was much too awkward and heavy to be worn on Naumkib feet, of course, but cut into pieces it might provide the makings for a couple of pairs of serviceable sandals. "If anything, I would think they would taste better than our neighbors."

While the chief and his warriors debated the deceased visitants' suitability for the cooking pot, other members of the tribe wandered up and down the waterline in search of other bodies. Among the searchers was a particularly tall warrior, tall even for a Naumkib, whose somber aspect was the subject of much good-natured gibing among his peers. In response to the frequent jokes made at his expense, Etjole would always smile tolerantly and nod. He was not one to spoil the fun of his hunting companions even when he was the butt of their entertainment.

"Help . . . me. . . ."

The words were barely audible, and for a moment Etjole Ehomba thought they were only subtle distortions of the surf-music, sprinkled upon his innocent ears like wind-blown foam. Having paused momentarily, he started to resume his walk, convinced he had heard nothing.

"Please . . . by whatever god you pray to . . . help me. . . ."

Not foam, not wind, but the dying utterances of a man very like himself. Halting, Ehomba looked northward along the shore with a tracker's experienced eyes, sweeping the rocks and sand for signs of life. Eventually, he found it—or what was left of it.

The man was younger than himself, sturdily built, and clad in the most elaborate garments anyone had yet seen on the bodies on the beach. His fine leather armor extended down to cover his upper arms and legs, but it had not been enough to preserve him. There was a great hole in his right side, through which glistening red flesh and pale white bone were clearly visible. Ehomba wondered how he had survived even this long with so deep a wound. It was ragged around the edges, clear evidence of a bite. Whatever had done it had bitten clean through the thick, tough armor. A big shark might have made such a wound, he knew. There were many sharks in the waters offshore from the village. Yes, it might have been a shark—or something else.

The man's hair was straight, shoulder length, and golden. Very different from the thick braids that were bound up in a tight bunch at the back of Ehomba's neck. He marveled at the wispy strands. Leaning forward, he wiped sea slime and sand from the pallid face. At his kindly touch, the other's eyes opened. They were a delicate, diluted blue, but not yet entirely dimmed, and they focused immediately on him.

"You . . . who are . . . ?"

"I am Etjole Ehomba, of the tribe of Naumkib. You and many others have been cast ashore on the beach below our village. Your companions are all dead." His gaze flicked briefly over the cavity in the younger man's torso. "You are dying too. I know a little medicine, but not enough to help you. Not even the old wise women of the village could help what I see. It is too late."

The stranger's reaction was not what Ehomba expected. The man's eyes grew suddenly, shockingly wide. Reaching up, he clutched the taller man's wool overshirt and used it to pull his ruined, bleeding upper body off the sand until his face was only a foot away from that of his finder. In light of the terrible injury he had suffered, the effort of will required to accomplish this feat was nothing short of astonishing.

Staring straight into Ehomba's eyes, he hissed in his odd, uneven accent, "You must save her!"

"Save her? Save who?" Ehomba's bewilderment was absolute.

"Her! The Visioness Themaryl of Laconda!" Remarkably, and with what invisible reserves of strength one could only imagine, the man was shaking Ehomba by the front of his overshirt.

"I do not know of what, or of whom, you speak," the herder responded gently.

Exhausted by this ultimate physical exertion, the wounded stranger collapsed back on the sand. He was breathing more slowly now, and Ehomba could sense Death advancing fluidly across the surf, choosing as its avenue of approach, as it so often did, its friend the sea.

"Know that I am Tarin Beckwith, son of Bewaryn Beckwith, Count of Laconda North. The Visioness Themaryl was my countess, or my countess-to-be, until she was carried off by that pustulance that walks like a man and calls itself Hymneth the Possessed. Many"—he coughed raggedly, and blood spilled from his lips as from an overfull cup—"many of the sons and masters of the noble houses of Greater Laconda took a solemn oath never to rest until she was returned to us and her abductor punished. To my knowledge, I and my men were the only ones to track the monster's ship this far." He paused, wheezing softly, praying for breath enough to continue.

"There was a battle this morning, on the sea. My men fought valiantly. But Hymneth is in league with the evils of otherness. He cavorts with them, delights in their company, and calls upon them to help defend his miserable self. Against such foulness and depravity even brave men cannot always stand." Once more the watery blue eyes, the life fading from them, fastened on Ehomba's own. "I pass on the covenant to you, whoever you are. I charge you, on the departure of my soul, to save the innocent Themaryl and to restore her to the people of Laconda. With her abduction, the heart has gone out of that land, and all who dwell within it. I, Tarin Beckwith, place this on you."

Ehomba shook his head slowly as he gazed down at the stranger. "I am but a simple herder of cattle and harvester of fish, Tarin Beckwith." He gestured with the tip of his spear. "And this is a poor man's land, spare of people and resources. Not a place in which to raise armies. I would not even know which way to begin searching."

Raising himself off the sand with a second tremendous effort, Beckwith turned slightly at the waist and pointed. Sunlight glistened off his visible intestines. "To the northwest, across the sea. There! Having defeated the only ones capable of following him, Hymneth the depraved will feel safe in returning now to his home. I am told it lies in the fabled land of Ehl-Larimar, which is far to the west of Laconda. Seek him there, or find another who will." Once more, clenching hands clawed at Ehomba's simple attire. "You must do this, or the innocent Themaryl will be forever lost!"

"You expect too much of me, stranger Beckwith. I have a family, and cattle to watch over and protect, and—"

Ehomba halted in midsentence. His encumbrance delivered, the life force spent, the spirit of Tarin Beckwith of Laconda had at last fled his body. Gently but firmly, Ehomba disengaged the insensible fingers from his shirt and laid the upper part of the destroyed body down upon the cool sand. It lay there, teal blue eyes staring blankly at the sky, as the herdsman rose.

It would be a privilege, he knew, to consume a chop cut from the flank of so brave and dedicated a man. When the time came for the sharing out of the food, he would make a point of making this claim to Asab.

As to the dead man's trust, there was nothing he could do about it, of course. He had spoken him the truth. There were family and herd and village responsibilities to look after. What matter to him the troubles and tribulations of a people from far away, or the carrying off of one woman?

Suarb and Deloog came running over. They were young men, not yet acknowledged elders, and they nodded to him respectfully as they knelt by the now motionless form at his feet. There was excitement in their voices, and their eyes were alight with the pleasure to be found in something new.

"Etjole, you found this one, but you do not take his belongings." Suarb eyed him uncertainly while Deloog gazed at the heavily embossed leather armor, openly covetous.

"No. I have no interest in such things. They are yours if you want them."

Elated at their good fortune, the two youths began to strip the body of useful material. As he yanked on a pants leg, Deloog watched the taller, older man curiously.

"These are fine things, Etjole. Why do you not take them?"

"I have been given something else, Deloog. Something I did not ask for and do not want, and I am not sure what to do with it."

The youths exchanged a glance. Ehomba was known for sitting and saying nothing for long periods of time, even when he was not guarding the herds. A peculiar man, for certain, but kindly and always helpful. The boys and girls of the village, and not a few of their parents, thought him peculiar, but nice enough in his own quiet fashion.

So the two young men did not make fun of him behind his back as he walked away from them, up the beach toward a point of rocks. Besides, they were too excited by their booty.

Working his way up into the rocks, Ehomba found a flat, dry place and sat down, positioning his spear in the crook of his right arm and resting his chin on his crossed forearms. Small waves broke themselves against the cool, gray stone. Farther up the coast, seals and merapes played in the surf, occasionally hauling out to dry themselves on the sun-warmed beach. The merapes would crack clams and abalone to share with the seals, who did not have the benefit of hands with which to manipulate rocks.

Out there, somewhere, lay lands so distant he had never heard of them, exotic and alien. A place by the name of Laconda, and another called Ehl-Larimar. A woman being taken from one to the other against her will. A woman many men were willing to die for.

Well, he already had a woman worth dying for, and two children growing up strong and healthy. Also cattle, and a few sheep, and the respect of his contemporaries. Who was he to go searching across half a world or more on behalf of people he did not know and who would probably laugh at his untutored ways and plain clothes if they saw him?

But a brave and noble man had charged him with the duty as he lay dying. As it always did, the sight of the sea and the waves soothed Etjole. Yet he remained much troubled in mind.

Half the day was done when finally he rose and started back to the village. All the bodies had been removed from the beach, leaving only the dark stains of blood to show where they had lain. Come high tide, the sea would cleanse the sand, as it cleansed everything else it touched.

That night there was a solemn feast in honor of the strangers who had died on the shore below the village. Everyone partook of the cooking, and it was agreed without dispute that wherever they had come from, it was a land of plenty, for their flesh was sweet and uncorrupted. As he ate of Tarin Beckwith, Ehomba pondered the unfortunate man's final words until those around him could no longer ignore his deep concern. Not wishing to lay his melancholy on them, he excused himself from the company of his wife and their friends, and sought out old Fhastal.

He found her by herself off to one side of the central firepit, sitting cross-legged against a tired tree while chewing with some difficulty on the remnants of a calf. Though white as salt, her hair was fastened in neat braids that spilled down her back, and she had decked herself out for the evening in her finest beads and long strips of colored leather. She looked up at him out of her one good eye and smiled crookedly. The other eye, blinded in youth, gleamed chalky as milk. Given her few remaining teeth, it was no wonder she was finding the meat tough going.

"Etjole! Come and sit with an old woman and we'll give the young girls something to gossip about tomorrow!" Her grin fell away as she saw that his expression was even more serious than usual. "You are troubled, boy. It clouds your face like smoke."

Crossing his own legs beneath him, he sat down beside her, waving off her offer of meat, broiled squash, or bread. "I need your wisdom and your advice, Fhastal, not your food."

Nodding understandingly, she picked at a strip of gristle caught between her remaining back teeth as she listened to him tell of his encounter with the dying stranger on the beach. When he had finished, she sat silent in contemplation for a long moment.

"The stranger placed this burden on you as he lay dying?" When Ehomba nodded, she responded with a terse grunt. "Then you have no choice." Idly she fingered the lightly browned slices of squash in her bowl. "Are you or are you not a man of conviction?"

"You know that I am, old woman."

"Yes, I do. So we both know what this means. You must finish this man's work. One who dies in another's arms is no longer a stranger. Like it or not, he bound himself to you, and in so doing, his mission was bound to you as well."

The man seated across from her sighed heavily. "That is also how I interpreted what happened, and it is what I feared. But what can I do? I am only one. This Tarin Beckwith had many warriors with him, and they were not enough to save him or allow him to succeed."

Fhastal sat a little straighter. "They were not Naumkib. They were from outside the stable world."

He was not persuaded. "They were still men. That is all that I am."

"No it is not." A gnarled fist the color of spoiled leather punched him several times in the upper arm. "You are Etjole Ehomba, herder, fisherman, father, warrior, and tracker. The best tracker in the village. Can you not track that which is not seen as well as that which is?"

"That is not so great a skill. Tucarak can do it, and so can Jeloba."

"But not as good as you, boy. You know that you must do this thing?"

"Yes, yes. Because this Tarin Beckwith, whom I do not know, put it on me as he died. This is not fair, Fhastal."

She snorted, her nose twitching. "Fate rarely is. If you want me to, I will explain it to Mirhanja."

"No." He uncrossed his legs preparatory to rising. "I am her husband, and it is my responsibility. I will tell her. She will not take it well."

"Mirhanja is a good woman. Give her more credit. She understands honor and obligation." She fumbled a slice of fried pumpkin into her mouth. "How old is your boy?"

"Daki will be fourteen years next month."

Fhastal nodded approvingly. "Old enough to do a turn or two looking after the herd in your stead. Time he started doing something useful. The little girl will have a harder time accepting this, but her tears will pass." Reaching down, she removed one of the many colorful fetishes that hung in bunches around her neck. It was a fine carving of a woman, done in the shiny gray horn of a stelegath. As he leaned forward, she slipped the cord from which it hung over his head.

"There! Now I can go with you. I have seen the Unstable Lands in my dreams, and now I can travel with you to see them in person."

He smiled fondly as he studied the figurine hanging from its cord of sisal fiber. "You mean that this image can go with me."

"Oh no, big handsome!" She cackled gleefully. "It is the image you are speaking to right now, the image that the village children make fun of and call names behind my back." She pointed to the necklace. "That is the real me."

For just an instant, he thought he saw something in her blind eye. Something flickering, and alive. But it was only a trick of the weak light, distorted by the cook fire.

"I will carry it as an amulet," he assured her, not wanting to hurt her feelings. Fhastal meant well, but she was a little crazy. "So that it will bring me luck."

"If you'd carry it somewhere else on your body, it might bring *me* luck." She laughed madly again. "I hope that it will, Etjole." She made shooing motions at him, like a mother hen guiding one of her brood of chicks. "Now then—go and see to your wife, so that you may lie with her before you leave. Make your farewells to your children. And be sure to stop by Likulu's house. She and the other women will gather some small things to give you to take on your journey. Meet me tomorrow by the stone lightning and I will set you on your way. I can do no more than that."

He straightened. "Thank you, Fhastal. With luck, I may be able to return this woman to her people and return home in a month or two."

He did not believe it as he spoke it, but that did not matter. Fhastal did not believe it either. Without discussion, they chose to connive in the illusion.

11

Mirhanja took it hard, as Etjole had known she would. He tried to explain slowly and carefully, not forgetting to include the confirming conversation he'd had with Fhastal, reminding his wife again and again why he had to go.

"If I did not do this thing, then I would not be the man you married."

Lying next to him, she reached over and hit him hard on the chest, a blow arising out of frustration as much as anger. "Better half a live man unconvicted than a whole one dead! I don't want you to go!" She pressed tighter against him, her thigh curling over his flat stomach. She was nearly as tall as he, but in this she was not exceptional. The women of the Naumkib were famed for their statuesqueness.

"I have to. He who betrays a dying man's obligation is himself dimmed forever in the sight of the heavens."

"But you don't want to go." She kissed him ferociously on the neck.

"No," he confessed as he turned to her in the bed, "I do not."

"Tucarak would not go. Not even Asab."

"I do not know that, and neither do you. But you do know me."

"Yes, damn you! Why must you be such a good man? You are going to try and save a woman you have never met, of a tribe you do not know, from a land no one has ever seen, for a man you knew only for a moment as he lay dying. I know the depth of a warrior's obligations, but can you not be even a little bit of a knave just for me?"

"You are so beautiful." He was running his fingertips light as a summer breeze over her forehead and back down across her hair, smoothing out the curls, trying to smooth away her fears as well. But despite his best efforts, they kept springing back up again, just like the curls.

"And you are a fool!" She placed gentle fingers on his lower lip. "And I am cursed because that makes me a fool's wife."

"Well then, Mrs. Fool, at least we are well matched."

"Promise me one thing, then." She looked over at him, her eyes moist. "Promise me you will not stay away long."

"No longer than is necessary—wife."

"And that while you are gone, when the nights are cold and lonely, you will not lie with the beautiful women of far-off lands, but will remember that I am here, waiting for you."

He smiled, and the love he felt for her poured out of him like water from a cistern. "No live woman could compare with even the memory of you, Mirhanja." He covered her then, feeling the warmth of her surge up and around him, and she sighed beneath him even as he wondered when next he might feel a part of her again.

Early the following morning Daki stood solemnly watching, maturing in the moment, but Nelecha would not let go of the leather strips that hung down and over his woolen kilt. For so slim a child she had a lot of energy, all of which she put into crying "No, no!" over and over, until her eyes were red from the weeping and her throat was sore. Eventually, reluctantly, hopelessly, she let herself be gathered up in her mother's arms.

He and Mirhanja had made their own farewell the previous night. Several of Ehomba's closest friends among the men of the village had come to see him off. He did not tell them he was going to meet Fhastal or they would have laughed at him. As it was, there was no laughter. Only firm handclasps and sympathetic waving of hands as he turned and started off along the coast path. They understood why he was going, but he could tell that, tradition notwithstanding, several among them disagreed with it.

"Asab could make you an exception. As chief he can do that," Houlamu had told him before he started on his way.

"Yes, but *I* cannot make myself an exception, and it is myself I have to live with the rest of my days," he had replied.

"A short life it's liable to be, too, in the Unstable Lands," his friend had muttered.

"I will track my way clear," he assured them.

"In the Unstable Lands? Where people are swallowed up by unreality, by things that should not exist?" Tucarak was dubious, his tone bordering on the spiteful. "Who comes back from those places? No one goes there."

"Then how can you say that no one can come back?" Ehomba challenged them, but try as they might they could not think of anyone foolish enough to have attempted such a journey. Not in recent memory.

As he crossed the point of rocks that led to the seal and merape beach, he paused to pick up a handful of the wave-washed thumb-sized gravel. The merapes preferred the purchase the sandless beach gave their hands, and the seals, their friends, went along with this choice. Carefully he dumped the handful in a small wool sack and put it into a pocket, then buttoned the pocket shut. Homesick in some far land, he could pull out the pebbles and they would remind him of the village, his friends, his family. Few of his fellow warriors would have understood. Already burdened with sleeping roll and leather backpack, no one else would have chosen to add ordinary beach pebbles to the load.

He looked back. The village was already out of sight, but he could see the fires from individual houses rising into the pellucid sky. Sight of his home, reduced to smoke. What would congeal out of the smoke that lay ahead? He pushed on.

No one knew when the bolt of lightning had turned to stone and embedded itself in the bank of the creek, but there was no mistaking its shape, or the way it made everyone's skin tingle and hair stand on end when walking over it. This phenomenon made it a favorite haunt of the village children, but none were running back and forth along its tormented petrified length today. It was too early for that kind of exploratory play.

As promised, Fhastal was waiting for him in front of the unnatural natural bridge. "Good morning, big handsome." She took notice of his pack, his best overshirt and kilt, the necklace of colorful, hand-painted and -drilled beads strung on a leather thong around his throat, the elongated spear he was using for a walking stick. In leather sheaths slung across his back were two additional weapons: the short sword fashioned from the scavenged jawbone of a whale that had been carefully lined on both sides with the inch-long, razor-sharp teeth of a great white shark, and the slightly shorter sword the village smithy, Otjihanja, had forged from one of the hundreds of lumps of nickel-iron that had fallen from the sky in archaic times and now littered the plain to the southeast of the village lands. "Ready to begin the thing, I see."

"As I must. As the covenant binds me to do." Despite his determination, he was already having second thoughts. The dying Beckwith's words were fading.

But try as the herdsman might to shut it out, the stranger's face would not.

She grinned knowingly, showing an alarming paucity of front teeth.

"You don't *have* to do this thing, Etjole. No one in the village will think the worse of you if you change your mind now."

"I will," he replied laconically as he looked past her. Beyond lay the barren north coast, and farther still the river Kohoboth, that marked the southern edge of the Unstable Lands. "The warrior Tarin Beckwith said that the woman Themaryl would be taken to a country far to the northwest, across the great ocean. How shall I cross it?"

"You must keep traveling north," the old woman told him. "Make your way through the Unstable Lands until you come to a place where the making of large boats is a craft, and take passage on one of them across the Semordria."

He looked down at her. "Is there such a land?"

"In my youth I heard tales of such kingdoms. Places where people live by knowledge that is different from ours. Not greater, necessarily, but different. It is likely you may find passage there. If not"—she shrugged—"you may freely return home knowing that you tried your best."

"Yes, that is fair enough," he admitted, content with her conclusion. "Obligations do not wait. Best I be on my way."

A gnarled hand grabbed his wrist. There was surprising strength in that withered arm. The one good eye stared up at him while the other seemed to turn in upon itself.

"You must come back to us, Etjole Ehomba. Among the Naumkib, it is you who stands the tallest. And I am not making a joke about your height."

"I will come back, Fhastal. I have a family, and herds to look after." Bending down to plant a kiss on the aged, parchmentlike cheek, he was startled when she shifted her face so that her lips met his. Her tongue dived into his mouth like a wet snake and he felt half the breath sucked out of him. As quickly as it had happened, she pulled away.

"Don't look so surprised, big handsome." The smile she gave him took forty years off her life. "I am old, not dead. Now then, be off with you! Discharge your obligation as best you can, and may the spirit of this Tarin Beckwith count itself supremely fortunate to have departed this world in your arms and not those of another."

He left her there, waving atop the little ridge of rocks among the ghost trees as merapes squabbled for seafruit on the pebble beach below. He watched until she turned and disappeared, beginning the long hobble back toward the village. It would have been interesting, he found himself thinking, to have known Fhastal in her youth.

Better to devote his thoughts to the journey ahead, he told himself. Resolutely, he turned away from the ridge, the village, and the only life he had ever known, and set his gaze and his feet firmly on the path ahead.

He passed the rest of the sheltered cove with its barking seals and chittering merapes lying on the glittering gravel just above the steep shore break. One of the merapes threw an empty oyster shell at him, but it landed well short of his legs. Funny creatures, the merapes. They could be playful or vicious, depending on their mood of the moment. Not unlike people.

Beyond the village lay untold stretches of empty coast, for his clan inhabited the last mapped settlement this far to the north. Traveling to the south he would have been in familiar territory. Though Wallab and Askaskos lay a goodly distance down the coast, their people and those of the village knew of one another, and engaged in regular commerce and trade. Beyond those villages was the larger trading town of Narkarros, and still farther the villages of Werseba, Lanos, and Ousuben. The farther south one journeyed, the more fertile the lands became, the better the pastures. But someone always had to live on the fringes of the known world, his father had told him more than once, and that choice had fallen long ago to the Naumkib.

North of the village the grass gave way to sand and rock in whose bleak confines only the hardiest plants could eke out an existence. Few animals lived there, and those that did had been rendered permanently mean and ill-tempered by their inhospitable surroundings. Expecting to encounter nothing specific, Ehomba was therefore prepared for anything. Where potential strife was concerned, he retained an entirely open mind.

That evening a gale rose up off the sea, indifferent and unfriendly. It blew all that night and the next day, forcing him to walk with a scarf over his face and his eyes locked nearly shut in a permanent protective squint. The harsh wind-blown grains blasted his face and scored his arms. But he was not to be so quickly defeated, and certainly not by mere weather.

"Go back to the open sea!" he yelled into the gusts more than once, raising his arms and shaking his spear at the ocean. Off to his left, the great flat green-black sweep of the Semordria roared its challenge, vast and cold. "Leave me be! I am only a man just begun on his journey, and this is not fair!"

The waves exclaimed on the shore and not even seabirds or the Soft Ones answered, but when he emerged the next morning from his makeshift shelter of blanket and driftwood, the wind had stopped. Given up, he decided with satisfaction, only to be replaced by a cousin of gentler mien.

Had he been traveling inland, the dense fog in which he now found himself enveloped would have created many problems. As long as he followed the coast, however, he could not lose his way, not even in the thickest mist. Not with the echo of the surf to guide him. If he kept it always on his left, for some distance yet it would guide him due north.

Using scraps and splinters of driftwood still dry from having been buried in the sand, he struck sparks off a convenient rock with his sky-metal sword and made a fire. Blanketed by the fog, the morning was chill. Tea and jerky were his breakfast, the tea warming him, the jerky providing his mouth with exercise in the absence of conversation. He sat huddled beneath his blanket, an island of life and warmth in the gray mist, sipping his drink and slowly chewing on the stubborn strip of dried meat. The smoke from his fire and the steam from his cup fought for space with the fog. In the mist-engulfed silence, all that could be heard beyond the dying crackle of the fire was the sound of unseen waves coming ashore on the shrouded beach.

Done with the frugal but adequate meal, he rolled his blanket tight and resecured it to the top of his pack. There was no need to scatter the ashes from the fire or douse them with water—there was little here to burn. No danger of a grass fire in the absence of grass, or of a forest fire in the absence of a forest. Orienting himself by the sound of the surf, he resumed his trek northward.

He did not know how far the impenetrable sea fog extended. No one did. For as long as the Naumkib could remember, theirs had been the northernmost settlement of the southern peoples. The perpetual fogs kept them from expanding northward, and probably kept people living to the north from moving south. He knew that he had to keep the sound of the ocean always close. Lose it, and he might wander around in the fog forever—or at least until his food ran out.

His expression set, he lengthened his stride. The fog clung damply to him as if trying to hold him back, but he pushed relentlessly forward, scattering it with sheer determination. North was where he had to go, and nothing was going to keep him from getting there.

111

The land did not grow steadily greener as he walked, but it became clear that the Earth was trying harder. Pockets of brush began to appear, and then clumps of smaller, more diverse vegetation that huddled close together beneath the protection of overhanging trees. Some he recognized, like the ivory-nut palms and salt-tolerant casuarina pines, while others were new to him. There was one tree in particular, with long spreading arms, that was ripe with both nuts curved like a courtesan's eyebrows and large purple fruit. Winged caterpillars gnawed on the round leaves, while flightless butterflies crawled along the branches in search of flowers or rotting fruit to suck.

In one grove where he stopped to drink from a small, comparatively clean pool, a troop of monkeys appeared overhead. They marched along the branch in single file, perfectly in step, following their leader. He wore a headdress made from the empty husk of a gourd. Necklaces of nuts and shells flopped against his hirsute brown chest. As was the nature of monkeys, all were armed. Several carried small bows and arrows, while the rest were equipped with tiny spears that had been whittled from hardwood sticks. There were no females or infants in the troop. Those, Ehomba knew, would be waiting back at a carefully chosen treetop bivouac for the males to return.

"Halt!" he heard the leader suddenly exclaim. Instantly, the rest of the troop assumed a fighting stance. As Ehomba stepped back from the edge of the pool, shaking water from his hands, he was careful not to reach for any of his own weapons. A dozen miniature bows were already trained on him.

Using his long arms and prehensile tail, the troop leader descended from the tree in a rush of anarchic branches, until he stood confronting the herdsman. Ehomba politely took a seat, a move that reduced his great height and left him eye-to-eye with the three-foot-tall monkey. Necklaces jangling, sharpened stick in hand, the troop leader approached warily to extend a limp hand, in the manner of edified monkeys.

"I am Gomo."

The herdsman gently enveloped the strong, limber fingers in his own. "Etjole Ehomba, of the Naumkib."

"I do not know that tribe of men." Overhead, the other members of the troop began to relax. Keeping their weapons close at hand, they spread out among the branches. Several began snacking on the moist, tasty leaves of the tree while others set about gathering the purple fruit, placing the dark orbs in crude sacks they carried slung over their narrow shoulders. The rest relaxed by grooming themselves or their neighbor.

Ehomba gestured loosely to the south. "I have come from down the coast, to fulfill an obligation to a man who died in my arms."

Gomo scratched vigorously at his tailbone. "Ah! Your path is chosen for you, then."

The herdsman nodded. "And what brings my small cousins to this place? The bounty of this tree?"

The monkey leader shook his head. "Bounty of a different kind, I hope. We are looking for help." Straining to see behind the human, he noted the strangely tipped spear and other unusual weapons lying on the ground. "You are a warrior?"

"A herdsman. But all the men of my village are also warriors. One never knows when raiders may come out of the interior, hoping for easy plunder." He smiled thinly. "They do not find it among the Naumkib."

"I understand what you say about human raiders," Gomo replied sagely. "That is a problem the People of the Trees do not have. We hold among us little that humans find of value."

"Difficult to maintain a herd in the treetops," Ehomba agreed. "Even a small steer or sheep would have a tough time grazing in the branches."

"Oh-ho!" Gomo doubled over and slapped his belly. Reflecting the laughter below them, the other members of the troop joined in, their raucous chattering momentarily drowning out every other sound in the grove.

When his chest and stomach finally stilled, Gomo turned serious once more. "Half a warrior would be more help to us than none." He scrutinized the human from head to toe with great deliberation. "And you are almost tall enough to make not a half, but two. You could help us."

Ehomba looked past him, gazing significantly northward. "I have told you where I am bound and why. My family waits for me to return. I have no time for side trips or excursions."

The monkey edged closer, bringing his pungent smell with him like a loose coat. "You are following the coast? North of here the trees thin once more and the country turns desolate. But inland it rapidly becomes greener, especially along the banks of the Aurisbub. That in turn flows into the great river Kohoboth. Upstream from their confluence lies the human town of Kora Keri, where one such as yourself would find rest, food, shelter, and information on the lands farther north that are a closed mystery to me and my people." He sat back, one hand on his spear-stick, his long tail flicking back and forth behind him. "Of course, if you already know all this, then I am wasting my time telling you about it."

"I did not." It was always wise, Ehomba knew, to be honest with a monkey. Unlike their human cousins, they could be sly, but only rarely were they intentionally deceptive.

"Our forest home lines this side of the Aurisbub. If you would help us," Gomo went on, "I myself would guide you to Kora Keri. Of course, you could continue on your way up the coast, but you would make much better time via the inland route, in the company of unlimited fresh water you would not have to carry on your back, all manner of available food, and a town for your immediate destination."

"You are right—I would."

"We would not ask you to stay among us more than a night or so."

"You mean a day or so."

"No." Gomo brooded on troubles unseen. "Our travails strike us at night, when we are at our weakest."

The herdsman sighed. "What is your trouble, Gomo, that you need the services of a warrior?"

Learned, limpid eyes looked up at him. "We are plagued, man, by a flock of slelves."

Ehomba nodded knowingly. "I have seen them, but they do not bother our flocks."

"No. They would not. Man and his weapons and warlike ways they shun, but of the People of the Trees they have no fear." Bitterness sharpened his words. "They come among us at night and steal our food. Several times now they have tried to take some of our children. The females are frantic, and we are all weary from lack of sleep. Sooner or later the slelves will wear us down, and then there will be tragedy instead of inconvenience." Too proud to beg, he lowered his voice.

"We cannot offer you gold or silver, Ehomba. Those are man-things and we do not keep them. I can promise only guidance, and gratefulness. I will understand if your obligation weighs too heavily on you to let you detour even a little from your predetermined path."

Ehomba considered the request, and the monkey seated solemnly before him. After a moment he rose abruptly, using his spear to lever himself upward. Startled, the members of the troop leaped about in a sudden, mad fit to regain their weapons. Their leader hastened to calm them.

"Peace! The man has something to say!"

Tilting back his head, the lanky herdsman peered up at the slim bodies within the branches. "Nothing is predetermined. I will help you— if I can."

His response inaugurated an even greater racket than before among the members of the troop. They leaped joyously from branch to branch, flung handfuls of leaves into the air, and did somersaults on narrow tree limbs without a single spill. When they began to quiet down, Gomo rejoined them, scampering up a trunk and swinging himself effortlessly back into the branches.

"This way, friend Ehomba." From his perch he used his spear-stick to point northeastward. "It is not far to the Aurisbub, and we need to hurry. In order to look for help, we had to leave the females and young in the care of juveniles and silverhairs. They will be wishing anxiously for us to return."

Ehomba nodded as he followed along below, occasionally glancing up into the branches to check the troop's direction. "Just don't expect me to travel through the trees. I am no monkey."

"No," Gomo agreed sadly. "Your kind has lost that ability and that freedom. We feel badly for the tribe of men."

Although the vegetation grew steadily denser as they moved inland away from the coast, there were still places where the troop was forced to drop to the ground and walk upright. Out of the trees, they were at their most vulnerable, and their alertness was correspondingly heightened. At such times they tended to shed their monkey bravado and cluster closer to the tall, well-armed human.

Once, they saw a patrolling leopard. A reversed female, her yellow spots were prominent against her black body. She only glanced in their direction. Of more concern was the herd of hairy elephants that lumbered past close on their southern flank. But despite the presence of young among them, the elephants, hot within their woolly coats, were interested only in reaching the river and assuaging their thirst. A couple of matriarchs bellowed in the troop's direction, raising both trunk and curving tusks, but did not swerve from their course. The troop paused briefly to let the herd get well ahead. It would not do to stumble into the migrating behemoths in the middle of the night.

The members of the troop shared their meager rations with the man in their midst, and he accepted the nuts and berries and fruit more out of politeness than necessity. Still, it was good to be able to conserve his own stores. One never knew when the future might prove less accommodating.

Eventually a line of taller trees appeared ahead, stretching unbroken from south to north. Birds and small dragons and squeaking pipperils flocked above it while rodents mowed the shorter grasses in long, disciplined ranks. Unlike the barren coast, this was clearly a region of abundance.

"Yonder lies the Aurisbub," Gomo told him as his troop broke into a gamboling trot. "We are a little south of where we should be. When we strike the river we will turn north, and soon I will be back in the bosom of my family."

"I wish I could say the same." Mirhanja's warmth was already a too-distant memory.

"I am no seer, Ehomba, and so cannot prophesy the end of your journey. But by traveling along the Aurisbub to the Kohoboth and then to Kora Keri, I *can* predict that you will achieve it sooner." He slipped a long, lanky arm around the human's thighs. "Come now. We are close to friendly faces and places."

The explosion of joy that greeted the appearance of the troop was something to see. Females and young came pouring, tumbling out of a clutch of trees that grew close to the river, setting up a din that had to be heard to be believed. The acrobatics the herdsman had witnessed earlier were as nothing compared to the circus that now ensued. The scene of reunion was one of utter and unrestrained monkey mania.

When families had been reunited and juveniles and oldsters relieved of their duties as guardians, Gomo introduced him to the members of his own family circle. For the rest of the day and on into evening, he was forced to tolerate the attentions of two incredibly energetic, playful youngsters. They clambered all over him despite periodic admonitions from their parents to cease and desist. For the young monkeys, it was as if a wondrous perambulating, talking jungle gym had wandered into their midst, exclusively for their enjoyment. At Gomo's urging, Ehomba would smack them off his head or shoulders when their antics grew too distracting. But he could not bring himself to do it often. They were small, innocent, brown bundles of pure unadulterated fun. The thought that if something was not done they might become food for marauding slelves was a sobering one.

There was very little moon that night as Ehomba sat in the crook of the orange-pod tree looking out at the silvered river and listening to Gomo chatter on beside him. Nearby, he could see monkey families settling down for the night, females clutching their infants close to their breasts, juveniles piled one atop the other, males sleepily doing their best to stay alert and on guard. In keeping with the beauty and tranquillity of the surroundings, it should have been a setting of pastoral contentment. Instead, unspoken threat saturated the air with tension.

"They always come from there." Gomo pointed. "From across the river. They must live in the taller trees on that side."

"At least you can see them coming." Years of standing watch over flocks day in and day out had sharpened Ehomba's night vision to the point where it was far more sensitive than that of the average person. Something flapped slowly as it made its way downstream, and he tensed momentarily before unbending: It was only a perffus, dragging the surface of the river for fish with its hooked wingtips as it glided along silently above the water. As he followed its progress, the flier's right wingtip suddenly dipped and jerked as it lanced a bug-hunting fish just below the gills. Quickly transferring the catch to its beak, it flapped mightily to straighten out and regain altitude. The last Ehomba saw of it was a flash of silver from the unlucky fish as predator and prey disappeared into the trees on the far bank.

But the movement there did not cease. Instead, it multiplied as a dark mass emerged from the wall of forest. It grew larger as it drew nearer, and in doing so resolved itself into individual shapes.

Gomo sounded the alarm. Half asleep, terrified females and infants were herded into the largest trees, where the bigger branches would offer some protection. Armed males gathered to protect them, while a strike force of the best fighters clustered around their leader. They would attempt to ward off the attackers before they could harry the more vulnerable members of the troop. The tribe's cries of panic and agitated chattering roused every animal along the river.

Ehomba clutched his spear firmly as he hunched down next to Gomo. The air around him was thick with the musky odor of the troop, but he hardly noticed it. As a herdsman, he had lived around and among animals all his life, and their smells did not bother him.

"It's them," Gomo murmured unnecessarily as he gestured with his spear-stick. "Why won't they just leave us alone?"

"You are easy prey." Ehomba seemed to become one with the tree, hardly moving. "I can see several problems with your defense already."

The troop leader's eyebrows lifted. A lesser individual might have construed the human's observation as an insult, but the desperate Gomo could not afford the luxury of indignity. "Is that so? What, for example?"

"No time. Tell you later."

In the absence of moonlight it was impossible to count the number of attacking slevves. They were more than a handful and less than a horde. Within moments they were in among the trees, diving at the troop, trying to reach the unarmed females with their infants. The monkeys screamed defiance, jabbing at the night fliers with their spear-sticks, firing feathered arrows at the dark shapes that darted between the branches. In the feeble light it was almost impossible to take proper aim at a target.

Ehomba fought alongside them, roaring the battle cry of his village and thrusting with his much longer spear even as he wondered what he was doing there. Then a shrill, piercing scream rose above the general cacophony and confusion, and he knew. An infant small enough to fit in the palm of his hand had been wrenched from its mother's arms by one of the attacking slevves. Piteous to hear, the wretched, hopeless cries of the little one were soon swallowed up by the noise of battle.

The herdsman was not as agile as his companions, but his great size gave a number of the invaders pause. It took several moments for them to realize he was no monkey, and in that time he wounded one aggressor and ran his spear through another. It fell to earth, tumbling over and over as it clutched at itself, mortally injured.

Then, just like that, it was over. The slevves withdrew back across the river, hissing and chattering among themselves, leaving the troop to count its losses. These consisted of the infant Ehomba had seen abducted and one old female who had been unable to free herself from the clutches of a pair of assailants.

An exhausted Gomo rejoined his human friend. "Two lost. Without you, my friend, it might have been much worse." He slumped heavily on the branch. "It will be worse. They will come again tomorrow."

"Why don't you just leave this place?" Ehomba asked him. "Move to another part of the river?"

The troop leader favored him with a jaundiced eye. "Don't you think we've tried that? The slevves track us, following our progress. To free ourselves from them completely would mean abandoning the entire length of the Aurisbub. It is a difficult choice. This is a good place, full of food. And there are no other troops here to compete with."

Ehomba nodded slowly. "I can understand your position."

"Yes. The living here is good. The water is clean and we have plenty to eat. It would be a paradise for us if not for the slelves."

Folding his arms over his chest, the herdsman leaned back against the trunk of the tree. "I admire anyone willing to stand up and fight for their chosen home. Tell me, Gomo, were the slelves here before you?"

The troop leader looked up sharply. "Whose side are you on here, man?"

"The side of those who do not steal children from their mothers." At this, Gomo relaxed. "But I have lived long enough to know that in such conflicts the truth is rarely as obvious and straightforward as either of the combatants would like others to believe."

"We offered you our assistance in return for your help in fighting the slelves. Slurs I can get for free."

"Don't be so sensitive, Gomo." Ehomba jabbed playfully at him with the butt end of his spear. "I have taken your side. But since I was very young I was taught always to examine both sides of a rock before picking it up. One never knows when there might be a scorpion on the other side." He straightened. "Now, let us see what these slelves of yours look like close up."

Instantly Gomo put aside his irritation with the tall human. "You have some ideas?"

"Perhaps," Ehomba replied noncommittally. "First I need to make sure of what I am dealing with."

The slelve he had speared lay where it had landed, sprawled on the grassy ground, one wing crumpled beneath it. With a total wingspan of more than six feet, it was an impressive creature. Covered in fine gray and beige fur, the humanoid body was slim and no bigger than a juvenile monkey. Two six-inch-long antennae protruded from the fuzzy forehead. The nostrils were wide and large, the ears pointed and batlike, and the great oversized eyes closed. A spear fashioned from sharpened wood lay nearby where the slelve had dropped it. Ehomba picked it up. Suitable for carrying by a flying creature with limited lift capability, it was made of a much lighter wood than the monkeys favored. But the tip was as sharp as a sewing needle.

Reaching down, he picked up the dead body in one hand. It weighed surprisingly little, much less than a monkey of comparable size. Much slimmer build, he saw, and bones that might be partially hollow. But the mouth was filled with needlelike teeth that were as sharp as the tip of the wooden spear, and the pointed nails on hands and feet hooked downward for grabbing and holding on.

"What do you think?" Behind Gomo, a clutch of males crowded close to listen. Several were bleeding from nasty bites and scratches. One

had a heavy bark bandage on his upper arm where a spear had penetrated the lean flesh.

Ehomba found himself staring across the river in the direction of the
trees where the invaders had disappeared. Tilting back his head slightly,
he studied the sky. Even though they had no idea what he was doing, the
assembled males copied his every move. Perhaps they thought imitation
would bring understanding. Monkey see, monkey comprehend, he
mused.

"You must have some relief from these depredations or you would
have been forced to leave this country by now. Do the slelves only attack
when the moon is sleeping?"

Gomo nodded slowly. "Mostly, though they will sometimes come
when there is as little as a sliver showing. It depends"—he choked back
emotion—"on how greedy they are feeling."

"Needy and greedy," added another member of the troop. Around
him, his companions gave voice to their fury and frustration.

"I see." The man in their midst turned from the river to gaze down
at them. "Then they will come again tomorrow night."

"In all probability." Gomo unloaded a vicious kick on the limp body
of the dead slelve. "It is the time of the month that suits them."

"Then we must make ready. We will need some things."

"You *do* have an idea." The troop leader's eyes shone with eagerness.

Ehomba nodded. "I think so. It cannot hurt to try it. If nothing else,
it will surprise them."

Gomo put a long-fingered hand on the herdsman's arm. "Tell us
what to do."

IV

After seeing to the setting of a night watch, Gomo and the other members of the troop retired to an uneasy sleep, leaving Ehomba to contemplate his plan in silence. If it worked, it might well free the troop from the depredations of the slelves forever. If not, he would try something else. Though he was dismayed at the delay in his journey, he had given his word that he would try to help. And he had told Gomo the truth in one other matter.

He didn't much care for a people who stole the children of others.

The following morning the monkeys responded to his directions with an alacrity that bordered on the hyperkinetic, rushing to and fro in response to instructions almost before he could finish explaining what he wanted them to do. As the intent behind his directives became clear, Gomo began to smile more and more frequently.

"I think I understand what you have in mind, man. You intend to make the slelves easier to see. So that we can make better use of our bows and arrows?"

"No." As he spoke, Ehomba watched the monkeys rushing to carry out his instructions. "That is not my idea at all."

The troop leader, who thought he had figured it all out, looked momentarily crestfallen. "Then I have to confess that I don't understand."

"You will." Ehomba raised his voice to a pair of peripatetic young males. "No, not there! Higher up! Yes, that's better." He returned his attention to Gomo. "That is, you will if it works."

His refusal to explain further left the troop leader pensive, but willing to wait.

Although it hardly seemed possible, the new night brought a darkness even deeper than that of the one that had preceded it. In the dead tree they had chosen for their frontline outpost, Gomo crouched next to Ehomba. Together they surveyed the line of trees that rose like a leafy stockade on the far side of the Aurisbub.

"A perfect night for the slevels," the troop leader whispered. "I would be surprised if they chose not to make another foray." His voice fell. "Especially after their success last night."

"If this works, that will be their last success." Ehomba was quietly confident.

"I pray that it is so. I am deathly tired of having to console mothers made vacant by the slevels."

"We will know soon if you will have to do so again." Ehomba raised an arm and pointed.

The dark mass came boiling out of the far treetops, forming an ominous smudge against the night sky that blotted out the stars. To the intently focused Ehomba it seemed bigger than the one the night before. His suspicion was confirmed by Gomo.

"There are more of them tonight. In addition to the one you killed, we slew several yesterday. They are not used to multiple losses. I think we made them angry." He concluded with a quietly triumphant gesture that was a recognizable obscenity to any primate.

"Probably you did," Ehomba agreed. "In addition, they know that I am here."

Gomo looked up at the human squatting stolidly on the branch alongside him. "You are not worried, or afraid?"

"Of course I am worried. I am always worried when I know that something is coming to try and kill me. But I am not afraid. The first time a little boy is guarding cattle at night and hears a distant dragon roar, he either loses his fear or is never sent to guard the herd again." In the darkness, he smiled at the monkey. "I am a good herdsman."

The troop leader nodded sagely. "I hope you will prove as good an undertaker." A hand came up to rest gently on Ehomba's knee. "For a human, you possess almost enough natural nobility to be counted a monkey."

"They're coming." Ehomba tensed. "Make ready."

"Everyone knows what to do. You briefed them thoroughly. My people will not let you down." With that final quiet assurance, Gomo went silent.

There were indeed more of the slevels than before. Their swooping, darting movements as they crossed the river suggested agitation as well as anger. To find a human in the monkeys' midst must have surprised them. To find one fighting on behalf of his fellow primates had surely left them enraged.

Onward they flew, brandishing their spear-sticks and small knives, intent this night not merely on abduction but on murder. Their collective demeanor suggested an intention to deliver a lesson to the monkeys: that resistance was futile, and that death would always be met with more death.

Rising from the branch on which he had been kneeling, Ehomba raised his spear above his head and waved with his free hand. "Here! We're over here!"

Like a dark river, the flush of slelves shifted in midflight to home in on the dead tree. Spears were drawn back in readiness for throwing. The high-pitched squealing of the attackers rose until it drowned out the sound of the river, of the forest.

Gomo held his ground, or rather his branch, silently, but several of the other armed members of the troop found themselves stealing nervous glances in the human's direction. What if his plan didn't work? they found themselves wondering. After all, it was a human and not a monkey plan, and everyone knew that the People of the Trees were vastly more clever and devious than any ground dweller. Still, none of them ran, as much out of fear of what Gomo would do to them if they did than from any terror of the approaching slelves.

Certainly Ehomba waited a long time, until the slelves were virtually upon them. Then, swinging his spear in a wide arc to clear a path through the first of the attackers, he shouted at the top of his lungs, "Now!" and scrambled down the tree trunk as fast as his clumsy human arms and legs would carry him.

His descent was not nearly as agile as that of his companions, but he still made it before the monkeys at the bottom removed the covers from their fire gourds and tossed the blazing containers against the base of the dead, lightning-hollowed tree. The troop had spent the previous day filling as much of the empty trunk as they could with a loose packing of dry leaves, twigs, flammable tree sap, and anything else that would burn fast and hot. They had done their job well. Converted almost instantly into a giant torch, the dead bole exploded in flame. Yellow-red tongues of fire erupted skyward, temporarily splashing the night with light that was brighter than that of morning.

Arrayed in the surrounding branches and on the ground, grim-faced members of the troop prepared to do battle. Their watering eyes struggled to adjust to the sudden, intense illumination. But if the human was right, the nocturnal slelves would have a much more difficult time handling the abrupt, unexpected flare of brightness. If his assumptions were correct, those attackers flying closest to the unexpected blaze ought to be momentarily but thoroughly blinded. The actual result, however, was different in a fashion quite unforeseen by the meticulous herdsman.

Gomo was gesturing madly with his spear-stick. "See! They are not blinded."

"No." Ehomba stood next to the troop leader and watched the tree-torch light up the night sky. "It is worse for them than that."

The monkeys waited for the fighting to begin. And waited, and stared in amazement.

Reacting like moths, the night-dwelling slelves found themselves irresistibly drawn to the towering blaze. Mesmerized, they darted up and down, in and about the length of the blazing tree. And like moths, an individual would swoop in too close to the conflagration, only to be consumed. One after another the slelves incinerated themselves, erupting one after another in a burst of flaming wings and charred bodies whenever they crossed into the critical zone.

Instead of finding themselves in a desperate fight for survival, the monkeys found themselves with time to cheer, jumping up and down and turning somersaults as they gleefully watched their enemies annihilate themselves in individual bursts of incandescent flame. A few of the slelves managed to resist the lure of the giant torch, but they were as blinded as Ehomba intended they should be. Fluttering dazedly toward the river, they flew into trees and branches, stunning themselves and becoming easy prey for the rancorous, vengeful monkeys.

It was all over within an hour. Near the end, the females and children emerged from the place of hiding where they had been sent for safety to cheer the final vestiges of the jubilant massacre. Ehomba took no part in this sorry business, preferring to stay on the sidelines and let the monkeys take out their frustrations on those who had for too many seasons stolen their children. When the troop was finished, not one slelve who had crossed the river was left alive.

Lingering behind, something barely glimpsed from the corner of his eye caught his attention. No member of the troop saw it, being fully engaged as they were in the slaughter of the surviving slelves. But Ehomba did. He froze, one hand stealing toward the sky-metal blade that hung ready for use against his back.

The bulging teardrop shape was a black smudge against the firelit sky. Two burning red eyes of pure vileness glared back at him above a mouth-slit that reminded him of a sword cut on ebony skin. When it parted slightly, the mouth shape bled malignance. As he watched, it darted through the air and took a bite out of the firelight. Not the fire itself, only the light. Slowly he slid the iron blade halfway from its scabbard, doing his best not to draw the nebulous entity's attention.

Then, on its own, it whirled and departed. Perhaps the light of the fire was too intense for it, he thought, or the taste not to its liking. In any event, it was not the illumination from the fire it was after but the light of triumph being expressed by the victorious monkeys. That was what its kind would truly delight in consuming. As soon as he was sure it was gone, he let the blade drop back into its sheath.

Something touched him. Turning sharply, he saw Gomo at his side. The troop leader had recoiled in response to the tall human's reaction. "What's wrong, friend Ehomba? You had the strangest look on your face just then. I have never seen you so tense, or so rigid."

Solemnly, the herdsman pointed in the general direction of the blaze. "I saw something by the tree."

Leaning slightly to his right, the troop leader peered past him. "I was looking in the same direction. I saw nothing."

"They are very difficult to see, for men as well as monkeys. It takes the eye of an experienced tracker. It was an eromakadi."

Gomo made a face. "I do not know that animal."

"It is not an animal. It is one of those creatures that lives in the spaces that fill the gaps in the real world. An eater of light. Not the kind of light that comes from the sun, or even from a fire like that." He pointed again at the flaming tree. "The eromakadi thrive on the light that comes from a new mother's joy in her babe, or an artist's delight in a new way of seeing the world around him. When they fixate on quarry, they are relentless. They are responsible for much of the misery in the world. We do not see them a lot in the south, where life is hard and there is little of glowing happiness for them to prey upon. The elders of my village know them, and from infancy all Naumkib children are taught how to recognize and deal with such creatures."

"I see." Gomo considered. "From what you tell me, I think I am glad I cannot see them."

"They are all around, but very sly and unpredictable. Some days they are themselves preyed upon by the eromakasi, the eaters of darkness, but this is uncommon. Unlike the eromakadi, the eromakasi seek to avoid confrontation." He turned toward the river. "It does not matter. I thought we might have to deal with this one, but it was quite a small specimen of its kind, and it did not stay long. Perhaps it smelled a greater happiness or inspiration elsewhere and went to seek it."

"I hope so," Gomo replied with feeling. "I dislike the idea of having to fight something I cannot see."

"It is very difficult, both for men and for monkeys. The next time you are severely depressed, or extremely unhappy, you can almost be certain that an eromakadi is close by, gnawing at your disposition."

Even though the night was warm and the heat from the burning tree prickly against his fur, Gomo shivered slightly. For all his disarming simplicity, it seemed that the tall human was in possession of knowledge that was denied to the People of the Trees.

The dead tree torch burned for another hour, and the embers that were its legacy glowed all through the remainder of the night, but as Ehomba had surmised, the surrounding jungle was too green and too damp to do more than smolder at the edges of the fire. The few nearby boles that did catch alight soon burned themselves out, the incipient blazes smothered by humidity, sap, and lingering dew.

Later, Gomo sought him out again, this time to offer congratulations. "Except for the eromakadi creature, which only you saw, it went much as you said it would, Ehomba."

"No," he replied reflectively, "not as I said it would. I thought they would be blinded. I did not expect them to be enraptured."

"Well, you expected them to be dead, and that is what they are." A spidery hand reached up to clap him on the side. "The People of the Trees are in your debt 'til the end of time!"

The herdsman smiled politely down at the troop leader. "Until I reach Kora Keri will be sufficient."

"It was something we would not have thought of. When we chose to remain in the trees while humans and apes went down to the ground, we forswore the use of fire." Gomo shook his head and stuck out his lower lip. "Fire and trees make a poor mix. Fire in trees is much worse." Using the tip of his spear, he tapped his friend on the shoulder. "That is the trade you humans made when you came down out of the trees. Freedom for fire."

"I suppose. I was not there at the time the decision was made so I was not given the choice."

"Oh-ho! A mastery of drollery as well as strategy. I will miss you, friend Ehomba."

"Perhaps, but your troop will not." He indicated the trees where males who had been prepared to die had joyfully reunited with their mates and offspring. The shapes and sizes and gruntings and chatterings of the reunion differed from what he would have encountered back in the village, but the tender domestic scene still left him feeling homesick. "They will be glad to see me gone."

Gomo turned to follow the herdsman's gaze and sniffed. "Yes, it's true. Humans make them uncomfortable. Especially tall, fighting humans like yourself." He looked back up at his newfound friend. "Where are you bound?"

"Finally? Truth to tell, I'm not sure of the exact location. For now, to the north. Hopefully to find someone to carry me across the Semordria to a land I have never heard of before—a place called Ehl-Larimar."

The troop leader frowned. "I've never heard of the place, either."

"A dying foreigner charged me with trying to save a beautiful woman from the embrace of a man she does not love or want."

Gomo considered the man's words, rubbing his chin with an index finger longer than that which could be found on any human. "Let me see if I understand: You have left behind your country and your family to go to a place you do not know, for a man you never knew, to fight an enemy you have never seen, on behalf of a woman you have never met."

"That is a very good summation, Gomo."

The monkey leader grunted. "And humans say we monkeys are stupid." He shook his head slowly. "Why are you doing this? If the fellow is dead, he no longer can trouble you."

"I am doing it because I have to. Because it is the kind of person I am," Ehomba explained frankly.

"You could turn around right now." Like hovering dragonflies, Gomo's fingers fluttered toward the south. "Say to anyone who asks why you are returning that you tried but could not get through. The dry lands stopped you, a river stopped you, an angry crocodile stopped you. No one need know otherwise."

"I would."

"Twaddle. An answer worthy of a hero. Or a fool." Hairy brows tried to mate as the troop leader leaned close and peered up into his friend's face. "I wonder. Which are you, Etjole Ehomba?"

"I don't know. Maybe both. Of one thing I am certain, though. It is in my nature to ask many questions. Before I am finished with this, that is one whose answer I will have."

Gomo nodded. "I hope you are not a fool. Fools die quickly and easily, with none to mourn them, and after what you have done for us this night it would grieve me to see you dead." Drawing back slightly, he straightened and smiled. "But in the end we are all dead. Tonight we live." He pointed to where other members of the troop were piling fruits, nuts, edible shoots and bugs in a delectable heap. "There will be a celebration. See? Preparations have already begun. If you think you humans know how to have a good time, then you have never partied with the People of the Trees! Come, Etjole Ehomba. Come and relax and forget your burden for one night! Tomorrow we will start upriver toward Kora Keri. Tonight, maybe we can help you forget who you are."

Ehomba rose from where he had been sitting and staring out at the river and the piles of incinerated slelves. What had the delicate flying creatures left on the other side of the river when they had flocked to attack the People of the Trees? Females and infants, now huddled in futile wait for their fighters to return? He strained, but could hear no sounds of wailing, no distant echoes of lamentation. It was as well. Too much death could cling to a man, like a bad odor no amount of soap could wash away. Turning to follow Gomo, he glanced down at a blackened corpse from which the wings had been singed and found himself wondering idly if it would be good to eat.

Gomo had not been bragging. The celebration began much as expected. What he had failed to mention was the monkeys' talent for seeking out fermented honey and fruit juices and combining them in ways no human had ever considered.

Ehomba awoke the following morning with a head that throbbed as if he had spent the night in the midst of a cattle stampede with the occasional steer using his skull for a football. His sorry condition engendered much good-natured jesting among the members of the troop. These chittering jibes and sallies he bore with his usual good humor.

The entire troop escorted him north. When Gomo had mentioned the location of Kora Keri, Ehomba had imagined he could find it himself simply by following the river north. But as he soon saw, it was not so easy as that. Numerous islands thick with jungle split the river into dozens of channels, not all of which flowed north. A wrong choice would send a traveler meandering in the wrong direction or, even worse, back the way he had come.

But the troop knew exactly where they were going. Following a road through the treetops that was invisible to him but wide and obvious to his companions, they pushed on past deceptive forks and mendacious tributaries, forging as straight a line as possible given the preponderance of dense vegetation and the occasional swamp. Without his active, agile guides Ehomba knew he might well have become hopelessly lost.

Of course, he could have continued as he had originally planned, turning west until he struck the coast again and then following it north. That would have kept him going in the right direction. But he would have missed Kora Keri and its amenities entirely.

River serpents broke the surface in the deeper channels. They posed no danger to the arboreal troop. Of more concern were the dragondines that skimmed low over the river. Whenever one of these swooped too near, the monkeys retreated into the trees where the leathery-winged fliers could not go and waited there until it had glided past. Yellow eyes glared balefully at the unreachable prey that taunted from the cover of entwined branches.

Before very many days had passed they reached a place where the river became a broad, slow, single channel. Descending from the branches, Gomo strode proudly to the grassy riverbank and dipped a finger in the murky liquid. Straightening, he turned proudly to Ehomba and pointed westward.

"We have reached the confluence of the Aurisbub and the Kohoboth. From here, the water flows west into the Semordria." Pivoting, he gestured in the opposite direction. "On the far bank a day's journey from here lies Kora Keri. You will have to find a way to cross the river. This is where we must leave you now to begin our journey back home. To a home that is safe now, where even children may feel free to play in the treetops and scamper along the water's edge."

Hands held high over his head, he waddled up to the herdsman and wrapped long arms around the human's waist. The powerful, slim arms gave a sharp, quick hug. "Good-bye, Etjole Ehomba. I will always think of you as a hero, because to believe you a fool would cause me too much pain."

Reaching down, Ehomba gave the troop leader's shoulder a friendly squeeze. "Believe me, it does my digestion no good to think of it either."

Raising his spear over his head with the shaft held parallel to the ground, he made sure his pack and weapons were secure against his back. Then, to the surprise and delight of the troop, especially the young ones, he plunged into the Aurisbub, showing Gomo that it was not necessary for him to find a way across.

Behind him, the female monkeys set up a lilting ululation that followed him as far as the middle of the river, where the coppery tonal palette of their combined voices became lost amid the swirling babble of running water. Here where the river was broad, the current was very weak. He was a strong swimmer, and the far shore was already looming near.

He grew gradually aware that he had company.

The frog was the biggest he had ever seen. Between its extended legs and its body it was at least as long as his arm. Dark green with black spots, it swam parallel to him on the surface, kicking once for every three strokes of his while tracking his progress with great bulging eyes. These were covered by some kind of transparent mask or goggles to which was attached an upward curving tube manufactured from some exotic, bright blue material. In addition, strange webbed footwear of the same matching blue substance covered the frog's feet, and it was clad in a false skin of some shiny turquoise-hued fabric.

"You swim well," the frog commented as it kicked along.

"What are you wearing?" Ehomba's arms pulled him through the water even as his legs pushed him forward.

"Mask, snorkel, fins, wet suit. I'm a great believer in redundancy, man. When others of my kind must turn away and flee, these let me get by in those places where the water turns to liquid methane." Behind the mask, one bulging eye winked knowingly. "There's good hunting in liquid methane, if you know where to look and don't let the cold get to you."

Ehomba rolled onto his back and continued kicking. "I've never heard of such a thing."

"There are many extraordinary places in the world where most folks fear to go, man. But not me." It grinned at him, but then it was always grinning. Like most frogs, this one couldn't help it. "A friend of mine is an eagle with no taste for amphibians. You ought to see his jet backpack."

"What manner of magic might that be?" Ehomba inquired. But there was no reply, for the outlandishly equipped batrachian had already arched its limber spine and dived, to be seen no more. The herdsman did not dwell on the strangeness of what he had seen or what the frog had said. There was indeed much that was odd in life, and a man who allowed it to trouble his mind would find his time on Earth forever dominated by nagging second thoughts about the stability of his cosmos.

His right foot struck something hard and unyielding, and for a moment he tensed. But it was only the bottom of the river, coming up to greet him. Emerging from the shallows, he looked back the way he had come. Though he could see clearly to the far bank, there was no sign of the troop. Having made their farewells, they had, as Gomo indicated they would, started on the way back to their southern forest.

Water dripped from him, drying as it fell, while he checked his gear to make sure nothing had been lost in the crossing. Assured that all was intact, he turned to the east and resumed walking. In the warm, humid atmosphere that clung to the river, the breeze created by his fast pace swept across his sodden clothes and helped to cool him.

He made a solitary camp that night by the river's edge. In the absence of the chattering, hyperactive monkeys, the silence that engulfed him was stupendous. The stars seemed to edge closer, as if interested in inspecting the lone man crouched next to the small fire, eating by himself in the darkness.

He thought he felt something brush against him. A chill like a thin stream of ice water ran down his back and he whirled, but if there was anything prowling the night, it was no more palpable than darkness itself.

He saw nothing. Taking a deep breath, he lay down and wrapped himself in his blanket. If something wanted to take him while he slept, there was nothing he could do about it. A man must sleep. He would rely, as always, on his tracker's intuition and alertness to awaken him if anything approached too near. Even an eromakadi, though he was not too worried about that.

After all, there was clinging to him no exceptional brightness, no radiant happiness, and therefore nothing to make him particularly attractive to those malevolent ephemera that haunted the margins of what most men falsely believed to be an immutable reality.

V

Morning brought renewed determination to press on. Just as Gomo had promised, the cultivated fields that marked the outskirts of the city by encircling Kora Keri like a verdant necklace soon came into view.

To say that the town was a colossal disappointment might have been too strong a conclusion, but at first glance it certainly was not what Ehomba had either expected or hoped for. In fairness to Gomo, the troop leader had never ventured an actual description of the municipality. He had only said that Ehomba might find useful directions or assistance there. It was good, the herdsman reflected as he walked toward the gate in the defensive mud wall that encircled the community proper, that he had hoped for nothing more.

From what he could see, Kora Keri had little to boast of but size. There were no towering temples, no marble palaces, no architectural marvels rendered in stone and brick. Though clearly a much poorer place than he had expected, the town was also far more populous. Plenty of activity was visible beyond the gate, through which a line of horse- and camel-drawn wagons, buffalo carts, giant cargo-carrying sloths, and pedestrians was slowly filing. A brace of husky guards checked bundles and packages, though for what manner of contraband Ehomba did not know. Fetching up against the back of the line, he patiently awaited his turn to enter.

"Well, a stranger stranger than usual." The guard rubbed at an itch beneath the brim of his tightly wound, bright blue turban and gawked at the tall herdsman standing before him.

"From the south, I would think." Approaching Ehomba, one of the other guards sniffed ostentatiously at the visitor. "This one stinks of sheep and cattle—and something else." He inhaled again and made a show of analyzing the aroma, like some degenerate oenophile pondering a particularly pungent vintage. "I've got it. Monkey! He stinks of monkey."

All five of the sentries on duty laughed while offering their own crude comments. One stepped up to poke the herdsman ungently in the ribs. "Tell me, herdsman: What are the hidden meanings of this distinctive perfume? Does it mean that when you are not consorting with sheep, you like to screw in the treetops?"

"You'd better watch your step in Kora Keri," another advised gleefully. "The whores here prefer hard coin, not bananas." Once more the mirth was general.

In response to this widespread jollity Ehomba offered no comment; he simply stood and waited patiently for a remark worth responding to. Wiping at his eyes as the laughter finally began to fade, the officer in charge confronted the traveler with something resembling formality. Behind him, the line waiting to enter the inner city was growing longer, and murmurs of impatience could be heard rising from drivers and tradesfolk.

"So then, monkey lover, what is your business here?"

"I am only passing through." Ehomba maintained a straight-ahead gaze and did not look at the guard.

"Passing through, eh?" The officer winked at his men, who were thoroughly enjoying themselves at the stranger's expense. "Passing through to where?"

"To the north," Ehomba explained candidly.

"Really? You'd best not go too far north. It is said there is big trouble brewing there." He took a step back and fingered the hilt of the sword scabbarded at his waist. "One gold piece entrance fee."

Ehomba frowned slightly. "I did not see anyone else paying an entrance fee."

The officer's expression darkened. "You need to look closer, then. Maybe there's something wrong with your eyes." His voice darkened. "If not, a little partial blindness can be arranged." Reaching down, he drew the sword partway from its scabbard.

The herdsman turned to meet the threatening gaze. "I do not want any trouble."

"Then don't go looking for it." With his other hand the officer extended an open palm. Nearby, his men tensed.

"I am a simple herdsman. I have mostly cattle and some sheep, but no coin. My village is a poor one."

The officer shrugged. "Not a problem. Turn around and go back to it."

Ehomba eyed the other side of the gate longingly. He could hear the sounds of a bustling bazaar, smell meat and vegetables being cooked in oil with exotic spices, understand many of the come-ons of unseen hawkers and barkers. "I have come a long way and am very tired. I need food and rest."

"Go ask your friends the monkeys to feed you!" suggested one of the sentries. His companions chuckled, but did not let down their guard.

"Maybe you have something you can trade." Not wishing to appear entirely unreasonable, the officer eyed the pack on the traveler's back. Even unprepossessing southerners, it was said, sometimes carried interesting goods and artifacts with them.

"I am traveling light as it is. I need everything I have," the herdsman protested softly.

"That spear, for instance." The officer gestured at the slender weapon in question. "Barbaric design and decoration, pretty useless in a fight, but perhaps worth something in the marketplace as a curio."

"As I said, I need everything I have."

"Oh, surely not everything." The officer winked at his men a second time, then took a step forward. His mouth twisted. "That point, for instance. What kind of stone is that?"

"It is not a stone." Lowering the spear, Ehomba indicated the dark brown, serrated seven-inch-long spearpoint. "It is a tooth that has been turned to stone. It comes from a creature that no longer walks the Earth. The wise people of my tribe believe that the spirit of its owner still inhabits the stone."

"Ah, good! A fine story to go with the weapon. Together they ought to be worth almost a gold piece." Extending a hand, he held tight to the haft of his sword with the other. "Give it to me." Immediately, his men spread out to prevent the reluctant traveler from fleeing.

Ehomba studied the circle of armed men. "Very well," he replied at last. "Here." Lowering the spear, he gave it a short thrust in the officer's direction.

Instantly, swords were drawn and the guard stepped back. What happened next was a matter of some debate among those farmers and traders who were lined up waiting to enter the inner city. Most saw nothing, whereas those in front insisted that, for the briefest of instants, something monstrous had appeared before the town gate. Something like a dragon, only much bigger, with a head the size of a bullock cart, eyes like Death itself, and enormous teeth curved like scimitars. It had startlingly tiny arms, a long, stiff tail, and, unlike any common dragon, it walked on two feet like a man.

It bent low over the aghast guards and growled, the sound coming from deep in its belly. At this the men flung their weapons aside and fled, all save one, who fainted on the spot. Eyeing the prone individual, the beast bent low and nudged it with gaping jaws. But before it could snap the man up and devour him in a single bite, Ehomba drew back his spear. There was a rushing noise, as of air escaping into a vacuum, and the monster seemed (so insisted a dealer in herbs near the front of the line who claimed to have witnessed the whole business) to vanish, sucked back into the point of a spear wielded by a tall southerner standing beneath the gate.

Back in the line, rearing horses and panicked pigs fully occupied the attention of their owners, so that not all eyes were fixed on the drama by the entrance to the city. Without saying a word, the traveler entered, striding purposefully off in the direction of the bazaar. In the sudden absence of guards there was a rush to follow, as people and goods scrambled to take advantage of the opportunity to avoid the irritating inspection that usually befell all those attempting to enter from outside. As for the story, it swiftly lost currency as a topic of conversation as people immersed themselves in the necessary business of the day.

Ehomba located a plain but clean inn whose owner, in light of the fact that business had been slow lately, reluctantly agreed to accept some of the colorful Naumkib trade beads the tall stranger carried with him in lieu of coin. Settling himself on a real bed for the first time since he had left home, Ehomba unpacked and spread his belongings out on the floor to air. The fist-sized cotton bag of glassy gravel from the beach north of the village he placed beneath the pillow, both to remind him of home and because the pillow was too smooth and soft to sleep on. Rolling over, he could smell the sea stench that still adhered to the sack of pebbles.

In this manner he fell into a soundless sleep, awakening with the sunrise as was his habit. After washing up and repacking his gear, he retired to the dining room. It provided breakfast in the form of sausages, toasted breads enhanced by an interesting variety of seeds and chopped nuts, butter, jams, eggs of varying size and color, and meats both cooked and cold. It was an impressive and necessary repast, and when the herdsman departed it was with the satisfaction of having received fair value for goods given.

Already the bazaar was teeming with traders and farmers and craftsfolk hawking their produce. Colorful canopies of woven fabric shaded the stalls and benches while signs in several scripts beckoned buyers from above dark doorways. Wealthier shopkeepers sold everything from rugs to rambutan, silver to snake oil, fish to fine filigree work. Pancake makers hovered over hissing grills, competing in batter and patter. A heavyset woman clad in a silken blouse and denim trousers tried to sell him long pants to replace his woolen kilt, while from a narrow doorway a scrawny young mongoose of a youth attempted to inveigle the tall herdsman into purchasing (or at least renting) one of several lithesome young ladies packed into the shadows behind him.

All around Ehomba there was sound and discussion, with only a minimal amount of fury. Another time, he would have lingered in fascination. But he was in a hurry, to fulfill his obligation and to return home. Having eaten, he was able to ignore the frenetic blandishments of the food vendors. What he did need was information on boats or, failing that, on the best route north.

Several queries led him to a multistory mud-brick building, where a dark dwarf at the entrance directed him up a tiled stairway to the third floor. Reaching the top, he turned down an open hallway. One side was exposed to the city and to the light, in contrast to the dark stairwell he had ascended.

At the end of the porch-hallway he found a portal barred only by a curtain of dangling beads. In response to his query, a voice from within bade him enter.

He found himself in a spacious room filled with shelves and dominated by a tinkling fountain of black and gray stone set near a far window. The stone was full of ancient animals that had been petrified, not unlike the tip of his spear. Moving close, he found he could sense their spirits, though they were not nearly as strong as the one that inhabited his weapon. Mostly they were of modest creatures that crawled and fluttered along the ocean floor.

The shelves and bookcases were filled to overflowing with specimens taken from the natural world, and with well-rubbed ancient books and scrolls. The room was very much the habitat of a scholar, well read and with extensive knowledge of the world beyond the town. He felt he had come to the right place.

"Be with you in a moment!" The voice came from a door set in the far wall. Finding an empty seat, Ehomba settled himself into it as best he could, taking care that the two swords slung against his back did not bump up against the embossed leather of the expensive chair.

A figure emerged from the unseen room beyond the doorway. It was not at all what Ehomba had expected. Extending a hand and favoring him with a cheerful smile, the young woman made motions for him to retain his seat.

"Good morning! I am Rael, of the school of Cephim. How may I help you?"

"I—please excuse my poor country manners. I was expecting . . ."

"Someone older?" Her eyes twinkled. "A superannuated, parchment-skinned man with a long white beard, perhaps? Or a lumbering fat woman with a crystal ball?" She laughed, and her laughter was the sound of summer waves lapping at a white sand beach. "I get that all the time. I'm sorry to disappoint you."

He tried not to stare. "I did not say that I was disappointed."

"Gentlemanly put. You are . . . ?"

"Etjole Ehomba. A herdsman from the south."

"Yes, I can tell that by your style of dress and your, um, bouquet." She settled herself behind a desk that was piled high with open books and specimens of insects, plants, stuffed birds, stones polished and rough, and colored glass bottles containing unknown liquids. "What do you need from me, Ehomba? Have some of your cattle gone missing?"

"No." She was teasing him now, he felt, and he determined to convey the gravity of his purpose to her in no uncertain terms. "It concerns an obligation put upon me by one who lay dying."

"Ah." Her mien grew serious and for the first time he saw, behind the unavoidable physical beauty and agile wit, a much deeper persona. "Tell me about it."

As he spoke, the air in the room seemed to chill slightly and the light pouring through the windows to darken. When he had finished, she sat in silence, eyes closed, contemplating all that she had just heard. When at last she opened them and focused on her visitor again, he noticed that they had changed color, shifting noticeably from blue to black.

"This is a serious business you speak of, Etjole Ehomba."

"Very much so, Rael."

"As to your question, there are boats that call regularly at Kora Keri. They ply the trade routes along the Kohoboth, traveling west with the current and returning eastward with the wind. But none that I know of would think of daring the wild currents of the Semordria. There are delta-based merchants who do leave the safe confines of the river. You might travel to its mouth in hopes of meeting one of them, but even they trade only along the coast. The idea of actually crossing the ocean would horrify them. They are interested in making money, not in noble exploration."

"I see," he replied resignedly. "Then I will have to continue northward until I find a captain and crew whom the notion of undertaking such a journey does not fill with terror."

She wagged a warning finger at him. "There is trouble in the north."

"So I have been told." Idly, he wondered if the gate guards had stopped running. At his feet, his spear stirred slightly, as if it were part of a cavernous mouth that was flexing in its sleep. "I do not fear trouble."

She eyed him intently, and he wondered at her purpose. With an effort, he forced himself to think of his wife. "What *do* you fear, Etjole Ehomba?"

He formulated a reply. "Ignorance. Prejudice. Eromakadi."

Her perfect eyebrows rose slightly. "So you are more than a mere herdsman."

"No. Nothing more." He waited silently.

After a moment, she grunted softly. "You are a tracker of certain things. I am a reader of certain things. I will give you instructions that will let you find the best route north, if you are determined to continue on. But first, for my interest, and because I like you, I will attempt to see what the future holds for you." Her expression conveyed a professionalism that worked hard to conceal a seething, underlying sensuality.

From a cabinet behind the desk she withdrew a crystal. Not round, as was the norm, but perfectly square. It was filled with embedded bits of other minerals. Rutilated quartz, he decided, or something even more exotic. Without waiting to be asked, he drew his chair close.

Setting the crystalline cube down on the desk between them, she began to make passes over its surface with her hands, caressing the transparent material with the tips of her fingers. Unwillingly, he found himself envying the stone. Within, the embedded shards of darker material twitched, shuddered, and began to move, realigning themselves according to cryptic patterns that meant nothing to him, but whose very activity he found fascinating. As near as he could tell, the stone cube was solid. Yet the deeply rooted inner crystals were clearly shifting their position within the rock.

The quartz cube grew cloudy as it embarked on a sequence of color changes. One moment it was morion, the next citrine, then amethyst, a squared succession of gemstone properties. Through it all Rael sat almost motionless, wholly intent on her task. Ehomba could only look on, equally entranced by the doer and the doing.

At last she looked up, closed her eyes, sighed deeply, and seemed to slump in on herself. The cube became colorless again save for the rutile and other inclusions. Opening her eyes, she blinked at him. Expecting a smile, he was disappointed.

"Go home, Etjole Ehomba."

He blinked. "What?"

"Go home." She laid one fine hand atop the cube. "It is all here. I saw it. Disaster, complete and entire. You are doomed to unremitting misery, your quest to failure, the rest of your life to cold emptiness. Unless you end this now. Go home, back to your village and to your family. Before it is too late. Before you die."

VI

Stunned, he sat back in his chair. Outside, the cacophony of the bazaar continued to rage raucously, the piquant odors of frying food still drifted up to the upper floors of surrounding buildings. But within the room something was different. Something had changed.

Despite her fervor, she was as beautiful as ever. Briefly, he wondered how that intensity of intellect might translate into physical passion. The moment passed, as circumstances compelled him to concentrate on other matters.

"I do not understand." He indicated the crystal cube. "What did you see in that thing to render so dire a warning?"

As she spoke, her eyes changed from black to green. "A woman of great—no, of supernal, beauty."

He pursed his lips. "That is not a sighting I would call a prelude to disaster."

"Then you know little of the real world, traveler."

His head dipped in barely perceptible acquiescence. "I cannot argue that. I am but a poor herdsman."

She eyed him shrewdly. "Are you, Etjole Ehomba? Looking at you, sitting here across from me, far from your animals and your village, I find myself wondering. A herdsman to be sure, and poor in the false coin of commerce perhaps, but there are other kinds of wealth, other means for measuring riches and the true worth of an individual. So, I wonder."

As always, he was uncomfortable when the subject was him. He gestured anew at the cube. "If your intent is to turn me from my chosen path, you will have to come up with a threat greater than the sight of a beautiful woman."

"My 'intent' is to do no such thing. I desire only to try and see what the future holds for you. The path you choose is your own, and only you can decide whether or not to walk it. Life is a noun, Etjole, and living it no more or less than a matter of adding adjectives." Her petite, fine-skinned hand brushed over the top of the cube. "I am here only to show you what adjectives may be added."

"The woman you saw is the Visioness Themaryl," he told her.

Her eyes widened. "So you have seen a little of the future yourself."

"Nothing of the sort." He crossed his arms casually over his chest and leaned back in the chair, rocking it gently. "It is the name of the woman abducted against her will, and was confided to me by the dying soldier Tarin Beckwith. It comes from my past, not my future."

"Well, it lies here in your future as well." The sensuous seer bent forward over the cube. "She is being held captive by a small man who commands great evil."

"Hymneth the Possessed."

"Yes." Rael frowned as she studied the rutilated innards of the crystal. "There swirls about him an air of great confusion. I cannot tell if he possesses this evil or is possessed by it."

"I would think the two would go together," Ehomba commented.

"As often they do, but the confusion and uncertainty here are profound beyond anything I have ever encountered before." She glanced up from the cube, and her eyes were a pale yellow, like those of a cat. "I am a strong woman, Etjole. Confident in my abilities, secure in my knowledge. But I would never, never consider challenging a power like this that I see here. Because its body is hidden from me and impenetrable to my arts, I can discern only its effects. There are many methodologies of evil, and this one exceeds my comprehension. It frightens me even to apperceive it. I don't think I want to look into it any deeper. I might come to understand how it works.

"If you continue onward and manage to confront this Hymneth person-creature, you will be utterly destroyed. Try as I might, I can foresee no other outcome." She sat back from the cube and closed her eyes. With her sigh, the air in the room seemed to surge around him and then relax, like a wave rushing onshore only to lose all its substance and energy to the thirsty sand.

"I would have hoped," he told her in a small masterpiece of under-statement, "for more encouraging words."

Her eyes opened. They were blue again. "I like you, Etjole Ehomba. Simple or not, smelly or not, it would trouble me to see you come to harm. But I can't stop you, nor would I if I could. Each of us chooses our own adjectives, our own modifiers. I choose to sit here, in this comfortable, sunny place, and parcel out my learning to those who will listen and pay. It's a good life." For the second time he saw the twinkle in her eyes. "I don't suppose I could convince you to stay with me a while. Given enough time, I might be able to talk you into saving your life."

Her body manifested itself in quiet ways that could not be ignored, not even when she was revealing matters of great import. He had been aware of it ever since she had entered the room. Now her gaze metamorphosed from penetrating to inviting, and the way she shifted in her chair produced sounds he could only hear with organs other than his ears. They were loud, and forceful, and they threatened to drown out his own inner voice.

"I can think of nothing that would please me more," he told her frankly, "if only I was not committed to fulfilling this obligation, and if I did not have a woman waiting for me in my house."

"Your house is a long way from Kora Keri, Etjole. Who is to say what your woman does to keep boredom from her door when you are not there?"

"I cannot worry about that." He rose. "I prefer not to create pain without foundation."

Smiling insidiously, she fondled the crystal cube. The inclusions within seemed to torque slightly in her direction. "I could look and try to learn the answer to that question for you."

He turned away from her. "I would rather not know."

The seer Rael sniffed, unable to mask her derision completely. "So you choose blissful ignorance. It strikes me a poor way to go into battle."

"Who said anything about bliss? And is this a battle I am fighting here? If so, whom am I battling? There is no one present except you and I, and I do not want to think that I am fighting with you."

Her lips, which in another time and place he would gladly have stilled with his own, tightened. "What a maddening man you are, Etjole Ehomba! You must pardon my forwardness. In my profession I am not used to dealing with men or women of principle. So I am having difficulty deciding what you are, and how to deal with you."

"I told you," he explained patiently, "I am—"

"A simple herdsman; yes, yes!" Rising abruptly from her chair, she turned away from him and stalked toward the rear portal. "A simple herdsman with an answer for everything. Worse, you are right." Whirling around, violet eyes blazing, she wagged a warning finger at him. "If you insist on pursuing the course you have chosen and succeed in following it to its end, you are going to die, Etjole Ehomba! Do you hear what I am saying; do you understand my words? You are going to die! What, finally, do you have to say to that?"

His voice was as calm and controlled as ever. "You have a very pretty finger."

Dropping her arm, she inhaled sharply. "I think you're right, and that I was wrong to ever think otherwise. You *are* a simple herdsman, uncomplicated and ingenuous. You're too naïve to be frightened. That— or you are the most subtle of sorcerers I have ever met." Her tone thawed. "Many are the men who have pursued me for months, years even, without success, but you have ensorcelled me in a matter of moments, and with me doing most of the talking at that." She shook her head slowly as she regarded him, a baffled look on her face.

"Who are you, Etjole Ehomba? What are you?"

Before he could reply yet again that he was but a simple herdsman from the south, she had spun on the heel of her slipper and vanished through the rear-facing beaded portal. The meeting was over. For an instant, he considered following her, to try to explain further, to do his best to assuage her upset and unease. But it might very well be dark in whatever back room she had vanished into, and the walls would certainly be closer to one another, his options for flight narrower. Nor was he entirely sure he would fight very hard to escape. Best not to place himself in a position where he might be forced to find out.

The entrance beckoned behind him. Leaving himself no more time to think, which might prove unsettling, or to feel, which could prove worse, he turned and departed.

It was only later, when he was safely back among the boisterous, jostling crowd in the bazaar, that he was struck by the realization that she had not charged him for his visit. Dipping one hand into a pocket of his kilt, he absently fingered the little sack of gravel from the beach near the village. The simplistic, repetitive activity always helped to remind him of the village and to strengthen his memories of home. The more he thought of the dazzling seer Rael, the more he needed that reinforcement. And if her words were to be believed, he had exerted as profoundly unsettling an effect on her as she had on him. Their lovemaking would have been volcanic.

But it was not to be. He pushed on through the crowd. There were preparations to be made. If, as she had told him, he would find no boat master in this country willing to attempt an ocean crossing, then he would have to seek farther north. That meant restocking the few basic supplies he could carry on his back. Salt, sugar, a few carefully chosen spices, some basic medicinal powders, and whatever else he could afford that might prove useful over the duration of an extended overland trek. If he was fortunate, he might learn of a caravan of some sort traveling

north and join them for guidance and mutual protection. But since he
could not count on doing so, he had to be prepared to press on alone.

Of the lands to the north of the Kohoboth he knew little, only what
village oldsters like Fhastal and Meruba mumbled around communal
campfires. Half and more of that might be as much sheer invention as
literal truth. Fhastal in particular could be exceptionally imaginative
when it came to telling tales of distant lands and strange peoples. He had
never paid more than cursory attention to such ramblings because they
had never functioned as anything other than stories, related for the entertainment of adults and children alike.

Now he struggled to remember what he could of those babblings,
hoping to winnow a few kernels of fact from the dross of speculation.
The region north of the Kohoboth was called the Unstable Lands. He
did not know why. Was it because knowledge of it was so limited, or were
there reasons more sinister? He would know soon enough, he realized.
In the absence of access to an oceangoing ship, that was where he had to
go next.

But first, restocking. And something else. He turned, heading back
toward the inn that had provided him with such good food and sleep.
Not because he was hungry, or even because he was ready to choose a
place to spend the night, but because of something the beauteous Rael
had told him. A small matter he intended to take care of even though
she would not experience the resolution of it.

He did not think that he smelled, but he was willing to take her word
for it. After all, she was a seer, and her word was to be believed, and
until he left Kora Keri behind he would be forced to suffer the company
of others whom he might not want to think the less of him. So he would
sacrifice, and have a shower.

VII

It was raining when he left town early the following morning, a drab drizzle the color of liquid charcoal that dampened his spirits if not his determination. An image appeared unbidden in his mind: of Rael, lying naked beneath silken sheets in a warm room, with the cool, clean rain-swept air pouring in through an open window, chilling the interior just enough to make the sheets a welcome accompaniment, bending them snugly across the bed, letting them outline the curves of her sleeping form with gossamer gentleness, almost as soft as . . .

He wiped water from his mouth and eyes and pulled the hood sewn to the back of his collar lower on his forehead. Using his spear as a walking stick, he exited the old part of the city via the northern gate. It was considerably smaller than the one that ingressed from the west, there being far less traffic to and from the northern reaches of the city than from east or west or from the south, where the town faced the river. The two miserable guards stationed outside ignored him. They were huddled together against the rain and wholly occupied with those trav-elers desiring entry. A glance showed that neither of them had been among the quintet that had, to their detriment, harassed him on his arrival days earlier.

Despite the drizzle, men and women were out working their fields, broad-brimmed hats and capes providing some protection from the weather. Kora Keri was a modest town, surviving both on trade and on the production of all manner of growing things. Though the soil was barely adequate, the river supplied a constant, reliable source of water. It was very different from home, where potable water was as precious as gold and the herds had to be moved periodically from water hole to water hole, pasture to meager pasture.

Watching the farmers at work in their fields as he strode past, he decided that he was glad he had not grown up in such a well-watered land. Too much ease made a man soft, and lazy. He was neither, nor were any of his friends back in the village. If necessary, they could survive in the harshest desert imaginable armed with only a digging stick and clad only in a loincloth. He allowed himself a slight smile, wondering if Rael had factored that knowledge into her predictions. The Naumkib had survived many disasters. Surely he could survive one.

Who knew? Perhaps this Hymneth the Possessed would prove amenable to reason, or even better, would have lost interest in his abducted lady by the time Ehomba reached the land where he held sway. Even beautiful women were known to bore powerful men eventually, and vice versa. The real trial Ehomba faced might consist solely of reaching the sorcerer's country—if indeed he was a sorcerer. For all her skill, Rael had seemed uncertain as to his true vocation, if not his nature.

Well, Ehomba would find out. He hoped he would not have to fight the fellow. Fighting was a waste of time when a man could be looking after his herds and raising his family. Perhaps this Hymneth was not possessed by evil, but only by unhappiness, or a choleric disposition. Ehomba was good at making friends. Most people liked him instinctively. With luck, so would this Hymneth the Possessed.

Water, mud, and saturated vegetable matter sloshed through his toes. Boots would have kept his feet dry, but he could not imagine wearing footgear that completely enclosed his feet. A man's soles had to breathe. Besides, the air was warm, and whatever liquid ran into the front of his sandals quickly ran out the back.

Gradually he left the cultivated fields and struggling orchards behind. The modest road he had been following shrank to a rutted track, then to a trail, until it finally disappeared in undisturbed grass that rose to his knees. Startled by his approach, birds and small flying reptiles exploded from cover to flee, squawking or hissing, in many directions. When he was hungry enough, he killed something to eat.

Several days out from Kora Keri, he reached a broad but very shallow river whose name he did not know. Wide sandbars protruded from water that ran clear over gravelly shallows. Unlike his crossing of the Aurisbub, here he confronted a watercourse that he would not have to swim.

Making sure his pack was secure, he hefted it a little higher on his back and was preparing to make his way down the gently curving bank when a voice hissed, softly but distinctly, "Man, I am going to kill you."

At first he could not find the source of the declaration. Only when he lowered his gaze markedly did he see the snake lying coiled in the grass where it gave way to the mud of the bank. It was ten or eleven feet long and a light lavender color, its scales shining brightly in the sun. No spots or stripes decorated its body, which helped to explain why he had not seen it. It was within easy striking distance of the place where he had put his foot. He knew that a poisonous snake that large would carry a lot of venom, and even though he did not recognize the type, he doubted its words no less than its intent.

Pushing his lips close together, he responded in the language of the legless. The snake's head drew back at his reply. Plainly it was not used to being addressed by a human in its own tongue.

"You sspeak the wordss that sslither. What kind of human are you that you do sso?"

"Just a herdssman, long brother." To show that he meant no harm, and that he was not afraid, Ehomba sat down on the side of the bank, letting his feet dangle over the edge. "There are ssome herdssmen who believe that a ssnake sshould be killed on ssight, to protect their animalss. Myssself, I do not believe in killing anything unless it iss for a much more sspecific reasson."

The snake's head lowered and it eyed the seated man with great curiosity. In his seated, relaxed position, Ehomba was quite helpless before the serpent, and the snake knew it. Realizing that it could kill the biped anytime it wished, the inquisitive reptile slithered closer.

"Enlightened, as well as articulate. What if I were to kill one of your animalss? How then would you ssee me?"

Ehomba shrugged, gazing out across the river as if he had not a care in the world, including the impressively venomous reptile that had approached to within an arm's length of his exposed leg.

"All creaturess have to eat. Myssself, I am very fond of meat. So I undersstand."

"Is that sso? I have heard that ssome humanss conssume only fruitss and vegetabless."

The herdsman smiled down at the serpent. "Long brother, we each of uss eatss what ssuits our belliess. As for myssself, I cannot imagine ssurviving on a diet of nutss and grass."

The snake hissed appreciatively. "I, too, long for ssomething warm and bloody to sslide down my throat. It iss the most deliciouss feeling. But you are human: You burn your food before you eat it."

"Not alwayss. It sso happenss that I myssself also enjoy the occassional tasste of raw flessh."

Uninvited, the snake slid the upper portion of its body onto

Ehomba's lap. It was heavy, and like the rest of its kind, as solid as a flexible steel cable. He could not escape now if he wanted to—but he did not want to. He was enjoying the conversation. Not all snakes were so voluble.

"What a remarkable human you are. I think maybe I will not kill you."

"I appreciate that. It would sspoil what hass otherwisse been a good day." Reaching down with one hand, he allowed the snake to slither onto it. Lifting it up, he found himself eye-to-eye with the business end of cold, smooth flesh. Personified by penetrating, slitted, unblinking oculi, Death loomed only inches away. For its part, Death regarded him cordially.

"Bessides," he added, "I am too large for you to sswallow anyway."

The serpent's tongue flicked out, delicately exploring Ehomba's lips. "You tasste good. Warm and wet. But you are right."

Gently, mischievously, the herdsman moved his hand from side to side, carrying the snake's head with it. The reptile did not object to the play. "Then why did you want to kill me?"

"You sstartled me. I don't like to be sstartled, esspecially when I am hunting. Alsso, I have not killed anything in many dayss."

"As far as that goess, long brother, I am hungry too." Lowering his hand, he let the snake's head slip back into his lap. "Would you sshare a meal with me? I will find ssomething of the right ssize to ssuit both our gulletss."

Raising its upper body three feet off the ground, the disbelieving reptile contemplated its unexpected new friend. "You would do thiss for me? After I promissed your death?"

Rising, the herdsman brushed dirt and mud from the seat of his kilt. "Why not? When I meet ssomeone else on the road I am alwayss willing to sshare a meal with them. That iss the right way of traveling."

"If thiss iss a trick, my brotherss will find you." The snake weaved back and forth as it spoke.

Ehomba smiled. "No matter. Your ssmall brotherss the wormss will have me one day regardless. Now come with me, and let uss ssee what we can find to kill. I am a good tracker."

"You have the advantage of height," the snake declared, "while I musst rely on ssmell, and on heat."

After several hours of searching, Ehomba found the spoor of a capybara and tracked it to an inlet of the river where a small herd of the giant rodents lazed in the warm shallows. Two juveniles provided more than enough food for both hunters. In deference to the sensibilities of his

companion, the herdsman ate his rodent raw. The serpent was appreciative.

"The ssmell of cooked meat makess me nauseouss." Though coiled
tightly next to the herdsman's campfire, the snake could not hide the
bulge that now dominated its middle. Swallowing the young capy had
been a slow process, and Ehomba had stood guard until the serpent had
finished. "I thank you for your courtessy."

"You're welcome." Ehomba chewed slowly on a strip of haunch. It
was greasy, as was all rodent meat, but not unflavorful.

"I want to give you ssomething, human. As thankss for your help in
hunting, and as a reminder of our friendsship. Ssomething very sspecial.
I ssee that you carry water with you."

The herdsman rested a hand on the leather water bag that was fastened to his pack. "I need it more than your kind."

"Bring it closse to me. I would go to it, but I am full."

Obediently, Ehomba removed the sloshing sack and placed it close
to the snake.

"Open it." Puzzled, the herdsman complied.

Moving forward, the serpent promptly bit down on the metal rim of
the bag. Ehomba could just make out the twin rivulets of poison that ran
down the grooved fangs to filter into the leather. When it had finished,
the snake drew back.

"I have meassured the dose carefully, man. Drink it sslowly, a little
at a time. By the time you have finisshed the last drop, you will be
immune. Not only to my poison, but to many other kindss." The scaly
head bowed, pointing groundward. "It iss my gift to you."

Gingerly, Ehomba used a patch from the repair kit that he carried to
reseal the two tiny punctures. Though dubious of the snake's claim, he
was willing to give it a try. He was not worried about swallowing the
diluted toxin. If the snake wanted to kill him, it could do so easily, at any
moment.

"Thank you for your gift, long brother." Leaning back on the pillow
of his pack, he let his gaze drift upward, toward the stars. "And now I
think we should ssleep."

"Yess." The serpent placed its head on its coils and closed its eyes.
"Try not to wake me in the morning, man. I will ssleep for sseveral
dayss."

"I will be quiet as a mousse," Ehomba assured it.

The sibilant hiss was already diffuse as the snake drifted off into
sleep. "I am quite, quite full. Sso pleasse: Do not sspeak to me of food."

VIII

True to his word, Ehomba made no noise at all when he awoke the following day. Ephemeral as a baby's breath on a cold morning, mist was rising from the shallow surface of the river. In the green-heavy trees on the opposite bank, a querulous parakeel screeched in solitary joy at having been granted another day of existence.

Gathering his gear about him, Ehomba parted from the serpent, reaching out to give it one final, friendly caress. Its skin was cool and dry to the touch. He had always marveled at town women who recoiled in horror from any snake, no matter how small or harmless, but who would without a qualm gladly dress themselves in snakeskin sandals or belt. The self-contradictions of his fellow man never failed to bemuse him. As for the serpent, it did not even stir, embalmed as it was in the arduous slumber of slow digestion.

Wading the gurgling, slowly running river, which at its deepest never climbed over his knees, Ehomba splashed as little as possible so as not to wake the snake—or any dozy, lurking river denizens. Slivers of silver shot past him as small schools of fingerlings twinkled like elongated stars around and past his legs. Their biology was not uppermost in his mind as he studied them thoughtfully. Unlike the great reptile he had left drowsing on the bank behind, Ehomba could still think about food.

He took an experimental sip from the water bag. The taste was slightly bitter, but not intolerable. At once, his heart began to race and a dull pounding thumped at the front of his forehead. But both faded quickly, leaving him much relieved. The snake had been true to its word.

He reached the far bank without incident. Soon the character of the landscape began to change radically. Instead of desert, or flat fertile plains, or river bottom, unchecked vegetation overwhelmed the land. He had entered true jungle, a riot of crackling greenery and noisy creatures. Such places had been only a rumor to him, as they were to anyone who had been raised in the dry, barren country to the south.

As he strode along beneath the towering boles he marveled at the variety and shapes of the growths that closed in around him. Who would have thought that the world contained so many different kinds of trees, so many varieties of vine, so many strangely shaped leaves? The plethora of insects that flew, crawled, and hopped within the forest was equally astonishing.

He had no trouble walking. The tallest trees spread their uppermost branches wide, blocking much of the sky and keeping the light from reaching the ground. There, the competition for life-giving sunlight was intense among seedlings and saplings. Gomo and his troop would love the place, he mused.

There was no trail. No traders came this way, no farmers tilled fields this far north of Kora Keri. He had to make his own way. That was a prospect that did not trouble him. It was something he had been doing all his life.

Brilliantly tinted birds whistled and sang in the branches, dragoneels cawed, and small, uncivilized primates rustled the treetops. While watching them, he kept a sharp eye out for snakes and insects on the forest floor, where downed logs and accumulating litter made it hard to see the actual ground. Stepping over a rotting log, he was careful to avoid the bristly fungi that had sprouted along its degenerating length. Some mushrooms and toadstools were toxic to the touch, he knew, while others provided shade to tiny intelligences whose whimsical approach to existence he did not want to have to deal with right now.

A second, larger log lay ahead and he had prepared to clamber over it as well—when he saw that it was not a log. Slowing his approach, he reached out to touch the mysterious barrier. To his left it extended as far into the forest as he could see, while in the other direction it eventually made a sweeping curve northward. A splotchy grayish white, it was gouged and battered along much of its inexplicable length.

At first he thought it was made of some kind of stone, but up close he could not find a place where individual sections had been mortared, cemented, or otherwise fitted together. The surface was rough but not pebbly. About five feet high and flat on top, it was slightly wider at the base, giving it a triangular shape.

Who had built such a redoubtable structure in the middle of the jungle, and why? Looking around, he saw no evidence of other construction; no crumbling temples, no imploded homes, no collapsed warehouses. The ground offered up soil, leaves, fungi, insects, dung, and other organic material, but except for the wall, there was not a hint of artificiality. Not a shard of rock, shattered lumber, or disintegrating brick. There was only the winding, smooth-sided, unaccountable barrier.

Despite the damage that had been done to it, it was largely intact, giving evidence of considerable engineering skill on the part of its makers. Turning to his right, he followed its length until he came to a place where a foot-high section had been gouged from the top. The exposed interior revealed fine gravel in addition to the compositing material itself.

The break offered a slightly easier place to cross. Looking down the length of the wall, he considered following the rightward curve until it no longer blocked his way north. Or, he thought, he could cross the wall here and save a little time. Placing a hand on either side of the break, he boosted himself up, put his feet down in the modest gap, and stepped through.

The air changed. The forest, abruptly, was gone. And the shrieking organisms that ignored him even as they surrounded him were like nothing he had ever seen before.

A lesser man would have panicked, would perhaps have gone running out into the howling herds to be instantly trampled to death. More poised than most of his kind, Ehomba froze while he tried to take stock of his surroundings. Facing the utterly unexpected, he knew, was not unlike confronting a rampaging mammoth. Best to stand motionless, appraise the situation from every possible angle, and hope the wind was against you.

Given the chaos into which he had stepped, it was not an easy course to follow.

The very air itself stank of unnameable poisons. Reflecting its composition, it was as brown as the backside of a brick kiln. Barely visible through the haze, buildings taller than Ehomba had ever seen or heard tell of towered into a blistering sky through which the feeble disk of the sun struggled to shine. Then he saw that the raging herds of wailing creatures that surrounded him on all sides were not animals, but vehicles.

Whatever pulled them was invisible to him. Their roaring was continuous and unrestrained. That, at least, was not surprising. Crowded together as tightly as any herd of wildebeest or brontotheres, their need to communicate with one another was obvious. Each held, locked away from the outside world, anywhere from one to a dozen people. Perhaps because they whipped past him at incredible speed, he was unable to tell if they were utilizing these remarkable means of transportation of their own free will, or if such a method had been forced upon them. Studying their faces as best he could, he strongly suspected the latter. Certainly few of them looked happy. Most wore masks of pure misery.

Many of their expressions turned to startled surprise as they shot past him. A few even turned to look back, which, at the velocity they were traveling, struck him as tweaking Death far too boldly. Several managed to yell something at him in passing, but he did not understand their words.

Though he was sure the people were traveling within vehicles, like wagons or oxcarts, they conformed to a pattern that more closely resembled organized animal migration. Half raced helter-skelter westward, while the other half sped past in the opposite direction. As for himself, he pressed hard against the wall that divided these two flows of people and vehicles lest he be run down. None swerved in his direction, the area immediately next to the wall apparently being inviolate or protected by some magic spell. Though it was not always so, he reminded himself, remembering the damage he had observed along its length. Not to mention the break through which he had vaulted.

A vehicle different from the others was coming toward him, from the west. As it approached it slowed and drifted over until it was operating in the otherwise unused region proximate to the wall. The top of the vehicle boasted bright flashing lights that reminded the herdsman of the aurora that could occasionally be seen on long winter nights, or the colors that experienced conjurors could bring forth out of seeming nothingness.

It stopped some forty feet away from him and two people emerged from within. They wore strange, flat clothing that except for the absence of scales was not so very unlike the skin of his friend the serpent. Finding the similarity unnerving, he began to back away from them. They responded with shouts and gestures that left him feeling even more uncomfortable.

When they broke into a run toward him, he had only a split second to decide which way to go. Realizing that to charge out into the ceaseless migration of vehicles was to invite a quick death, he turned the other way and in a single bound, cleared the wall back the way he had come. If nothing else, it would separate him from the onrushing snake men. Behind him, he heard them yell.

He landed solidly on cushioning soil, decaying leaves, and other forest detritus. Almost as startled as he had been the first time, he whirled to look behind him. All that could be seen was dark green rain forest, stretching endlessly in all directions until it closed off every horizon. All that remained of his unsettling experience was the wall, which continued as before to run in a white line to the west and northeast. That, and his memory of the experience.

A hand reached out and grabbed him firmly by the shoulder, strong fingers digging deep into his flesh. Jerking around sharply, he saw that one of the men who had been running toward him and shouting was leaning through the break in the wall. His face was red with anger and excitement, and the peculiar headgear he wore lay slightly askew on his skull. Glaring furiously at Ehomba, he mouthed incomprehensible words as he started to pull on the herdsman's arm. Ehomba started to reach back over his shoulder for one of his swords.

Then the man glimpsed the forest behind his quarry, saw the soaring trees, the arcing vines, the struggling rain-forest plants and saplings. Heard the musical chorusing of the canopy creatures, smelled the pungent odors of decaying vegetation, inhaled the oxygen-rich air, and fainted.

Ehomba was never sure whether the man slid back over the wall or was pulled back, perhaps by his companion. Regardless, he did not reappear. Letting loose the haft of his tooth-lined sword, the herdsman turned away and resumed his hike along the wall. A couple of times he looked back uneasily, but there was no sign of his former pursuers.

No wonder he was traveling in what were known as the Unstable Lands, he reflected. Crossing the wall had seen him, for a few brief, unpleasant moments, stranded in another country. No, he corrected himself. In another world. One that, while superficially fascinating, he had no desire ever to revisit.

He eyed the wall, a constant companion on his left. If he jumped it again would he once more find himself in that same choking, clangorous place? It was a conundrum he had no desire to resolve. As for the hapless inhabitants of that world, none of them sprang forth to confront him again. Perhaps the wall, or the section of it that was easily crossed, was more readily accessed from Ehomba's side.

When the wall finally disappeared, leaving him free to turn in any direction, it did not sink into the soil or rise magically into the sky. It simply stopped. Frowning at the abruptness of it, he cautiously examined the terminus. Long, ribbed bars of metal as thick around as his thumb protruded from the end, giving it an unfinished look. Perhaps that was its status in that other world—incomplete. Mischievously, he plucked a large toadstool from the fallen log on which it was growing nearby and placed the beige-hued fungal disk carefully between two of the metal bars. That should give the inhabitants of that other world something to think about, he resolved with a grin.

Leaving the jagged terminus of the wall behind, he continued on his way. From now on, until he left the Unstable Lands, he would be careful what artifacts he handled, what doors he entered, and what walls he leaped.

The rain forest grew denser, packing in tight around him, the trees pressing together, impenetrable undergrowth more prevalent. Clouds gathered, turning the visible sky the color of wet soot. Without the setting sun to guide him, it became more difficult to maintain his bearings.

Unsheathing the sky-metal sword, he hacked a large arrow into the bark of a nearby tree. With its thin, greenish outer covering thus distinctively incised, the much paler inner wood was revealed. Yellowish white, it would be visible from a distance. Letting the blade hang at his side, he strode on.

He was preparing to blaze another tree when a glimpse of pale not far in front of him made him hesitate. Hurrying forward, he found himself staring at the same arrow mark he had incised only moments ago. The edges of the cut were still fresh. Turning a slow circle, he studied the intense verdure that engulfed him on all sides. It was impossible to tell one growth from another. Angles blended together, and one bush looked much the same as its neighbor. Amidst all the greenery, only the blaze mark on the tree stood out distinctively.

He would have bet a whole steer that he had hewed to a straight line through the forest, but the marked tree gave lie to that claim. There was no questioning it: Somehow, he had become turned around and walked in a circle. He was back where he had been not long before.

Even though he had seen no one for days, he took the precaution of adding a straight line beneath the arrow. Sheathing the blade, he walked forward. Every few seconds he paused to look back, until the blazed tree was no longer in sight. Satisfied, he continued onward, marking his progress carefully. If not in a perfectly straight line, he was certainly walking north.

A flash of diminishing light illuminated a trunk and his eyes widened. He did not panic. That was a concept known to Etjole Ehomba only through example. It was not an emotion he had ever experienced personally. If ever he was going to, though, now was probably an appropriate time.

There was the tree again, the hewn arrow shape stark on its side, the secondary straight cut gleaming prominently beneath it.

Consider every possibility, he told himself slowly. Ask the necessary questions, beginning first with the most obvious. That was what he had been taught to do as a youngster, whenever a cow or sheep went missing. The chances that the animal had been carried off by a giant bird of prey or an invisible spirit were invariably less likely than the probability that it had wandered off and become stuck in a ravine somewhere, or was lying ill from eating madroot.

Ehomba was not tormented by invisibilities of enigmatic purpose, nor had he eaten anything whose hallucinogenic potentialities he was not reasonably sure of. Therefore, this was the same tree he had already encountered twice this evening. Therefore, despite his certitude, he was still walking in circles.

No, he corrected himself. It was the same tree, definitely. He had been walking in circles, *possibly*. Approaching the greenish-barked bole, he prepared to make another mark on its side.

Overhead, branches rustled. "Don't you think that's about enough? Or does mutilating me give you some sort of twisted pleasure?"

As one might expect, Ehomba stepped back quickly. His eyes roved the trunk, but he could espy neither eyes nor mouth, nor any other recognizable organ. There were only branches, and leaves, and the voice in his head. The tree looked like nothing but what it was. Am I really hearing this? he thought uncertainly.

"Of course you're hearing it. Did you 'really' cut me?"

"I am very sorry." The herdsman spread his arms wide and bowed his head. "I did not mean to cause pain. It has been my experience that most trees are not so sensitive as you."

"Oh really? And how many trees have you asked, before you sliced into them?"

"Truth to tell, tall forest dweller, not a one. But in the land I come from, trees are rarely cut. There are very few of them, and so they are treasured for their shade and companionship." He gestured at the surrounding forest. "I can see more of your kind from where I stand right now than grow within many leagues of my home."

"A poor land that must be, to be so treeless." The growth sounded slightly mollified. "Most of your people are far less sensitive, though admittedly few of them pass this way. Most that do never leave the Unstable Lands. They become lost—or worse."

"That is why I made the marks." The herdsman hastened to defend, or at least to explain, his actions. "So I would not pass the same place twice. But it seems that I have been walking in circles, because this is the third time I have come back to you."

"Nonsense," the tree replied. "You have been following an almost perfectly straight route north, and as a consequence I have had some difficulty catching up with and passing you."

So it was the same tree, Ehomba reflected, but it had not stayed in the same place. "Trees cannot move."

"For a man who confesses to coming from a land where few trees live, you presume to know a great deal about them." There followed a great rustling and shaking of branches and vines, whereupon the tree promptly rose a foot or so off the ground and skittered forward several feet. Plopping itself back down, it reestablished its root system and regarded the man.

"I withdraw my statement," Ehomba commented promptly.

Branches bent toward him. "Because of your lack of knowledge of and experience with trees, I forgive you your actions. But a warning: No more casual incising to mark your way. In the lands ahead live plants less benign or forgiving than myself."

"I appreciate the warning." Ehomba glanced at the cuts he had made. Sap was already beginning to ooze over the wounds as a first step in healing the marks. "Again, I am sorry."

"Good. Remember how much you value the trees in your own country, and accord my brethren here the same respect. In return, they will keep you cooled, and sometimes fed."

Ehomba nodded, turned, and nearly fell as he stumbled to avoid stepping on a tiny shoot that was poking its minuscule green head out of the damp rain-forest soil. After all, it was something's offspring, and if the example of the tree was to be believed, the vegetation hereabouts was exceedingly sensitive. What with watching for dangerous animals, he had enough to do without riling the forest itself.

In the depths of the jungle there was no wind, but his unfamiliarity with the high humidity was largely canceled out by his natural affinity for hot climes, so that he sweated continually but not excessively. Anyone from a more temperate climate would surely have collapsed from the combination of heat and humidity. Ehomba drank from his water bag and kept walking. With each swallow his body shuddered a little less.

As evening drew into night, he encountered a surprise: a stone. The flat slab of grayish granite protruded like a crude spear point from the moist earth. When journeying through a realm of dirt and decomposing organic matter, it was always unusual to find exposed rock. The smooth, immutable surface reminded him of home, where there was no shortage of rocks but a considerable paucity of thick soil.

Slipping free of his backpack, he laid it carefully down on the dry stone, laying his spear alongside. For the first time in days he allowed himself to do nothing: not to worry about what lay ahead, or about how he was going to find his way out of the jungle, or what he might encounter when he did. He did not concern himself with Tarin Beckwith's dying request, or how he was going to supplement his limited food supplies, or what dangers the Unstable Lands might still hold. He relaxed in the company of the rock that needed only direct heating to make it feel exactly like the rocks he had left back home.

Astonishing, he mused, the simple things that one misses. We take our environment, our surroundings, for granted, until we are forced to survive in completely different circumstances. He would never have thought he could miss something as straightforward and commonplace as rocks.

If the sky were green, though, he knew that he would miss the blue. If sugar turned bitter, he would miss the sweet. And if he someday turned old and mean, he would miss himself.

Finishing a simple meal, he stretched out on the broad palm of granite and lay back, wishing he could see the stars. But until he emerged from the great rain forest of the Unstable Lands he would have to be content with a roof of green, and with the soaking precipitation that arrived every morning in advance of the sun, like a trumpeter announcing the approach of a king.

IX

The Lord of the Ants

This is a story that is told to every member of the colony on the day when they slough off the last vestiges of pupahood and graduate to the status of worker, attendant, or soldier. It concerns a most momentous event in the history of the colony, one that occurred not so very long ago, which affected the future of everyone from the Queen herself on down to the lowliest worker toiling in the refuse beds.

No one could remember when the war with the Reds had begun. They had come raiding from beyond the big log to the east and had surprised the outpost guards. But providentially, a small column of workers returning with food had espied them sneaking forward through the forest litter and had raced homeward to spread the alarm. All save one pair were run down and dismembered, but those two who made it back alerted the rest of the colony, their agitated pheromones preceding them.

That warning, fleeting as it was, gave the colony time to mobilize. Quickly, soldiers were dispatched to the main entrance while the largest workers took up positions in front of the secondary portals. When it came, the attack was relentless. Holding sturdy defensive positions, however, allowed the members of the colony to keep most of the invaders from penetrating to the nursery. While some pupae and eggs were lost, it was nothing compared to the devastation that might have occurred had the survivors of the foraging party not been able to sound the alert.

That was the beginning of the war. Establishing themselves in a hollow at the base of a great tree on the other side of the fallen log, the Reds continued to make periodic depredations on the colony. In turn, the All-blacks not only defended themselves vigorously but launched zealous reprisals against the Red colony. Pupae and eggs from both brooderies were regularly carried off, to be raised as slaves of the kidnapping colony with no loyalty to or regard for their place of birth. This was in the natural way of things.

Then occurred the remarkable event that is the subject of this recounting.

It was not long after a typically ferocious morning's battle that the visitation was first remarked upon. Ordinarily, such intrusions from the outside world are ignored. Ants pay no attention to them, and they pay no attention to us, and the world continues as before. But this time, something was different.

Instead of passing through with great speed and indifference, like a passing cloud, the visitant paused. Not only paused but stopped, stretching all of its great length on the nearby rock upon which, unlike all the surrounding earth, nothing grows or can be grown. It stopped, and consumed food common to its kind, and lay there at rest.

Scouts duly communicated this information to the Queen and her personal attendants and advisers. It was a matter of some interest, but hardly a profound imposition on the daily routine of the colony, until Imit took an interest. I have mentioned Imit the Unique before. A most unusual ant, he had an exceptionally large head, bigger even than a soldier's but without the soldier's great scything jaws. Most remarkable of all, he was a drone who did not die subsequent to the annual mating flight.

Yes, I know that sounds impossible, but it is the truth. Anyone in the colony can attest to it. He did not succeed in mating with the chosen Queen, he shed his wings as was normal, but he did not wither and expire. Instead, he was made a special adviser to the Queen, as befitted his truly singular status within the colony. When I was but newly emerged, I myself waited on him in the royal chamber.

It transpired that Imit had a plan, which he proceeded to communicate to the Queen and to her other advisers. As to its efficacy, the most enthusiastic were dubious at best, while those who were skeptical bordered on the contemptuous. But seeing little risk to any but a few expendable workers and Imit himself, the Queen bade him to proceed, in the hopes that where incredulity prevailed, a benevolent destiny might intervene.

So it was that Imit requisitioned a column of workers who loaded themselves down with supplies from the colony's storage chambers and proceeded southward toward the reclining visitant. It was there that the drone proceeded to embark upon an enterprise so bold, so daring, so unmyrmecological, that those who attended him could scarce believe it.

That it was accomplished through the inculcation of the black arts no one could doubt, for it was whispered often and openly that Imit had the command of forces and resources denied even to long-lived Queens.

Without knowing how it was done, all present were able to swear that the thing happened. Somehow, despite the impossible disparity in sizes, Imit succeeded in attracting the attention of the visitant. And not only did he attract it, but a rudimentary form of communication, or at least of mutual understanding, was established. It is, and was, beyond the comprehension of common workers like me and thee, but although I was not present for the momentous happentance, I was able to talk later with those who were, and they assured me that there was no mistaking what had occurred.

After establishing contact, Imit made obeisance to the visitant, subsequent to which the gifts of sugar carried by the column were presented as offerings. No one was more surprised than the workers who had done the carrying when the visitant responded. Not only responded, but consumed the gifts with apparent enjoyment. When the last of the presents had been handed over, Imit boldly approached the visitant itself, thus demonstrating either remarkable courage or blind stupidity. To this day, not one of those who was present for the encounter is prepared to say which description would be appropriate. Myself, I tend to think a little of both.

Those proximate were able to understand nothing of the exchange that took place, but when it had concluded, Imit related to them all that had transpired, thus explaining both his purpose and his intent. He aimed to enlist the visitant as an ally in the war against the Reds, utilizing not only its immense physicality, so far beyond that of even thousands of ants as not to be believed, but the shock value of its mere presence, to deal our enemies such a blow as they would never recover from. It was a notion as radical as it was daring, beyond the conceiving of anyone but an ant as peculiar as Imit.

Returning to the colony, the details of this incredible encounter were related to the Queen. Though wary and incredulous, she and her advisers were unable to dismiss the reports of both Imit and the workers who had witnessed the historic encounter. Furthermore, the temptation was too great, the opportunity too exceptional to be dismissed out of hand. It was resolved to proceed, but with as much caution as possible.

Imit was authorized to return to the visitant with a much larger gift of sugar, with the promise of at least half the colony's stores if it would consent to the alliance. Much pleased with himself, Imit set off at the head of a multiple column of workers, carrying the finest, most completely refined sugar the colony could produce. They were escorted on both sides by grim soldiers prepared to give their lives to fend off any attack. The presence of so much sugar was, after all, a temptation not only to enemy ants but to a great many of the forest's inhabitants.

They reached the rock without incident, the visitant seated thereon becoming visible long before the rock itself. Imit stated later that it appeared bemused, though how he could interpret such an entirely alien expression was and is the subject of much derision. Regardless, the column approached, intending to deliver its presents with as much fanfare and ceremony as Imit could muster. It was only when they began to mount the rock that they found themselves shocked into immobility.

Arrayed on the far side of the outcropping were several brigades of Reds, drawn up in neat columns opposite the visitant's enormous foot. When Imit and his troop arrived, these representatives of our sworn enemy were in the process of divesting themselves of a great load of processed sugar, which they placed in an ever-growing pile at the foot of the visitant. Directing them in this farcical protocol was a Red ant with a strangely swollen head and oddly deformed antennae.

It seems that the Reds, too, had among them a male anomaly who had mastered the arcane, and who had independently and coincidentally hit upon the same notion of making an ally of the visitant as had Imit.

As for the visitant itself, it clearly made no distinction between Red ant or All-black, and was content and no doubt even delighted to receive free sugar from both of them. Certainly it consumed the sweets offered up to it by the Reds with as much gusto and enthusiasm as it had those presented by us. No doubt the same thoughts were occurring to Imit's crimson equivalent, for it is reported that he looked every bit as startled as Imit by the unexpected confrontation.

One thing that all who survived can agree upon without dissention is that which happened next. Espying the obtruding Reds, Imit immediately gave the order to attack. Internal commands among the Reds followed at approximately the same time, with the result that the lower portion of the rock was soon engulfed in hostilities. Sugar was forgotten, as was their purpose in going to that place, as old enmities rose to the fore.

The trouble was, that in their haste to attack and dismember their enemies, everyone forgot that the visitant was not merely an available agent of change, but one with a purpose and mind of its own. As All-black and Red alike swarmed over its feet and possessions, the visitant reacted with the energy and fury that each side had hoped to procure for their own. Only instead of displaying an affinity for the members of either colony, the visitant proceeded to look solely and actively after its own intrinsic interests.

Rising not to the height of a tree but exhibiting considerably more mobility, the visitant proceeded to hop about, flailing away with its gigantic upper legs at any ant unlucky enough to come within reach. When it landed, its weight shook the earth and dozens of Reds and All-blacks died beneath its immense feet. It continued to dance about in this manner, indifferent now to the precious, scattered stocks of sugar, intent only on ridding its own colossal form and the rock on which it had been sitting of all intruders regardless of color or allegiance.

Many hundreds died that morning, smashed by huge hands or stomped to death beneath feet each of which weighed more than most of the colony. Only a few on either side survived the carnage and returned to their respective colony to relate what had happened. Imit was among them. You all know what happened to him.

After offering explanations as best he could, and apologizing for stepping beyond the bounds of what an ant ought to do when confronting the rest of the world, he was ordered ritually dismembered by the Queen and her advisers, a task that watching soldiers attended to with considerable enthusiasm. One might suppose that the same fate befell his Red counterpart, assuming that he survived.

As for the visitant, it was observed not long thereafter gathering up its exotic belongings and departing to the north. There followed the Second Battle of the Rock, but this time the objectives were clear to all who participated. Perhaps out of indifference, perhaps as a gesture of contempt, the visitant had left behind the sugar that both sides had offered up as bribe and tribute. No one could say, no one knew, because the only one among the All-blacks who might have been able to find out had been slain by order of the Queen.

Safe to say that while many more died, we recovered at least half the sugar and perhaps a little more, so on balance the day might be accounted a victory for the colony. Discounting the hundreds who perished in both battles, of course. Regarding the visitant, it has not been seen since. Nor do the Queen's advisers think it ever will be again.

Myself, I sometimes regret not being privy to the clumsy conversation that took place between the visitant and the remarkable if imprudent drone Imit. To actually communicate with so alien a creature, one so inconceivably much larger than ourselves, must be a wondrous and terrifying thing. Who can imagine what its perspective might be, how different from ours its view of the world? I think I would have the courage to try it, if I but possessed the ability. I think I would, but cannot really say. For who can envision standing before a titan and engaging it in small talk?

Now then, what lessons are there to be learned from this story? You, in the back, with the one antenna shorter than the other. No, it does not speak to us of the folly of trying to engage allies who are different from ourselves. I venture to say any outside help against the Reds would be gratefully accepted, even after Imit's luckless encounter with the visitant.

No, what there is to be learned is this: First, do not expect reciprocity from the giving of gifts; second, remember always that just because your prayers are answered it does not mean that your enemy does not have a similar pipeline to heaven; and third, request of the gods all that you will, but never forget that the gods themselves may have an agenda all their own—one that does not include insignificant creatures such as yourself.

That is enough for one day. There is the work to be done: foraging to help with, eggs to be brooded, pupae to be rotated and attended to, and perhaps a raid on the Reds to be planned. There is no room in the colony for those who do not perform their assigned tasks. Here, the lazy are dismembered and consumed. The gods are out there, yes, and when carrying a leaf larger than yourself or moving rocks from the entrance you may call upon them for assistance all you wish, but never think for an instant that they have the slightest interest in helping poor little you, or any of our kind.

X

If he was hoping for the jungle to thin out or the terrain to become easier, Ehomba was sorely disappointed. Not only did the density of the enveloping vegetation increase, but the relatively flat countryside gave way to ripples and then folds in the Earth. Soon he was not only walking but climbing and descending, pushing himself up one growth-infested ridge only to face the prospect of slipping and sliding down the far side to confront the equally difficult base of another.

Muttering under his breath as he advanced, he looked longingly and more than once at the rivers that sluiced through the narrow gorges between the ridges. But it was useless to consider utilizing them as a way out of the difficult country in which he now found himself. The streams were too shallow, rock-riven, and narrow to be navigable, even if he was willing to take the time to build a raft. Besides, they all ran from east to west, racing toward the distant sea, while his obligation pushed him ever northward.

At first he thought it was simply more of the mist that trailed from the tops of the green-swathed ridges, but on closer inspection he saw that it was thicker than the rising forest-steam and that it behaved differently as it rose, crawling upward through the saturated air with a purpose foreign to mere fog. He knew it could not be smoke from a fire: Nothing left out in this sodden clime would burn. Whatever fuel was combusting on the side of the ridge he was climbing had to have been gathered and dried specially and specifically for the purpose.

He considered whether to ignore it and continue upward on his chosen course. What kind of hermit would elect to live in so isolated and difficult a terrain he could not imagine, but such individuals were inherently antisocial at best. But he was curious—curiosity being his defining characteristic, insofar as he could be said to have one—and so after a moment's hesitation he turned to his left and began making his way through the trees toward the narrow column of smoke. He approached cautiously. If from a distance the instigator of the fire looked unfriendly, Ehomba would simply avoid initiating contact and continue on his way.

The unprepossessing hut was perched on a bump on the ridge, commanding a fine view of the enclosing jungle in three directions. Fashioned of rough wooden slats, bamboo, and thatch, it was encircled by an almost elegant and inviting porch, a fine place on which to sit and watch the sunset—mist and fog permitting, of course. There were a couple of bentwood rocking chairs and a small table, and well-tended flowers bubbled from wooden planters set on the decking and atop the railing. Hermit or not, the hut's owner was horticulturally endowed. A pair of small, iridescent purple songbirds flared their tiny arias from the confines of a handmade wooden cage. Far from being hostile or antagonistic, the isolated abode appeared calculated to draw a traveler in, as if frequent guests were expected.

Approaching along a narrow animal trail, Ehomba kept a tight grip on his spear. By asking many questions of his elders when he was a child he had discovered early on that in the desert, appearances were often deceiving. Many dangerous plants and animals were masters of camouflage. The brightly colored flower concealed toxic thorns, the garish pond frog poison glands within its skin, the slight bump in the sand a deadly snake. He had learned to warn himself within his mind: What looks like one thing can often be another.

So it was with the hut. Eager as he was for some company and converse after many days alone, he was not about to go barging in on anyone who willingly chose to live in such surroundings, cheery flowerpots, rhapsodic songbirds, and shady confines notwithstanding.

When he drew near he slowed and stepped off the trail and into the surrounding brush. Advancing stealthily, he approached the hut not via the steps that led onto the porch but from behind. If his choice came to be remarked upon he would be happy to explain the reasoning behind it. Living in isolation, the owner should understand.

Voices. There were two: one strong and persistent, the other querulous and a bit shaky. Occasionally the latter would strengthen for a sentence or so, only to weaken with the next phrase. From his position outside it was hard for Ehomba to tell if they were arguing or having a normal discussion. Both voices sounded human, at least. In the Unstable Lands he supposed that one could never be sure. On the other hand, being human was no guarantee of anything. Had he not recently dealt with a snake more honorable than many of his own kind?

Advancing silently through the forest, he crept to the rear of the hut. There were several windows there, which surprised him. He would have thought that anyone building in such a place would want to keep the less appealing denizens of the jungle at bay by restricting their access to the interior insofar as was possible. But all the windows were open to the forest.

Raising his head slowly until his eyes were over the sill, he peered inward. He was looking at a large, comfortable room with access to the porch visible on the far side. Seated on mats on the floor were two figures: a man about his own age and another with his back to the window. As he stared, the man facing him caught him looking in and shot him a glance, though whether of helplessness, surprise, or warning Ehomba could not say.

Somehow the other figure simultaneously became aware of his presence. Perhaps it noticed the direction of the other man's gaze. Without turning, it announced in a tenor voice smooth as the syrup the women of the village made from distilled honey, "Come in, traveler. You are welcome here."

Ehomba hesitated. The other man was still staring at him. An urge to turn, and to run, welled up sharply within the herdsman. But that inviting voice was compelling and besides, as always, he was curious.

Walking around the hut from back to front, he mounted the porch steps and entered. Like the windows, nothing barred the doorway. It was a portal without a barrier. Like the rest of the hut, it was enticing.

"Come in, come in!" The larger figure seated in the rear of the main room beckoned encouragingly. As he entered, Ehomba noticed that the man already present continued to stare at him. "Take a seat."

Ehomba remained standing. "I do not want to interrupt a private conversation."

"Not at all, not at all." The figure in back smiled, though it was a doleful sort of smile, the herdsman thought. It was a ghost of an expression from which all honest sentiment had fled; a shell, a shadow, from which all real contentment had been wrung like washwater from a rag. Nevertheless, he took a seat, crossing his legs beneath him and setting his spear to one side.

As soon as he did so, the other man present let out a groan. "Well, that's beggared it! We're both done for now." He dropped his head.

"Done for?" What odd manner of speech was this? Ehomba wondered. Up close, he considered the other occupants of the room more closely.

The man seated on the mat next to him was of average height, with heavily knotted legs and a stocky, muscular upper body. His black hair was long and tied up in a tail in back while his facial features were like none the herdsman had ever seen before, with narrow eyes and small nose set above a wide mouth. The face was inordinately round in contrast to the athletic build and the forehead high and intelligent.

He wore light leather armor that must have been a burden in the jungle heat. Beneath it could be seen a white shirt of some silken material. Below the waist the man was clad in very little: a loincloth that was bound up between his buttocks over which protective leather straps hung no farther than midthigh. This unusual raiment was matched by its owner's disposition, which was dyspeptic at best.

"Why couldn't you have just run?" he was muttering. "Didn't you see me trying to warn you off when you were peeping in the window?"

"I was not peeping," Ehomba explained decorously with a glance in the direction of the master of the house. "I was reconnoitering."

"Well, it sure as Gibra didn't do you any good. You're in here now, and he's got you, too." The speaker nodded in the direction of the third occupant of the room.

Unperturbed, Ehomba turned toward their nominal host. "Is what he says true?" he asked quietly. "Do you have us?"

"Oh, most certainly," the other replied in his lugubrious voice. "Once caught, none can escape me."

"That is strange. I do not feel caught."

"Don't worry about it. You are."

The speaker was not entirely human, Ehomba saw. Or perhaps he was merely representative of a type of humanity the herdsman had not previously encountered. One thing Ehomba was ever conscious of was his unabiding ignorance. That was why he asked so many questions. The habit had frequently driven his elders to distraction.

The squat shape confronting him was massive and blocky, rather like a squeezed-down, compact version of a true giant. It had a lantern jaw and dark, deep-set eyes. Perhaps its most notable feature was its great mane of red and gold hair, which swept back from not only the forehead but the cheeks to flow in a single continuous hirsute waterfall over its shoulders and back until it touched the floor. The nose was crooked and the upper body much too big for the lower, as if it had been grafted onto hips and legs from another person entirely. Ehomba would have called the face apelike had such an appellation not been denigrating to the monkey. It was ugly—there was no getting around it—but not grotesque. There was even a bizarre, alien warmth to it.

It did not warm the man seated next to him, however. "Don't feel caught, eh? Try getting up."

Ehomba attempted to comply, only to find that he could not rise from the mat. Looking down, he saw that the tiny fibers upon which he was seated were anything but inanimate. They were twitching and rustling in spasmodic silence. A fair number already gripped his lower legs and sandaled feet, but not by wrapping around them and holding them down.

They were boring into them, skin and sandals both.

Looking to his left, he saw that his neighbor was suffering from the same affliction. He was as tightly fastened to the mat as if he had been rooted there. Which was, in fact, precisely what was happening to him.

After waiting a moment for realization to strike the newcomer, the stocky figure extended a hand. "Too bad for you, but I can't deny that it's nice to have some company." He nodded curtly in the direction of their host. "I was fed up with being able to talk only to him."

"Tut," murmured their hairy host, "surely my conversation is not so intolerable."

"Of course it is, but I suppose you can't help it." Despite circumstances that were obviously less than conducive to casual joviality, he grinned as he looked back at Ehomba. "I'm Simna ibn Sind. I come from a country that's far to the northeast of here. And I sure wish I was there now."

"Why aren't you?" the herdsman asked him.

Simna looked away, still grinning. "Dispute seems to dog me the way a sweat bee pesters a runner. I find that I have to keep moving in search of outer as well as inner peace."

"Have you ever found it?"

The fine-featured face looked around sharply. Then the smile widened. "Not yet, but I understand that it's a condition devoutly to be desired. I'd hoped someday to be able to appreciate more than just the theory."

"I am sure that you will."

"Don't you get it, uh . . . ?"

"Ehomba. Etjole Ehomba. I am a herdsman from the south."

"Yeah, well, it's time to stop deluding yourself, friend. You're stuck here just like I am, and neither of us is going anywhere. We're going to sit here until we rot."

"Of course you are." Their host was most agreeable. "That is what people do in my company. That is what everything does in my company." He sighed resignedly. "I do so wish others wouldn't take such a negative view of what is after all a most vital and necessary process." The great-maned head shook slowly. "So few stop to consider what kind of place the world would be without me."

"And what is that?" Ehomba inquired with interest. "What are you? Who are you?"

"I thought you might have guessed by now, traveler." Again the intimation of an imitation of a smile. "I am Corruption."

"I see. By whom were you bribed?"

"No, no; you don't get it, do you?" A man of short sentences and peppery disposition, Simna looked disgusted. "He's not corrupted. He *is* Corruption. Take another look around you. Take a good look."

Ehomba did so, and found that by squeezing his eyes tight together, certain aspects of his surroundings that had heretofore escaped his notice suddenly stood out in stark contrast to what he had initially believed he was seeing.

All those colorful flowers growing in planters and pots on the porch, for example. Gazing at them afresh, he saw now that they were wilted and dying; the petals wrinkled as the faces of old, old men, the stems shivered with disease. The stench of decay permeated the hut. Instead of a woven mat, he was sitting on a heap of moldering dung from which emerged the tendrils of corrupted fungi that were ever so slowly drilling into his feet and lower legs.

As if his eyes had suddenly refocused, he saw the hut in a new light, a dark and decomposing one. The walls were not made of wood, but of some crumbling earthen material resembling peat. Instead of thatch, the roof was composed of the yellowed bones of long-dead animals—and other things. And their host . . .

Pustules and boils covered the heretofore smooth skin while the great mane of hair was in reality a compact herd of composting worms that writhed and twisted slowly around and through the stolid skull. A palpable fetidness that oozed from every pore made the herdsman glad he had not eaten since morning, and then very little. Yet for all the quiet horror of his revealed self, Corruption exhibited no excitement at his new guest's realization, belched no bellow of putrefying triumph. He remained quiet and courteous. Ehomba found this only natural, patience being an important component of the nature of corruption.

"What do you want from us?" he inquired of their host.

Eyes that seethed like the sewage system of a great city turned to him, and maggots spilled from cracked lips. "What your friend said: for you to rot. Don't feel singled out or put upon. It is what I want everything to do." Around him, the hut moaned as the molecules of which it was made slowly collapsed.

"I am afraid I do not have time for it," Ehomba responded. "I have an obligation to fulfill and responsibilities to others."

Cackling laughter bubbled up from noisome depths and the rankness of the room pressed close around him. On his left, Simna turned his head away from their host and gagged. He did not throw up only because he had done so earlier. Repeatedly.

"You have no choice in the matter." Corruption was insistent. "You are rotten. All men are rotten. So is the rest of the world. It is true that I am spread thin, so it is a particular pleasure when I can give personal attention to individuals. I must say that I admire your calm. You will make a fine and entertaining guest until your tongue rots in your mouth and your lungs begin to putrefy."

"I think not."

Reaching back over his shoulder, Ehomba unsheathed the sky-metal blade and drew it across the tendrils that were growing into his sandals, feet, and legs. Normal steel they would have resisted, but against an edge drawn from the absolute purity of space they had no resistance. Corruption's dull eyes were incapable of registering surprise, but they focused more intently on the tall man who now straightened atop the pile of dung.

"Hey bruther, don't forget me!" Simna ibn Sind struggled against his own fungal bonds. Bending over, Ehomba rapidly and efficiently cut him loose. The garrulous traveler rose gratefully and removed one of a pair of swords from a single scabbard slung across his back. Corruption looked on, unperturbed.

"Right now, that's for you, you pile of shit!" As an opprobrium to Corruption, it was not very effective, but the apoplectic Simna was too excited and angry to hazard a more effective imprecation. Bringing his sword around and down in a swift arc, he swung at their host's head.

The blade struck the neck and stuck there. Teeth clenched, Simna tried to pull it free, to no avail. As the two men looked on, rust bled from Corruption's neck, crawling up the flat of the fine blade like water through a straw, turning the gleaming steel a dull red-brown right up to the bone haft. Bone and metal disintegrated simultaneously.

Taken aback but still full of fight, the emancipated traveler drew his second weapon and crouched warily. "Clever it is then, but I warn you: I'm not going to rot quietly."

"Everything rots quietly." Corruption placed the tips of moldering, sausagelike fingers together. "Whatever you do will only put off the inevitable."

"That is true," observed Ehomba.

Simna turned on him quickly, eyes a little wider, stance more tense than a moment before. "Hoy, what's that? You agree with this perversion? Whose side are you on, anyway?"

"The side of life," Ehomba assured him, "but that does not mean I cannot see things as others see them." He met the putrid gaze of their host without flinching. "Even Corruption."

"You are a man of the Earth." The thickset figure was bloating before their eyes, swelling with gas and putrescence, threatening to explode all over them. "I will miss your company."

"And I will not miss yours." Reaching into a pocket of his kilt, Ehomba felt of the beach pebbles there. They were not all he had brought along to remind him of home. What he wanted, he remembered, was in his other pocket.

He came out with a handful of . . . dirt. Simna stared at it in disbelief. "What are you gonna do with that? Offer to plant some mushrooms? This is a helluva time to be thinking about gardening!" He clutched the handle of his blade tightly in both hands, knuckles whitening.

Eyes that had become pools of scummed-over sewer seepage focused on the handful. "Even small contributions to the state of decomposition are always welcome. But it will not buy you your freedom."

"The Naumkib do not pay bribes." So saying, Ehomba threw the dirt at their implacably malodorous host.

It struck where the ballooning chest had been—with no apparent effect. The crouching, poised Simna was openly contemptuous. "Well now, that was useful! What was that you were trying to do, force him to take a bath? It's done nothing at all."

The herdsman did not comment, just stood and watched as Corruption continued to swell. And swell, and swell, until he filled half the hut. Now it was Simna's eyes that widened.

"I think—I think maybe we ought to get out of here and reflect on the situation from a distance, bruther." He turned to run. Though curious, Ehomba recognized the sense of the other man's aside and turned to join him. Within the room, the stench of rotten eggs had become overpowering.

They reached the door just as Corruption exploded, spewing every imaginable kind and variety of filth and muck in all directions. This mephitic fusillade struck them from behind as they threw themselves out the door and onto the porch. The discharge would have swallowed them up had not the wood of the porch been rotted through. It collapsed beneath their weight and they tumbled onto the heavily vegetated slope below. Decaying bushes broke under their fall, cushioning their descent.

Healthy growths would have cut and torn at them. Corruption, Ehomba mused as he rolled to a halt, really did have its uses.

Simna was up and on his feet, sword in hand, with commendable speed. He stared up at the hut through the gap their bodies had made in the rotted porch. Very little was left of the building, most of the walls and all of the roof having been blown away by the explosion. What was left was encased in a coating of solid—well, corruption. Above them, nothing moved.

Breathing hard, Simna turned to look at his taller companion. Ehomba had picked himself up and was wiping distastefully at the mire with which he was covered. When he saw Simna staring at him, panting slowly and evenly, he smiled.

Simna grimaced huffily. "What in Gorath are you squinting at, traveler?"

"You are a mess." Ehomba's smile widened.

The other man looked down at his coat of exceptional filth. When his gaze rose again, he too was grinning. "S'truth, I am, aren't I? And you—if you sought refuge in a pig sty, the hogs would throw you out and hold their noses while doing it!" He started to chuckle.

"I have no doubt," Ehomba admitted.

The swordsman nodded upward. "That wasn't dirt you threw at our late unlamented host, was it?" Eager curiosity burned in his expression. "It was some kind of magic grit, or powdered thrall. Are you a sorcerer?"

Ehomba shook his head dolefully. "I am only a herdsman, from the south."

"Yeah, yeah, so you said. But what was that stuff?"

"Just as I explained: dirt." Ehomba eyed the obliterated hut speculatively. "But it was clean dirt, free of corruption, from my home village. In a desert country, soil that is good enough to grow food in is revered. It is a precious thing, and looked after with care. For what is more magical than the ability to bring forth food from the bare earth?" He nodded up the slope. "I kept it with me as a remembrance of my home. It came from a small plot that my wife tended that had been many times blessed by Oura, the mother of Asab, our chief. She is a wise woman, and skilled in the ways of the earth. I did not think its purity would suit Corruption."

"Suit him? By Girun, it gave him a damned bellyache, it did!" Simna started upward, fighting the slippery slope with renewed energy. "Now let's get after it."

"Get after it?" The herdsman frowned. "Get after what?"

"Why, his treasure, of course." Simna eyed him as if he had suddenly gone daft. "Everyone knows that wherever Corruption lingers for very long there is treasure. There are all kinds of corruption, you know. Somewhere up there should be a hoard of riches amassed from the morally corrupt, from crooked magistrates and bent politicians and back-door guards."

Ehomba wanted nothing to do with any treasure that had been gathered by Corruption. But as always, his curiosity tugged at him more powerfully than common sense. "I thought you were traveling in search of inner peace?"

Using broken stems and branches to pull himself up the steep slope, Simna ibn Sind smirked back at him. "Gold pieces first, my friend. Inner peace later."

"I do not agree with your priorities," Ehomba grumbled as he followed behind.

The shorter man leaped slightly to grab a thick root protruding from the hillside. With the agility of a gibbon, he pulled himself up and continued ascending. "You saved my life, Etjole. So I'm not going to argue with you. But I give you fair warning right now: Whatever happens, don't ever try to get between me and treasure."

"I have no interest in treasure," the herdsman replied softly.

"Hoy, right, that's what they all say."

But as he continued to climb, the compact swordsman was less sure of himself, just as he was less than certain of his quiet-voiced companion. An odd duck for sure, he thought. The concern did not linger. There was treasure to be unearthed and he was going to find it—even if it meant digging through untold layers of exploded, accumulated foulness.

XI

They found nothing in the hut, but there was a slanting cave behind it that was high enough for a man to enter, if he bent slightly. Remarking that corruption burned well, Simna fashioned torches for them both and started in. Ehomba was content to follow. If anything, the stench in the enclosed tunnel was even worse than that without, but nothing could compare with the odor that had momentarily filled the air during the detonation of Corruption himself.

"Who told you there would be treasure here?" Ehomba kept his attention on the well-slimed floor instead of his eager companion.

"You hear things." Simna kept flashing his torch from side to side to ensure nothing was overlooked. "Besides, doesn't money always follow corruption?"

"I would not know," the herdsman replied frankly. "There is none of it in my village, nor among my tribe."

" 'Tribe,' " Simna muttered. "Hoy, that figures. You're not exactly a sophisticate from the big city, are you, bruther?"

"Kora Keri is the biggest town I have ever seen, and that only recently."

"Well, lemme tell you, Etjole—I can call you by your friendly name, can't I?"

"You just did," Ehomba pointed out pragmatically.

"Etjole, if there's one thing I know, it's corruption." If it occurred to Simna that admitting to this body of knowledge might reflect less than favorably upon him personally he gave no sign that he realized it. "And believe me, money follows it the way a honey badger tracks bees." His torch swept back and forth, the swinging flame leaving behind a wake of flickering light. "It's got to be here somewhere. It's got to!"

"Perhaps that is what you are looking for up ahead."

"What?" Simna had been gazing back at his companion. Now his attention shifted forward. Raising his torch as high as the tunnel would allow, he saw what he had hoped to find glittering back at him.

The gold was piled higher than a man, higher even than one as tall as the rangy herdsman. Coins, bracelets, rings, chokers, tiaras, bullion, slabbed bars, goblets, plates, and all manner of other devices lay in a single imposing heap, as if casually discarded during a trash pickup. Peering from the small mountain of gold like iridescent insects were jeweled earrings and buttons, rings and wristlets, and all manner of elaborately carved lapidary decorations.

Eyes wild as a mad kudu, Simna ibn Sind had prepared to take a flying leap onto the golden hillside when he felt a hand restraining him. Attempting to shake it off, he was startled by the strength of the grip. Tough and well built himself, he quickly became frustrated at his inability to loosen that unyielding grasp.

Cobalt blue eyes flashed at Ehomba. "What's the idea, bruther? Let me go! Or are you going to stand there like a disapproving priest and tell me you have no love for gold yourself?"

"Actually, I do not," Ehomba told him, quite honestly. "It is you I am concerned for."

Licking his lips in anticipation, Simna's gaze darted between his eccentric friend and the kingdom's ransom that dominated the chamber. "Don't worry about me. This will fix anything that's wrong with me."

"When I was young," the herdsman went on, still keeping a firm grip on the other man, "I learned that many delicious-looking fruits are safe from grazing animals despite their enticing appearance because they contain one form or another of deadly poison." He nodded at the hoard. "Here is the treasure of Corruption. Think a moment, my friend, on what we have just seen. Corruption corrupts everything it comes in contact with. The instant our eyes and minds cleared we saw that his house was corrupted, the furniture within was corrupted, everything that grew inside and nearby was corrupted. What makes you think this is any different? The fact that it is shiny?"

"C'mon, Etjole! This is gold, and jewels! Not plants or wood."

"It is the provenance of Corruption."

"Let go of me." The swordsman struggled furiously in the other man's grasp. Eventually, one flailing hand encountered the knife sheathed at his waist. "Let me go or by Gwetour . . . !"

Ehomba released him. Simna staggered a moment before regaining his balance. "Take it if you will, then," the herdsman said, "but do me one favor first. Pick only one piece, one coin, and examine it closely before you hurl yourself upon the rest."

Simna squinted at the tall southerner. "That'll shut you up?"

Ehomba nodded, just once. "That will shut me up."

"More than worth it, then." Pivoting, the slim swordsman bent and chose a coin from the bottom edge of the pile. It was a fine coin, lustrous as the day it was minted, with the silhouette of some obscure emperor stamped on one side and an obelisk surrounded by cryptic symbols on the other. Simna turned it over and over between his fingers, flipped it into the air, and caught it with the insouciance of an experienced juggler.

"There! Satisfied?"

"Let me see." Ehomba leaned forward and the other man held the golden disk out for him to inspect. "Yes, it is a large coin, and based on what little I know about such things, real gold."

"Of course it is!" Simna did nothing to try to hide his contempt and impatience. "What else did you expect?"

"I was not sure. Something like what is happening to your hand, I think."

"Something . . . ?" The swordsman blinked and looked down at the coin in his palm. "What are you babbling about?"

"Beneath the coin. See?"

Simna squinted, and then his eyes widened. With a yelp as if he had been stung by a hornet, he flung the coin away from him with a spasmodic twitch of his arm. Holding his wrist, he gaped open-mouthed at his hand.

A neat hole the exact diameter of the coin had appeared in the flesh. The edges of the quarter-inch-deep wound were black and festering. White pus oozed from the center and a mephitic miasma arose from the rotting meat. It was a stink with which both men were by now all too familiar.

"Ghontoh!" Simna exclaimed. Still tightly clutching his wrist, he started to tremble as he looked back over his shoulder at the gleaming, beckoning golden hillock. "If I'd gone and jumped onto that, buried myself in it like I wanted to . . ." He left the rest of the thought unvoiced even as he tried to expel the synchronal vision from his mind.

Ehomba had slid his pack off his back and was rummaging through it. When he rose from the inspection, he had a small piece of sealed bamboo in one hand.

"Here," he said gently, "let me see it."

Shakily, the swordsman held out his ulcerated palm. The herdsman examined it thoughtfully for a moment, then unsealed the bamboo.

Pushing a finger inside, he smeared it thoroughly with the milky sap the container held and proceeded to rub this across the injured man's open palm. After repeating the treatment several times until the wound was thoroughly invested with the sap, he resealed the bamboo vial and replaced it in his pack.

"Give me your other arm," he directed Simna. The swordsman obeyed without question. Ehomba promptly tore a long, winding strip from the sleeve of the other man's shirt.

"Hoy, that's Bakhari silk! Do you know what that costs in a Thalussian marketplace?"

Ehomba eyed him darkly. "Which is more important to you, Simna—your shirt, or your hand?" Wordlessly, he began to bandage the circular lesion with the silken strip. The swordsman did not comment further.

Satisfied, Ehomba stepped back and examined his handiwork. "The dressing should be changed every three days. If you keep the wound clean, it should be healed in a week or two."

"A hole like that? Are you crazy? Even if that goo you smeared on it is worth anything, it'll take at least a month for the flesh to replace itself."

"Oura is mistress of many unguents and salves. I have seen her reduced sap from the leaves of the kokerboom tree save a child from a mamba bite." He offered the other man a thin smile. "Of course, if you think you can do better, you are welcome to do so. Perhaps immersing it in gold bullion would be more to your liking."

"I never met a herdsman with a sense of humor," Simna grumbled. His tone changed quickly. "That's the second time you've saved my life. How am I ever supposed to repay you?"

With a shrug, Ehomba turned. He was more than ready to leave the tunnel. He had been ready to leave before he had entered it. "I know that had our situations been reversed, you would have done as much for me."

"Oh, sure, hoy, absolutely." The swordsman nodded too vigorously. "I would've done so without a thought, bruther!" Holding his torch in his good hand, he followed Ehomba as they started out of the stench-filled cavity. "I guess you're not as green as you look. For a start, I expect you know more about certain kinds of corruption than me. Organic corruption, anyway. Meself, I'm more conversant with the societal variety. I just didn't think there'd be that much difference between the two. Urban corruption wouldn't have rotted a hole in my hand."

Ehomba glanced back at him, only half his face visible in the enveloping darkness. "Perhaps not, but presented with such a circumstance I would have a worry for my soul."

Simna trailed behind in silence for a while before venturing to inquire uncertainly, "Are you sure you're just a herdsman?"

"Cattle and sheep, with the occasional moa," Ehomba assured him. "I miss them even as we speak."

"Hoy, well, better you than me, bruther. Meself, I prefer the companions of my days and nights slimmer, smoother, and better smelling. Watch your step," he added solicitously. "Remember that big rock that sticks out of the floor near the entrance."

They emerged into sunlight that, mist-shrouded and dimmed as it was, seemed brighter than any either man had ever encountered before. Without a word, Ehomba turned to his right and began to make his way along the flank of the mountain, keeping to the open spaces in the rain forest while heading north.

"Hoy, wait a minute!" Surprised by the abruptness of the other man's departure, Simna ibn Sind hurried to catch up to him. "Where are you going?"

Without slowing or looking back at the swordsman, who continued to pace him, Ehomba replied succinctly, "North."

"North?" Simna echoed. "That's it? Just 'north'? North to where? North for what?" Somewhere nearby a flock of very large and throaty birds trilled in chorus like a carillon of silver bells.

"Just north." The herdsman stepped over a root that hugged the ground like a petrified snake. "You would not believe my purpose if I told it to you."

Licking his lips, Simna pressed close on the other man's heels. "Okay, okay, look—I'll tell you what I was really doing here, and then you tell me, okay? We'll each tell the other the truth." He eyed the tall herdsman eagerly. When no response was forthcoming to his offer, he added enthusiastically, "I'll go first.

"You say that you're going north? Well, I was heading south. Way south. Further south than a sensible man might be expected to want to go." He took a deep breath, framing his imminent revelation. "I'm looking for Damura-sese."

Surrounded by steep jungle, Ehomba halted and peered over at the swordsman. "That is too bad. I happen to be from the south, and as a southerner I can tell you that there is no such place as Damura-sese. All that exists of it is the name. I have heard about it all my life, and I can tell you with complete confidence that no such place exists on the face of this Earth."

Simna's expression turned sly. "Ah, but that's what they all say. I figure it's because anyone who knows anything about the place wants to keep it a secret until they can mount an expedition to find it for themselves." He slammed his closed fist against his chest. "Well, I'm an expedition! I'm going to find it, and all the riches the old legends say it holds, and buy myself a khanate or a kingdom. And then when the norics who've been hounding my heart come looking for me, I'll send a battalion of my household cavalry to harry them into the nearest river."

Ehomba listened to all this in silence. "Better to secure yourself an honest and stable position with some noble courtier, or learn a distinguished trade. You might even consider farming." His eyes seemed to change focus, to see far off into the mist-murky distance. "There is much to be said for working in close contact with the earth."

"You keep close to it." Simna tersely jerked a thumb back the way they had come. "Didn't you get close enough to the earth back there?"

"That was not the earth, but its dross." Again he looked over at his companion. "I tell you there is no Damura-sese, Simna ibn Sind. There are only stories that mothers use to amuse their children and see them off to sleep. That too is a sort of magic, but not the kind you seek. If you think you will make your fortune by finding it, you might as well try to market your dreams."

"Don't try to talk me out of it, because you can't." The swordsman pushed through a line of leafy branches, keeping a careful eye out for stinging insects as he bashed his way through. "Okay, now I've done my part and told you of my intentions. Now it's your turn. And since I've been pretty forthcoming, I think you owe me more in the way of detail than 'I'm going north.' "

Ehomba sighed heavily. Good-natured though he might be, the swordsman was tenacious as a leech. Clearly he was not going to let the matter rest until he heard something that would satisfy him. So the herdsman explained his purpose, and his intentions, in making his way northward, eventually to take ship to the unknown west.

Simna listened to it all in silence, occasionally nodding sagely as Ehomba made his points. When the herdsman finished, the swordsman grinned crookedly up at him and commented, "That's some story." He sidled closer and lowered his voice, as if there were someone besides bugs and birds present to overhear. "Now really—what are you up to? You're after treasure too, aren't you? Everyone's looking for treasure. Or you've been given some secret assignment by a high wizard, or better yet, by a banker. There's a lot of gold at stake here. I can tell. There has to be, or you wouldn't have come this far and gone through everything that you have already." He gave the taller man a comradely nudge in the ribs. "Come on, Etjole. You can tell old Simna. What are you after, really?"

Ehomba did not look over or break stride. Another steep-sided ridge loomed ahead, clad in its familiar coat of rain-forest green. "What I told you was the truth. The whole truth. There is nothing else."

The swordsman chortled aloud. "You're good, I'll give you that. One of the better liars I've encountered in my time. But not the best, not by a long shot. See, I've been around, Etjole. I can tell when a man's having me on and when he's telling the truth just by studying the way his cheeks twitch and his lips quiver. I look them right in the eye and I can tell. You're good, but you can't fool me."

Stolid and determined, Ehomba strode on. "You are right," he replied imperturbably. "I cannot fool you. You are too perceptive for me."

Simna beamed, well pleased with himself. "See? I knew better! Now then, what is it that you're on to? A sunken merchant vessel laden with scarce trade goods? A spice merchant's caravan on its way from far Narinchu? A pirate's abandoned lair, or jewels guarded by the spirit-wraith of a dead queen?"

"Something like that," Ehomba replied noncommittally. The ridge ahead looked less imposing than the last several he had crossed. Perhaps the mountains were beginning to subside. It would be good to travel on level ground once again. He was tired of climbing.

Simna pouted. "Fine then! Be that way. Keep the truth to yourself. I'm sure you'll tell me when the time comes."

Frowning, Ehomba looked over at him. "Tell you? Do you think you are coming with me? I thought you were bent on finding Damura-sese?"

"One expedition at a time," the swordsman replied. "Truth be told, bruther, when speaking of directions, 'south' is pretty generalized and offers little in the way of direction. You, on the other hand, seem to have a definite destination in mind."

"Not as definite as you seem to believe." Ehomba kicked aside a fallen branch that was decorated with spotted blue liverworts.

"More definite than mine, anyway. Wherever it is, Damura-sese isn't going anywhere. So I had this notion that I might tag along with you for a while." He indicated the knife at his belt and the remaining longsword slung against his back. "I can hold my own against any half dozen men in a fight, keep a dragon at bay, satisfy three women at once, outdrink the biggest primate in a tavern, and ride all day and all night while asleep in the saddle. I'm a boon companion with more stories to tell than any two professional guides, better songs than a tintinnabulation of troubadours, and I won't run out on a man in a tight spot. You'll do well to keep me in your company."

Ehomba could not repress a slight smile. "If you can handle that sword as well as you do your tongue, truly you would be a good man to have at one's back in a fight. But I do not need, or want, any company."

"Oh." Simna was momentarily crestfallen. But his irrepressible good spirits rapidly returned. "Want to keep all the treasure to yourself, eh?"

The herdsman's gaze rolled heavenward. "Yes, that is it. I want to keep all the treasure to myself."

"Well, don't worry. I'll only expect for what I'll earn. So you won't mind if I keep company with you for a little while?"

"It may be more than a little while," a somber Ehomba informed him. "As to you 'tagging along,' much as I might wish to do so, I cannot very well prevent it. I think you are like malaria: It can be made to go away for a while, but it always comes back to make a man sick and uneasy."

Simna lengthened his own jaunty stride. "Flattery'll get you nowhere, cattle-man. So this fortune you're on the trail of, how big is it? Are we after gold, or works of art, or what?"

By evening Ehomba was almost ready to use the spear on his tirelessly garrulous new companion, but he was too weary. Simna ibn Sind prattled more than a convocation of women gathered for the village's annual coming-of-puberty ceremony. The herdsman finally compared it to a forlorn steer bulling in the fields. Eventually and with an effort of will he was able to largely tune out the drone of the peripatetic swordsman's voice.

Briefly, he considered abandoning the man while he slept. Attractive as he found the imagery, however, he could not quite bring himself to do it. Since he could not courteously lose the fellow, he decided that he would have to find some way to tolerate him. The prospect did not concern him overmuch.

Once they had trudged another couple of hundred leagues or so north without encountering any sign of treasure, he decided, Simna ibn Sind would undoubtedly dissolve their little company of his own accord.

XII

His supposition was correct. Not about Simna ibn Sind, but about the lay of the land ahead of them. There were more jungle-clad ridges, but they continued to grow smaller and less difficult to surmount, the rain forest that flourished on their flanks thinning out even as the knife-edged ridge tops became more manageable.

Then, without warning, there were no more tree-crowned summits to ascend.

They found themselves standing on the last ridge top looking out upon a sea of grass that stretched, utterly unbroken, to the northern horizon. No rocky knoll poked its stone-crowned head above that perfectly flat green-brown plain. Not a single tree thrust its trunk or lofted its branches over the endless emerald sward. Unobstructed sunlight did not glint off isolated lakes or ponds, or flash from the mirrored surface of some lazily meandering stream. There was nothing, nothing but the grass.

"The country ahead looks like it's going to be easy to cross but difficult to hunt in." Simna held his chin in his hand as he studied the terrain spread out before them.

"It may not be so easy to cross, either," Ehomba commented. His eyes glistened. "What wonderful country!"

His companion gaped at him. "Wonderful?" He stretched out an arm to encompass the endless overgrown meadow. "You call that wonderful? There's nothing there but Gopuy-bedamned grass!"

Ehomba looked sideways at Simna. "I am a herdsman from a dry country, my friend. To one responsible for the well-being of cattle and sheep, forced to move them from place to place just to keep them from starving, this would be an earthly kind of paradise. Not all people see riches only in gold."

The swordsman eyed the tall southerner tolerantly. "You really *are* a simple guy with simple needs, aren't you?" Ehomba nodded, and the other man responded with a sly, knowing smile. "I've got to hand it to you, Etjole. I've crossed paths with some shrewd, closed-mouthed types in my time, but you're right up there with the best of them! How long do you think you can fool me with this 'simple herdsman' routine? Grass my ass! We both know what you're after, and you're not going to get rid of me that easily! It'll take more than cheap, obviously phony claims of ignorance to fool Simna ibn Sind!" He edged nearer.

"Come on, Etjole—you can tell me now. What is it you're after, really? A lost city like Damura-sese, only even richer? A bandit's abandoned cache? Clandestine merchant gold?"

Ehomba sighed tolerantly. "It is a shame, Simna. Having so narrow a vision, you must miss much of what goes on in the world. You are like a horse with blinders."

Annoyed, the swordsman stepped back. "Okay, okay. So don't tell me. I know you must have your reasons, and that you'll make everything clear when the time comes."

"Yes," Ehomba assured him candidly, "everything will become clear when the time comes." He started down the slope. The last slope, for which he was grateful. Clambering over the jungle-wrapped ridges had been as tiring as it was dangerous. Seeking to change the subject, he said, "I would think you would know this country. Did you not come from here?"

Simna shook his head. Extraordinarily agile, he had an easy time picking his way down through the last trees. Where Ehomba had to step carefully, the stocky swordsman would simply hop or leap to the next clearing.

As they descended, the grass grew nearer—and taller. And thicker, and taller, until it became clear to both men that the country ahead was no ordinary veldt, and the grass they were approaching almighty unlike its humbler cousins elsewhere. They were unable to appreciate its true dimensions, in fact, until they were standing at the very bottom of the ridge.

"Nine feet high." A contrite Simna stood before the wall of solid green. "Maybe ten. How in Gerooja are we going to get through *that*?"

Stolid as ever, Ehomba regarded the seemingly impenetrable barrier. "We have blades. We will cut our way through. Make a path." He nodded skyward. "I can navigate by the stars. A lone herdsman out in the pasturelands learns early how to do so."

"That's all well and good, it is," Simna snorted, "but do you recall the panorama from the top of the ridge?" He nodded back at the slope they had just descended. "This extends farther than a man can see." Taking a couple of steps forward, he felt of the nearest blade of grass. Soft and fibrous, it was as thick and wide as his hand. "You know how long it will take us to cut a league or so deep into this? If the plain reaches beyond the horizon, it could take us months just to cut a path halfway through. And what are we going to eat while we're doing it? I'm no grazer."

"There must be game," Ehomba commented. "Surely so much rich forage does not go unutilized."

A skeptical Simna waved at the wall. "Hunt—in this? How can you hunt something that might be standing right behind you without being visible? And anything that does live in there is bound to travel through it faster than a man."

"What would you have us do?" With his spear, Ehomba gestured toward the top of the ridge. Back the way they had come. "Retrace our steps? Over every ridge and canyon? Or go back the way you came, toward the east?"

"I didn't say that." A frustrated Simna slumped down on a moss-covered rock and cupped his head in his hands. "Of course not. An ibn Sind never retreats. But I don't like our prospects for advancing, either."

"We could camp here until inspiration strikes."

The swordsman managed a weak grin. "You mean like a rock to the head? If I thought it would do any good, I'd take the blow myself." He eyed the unbroken, ten-foot-tall rampart of green. "I can resign myself to the necessary cutting. It's the problem of finding food that worries me."

"We will manage." Reaching back over his shoulder, Ehomba unsheathed the sky-metal sword, the exposed blade gleaming grayly in the muted sunlight and glinting off the strange, sharp, parallel lines etched into the metal. Bringing back his arm, he prepared to begin the arduous task of cutting a lane through the overgrown veldt.

"Just a moment there, if you please."

Pausing with the blade held over his head, the herdsman turned toward the sound of the voice. So did Simna, who had been steeling himself to join in the path-cutting effort.

Emerging from the towering greensward just to their right was a man—or a close relation. Stepping out from between two ten-foot-high blades, he turned to confront them, sharp-eyed and unafraid despite his small stature. He was maybe three feet tall, slim to the point of emaciation, with high pointed ears, eyes that were small round circles of intensity, a bare snub of a nose, and a cone-shaped head that more than anything else resembled small blades of grass slicked up in the manner of some dandified courtier and glued together to form a perfect point. He wore nothing but a green loincloth that had been braided from strips of grass, and went barefoot. Fastened to his loincloth by a single loop was a comparably sized scythe of sharpened bone.

Like his loincloth and his surroundings, he was bright green, from pointy head to tiny-toed foot. No wonder they hadn't seen him until he had elected to emerge from hiding. Looking upon him, Ehomba decided their visitor might be a hundred years old, or two, but certainly no less than fifty. Of course, he was using the only referents he knew, which were human. The small green manikin was surely something else.

This their unexpected visitor proceeded to confirm, in prompt response to Simna's diplomatic inquiry of "What the hell are *you*?"

The figure drew himself up to his full, if unimposing, height. "I am Boruba-Ban-Beylok, sangoma of the Tlach Folk, the People of the Grass." He glared at Ehomba. "The grass gives life, the grass gives protection, the grass is the carpet on which the world treads. We do not take indifferently to its wanton cutting."

Hand on sword hilt, an uneasy Simna studied the impenetrable wall of high green and wondered if the blade might have found itself cutting down something more mobile and less indifferent than grass. There could be a hundred tiny green warriors hiding in there, a thousand, and he would not have known it. His senses were acute, but he saw and heard nothing. As near as he could tell, the only intruder that was rustling the grass was the wind. But he was on full alert now, trusting in his unassuming companion to defuse the situation. Simna was smart enough to know when to keep his mouth shut, aware that his chronic intemperance was more likely to exacerbate than ease the confrontation.

Ehomba lowered his blade but did not put it up. Instead, he let it hang loose from his right hand. "I was not being wanton." With his other hand he gestured at the green escarpment. "We are traveling to the north. The grass is in the way. If we could fly, we would choose that method of travel. But we are only human, so we must walk. To walk, we must make a path."

Boruba-Ban-Beylok shook his head disapprovingly. "Human you are, to think always of going through things. Never around."

"Very well." Ehomba was perfectly agreeable. "We will not cut the grass." Simna stared at his friend, but continued to keep his opinions and suggestions to himself.

Approaching the greensward, the herdsman pushed one blade of grass aside. Another was immediately behind it. "Show us how."

"You mock me," the little green sangoma snarled. Or at least tried to snarl. Like the rest of him, his voice was not very deep.

"Not at all," Ehomba replied. "I do not know how to go around the grass. If that is what you wish us to do, show us how. We will be glad to comply." He swung his blade in a short arc. "Cutting grass of any height is hard work. I would be delighted to be able to avoid it."

"And so you shall," the sangoma informed him, "if you can answer for me three riddles."

With a heavy sigh, Simna resumed his seat on the rock. "I knew there was a catch in this somewhere. When you're dealing with sangomas and shamans and witch doctors and spirit women, there's *always* a catch." Resignation underlay his words. "Sometimes it's deeds that have to be performed, or a magic crystal that needs recovering, or a sacred icon that has to be returned to its altar. Or bridges to be crossed, wells to be plumbed, cliffs to be scaled—but it's always something."

"What happens if we cannot answer your riddles?" Ehomba asked quietly.

The sangoma took a short hop forward. He was smiling now. "Then you'll have to go back the way you came, you will. Have to go back, or a fate worse than any you can imagine will spring out at you from between the very blades of grass you seek to pass and rend you to fragments small enough for the beetles to feast upon, rend you with fang and claw and poison stinger."

Alarmed by this augury, Simna rose and retreated until he could stand with his back against a solid rock that protruded vertically from the base of the ridge. He held his sword at the ready and redoubled his continuous scrutiny of the green barrier.

If Ehomba was at all taken aback by the naked threat, he did not show it. "Ask your three riddles, then, Tlach-man."

Clearly enjoying himself and his role as ambassador of confrontation, Boruba-Ban-Beylok rubbed tiny green hands together as he primed himself. As they made contact with each other, the sliding palms generated a sound like bark being sanded. The sky did not darken and thunder did not roll—the Tlach sangoma was not a very big sangoma, after all—but the crests of the nearest grass blades tilted forward as if eavesdropping on the proceedings, and the rustling within momentarily grew louder than the slight breeze alone could have inspired.

"Listen close, listen careful, human." Trenchant green eyes stared deeply into Ehomba's. "First riddle: In the morning comes the sun, in the night comes the moon. But what comes at midday and is midwife to both? Riddle second: A fish is to a frog as a heron is to a crow. What is a Tlach to? Third riddle and last: The name of a man is how a man is

known to others, but by what other means may he introduce himself?"
With a confident smirk, the sangoma rested his hands on skinny green-
skinned hips and waited for the tall trespasser to respond.

Observing scene and byplay, Simna had already resigned himself to
finding a way back through the mountains. Sick as he was of climbing
and descending, of fording rock-filled jungle streams and fighting off
bugs and thorns, he struggled to accommodate them in his mind. Because it was clear that his simple, kindly friend, while a boon companion
and pleasant fellow, was no towering intellect. In contrast, Simna was
highly conversant with puzzles and conundrums of many kinds and origins. Quick-witted as he was, though, the solution to the three riddles of
the Tlach was beyond him.

He eyed the impossibly lofty wall of grass apprehensively. If as
seemed certain Ehomba failed to answer the riddles and they attempted
to press on through the high veldt, Boruba-Ban-Beylok had all but promised them encounters with apparitions unpleasant. He studied the green
escarpment intently, searching for signs of the brooding monstrosities
the sangoma had assured them were lurking within, waiting for the right
moment to spring upon unfortunate travelers. Just because he could not
see anything did not mean there was nothing there. If it was green, like
the sangoma, it could be standing right in front of them while remaining
virtually invisible.

Ehomba stood quietly as he pondered the Tlach's questions. Then
he slowly raised the sky-metal blade he was holding and silently aimed
the point at the sangoma's chest. Simna tensed, while Boruba-Ban-
Beylok eyed the much bigger man warily but did not turn and run.

"You cannot imagine what fate will befall you if you harm me," he
growled darkly.

"I do not intend to harm you, but to answer your riddles." The
herdsman advanced the tip of the sword ever so slightly nearer the
sangoma's throat. "This blade is forged from metal that fell from the sky.
See how strangely the sunlight shines on it? That makes it midwife to
both the sun and the moon. As to your second riddle, a Tlach is close to
Death, if he should come too close to such a blade. And it answers your
last query as well, for with this sword I provide another way of introducing myself than by using my name." With surgical precision, he touched
the sharp point of the weapon to the sangoma's neck, dimpling the green
flesh just above the bulging Adam's apple.

"Boruba-Ban-Beylok, sangoma to the Tlach, meet the metal that
comes from the stars."

The sangoma swallowed—not too hard, lest he awkwardly impact
the location of the blade. Behind them both, Simna put a hand on the

hilt of his own weapon as he tried to divide his attention between the two figures and the still quiescent wall of grass. At any moment he expected something huge and horrific to spring forth from between the stems. But the greensward remained still.

"Am I supposed to offer a greeting in return?" Eyes narrowing, the sangoma fixed the contentious interloper with a threatening stare. "I warned you. Now you must accept the consequences."

"I am prepared to do that," Ehomba assured him. "That is why I am still standing here holding this weapon at your throat instead of running away. I have never run from a confrontation in my life, and I do not intend to start now." He nodded at the grassy escarpment. "I have vowed to travel north until I can find a ship to take me westward across the Semordria, and north I will go in spite of spew, spirits, or spiteful sangomas."

Simna stretched as he tried to see over the tops of the grass. "Etjole, something's coming! I can hear it." He inhaled sharply. "And smell it."

"What is it, Simna?" The herdsman's blade did not waver. Boruba-Ban-Beylok was starting to smile.

"Can't tell. Animal of some kind. No—animals. More than one, less than a dozen. Big." He drew his sword. "If we're going to make a stand, we'd do better to find a cave to fight from, or at least higher ground."

"No." Ehomba kept his attention on the small green man standing before him. "I stay here. Climb to safety if you want."

Simna stood with his back against the protruding rock, torn among common sense, personal desires, and admiration for the stupidly brave herdsman. The internal conflict found him in an agony of indecision.

"You know I can't do that! You saved me from Corruption, not once but twice. I can't run out on you!"

Ehomba nodded agreeably. "Good for me. Then stand, and be ready." He met the sangoma's stare with an unwavering gaze of his own. Startled by its unexpected depth and intensity, the Tlach stumbled slightly before recovering his balance.

"A herdsman, you say you are? Are you sure?"

Ehomba's tone was rock steady. "In the pastures a man must learn to stare down predators that threaten his herds and flocks. When one is used to doing that, locking eyes with another man-thing is never very intimidating."

Something large and heavy was smashing its way through the grass toward them. In spite of himself, Ehomba turned to look in its direction. Boruba-Ban-Beylok sniffed expectantly.

"Now you will learn the folly of challenging a sangoma of the Tlach!

Your death approaches. Prepare yourself, herdsman! And don't say that I didn't warn you."

"They're coming!" Leaping from his rock, an agitated but determined Simna took up a defensive position alongside the herdsman's back, facing the green wall with his sword held firmly in both hands. "Whatever it is, is coming!"

The grass parted and a glowering brown face glared down at the three bipeds. A second facade, splotched with white, emerged nearby. Two flat-surfaced, sharp incisors protruded downward from the upper jaw, each longer than Simna ibn Sind's body. Black convex eyes stared down at them while the upthrust ears were each as big as a good-sized steer. The fur that covered each animal was thick and silky, and the round, compact bodies traveled on gigantic, immensely powerful feet.

Ehomba stared back while a gargling sound emerged from the throat of the startled Simna. They were hares, the herdsman saw immediately.

Hares as big as elephants.

XIII

Neither man laughed. Expecting something toothier, they nonetheless did not lower their guard for a moment. A small hare could bite off a man's finger, while a larger one like those that inhabited the Naumkib country could knock the wind out of a person with a single kick, or do real damage if such a blow struck a vulnerable area. Hares the impossible size of those they now confronted should be capable of biting a horse in half or kicking down a castle wall. Though not what was expected, they were no less potentially lethal.

Ehomba wondered at his own surprise. In a country of tree-high grass, what could be more natural than to encounter grass-eaters of equivalent size?

He was watching the triumphant sangoma carefully. He had not seen the little green man trace any arcane symbols in the air, nor had he been heard to enunciate any mysterious phrases. His voice had not been raised in alarm, nor had he uncorked a gourd or bottle of concentrated musk. Therefore the appearance of the titanic hares was most likely a consequence of their mere presence in the area, and a natural curiosity about the source of human conversation. The boastful sangoma might know their ways, but he had done nothing thus far to indicate that he commanded them.

Which did not make their present situation any less potentially perilous. With an admirable effort of will, Simna held his ground when his natural instinct was to run for cover among the rocks behind them. That, Ehomba suspected, was what Boruba-Ban-Beylok had intended to do the instant the hares made their initial appearance. With his small size and knowing the ways of the new arrivals as intimately as he surely did, he was doubtless counting on finding a place of safety long before the travelers did, leaving it to the hares to finish off the unbelievers.

Ehomba put up his sword. Using his spear as a walking stick, he marched straight toward the nearest of the immense leporids. Still holding his own weapon out in front of him, Simna made a grab for his tall friend—and missed. He did not follow.

"Etjole, are you crazy? They'll bite off your arms—or your head! They'll stomp you into the earth! *Etjole!*"

Ignoring the well-meaning swordsman's warnings, Ehomba approached until he was within paw-length of the nearest hare. Glowering, it leaned toward him, both front paws extended. It could easily pin him to the ground, or pick him up and, with a single snap, bite off his face.

Now, it is said that there is no talk among hares, and that they reserve all such ability for their death throes, for as everyone knows, the scream of a dying hare is as piercing and soul-shattering a sound as exists in nature. But most men know nothing of the lives of such creatures, for they are familiar with them only as garden pests, or a possible dinner. Not so with Etjole Ehomba, and not by accident or chance.

The great ears inclined forward to listen to the softly speaking herdsman. With a single short hop that caused it to emerge entirely from the grass, its white-faced companion moved intimately close. Both enormous leporids remained quite still as Ehomba whispered to them. Only their whiskers and oversized nostrils moved, quivering without pause.

Boruba-Ban-Beylok was positively beside his diminutive green self. "What are you waiting for? Kill them! Kill them both! They are intruders, interlopers, blasphemers! Tear them to pieces, crush their bodies beneath your great feet! Take them up and hurl them—"

He broke off as the point of Simna ibn Sind's sword replaced that of Etjole Ehomba at the front of the sangoma's green-skinned throat. The stocky swordsman was grinning nastily. "Here now, bruther, that's about enough noise-making out of you, don't you think?" He glanced significantly in the direction of the soft-voiced conversation that was now taking place between prodigious hares and easygoing herdsman. "We wouldn't want to interrupt a friendly chat between man and beast, now, would we?"

Ignoring the presence of the sword as much as it was possible to do so, a goggle-eyed Boruba-Ban-Beylok gawked at the unreasonable trio, the two huge hare heads bent close to the tall intruder so as not to miss a single word of his gentle discourse.

"No—it's impossible! No man may talk with the great grass-eaters! Such a thing cannot be!"

As time continued to pass without the immense herbivores attacking, Simna grew increasingly at ease. "You have eyes, don't you, wise man? Tiny, beady, nasty eyes, but eyes nonetheless. Believe it: It is happening." He nodded in the direction of the most unlikely conversation. "My country friend there may sometimes smell of cattle piss and sheep droppings, but he is just full of surprises."

"This can't be happening." Moaning, the distraught sangoma dropped to his knees.

Moments later Ehomba broke off the talk and rejoined the other two. Behind him the great hares waited, following his progress with their bottomless eyes, noses twitching, whiskers as long as a man's leg quivering. The white-faced one turned away and began to gnaw at the nearest grass stalk. The green span disappeared into the oversized, mechanically grinding mouth as neatly as a log into the maw of a sawmill.

Fully aware that his life was on the line, Boruba-Ban-Beylok gazed up at the solemn-faced herdsman. "Don't kill me, warlock of an unknown land! Please don't! My people need me. They rely on my knowledge and skills to help them survive in the grass. Without me they will panic and perish."

"I doubt that," Ehomba replied. "I have no doubt that you are a person of importance among your tribe, and master of some small competencies. But I think they would manage to find another to take your place."

"Too right, bruther." Nodding agreement and smiling wickedly, Simna shoved the point of his sword more firmly against the green man's neck.

"However," Ehomba went on even as he rested his free hand on the swordsman's arm, "I will kill another only to defend myself, and that is no longer necessary."

"Awww." Openly disappointed, Simna reluctantly drew back his blade. The air went out of Boruba-Ban-Beylok. Then he rose and gestured in the direction of the hares, who were both now munching contentedly on the towering grass, indifferent to the small drama being played out in their vicinity.

"How?" he asked simply. "I have never seen or heard of such a thing, magician."

"As soon as I saw what kind of creatures were threatening us, I was no longer worried. And stop calling me that." A touch of irritation crept into the southerner's voice. "I am a herdsman; nothing more, nothing less."

"As you say, mag—herdsman. You were not worried? You are the first interloper I have ever encountered who was not terrified by the very sight of the giant browsers."

"That is because I know them," Ehomba explained. "Or rather, I know their kind. You see, I come from a dry country, and in dry country there is always constant competition for pasturage. Left to themselves, cattle will compete with sheep. There are also the wild animals: the antelope and the rhinoceros, the mice and the meerkats, the bushbuck and the brontotherium, the gerbil and the gormouth."

Simna's brows drew together. "What's a gormouth?"

"Tell you later." To the sangoma he added, "In the face of such endless competition for forage a herdsman can do one of two things: poison and kill those that compete with his herds for food, or try to work out some kind of mutually acceptable arrangement that satisfies all."

"And you," the sangoma asserted, "you are a compromiser."

Ehomba nodded. "The Naumkib are not a violent tribe. Our herds and flocks share with the oryx and the deer. They understand this, and so do the animals we claim for our own. To maintain this peaceful arrangement it is sometimes necessary for the parties involved to ratify and adjust, to discuss and debate. The talking of it is delegated to those of us who possess some small skill in conversation."

"And you," Simna declared bluntly, "you talk to hares."

"Yes." The herdsman nodded once. "I talk to hares." He glanced back over his shoulder at the quietly browsing brown behemoths behind them. "Among the Naumkib there is a saying for each species, for each of the grazing kind we have learned to deal with. For the hare it is 'Speak softly and carry a big carrot.' Unfortunately, I have no carrots to offer these, but I think it would not matter. To impress these would take a carrot the size of a sago palm.

"But they recognize a conciliatory spirit, and being of a nonviolent nature themselves, were quick to respond to my overtures." He looked down at the green hominid, who, while still wary, had managed to cease trembling. "I do not know if it is natural to your tribe, Boruba-Ban-Beylok, but you, at least, should learn some hospitality."

Immediately, the sangoma dropped to his knees and placed his forehead and palms upon the ground. "Command me! Tell me what it is you need of me."

"Well now, that's more like it, bruther." Strutting back and forth while picking at his teeth with the point of his sword, Simna considered the offer. "For a start we—"

"We need nothing from him," Ehomba declared, interrupting. "I take nothing from someone who is offering under duress."

"Duress? What duress?" Simna demanded to know. "I've drawn back my sword, haven't I? Besides, what's wrong with taking from someone who's under duress? D'you think he'd not do so if given the chance?"

"I do not know," the herdsman replied softly. "I know only that I am not him."

"Well, I ain't him neither," Simna protested, "but I do know that finding a way through this bulwark of bastard grass is going to be Gimil-bedamned difficult, and that he probably could show us the way!"

Eagerness shining from his face, the sangoma rose quickly to his feet. "Yes! I can have several of our youth guide you! Otherwise you will quickly become hopelessly lost and wander about until you perish." He waved an arm at the green barrier. "In the grass there are no landmarks, no way to determine direction. Even at night, the tops of the blades will shut you in and keep you from seeing the stars. Nor can you climb to find your position. The upper edges of the blades are too sharp, and can cut a person to shreds." He tapped his chest.

"Only the Tlach know the way, and are small enough to slip easily between the blades."

"We appreciate your insights," Ehomba informed him, "but we must move quickly. Therefore your offer is declined."

Sword hanging at his side, Simna gaped at his friend. "Declined? You think we're going to be able to travel faster through that mess without a guide?"

"Yes." Turning, Ehomba smiled reassuringly at his bemused companion as he started back toward the browsing hares. "And we are not going through the grass—we are going over it."

"Over—oh no, not me! Not me, Etjole!" Simna started backing away, toward the familiar, comforting, unmoving rocks. "If you're thinking what I think you're thinking . . ."

Reaching the haunch of the nearest hare, Ehomba turned to look back at him. "Come, Simna ibn Sind. I have a long ways yet to travel and therefore no time to waste. Is it so very different from mounting a horse?"

"I don't know." Uncertain, unsure, but unwilling to be left behind, Simna reluctantly took a step forward. "I've always had a decent relationship with horses. My own relationship with hares has been solely at the dining table."

"I would not mention such things around them." Placing his left foot on the brown hare's right, Ehomba stepped up. Using the long fur as a convenient hand-hold, he pulled and kicked his way upward until he was sitting on the broad chestnut shoulders just behind the great head. The enormous, towering ears blocked much of the view forward, but there was nothing to see anyway except the endless, monotonous field of grass.

"Why not?" Making an easier if more hesitant job of it than the herdsman, the always-agile Simna boosted himself into an identical riding position on the neck of the second elephantine hare. "You're not going to tell me they can understand us?"

"Not our words, no," Ehomba informed him, "but they are good at sensing things. Feelings, emotions, which way a predator is likely to jump. Helpless as the majority of them are, they have to be." Leaning forward, he spoke into the nearest ear. He did not have to whisper. With auditory apparatus the size of trees, the hare could have heard him clearly from the top of the final jungle-draped ridge.

With a turn and a leap, they were off, Ehomba holding tightly to the thick neck fur and maintaining his usual contemplative silence, Simna howling and protesting at every bound. With each mighty hop they cleared tracts of grass that would have taken men afoot many difficult, sweaty minutes to traverse, and with each jolting landing Simna ibn Sind seemed to find a new imprecation with which to curse the extraordinary method of travel.

They were not alone on the veldt, nor were the Goliath hares the only oversized creatures to be seen. The wind-whipped, emerald green food source was host to an abundance of equally remarkable creatures. At the apex of every gargantuan leap they could see down and across the soaring grassland. Tree-sized blades twitched where hippo-sized mice gnawed at fallen seeds. Caterpillars as long as dugout canoes felled stems like nightmare loggers at work in an unripened forest. Earthen ramparts that would have made any siege engineer proud were the work not of attacking or defending armies, but of bull-like moles and gophers that burrowed prodigiously beneath the rich soil.

Once they were attacked by crows the size of condors. Unceasing in their search for an easy meal, the black-feathered robbers struck boldly from all sides—not at the hares, which were far too big to serve as prey for them, but at the far smaller riders clinging to their backs. Simna had his sword out as soon as he saw the first bird approach, but he never had the opportunity to use it.

Sharp, barking caws and *cut-cut*s sounded on his right. Using his legs to maintain his seat, Ehomba was sitting up straight, hands cupped around his mouth in a most unusual fashion, and shouting back at the marauding crows as good as they were giving. To hear those clipped, guttural caws coming from his mouth was an entertainment any prince would have paid to witness. Simna got it for free. Given the seriousness of the circumstances, his commentary following the crows' departure perhaps ought to have been less acerbic.

"Wait, don't tell me!" The swordsman made a great show of analyzing in depth what had just transpired. "I know, I know—you can talk to crows, too."

Untutored herdsman though he might be, when it came to unfettered sarcasm Ehomba was not above responding in kind. "You are very observant."

Holding tight to the neck fur of his hare, Simna reserved his rejoinder for the moments when he and his mount were sailing freely through the air above the grass. "So you've convinced me. You're *not* a sorcerer. You're just the world's greatest talker. What else can you talk to, Etjole? Turtles? Nightingales? Dwarf voles?"

"In my country there are many crows," the herdsman responded without a hint of guile. "Living there is as hard for them as for hares or cattle, men or lizards. It is . . ."

"A desert country, a dry country, difficult and bleak—I know, I know." Simna returned his gaze to the unbroken swath of green that still stretched out in every direction before them. "Not that I'm complaining, mind. I've always been adept at the languages of man, but never bothered to try learning those of the animals. Maybe it's because I didn't know they had languages. Maybe it's because no one I ever met or heard tell of knew that they had languages."

"It sounds to me," his companion called across to him, "like you have spent most of your life around men who only talked and did not listen."

"Hah! Sometimes, they don't even talk. They just swing things, large and heavy or slender and sharp. I'll make you a deal, bruther. You take care of talking to the dumb animals we encounter, and I'll take care of talking to the men."

"Fair enough," Ehomba agreed, "but there is one thing more you will have to help me with."

Simna glanced over at his friend. "What's that?"

"How does one tell which is which?"

Onward they raced through the high green veldt, their mounts seemingly tireless, covering great difficult distances with each bound. Until, at last, it seemed that they were tiring. They were not. It was the universal perspective that was being altered, not the enthusiasm of the hares.

The first indication that something had changed came from Simna's observation that they were covering shorter and shorter distances with each bound. This was immediately confirmed by Ehomba, who was the one to point out that the hares were jumping as frequently and as powerfully as ever. It was not that they were covering less and less distance with each leap, but that they were covering less proportionately. Because with each hop now, they were growing smaller and smaller.

The hares shrank to rhino size, then to that of a horse, then a calf, at which point they could no longer support their human riders. After a very bad moment during which he thought he was shrinking as well, Simna realized that he and his companion were not changing in size. It was only the world around them that was changing.

They followed the hares forward until both fleet-footed creatures were reduced to the size of those that Simna knew from his travels in his own homeland and other countries: small brown furry creatures that barely came up to the middle of a man's shin. Their noses still twitched, their whiskers continued to flutter, and in every other aspect they were unaltered, even to the white splotches on the face of his own former mount. But the journey had reduced them from giants to the reality of the world he had always known. The real world, he decided—though in the company of a singular individual like Etjole Ehomba, who was to say what was real and what imaginary?

Along with the hares, the grass too had been reduced in size until the tops of the highest blades rose no higher than his waist, with a few isolated, more productive patches reaching to his shoulders. The taller Ehomba could see easily over even these.

Bending, the herdsman made unintelligible sibilant sounds to the two hares, who listened attentively. Following a light pat on the head of each, they turned and scurried back into the grass from whence they had all come.

Simna watched them go. "What will happen now? As they travel south will they start to return to their former extravagant size?"

"I believe so." Ehomba was trying to follow the progress of their mounts, but his efforts were defeated by the dense growth that closed in behind them. When not in their exaggerated state, small hares needed to be ever vigilant. Once back in the veldt of the giants, he reflected, they would be safe once again. Tilting back his head slightly, he glanced at the sky. Unless, of course, there soared among the clouds in the region they had just fled hawks and eagles that reached proportionate size. Such a winged monster would put all the tales of rocs and fire-breathing dragons to shame. What a wonder it would be, though, to see such a creature! An eagle with the wingspan of a nobleman's house!

He was glad they had been spared that particular marvel, however, because it would have meant that the monster would surely also have seen them.

Walking north, it was not long before they came upon a kopje, a rocky outcropping rising from the surrounding veldt. At its base was a small pool, not so shallow as to be too hot, not so stagnant as to prove distasteful. By mutual agreement it was decided to make camp there for the night.

When Ehomba announced that he would build the fire, Simna waited and watched eagerly for the herdsman to generate sparks with the tips of his fingers, or blow flame from his nostrils, or conjure it out of the thin dry air with closed eyes and staccato chant. He was sorely disappointed. The fire was started with flint and dry grass and much careful blowing on the tiny wisp of smoke that resulted.

Perhaps the tall herdsman was nothing more than he claimed to be: a simple master of cattle and sheep with an unusually adept skill at multispecies linguistics. One who would maintain that assertion even under torture or threat of death. He would have to, Simna knew.

Otherwise others might find out about the treasure he was after.

Smiling to himself, knowing that he knew the truth no matter what the disarmingly personable southerner might claim, Simna prepared for the coming night. Let the "herdsman" think that his traveling companion believed his fictions. Simna knew better, and that was enough for now. When the time came, he would confront his laconic companion more forcefully.

As forcefully as was necessary to ensure that he got his full share of what they were after. Whatever that was.

XIV

With the blackness that follows the day pulled over them like a speckled silk veil, the two men crouched around the fire taking turns trying to identify the sounds of the night. Occasionally, they argued. More often, they agreed. Ehomba was impressed by his well-traveled companion's range of knowledge, while Simna appreciated the acuity of his tall friend's hearing.

Not that it was always necessary to strain to hear the murmurings of the night creatures. A well-spaced assortment of screeches, yowls, roars, bellows, hisses, and whistlings surrounded them. A few they were able to identify, while the perpetrators of the majority remained as unknown as if they had come down from the dark side of the moon.

Once, the clear, still air resounded to the sounds of horrific conflict between unseen combatants. The noise of battle died away without any concluding scream, suggesting that the fighters had resolved their nocturnal dispute in nonfatal fashion. Not long thereafter, a high-pitched, lilting song that tinkled like running water made melody drifted across the grass, beguiling all within range, man and beast alike. And as they were about to retire, a small blue serpent whose back sported a pattern of pink diamonds slithered silently through the lonely encampment, passing directly and disinterestedly beneath Ehomba's ankles before disappearing back into the grass.

Simna rose abruptly at the sight of it and started to reach for his sword. When he saw that his companion was not only not afraid of the scaly intruder but actually indifferent to it, he slowly resumed his crosslegged seat on the ground.

"Do you talk to snakes, too, bruther?"

"Occasionally." The herdsman sipped from a leather water bag. "They have much to say."

"Really? It's been my experience they just bite, kill you, and go on their way."

"They should be forgiven the random burst of temperament. How would you like to go through life without legs or arms? Considering how unfairly Fate has dealt with them, limb-wise, I have to say that I find them admirably restrained." Finishing his drink, he recorked the container and set it aside. "Under the circumstances, I think I would find myself wanting to bite everything in sight, too."

"You know what your talent is, Etjole? In case you didn't know, I've just decided for you." Simna was preparing to turn in. "You sympathize with everything. You know what your problem is?"

"No. You tell me, Simna ibn Sind. What is my problem?"

The itinerant swordsman pulled the thin blanket up over his legs and torso. Upon it, a grieving maid had embroidered her feelings for him in certain and graphic terms.

"You sympathize with everything." With that he rolled onto his back and opened his eyes to the dark heavens. Everyone knew that the grains of sandy material that filled one's eyes and induced sleep were actually made of star-stuff. While lying beneath an open sky, this material would gradually sift downward to fill the corners of a man's eyes and gift him with a sound and healthful night's rest. Knowing this, Simna had never been able to understand how people were able to sleep indoors. No wonder so many of them tossed and turned uneasily in their beds.

The fire was burning low. A single distant but penetrating roar of particular resonance briefly jarred him, but he was too contented to let anything disturb him for long. They had crossed the seemingly impossible high veldt without injury or difficulty, saving weeks of difficult walking through dangerous country. He was traveling in the company of a mysterious but pleasant and unthreatening foreigner who was going to lead him to a trove of untold riches. True, this individual possessed abilities he refused to acknowledge until the time came to make use of them, but Simna had seen fakirs and magicians at work before, and was not intimidated by their ruses. Not even by those of one who could talk to animals. He was certain he was ready for whatever surprise his traveling companion might choose to spring next.

No he wasn't.

It was the light that woke him. Stealing in under his eyelids, prying at them with insistent photons, raising both his lids and his attention. The explanation was simple and natural: The sky had become lit by a rising full moon. Smacking dry lips, he prepared to roll over, away from the light in the sky. As he did so, he opened one eye to check on the position of the night's light. At the same time it occurred to him that there had been only a sliver of moon the night before, and that it was usual for the moon to move with stately and regular procession through its phases and not to jump from one-eighth full to wholly rounded.

He was wrong. The light did not come from the moon. He sat up, the thin but warm blanket sliding down to his thighs, his eyes now fully open and alert.

The campfire had been reduced to a pile of coals from which curls of smoke continued to rise, taking flight into the night and making good their escape from the company of man. Ehomba sat cross-legged on the other side, staring not at the sky nor at his companion but at the intense glimmering that was drifting, will-o'-the-wisp-like, in front of him. No random, irregularly shaped glob of luminance, the light had form and shape.

What a form, an enchanted Simna thought dreamily, and what a shape.

It hovered in the air before the herdsman, draped in tight folds of silk in many shades of blue flecked with silver stars and laced with pearls and aquamarines. Though long of sleeve and skirt, the binding of the royal raiment was such that he could see the curves that folded upon curves. It was at once entirely modest and unrelievedly arousing.

The young woman who was thus encased, like a spectacular butterfly about to be born from a glistening cocoon, had skin the color of love and smooth as fresh poured cream. Her eyes were bluer than the silks she wore, and they sparkled more brightly than any diamond sewn to her gown. In striking contrast to the color of her skin, her hair was impossibly black, wavy filaments of polished onyx that spilled down her back and around her shoulders, as if a portion of the night itself had attached itself to her being.

She was staring not at the unmoving, attentive Ehomba, but off into the distance. Her expression was resigned, determined, wistful. What she was looking at Simna could not imagine. He knew only that he would, without hesitation, have given his very life to be the subject of that stare.

Something made her frown, and as she did so the light in which she was enveloped curdled like souring milk. A second presence stepped into the ragged splotch of efflorescence. It was huge, monstrous, and overbearing.

You could not see the eyes, concealed as they were within the depths of the horned helmet. Spikes and scythes protruded from the rough-surfaced black metal. Below the helmet began the body of a wrestler and a giant, immensely powerful, the muscles themselves occasionally visible beneath flowing garments of purple, gold, and crimson. The cape that trailed behind the figure, which Simna estimated to be close to eight feet tall, was decorated with the most horrible visions of hell, of bodies being torn limb from limb by demons and devils, all of whom were performing their dreadful activities under the supervision and command of that same towering, helmeted figure.

As both men looked on, there in the night in the middle of the veldt, the giant put a massive, mailed hand on one flawless bare shoulder. Instantly the woman whirled, her far-off look abruptly replaced with one of utter loathing and revulsion. Her reaction did not seem to trouble the giant. Though she did her utmost to remove his clinging hand, at first shaking and then grabbing at it, she was unable to dislodge the mailed grip even when pressing both hands and all her weight upon it.

Until now Simna had sat motionless, enthralled by the vision and the distant drama of what he was seeing. But suddenly, the giant was looking past the woman held in his bruising, unyielding grasp. Looking beyond the room in which he and his prize stood, beyond even the building where his prisoner was bound in unwilling consort.

He was looking straight at Etjole Ehomba, a herdsman from the dry, desiccated lands to the south.

With a bellow of outrage that dwarfed anything that the veldt had produced, the figure brought its other hand forward. Something that was the consequence of an unholy union between fire and lightning sprang from the mailed palm, leaping toward the seated southerner. Ehomba ducked instinctively and the blast of luminescent diablerie passed over his left shoulder to strike the center of the dying campfire.

Those flames that remained within fled in terror of a greater fire than they could know. As the air screamed, the very molecules of which it was composed were torn and rent. The image of giant and entrapped beauty collapsed in upon itself, twisting and crumpling like a sheet of paper in the trembling fingers of a scandalized warlord. And then it was gone: giant, empyreal prisoner, and the light that had framed them, leaving behind only the veldt and the scandalized night.

Not a sound emanated from the surrounding leagues of grass. It was as if the earth itself lay stunned by the apparition. Then, somewhere, a cricket resumed its violining. A frog croaked from within its prized puddle. Night birds and insects resumed their timeless chorus.

Aware that he had neglected to breathe for a while, Simna ibn Sind inhaled deeply. The perspiration in which he was drenched began to dry and cool on his body, causing him to shiver slightly. Shunting aside his blanket, he crawled over until he was beside his companion. It took a moment, because he had to avoid the foot-deep, smoking ditch of scorched earth that occupied the place where their campfire had been and that now drew a line in the soil between them. It stank of carbonized malignance and inhuman venality.

"Pray tell, bruther, what that was all about? And in the same breath, deny to me one more time that you are a sorcerer."

Ehomba looked over at him and smiled tiredly. "I have told you, friend Simna, that I am but a simple herdsman. Believe me, I would rather be lying with my wife than with you, listening to my children instead of the growls and complaints of strange animals, and in my own bed than here in this alien land. But through no wish or desire of my own, I have become involved in something bigger than myself." Turning away, he looked at the patch of sky where the phantasm had appeared and subsequently burned itself out.

"I did not conjure up what we just saw. I did not call out to it, or beckon it hither, or ask it to appear before me. I recited no litany, cast no spells, burnt no effigies. I was having trouble going to sleep and, having trouble, thought to sit a while and contemplate the majesty of the sky." He shrugged so lackadaisically that Simna almost believed him.

"So that just 'happened'?" The swordsman waved at the space in the sky where the figures had appeared. The air there still shimmered and smoldered like distant pavement on a scorching hot afternoon. "You did nothing to make it happen?"

"Nothing." With a heavy sigh Ehomba lay back down on the comforting earth. "I was sitting, and it appeared before me. The auguries of a dead man, Simna. The burden of Tarin Beckwith of Laconda, North." He nodded at the disturbed patch of atmosphere.

"I believe that the woman we saw was the Visioness Themaryl, and the frightful figure that appeared behind her must perforce be her abductor, Hymneth the Possessed. She fits the allusion of comeliness the dying Beckwith described to me, and he no less the likeness of concentrated animus. How or why they should appear to me now, here, in this isolated and unpretentious place, I cannot tell you."

Simna nodded and was silent for several moments. Then he commented, "You really don't know what you're getting into, do you?"

"I never worry about such things. We are all fallen leaves drifting on the river of life, and we go where the current takes us." The herdsman looked up at his friend. "Do you worry?"

The swordsman let his gaze rove out across the veldt. "I try to. I like to have some idea what I'm in for." Pulling his gaze away from the veldt and whatever was out there, he looked back over at the herdsman. "That must be some treasure he's guarding."

Frustrated, Ehomba rolled over onto his side. "If what you just saw and experienced is not enough to convince you that I am not doing this for treasure, then it is certain nothing I can say will convince you otherwise."

"Oh, don't get me wrong," Simna declared. "The woman is certainly worth saving." He whistled softly. "There are all kinds of treasure, even some that come wrapped in silk. Speaking of which, did you happen to notice that—"

"You are an impossible person, Simna ibn Sind."

"I prefer incorrigible. All right, so my intentions are base. But my objectives are noble. I'll help you rescue this Visioness Themaryl, if you're bound and determined to return her to her family as you say you've sworn to do. But as my reward, or payment, or whatever you wish to call it, I claim for myself any gold or jewels we can plunder along the way."

In the darkness, Ehomba smiled in spite of himself. "You would pit yourself against the figure we saw, against this Hymneth the Possessed, for mere wealth?"

"Take it from me, Etjole—there's no such thing as 'mere wealth.' So he's big and ugly and can throw sky fire from his fingertips. So what? I'll bet he bleeds like any man."

"I would not count on that. But I admire your bravery."

"I've found that in the face of danger, greed is a wonderful motivator, Etjole. I suppose you're fortunate that you're immune to it."

"I did not say that I was immune. It is just that we covet different things, you and I."

"Fortunate for me, then." Rising, the swordsman returned to his resting place and once again drew the embroidered blanket up around his body.

His companion was not quite ready for sleep. "Simna, have you ever contemplated a blade of grass?"

Already drifting off, the exhausted swordsman mumbled an indifferent reply. "Look, I'd rather believe that I'm traveling in the company of a sorcerer than a philosopher. You're not going to philosophize at me now, are you? It's late, it's been a tiring time, and we need to get an early start tomorrow morning to cover as much ground as possible before the sun rises too high."

"You should look forward to walking when the sun is high. It keeps the snakes in their lairs. In the cool of morning and evening is when they like to come out."

"You're sure of that, are you?" Something brushed the swordsman's exposed left arm and he jumped slightly. But it was only, to his relief, a blade of grass being bent by the breeze.

"That is what they tell me."

"Hares I can accept, but snakes? Not even magicians can talk to snakes. Snakes have no brains."

He could almost see Ehomba scowling in the darkness. "I am sure there are many in this place, and I hope none of them overheard that."

"Hoy, right," Simna snorted softly.

"There is the universe we live in," the herdsman went on, as if the colloquial conviviality of serpents had never been a question under discussion, "and then there is a blade of grass." In the deepening shadows Simna saw his companion pluck a young green shoot from the ground and hold it above his reclining head, a tiny sliver of darker blackness against the star-filled sky.

"A wise man of our village, Maumuno Kaudom, once told me that there is a world whole and entire in everything we see, even in each blade of grass, and that if we could just make ourselves small enough we could walk around in it just as we walk around in this world."

Rolling his eyes, Simna turned over on his side so that his back was facing his suddenly talkative friend. "Just assuming for a minute that your wise man knew what he was talking about and that he wasn't speaking from the effects of too much homemade beer or garden-raised kif, and that you could 'walk around' inside the 'world' of a blade of grass, why would anyone want to? Everything there is to see in a grass blade can be seen now." Reaching out from beneath his blanket, he ripped a small handful of stems from the soil and flung them over his side in the direction of his prone companion.

"Catch, bruther! See—I fling a whole fistful of worlds at you!"

A couple of the uprooted blades came to rest on Ehomba's face. Idly, keeping his attention focused on the stem that he was holding, the herdsman flicked them aside. "One world at a time is enough to ponder, Simna."

The swordsman rolled back to his original position. He was weary, and had had about enough learned discourse for the evening. "Good! At last we're in agreement on something. Concentrate on this one, and forget about grass, except for the leagues of it we must march through tomorrow."

"But, think a moment, Simna."

The other man groaned. "Must I? It hurts my head."

The herdsman refused to be dissuaded. "If Maumuno Kaudom is right, then perhaps this world, the one we inhabit, is to some larger being nothing more than another blade of grass, one among millions and millions, that can be held up to contemplation—or flicked aside in a moment of boredom or indifference."

"They'd better not try it," the swordsman growled. "Nobody tosses Simna ibn Sind aside in a moment of anything!"

Gratifyingly, it was the last thing Ehomba had to say. The silence of the night stole in upon them, pressing close on the sputtering embers of the dying campfire until it, too, went silent. In the rising coolness of the hour the enormity of what Ehomba had been saying eased itself unbidden into Simna's thoughts.

What, just what, if the old village fakir his friend had been talking about was right? He wasn't, of course, but just—what if? It would mean that a man's efforts meant nothing, that all his exertions and enthusiasms were of such insignificance as to be less than noticeable to the rest of Creation.

Reaching down, he fingered another blade of grass that was struggling to emerge from the soil just beyond the edge of his blanket. Fingered it, but did not pull it. He could have done so easily, with the least amount of effort imaginable. Curl a finger around the insignificant stem and pull. That was all it would take, and the blade would die. What did that matter in the scheme of things? They were surrounded by uncountable billions of similar blades, many grown to maturity. And if this one was pulled, two more would spring up to claim its place in the sun.

But what if it contained a world, a world unto itself? Insignificant in the design of Creation, yes, meaningless in the context of the greater veldt, but perhaps not so meaningless to whatever unimaginable minuscule lives depended on it for their own continued existence and growth.

Absurd! he admonished himself. Preposterous and comical. His finger contracted around the blade even as his lips tightened slightly. It hung like that, the slightly sharp edge of the blade prominent against the inner skin of his forefinger.

Slowly, he withdrew his hand. The blade remained rooted in the earth. It was nothing more than that: a single finger-length strand of grass. No horse or hare would have been as forgiving, no hungry kudu or mouse would have hesitated before the small strip of nourishing greenery. But Simna ibn Sind did.

He was not sure why. He was only sure of one thing. The next time he and his impassive traveling companion were lying in some empty open place preparing for sleep, he was going to cram his bedsheet, or blanket, or if need be clods of earth, into his ears so as not to have to listen to what the herdsman had to say. It was an evil thing to play with a man's mind, even if, as it appeared, Ehomba had done so unintentionally.

Blades of grass as individual worlds! This world as nothing more! What lunacy, what folly! Fortunately he, Simna ibn Sind, was immune to such rubbish. Slipping his forearms beneath his head to support it, he turned onto his belly and tried to get comfortable. As he did so, he found himself wondering how many blades of grass he was crushing beneath his chest. His closed eyes tightened as he vented a silent, mental scream.

Tomorrow he would do something to unsettle Ehomba twice as much as the herdsman had unsettled him. That promise gave him something else to think about, to focus on. With visions of cerebral revenge boiling in his thoughts, he finally managed to drift off into an uneasy, unsettled sleep.

When he woke the following morning his good humor had returned, so much so that all thoughts of retaliation had fled from his mind. Sitting up on his blanket, he stretched and let the rising sun warm his face. Ehomba was already up, standing on the other side of the campfire staring into the distance as he leaned leisurely against his long spear. Staring north, where they were headed.

A humble man, the condescending Simna mused. Some would say single-minded, but it was as easy to think of him as highly focused. As he prepared to rise from where he had been sleeping, the swordsman happened to notice the skin of his left forearm. As he did so, his eyes bugged slightly.

A neat line of red spots ran from wrist to elbow. Some were larger than others. All were grouped in twos. The pattern was plain to see. What sort of biting insect would make such marks? He rubbed his hand over the pale splotches that were already beginning to fade. They did not itch, nor had whatever had made them penetrated the skin.

The repeated double pattern reminded him of something, but for a long moment he could not remember what. Then it struck him: They were exactly the kinds of marks the fangs of a snake would make.

Hopping back onto his blanket (as if that would provide any refuge or protection!) he looked around wildly. When he bent low he found that he could make out marks in the grass and the dirt. Many marks, familiar patterns in the ground, as if he had been visited during the night by a host of serpents. A host who had left their signs upon him as a warning, and a commentary.

Straightening, he scrutinized the surrounding grass, but could see nothing moving. Only the tips of the blades disturbed by the occasional morning breeze, and the flitting of hesitant, busy insects.

"All right," he called out to the open veldt, "I apologize! Snakes *do* have brains! Now leave me be, will you?"

With that he turned to see Ehomba staring back at him.

"Well," he groused as he snatched up his blanket and shook it free of dirt, grass, litter, and assorted would-be biting fellow travelers no bigger than the motes of dust that swirled in the air, "what are *you* laughing at!"

"I was not laughing," Ehomba replied quietly.

"Ha!" Roughly, the swordsman began rolling his blanket into a tight bundle suitable for travel. "Not on the outside, no, but on the inside, I can hear you! You're not the only one who can hear things, you know."

"I was not laughing," Ehomba insisted in the same unchanging monotone. Turning, he gestured with his spear. "That way, I think. More inland than I would like to go, but I think there may be water that way. I see some high rocks."

Pausing in his packing, Simna squinted and strained. Despite the best efforts of his sharp eyes, the horizon remained as flat as the beer in the last tavern he had visited. But he was not in the mood to dispute his companion. It was too early, and besides, Ehomba had already proven himself more right than wrong about the most extraordinary things. When a man was right about visions of ultimate beauty and terror, much less about snakes, it made no sense to squabble with him over the possible presence of distant rocks.

Shouldering their kits, the two men struck off to the north, heading slightly to the east. As he walked, Simna found himself apologizing to the young shoots of grass on which he unavoidably stepped, and followed each apology with an unvoiced curse in his companion's direction. The red spots on his arm were nearly gone, but that did not keep him from carefully inspecting any open places in the grass ahead before he strode through them.

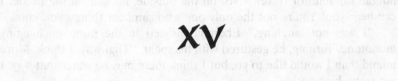

"Screaming."

"What?" Simna had been watching a small flock of brilliantly colored parrots chattering and cackling in a nearby tree. The unprepossessing tree itself was as worthy of attention as its noisy, joyfully bickering occupants. In the open veldt, it was worth marking the location of anything above the height of a mature weed for use both as a landmark and a possible camping site.

"I hear screaming."

Maybe his eyesight was not as keen as that of the herdsman, but there was nothing wrong with Simna ibn Sind's hearing, which was sharp from untold nights of listening intently for the creak of doors or windows being stealthily opened, or for the ominous footsteps of approaching husbands. The instant that his tall companion had drawn the swordsman's attention away from the tree, he too heard the rising wail.

His brows drew together. "It's coming at us from the east, but I don't recognize it. If it's some kind of beast, it's a mighty great huge one to make itself heard at such a distance."

Ehomba nodded solemnly. "I have an idea of what it might be, but this country is strange and new to me, so we will wait and hope it draws near enough for us to make it out."

His friend spun 'round to face him. "Draws near! We don't want it to draw near, whatever it is. We want it to go away, far away, so that we don't hear it anymore, much less set eyes on it."

The herdsman glanced down at the other man. "Are you not curious to see what it is that makes such a consistent and ferocious noise?"

"No, I am not." Simna kicked at the grassy ground. "I am perfectly happy to avoid the company of anything that makes consistent and ferocious noises. If I passed the rest of my life without ever seeing anything that made consistent and ferocious noises, I would be well content."

"I am surprised at you, Simna." Once more Ehomba turned his attention eastward. "I am always questioning things, wanting to learn, needing to know. I am afraid it made me something of a pest to my mother and an enigma to my father. The other children would taunt me whenever I wanted to know the name of something, or the meaning, or what it was for. 'Curiosity killed the catechist,' they would tell me. Yet here I stand, alive and well—but still boundlessly ignorant, I fear."

"I wouldn't disagree with that," Simna muttered under his breath. The roar from the east was growing steadily louder. The problem now was not how to hear it, but how to avoid it. His gaze fell on the kopje. "Unless it's some harmless but large-throated creature coming toward us, we ought to be prepared to deal with it. For once we have the opportunity of some cover, however slight." He nodded in the direction of the prominent rock pile. "I suggest we avail ourselves of it."

"Yes." Ehomba smiled at him. "A question may be as easily answered from a position of safety as from one of exposure. You are full of good common sense, Simna."

"And you are full of something too, bruther Etjole." Putting a hand against the taller man's back, the swordsman gave him a firm shove in the direction of the granite outcropping. "But I am growing fond of you nevertheless. I suppose there is no accounting for one's taste."

"Even if I am not leading you to great treasure?" The herdsman grinned down at him as together they loped toward the looming rocks.

"Save your fibs for later, bruther." Despite his inability to match Ehomba's long stride, Simna easily kept pace with his companion.

Several small, yellow-furred rodents scurried for holes in the rocks as the men drew near. From the far side, a large bird rose skyward in a spectacular explosion of iridescent green and blue feathers, two of which trailed from its head and exceeded the rest of its body in length. Though it had the appearance of a songbird, its call was as rough and jagged as that of a magpie.

There were no caves in the rocks, but they found a place between two great sun-blasted whitish gray stones that was large enough to accommodate both of them side by side. While the depression did not conceal them completely, it afforded a good deal more protection than they would have had standing out on the open plain.

"See!" This time it was Simna who reacted first, rising from his crouch and pointing to the east. "It's coming. At least, something's coming." Shielding his eyes from the blazing sun, he squinted into the distance.

"It certainly is." Ehomba gripped his spear tightly. "And it is not an animal."

By this time the distant screaming had risen to a level where both men had to raise their voices slightly in order to make themselves understood to one another.

"What do you mean it's not an animal? What else could it be?"

"Wind," Ehomba explained simply.

Simna frowned, then listened closely, finally shaking his head. "That's no wind. I don't know what it is, but it's alive. You can hear the anger in it."

Crouching nearby, using the smooth rock for support, Ehomba leaned his spine against the unyielding stone. "What makes you think, my friend, that the wind is not alive, and that it cannot feel anger?" He gestured. "Not only does this wind sound angry, it *looks* angry."

The screaming grew still louder, rising with its increasing proximity. Then the source of the shrieking came into view, making no attempt to hide itself. It was like nothing Simna ibn Sind had ever seen, not in all his many travels. Frightful and formidable it was to look upon, a veritable frenzy of malice galloping across the veldt toward them. It displayed every iota of the anger the swordsman had heard in its voice, confirming all he had suspected. But to his wonder and chagrin, Ehomba's explanation proved equally correct.

The fiend that was racing toward them, howling fit to drown out a good-sized thunderstorm, was wind indeed, but it was unlike any wind Simna had ever seen.

That in itself was extraordinary, for the wind rarely manifested itself visually. Usually, it could be felt, or heard. But this wind could also be seen clearly, for it took upon itself a form that was as appalling as it was imposing. Rampaging across the veldt, it ground its way in their general direction even as it wound deliriously inward upon itself. Nor was it alone. Again Simna squinted eastward. No, there could be no mistake. Unlike the winds he knew, this one was advancing purposefully and in a decidedly unerratic manner.

It was chasing something.

"There's something running from it," Simna called out as he put up his sword. Of what use was steel against an unchecked force of Nature?

"I see it," Ehomba avowed. "It looks like some kind of cat."

"That's what I thought." His companion nodded agreement. "But it doesn't look like any kind of cat I've ever seen before."

"Nor I. It is all the wrong shape. But it is definitely running from the wind, and has not merely been caught out in front of it. See how it swerves to its right and the wind demon turns to follow it?" He turned away briefly as a rising gust sent particles of dust and fragments of dry grass smacking into his face.

"Not again!" Simna pointed over the rocks. "What kind of demonic hunt is this? Whoever heard of wind deliberately chasing a cat—or any other creature, for that matter?"

He expected the ceaselessly surprising herdsman to say, "I have seen . . ." or "In the south I once knew of . . ." but instead the tall spear carrier simply nodded. "Certainly not I, Simna."

"You mean you haven't experienced everything, and you don't know all there is to be known?" the swordsman responded sardonically.

Ehomba looked over at him, now having to shield his eyes from blowing debris. The wind was much closer, and therefore that much more intense. "I have tried to tell you on several occasions, Simna, that I am the most ignorant of men, and that everything I know could fit in the bottom third of a spider's thimble."

"I didn't know spiders used thimbles."

"Only certain ones." This was said without a hint of guile. "They have sharp-tipped feet, and it is the only way they can avoid pricking themselves when they are weaving their webs." Keeping low, he looked back out across the rocks. "The cat is exhausted. You can see it in its face. If something is not done, the wind will catch it soon."

"Yeah, you can see how its stride is growing slo— What do you mean 'if something's not done'?" As warning signs flared in his brain, Simna eyed his friend with sudden wariness.

His worst fears were confirmed when the herdsman rose from his crouching position and moved to abandon the comparative safety of their rocky alcove. "Wait a minute, bruther! What do you think you're doing?"

Standing atop the bare granite, Ehomba looked back at the other man, that by now familiar, maddening, doleful expression on his long face. "There is something strangely amiss here, my friend, that has led to a most unequal contest. I am by nature a peaceful fellow, but there are a few things that can rouse me to anger. One of these is an unequal fight." Lowering his spear, he stretched it out in the direction of the advancing wind and its failing prey. "Such as we see before us."

Simna rose, but made no move to follow the taller man. "What we see before us, bruther, is a contest of unnatural will and unreasoning Nature in which we are fortunate not to be a part. Leave circumstances alone and get back under cover. Or would you think to debate with a thunderstorm?"

"Only if it was a rational thunderstorm," the herdsman replied unsurprisingly.

"Well, this is no rational wind. I mean, just look at it! What are you going to do—threaten it with harsh language?"

"More than that, I hope." Gliding easy as a long, tall wraith across the rocks, Ehomba made his way down the slight slope of the kopje toward the onrushing disturbance. Behind him, Simna cupped his hands to his lips in order to make himself heard above the ever-rising howl.

"All right, then! If suicide is your craving, far be it from me to interfere!" As Ehomba bounded off the last rock and down into the grass, the swordsman's voice became a shout. "But before you die, at least tell me the location of the treasure!"

Perhaps the herdsman did not hear this last. Perhaps he did, and simply chose to ignore it. Looking back, he raised his spear briefly over his head in salute, then turned and jogged out into the grass, heading directly into the path of the onrushing cataclysm.

If the exhausted cat saw him, it gave no sign. Nor did it react by changing its course and heading in his direction. Why should it? What could one mere man do in the face of one of Nature's most frightening manifestations? Lengthening his stride, Ehomba hurried to intercept the storm's quarry.

Certainly it was the strangest and yet most magnificent cat the herdsman had ever seen. Jet black in color, with yellow eyes that burned like candles behind the old magnifying lenses of a battered tin lantern, it had the overall look and aspect of an enormous male lion, complete to inky black neck ruff. But the heavy, muscular body was too long and was carried on absurdly elongated legs that surely belonged to some other animal. An unnatural combination of speed and strength, its lineage was a mystery to the curious Ehomba. From having to guard his flocks against them, he knew the nature and countenance of many cats, but he had never seen the like of the great black feline form that came stumbling toward him now.

While its pedigree remained a mystery, there was no mistaking its intent. It was trying to reach the shelter of the kopje. Given the speed at which it was slowing, Ehomba saw that it was not going to make it.

Breaking into a sprint, he raced to insert himself between the faltering cat and the pursuing tempest. Once, he thought he heard Simna's anxious cry of warning rising above the growling wind, but he could not be sure of it. As he drew near, the great cat stumbled again and nearly fell. It was not quite ready to turn and meet its apocalyptic pursuer, but from studying its face and flanks Ehomba knew it had very little strength left in those extraordinarily long legs.

Spotting the approaching human through its exhaustion, the cat followed him with its eyes, eyes that were strangely piercing and analytical, as Ehomba slowed to a halt between it and the storm. Standing tall as he could, willing himself to plant his sandaled feet immovably in the solid earth, the herdsman confronted the storm and threw up both hands.

The storm did not stop—but it paused. Not intimidated, not daunted, but curious. Curious as to what a single diminutive human was doing placing itself directly in the storm's unstoppable path.

It towered above him, reaching into the clouds from where it drew its strength, a coiled mass of black air filled with flying grass, bits of trees that had been ripped from their roots, dead animals, soil, fish, and all manner of strange objects that were foreign to Ehomba's experience. It was wind transformed into a collector, running riot over the landscape gathering into itself whatever was unfortunate enough to cross its path. In shape it most nearly resembled far smaller wind-cousins of itself that the herdsman had seen dancing across the desert. But those were no more dangerous than a momentary sandstorm that nicked a man's skin and briefly rattled his posture. This was to one of those irritating dust-devils as an anaconda was to a worm.

Not surprisingly, its voice was all breathiness and barely checked thunder.

"What is this? Are you so anxious to end your life, man, that you presume to confront me? Before I suck you up and drink you like a twig, I would like to know why." It held its position, neither advancing nor retreating, swirling in place as it glared down at Ehomba from a height of hundreds of feet.

"I do not know what sort of deviate contest you are engaged in with this poor animal." Ehomba gestured back at the great cat, who had paused to try to gather its strength and lick at a cut on its left flank. "But it is a patently unfair one, for you have all the sky to draw upon for energy while it has only legs and muscle."

A gust of wind blew in the herdsman's face: a tiny gust, a mere puff of air, really—but it was enough to knock him from his stance, and make him stumble.

"I was told of the creature's boasting," the tornado replied, "that it claimed it could run faster than the wind. So it was he who set the challenge, and not I."

Ehomba turned to eye the cat questioningly. Undaunted by either the herdsman's stare or the column of frenzied air hovering behind him, it replied in a voice that was notably less barbaric than those cat-tongues with which the southerner was conversant. How and where it had learned to speak the language of man was a matter for further discussion, under less adverse climatic conditions.

"The wind demon speaks the truth. I did say that." Yellow eyes rose past Ehomba to fixate on the column of air. "Because it's true. I am faster than the wind."

"There! You see!" Screaming, the storm corkscrewed violently against the Earth. "As weather goes, I am among the least patient of its constituents. How could I let such an impertinent claim go unchallenged—or unpunished?"

The calm before the storm, Ehomba queried the cat. "I mean no offense, or disrespect, but you will pardon me for saying that given the current state of affairs it does not appear to me, anyway, that you are faster than the wind."

"I am!" Turning to face both the herdsman and the storm, the cat was spent but unbowed. "But I am only flesh and blood and cat-gut." It glared furiously at the towering, watchful column. "I can and did outrun it, for a day and a night. It tried, but could not catch me. But, unlike it, I need to stop to feed, and to drink, while it can draw sustenance directly from the clouds themselves. Its food follows it, while mine wanders, and does its best to avoid me."

"Sensible food," Ehomba murmured knowingly.

The cat took a faltering but proud step in his direction. "This twisting thing refuses to accept the result of that day. Now it pursues me with murder in mind."

"Nature does not like to be embarrassed," Ehomba explained quietly. He turned back to confront the waiting storm. "Is what the cat says true?"

"A day, two days, a month—what does it matter? Nothing can outrun the wind!"

"Not even for a day and a night?" The herdsman cocked his head to one side and eyed the writhing tornado.

"This is not a matter for discussion!" The wind that blasted from the swirling pillar of constipated atmosphere threatened to implode Ehomba's eardrums. "I am fastest, I am swiftest, I am eternally triumphant! And now you, man, will die too. Not because you anger me, not because you take the side of the blasphemer, but simply because you are here, and unlucky enough to be in my way. I will rip your limbs from your torso and scatter them within my body like the summer flowers that decorate the shores of distant rivers, and I will not feel it."

"You know," Ehomba replied as he reached back over his shoulder for a sword, "not only are you not the fastest, but you're not even the greatest of winds. Against the greater gales you are nothing but a wisp of air, a summer zephyr, less than a child's sneeze."

"You are brave," the storm told him, "or demented. Either way it makes no difference. The death of a madman is still a death. Upon the face of the Earth nothing can stand against me. I cut my own path through typhoons, and dominate storms strident with thunder or silent with snow. Tropical downpours part at my arrival, and williwaws steal in haste from my sight." It resumed its advance, tearing up the ground before it.

Unable to run anymore, its hind legs paralyzed by muscle cramps, the cat could only stand and watch as Ehomba held his ground, plunged his spear point down in the dirt, and with both hands held the dull gray sword out in front of him. The storm is right, fatigued feline thoughts ran. The man is mad.

The tornado could not laugh, and if it could, the difference between laughter and its habitual ground-shaking howl would not have been perceptible. But it did manage to convey something of amusement.

"What are you going to do, man? Cut me? Take a bite out of my air?"

"You are right, storm," the herdsman yelled back. "Nothing can stand against you—on the face of the Earth. But anyone who looks at the night sky knows that this is not the only Earth, that there are many others out there in the great spaces between points of light. Hundreds, perhaps. I have spent many nights looking up at them and thinking about what they might be like, and have talked often about it with the wise men and women of the Naumkib."

A glow was beginning to emerge from his sword, but it was unlike any glow the cat had ever seen. Neither yellow, nor white, nor red, it was a peculiar shade of gray, a cold metallic radiance that was traveling slowly from the tip of the weapon toward its haft. Silent now, the cat stood on tottering legs and stared, its pain and exhaustion completely forgotten. There was a wonder taking place before his eyes, and he wanted to miss none of it.

"The wise ones say that the Great Emptiness that spreads over our heads, even over yours, is not as empty as it appears at night. It is full of incomprehensible but miraculous things. Bits of forgotten worlds, the memories of long-lost peoples, energies greater than a veldt fire, beings vaster and more wise than a woman of a hundred years. All that, and more."

"I am not impressed or dissuaded by the ravings of madmen." The tornado inched closer, teasing the grass, toying with the lone human standing before it.

By now the gray glow had enveloped the entire sword, which was quivering like a live thing in the herdsman's powerful grasp. Ehomba held it high, presenting its flat side to the surging column of tormented air.

"Then be impressed by this. Storm, meet your relations, your distant cousins and brothers and sisters—the winds that blow between the stars!"

XVI

Had he been able to, a dumbstruck Simna would have shut his eyes against the blast that came out of the herdsman's sword. But he could not. The thread of intergalactic cyclone blew his eyelids up toward his forehead and kept them there. It caused the grass for leagues in every direction to bow down away from it, and knocked the muscular black cat right off its feet as easily as if it were a house kitten. Rooted as they were in the ground from which they sprang, the very rocks of the kopje trembled and threatened to blow free, and the sky was instantly cleared of birds and clouds for a hundred miles around.

Fortuitously trapped within the rock-walled alcove like a bee in its hive, Simna found himself pinned flat back against the rocks, his arms spread out to either side of him, and knew that he was experiencing only the feeblest of side effects from the wind his friend had called forth. Knew because the strength of that wind, its full force and energy, was directed straight out from the sword, directly at the inimical advancing storm.

It was an unnatural wind not only in its strength. It brought with it an intense biting cold that threatened to freeze his skin as solid as a shallow lake in the taiga, and an odor—an odor of alien distances that clotted in his nostrils and threatened to blunt his sense of smell permanently.

Crackling with energies exotic and inexplicable, the wind from between the stars struck the tornado foursquare in the center of its boiling column—and ripped it apart. Overwhelmed by forces beyond imagining, from beyond the Earth, brought forth through the medium of a sword forged from metal that itself had been subject to the whims of the inter-galactic winds, the mere column of air could not stand.

With a last outraged howl it came asunder, fell to pieces, and col-lapsed in upon itself. The great pillar of conflicted energy blew apart, hurling its internal collection of dead fish and broken branches and river beach sand and the limbs of the unfortunate dead flying in all directions. As the radiance from the sword faded and the unearthly wind it had called up died with it, Simna was released from his imprisonment and allowed to slump to his knees. Something smacked against the stone where his head had been pinned only moments before, and he turned to see the upper half of a carp lying on the rocks where it had fallen.

The boiling clouds from which the tornado had derived its strength shattered silently, their constituent parts dissipating into the resultant blue sky. In a little while all was as calm and peaceful as it had been before the storm's arrival. Lizards emerged from their dens in the rocks, small dragons took wing and resumed their singing in concert with the birds, and vultures appeared as if from nowhere to feast on the widely strewn, discarded contents of the tornado's belly.

Taking a deep breath of uncommitted air, Ehomba slipped the sky-metal sword back into the scabbard lying flat against his back and turned to reflect on the cause of all the commotion. The huge black cat was sitting on its haunches in the grass, which was only now beginning to spring back to the vertical from the effects of the deviant wind. Licking its left paw with a tongue thicker than the herdsman's foot, it was groom-ing itself silently, working its way from nose back to mane.

It did not let Ehomba's approach interrupt its labors. "You saved me."

"You speak well in a tongue not widespread among your kind."

"Humans presume to know too much about cats." A paw that could easily have taken the herdsman's head off with one swift stroke daintily combed through the long black ruff that formed the fluffy mane. Claws like daggers isolated individual hairs.

"That is certainly true. I am Etjole Ehomba, of the Naumkib." When silence ensued, he added as he leaned on his spear, "What am I to call you?"

"Gone, as soon as I can get myself cleaned up." The stroking paw paused and piercing yellow eyes met the herdsman's. "I am a litah."

"A litah," Ehomba echoed. "A small name for so big a brute."

"It is not a name." The cat was mildly annoyed. "It is what I am. My father was a lion, my mother a cheetah."

"Ah. That would explain your lines, and your legs."

Brows drew together like black ropes thick as hawsers. "What's wrong with my legs?"

"Nothing, not a thing," Ehomba explained hastily. "It is just that it is unusual to see such a combination of speed and strength in one animal."

"A lot of good it did me." Grumbling and rumbling, the litah set to work chewing on his hindquarters.

"What did you expect?" Out of the corner of an eye, Ehomba saw Simna ibn Sind approaching, slowly and cautiously. "For the wind to play fair?"

The litah turned back to him, his tongue scouring around his snout. "Animals as well as humans always expect too much of Nature. I was truthful, but tactless. I admit I did not think the wind would take it so much to heart, if heart it can be said to have had." Bright eyes glanced heavenward, searching the sky behind Ehomba. "You are a sorcerer."

"See? See?" Coming up alongside the herdsman, Simna chimed in his agreement with the cat's assertion. "I'm not the only one."

Ehomba sighed tiredly. "I am not a sorcerer," he told the litah. "I am only a herdsman from the south, bound by an obligation set upon me by a dying stranger to travel to the north and then to the west in hopes of helping a woman I do not know."

The litah grunted. "Then you are right. You are no sorcerer. Any wizard, human or animal, would have better sense."

Simna drew himself up proudly next to his friend. "He won't admit to it, but he's really after treasure. A great treasure, buried somewhere in the lands across the western ocean." Beside him, Ehomba was shaking his head sadly.

"I have no use for treasure," the litah growled softly. "I need water, and sex, and a place to sleep. And meat." With this last, he eyed Simna thoughtfully.

"Now wait a minute, whatever your name is." Putting his hand on the hilt of his sword, Simna took a step backward. In addition to putting a little more distance between himself and the cat, this also had the effect of placing him slightly behind the herdsman. "My friend here just saved your life."

"Yes, curse it all." Idly, the cat inspected the claws of his right foot, holding them up to his face as he studied the spaces between for thorns or bits of stone. "Since humans cannot talk without having names to address, and since you already know me as a litah, I suppose you may as well call me Ahlitah as anything."

"Very well—Ahlitah." Ehomba eyed the great black feline uncertainly. "But why 'curse it all'? Most creatures express gratitude and not irritation when someone saves their life."

The heavy paw descended and the brute rolled over onto his back, rubbing himself against the grass and the ground with his paws flopping loose in the air. A wary Simna was not yet reassured, and continued to keep his distance despite the kittenish display.

"I suppose it's not in my nature. Therefore I am not especially grateful. I am, however and unfortunately, indebted. This is a legacy that both my lines are heir to, and I am sadly no different." Concluding its scratching, the cat twisted with unnatural quickness back onto its feet and began to pad toward Ehomba. The swordsman held his ground, as did Simna—behind him.

"Easy now," the swordsman whispered. "This Ahlitah's idea of gratitude may be different from our own."

"I do not think so." The herdsman waited, hand on spear, its butt end still resting unthreateningly on the ground.

The great cat finally halted, its face less than inches away from Ehomba's own. Its jaws parted slightly, revealing major canines more than half a foot long. From between them emerged a giant pink tongue that proceeded to slather the herdsman's face in drool from chin to hairline. The tall southerner gritted his teeth and bore the infliction. The sensation was akin to having one's face rubbed hard in the sand.

Taking a step backward, Ahlitah dropped to one knee and bowed his massive, maned head. "For saving my life—even though I didn't ask you to interfere—I swear allegiance and fealty to you, Etjole Ehomba, until such time as you have successfully concluded your journey, or the one or the both of us die. This I vow on the lineage of my father and of my mother."

"Oh now, that's not necessary," the herdsman responded. From behind, Simna nudged him in the ribs.

"Are you crazy?" The swordsman had to stand on tiptoes to place his lips close enough to whisper into his companion's ear. "He's offering his help, Etjole! Willingly! When looking for treasure, it's always best to have as many allies as possible."

"It is not willingly, Simna. He is doing so out of a sense of enforced obligation."

"That's right," concurred the cat, who easily overheard every whispered word.

Simna stepped back. "And what's so wrong about that? Seems to me I know someone else who's doing something against his will in order to carry out an unsought-after obligation."

Ehomba's brows rose slightly as he regarded his friend. "Contrary to what many people believe, too much common sense can be bad for a man."

"Hoy?" Simna grinned challengingly. "For me—or for you?"

The herdsman returned his attention to the watching four-legged blackness. "I do not like the idea of having in a moment of danger to rely on another who accompanies me unwillingly."

Yellow-bright eyes flared and enormous teeth made their second appearance in the form of an exquisitely volcanic snarl. "Do you doubt the steadfastness of my vow?"

"Oh no, no, we would never do that!" An anxious Simna forcefully jogged his friend's arm. "Would we, Etjole?"

"What? Oh, sorry—I was thinking. No, I suppose you should be taken at your word."

Teeth disappeared behind thick folds of lip. "How very magnanimous of you," was the acerbic response.

"But this is not necessary. I did not help you with the intention of indenturing you to me. Maybe it would be best if you simply returned to your home."

The litah began to pace back and forth, looking for all the world like an ordinary agitated house cat made suddenly gigantic. "First you doubt my word, now you scorn my help."

Ehomba did his best to appear reassuring without sounding condescending. "I speak to you out of neither doubt nor scorn. I am simply saying that your assistance is not required."

"But it is, it is!" Throwing back his head, Ahlitah let out a long, mournful howl that was a mixture of melancholy and roar. It was at once impressive, terrifying, and piteous. When he had finished, like a tenor at the end of a particularly poignant aria, he fixed his gaze once more on the empathetic herdsman.

"Don't you see? Until I have repaid you in kind for what you did for me—without your being asked, I might add—I can't proceed with a normal life. I couldn't go on with that burden resting heavy on my heart and thick in my mind. However long it takes, whatever the difficulty involved, I have to discharge it before I can again be at rest."

"For Gudru's sake, Etjole," Simna whispered urgently, "don't argue with him. Accept the offer."

"Your annoying friend is right." Sitting back, Ahlitah scratched vigorously at his belly with a hind foot. "If you send me away, you not only shame me, you spray on my soul. You say to me that my offer of all I can give is worth nothing." Scratching ceased as the great cat resumed its pacing. "You reduce me to the level of a jackal, or worse, a hyena."

"Oh all right!" Fed up, Ehomba waved a diffident hand in the litah's direction and turned away. "You can come along."

The cat dipped its head, its long black mane falling forward like a courtier's cape. "I cower before your unfettered magnanimity, oh maestro of the condescending arts."

"If you want to do something for me," the herdsman responded, "you might lose some of that feline sarcasm."

"Sorry. It's in a cat's nature to be sarcastic."

"I know, but yours seems in proportion to your size. Over time, I see it growing tiresome."

Teeth flashed in a grinning display. "I will try to restrain my natural instincts. Given present company, that may prove difficult."

"Do your best," Ehomba instructed his new companion curtly. He looked back at the kopje. "It has been a wearying day."

Simna let out a muted guffaw. "That's me bruther—master of understatement."

"We might as well rest here until tomorrow."

"Agreed." The litah turned and began to walk away.

Simna called after him. "Hoy, where are you going? I thought you were with us?"

The cat looked back over its maned shoulder. "I am going to find something to eat, if that's all right with you. Maybe a human can live on anticipation and fine words, but I cannot."

"Don't get testy with me, kitty," Simna shot back. "I'm as hungry as you are."

"As am I," added Ehomba. "If you truly want to be of assistance, you could bring back enough for us all to eat. We will make a fire."

"I'll enjoy the warmth," Ahlitah growled back. "We cats quite like fire. We're just not adept at fabricating it." He sniffed derisively. "You, of course, will want to use it to burn perfectly good meat." Turning, he surveyed the veldt. "I will be late, but I will be back."

"Why so?" Simna's expression became a smirk. "Are you like the male lions that let the females do all the hunting?"

Sliding smoothly through the grass, the litah did not deign to look back. "Idiot. Male lions hunt often and perfectly well—at night. During the day our dark manes are highly visible through the yellowed or green grass and give our presence away. That is why the females run the day hunt. For the same reason, I am a better night hunter than any lion, and can bring down larger prey than any cheetah."

Ehomba moved to stand behind his friend. "Do not taunt him. He is unhappy at having to accompany us. If a man has one bad moment and strikes out at you, your face may suffer a bruise." He nodded out into the veldt. "If *that* one has a bad moment, he is liable to take off your head."

"Aw, he's all right," Simna insisted. "He's obligated to you, and I'm your friend, so he won't let harm come to me."

"Probably not as long as I am alive, no. So it is in your best interest to see that I stay healthy."

"Hoy, that's always been in my interest." Simna grinned broadly as together they turned toward the kopje. "If anything were to happen to you, I'd never find the treasure. Not," he added in haste, "that I'd want anything to happen to you even if there was no treasure."

"There is no treasure," Ehomba replied forthrightly.

The swordsman clapped the tall herdsman roughly on the shoulder. "Yeah, right—what a kidder! I'll bet among your fellow villagers you're considered a real comedian."

"Actually, I believe they think I am rather dry and somber." He smiled hesitantly. "Of course, I do not think so, nor do my children or my wife." His expression twitched momentarily. "At least, I do not think she does."

XVII

There was enough dry wood to make a fire on the kopje, but not a large one. Raised above the surrounding grass on the rocks, the blaze would still be visible for quite a distance. Even so, Simna especially was beginning to doubt the truth of the litah's words as evening gave way to night and there was still no sign of their erstwhile ally.

"Maybe he decided he wasn't so indebted after all." Using a long stick, the swordsman stirred the vivacious embers that winked at the bottom of the fire. "Maybe he met an obliging pride, or a lone female in heat, and decided some things were more important than tagging along with us."

"I do not think he would leave like this. He was very adamant." But as the night wore on and the moon came to dominate the speckled bowl of the sky, Ehomba was less certain.

"He's a cat. A prodigiously talkative one, 'tis true, but a cat still. Cats set their own agendas, and big or small, those rarely include tending to the needs of humans."

"Listen." Ehomba froze suddenly, his face highlighted by the glow of the campfire.

Simna was immediately on guard. "What is it? Not more wind, I hope." Visions of angry wild relatives of the demolished tornado appearing in the middle of the night to wreak vengeance on those who had murdered their brother swept through his thoughts.

"No, not wind. Something moving through the grass."

Ahlitah was almost upon them before the flickering blaze cast enough light to reveal even the outline of his massive form. In his jaws he carried the limp, bent body of a wandala, a medium-sized antelope whose horns had spread wide and thinned out until they formed a great membranous sail attached to the skull. Using this the animal could tuck its short, fragile legs beneath it and in a good breeze literally fly across the tops of the veldt grass, flattening its body to assume a more aerodynamic shape.

The successful hunter unceremoniously dumped his offering onto the rocks alongside the fire. "Here is meat. You may have the flanks. I know humans are fickle about what portion of animal they eat."

"Hoy, not me." Drawing his knife, an eager Simna set to work on the carcass. "When I'm hungry I'll eat just about anything."

"Yes, I see that. But then, one would never mistake you for the fastidious type." Settling himself down on the other side of the body, Ahlitah began to eat, ripping dainty chunks out of the hindquarters of the dead wandala.

"You were late," Ehomba declared accusingly. "We had begun to wonder."

Blood stained Ahlitah's muzzle as he looked up from the other side of the cadaver. "I had to wait until it was dark enough for the night to hide me. When I stand or stalk, I am taller than any other cat. Better a certain kill that takes time than a quick one that fails." Lowering his head, he thrust his open jaws into the wandala's soft belly. The ragged percussion of bones breaking drifted out across the veldt.

"This situation makes for an interesting puzzle to contemplate," the litah announced later, when cat and men had finished eating. "Here we sit, as companions if not as friends. I kill for you. But if we were in your homeland to the south, I would be hunting your herds and flocks, and you would be trying to keep me from doing so. Trying to kill me, if it became necessary."

"That is true." Ehomba watched Simna slice steaks from the side of the dead antelope, the easier to pack them for carrying. "Oftentimes it is not personal preference that makes friends and enemies, but circumstance." This time it was he who mustered the feral gaze, peering deeply into the eyes of the litah. "It is a good thing I trust your word, for fear you might try to eat me in my sleep."

"And I yours," Ahlitah replied, "or I might worry about you acting like just another man, ready to leap to murder at the first opportunity and skin me for my valuable coat. How fortunate that we have such trust in one another."

"Yes. How fortunate."

Just because Ehomba could survive comfortably on little food did not mean that he was averse to a filling meal. Knowing that the meat would not keep for very long and that they had no time to spare to jerk it, they ate their fill of delicious wandala. Nothing was left to waste, not even the marrow of its bones, as Ahlitah possessed an appetite to match his size. When the unlikely trio finally drifted off to sleep, more than content, it was with an ease in mind and body none of them had known for days.

Except Simna. Troubling thoughts woke him several hours before dawn. Nearby, Ehomba lay on his side beneath his blanket, his back to the swordsman. On the other side of the vanquished campfire Ahlitah snored softly, his shadowed bulk like a storm cloud that had, silent and unnoticed, settled to earth for a moment's unnatural rest.

He had seen Ehomba utilize the power of the sword smelted from sky metal, but until the fight with the spinning storm cloud he had never imagined the extent of that power. What not could a man do who possessed such a weapon? The herdsman had declared that, just as its substance was not of this world, so it had powers that were not of this world. Certainly whoever wielded it could defeat more than clouds and Corruption.

Sitting up, he gazed out across the veldt. Distant moans and occasional sharp barks broke the stillness of the night, but nothing troubled them on their isolated stony outcropping. Ehomba had yet to vary from his path northward. He, Simna, had come from the east. What if he were to return that way? Would the herdsman try to come after him, or would he accept what had transpired, absorb his loss, and maintain his course? How valuable was the sword to him, how important to his journey? A wondrous weapon it was, true, but it was only a sword. Simna would not be leaving him weaponless. Ehomba would still have his spear, and his other sword, not to mention the protective, intimidating company of the litah.

Visions of conquest swam through the swordsman's tormented thoughts. He had never been what one would call a greedy man. Acquisitive, yes, but hardly rapacious. Overlordship of a small city would be sufficient to satisfy his desires. With the sky-metal sword in hand, what minor nobleman or princeling would dare stand before him? Again he gazed at his lanky companion's sleeping form. Ehomba was a generous soul. Surely he would not begrudge a good friend the loan of a wanted weapon.

By Giopra, that was it! Not a theft, but a loan, a borrowing! A temporary adoption of a singular arsenal, to be returned as soon as vital objectives had been achieved. As he slipped silently from beneath his blanket, he reflected on the worthiness of rationalization. The herdsman would understand. Humble and unsophisticated he might be, but he was compassionate as well. While he might not feel the need to take control of a town or trade route himself, surely he could empathize with the preoccupation of another to do so.

Advancing more quietly on hands and knees than a beetle on its six legs, he made his way over to where his friend slept. With his back to the humans, Ahlitah did not stir. The sky-metal sword lay alongside its tooth-lined bone companion and the strangely tipped spear, all three within easy reach of their owner in case of emergency.

Ever so gently, as though he were handling a king's newborn infant and heir, Simna slipped his right hand beneath the fur-covered, quaintly beaded scabbard. It was heavy, but not unmanageably so. At any moment he expected the herdsman to turn over, or rise up, and innocently ask what the swordsman was doing with his property. But Ehomba never stirred. He was worn out, Simna knew. Exhausted from his battle with the elements. Poor fellow, the best thing for him would be to forget all this nonsense and return home to his family and his cattle, his flocks and his friends. He might have the fortitude for this kind of journeying, but he most surely did not have the zeal.

If it induced him to turn back, Simna decided virtuously, then by borrowing the sky sword he was actually doing his friend a favor. Probably saving his life, yes. Certainly the herdsman's family would thank him for it.

Returning to his blanket with the sword gripped firmly in one hand, he prepared to gather up his kit. The moon would guide him eastward, and by the time Ehomba woke, Simna would be well out of sight and on his way. He could move fast when the occasion demanded.

But before departing, best to make sure he could make use of the weapon. Though Ehomba continued to insist he was no magician, Simna would look the prize fool going into battle someday with a sword he could not draw. If he could but remove it from its scabbard, that would be enough to reassure him that its owner had cast no locking spell on it.

Gripping the handle, he gave an experimental tug. The polished metal was slick against his palm, and the oddly etched blade slid effortlessly upward. The smooth, gray edge with its peculiar right-angle markings gleamed dully in the moonlight. No problem there, he saw appreciatively.

One series of cross-hatched markings in particular caught his eye. They looked a little deeper than the others, though by no means deep enough to threaten the integrity of the blade. They drew his attention to smaller markings still, and others still smaller, until he felt that he was looking into the very elementals of the metal itself.

Suddenly the parallel scourings flew apart. It was as if he had been staring at a painting, a painting rendered entirely in gray, only to be drawn in, sucked down, cast helplessly into a gray metallic pit. Now the picture's frame was flying to pieces all around him, and he found himself falling, kicking and flailing helplessly at ashen emptiness adrift in a leaden vacuum.

Fiery globes of incandescent energy rushed past him, singeing his skin and clothing. Around these colossal spheres of coruscating hellfire spun worlds whole and entire, swarming with life-forms more fantastic than the word spinnings of any storyteller. Immense, billowing clouds of luminous vapor filled the spaces between the fire globes and their attendant worlds, along with tailed demons and rocks that seemed to have been launched from God's own slingshot.

And in the middle of it all was he, tumbling and kicking, screaming at the top of his lungs even though there was no one to hear him. Not that it mattered, because despite his frantic efforts, no sound emerged from his throat. Perhaps because there was no air in his lungs with which to make sounds. As this new horror struck home he began to choke, gasping for the air that was not there. His hands went to his throat, as if by squeezing they could somehow force nonexistent air into his straining, heaving chest.

Something pushed at him, rocking him even as he fell. Invisible hands—or claws, or tentacles—were wrenching at his body, threatening to divert him from his endless eternal fall to a place where unfathomable horrors could be wreaked on his impotent person. Screaming, crying, he kicked at the unseen presence and flailed at it with his hands. Though he could see nothing, his extremities made contact with something.

He was struck across the face, the blow stinging but not hard enough to draw blood. Dimly, distantly, he felt he heard a voice calling his name. Gojura, the Lord of Unknown Places, or some other deity? He was in no shape to meet his sister's daughter, much less a god or two. Not that he had any choice. Beyond caring, long past mere fear, he opened his eyes.

Ehomba was leaning over him, looking down into his friend's tormented face. The herdsman's expression was full of sympathy and concern, notwithstanding the fact that he held one hand upraised and poised to strike downward.

A gruff, inhumanly deep voice somewhere off to his left growled, "There—he's around. No need to hit him again. Unless you're simply in the mood." The speaker sounded sleepy, and bored.

Ehomba lowered his open palm and sat back. Feeling of his body to assure himself it was still intact, the swordsman sat up. Around him were darkness, night sounds, veldt smells, and wistful moonlight. The comforting solidity of the kopje's naked rock chilled his backside.

Relieved, the herdsman leaned away from his friend. "You were having a bad dream, Simna. Bad enough to wake us. You were kicking and screaming in your sleep as if something was after you. What was it?"

"I . . ." The swordsman put a hand to his perspiring forehead. "I'm not sure I remember, exactly. I was falling. Not into something, but through it."

"That is interesting." Yawning, Ehomba slipped back beneath his own blanket. "What were you falling through? The sky, or maybe the sea?"

"No—not either of those." Suddenly Simna tilted back his head, craning his neck as he stared open-mouthed at the night sky. "I was falling through everything. I—saw everything. Well, maybe not everything, but an awful lot of it." He lowered his head. "As much of everything as I think I ever want to see."

Lying prone beneath his blanket and tucking it up around him, Ehomba nodded drowsily. "I can understand that. To see everything would be too much for any man. It is hard enough to look at and make sense simply of that which is around us. Myself, I am content simply to see something. I have no wish to see everything."

Simna nodded without replying as he slowly settled himself back beneath his own blanket. As he did so, his gaze inevitably returned to the dome of the night sky and the tiny points of light that twinkled in the darkness. He knew what they were now, and shuddered. Few men are capable of dealing with the world around them, he mused, so how could anyone be expected to handle the immensity of everything else? Certainly it was too much for him.

It had been a terrible dream, but an efficacious one. From now on he would leave strange weapons alone, no matter how much they might tempt him. Even if they belonged to someone who was simply a fortunate herdsman and not a sorcerer. He was lucky he had only dreamed about stealing—um, borrowing—the sky-metal sword. Had he tried to take possession of it, the harrowing visions he had experienced while sleeping might have become real.

Turning away from the no longer amicable sky, he lay on his side gazing in Ehomba's direction. Tomorrow they would resume their northward trek. With luck they would come to a river that could carry them to the sea, where they would find a town at which seaworthy vessels called. They would book passage westward, to the fabled lands of Ehl-Larimar, where dwelled Hymneth the Possessed, and the treasure he knew in his soul must be at the heart of the poor herdsman's quest.

As he lay still, his head resting in the cup of his right hand, he saw that Ehomba's weapons were no longer neatly aligned on the smooth rock above his head, but had been put askew. Perhaps the herdsman had disturbed them in his haste to awaken and free his friend from the anguish of his nightmare.

Ignoring the feathered spear and the tooth-edged sword, he found his gaze drawn inexorably to the scabbarded blade of wondrous sky metal. It seemed to be partly drawn, just enough to expose an inch or so of the metal itself. The Widmanstätten lines etched into its side caught the moonlight and twisted it the way a child would knot a rope. A nimble pain shot through part of his forehead as he felt his left eye poked with too-sharp perception.

He rolled over quickly and closed his eyes tight, resolving to look upon nothing save the inside of his eyelids until dawn renewed both the day and his trust in the authenticity of existence. Some dreams drifted too close to reality, and some realities too close to dream. In the company of a perambulating curiosity like Etjole Ehomba, he decided, it was important for one to concentrate with unwavering determination on the path between the two, lest one's world suddenly slip out of focus.

Opening his eye just a crack, it was filled with a flash of light. For a dreadful moment he was afraid it was one of those hellish globes of fire he had seen floating in emptiness. Almost as quickly as he started to panic, he relaxed. It was only the glint of moonlight off a chip of quartz embedded in the rock close to his face.

He closed his eyes again, and this time did not open them until the sun began to sneak its first rays over the eastern horizon.

XVlll

Morning arrived not with the ease of awakening with which Ehomba was most comfortable, but with a thunderous declaration of life that had both him and Simna ibn Sind erupting from their place of sleeping. Initially panicked, the men relaxed when they saw it was only Ahlitah, greeting the arrival of the sun with an ardent bellowing that all but shook the rocks beneath them as his robust roars detonated against the vast expanse of the veldt.

"Must you play the lord of all roosters?" Exhaling sharply, Simna sat back down on the smooth, cool granite.

Standing with his forefeet on the highest point of the kopje, the litah turned his great black-maned head to glower down at him. "I am king of this land, and must so remind my subjects every morning."

"Well, we're not your subjects," Simna snapped, "and we'd appreciate it if while we're traveling in each other's company you maybe just waved to your subjects every once in a while."

"Yes." Ehomba was already packing to depart. "I am sure the mere creatures who inhabit the veldt already recognize your suzerainty, and that it is not necessary for you to remind them of it quite so loudly every morning."

"Oh, I do beg your pardon. From now on I'll do it like this." Looking away and throwing back his head, the massive jaws parted and Ahlitah let loose as resounding a meow as Ehomba had ever heard.

"Much better," Simna commented tartly.

"I am so pleased that you approve." Tomorrow morning, the great cat vowed, it would roar again as loudly as ever—making it a point to place his lips directly opposite one of the stocky swordsman's ears as he did so.

But he would not argue the point now, when they were about to set off for a portion of the veldt that was new even to him. While he was embarrassed at having to keep company with humans, a part of him was anticipating the forthcoming opening up of new territory. He looked forward to meeting the inhabitants, and to eating some of them.

As they descended the kopje, which had proved to be an agreeable refuge in the midst of the all but featureless veldt, Ehomba found himself again questioning the suitability of his companions. Given alternatives, he would have chosen otherwise. One was inhuman, tremendously strong, but reluctant to the point of apathy. He wondered how he was going to be able to rely on someone to watch his back who would do so only out of a sense of enforced obligation.

His other associate was fearless, wily, experienced, and tough, but interested in only one thing: the domineering illusion of false wealth. Again, not the truest motivation for standing behind someone in need. Still, he supposed it was better to have them at his side than not, to have company and companionship in strange country than to be traveling alone. If nothing else, it gave potential enemies someone else to shoot at. For all his unrelenting babble about treasure, Simna ibn Sind would prove useful if he took but one arrow meant for Ehomba. And Ahlitah the same if he did nothing at all but stand still and frighten off a single stealthy assassin.

Yes, it was better to travel in the company of an entourage, however small and however uncommitted. They would be of no use against someone as overawing and powerful as this Hymneth individual, but if they could simply help him to achieve that final confrontation then all would be worthwhile. Until that ultimate moment he would suffer their company, dealing with Simna's endless harping about treasure and Ahlitah's incessant muttering.

Another day's walking brought them within sight of a line of trees. This was greatly to Simna's liking since, as he put it, he had seen enough grass and weeds to last a million cattle the rest of their lives, and him not able to eat a blade of it. Ahlitah was more circumspect.

"Trees make good places to hide behind."

"Maybe in the veldt, where trees are few and far between." Simna was leading the way. "In lands where they're the rule rather than the exception, they're no more dangerous than taller grass."

But the trees did hide something: a river; broad, murky, and of indeterminate depth. Ehomba resigned himself to another swim.

"Don't be in such a hurry." Simna was leaning over the bank. It was a short drop, less than a foot, to the water. There was no shoreline, no beach of sand or mud. Short, stubby grass grew right up to the water's edge. "It *looks* shallow."

"Fine," commented Ahlitah. "You try it first."

The swordsman nodded at the big cat. "Your legs are longer than mine, but if you're that afraid of water, then I'll break trail for you."

Making sure that his pack was secure against his back, Simna stepped off the bank. The water barely reached to the tops of his ankles. Turning, he spread his arms and smiled.

"See? No swimming, Etjole. The bottom has the feel of fine gravel. We can walk across." He kicked water in the direction of his friends, causing Ahlitah to blink and turn his head away momentarily.

Snarling softly, the great black shape hopped gingerly into the moderate current. Water ridged up slightly against his ankles before continuing to flow westward around them. A disappointed Ehomba followed. Had the river been deeper, he would have entertained notions of building a raft and following it west to the ocean. He missed the sea very much. Surely they were far enough north now to resume walking up the coast. But any raft made large and strong enough to carry them for any length of time risked running aground every few yards in such shallows. Northward they would have to continue to trek.

He fingered the sack of pebbles that rested heavily in the pocket of his kilt, remembering the beaches back home, the way the cold water foamed and danced whitely over sand and rock. As always, in helping to bringing back memories, the sheer tactility of the rough gravel in the little cotton bag helped to soothe his thoughts and ease his mind.

Once, something that was softer than stone but harder than water bumped into his right foot. Glancing down, he made out an indistinct, elongated shape hurriedly darting upriver away from him. A freshwater eel, perhaps, startled by the presence of something long, straight, and moving through the water that was not a drifting tree branch. Some eels could give a man quite a nip. Thereafter he paid more attention to the water swirling around his ankles.

Halfway across, the strangest thing began to happen. It could not be explained any more than it could be ignored. While the river itself grew no deeper, patches and pockets and globules of water began to come into sight above the actual surface. At first they were no bigger than a man's fist, but soon much larger blobs began to appear. The largest were the size of small ponds.

At their highest, these individual drifting sacs of liquid were as tall as the trees that were now visible on the opposite bank. Some had transparent undersides while others were dark with accumulated muck and soil. Water lilies, reeds, and small bushes grew from these individual pockets of aerial swamp. Some plants put down roots that traveled through the intervening air to suck nourishment from splotches of water floating in midair beneath them. Wind roiled their surfaces just as it did that of the shallow river beneath.

Sometimes two wandering patches of water would flow slowly into one another and merge to form a larger pond shape. Elsewhere, ample globules would slowly break apart to form two or more separate aqueous bodies. It was quite the most extraordinary landscape any of the companions had ever encountered.

Ducking beneath a floating raft of pond weed as big as a boat, Simna jabbed a finger upward and pulled it free. The bottom-side surface tension stuck to his finger for an unnaturally long moment, clinging to the skin more like clear glue than water. Then the contents of the floating pond began to drain out through the finger-sized gap, as if the swordsman had punched a hole in a transparent, thin-skinned balloon.

Fascinated, they watched as water grass, tadpoles, struggling fry, black-shelled snails, and other inhabitants of the airborne pond spilled out into the river below. After a minute or two of free flow, the hole was blocked and sealed by a clump of soil that formed the root-ball of a water hyacinth. Amazed and delighted by the aqueous phenomenon, they resumed their crossing.

The river never bulked up against a far bank so much as it spread out to form a vast, shallow lake whose extent they probably could not have determined even if the view northward had not been blocked by more and more of the free-floating aerial ponds and lakes. Not only were these becoming larger, but they were also growing considerably more numerous, as if drawing strength and sustenance from the boundless, shallow inland sea beneath.

Of more immediate concern, the travelers began to encounter places where the underlying river-lake itself deepened. It was difficult enough to keep moving forward while avoiding masses of drifting water that rose higher than a man's head. Doing so while stumbling into hidden cavities that brought the water up to one's neck was not only harder, but frightening. In such an environment it was technically impossible to keep one's head above water, because individual blobs of water were constantly drifting past at levels higher than one's hairline.

Within an hour they were having to duck beneath a small airborne lake that completely blocked their path in all directions. Hunched over, Ehomba was more wary of the great mass of water that hung just above his head than he was of the foot or so they were sloshing through.

"No experiments here," he warned Simna. "Do not stick your finger into the water hovering above us. If it were to break and all come down in a rush, we would surely drown."

"Don't worry." The swordsman was walking next to him, bent over and eyeing the underside of the great shimmering mass uneasily.

They passed out from beneath it without incident, but were then forced to advance single file down a narrow corridor between two twenty-foot-tall bodies of free-floating swamp. The dark green walls that hemmed them in on either side were in constant, if lugubrious, motion, bulging and rippling with a great volume of water constrained only by thin, transparent walls of unusual surface tension.

"Guela!" Simna, who had momentarily taken the lead, suddenly let out an exclamation of surprise and stopped short. Behind him, Ahlitah let out a warning snarl. A concerned Ehomba stopped short of the cat's flicking tail.

"What is it, what's wrong?"

"Look to your left." The great cat was pressed up against the floating swamp-sac on their right, his eyes focused in the indicated direction.

The crocodile that swam slowly past at eye level with the travelers was at least twenty feet long and weighed close to two tons. Its huge armored tail swayed slowly from side to side, propelling it languidly through the murky water. As it swam past, one eye swiveled to meet Ehomba's. The slitted yellow orb tracked the man standing next to the side of the aerial pond for a long moment. And then the hulking reptile was gone, turning back into the distant depths of the floating lake it called home.

"I don't understand." Simna's tone betrayed his lingering tension. "Why didn't it have a go at us? It could have broken out easily."

Ehomba considered. "We are making our way through air, not water. Perhaps it did not see us as part of its environment. Who can imagine how the creatures that have learned to live in such a remarkable place have developed? Possibly they consider each individual bubble of water, whether as big as a lake or small enough to fit in a bucket, an isolated world whose boundaries are not to be tampered with." Looking away from the dark green water that hemmed them in on either side, he tilted back his head to regard the narrow band of blue sky that still held sway directly overhead.

"Even our world could be like that. Stick a finger up high enough, hard enough, and you might puncture the lining of the sky and let all the air escape out into nothingness."

"That's ridiculous!" With a snort of derision, Simna turned away and resumed walking. But for a while thereafter, every so often he would sneak a glance at the clouds and resolve to suppress any impulse to make sudden, sharp gestures upward.

They emerged safely from between the two large bodies of floating water only to find themselves surrounded by a dense population of smaller but still sizable globules. While some of these were clear and contained nothing larger than small cichlids and kindred swimmers, others were opaque with flourishing plant life, crustaceans, shellfish, and aquatic reptiles. Though still able to advance, their progress was slowed by having to walk around or duck under the proliferating floating bubbles.

Once they had to wade right through a drifting airborne pond too wide to walk around. As they did so, they experienced the most peculiar sensation of being soaked from sole to ankle, then dry up to their waists, and then wet again up to their necks. By lowering their packs so that they temporarily rode not on their shoulders but on their hips, Ehomba and Simna were able to keep their gear dry despite the double immersion.

All day they trekked through the unprecedented landscape, ducking beneath, walking around, or hopping over individual intervening patches of water, until the sun, a welcome harbinger of the normal world, began to set. Certainly it was a most curious place to make a camp.

Simply choosing a suitable site presented unique problems of its own. Standing in six inches of water with not a suggestion of dry land visible in any direction, the prospect of a fire was out of the question, much less any thoughts of lying down and keeping dry. Big as he was, Ahlitah would have no trouble keeping his head above water during the night, but it was not inconceivable that Ehomba or Simna could roll over in their sleep and drown. Furthermore, soaking themselves to the skin for an entire night was not the best way of ensuring continued good health.

"Gembota, but this is awkward." Muttering to himself, Simna sloshed through the tepid shallows in search of someplace to drop his pack, and found none. "What are we going to do until morning?" He eyed the great cat's broad back speculatively. Correctly interpreting the swordsman's appraising stare, Ahlitah lifted a massive paw and shook his head.

"Put it out of your mind, little man. No one sleeps on me. Up against me, perhaps, for mutual warmth, but only if I am in a sociable mood. But on my back, never. It would be demeaning."

"We have to do something." A peevish Simna kicked at the omnipresent water. "We can't lie down and safely go to sleep in this. Never mind that we'd wake up sodden through and at risk of catching a fever. Isn't that right, Etjole? Etjole?"

Ehomba's attention was concentrated elsewhere. Instead of looking at their feet for a campsite, he was looking up. Specifically, at a small irregularly shaped hovering pond, the center of which boasted a small sandy island from which grew a trio of juvenile casuarina pines.

"Up there?" Simna sloshed over to stand alongside his tall friend. "But the island is floating. Put the three of us on it and our weight will make it sink to the bottom of this watery mass."

"I do not think so." Ehomba continued to study the drifting aerial pond. "If weight was going to do that, I would think the heaviness of the soil itself would be enough to sink it. And there are the trees it supports—not giants, it is true, but not saplings, either. I think we should give it a try.

"Besides, what is the worst thing that could happen? The island will sink beneath us and we will fall into the pond."

"And drown," Simna added. "That's a little too much of a 'worst thing' for me."

"We would not drown," Ehomba assured him. "Even if we sank to the bottom, all you would have to do is rip a hole in the pond's underside and all the water would come spilling out, along with the fish, and frogs, and plants, and us."

Simna was still dubious. "It doesn't make any sense. If I can poke a hole in the wall of one of these deluded bodies of water, why don't fish and salamanders and snails and tree roots do it all the time?"

"An adaptation to where they are living, I imagine." The herdsman pursed his lips as he regarded his friend. "We hike through a land where the lakes and ponds and puddles all float about away up in the air, where you can walk around and beneath them, and you wonder about such matters?"

Though still reluctant, Simna was willing to be convinced. Besides, the only alternative promised a night of little sleep and unrelenting wet. He glanced over at the patient Ahlitah.

"How about it, bruther cat? What do you think?"

Their feline companion shrugged, his ebony mane twitching as he did so. "Why put it to me? I am only a nomadic quadrupedal carnivore of commingled ancestry. Aren't humans the ones who are supposed to have the big brains? That's what you're always saying, anyway. Or are you experiencing some second thoughts about your own cerebral propaganda?"

A bemused Simna turned back to Ehomba. "Ask a simple question, get a biting discourse. All right, I guess it can't hurt to try. One way or the other, it looks like we're gonna get soaked. The question is, for how long?" He glanced upward. "It's getting dark, and I don't fancy trying to find a better spot in the middle of the night. Not in this muck."

"That is good." Turning, the herdsman positioned himself next to the transparent wall of the hovering pond. "Because you get to go in first."

"Me? Why me?" Simna hedged.

Looking back over his shoulder, Ehomba eyed his stocky friend considerately. "If you want me to go, you get to boost me up."

"No." The reluctant swordsman scrutinized the watery wall. "I'll go."

Scrambling up Ehomba's legs and back as the herdsman braced himself against the transparent wall of water, Simna was soon balancing on the herdsman's shoulders. Gripping the upper rim of the pond, he pushed down and up. The rubbery wall gave a little, sending small fish scurrying in the opposite direction and letting water spill through the depression created between Simna's downward pressing hands. Then the swordsman was up and over the rim, swimming for the central island while doing his best to keep his kit as dry as possible.

Together, man and litah watched as Simna hauled himself out on the island and stood up, shaking water from his limbs like a slow dog. Experimentally, he jumped up and down a couple of times.

"Well?" Ahlitah growled impatiently.

"The ground gives a little, like a wet mattress, but I don't think it's going to sink under us. Come on over." Turning, he carried his pack inland and set it down beneath one of the shady pine trees.

Ehomba turned to eye his remaining companion questioningly. Grumbling but complaisant, the cat advanced and placed itself next to the bottom of the watery mass.

"Tread easily, Etjole Ehomba. No man who was not a meal has ever done this before."

"I will step lightly," the herdsman assured him. So saying, he placed a foot on the litah's right thigh and stepped up onto his back. From there he was able to pull himself up and over the rim of the pond into the water.

It was a short, easy swim to the island, where Simna was trying to dry himself with some large leaves he had scavenged. Wading out of the water, Ehomba settled down nearby and began to fumble inside his own pack. A violent splash made him look up. Ahlitah had negotiated the intervening height in a single effortless leap and was paddling toward them, his magnificent head held as high above the water as he could manage.

"One thing's for sure." Removing his leather armor and undershirt,

Simna hung them over a casuarina branch to dry. "If we can get a fire started here, we can let it burn high all night without having to worry about it spreading. Hoy—have a care, there!"

He threw up his hands to shield himself and Ehomba turned away as Ahlitah shook vigorously, sending water flying from his fur. A marinated cat was a comical sight, Ehomba knew, even as he was careful to keep his expression perfectly neutral. He was not certain that Ahlitah's pithy sense of humor extended to amusement at his own loss of dignity.

As it turned out, they were able to start a fire, but only a small one. Still, the additional warmth was welcome more for its aid in drying out their clothes than for their bodies.

"Not that this is very useful." Simna was lightly toasting his underwear over the cheery blaze. Nearby, Ehomba was filleting the fish Ahlitah had scooped out of the pond with a couple of leisurely swipes of his huge paws. "We're only going to have to drench ourselves again tomorrow when it's time to leave and move on."

"Perhaps not." Ehomba, as he so often did, was looking not at the swordsman but past him. And as he so often did, Simna followed the direction of the tall herdsman's gaze and saw nothing.

"Why? Why not?" His expression brightened. "I know! You're finally going to do some real magic and float us out of here! Or call up a boat—no, that wouldn't work in water as shallow as that which covers the real ground below."

"I have told you," an exasperated Ehomba replied, "I cannot do magic."

"Yeah, right, sure." The swordsman winked at Ahlitah who, head resting on crossed forefeet, did not respond. "Then if not by magic, how are you going to keep us from having to get good and wet again?" He gestured at their surroundings. "Going to drain the pond with us in the middle of it? I'm not sure that'd be such a good idea. The wondrous envelope that holds this water aloft might collapse in upon us, wrapping us up like a holiday present and suffocating us in the bargain."

"I am not sure exactly what I am going to do. I was thinking of assaying some engaging conversation."

"Really?" The other man swept his right arm around in a broad arc to encompass every inch of their aqueous surroundings. "With whom? Fish?"

"Something like that." Turning away, the herdsman resumed wringing water from his kilt.

Simna grunted and looked over at the sleepy Ahlitah. "He's going to talk to fish. Me, I don't see the use of it."

"*Can* he talk to fish?" the cat asked curiously.

The swordsman stole a glance in his companion's direction. "I dunno. He's a funny sort, is Etjole. After we first hooked up together he told me a story about him spending time with some monkeys. I thought it was just that: a story. But the better I get to know him, the more I'm not sure."

"So you think you know him?" The litah's massive jaws gaped in an impressive yawn.

Simna shrugged confidently. "Sure I know him! He's a sorcerer, see? Only he won't admit to it. Hunting after a great lost treasure he is, and I aim to help him acquire it in return for a share. He'll probably cut you in on the haul, too."

"And what would I do with the bastard currency of human exchange? A warm place to sleep, plenty of game—preferably old and slow or young and stupid—and a pride of willing females one of whom is always in heat, and I would have all I could ask for. I am immune from and indifferent to the driving need that you humans suffer from to accumulate things. Spending so much time in accumulating, you forget to live." He yawned again. "Your friend, however, is a breed of human I have not met before."

"By Gwantha, he's a new breed of human to me as well," the swordsman confessed.

"Then who knows? Maybe he can talk to fish." A guttural cough emerged from the muscular throat as the big cat closed his eyes and rolled over onto his back, all four paws in the air. "Me, I would rather eat them than talk to them."

"Don't see what good it would do us anyway," Simna muttered uncertainly. "Even if he could arrange for us to ride, what fish would be big enough to carry you? And every time we reached the far side of one of these lunatic floating blobs of water we'd have to get off our fishy mounts, scramble over the side, climb up into another and find new fish in the new pond to carry us. Be quicker to walk—provided the water covering the real ground doesn't get any deeper." He concluded with a deep breath: "Well, best to leave it to Etjole. He's the brains here."

Eyes shut tight, the drowsing litah barely responded. "Among the humans, anyway."

XIX

They have been watching us for a long time. Ever since we crossed the river, I think."

"What?" Suddenly alarmed, Simna left off repacking his kit and looked around wildly.

Ahlitah lifted his head, nose in the air, nostrils working. "I see nothing. But I do smell something—unusual."

Without moving from where he was standing, the now wary swordsman turned a slow circle. Beyond the island in the floating pond and outside its transparent boundaries, hundreds of additional bodies of water drifted independent of one another, some the size of small lakes, others mere globules no bigger than a child's ball. Some squeezed together until their mysterious transparent envelopes merged to form a larger aqueous mass while others wrenched apart until they separated into two or more distinct hovering bodies. He tried to let his gaze touch every one of them, but nowhere did he see anything out of the ordinary.

"There's nothing out there," he declared conclusively. "Nothing but fish and frogs, newts and waterbirds."

"No, you are wrong." One hand shielding his eyes from the mist-shrouded sun, Ehomba was standing at the water's edge staring off to the east. "There is something else. Something greater."

"They're coming closer." Head back, nose in the air, Ahlitah was inhaling a scent still too subtle for human nostrils to detect.

"Where, by Gheju! I don't see anything, and I don't smell anything! Except you two." Frustrated, Simna stomped up and down the tiny beach, sending tide-zone insects and crustaceans scrambling for cover from the footprints he left in the soft soil.

They came from beneath the rising sun, distant dots at first that soon matured into rising and falling arcs of glistening pink, as if the morning had decided to hesitate in its brightening and mark the pause with a series of rose-hued commas. With the precision of experienced acrobats they advanced by leaping lithely from one hovering body of water to the next, sometimes entering those nearest the ground, then ascending skyward from pond to pond as if climbing a watery ladder. This they did effortlessly, soaring from floating lakes to drifting ponds in spite of the fact that a single missed leap would in all probability result in the slow, unpleasant death of the jumper. Because while they could live out of water, they could not do so for very long.

"Dolphins!" Simna exclaimed. "Here?"

"Yes, here," Ehomba murmured. "They have sharp eyes, and even sharper hearing, and ways of seeing the world at distances greater than either eyes or ears can match."

"But dolphins are creatures of the sea," Simna protested as he watched the school continue its approach, leaping from one drifting body of water to the next.

"Not always," rumbled Ahlitah. "I have seen these very same, or their relations, playing in the rivers that crisscross the veldt."

"There are sea dolphins and freshwater dolphins," Ehomba informed his friend.

"I guess there are," admitted Simna. "Strangely colored they are and—" He broke off, frowning. "Wait a minute. You've been telling me that you come from a desert country. Now you're saying that you know all about the different kinds of dolphins, even those that live in fresh water. Deserts aren't known for a surplus of deep rivers. How do you know so much about this kind of water dweller?"

The herdsman smiled gently down at his friend. "The dolphins of the sea know well their inland relatives. Where river meets ocean they often meet and talk, and sometimes exchange matings. I know about the river dolphins because the sea dolphins told me of them."

"Ah. So you don't talk to fish. You talk to dolphins."

"No. No man talks to dolphins. It is up to the dolphins to talk to men."

"And they just happened to settle on you?" Simna eyed the tall southerner slyly. "Why would that be, Etjole? Because you are making all of this up to keep from confessing what I've known all along? That you are a sorcerer?"

"Not at all, Simna. They talk to me because I like to take long walks by myself along the beach, and the shores of my country are desolate. The currents there are swift and cold. There are men who kill dolphins, for food and to keep them from competing for the catch. I would never do such a thing. How can one eat another who is known to be kind as well as intelligent?"

Behind them, Ahlitah licked a paw. "I've never had any trouble with that."

"Well, I could never do such a thing. I believe that they can sense a kind and kindred spirit. I have been talking to dolphins since I was a child."

"So you called them to us?" Simna wondered uncertainly.

"Nothing of the kind." Raising his gaze once more, Ehomba monitored the school's advance. They were quite near now, slowing as they debated which floating globules to use to make their final approach. "I doubt they have seen many humans in this place before, or perhaps none at all before us. Naturally curious as they are, I believe they have simply grown too interested in our presence here to stay away any longer." He began walking backward. "You should step away from the water."

"Why?" Then Simna noted the enthusiastic splashes the oncoming dolphins were making and hastily gathered up his gear, moving it to higher ground among the trio of casuarinas.

The dolphins arrived singly and in pairs, leaping magnificently from a second pond into the one where the travelers had spent the night. There were a dozen of them, including a quartet of youngsters. They took up much of the available water, forcing the indigenous inhabitants up against the transparent skin of the hovering pond or close inshore as the invaders dashed in energetic circles around the island, squeaking and barking joyously. With their bright pink coloration they resembled strips of flame shooting through the water.

If it was a form of ceremonial greeting, it was a dizzying one, as Ehomba and his companions struggled to follow the streamlined racers' progress around and around the little island. Eventually the new arrivals tired of the game and settled down to hunting out the fish and other pond dwellers who were trying to hide in the crevices and roots of the island.

One of the dolphins did not. Instead, it swam slowly toward the three travelers with effortless strokes of its broad, flat tail. Its head was different from those of its seagoing relatives, being narrower and with a prominent forehead in back of the long beak. Turning slightly to her left, she raised her head out of the water and parted tooth-lined jaws.

"I am Merlescu, Queen of the High River School and of the central district of the Water-That-Flies. Who are you?" Dancing eyes tracked their every movement.

Simna leaned close to whisper up at his tall friend. "No wonder you can talk to them. They speak perfectly."

"Of course we speak perfectly!" declared the queen. "Why would you think otherwise, man?"

"Oh, I dunno. Maybe because I've never before heard your people do anything but squeak like oversized finned mice."

It was hard to tell if Merlescu was smiling, because her kind were always smiling. Inherited physiognomy made any other expression impossible.

"It suits us to speak our own language around humans and to keep them ignorant as to our true abilities. Except," she added as she turned to face Ehomba, "a very few. You, man, have about you a kind and sympathetic aspect."

"Oh really?" Simna made a show of inspecting his companion's face. "He looks pretty ordinary to me."

"What are you doing in the land of the Water-That-Flies?"

"We are making our way north," Ehomba explained, "so that we may eventually book passage on a boat going to the dry territories that lie to the west."

"So very far!" Pivoting on her tail, she squealed at her school, whose members replied with energetic squeaks and chirps. Looking back at the travelers, she professed, "I have never met anyone who has crossed the ocean. Not even others of my kind—though there was one who insisted she had talked to one who had talked to one who had done it. What drives you three to undertake so extensive and dangerous a journey?"

"An obligation," Ehomba told her.

"Treasure," added Simna.

"The tall idiot had to go and save my life," fumed Ahlitah.

Merlescu nodded, a gesture that dolphins often used among themselves, particularly when there were no humans around to witness it. "I see that your motivations are as diverse as your appearance." Turning her body around, she gestured with a fin. "Many, many days of difficult travel stretch out ahead of you before you will come to the end of the Water-That-Flies. This is country best suited to those with fins, or with wings. Not to those with awkward, many-jointed legs. North of here the Water-That-Flies becomes denser still. You will find very few places where you can slip between."

"I wanted to ask you about that." Walking right up to the water's edge, Ehomba sat down and stretched out his legs. Merlescu swam close enough to rest the tip of her beak on one of his bare ankles. Behind them, Ahlitah found himself contemplating a large and easy meal until Simna jabbed him hard in the ribs. The great maned head whirled on the human, but the swordsman, more familiar now and therefore more comfortable with the great cat's moodiness, did not flinch.

"I see what you're thinking, kitty. Don't. Can't you see that Etjole's working his magic on our behalf?"

"What magic?" The litah growled softly. "They are only talking."

"Ah, but that's how our friend Etjole works his magic. With words. At least that's the only way I've been able to catch him working it so far."

"Of what possible use to us can talk with these water dwellers be?"

"I don't know," Simna readily admitted. "But this I do know: Etjole wouldn't be wasting his time doing so if he didn't think we would benefit in the end. So let's just sit on our natural instincts for a while and see what develops, shall we?" Experimentally, he prodded the litah's belly. "This morning you ate more fish than both of us put together. Surely you're not hungry again already?"

"Watch your hands, man. You presume a familiarity that has not been granted." Settling himself back down on all fours, Ahlitah concentrated intently on the verbal byplay taking place between human and dolphin. "I am not hungry. I just felt like killing something."

"Well, my furry friend, hold that thought." Ignoring the big cat's warning, the swordsman leaned up against the muscular flank, using it for casual support. "I have a feeling that before this little excursion is done you will have more than one opportunity to indulge it."

Merlescu drew back slightly, sliding deeper into the water. "That is a fine proposition for you, man, but what do we get out of it? You ask much in return for nothing."

"I would never propose anything so one-sided." The seated Ehomba was quick to reassure her. "Your rewards for helping us will be many. For one thing, you will be rid of us and any lingering worries our presence in your territory may cause you. More importantly, you will have that rare chance to work together in a manner I know your kind delights in but can only rarely experience. It will require great precision and timing on the part of you and all the members of your school." He looked away and shrugged indifferently.

"Of course, if you are not the kind of school that delights in this type of activity, we can always try to make contact with another. It may be that you and yours are not up to the challenge. If so, I will understand. After all, that which is elementary is for those whose focus is forever on taking it easy."

"What, what?" Backing off, the greatly distressed dolphin churned the water as she spun in a tight circle. After several moments of this she reapproached the shore and spat a mouthful of dirty pond water straight into Ehomba's face. Simna straightened and next to him he could feel

Ahlitah's muscles tense, but the herdsman did not appear in the least perturbed.

Calmly, he wiped water and plant matter from his dripping face. "That is not an answer. Can you do it?"

"Can we? Can we?" She took up another mouthful of water and for a moment Simna thought she was going to drench his friend again—but she did not. Slowly, the water trickled from her jaws. "It is not a matter of can we, but will we."

"I refuse to concede the point without proof. Will you?" Ehomba leaned forward and squeaked something at her. "It will be great fun—if you can make it happen."

"It is not up to me. We of the water do not work things as humans do. Not even queens." Turning and squeaking, she swam out into the deeper water of the pond, calling the members of the school to her. While they convened in a mass of squeals and barks, Simna sidled over to his friend. Ahlitah pretended disinterest as long as he could, but soon he too was standing within leisurely hearing range of the tall herdsman.

"What did you ask of them?" The swordsman kept his eyes on the garrulous, squawling dolphins.

"To help us," Ehomba explained honestly.

"Help us!" Ahlitah grunted. "How can such as they help us? Without filling our bellies, I mean."

"Remember what I said previously about engaging conversation?" Ehomba nodded toward the dolphins. "I have just had some. Be patient until they are finished with their squabbling."

So Simna ibn Sind and Ahlitah squirmed silently and waited to see what their lanky friend was about, wondering how it might involve the three of them with a pack of obstreperous, noisy water dwellers who were not fish but not human, either.

After what seemed like hours of raucous argument the school broke up, its members resuming their former activities of hunting, playing, mating, and chasing one another around and around the single island. Merlescu swam slowly back to land. Leaning back so that she was floating upright in the water, she once again addressed herself to Ehomba. But her words and her gaze encompassed all three of them.

"We will need to find some vines." As she spoke a trio of adults leaped clear of the pond, across the intervening open space, and into another, larger drifting body of water beyond. "This may take a little time." With that she turned her head and slipped back beneath the surface.

"Vines?" Simna frowned at his friend. "What do we need with vines?"

"I am not even marginally vegetarian," Ahlitah added.

"Have you ever wondered what it would be like to swim to the bottom of a pond and be able to stare right through the bottom? It must puzzle the fish." Stripping off his kilt and shirt, Ehomba kicked off his sandals and dove, naked and none too gracefully, into the water. A pair of the younger dolphins promptly swam up to him and, chattering and squeaking, began a game of tag with him as the divider between.

"Will you have a look at that." Simna was grinning and shaking his head even as he began removing his own accoutrements. "I suppose any chance to get clean is a welcome one."

"Not at all." Lying down on his side, the litah promptly dropped his head onto the soft earth and closed his eyes. Simna eyed the big cat disapprovingly.

"Going to sleep again?"

One piercing yellow eye popped open to fix him in its glare. "When not hunting or screwing I usually spend eighty percent of my time sleeping. It's what we big cats do. And we do it well." The eye closed and Ahlitah rolled over so that his back was facing the human. "Go soak yourself, if you must. It's a human thing."

Simna started to turn away, then paused. An entirely impish smile spread across his face. Searching until he found what he needed, he walked to the water's edge, knelt, and then retraced his steps, tiptoeing up to the back of the cat.

The litah's roar as the swordsman dumped the contents of the hollow gourd onto the big cat's slumbering face shook the transparent epidermis of the pond and caused cones to fall from the shading casuarinas. With a whoop of delight, Simna had spun around and raced for the water. He had just enough of a lead to beat his pursuer to the pond.

His face twisted into a black rictus of pure ferocity, Ahlitah paced rapidly back and forth along the shore. "You've got to come out sometime, little man. When you do, I'll twist you up so tight you'll have to drink your own piss!"

"Just as I've always suspected." Treading water, Simna made faces at the outraged feline. "The bigger the cat, the smaller its sense of humor."

His eyes bugged and his expression was radically altered when, with a warning roar, the litah suddenly crouched and sprang directly toward him. Ducking, the swordsman kicked frantically for the bottom of the pond.

Massive paws dug at the water, but not for long. Soon Ahlitah was bucking and jerking as first one dolphin then another prodded him from below with their snouts, or blew bubbles beneath his belly. A smiling Ehomba joined in, and the big carnivore's initial outrage was soon forgotten as humans, dolphins, and cat churned the surface of the pond to joyful froth.

It was midafternoon before the absent trio of water dwellers returned from their scavenging. Held in their mouths and wrapped around their upper bodies were long lengths of strong vine, some green, the rest brown. Ragged ends showed where sharp teeth usually employed in the catching of fish had torn the tough lengths of plant matter free.

While Merlescu and Ehomba conversed softly, man face-to-face with dolphin in the water, Simna and Ahlitah hauled themselves out onto the edge of the island to dry their bodies in the sun.

"All right," Simna puffed, "you win."

"Win what?" Alongside him, the great cat was even more fatigued than his human companion.

Simna looked to his left, gazing across sand, gravel, and grass. "I retract my earlier allegation. You do have a sense of humor."

The litah was sitting up and cleaning itself with one paw, attempting to aid the sun in removing as much water as possible from its ebony coat. "Of course I do. But fair warning, man: Have a care when you trifle with a cat's dignity."

"Hoy, I allowed as how you might have a sense of humor. Nothing was said about dignity."

They verbally lunged and riposted in that vein until Ehomba rejoined them, pond water coursing in long rivulets down his lean, muscular form. "Our friends will make ready. I have to help them." Tilting back his head, he studied the sky. "We will have to spend another night here and leave in the morning." His gaze dropped to his companions. "They will help us."

"How?" Simna let out a querulous snort. "By tying vines around us and dragging us from one floating pond to another?"

"You will see." Turning, he loped back into the water.

Simna wanted to find out what the herdsman and the dolphins were up to, but he was too tired from all the water play. Maybe Ehomba's occupation was the key, he mused. Perhaps the vines were to be used as whips, to urge and guide the dolphins as the school towed the three travelers from lake to lake. With a mental shrug, he closed his eyes.

Despite his ever-present skepticism, he had come to have a certain confidence in Ehomba, even when he did not always have a clue as to the herdsman's intentions.

He was awakened by a delphinic din of ear-splitting proportions. It sounded as if every member of the school was squealing and squawking at the top of its capacious lungs. Rising from beneath his blanket, he saw that Ahlitah was standing at the water's edge watching as Ehomba and the dolphins organized themselves for departure.

Dressing quickly, he hurried to join them. It took only a moment to see what was intended and finally to ascertain the purpose of the scavenged vines.

Secured around each dolphin's head in a crude bit and bridle arrangement, each set of vines terminated in a pair of reins that ranged from four to six feet in length. Belting his skirt of leather armor, Simna moved to stand next to the watchful Ehomba.

"What are we supposed to do with those? Grab hold and hang on while they drag us from lake to lake? I didn't know their jaws were that strong. It's going to make for awkward traveling."

"Yes," agreed Ehomba readily, "but not in the sense that you think." He nodded at the nearest brace of eager dolphins. "The reins are not for hanging on to, but for balance."

"Balance?" Simna's brows drew together, as confused as the rest of him.

"Like this." Stepping out into shallow water, Ehomba proceeded to demonstrate.

Watching him balance himself with one foot on the back of each dolphin, using their dorsal fins to brace his feet while holding a rein in each hand, both swordsman and cat were astonished at the speed and grace the dolphins displayed as they raced around the circumference of the island and the confines of the pond with the human on their backs. After several such high-spirited circumnavigations, they sped into shore and deposited their passenger next to his friends. So skilled, so controlled, had been the dolphins' run that the herdsman was barely damp.

He handed the ends of the reins to the suspicious swordsman. "Here, Simna. You try it."

The shorter man held up both hands. "Oh no. Not me."

"Hmph!" Wearing his inherent haughtiness like a crown, Ahlitah promptly padded forward. Two more dolphins arrived and positioned themselves. Holding the reins firmly in his jaws, the big cat stepped forward and allowed the two dolphins to convey him effortlessly around the island, riding their backs as easily and magnificently as any carved figurehead ever rode the prow of a ship.

Simna eventually did as well. Despite his initial skepticism about the unique means of travel, he was too experienced a horseman to incur a spill from the striking double mount. Thus familiarized with the behavior of their slick-skinned chargers, the travelers gathered up their gear and took up their riding positions.

"Ready then?" Merlescu queried in her high-pitched yet elegant voice. Satisfied by an expectant vocal melange of squeaks, snarls, and shouts, she threw herself forward into the water and kicked violently with her tail. "Then—let's go!"

There were none to witness the departure but fish and salamanders, frogs and birds, but even they must have been impressed by the sight of an entire school of dolphins soaring as if a single entity from one floating pond to the next—especially with two humans and one great black cat riding upon their arching backs. The splash as they all hit the surface of the next airborne body of water more or less simultaneously was impressive. Water would cascade over the sides of the transparent enclosure thus struck, spilling into smaller pondlets of water and the vast, shallow, freshwater sea that covered the actual ground below.

In this manner the travelers progressed, their fingers wrapped tightly around green reins, their feet planted firmly behind rubbery fins, their legs and joints braced for the relief of each takeoff and the shock of each watery landing. From pond to lake, lake to pond they advanced, never in a perfectly straight line, but always crisscrossing and hip-hopping and hopscotching more or less northward.

With the assistance of the acrobatic, leaping dolphins they covered miles instead of yards, resting and camping on those lakes and ponds that boasted dry land, helping their finned friends to round up and catch enough fish to satisfy all. The humans supplemented their diet with everything from berries to watercress, while Ahlitah proved he was not above eating even snails and crawfish—though filling his belly, they did not offer much of a challenge in the way of a hunt.

Once they encountered a place where no proximate body of water large enough to accommodate the dolphins and their passengers loomed near. Simna was convinced they would have to waste time backtracking and then searching to east or west, but at the last moment Ehomba did something with the reins of his mounts. It was very subtle, and the swordsman was not entirely convinced he had seen anything at all, but it left him with something to ponder while he fought to balance himself on the back of his own steeds as they soared over the liquidless gap. They did just make it to the next, seemingly too-distant hovering body of water, their tails slapping down on the rim of the thin, transparent wall, their squeals of triumph and delight echoing in his ears.

Ehomba had urged them forward with words, Simna decided. Words, or a suggestion, or orders to alter their angle of approach. Or— something more.

There had been no flash of lightning, no burst of alchemic effulgence. Just a barely perceptible flutter of long-fingered hands. The hands of a musician, Simna had mused on more than one occasion. Or hands that could cast spells.

Without preparation, or magic powder, or wand or crystal orb? All Ehomba had was a spear and two swords, and while they rode the backs of the dolphins, those devices rode high and secure against the southerner's back. Simna shook water from his eyes. Was his tall, soft-voiced friend sorcerer or no? More often than not, he found himself absolutely confused on the matter.

He could not spare the time to cogitate too deeply the conundrum that was Etjole Ehomba. At the moment he was too busy toiling to keep from falling off.

XX

Many days passed before the floating, airborne ponds and lakes began to grow dangerously infrequent. The dolphins had to work harder to clear longer and longer gaps between the drifting bodies of water. After a while it became impossible to maintain a reasonable northerly heading. Too much energy was being expended on leaping from side to side instead of forward, like a sailing ship forced to tack into a steadily decreasing wind.

There finally came a day and an hour when Merlescu and Ehomba agreed that the time had come to call a halt and make an end to the joyous and fruitful relationship they had established. Neither wished to risk pressing on until one of the hardworking dolphins fell short of its goal and had to be raised bodily by the travelers back into the nearest, lowest body of deep water. That Ahlitah by himself could accomplish this no one doubted, but any dolphin missing a jump who fell to the ground would not find its fall adequately cushioned by the six inches of water there. Neither the travelers nor Merlescu desired to see that happen.

For their final farewells they chose a pond large enough to aspire to be a lake. Its rippling, curved underside hovered no more than a foot or so above the surface of the endless shallow swamp that covered the ground. The school clustered close along the water's edge, looking on and offering encouragement as the travelers clambered over the side and, one by one, dropped to the pale, tepid shallows below.

Terse but heartfelt good-byes given, the dolphins turned and, as one, began their return journey southward, heading for the heart of the land of suspended lakes. The travelers watched them go until the last pink, curving back had arched out of sight.

Simna gestured at the dripping length of thin, tough vine Ehomba had been utilizing as a rein for days. It was wrapped in coils around the southerner's shoulder. "What do you plan to do with that? Rope us a couple of frogs to ride the rest of the way?"

"No. But I have a feeling we may eventually have to use it to rope something." With that he started off, heading due north. Simna marveled at the herdsman's ability to tell direction from an empty sky the way a thief senses a heavy purse concealed within many folds of garment. He followed without question while Ahlitah splashed primly alongside, occupying himself with scanning the languid shallows for edible mollusks and crustaceans.

By the morning of the next day they had reached a place where the vast, shallow river bay that underlay the hovering ponds had been reduced to streaks of fading dampness in the sand. Behind them, glittering and glistening like pearls hung on invisible cords, the floating ponds and lakes stretched south to the main body of the river and the veldt beyond.

Ahead lay gravel plains dotted with low scrub and clusters of bizarrely shaped succulents. Half a day's march later found them confronting a desert. The first dunes lifted smooth-sided yellow-brown flanks toward the deep blue sky.

"More fine country!" Simna spat and watched as the dry grains rapidly soaked up his spit. "I long for the green fields and leafy forests of home." The disgruntled swordsman looked up at Ehomba. "At least you'll be comfortable."

"What, in this?" The herdsman indicated the desiccated terrain that lay before them.

"Hoy, haven't you told me that you come from a desert land?"

"No, I have not. Dry, yes. Desert—well, to some I suppose it is. But where I come from there are mountains crowned with trees, and valleys that fill with grass and clover and flowers, and springs that nourish small lakes and give rise to flowing streams." He nodded northward. "I see none of that here. Right now, the only thing about this place that reminds me of home is the temperature." He looked to his right.

"Are you suffering, my four-legged friend?"

"Not at all. Not yet, anyway." Ahlitah was panting, the splotched dark pink of the heavy, thick tongue shockingly bright against his black lips. "I know that when the sun is up I get hotter than my kin because of my color, but I have grown used to it."

"We're going to need plenty of water." Grim-faced, Simna surveyed the ground ahead. "No telling what we'll find out there."

"That is what I kept this for."

Turning, Ehomba retraced their steps until he halted before a very small pond. Floating a yard or so above the ground, it contained no central island, no visible soil of any kind. Reflecting its diminutive size, only minnows darted in its depths.

Unlimbering the coil of vine from his shoulder, he turned to his companions. "Come and help me secure this."

"Secure it?" Simna started toward the other man. "Secure it to what? And why? You're not thinking of somehow bringing it with us?"

"And why not?" Ehomba challenged him as he began to measure out the length of vine around the circumference of the pond. "Can you think of a more reliable source of water, or a better container?"

"I know it's small compared to many we've seen." The swordsman bent to help with the vine. "But it's still a lot bulkier and heavier than a couple of gourds slung over the shoulder. What makes you think we can move it, anyway?"

"It will move," Ehomba assured him. "Now when I tell you, pick up that side of the vine and press it tight against the water wall."

It took work and a while—the vine kept slipping against the smooth exterior of the pond—but eventually they had it snugged tight. The green rope dug slightly into the sides of the drifting pond but did not break through. Strange to think of water having skin, Simna mused. With his knife they split the free end of the vine in half. He took one end and Ehomba the other, and together they put their weight into it and pulled.

The pond did not budge until Ahlitah, with a snort of disdain, grabbed the vine in his teeth and tugged. Once set in motion, the pond moved easily, traveling as if on an invisible greased pad. As soon as it had acquired some momentum, one man could drag it behind him. It glided through the air more freely than they had any right to expect.

"We will drink our fill until it is half empty," Ehomba declared, "and that will make it even easier to pull. Meanwhile we will be able to sip more lavishly than any desert would normally allow."

Putting out a hand, Simna pushed against the side of the pond. He was careful not to poke it with a finger. The cool, transparent epidermis dimpled at his touch before springing back to its original shape. It took several seconds to complete the process and return to normal, the marvelous container reacting not unlike an old man's skin.

"Drink our fill? By Ghothua, we can have a bath!"

Ehomba regarded him with distaste. "You would swim in your drinking water?"

The swordsman blinked ingenuously. "Sure, why not?"

"Why not indeed," added Ahlitah supportively. It was the first time he had agreed with Simna on anything.

Ehomba simply shook his head. "It is true what the migrating traders say. Civilization and civilized behavior are matters of perspective."

"Aw, our customs are just different, Etjole." Simna gave the herdsman an amiable slap on the back, marveling as always at the dryness of the southerner's attire. No matter the time of day or the temperature, he never seemed to sweat. "If it'll ease your mind, I promise not to swim in your drinking water."

"I would appreciate that." Like his companions, Ehomba was enjoying the easy walking. For the first time in many days, the ground underfoot crunched instead of sloshed.

They kept to the dry, dusty washes that ran like rocky rivulets between the dunes. Soon these were towering overhead, their sandy peaks rising to heights of a thousand feet and more. Yet between them, in shadowed and sheltered places, desert plants thrived on subsurface sources of moisture.

Besides the more familiar bushes and small trees with their desert-adapted miniaturized leaves and green bark, they encountered the most extraordinary miscellany of cacti and other dry-country plants. Some had spines that were curved like fishhooks, while others boasted spikes fine as hair, rust-red in color and threatening. Towing their floating water supply behind them, the travelers were careful not to brush up against any of these. In Ehomba's experience, such plants not only stung, but many also carried poison in their quills. Overhead, small, fringed dragonets soared and circled like tatters of torn tent, their outstretched membranous wings keeping them effortlessly aloft as they watched the progress of the trekkers below. Enamored of carrion, they would track isolated wayfarers of any species for days, hopeful and expectant.

Ehomba's companions trudged along, sometimes locked in their own private silence, sometimes chattering briskly either to him or to one another. What an odd trio of travelers we make, he meditated on more than one occasion. None of us really wants to be here. I would rather be home with my wife and children, Ahlitah would surely prefer the company of other great cats, and Simna doubtless misses the fleshpots and garish excitements of more populous surroundings.

Yet here we are: I because I made a promise to a man now long dead, whom until he lay dying in my arms I did not even know. Simna because he thinks I am a sorcerer on the trail of treasure. And the litah because I had the audacity to save his life.

I should go home. Abandon this foolishness. Calving season is over and the cows and ewes have dropped their young, but summer does not last forever. There is much to be done before the cold winds come ashore.

Yet Mirhanja would not want for help, he knew. The Naumkib looked after their own. And his friends and fellow villagers understood the nature of his obligation. None of them would complain at having to help the family of an absent husband. Not for the first time, he was glad he was Naumkib. In other tribes, he knew, an extended absence such as his would water the flowers of resentment.

How he missed the sea! Its heavy perfume, the rolling chorus of the waves fondling the shore, the uncompromising purity of its rejuvenating embrace. He even missed its taste, blunt and salty and steadfast in its distillation of every part of the world. Around him desiccation had reduced the good earth to powder, useful for taking the hair off a hide preparatory to tanning but little else. Unlatching the flap that covered the right-hand pocket of his kilt, he kneaded the sackful of beach pebbles between his fingers, listened to them grind against one another, hearing the sounds of the ocean at night resonate between his fingers.

Days that could have been hotter and gratefully were not were broken by chilly nights during which distant creatures howled and screamed at the moon. Twice it rained lightly, not only cooling the travelers but also partially replenishing their drifting bubble of water. All things considered, the journey through the dunes was proving difficult but not harsh. No one had succumbed to the heat, no one had been bitten or stung or acquired an armful of cactus stickers.

The days would have passed more rapidly, however, if they had had some idea how far they still had to go before emerging from such desolate country. Though not overtly hostile, the land through which they were traveling rapidly grew dull and uninteresting. Even the appearance of a spectacular new succulent no longer drew more than a casual comment or mumbled observation.

"I saw something."

Head down, tongue hanging out, Ahlitah growled testily. "None of us are blind. We all see many somethings. It is hardly reason for excitement."

"No." Simna had halted in the middle of the wadi and was shading his eyes as he peered ahead. "This was moving."

Ehomba was more charitable. Stopping alongside the swordsman, he leaned on his spear and tried to follow his friend's line of sight. "What did you see, Simna? A rabbit, perhaps? Roast rabbit would be good."

"Rabbit or rat, I'd thank you for either." Drawing in its tongue, the litah licked dry lips. "I'm hungry."

"You are always hungry." Ehomba spoke without looking over at the great cat. He was striving to see whatever Simna had seen.

"As Gwyull is my witness," the swordsman insisted tersely, "it was no rabbit. No rat, either."

"Then what?" the herdsman prompted him.

Lowering his shading palm, Simna looked uncertain. "I don't know. It was there for an instant, and then it was gone."

"Like any story." With a snort, Ahlitah resumed padding forward, his big feet kicking up dust at every step.

Camp that night was uninviting, but in the absence of any kind of shelter it was the best they could do. Ruddy dunes towered all around them as they spread themselves out on the floor of the dry ravine. Ahlitah was less grumpy than usual, thanks to the den of rodents he had sniffed out and promptly consumed. For a veldt master used to bringing down and killing much larger prey, this hunting of rats and mice was demeaning, but an empty stomach in need of meat does not discriminate against the nature of whatever the throat elects to provide.

As they unrolled their blankets on the hard, unforgiving ground, they were more grateful than ever for the floating pond Ehomba had thought to bring along. Half empty now, it was easier to tow. Everyone drank from it, so everyone shared in the pulling.

Overhead, a swelling moon promised good night walking should they choose to exercise that option. It was something to consider if the heat grew intolerable. Lying on his back, listening to the cautious scurrying of nocturnal insects and those rodents who had escaped Ahlitah's attentions, Ehomba put his hands behind his head and tried to envision what Mirhanja was doing at that same moment. Lying in their bed, most likely, in the posture she usually favored for sleeping: on her left side, with her back toward him, her knees bent up toward her smooth belly, the knuckles of one hand resting just below her slightly parted mouth giving her an incongruously childlike appearance.

Except there was nothing behind her in the bed now except cool night air. The body, the man, who should have been there, was lying on the rocky floor of a dry ravine far to the north, dreaming of her as he hoped she was dreaming of him.

Soon, he promised himself. We will reach a large town with a harbor, and I will travel on a boat across the sea to deal with this Hymneth person on behalf of the man who died in my arms. And then I will come back to you, covered not in glory, which I do not seek, but in the satisfaction and the inner contentment no crown or generalship can match. *Soon.*

Pursing his lips, he blew a silent kiss at the moon, turned over, and went to sleep with an ease no king or soldier could equal.

XXI

It was cold when Simna ibn Sind awoke. Blinking, he yawned silently at the polished bowl of night that filled the sky between the dune crests. While it was beginning to set, the nearly full moon still threw enough light for a man to see clearly by, if not enough to enable him to read. Simna had never been much for reading and was glad he was traveling in the company of individuals of similar mind. Certainly Ahlitah, despite his exceptional if acerbic linguistic talents, was no peruser of books and scrolls. He was less certain about Ehomba, but the untutored, unsophisticated herdsman did not strike him as much of a scholar. A master of magics perhaps, but no great reader. Certainly in the time they had spent together thus far he had never expressed any great longing for the printed page.

He grinned at the thought of Etjole standing watch over his cattle and sheep, balancing himself with his spear as he alternated standing first on one leg and then on the other, with weighty tome in hand. The spear fit the image; the book did not. He comforted himself with that thought. Simna had little use for scholars. They tended to look down on an honest, hardworking man, and whisper about him behind his back.

Something nudged his right thigh, and he froze. Probably some harmless creature of the dunes come exploring under cover of night. A large desert beetle, black and preoccupied, or one of Ahlitah's scurrying snacks unwittingly tempting fate. But the drylands of his native country were home to their share of less benign nocturnal creatures, and in terrain as harsh as this there were bound to be hunters of the dark that used poison and fang and sting.

So he moved only his neck and head as he rose slightly to see what was repeatedly thumping his thigh through the blanket. Even with the slight movement he expected whatever it was to react: either by turning and racing off or pausing in its activity or skittering away from the movement and retreating in the direction of his feet.

He did not expect it to look back at him.

The warrior's diminutive form was clad in rough brown fabric woven from sisal or some similar plant. From fringed pants that reached to just below the knobby knees, short legs protruded, terminating in disproportionately large, splayed feet that were bare of any covering. The correspondingly undersized arms were gnarled and muscled. In his right hand the tiny fighter held a slim spear or lance. Bits of carved bone gleamed whitely against cuirass and shirt, serving to decorate as well as armor the upper body.

The head was a slightly squashed oval instead of round. Commensurate with the rest of the squat body, it gave the warrior the appearance of one who had been stepped on and had his whole self compressed and flattened out. The mouth was inordinately wide, the lips thin to the point of nonexistence, the eyes deep-set and intelligent. An oversized cap of finely woven natural fiber flopped down over the forehead. As a wide-eyed, motionless Simna watched in fascination, the soldier pushed the thick front of the cap farther back on his head, revealing the first tight curls of red-gold hair beneath.

His ears were remarkable: oversized, protuberant organs that stuck out from underneath the cap and rose to points higher than the head. They were also immoderately hairy. Unlike the curls that emerged from beneath the rim of the heavy cap, these hairs were straight as needles. But they were equally red.

Softly snapping something in a tongue Simna had never heard before, the warrior gestured brusquely with the lance. Taken in concert, the meaning of his tone and movement were unmistakable. Slowly, Simna sat up and raised his hands. He was wary, but far from intimidated.

After all, the fearless fighter was only five inches tall.

As soon as Simna complied with the order, his captor advanced toward him on his mount. This was a running bird of a kind that was also new to the swordsman. A mottled, spotted brown with flecks of white, it had a very long, broad tail, a slim bill, a tall topknot, and a highly intelligent gaze. Whenever it moved forward, its head dipped, the long tail stretched out behind it, and the topknot flared upward like a weathervane taking the mood of the wind.

Seated on the bird's back, the diminutive soldier rode on a perfectly miniaturized saddle. From bridle to stirrup, every fragment of avian tack was downsized to the point of airiness. An intrigued Simna noted that the arrangement would preclude any possibility of flight. Apparently the warrior's mount was a bird that preferred running to flying.

"I give up." He raised his hands even higher. "You've got me."

"Soh," the wee fighter responded curtly, "you speak *that* language." His voice was not as high and thin as Simna would have expected. Raising his six-inch-long lance over his head, he stood up in the stirrups, turned in the saddle, and ululated loudly.

Ehomba awoke to find the camp invaded by forty or so of the bantam night riders. The intruders darted back and forth in the quick, short bursts of speed that characterized their mounts' natural agility. They looked and acted quite confident—until Ahlitah yawned and stood up. Eyes drooping and tired, the great cat frowned at the intrusion, sniffed once, and opened oculi that were two yellow moons flanking the night.

"Ah, how considerate—a midnight snack."

"Back, get back!" The warrior who had awakened Simna was screeching frantically at his comrades. Observing the retreat, the swordsman discreetly lowered his hands. There had really been no reason to raise them in the first place, and besides, his shoulders were getting tired.

Swinging his legs out from beneath the blanket, Ehomba sat up and contemplated their visitors. He addressed them with the same respect he would have accorded a squadron of full-sized men, even though the arrivals were neither full sized nor men.

"I am Etjole Ehomba. These are my traveling companions, the swordsman Simna ibn Sind and the litah Ahlitah." He eyed the big cat disapprovingly. "Put your tongue back in your mouth. Guests are not for eating."

"Hmph." Disappointed, the litah slumped back onto his belly. "My late-night entertainments are more fun than yours."

The diminutive callers gradually relaxed. Trotting forward on his feathered mount, the one who had awakened Simna confronted the herdsman. "I am Loswee, Son of the Patriarch Roosagin, of the Swick—the People of the Sand." His gaze narrowed and the hairy oversized ears inclined ever so slightly forward. "You are not agents of the Dunawake?"

Herdsman and swordsman exchanged a glance while Ahlitah remained relaxed, unmoving, and uninterested. Long legs crossed, Ehomba looked back down at their interrogator. Loswee's mount was pecking curiously at the underside of the southerner's well-worn leather sandal.

"What is a Dunawake?"

"Not 'a' Dunawake," the miniature warrior corrected him. "*The* Dunawake." In the subdued silver shimmer of the moon, his shudder was clearly visible. "I don't even like to consider the possibility that there might be more than one." Wide eyes looked up at the infinitely larger visitor.

"The Dunawake is a Terrible. There are many Terribles in the world, but the Dunawake o'ertops them all. You can't fight it. All you can do is get out of its way. And you'd better get out of its way, or you'll be mushed. Obliterated, my friend, even such giants as yourselves, as deftly as I would pulp a sweet ant. So we move. It's aching and arduous work, but we have no choice. There are those who are not as skillful or agile as we, and these suffer the unmentionable fate that befalls all victims of the Dunawake." He sat a little straighter in his avian saddle. "So far we have succeeded in keeping ahead of it. We Swick are quick.

"We would fight it, if we had the weapons. But spears and arrows are less than raindrops to the Dunawake. We need something stronger."

Simna considered. "Bigger spears, bigger arrows?"

Loswee's gaze narrowed, tugged down by heavy brows, and Ehomba was quick to intercede. "You must excuse my friend. His muscles and his determination are both stronger than his imagination. What would you need to fight this Dunawake?"

"Magic," the Swick replied promptly. "Magic such as you possess."

Ehomba blinked. "We have no magic. I am a herder of cattle and sheep, my friends unpretentious wanderers. We are not magicians." He was aware that Simna was watching him as closely as was Loswee.

"If you are not magicians," the Swick countered, pointing with the tip of his spear, "then how do you explain that?"

He had singled out the half-full pond that hovered behind the travelers. A few minnows still swam in its reduced depths.

Ehomba smiled gently. "We did not conjure the floating water, nor can I explain it. We found it and many thousands like it in a land to the south of here, and brought it with us so that we would have enough to drink in this dry country. You could do the same."

"To the south, you say?" Loswee reflected. "This is as far south as the Swick have ever come. And we would not have done so had the Dunawake not forced the journeying upon us." He squinted at the pond, which was tied to a rock outcropping so that it would not drift away during the night. "I'm not sure I believe you. I think you have more magic than you're admitting to."

Ehomba shook his head. "I wish you were right and I untruthful. There have been times when I could have done with a little magic."

Turning in his saddle, Loswee barked something at his squadron of armed fighters, then turned back to Ehomba. "Perhaps after we have talked further, you will feel like being more forthcoming."

"We have no objection to talking," Ehomba assured him noncommittally.

"Good. I see that you are traveling light, so you must be ready for a real meal."

"Giquina knows that's true!" Simna agreed heartily.

Ehomba frowned at his friend. "Look at this country, and the size of these people. They cannot have much to eat, far less anything to spare for visitors of our size."

"On the contrary," Loswee proudly disagreed, "we have more than ample stocks. We don't lack for food, and we'll be pleased to share. If not magic, then maybe you can give us some advice. Having come from the south, you must at least be the bearers of new ideas." Extending his arm, he pointed with his spear. "It's not far, and I promise you will be warmer in the castle than out here in this ravine."

Ehomba beckoned to Simna, and the swordsman was at his side in an instant. The two men conferred briefly.

"What do you think?" the herdsman asked his friend.

Simna exhaled softly. "Any free food, however small the amount, is welcome. Especially if I don't have to carry it. If they mean treachery, then their brains are as small as their fingers. You or I could probably give their whole army a good fight, and Ahlitah would simply stomp them at his leisure. Since I don't see them being that stupid, I expect that their offer is genuine."

Ehomba nodded. "Those are my thoughts as well." He turned back to the bird rider and smiled. "We accept. Give us a moment to gather our things, and to untie our water, and we will come with you."

"Excellent!" While Loswee's mount could not rear back in the manner of a horse, it could mirror its rider's enthusiasm by hopping about jerkily. "Wherever else you go and whatever else happens to you, you will never forget Swick hospitality."

The riders waited patiently for the travelers to collect themselves. A number occupied themselves hunting along the base of the dunes for edible insects and plants. But they had little time for scavenging, because Ehomba and Simna were packed and ready to go within a very few minutes. Ahlitah, of course, was always ready.

The Swick troopers led the way down the gulch. Expecting to have to moderate their pace so as not to overstride their diminutive hosts, the travelers found themselves having to hurry to keep up, so swift were the Swick's feathered earthbound mounts. They hardly had time to take note of their surroundings as the line of mounted warriors turned down a much narrower wadi between massive slopes of sand, and then just as rapidly down another.

Panting, Simna looked uneasily back the way they had come. "All these dunes look alike. Many more of these twists and turns and we'll never be able to find our way back to the main canyon."

"What makes you think it was the main one?" Ehomba was striding along easily beneath his pack. "Another day or two's walk and it might have become as narrow and winding as this one." He spared a glance at the sky. "At least we are still moving in a more or less northerly direction."

"Hoy," the swordsman agreed with a nod. "Didn't they tell us that's where this Dunawake was coming from?" He surveyed the encircling dune walls uneasily.

"Relax, my friend. I do not think they would run us right at their nemesis without any warning. I think they are taking us to their community, as they promised."

The swordsman squinted ahead, past the double line of mounted Swick speeding along in front of them. "I'm looking for tents or huts, but I don't see anything yet."

He still saw nothing when the troop piped to a halt and Loswee trotted back to alert them. "We have arrived. Welcome to the castle."

Simna's eyes widened as he surveyed the moonswept sand. A few ragged bushes puffed branches into the night sky. It was almost morning and he was freshly tired. Too tired for jokes.

"Castle, is it, wee bruther? I see no castle. I see not even an outhouse."

"Come around this ridge of sand." Oblivious to the swordsman's sarcasm, Loswee beckoned for them to follow. To their left, the rest of the Swick troop lined up, wing to wing, forming a guard of honor. The travelers, after securing their floating water supply to a well-rooted nearby bush, marched on past, trailing Loswee.

The entrance was far larger than any of them had expected, a dark, gaping hole in the side of the dune. Why the shifting sand did not spill down to cover it they could not understand. Though it was difficult to tell anything for certain in the dim light, it was clear that something was holding the sand above securely in place and keeping it from tumbling down to block the opening. Provided that he advanced in a hunting crouch, it was even large enough to admit Ahlitah.

While the mere existence of the unnatural ingress was unexpected, it hardly harmonized with Loswee's description.

"I was wrong," Simna declared churlishly. "It *could* serve as an outhouse."

"Come inside." Unperturbed and at ease, Loswee led the way.

Equally as remarkable as the undisturbed, unblocked entrance was the depth to which it penetrated the dune. Bending double to keep from bumping his head against the ceiling of the tunnel, Ehomba and his companions were uncomfortably aware of the many tons of loose sand that loomed overhead. But though walled with the same grains that constituted the shifting slopes outside, the tunnel showed no signs of instability.

After a while, the soft babble of many voices became audible. Light appeared ahead. Loswee straightened in his saddle, a miniature portrait of satisfaction as he chirped to his soldiers.

"Heigh up back there! Ware your posture!" In a less martial tone he explained to his guests. "We are coming into Barrick, and the castle is waking up."

Simna grunted. "Good for it. Me, I'm going to sleep."

Close behind him, Ahlitah growled warningly. "This better be good. I didn't trot all this way for a breakfast of beans and berries. On the other paw," he added after a moment's consideration, "some of these Swick look quite nutritious."

"Ahlitah!" Looking back past his hunched-over shoulder, Ehomba glared at the big cat. "We are guests here. Mind your manners."

"Hoy that, long bruther," Simna admonished him. "Etiquette's not my style, but even I know the idea's to dine with one's hosts—not on them."

"But I'm *hungry.*" Irked by the early morning run, the hulking feline did not try to conceal his displeasure.

He forgot it, as they all did, when the tunnel made an abrupt turn to the left and they found themselves gazing at last upon the castle itself. Outside, it would have been a wonder. Here, in the deep heart of the dune, its existence was nothing short of miraculous.

Simna's anticipated tents and huts were nowhere to be seen. Instead, it was a true castle that rose before them, complete to external battlements and towers, minarets and multiple keeps. Off to the right were commodious stables where the prized running birds were quartered. In place of miniature wagons, cleverly made sand sleds were parked neatly side by side, and blacksmiths were arriving to begin the day's work with tiny bundles of wood and bands of black iron.

As they entered, advancing down a central avenue just wide enough to accommodate Ahlitah's bulk, awakening Swick appeared on the innumerable side streets to gawk at them. Smoke rose from dozens of cooking fires, trailing out tall, crooked chimneys as it curled toward the high dome of the great artificial cavern that had been hollowed out of the inside of the dune. Holes bored in the ceiling drew the smoke, allowing it to find a way out.

Pens held captive food animals: mice and rats, lizards and snakes. There were tanneries and slaughterhouses, farms exuberant with domesticated mushrooms and other edible fungi, kitchens and schools, workshops and apartments. Ehomba marveled, Simna was struck dumb, and even Ahlitah, though he gave little sign of it, was impressed. Expecting to find an unpretentious encampment, they found themselves instead in a veritable underground city. Prepared to deal with a few dozens of Swick, they instead were confronted by the People of the Sand in their teeming hundreds, perhaps thousands.

Looking past the main castle, Ehomba found that he could not see to the far end of the chamber, so extensive was the excavation. There were side galleries as well, similarly quarried from the dune, that were home to still more of the same. And everywhere rose miniaturized battlements and towers from which hung innumerable flags and decorations. Despite its reduced size, the citadel had been constructed on a grand scale, notwithstanding its implausible location or the diminutive size of its inhabitants.

He found himself smiling at no one in particular. In actuality, he was thinking of Daki and Nelecha. Because they would prize this place as no one else could.

Who else but children could truly appreciate the grandest of all sand castles?

XXII

They wondered what held it all together, much less kept the dune from collapsing in upon them, until they saw the first of many eternally busy construction crews. Secure in their saddles, Swick engineers directed dozens of domesticated slugs and snails as they worked at maintaining and adding to the buildings and walls.

Moving more swiftly than Ehomba had ever seen their kind travel, these humble creatures spread thick, viscid trails wherever they went. Other Swick riding large, sucker-toed geckoes followed behind, using long-handled brushes to spread and position the natural glue before it could harden. Looking up and to the side, he observed one crew working on the ceiling, the Swick hanging upside down in their saddles and harnesses.

Reaching over, Simna felt a nearby castle wall. Though nothing but fine yellow-red sand that glistened in the light of the many town lamps, it was firm and rigid to the touch.

Loswee was watching him. "Go ahead—try it."

Simna hesitated, then pushed hard with a finger, and then with his entire hand. To his astonishment, the wall held firm against his giant's push.

"You could stand on it." Loswee's words were suffused with pride. "The Swick build thick."

They were coming to a central square. Beneath their feet, sand sifted by color and brilliance had been collected in minuscule molds. Framed and then glued in place, it gave the plaza the appearance of having been paved with multicolored stone. Tall buildings topped with cylindrical towers rose around them, some soaring to heights that would enable a

Swick to look down even on Ehomba. Overhead, the dome peaked at twenty feet, allowing the visitors to stand freely.

Multiple street lamps formed a glowing necklace around the plaza, whose fringes were now filling with curious Swick anxious for a look at the giant guests. The mounted warriors of Barrick filed away through a gate off to the right, leaving only Loswee behind. Trotting up to Ehomba's feet, he tilted back his head and raised his spear in salute.

"I go to announce your presence to the Elected and to arrange for your proper reception. I will be back in a moment." With that he turned and sped off, his mount sprinting out of sight in seconds.

The travelers settled down to wait, Ahlitah pacing three tight circles before settling down against himself. Looking out at the inquisitive Swick staring back up at them from the edges of the plaza, the swordsman whispered to his phlegmatic companion, "Wonder what he meant by 'proper reception'?"

"I would imagine food, like he promised." Ehomba looked around sharply to face his friend. "I thought you did not believe that these people posed any threat to us."

"That was when we were outside, bruther." Simna studied their surroundings, which were much more spacious than the entrance tunnel but still confining. "In here, we're trapped. Any folk that can train snails to do masonry for them could have all sorts of surprising tricks up their smelly little sleeves."

Ehomba chuckled softly. "You are too suspicious, my friend."

"Hoy yes. I'm also still alive."

"And noisy." Behind them, the litah fully extended his remarkably long legs and stretched. "Why don't you shut up for a while?"

"Long bruther, why don't you—" Simna started to retort, but he was interrupted by the return of Loswee.

"That did not take very long," Ehomba ventured in greeting.

The Swick officer dismounted, leaving his bird tethered nearby. "Arrangements are being realized even as we speak. Prepare yourselves for a true Swick feast, my friends! The bites may be small, but you will find the quality and satisfaction unsurpassed."

Breakfast arrived on sand sleds pulled by teams of running birds yoked in pairs. And arrived, and kept on arriving. Where the Swick stored such copious quantities of food Ehomba did not know, but despite his unease he accepted Loswee's assurance that the banquet would in no way impoverish the community or impact adversely on its stores.

There was finely cooked and flavored meat, the origins of which Simna chose not to question. There were wild berries and nuts, desert melon, and a dozen different varieties of edible fungi, all basted and broasted and sauced to a turn. There were insects, cooked crisp in oil, and even cracker-sized loaves of bread made from wild grains. After days of living on jerked antelope and fish and what they could scavenge from their surroundings, the travelers soon put aside all pretense at politeness and gladly gave themselves over to Loswee's invitation to indulge.

When tankard-sized barrels of home-brewed beer appeared, Simna was all but ready to apply for transient citizenship.

"Not such a bad place, by Gyofah." Wearing a contented smile, he surveyed their splendid if shrunken surroundings. "A man could get used to it, if they put in a few windows."

"I believe the idea is to hide from danger," Ehomba commented dryly, "and not give it a way to look in." He considered the endless and apparently untiring line of heavily laden sleds that continued to funnel food and drink to him and his companions. "I am so full I can hardly keep my eyes open. I wonder if one of us should stand guard while the others sleep?"

Simna tossed back a cup-sized barrel of beer and blinked at him. "Now who's being suspicious? I thought you trusted these people."

"I trust everyone to a degree, but in a new country among unknown people it is better to trust no one completely. Not at first."

"So maybe you're smarter than your sheep after all." The swordsman grinned.

"Go ahead and rest." Both men turned to where Ahlitah lay on his side, having eaten his fill. The great cat's eyes were shut tight. "My kind sleeps long but lightly lest we miss the footsteps of passing prey. Trust me. If our hosts prove duplicitous, I will be up and on my feet in an instant."

"Remarkable," Simna murmured.

One yellow eye popped halfway open. "That I should rest so lightly?"

"No. That you'd use a word like 'duplicitous,'" the swordsman replied. "What's it mean, anyway?"

"One who articulates with the apposite orifice." The eye closed. "Shut up and go to sleep."

"Might as well." Stretching out prone on the paved plaza, Simna found himself regarding the domed sand ceiling. "Can't tell whether it's day or night in here anyway. Can you, Etjole?"

But the herdsman, never one to waste the opportunity, was already locked fast in slumber.

In the morning they were taken to another part of the underground castle-city to see how the Swick were able to extend and expand their living space. The method was not at all what Ehomba had envisioned. There were plenty of shovels in evidence, and teams of birds hauling away sled-loads of excavated sand, and slug and snail supervisors shoring up the finished walls, but the initial removal was accomplished not by digging but by a small choir around which the rest of the engineering activity centered.

"I wondered how you had managed to burrow all this out." Ehomba gestured around him. "If I had tried to do so, fresh sand would simply spill into any hole I tried to dig."

"See," Loswee advised him. "They are working on extending that small service tunnel."

The choir faced a small hole in the wall. As the visitors looked on, the choir master raised his stubby arms and brought them down. Simple, single notes poured from several dozen petite Swick throats. High and sharply pitched, the consequent tone was astonishingly loud to have been produced by such downsized lungs.

As the travelers looked on in bemusement, the sand in the back of the hole began to disappear. No, Ehomba noted as he bent over for a closer look. Not disappear. It was retreating, compacting away from the singing as if propelled by an invisible shovel. As the tunnel deepened and widened, the slime spreaders moved in to cement and stabilize the new walls. Meanwhile, the choir continued to pour forth high, extended notes. Among the Naumkib Ehomba was reckoned a fine singer in his own right, but at his best he could not have matched the staying power of the weakest of the Swick singers. Not only natural talent but also much strenuous vocal training was being put to use.

"Where is the sand going?" he asked their host. Eyeing him, Simna shook his head sadly.

"Who cares? Do you always have to ask questions? Must you know everything? Do you have any idea how exasperating that is to those around you?"

"Yes, hopefully. I know but cannot help it," the herdsman replied.

"The sand is not going anywhere." Loswee ignored the byplay between his guests. "Look more closely. The same number of grains are present. It is the air between them that is being disappeared. Have you ever slid down a dune and listened to it roar?" Ehomba nodded while Simna shook his head energetically. Ahlitah ignored them, bored with the entire matter and wishing they were back outside.

"That roaring," Loswee went on, "is caused by the movement of air trapped between the particles of sand. Our singing disturbs the air and pushes it out from between the grains. The sand that remains behind becomes consolidated. This not only opens up living space but helps to stabilize the sand. Our masons complete the task of stabilization before air can seep back between the grains and expand the pile or wall once again."

"Sounds like magic to me," Simna avowed.

"Not at all," Loswee countered. "It is simply sound engineering, in every sense of the term."

"It is a wonderful thing." Ehomba was openly admiring. "Of what other marvels are the Swick masters?"

"Come and I'll show you." Loswee led them back toward the plaza.

They were shown the vast underground storehouses and fungi farms, the workshops where Swick craftsfolk turned out superb works in leather and in fabric woven from desert fibers, the narrow-bore but deep wells that brought cool water up from unsuspected pools deep beneath the dune, and the extensive stables for the care and breeding of running birds and other small domesticated creatures. A dark seep at the end of a tunnel so long and low they could not enter produced an endless supply of fine black oil that kept the lamps of the community burning around the clock.

"This country is full of such seeps," Loswee told them. "I think there must be enough of the black liquid here to fill all the lamps of the world."

Ehomba's nose wrinkled at the thought. "It smells badly, though, and it stains clothes, and animals could become trapped in it. Give me a clean wood fire any day."

"Same here," agreed Simna readily. "The stuff's not good for anything else anyway. I say take what you need for your lamps and leave the rest of it in the ground."

"That is what we do." Loswee turned back toward the main square. "You have seen much in a short time. I am hungry again myself."

Simna rubbed his hands together. "I wouldn't have thought a man could get fat on such small portions, but your cooks are as adept as your singers."

It was as they were finishing the midday meal that Loswee reappeared to confront them in the company of half a dozen senior Swick. These Elders had long, curly white whiskers emerging from their chins, like gypsum helectites protruding from a cave wall, but not one could boast of sufficient chin hair to be labeled the father of a real beard. The two females among them had manes of scraggly white hair corkscrewing down their backs. Instead of the familiar Swick attire of shorts and upper garment, these respected seniors wore voluminous cloaks whose hems scraped the ground.

Despite their impressive appearance, both individually and as a group, it was still Loswee who did the talking. Ehomba found himself wondering if the Swick warrior had volunteered for the position of go-between or if he had been delegated to the task. Whatever the truth of the matter, he did not act like someone laboring under a compulsion.

"These are members of the Council of Elders," he explained. The half dozen senior Swick promptly kowtowed spryly. "As the first among Swick to encounter you, I have been asked by them to beg your help."

Leaning to his right, Simna whispered to his companion, "Hoy—here it comes. I knew all this food and friendship had to come with a price."

"Hush," Ehomba admonished him softly. "Let us see what they have to say." Louder he responded, "What kind of help?"

For such a small warrior, Loswee could muster an impressively steely gaze. "We want you to fight the Dunawake."

"I knew it," muttered Simna sourly as he put down his latest barrel of beer.

As always, Ehomba's tone remained unchanged. "You said that magic was necessary to battle this creature. We told you before you brought us to your castle-town that we had no magic. Nothing has changed since we first talked."

Loswee's demeanor began to show some cracks. "When I said that we wanted to beg your help I was being truthful. The Dunawake is very close and comes nearer every day. You have seen how much work has gone into the building of our home here. Can you imagine the effort involved for people our size?"

Ehomba nodded slowly. "I think I can."

"I told you outside that we cannot fight the Dunawake, that we can only try to keep ahead of it." He gestured expansively, taking in the central square, the surrounding towers and buildings and shops. "How many times do you think we have had to move? How many times do you think we have had to rebuild our homes starting outside the face of a virgin dune?" When none of the visitors responded, Loswee quietly informed them, "This castle in whose center you sit, this thriving community wherein we dwell, is our forty-fifth. Forty-five times we have raised a castle-town like this, and forty-four times we have had to abandon it and move on, to keep clear of the Dunawake."

Ehomba did his best to imagine the effort of which Loswee was speaking, the heartbreak of picking up and moving everything, down to the last miniature shovel and hearth. Of hurrying off through the desert between inhospitable dunes that were hills to him and his friends but gigantic sand mountains to people the size of the Swick. Of starting again from scratch, with the first choir singing out the first hole in the base of a fresh, untouched dune.

Of doing it forty-five times and now having to face the unholy prospect of doing it for a forty-sixth.

He took in the wondrous construction surrounding them, all of it fashioned from nothing more than laboriously worked sand. Contemplated the humming, thriving community, alive with craftwork and farming and art. Considered, and tried to envision abandoning it all to inevitable ruination and starting over again from nothing.

His gaze returned at last to the waiting Loswee. "I am sorry, but we cannot help you."

Simna looked momentarily startled, then relieved. Clearly, he had been expecting a different sort of response from his friend. Behind them, Ahlitah rolled over and snored.

Loswee accepted the response gravely. "Outside, you agreed that if not help, you might be able to give us some advice."

Ehomba shrugged diffidently. "I said 'might.' Loswee, I do not know what to say. You told us that magic was needed to fight this Dunawake, and I replied that we had no magic. I am sorry to say that we have no advice, either. We do not even know what a Dunawake is. Believe me, I feel terrible about this. Men I know how to fight, and animals, and even certain circumstances of nature, but not a Dunawake. I have never heard of one, seen one, or had it described to me."

"Perhaps if you saw it you would know how to respond." Backed by his silently watching Elders, Loswee was unwilling to drop the matter.

"I do not see why. And if it is as dangerous as you say, and we confronted it without knowing how to respond or react, I imagine we would probably die. I do not want to die. I have an obligation of my own to fulfill that does not, regrettably, include the Swick, and also a family that I am missing more than I can say."

"Also friends," Simna added quickly.

"Yes, even that." Ehomba took a long, deep breath. "I am sorry, Loswee. For you and for your people. But it is not like you are unused to moving."

"It never gets easier," the Swick soldier told him. "But if there is nothing you can do, there is nothing you can do. These Elders and I will convey your response to the rest of the Council." Behind him, the senior Swick genuflected once again. They had spoken, and having had their say, now added not a word. "Finish your meal," Loswee advised as he turned away.

This the visitors proceeded to do: Ahlitah quietly, Simna without a thought, and Ehomba with perhaps one or two—but they were fleeting. He could not change the world, and in actual fact had no desire to try.

If their hosts in general or Loswee in particular held any resentment against the travelers for their refusal to help in the endless ongoing battle against their nemesis, they did not show it. The rest of the day was spent touring other parts of the remarkable underground complex and in learning more of Swick culture. It was ancient but not widely known, in large part because of the perpetrators' secretive style of living.

"There are other dunes in other desert parts of the world where our distant relations thrive," Loswee informed them, "and the human beings who live in close proximity to those dunes are completely unaware of our presence nearby. They see tracks in the sand, but the tracks are those of the birds and other animals we make use of."

"You are a very resourceful people," Ehomba admitted respectfully.

"Yes," declared Loswee with pride. "Our lands have always been safe from all trespass except that of the Dunawake, though I fear that someday this may change."

"Why's that?" inquired Simna, only half interested.

Loswee turned quite serious. "Humans have a great love for lamps, and our land floats on the liquid they use to fill them. I am afraid that one day they may come to take it, smashing down the dunes and trampling the plants in the ravines and wadis."

Ehomba looked up at the sand ceiling overhead. "Not these dunes," he commented reassuringly. "They are too big, and this land is too remote."

"I hope you are right, my friend." Loswee sighed, the diminutive exhalation comical in the enclosed space, like the wheezing of a mouse. "I am more sorry than I can say that you are not the magician we had hoped for."

"So am I." It cost Ehomba nothing to agree. Sympathy was cheap.

"I know that you must be on your way." The tiny fighter summoned up a smile. Given the width of his mouth, it nearly split his broad, flat face in half. "At least you have had the chance to experience Swick hospitality. That is a treat few human beings have enjoyed."

"We are grateful." As a courtesy, Ehomba dipped his head slightly. "We will take away good memories with us."

"And I, if not the Elders, will remember you fondly." It seemed impossible that Loswee's smile could grow any wider, but it did, defying the boundaries of his face. "Tomorrow morning I myself will conduct you back outside, and show you the easiest way to the north. Follow my directions, and you will not find yourselves pinched by the dunes and having to slog your way through sand. There is a particularly wide and flat gulch that runs all the way through this country. Keep your feet on it always and you will soon find yourselves once more in a land of green trees and running water."

"How far from there to the nearest river or seaport?" Ehomba asked him.

Loswee spread his small hands apologetically. "That I can't tell you. We Swick keep to the sand country, where we can live in peace and solitude among our dunes. Not all people are as understanding or kindly toward others as yourselves. Believe it or not, there are some who like to hurt anything and anyone who is smaller than themselves simply because they can."

"The world is full of bullies," Ehomba agreed. "I understand your desire to maintain your privacy. When people are squabbling over nothing, as often seems to be the case, I myself prefer the company of cattle."

"Tomorrow, then." Loswee backed away. "Sleep well, my friends, and dream of Swick choirs singing back the stars."

XXIII

The travelers awoke refreshed and relaxed, ready to resume their interrupted trek northward. After a final, sumptuous breakfast, Loswee himself escorted them away from the inner castle, through the rest of the town, and into the main tunnel that led to the world outside.

After the time they had spent underground, the unfiltered directness of the desert sun stung their eyes. They had to retreat back into the tunnel and reemerge gradually. It took almost half an hour before their eyes could once more handle the harsh clarity of the blue sky and the sun reflecting off the surrounding dune faces.

There was no shaking of hands as was the custom in Simna's homeland, nor clasping of forearms in the fashion of the Naumkib and related peoples, nor even licking of faces as was common among Ahlitah's feline tribe. Loswee simply raised a hand in farewell, then turned on his bird and rode back toward the tunnel that led to the wondrous subterranean world of the Swick.

But not before leading them around the base of the great dune whose unsuspected secret was the flourishing inner community it concealed. There, radiating out from a small salt pan, three waterless meanderings wandered off in search of the far distant sea. Pointing to the one in the middle, Loswee informed them that if they followed it, not only would it broaden into a wide, easily hiked desert highway, but eventually it would lead them into greener and more populated country. From there they would doubtless have better luck finding the oceanic transportation they sought.

Towing their diminished but still significant water supply behind them, they thanked the diminutive Swick warrior before starting off in the indicated direction. True to his word, the narrow wadi soon expanded into a sun-blasted, relatively gravel-free promenade that promised easy access to wherever it led.

By late afternoon, enough clouds had gathered to provide some surcease from the intolerant sun. This was not enough to assuage the mood of the valiant swordsman, who without anything specific to complain about was feeling decidedly peckish.

"If we were back among the Swick it'd be lunchtime about now." Adjusting his pack so that it rode a little higher on his shoulders, he squinted at the cloud-masked sky.

From his position in the lead, Ehomba looked back at his companion. "Would you have ever left? I was afraid that we had overstayed our welcome as it was."

"Of course I would've left, bruther. The food was good, for sure, but the appearance of the local ladies was not only a tad gruesome for my taste, they were also most proportionately incommodious."

The herdsman was left shaking his head. "What a wastrel you are, Simna ibn Sind. You have built nothing with your life."

"As opposed to you, with your nagging cattle and daggy sheep? If that's a legacy for a man to be proud of, I'll take cinnamon."

"Excess!" Ehomba actually raised his voice slightly. "Your life is all about excess, Simna. Useless, wasting, scattergood excess."

"And yours is about nothingness, Etjole. Empty, barren, sterile nothingness!"

"Barren and sterile, is it? I have a most beautiful wife, and two handsome, strong children to care for me in my old age."

Simna would no more back down from a verbal challenge than from a physical one. "And when I claim my share of treasure I'll buy a harem to care for me, and guards, and the best physicians. That I'll enjoy while you toss and rot as old women chant lamentations over your withered, dying body."

"You may be right about that," Ehomba conceded, "but therein lies a difference between us."

"And what's that?" riposted the swordsman belligerently.

Ehomba held his head high. "Having already acquired my treasure, I have neither the need nor the desire to claim another."

"What treasure?" Simna made a face. "Your 'beautiful wife'? I've had, and will have, dozens, hundreds more of the most beautiful. Gold, you know, herdsman, is the most potent aphrodisiac of all."

"It will not bring you love," Ehomba shot back.

"Hoy! Love!" The swordsman laughed aloud. "Highly overpriced as well as overrated. Keep your love, bruther, and I'll have my harem."

"That is where you are wrong, Simna. If you are not careful, *it* will have *you.*" Angry, he lengthened his stride, forcing the stubbier swordsman to have to hurry to keep up with him.

"Is that so?" Simna really had no idea what his companion meant by the comment but was unwilling to leave him the last word. "I can tell you from experience that—"

"Scat on your experience! Be *quiet*!" Having viewed the entire argument with jaundiced detachment, Ahlitah had lifted his great maned head high into the clear, overheated air and was listening intently. Ehomba and Simna immediately put their discussion on hold as they tried to detect whatever it was that had alarmed the big cat.

For alarmed he was, or at the very least, suddenly wary. It was manifest in his posture: every muscle tense, every sense alert. Both men looked around uneasily but could see nothing out of the ordinary. A lizard with unusually broad, flat feet scampered up the face of a dune to get away from them. White-breasted dragonebs circled on silent wings high overhead, hoping and waiting for one or more of the party to drop. Isolated insects buzzed about the fragmentary plants that clung to the dry ravine or fought the fringes of encroaching dunes. There was no noise, not a sound, as if the very constituents of the air itself had stopped moving. The stillness was as profound as stone.

Then a slight breeze picked up, ruffling the paralysis. The world, after momentarily holding its breath, seemed set in motion again. For an instant, Simna would not have been surprised to see one of the violent corkscrew storms they had battled on the veldt emerge from hiding behind one of the towering dunes. But all that showed itself was a pair of iridescent blue butterflies with white wing spots, flitting and fluttering about a common axis of anticipated procreation. That, and the slightly darker-hued sand that was blowing around the far corner of the dune on their left.

Except—far more sand was sifting from west to east than the barely perceptible breeze should have been capable of moving.

It was the color of powdered rust, stained with a hint of decay. Yellow blotches appeared here and there as the sand drift continued to increase. Now a small ridge a foot or two high where it was emerging from behind the motionless bulk of the other dune, it continued to pile up across the wadi. The first scouting grains had already crossed completely to the other side, leaving behind a rising, widening seam of dark reddish sand.

Ahlitah continued to sample the air, but it was Ehomba who called a halt. "That is odd."

A frustrated Simna was searching their immediate surroundings for a nonexistent danger. "What is?"

"That rising ridge of sand." The herdsman pointed.

Simna glanced distractedly at the unthreatening maroon granules that were drifting across their path. "I see a line of blowing sand. Nothing odd about that."

"Not in and of itself, no." The herdsman gripped his spear a little tighter. "But by its actions it heralds an approaching darkness. Not an eromakadi, an eater of light that can only be slain by an eromakasi, but some kind of more physical, less subtle relation."

"Hoy, what are you jabbering about, long bruther?" What he could not see made Simna more nervous than any visible opponent, no matter how menacing.

Adding to the swordsman's discomfort, Ehomba took a step backward, acting for all the world as if he were actually retreating from something. "The reddish sand advances—but the sand in front of it and across from it does not move." He glanced meaningfully at his friend. "Since when does the air select its wind-borne freight with such care?"

Simna's expression contorted as he mulled over his companion's words—and suddenly he saw the blowing, drifting red sand in a new light. It was true, only the sand the color of rust rushed and rambled across the width of the wadi. Before it and behind it, not a grain was stirring. That was peculiar, all right.

It was also more than a little frightening.

"Maybe we'd better go back." He had already started backing up. "Loswee's directions aside, there must be another way north. One that doesn't involve confronting animate sands."

Retreating, he bumped into the litah's behind. But the great cat did not growl at him. He was holding his ground, facing back the way they had come.

"I'm afraid it's too late for that, man." A rising breeze stirred his jet black mane.

A second stream of reddish sand was whisking across the ravine behind them, cutting off their only retreat. Simna gaped at the steady flow and the rising dike it was creating.

"For Grentoria's sake, it's only sand! A man could still clear it in a single bound!"

"Maybe," Ehomba conceded, "if all it did was continue to blow from west to east." Turning, he gestured sharply with the toothed tip of his spear. "That way, quickly! Up the side of the dune!" Obeying his own words, he started up the slick, difficult slope. Glancing methodically from left to right, Ahlitah followed, his broad footpads having an easier time with the difficult terrain than the sandaled human.

Simna trailed behind, cursing with every step the sand that slid away beneath his feet and made upward progress a strenuous ordeal. Seeing that the mysterious wall of red sand was now ten feet high at either end of the gulch and still rising helped to spur him on.

They were halfway up the side of the accommodating dune when the sky began to darken and a voice boomed behind them. It was the lament of something that was less than a beast and more than a natural phenomenon, the unnaturally drawn-out moan of a fiend most monstrous and uncommon. With their feet planted ankle deep in the sand the fleeing travelers turned, and saw at last what had so subtly tried to ambush them by trapping them within the ravine.

It looked for all the world (or any other) like just another dune.

Except it was taller, and darker. Angry-red darker. And it advanced not in the manner of a living creature, but in the fashion of dunes, by shifting that which composed its near side forward, so that it in turn pulled the center. The center drew the rear portion forward, rolling on over the middle, and so continuing the cycle. Back become middle become front, like a slow wheel spinning about a central axis; endless, eternal, indomitable.

It had no arms and then a hundred, no feet but one that was as wide as the base of the advancing dune itself, like the great lumbering foot of some muscular mollusk. Everywhere and all of it was sand, dark red like all the rust that had ever afflicted all the metals of the world rolled and bunched and squeezed up together into a single swiftly shifting pyramid of revenge. Loswee had spoken of roaring dunes, and indeed there were some such in Ehomba's own country. But never before had he heard of, or encountered, a dune that howled and moaned and bellowed like some sky-scraping banshee unwillingly fastened to the Earth.

And in the midst of all that displaced geologic fury, two-thirds of the way up the face of the oncoming mountain, were two eyes. An abyssal, lambent red, they pulsed like fires from deep within the sand, inclined forty-five degrees in opposite directions, and focused fixedly on the three fleeing travelers. Why they, foreigners in a foreign land, should inspire such rage and determination on the part of the Dunawake, none of the three could say. Perhaps the monster raved and raged from a deep-seated need to exterminate whatever life it encountered within the dunes, no matter its origin.

Already, several small mammals and reptiles had been caught and smothered beneath the advancing skirt of sand, too slow or too blinded by blowing particles to flee in time. The same fate now threatened those trying to scramble clear of its reach. Blasts of maroon sand stung their backs while granular tendrils clawed at their legs. High on the face of an indifferent, inanimate dune, they were temporarily safe as long as they stayed above and ahead of the abomination's advance.

But the Dunawake was bigger than the dune they were climbing. If it continued to flow forward it would eventually engulf the sandy prominence, overwhelming both it and them. Ehomba knew the far side would provide no refuge. Not when their abrasive pursuer could send arms of sand racing around the base of the dune whose summit they were about to reach. They were trapped. They could only continue to climb until they reached the top, there to wait until the steady advance of the Dunawake overwhelmed them on their final perch.

Struggling upward as his sandaled feet sank inches deep and more into the unstable slope, Simna drew his sword and slashed repeatedly at the thin red tendrils that were clutching at his legs. As he cut and hacked away, handfuls of sand went flying in all directions. What held them together, what made of tiny individual particles a coherent and persistent entity, he could not imagine. Who would have thought that unadulterated rant would make so effective a glue?

For every clutching sandy offshoot he scattered, another crept upward to take its place. Noting the dispersing effect of his methodical, skillful sword strokes, he felt he could eventually cut the Dunawake down to size. Why, at the rate his sword was strewing sand to left and right, the monster would run out of granules with which to form grasping tendrils in not less than a couple of million years! Unfortunately, his arm was already growing tired.

Sorely vexed by the streamers of sand that flogged his heels, Ahlitah whirled repeatedly to bite at the sinuous red tormentors, pulverizing them within his massive jaws. But biting and spitting were ultimately no more effective than Simna's sword-work. Furthermore, with each snap the great cat had to spit out a mouthful of hot, red sand. He would have much preferred to battle an opponent with some taste.

"The sword!" Sweating profusely as he struggled up the tenacious incline, Simna yelled at his tall companion. "Use the sword of sky metal and blow this Dunawake to bits!"

Looking back down at his friend, Ehomba shouted above the advancing shriek of animate sand treading corybantically upon itself. "It will not work! I can fight wind with wind, but rock and soil and sand are a weightier proposition."

"Try!" With an effort more of will than of muscle, the swordsman used some of his rapidly failing strength to accelerate upward, until he was standing alongside his friend. Wind squeezed forward by the advancing Dunawake tore at their garments and wilded their hair. "If you can't beat it, maybe enough wind in its face will discourage it."

They were nearly to the top. "Feeding the wind off a dune face only encourages it. Its strength lies in its coherence. You have seen how it may be cut and broken on the sword."

"Hoy!" Simna agreed as they reached the crest of the dune together. Ahlitah turned and snarled, mane streaming backward in the hot, stifling wind, defying the elements both natural and unnatural. "And if Gupjolpa would give me ten thousand swordsmen we'd beat it back as surely as this hot air scours my flesh. But there are only two, me and thee, and you won't fight."

"I did not say that." Having swung his backpack around to rest against his chest, the herdsman was busy within its depths. "I suggested that it was futile to use the sword."

Simna looked back and down. Already the raw red sand of the Dunawake was three-quarters of the way up the side of their inadequate asylum and climbing fast. "Well you had best find something to use, by Gostoko, or in minutes we'll all the three of us be good and buried, leaving nothing behind but our memories."

"Ah." Straightening, Ehomba withdrew something from the interior of the pack. Simna's hopefulness was replaced by disbelieving eyes and lowered jaw. In his right hand his good friend, his resourceful friend, his knowledgeable friend, held—a rotund, stoppered clay flask smaller than his fist. A single thin cord secured the rubber stopper to a ring carved in the side of the bottle.

The swordsman struggled to remain calm. "Poison?" he inquired hopefully. "You're going to poison it?"

"Do not be an idiot." Closing up his pack to keep out the swirling sand, Ehomba turned to face the rising, oncoming hulk of the Dunawake. Absently he juggled the clay bottle up and down in his open palm. "You cannot poison sand. I told you, to affect it you must impact its integrity."

"With that?" Simna gestured at the bottle with his free hand. "Well then, by Gwipta, what's in the pharking phial if not poison?"

Ehomba did not take his eyes off the oncoming Dunawake nor the tide of red granules that would soon be lapping at their feet. Behind them, more rivers of red sand were creeping up the backside of the dune, further extirpating any lingering hope of flight.

"Whater," he replied simply.

Striving to retreat farther, Simna found himself slipping down the eastern, back face of their dune. "Water?" he mumbled, more like a drowning man than a moribund one.

"No." Ehomba gestured at the pond remnant Ahlitah had dragged up the dune face with them. "That's water. This is whater."

Feeling more than a little taste of panic in his mouth, the baffled swordsman looked on as the herdsman carefully removed the stopper from the clay flask. The crest of the red dune was now very close to overtopping and swamping the dune on which the travelers stood. The glowing, fiery eyes had slipped up the face of the oncoming mountain so that they were now nearly level with Ehomba. Sliding farther down the backside of the crest, Simna bumped into the litah. The big cat snarled at him but held his ground, using his much greater weight and all four feet to keep them from tumbling down the steeper, unstable slope.

Above, they saw the herdsman lower the point of his spear and rap the bottle sharply against it once, twice. The clay cracked but did not come apart. Then Ehomba drew back his right arm and threw the fractured container directly into the face of the swollen, howling Dunawake. As he did so, the shattered bottle came apart, its contents spilling onto the hissing red sand. Simna strained to see, but it looked like the bottle contained nothing more than a swallow or two of water. Or whater, as his friend had insisted.

A mammoth curl of sand rose high, higher than the dune peak, pausing before surging forward to crush the stoic herdsman and his companions beneath its hot, smothering weight. And then a strange thing happened. Simna, for one, was not surprised. He had already had occasion to observe that in moments of difficulty, strange things had a tendency to transpire in Etjole Ehomba's vicinity, and that at such times it was a good idea to be on the herdsman's beneficent side.

The unimaginable tons of sand that comprised the malevolent structure of the Dunawake began to shiver.

XXIV

It was a most peculiar sight, to see sand shiver. First the dune face and then the entire scarlet mass commenced to tremble, shaking and quaking and shuddering in place. Ahlitah's lower jaw fell, revealing huge canines in a gape of amazement instead of threat. Simna stared grimly, wondering how his tall friend had managed to freeze an entire dune with one tiny bottle of water. Only it was not water, he reminded himself. It was whater, whatever that might be.

But he was wrong. The Dunawake was not freezing, not turning from sand to ice or anything comparable. What it was doing was coming apart, shaking itself to pieces. How something that was already composed of billions of tiny grains could come to pieces was yet another wonder that the awe-struck Simna had no time to ponder.

What was happening before their eyes was that the Dunawake was shivering itself into its individual components. A small dune of pure quartz began to rise alongside a sibling dune of feldspar. Next to them a glistening cone of mica rose from the desert floor, and beside it granulated black schist heaped up in dark profusion. There were other colors and cones, stacks and mounds, to which Simna could not put a name. Their identities did not matter to him. What was important was that none of them moved, and none glared up at him out of baleful, pulsing red eyes.

The once fearsome Dunawake continued to tremble and quiver until it had shaken itself apart. Where it had once loomed there now rose a dozen separate dunes far more modest in size, each composed of a single different, unadulterated mineral. The herdsman's companions climbed the short distance back up the east face of the dune from where they had sought refuge to rejoin their friend.

Thin as a stick stuck in a child's mud pile, tall and straight as a tree rooted in the depths of the earth, Ehomba was standing at the very apex of the yellow dune staring down at the disassociated remnants of the Dunawake. Wind whipped his shirt and the hem of his kilt. Had he suddenly raised his arms to the sky and drawn down lightning from nothingness Simna would not have been surprised. Nothing of the sort happened, of course. As the subject of the swordsman's stare would have been the first to remind him, he was nothing but a simple herdsman.

Coming up alongside him, Simna grabbed his friend's arm as together they gazed downward. "Tell me now you're no sorcerer, Etjole Ehomba. Tell me now to my face that you're not a man who can work magicks!"

"Sorry to disappoint you yet again, friend Simna, but I am not." Lips firm, jaw set, the laconic southerner looked down at his disbelieving companion.

"Oh, I see. And how, then, do you explain what you just did?" He nodded at the dozen or so new, unalloyed dunes that rose from the desert floor below where they stood.

"That was not me," the other man protested humbly. "It was the whater that did that."

"Perhaps we would understand better," Ahlitah put in from behind him, "if you told us what this 'whater' is? Or was."

Ehomba nodded agreeably. "Before I set out on this journey, the women of my village gave me several things to carry with me, to help me along the way. Old Fhastal, clever Likulu, bright-eyed Omura; even my own woman, Mirhanja, helped. It is a tradition among the Naumkib that when a warrior leaves for any length of time, the women get together to bundle useful items for him to take with him." His gaze angled downward once more, toward the remnants of the Dunawake. "Sadly, that was my only bottle of whater." He started down the dune, positioning his body sideways as he descended, the better to balance himself against the shifting sand.

Simna simply walked straight down, paralleling his friend and exhibiting the remarkable physical poise of which he was capable. The four-footed Ahlitah, of course, had no trouble at all with the steep slope. Not nearly as agile as his companions, Ehomba stumbled several times in the course of the descent.

"This whater," the cat asked, "what does it do?" The maned head nodded tersely in the direction of the neatly disassociated dunes. "What *did* it do?"

"It was for purifying water." Ehomba stepped over a rock that protruded from the lower dune face. "The women say that one drop of whater will make an entire basin of water fit for drinking. It purifies liquid by separating out all the dirt and scum and little bugs we cannot see from the water itself."

A much puzzled Simna wore a deep frown. " 'Little bugs we cannot see'?"

Herdsman and cat ignored him.

"So that's what you did to the Dunawake," Ahlitah mused aloud. "You 'purified' it."

"Into its individual parts." They were almost down, stepping back onto the hard, unyielding, blissfully motion-free bed of the ravine where the monstrous apparition had almost had them trapped. "In this instance, the sum of the parts is much less than the whole. A man would be no less," he added thoughtfully, "if he were similarly purified. Skeleton here, blood there, muscles in one pile, and organs in another."

Simna's mouth twisted. "Now there's a pretty picture. Remind me not to go sampling the contents of any other bottles you happen to be carrying."

"That was my only whater." Ehomba gestured at the half-full floating pond Ahlitah continued to tow. "We had better hope we always find good water from now on, because I have nothing left with which to launder the undrinkable."

"You did the right thing, Etjole. By Girimza, you did!" The swordsman clapped his friend reassuringly on the back. "Clean water's no good to a corpse."

"Hold up." Ahlitah lifted a paw and sniffed the air. "We are still not alone here."

Startled, Simna reached instinctively for his sword even though it had proven ineffectual against their last opponent. Then he relaxed. Relaxed, even though he was no less disconcerted.

Ehomba handled the unexpected confrontation with his usual sangfroid, smiling and nodding at the figure that now blocked their path.

"Hello, Loswee. I did not expect to see you again."

As the Swick's feathered mount advanced toward the travelers, a dozen other miniature mounted warriors trotted out from their place of concealment behind a pile of sand-swept rocks. Brightly tinted pennants flew from the tips of their lances, and they were clad in decorative ceremonial armor.

Leaning forward in his saddle, Loswee stared at the travelers for a long moment before sitting back and gesturing at something behind them. "For not-a-magician you seem to have not-dealt pretty well with the is-no-more Dunawake."

"It wasn't him," Simna interjected sarcastically. "It was just a bottle of whater that did that."

"Thum," murmured the Swick fighter. "It would be pointless for me to argue with you about your true natures. The People of the Sands do not care. What matters is that the Dunawake is done and the dreadful, persistent threat of it has been removed. For this deed you will live forever in the hearts of the Swick. One last time, I salute you."

He raised his lance as high as if he wished to pierce the sky itself. Behind him, his resplendent escort echoed the gesture. Five times they did this, each time giving forth a piercing ululation that seemed to rise up from the depths of the surrounding sand itself. Then they turned to go.

"Strange the ways of coincidence, is it not?" Ehomba watched the long tail feathers of the warriors' mounts bob up and down as they filed back behind the rocks from where they had emerged.

"What?" A bemused Simna turned to look up at his friend. "What coincidence?"

With a sigh, the herdsman started forward, formally resuming their trek northward and using his spear for support, like a tall walking stick. "The little people wanted us to fight the Dunawake for them. We refused, and so after wining and dining us they graciously bid us on our way. They even told us the easiest way to go to reach the lands to the north. Told us even though we did not ask directions from them. Soon after leaving, we run right into the Dunawake." Glancing over at the swordsman, he did something Simna had not seen him do very often. He laughed aloud: not only with his mouth, but with his eyes.

"Face it, my friend. We have been played the way a master musician plays his flute."

Simna's expression darkened. "Are you telling me, bruther . . . ?"

"That we have been the victims of a Swick trick." And the herdsman chortled afresh.

Realization landed on the swordsman like the news of an unwanted pregnancy. "Why, those miserable little, lying-lipped, arse-mouthed, flat-faced fuggers!" Raising his voice, eyes wild, Simna drew his sword and rushed toward the pile of rocks where the diminutive warriors had disappeared. "I'll kill you all! I'll cut off your hairy ears and feed them to the scorpions!"

With an indifferent snuffle, Ahlitah changed direction until he was pacing the long-striding Ehomba. "He doesn't get it, does he?"

The herdsman shrugged diffidently. "Simna's a good man. He is just a little impulsive."

"A little too human, you mean." The big cat sniffed derisively. The penetrating yellow eyes of a great feline predator peered into Ehomba's face from only a foot away. Hunting, searching. "And you?"

The herdsman pursed his lips. "I do not follow you."

"What are you, Etjole Ehomba? Are you all human? Or is this a mask you choose to wear to fool the rest of us? I am thinking that the Swick are not the only ones who are good at tricks."

The rangy southerner smiled comfortingly as he poled the hard ground with the butt of his long spear the way a sailor would dig his paddle into water. "I am only a man, Ahlitah. I am only what you see here walking beside you."

"I will accept that—for now." With that, the litah moved away, the hovering pond bobbing along behind him as he put a little distance between them. Ehomba watched him with interest. For one who slept as long and often as the litah, very little escaped the big cat's notice.

Simna ranted and raged among the rocks for only a moment or two before resigning himself to the fact that his intended quarry had fled. More than fled, they had disappeared, utterly vanished from sight. Even the footprints of their mounts had evaporated like mist in the desert air. Muttering to himself as he resheathed his sword, he rejoined his companions.

"The little buggers are fast, but I didn't think they were that fast." He shook an angry fist at the dunes and wadi behind them. "What I wouldn't give for one small gray neck under my fingers!"

"Yes, they are fast." Ahlitah's black lower lip curled upward. "That'd make it a quick slick Swick trick, wouldn't it?"

"Oh, shut up, you imprecise venter of stinking bodily fluids!"

Still grinning in its sly cat fashion, the litah did not respond.

"They did what they felt was necessary for their survival." Ehomba tried to mollify his companion.

"Their survival?" The swordsman jabbed a thumb into his chest. "They didn't give a sparrow's fart for *our* survival!"

"The grand welcome they gave us, mere passing strangers. The escorts and the tours, the singing and the feasts, giving freely, even extravagantly, of their food and drink. Did you think that was all done out of impulsive friendship?"

Simna's anger dissipated as he considered the herdsman's words. Eventually, he nodded agreement. "Yes, you're right, Etjole. I, of all people, should have known better. I suppose it was their size that fooled me. Who would have guessed that their appetite for treachery was as great as their ability to build structures out of sand?" With that admission the last of his fury fled as effortlessly as it had originally consumed him, and he was his old self again.

"Clever little dumplings, weren't they? I'll know better next time. From now on I, Simna ibn Sind, won't accept hospitality from a mouse without first questioning its ulterior motives."

"I understand why they did what they did."

The swordsman glanced up at his friend. "You take their side? 'What they did' nearly got us killed!"

"I know. But if it was my village at stake, my family, all my friends, everyone I had ever known, I would also do whatever was necessary to save it. At such times, under such circumstances, expediency always takes precedence over honor."

Simna drew himself up to his full height. "For a true hero, nothing takes place over honor!"

"Then you can be the hero, Simna. I want only to discharge my obligation and return as quickly as possible to my family and to my village. That is what is important to me. That is what I have built my life around. Not abstract notions of what may or may not be considered acceptable behavior among those I do not care for and do not know." He nodded back the way they had come, back toward the silent dunes and their sand-locked, unseen mysteries. "That is how the Swick believe. I cannot condemn them for acting exactly as I would have under similar circumstances."

The swordsman snorted. "Then you'll never be a hero, Etjole. You'll never ride in triumph through the streets of a great city, acknowledging the acclamation of the crowd and the eyes of pretty women. You'll never be a noble in your own land, much less a king lording it over others."

The lanky southerner was not in the least offended by his companion's dismissive summation. "I have no desire to lord it over even my children, friend Simna. As for drawing the eyes of pretty women, I have never thought myself the type to do so, and would not know how to react if I did. Besides, I already have the eyes of the one woman who means anything to me. As for riding through the streets of a great city, I am content to walk, and am satisfied in place of cheers to receive the occasional 'Good morning' and 'How are you?' These things are enough for me."

"You have no ambition, bruther," the swordsman groused at him.

"On the contrary, my friend, my aspirations are considerable. I desire greatly to live a long and healthy life in the company of my woman, to see my children raised up strong and of kindly mien, to have always, or at least most of the time, enough to eat, to continue to be able to watch over my animals, to enjoy the company of my friends and relations, and to walk once again along the edge of the sea, listening to its song and smelling of its perfume." His eyes glistened. "That, I think, should be enough for any man." Slipping his free hand into a pocket, he felt of the pebble-filled cloth bag there, wondering how much of the sea-smell still clung to the shiny rock fragments.

They walked in silence for some time before a wide grin came to dominate the swordsman's face, wiping out the indifference that had been extant there. "Hoy, now I see." He shook his head and guffawed delightedly. "Oh, you're good, good it is you are, Etjole Ehomba! You had me going for a while there. It's a clever, clever magician you are, but you can't fool me! Not Simna ibn Sind. I've been tested in the market-places of wily Harquarnastan, and gone toe-to-toe with the shrewd and shifty barkers of the Yirt-u-Yir plateau. But I'll grant you this: You're the subtlest and sneakiest of the lot!" He executed a joyful little pirouette, dancing out the delight of his personal revelation. Ahlitah looked on with distaste.

" 'Have enough to eat.' 'Walk along the edge of the sea.' Oh surely, sorcerer, surely! As a cover it's brilliant, as a mask unsurpassed. No one will think anything more of you, humble master of steer and sheep that you are. What a masquerade! Better than pretending to be a merchant, or storyteller, or unoffending pilgrim." While walking backward in the direction they were headed, he executed several mock bows, making a dance of it as he repeatedly raised and lowered his head and his out-stretched arms.

"I concede to you the title Wizard of the Incognito, o masterful one! Herder of goats and sovereign of infants; that shall be your designation until the treasure is ours." Resuming his normal gait, he fell in step alongside his friend while Ahlitah padded along opposite. "You *almost* had me fooled, Etjole."

"Yes," the herdsman responded with a heartfelt sigh, "I can see that you are not a man to be easily deceived." He focused on a lizard that was scampering into a burrow off to their left. It was blue, with bright pink stripes and a yellow-spotted head.

"Just so long as you realize that," Simna replied importantly. "Hoy, but I'll be glad to get out of this desert!"

"The desert, the cleanness and the dunes, is all beautiful."

"Speak for yourself, devotee of dry nowheres."

"Yes."

Lifting his head, the litah let loose with a long, mournful *owrooooo*. It echoed back and forth among the dune slopes, escaping their sandy surroundings far faster than could they. When it was finished, the big cat eyed his human companions. "In this I side with the swordsman. I love tall grass and shady thickets, running water and lots of fat, slow animals."

"Then why are we lingering here?" A cheerful, composed Simna looked over at the great black feline. "So this long-faced drink of dark water can set the pace? If we let him determine it, we'll find ourselves dawdling in this accursed country until the end of time." With that he broke into a jog, stepping easily and effortlessly out in front of the others.

Despite the burden imposed by the hovering pond he was towing, Ahlitah stretched out his remarkable cheetah-like legs and matched the man's pace effortlessly. Ehomba watched them for a moment before extending his own stride. It would be useless to tell them that he had wanted to move faster all along, but had held himself back out of concern for their welfare. It was better this way, he knew. Healthier for Simna to have made the decision.

He did not smile at the way events had progressed. There was no particular gratification in knowing all along what was going to happen.

XXV

The Tale of the Lost Tree

The tree did not remember much of what had happened, or even when it had happened. It was all so very long ago. It had been nothing more than a sapling, a scrawny splinter of wood only a few feet high, with no girth to shield it from the elements, no thick layer of tough bark to protect it from marauding browsers.

Despite that, it had thrived. The soil in which it had taken root as a seed was deep and rich, the weathered kind, with ample rain and not too much snow. It had neither frozen in winter nor burned in summer. Though it lost leaves to hungry insects, this was a normal, natural part of maturing, and it compensated by putting out more leaves than any of the other saplings in its immediate vicinity. As a consequence of insect infestation, several of the others died before they could become more than mere shoots.

The tree did not. It survived, in company with several of its neighbors. In spite of the fact that they had all taken root at the same time, two of them were taller. Others were smaller.

Growth was a never-ending struggle as they all strove to gain height and diameter. Though ever-present and never ceasing, competition from others of their kind was silent, as was the nature of trees. In its fourth year one of its neighbors fell prey to hungry deer during a particularly long and cold winter. They stripped the bark from the young growth, leaving it naked and unprotected, and when spring next came around it was easy prey for boring beetles. Another succumbed to the benign but deadly attentions of a bear with an itch. Scratching itself against the youthful bole, it snapped it in half, leaving it broken and dying, its heartwood exposed to the callous, indifferent elements.

But this tree was lucky. Large animals left it alone, insects found others in the vicinity more to their liking, birds chose not to strip its young twigs for nest-building material. Every spring it budded fiercely, fighting to throw out new leaves and to photosynthesize sugars before they could be consumed. Every winter it lay dormant and still, hoping the migrating herds would leave it alone.

Then, just when survival and long life seemed assured, disaster struck.

It happened late in autumn and took the form not of anything with blood in its veins but of a vast and powerful storm. The terrifying weather swept up the coast of the land where the tree grew, destroying everything in its path that was unable to resist. Even some of the great old trees that formed the bulk of the forest mass where the tree lived were not immune. Unprecedented winds roared down off the slopes of the western mountains, descending like an invisible avalanche. As they fell, the winds picked up speed and volume.

Trees that had stood for a thousand years were blown over, their roots left exposed and naked to the world. Others lost dozens or even hundreds of minor branches and many major ones. The forest floor was swept clean as leaves, logs, mushrooms, insects and spiders, even small animals, were sucked up and whirled away.

The sapling held fast as long as it could, but its shallow, young roots were no match for the unparalleled violence of the storm. It found itself ripped up into the sky, where it joined the company of thousands of tons of other debris. Since the storm had struck in autumn, the tree had already shut down in anticipation of the coming winter. Sap was concentrated in its heartwood, waiting for the warmth of spring to send it coursing freely once more throughout the length and breadth of the young growth.

Now it was at the mercy of the berserk elements, which tossed and flung it about as if it weighed even less than its slim self. How long it was carried thus, over water and field, mountain and plain, the sapling did not know. It might have been an instant or a month. A tree's sense of time is very different from that of most other living things.

Then it felt itself falling, tumbling crown over root, spiraling toward the ground. Nature is rife with examples of extraordinary accidents, and the fall of the tree was one of those exceptions. It landed not on its side as would have been expected, nor on its crest. It struck the ground with its slender trunk exactly perpendicular to the earth. Bare roots slammed into and partially penetrated the loose-packed surface, giving the tree immediate if uncertain support.

Expelled from the tail end of the swiftly moving storm, the tree shuddered in its farewell gusts but did not fall. The tempest continued on its way, wreaking devastation to the east and leaving the tree behind. It was surrounded by other debris that had been abandoned by the weather, but most of it was dead. That which was not soon died and began to decompose.

Only the tree survived. Along with wind, the storm had contained a great deal of water, which fell along its path as heavy rain. The soil in which the tree had providentially landed upright was now saturated, so much so that the sapling's roots were able to draw from this source for many months after its unwilling transplantation.

Against all odds, its roots took hold in the alien ground. Where winter had been approaching in the tree's homeland, it was summer where it had landed. Sap began to flow well in advance of the date determined by the tree's biological clock. This perturbation also it adapted to. Buds appeared on those branches that had survived the storm's wrath. Leaves sprouted and unfolded wide, drinking in the strong, unobstructed sunlight of their new home.

In this new land there were far fewer insects, and so the tree was able to grow even faster than was normal. Over the years its branches thickened and its trunk put on weight. It spread its arms wide to shade the ground on which it stood. This helped to preserve the rain that fell seasonally and rarely, much more so than in the land where the tree had first sprouted.

But beneath its roots lay a consistent, subterranean supply of water. This the tree tapped with roots that bored deep, assuring it of proper nourishment no matter how infrequent the annual rains. With no other growths in its immediate vicinity, it had no competition for nutrients. Only the sparseness of the land itself kept it from growing to even greater proportions.

Inherently unambitious, over the years and the decades and even the centuries, the sapling flourished and matured into a fine, tall specimen of its species, with numerous major branches and a trunk whose diameter far exceeded that of its parent. As the centuries unfolded, it observed the comings and goings of hundreds of creatures, from small beetles that tried and were unable to penetrate its dense, healthy layer of bark to migrating birds and other flying creatures that found grateful refuge in its branches. Occasionally, intelligent beings would pass by, and pause to enjoy the shade it gave freely, and marvel at its unexpected splendor.

Unexpected, because the tree was alone. Not only were there no other trees of its kind in the vicinity, there were none anywhere in sight. With none of the particular insects that were needed to pollinate its flowers, its seeds did not germinate, and so it was denied the company even of its own offspring. No lowly bushes crowded its base to make use of its protective shade, no flowers blossomed beneath its branches. There were not even weeds. There was only the tree, spectacular in its isolation, alone atop the small hillock on which it grew. An accident of nature had condemned it to eternal hermitage.

But a tree cannot die of loneliness. Every year it put out new leaves, and every year it hoped for the company of its own kind. But there were only visiting insects, and birds, and the occasional small animal, or travelers passing through.

Three such were approaching now, and an odd trio they were. Though it had no eyes, the tree perceived them. Through sensitive roots that grew just beneath the surface it sensed the vibration of their coming. It knew when they increased their pace, and felt when they slowed and stopped beneath it.

Two of the travelers immediately sat down at the base of its trunk, leaning their backs against its staunch solidity. The tree supported them effortlessly, grateful again for some company. Such visitations were rare and welcome. Lately, the tree had come to treasure them even more.

Because it was dying.

Not from senescence, though given its long lineage that would not have been unnatural, or even unexpected. Despite its great age it was still inherently healthy. But its roots had exhausted the soil in the immediate vicinity. Despite the extent and depth to which they probed, they could no longer find enough of the nutrients vital to the tree's continued health. The land in which the tree had taken root so long ago was simply not rich enough to support more than another decade or two of continued healthy life. And with no other vegetation nearby to supply new nutrients through the natural decomposition of leaves and branches and other organic matter, there was nothing to renew the supply the tree had mined when it had been planted atop the small rise by the ancient storm.

So it sat quietly dying and contemplating the world around it. There were no regrets. By rights it should never have reached maturity, much less lived a long and healthy life. Trees were not in the habit of regretting anyway.

It savored the presence of the travelers, silently delighting in the pleasure they took from the shade it provided against the hot sun, the support it gave to their tired, sweaty backs, and the use they made of the seeds that lay scattered all about. Most creatures found those seeds delicious, and these visitors were no exception, though there was one among them who refused absolutely to partake of the free feast. Apparently, despite the protein they contained, such vegetable matter was not to its liking.

No matter. Its companions gorged themselves. What they did not eat on the spot they gathered up and packed away for future consumption. All this activity the tree marked through its receptive roots, glad of active company on a scale it could easily sense. It had been a hale and robust life, but a lonely one.

Unlike many of the tree's visitors, these travelers were among those who employed a language. This was normal, since all motile visitors possessed a means for communicating among themselves. The insects used touch and smell, the birds song and wing, but spoken language was of the most interest to the tree. Sensed by its leaves, the vibrations words produced in the air were always novel and interesting. Though the tree could not understand a single one of them, that never stopped it from trying. It was a diversion, and any diversion in its lonely existence was most welcome.

Taking turns, all three of the travelers urinated near the base of the tree. This gift of water and nitrates was much appreciated, though the tree had no way of thanking the disseminators openly. It tried to provide a breeze where none existed, but succeeded only in motivating a few of its leaves. The travelers did not notice the movement. Even if they had, it's doubtful they would have remarked upon it.

They seemed content with the shade, however, and that pleased the tree. It was happy it could give back some of the pleasure the travelers were providing through their company. Had it a voice, it would have trilled with delight when they decided to spend the night beneath its spreading boughs. Curled up near the trunk, they relaxed around a small fire they built from fallen bits and pieces of the tree itself. The tree felt the heat of the flames but was not afraid. The travelers kept the fire small, and there was nothing around to make it spread.

In the middle of the night one of the visitors rose. Leaving its companions motionless and asleep, it walked a little ways out from their encampment until it stood beneath the very longest of the tree's branches. This pointed like a crooked arrow to the south, which direction the traveler stood facing for a long while. The moon was up, allowing him to view dimly but adequately his surroundings. But he looked only to the south, his stance barely shifting, his gaze never varying.

After what was for his kind a long while but which to the tree was hardly more than an instant, he turned slowly and walked back toward the encampment. But he did not lie back down on the ground. Instead, he walked slowly and contemplatively around the base of the tree, peering up into its numerous branches, studying its leaves. Several times he reached out to feel of the rippling rivulets that gave character to its cloak of heavy bark, caressing them as gently as he might have the wrinkles on an old woman's face.

Then he began to climb.

The tree could hardly contain its joy. The feel of the traveler's weight against its body, the sensation of fingers gripping branches for support, the heavy placement of foot against wood, was something it had never felt before. In all its long and insightful life, no other traveler had thought to ascend into its upper reaches. It relished every new contact, every fresh vibration and touch.

Eventually, the traveler could ascend no higher. Up in the last branches that would support his weight, he paused. Settling himself into a crook between two accommodating boughs, he leaned back, resting his upper back and neck and head against one unyielding surface. With his legs dangling and his hands folded over his belly, he lay motionless, contemplating the moonlit horizon. All his work and effort gained him a perch that allowed him to see only a little farther to the south, but to the traveler this seemed enough.

He spent the night thus, nestled in the upper branches of the hardwood, and it was difficult to say who luxuriated in it more: traveler or tree. When morning came his companions awoke and immediately rushed about in panic, wondering what could have happened to their friend. He let them agitate for a while before announcing himself. They reacted with a mixture of relief and anger, generating vibrations whose meaning was transparent even to the tree. It might have chuckled, had it possessed the means.

They gathered together beneath the heavy boughs to ingest nourishment. This was done in the manner of motile creatures, at incredible speed and with little regard for the pleasure of slow conversion. Careful consumers, they left behind very little in the way of organic scrap that might have nourished the tree. It did not mind. The company they had provided was worth far more to it than a few bits of decayable plant or animal matter.

When they had finished, they gathered up their belongings and struck off to the north. As with every visitor it had ever had, the tree was sorry to see them go. But there was nothing it could do about it. It could not cry out to them to stay just one more night, or wave branches at them in hopes of drawing them again to its base. It could only sit, and meditate, and pass the time, which is one of the things trees do best.

Before departing, each of the travelers had performed an individual farewell. A final gesture, if not of good-bye, then of acknowledgment of the comfort the tree had given them. The largest among them raised a hind leg and made water again, forcing it out at an angle that actually struck high up on the tree's trunk. As before, it was thankful for the small contribution, though it was not nearly enough to provide the quantity of vital nutrients it required for continued healthy life. The second traveler plucked a leaf from a low-hanging branch and placed it in his hair, over one ear, as a decoration.

The one who had spent the night high up in the tree's branches walked up to the base of the trunk and pressed his body against it. Spreading his arms as wide as possible, he squeezed tight against the bark, as if trying to press his much softer substance into the wood. Then he drew back, turned, and rejoined his companions. The tree felt the vibrations of their footsteps fade as they strode off to the north. It tuned itself to its most sensitive rootlets, drinking in the motion of their passage until the last faint trembling of animate weight against earth had gone.

Once more, it was alone.

However, it did not feel the same as before. When the one traveler had pressed himself tight against the trunk it was as if a part of himself had entered into the tree. Xylem and phloem quivered ever so slightly as a subtle transformation began to race through the tree's entire self.

It was as if the solid ground beneath its roots were giving way. Not for hundreds of years had the tree experienced the sensation of falling. But it was doing so now. Whether it was penetrating the ground or the ground was moving away beneath it the living wood had no way of telling. It sensed only that it was descending, not in the manner of a dying tree falling over, which was the only natural kind and style of falling it contained in its cells' memory, but straight down, without damage to branches or leaves.

It fell for what seemed like a very long time. Fell through the soil that had supported it, then through solid rock, and finally through rock that was so hot it was as liquid as water. The tree knew it should have been carbonized, burned to less than a cinder. Miraculously, it was not. It passed on through the region of molten rock as easily as, as a sapling, it had passed through wild, frivolous air.

Still sinking, it reached a region where everything was hot liquid, where the pressure of its surroundings should have crushed and shattered it. Nothing of the kind happened. Instead, it began to rotate, turning slowly, slowly, until it was facing in the exact opposite direction from the one in which it had spent its entire life. Meanwhile, motion never ceased entirely. It continued to sink. Or perhaps now it was rising. Or possibly it had always been rising, or sinking. The tree did not know. It was confused, and bemused, and although it had no means to show such emotion, the sensations were very real to the tree if not to the rest of the world.

Upward it went, or downward. It could not tell, could sense only the movement of motion. Through more of the molten rock, and then through solid stone, until it once again felt the cool, moist embrace of nourishing soil. But it was soil unlike that in which it had grown. Rich soil, thick and loamy, opulent with every kind and sort of nutrient. A veritable feast of a soil.

And then, air. Cool against its leaves, no longer hot and burning. Comforting and damp, encasing each leaf and branch in a diaphanous blanket of invisible humidity. Moving still, rising until the lowest branch was exposed, and lastly the base of the trunk.

Until finally, ascension ceased, leaving it free and exposed to entirely new surroundings. Around it the tree sensed other trees; dozens, hundreds. Smaller growths, and flowers, and grasses in their aggregate profusion. Birds different from those it had known quickly took perch in its outspread branches, and new kinds of animals began to inspect its base. It welcomed even the threatening explorations of active, dangerous insects. Anything that was new, and fresh. If a tree could have been overwhelmed by a surfeit of new sensations, it would have happened then and there.

Except the sensations were not new. Not the atmospheric conditions, not the birds, not the bugs. Certainly not the soil. Not new—simply very old, and all but forgotten. Not quite, though. Trees do not have memory. They *are* memory, in hard wood and soft presence. The tree was no different. It remembered.

This place, this grove: almost destroyed by a once-in-a-thousand-years storm. Renewed now, rejuvenated by time and nature's patience. The tree was back.

It had come home.

How and by what means it could not say, because it had nothing to say with. But it knew, as it knew the air, and the soil, and the vibrant mix of creatures that dwelled in the vicinity. Its wind-borne journey as a sapling had carried it over half the surface of the Earth. In the equally inexplicable course of its return, it had passed through the very center.

Long-starved roots sucked hungrily at the rich, fertile soil, commencing the slow process of replenishing the tree's nutrient-starved cells. In such bountiful surroundings the tree would have no trouble reinvigorating itself. It would not die but would continue to live, perhaps for another hundred years, possibly even longer. For this it did not know whom or what to thank. It knew only that it was going to survive.

Not only in the company of other trees, but trees of its own kind. All around it, hardwoods belonging to the same tribe thrust sturdy trunks skyward and threw out branches to all points of the compass. Birds nested in their boughs and small mammals and reptiles scampered among them. In this forest bees and wasps and bats and birds lived in plenty, more than enough to ensure thorough pollination of any plant that desired to reproduce. The tree would, after all, not die without having given a part of itself over to new life.

Renewed, the tree regretted only one thing, insofar as a tree could have regrets. Somehow, deep within its heartwood, within the solitary spirit that was itself, it knew that everything that had happened, the silent impossibility of it, was all tied in to the final, farewell hug that singular traveler had performed before he and his companions had taken their leave. How mere contact could have initiated the remarkable sequence of events that had led to the tree returning home the tree did not know, but it was the only explanation.

Or perhaps it was not. Refreshed and renewed, it had plenty of time to consider the conundrum, to stand and contemplate. It was the thing that trees did best, and this tree was no exception. If it came into an answer, that would be a good thing. If it did nothing more than continue to stand and grow and put forth leaves and seeds, that would be a good thing too.

It regretted only that it would never see that traveler again, and therefore could not give him a hug back.

XXVI

Ehomba glanced over his shoulder, but they had been walking for some time and there was nothing to see behind them that was not also in front of them. Sand and rock, rock and gravel.

"I still cannot get over that tree." The herdsman stepped over a small gully. "Standing out there all by itself, with nothing else growing around it, not even a blade of grass. And I have never seen that kind of tree before."

"I have." Simna kicked at a small red stone, sending it skipping across the hardpan floor of the wadi down which they were walking. "To the north of my homeland. There are lots of them there. They're nice trees, and as you found out, their nuts are delicious."

"They certainly are," the herdsman readily agreed.

Alongside him, still towing the remnants of their floating pond, Ahlitah snorted. "Omnivores! You'll eat anything."

"Not quite anything," Simna shot back. "I find cat, for example, stringy and tough."

"But why was it there?" Ehomba was reflecting aloud. "Obviously so far from where its kind of tree normally grows, all alone on top of that small dune? It must have some important meaning."

"It means somebody else traveling through this Gholos-forgotten land dropped a seed or two, and unlikely as it may be, one took root on that knoll." The swordsman was not sympathetic to his tall companion's interest. "You ask too many questions, Etjole."

"That is because I like answers."

"Not every question has an answer, bruther." Simna avoided the disarticulated skeleton of a dead dragonaz. Fragments of wing membrane clung to the long finger bones like desiccated parchment.

Ehomba eyed him in surprise. "Of course they do. A question without an answer is not a question."

The swordsman opened his mouth, started to say something, then closed it, a puzzled look on his face as he continued to stride along. It was early, the sun was not yet at its highest, and the increasing heat disinclined him to pursue the matter further. Not wishing to clutter up the place with another of the herdsman's inexplicable commentaries, he put it clean out of his mind, a process that with much practice he had perfected some time ago.

Days passed without incident. Game began to reappear. Not in profusion, but sufficient to satisfy Ahlitah's appetite as well as that of his less voracious companions. Standing sentinel over abating desert, date, coconut, and ivory nut palms began to appear. Other, smaller flora found protection at the foot of these taller growths.

When the travelers began to encounter otherwise dry riverbeds that boasted small pools in their depths as well as more frequent traditional oases, Ahlitah kicked off the shackles he had been using to tow the remnants of the floating pond. It was nearly drained anyway, and he was tired of the constant drag on his shoulders. Despite the escalating ubiquity of freestanding water, the ever cautious Ehomba argued for keeping the pond with them as long as it contained moisture. For once, Simna was able to stand aside and let his companions argue.

Ahlitah eventually won out, not through force of logic but because he had simply had enough of the ever-present pond. Simna watched with interest to see if the herdsman would employ some striking, overpowering magic to force the big cat to comply, but in this he was disappointed. Ehomba simply shrugged and acceded to the cat's insistence. If he was capable of compelling the litah, he showed no sign of being willing to do so. Simna didn't know whether to be disappointed or not.

They continued on. Once, when water had been scarce for several days, Ehomba muttered something to the big cat about performing reckless acts in unknown countries. Ahlitah snarled a response and moved away. But this scolding ended the next morning when they found a new water hole. Fringed by bullrushes and small palms, it offered shade as well as water once they had shooed away the small diving birds and nutrias.

After that, Ehomba said nothing more about water and the need to conserve it. This left Simna sorely conflicted. If the herdsman really was an all-powerful wizard traveling incognito, why would he let himself lose an argument he clearly felt strongly about to a mere cat? And if he wasn't, how then to explain the sky-metal sword and the vial of miraculous whater? Was he really dependent for such expertise and achievements on the work of a village blacksmith and a coterie of chattering women? Where sorcery was concerned, was he after all no more than a vehicle and venue for the machinations of others?

Or was he simply so subtle not even someone as perceptive and experienced as Simna ibn Sind could see through the psychological veils and masks with which the tall southerner covered himself? Much troubled in mind, the swordsman trudged on, refusing to countenance the possibility that he might have, after all, allied himself to nothing more than a semiliterate cattle herder from the ignorant south.

Ehomba's reaction to the palace that materialized out of the east was anything but reassuring.

Simna saw it first. "It's a mirage. That's all." After a quick, casual glance, he returned his attention to the path they were following northward.

"But it is a striking one." Ehomba had halted and was leaning on his spear, staring at the fantastical phantasm that now glimmered on the eastern horizon. "We should go and have a look."

What manner of dry-country dweller was this, Simna wondered, who sought to visit something that was not there? "And just how would we go about doing that, bruther? I'm thinking maybe you've been too long on the road and too much in the sun."

Ehomba looked over at him and smiled innocently. "By walking up to it, of course. Come." Lifting his spear, he broke away at a right angle to their course.

"I was joking, by Geveran. Etjole!" Exasperated, and starting to worry if his tall friend really was suffering from the accumulated effects of too much sun, the swordsman turned to the third member of the party. "Cat, you can see what's happening. Why don't you go and pick him up by the scruff of his neck and haul him back like you would any wayward kitten?"

"Because his scruff is furless and I'd bite right through his scrawny neck, and also because I think I might like to have a look at that mirage myself." Whereupon Ahlitah turned right and trotted off in the wake of the departing herdsman.

Aghast, Simna called after them. "Have you both lost what little sense you possess?" He gestured emphatically northward. "Every day brings us nearer some kind of civilization. You can practically smell it! And you want to go chasing after mirages? By Gwiquota, *are you two listening to me?*"

Sputtering inventive imprecations under his breath, the swordsman dropped his head and hurried to catch up to his companions. He calmed himself by determining that while it was a waste of time, the diversion wouldn't waste much of it.

But he was wrong.

"Interesting," Ehomba observed as they neared the object of their detour. "A real mirage. I have heard of them, but I never thought to set eyes on one."

Simna had caught up to the others. "What do you mean, 'a real mirage'? Is that as opposed to a fake mirage? Have you gone completely balmy?"

"No, look closely, my friend." The herdsman raised his spear, which when walking he often held parallel to the ground, and pointed with the tip. "An ordinary mirage would be fading away by now, or retreating from us. This one does not wane, nor does it drift into the distance."

"That's crazy! Anyone knows that—" Simna broke off, his brows drawing together. "Offspring of Gupzu, you're right. But how . . . ?"

"I told you." Ehomba continued to lead the way. "It is a *real* mirage."

Right up to the palace gates they strode, tilting back their heads to gawk up at the diaphanous turrets and downy-walled towers. From their peaks flags of many lands and lineages streamed in slow motion, though not a whisper of a breeze stirred the sand and soil beneath their feet.

Stopping outside the great gates, which were fashioned of pale yellow and pink wood strapped with bands of pallid blue metal, they weighed how best to enter. Simna continued to refuse to acknowledge the evidence of his own eyes.

"It's impossible, bedamned impossible." Reaching out, he tried to grab one of the metal bands. His fingers encountered only the slightest resistance before penetrating. It was like trying to clutch a cloud. Drawing back his fingers, he stared down at the handful of blue fog they had come away with. It lay in his palm like a puff of the finest dyed cotton. When he turned his hand over, the vapor floated free, drifting lazily down to the ground. There it lay, at rest and unmoving, a small fragment of mirage all by itself.

"Impressive walls," he found himself saying softly, "but they wouldn't stand much of a siege."

"This is a special thing." The herdsman advanced and the gate could not, did not, stop him. He walked right through, leaving behind an Ehomba-sized hole, like a cookie cutout of himself. Instantly, the opening began to close up, the wall to re-form behind him. Ahlitah followed, making an even larger breach through which Simna strolled in turn, a disbelieving but triumphant invader.

They found themselves in a hallway whose magnificence would have shamed that of any king, khan, or potentate. Pillars of rose-hued cold fire supported a mezzanine that appeared to have been carved from solid ivory. Overhead, the vaulted ceiling was ablaze with stained glass of every imaginable pastel color. It was all vapor and fog, the most elegant effluvium imaginable, but the effect was utterly stunning. Marveling at the delicate aesthetics of the ethereal architecture, they strode in silence down the vast hallway. Beneath the pseudo–stained glass, the color of the light that bathed their progress was ever changing.

"So this is what the inside of a mirage looks like." Though there was no compelling need for him to do so, Simna had lowered his voice to a whisper. "I never imagined."

"Of course you didn't." Ehomba strode easily alongside his friend. His sandaled feet made no sound as they sank slightly into the floor that, instead of tile or marble, was paved with mosaic ephemera. "No one could. The inside of a mirage is not for human imagining, but for other things."

Simna's eyes widened as he espied movement ahead. "It's not? Then how do you explain that?"

At the end of the overpowering hallway was a throne, eight feet high at the back and decorated with arabesques of rose-cut gemstones. Pillows of lavender- and orange- and tangerine-colored silk spilled from the empty dais to form a rolling wave of comfort at its feet. Sprawled and splayed, reclining and rolling on this spasmodic bed of dazzling indulgence, was a clutch of sinuous sloe-eyed houris of more color and variation than the pillows they lolled upon. There was not a one who would not have been the pride of any sultan's harem or merchant's front office.

Giggling and tittering among themselves, they rose in all their diaphanous glory to beckon the visitors closer. Their gestures were sumptuous with promise, their eyes the lights of the passion that dances like a flame at the tip of a scented candle: concentrated, burning, and intense. For the second time since he had begun his journey, Ehomba was tempted to forget his woman.

Simna suffered from no such restraints. Eyes alert, every muscle tense, a grin of lust on his face as pure as the gold he hoped to find, he started forward. One houri in particular drew him, her expression simmering like cloves in hot tea.

Blackness blotted out the enticing, serpentine vision. The blackness had four feet, unnaturally long legs, and muscles bigger around than the swordsman's torso. Simna started to go around it, only to find himself stumbling backwards as a massive paw smacked him hard in the chest. More than his sternum bruised, he glared furiously at the litah.

"Hoy, just because there's no cats here, don't go trying to spoil my fun!"

"There's no fun here, genital man." Ahlitah was staring, not at him, but at the hazy, vaporous side corridors that flanked the hallway. The ostensibly empty corridors. "Get out."

"What?" Two surprises in a row were almost more than Simna could handle. Ehomba stood nearby, not commenting, his gaze shifting repeatedly from the now frantic demimondaines to the litah.

"Get out. Get back, get away, retreat, run." As he delivered these pithy admonitions, the great cat had turned to face the vacant throne and was backing slowly up the hallway, his massive head swinging slowly from side to side so as to miss nothing.

Hesitant, but for the moment persuaded more by the cat's behavior than his words, Simna complied, keeping the litah's bulk between himself and—nothing. Or was that a flash, a flicker, a figment of movement there, off to his left? And another, possibly and perhaps, on the far side of the hallway, dancing against the evanescent wall?

Ehomba had joined in the retreat. More importantly, he held his spear tightly in both hands, extended in fighting posture. Together and in tandem, the visitors backed steadily away from the dais and its languorous promise of phantasmal carnal bliss.

"I still do not see anything," the herdsman murmured tightly.

"Hoy, cat, what are we—"

Simna's query was interrupted as Ahlitah rose on his hind legs and slashed out with his right paw. The blow would have taken off a man's head as easily as Simna could pull a cork from a bottle. Four-inch-long claws tore through an unseen but very real something, ripping it where it stood. The two humans saw only reflections of the destruction, flashes of bright gold in the air in front of the cat. Something that was all long, icy fangs and shredded, glaring eyes howled outrage that echoed off the enclosing walls. Tiny individual droplets of wet, red blood appeared from nowhere to fall as slow scarlet rain, crimson bubbles suspended like candy in the cloying atmosphere of the hallway. The mist-shrouded floor sucked them up greedily, hungrily. Thin, skeletal tendrils of the tenebrous surface under their feet began to curl and coil upward, clutching weakly at the travelers' ankles.

Whirling and roaring like the tornado he had once challenged to a race, Ahlitah snapped viselike jaws on something that had fastened itself to his back. An inhuman high-pitched scream split the sugar-sweet air, and fresh reflections emitted a second shower of rapidly evaporating blood. Simna had his sword out and was looking to cover the litah's rear, only there was nothing to cover against. Strain as he might, he could see nothing moving save his friends and the delicate feminine visions that seemed restricted to the vicinity of the magnificent, forsaken throne.

"Gronanka—show yourselves—whatever you are!" Close to him Ehomba was swinging the point of his spear from left to right and back again, sweeping it in a deadly arc over the floor as they continued their withdrawal. "Do you see anything, Etjole?"

"Not a thing, my friend!" Alongside them, two immense paws came together with a thunderous clap, and a third something unseen died. Ahlitah's eyes were wide and wild as he dealt death to the invisible. And all the while the floor continued to scrabble and clutch at their feet with futile fingers of fog.

Two of the gesticulating, moaning houris left their pillows and came running toward them. Their arms were outstretched, their eyes pleading. They wailed and moaned in languages unknown to either man, but there was no mistaking the desperation in their gestures, the imploring in their eyes. They were beseeching the visitors to take them along, to remove them from the mirage in which they dwelled in unsolicited, unwanted, unloved luxury.

Something bellowed angrily and slapped at them, sending them flying backwards to land among the satiny fluff and froth-filled cushions that hugged the dais. Helplessly they lay there, sobbing softly among their intimates, turning their flawless faces away or dropping their heads into their hands.

Meanwhile, the apprehensive, uneasy visitors continued their steady retreat. Having picked up the pace a little, the two men strained every sense they possessed in search of assailants they could not see while Ahlitah continued to rage and destroy corposants that could not be made visible but that could bleed.

They backed right out of that grand and sumptuous hallway, right through the walls of wisp that enclosed the delirium palace, until they were standing once more upon dry sand and rock. The splendid battlements and spires rose high above them, masking but not blotting out the sky.

"Now—run!" Ahlitah commanded.

Turning, they sprinted away from that place as fast as their inadequate human legs would carry them. Though he could have fled westward at ten times the speed, Ahlitah trailed behind, often looking back over his shoulder to make sure they were not being pursued.

But a mirage cannot follow. Sooner than Ehomba would have expected, the litah slowed. "It's all right now. It's going away."

Out of breath, they turned and stared. In the distance the fleecy, resplendent palace was fading from view, waning like a new moon obscured by clouds until, like a final shimmer of heat pinched between earth and sky, it vanished from sight.

Simna sank to one knee, struggling to catch his breath. "What—what were we fighting in there? I never saw anything."

"Eupupa." Through his hands, Ehomba rested his weight on his spear. "I have heard of them, but never before encountered any."

"How would you know if you had?" Taking an especially deep breath, the swordsman straightened and sheathed his untested sword.

"I am told you can feel their presence around you. They live in the empty, dry places of the world. Only rarely do they come out of the mirages that are their homes. But on a long day, when the sun is high and hot, I am told you can feel them investigating your body, swimming around your cheeks and your chest, coming right up to you to peer deep into your eyes. Outside their mirages they have only the power to cloud one's thinking. Have you never wondered why so many people who are lost in the desert die only a day, or an hour, or sometimes less than that but a few feet from water, or help?" Looking away, he gazed back at the now ordinary, unmarred horizon.

"The Eupupa do that. They make you dizzy, and stare into the depths of your eyes until they have disoriented you, so that you stumble away from water instead of toward it, or walk in circles, or ignore the signs that would lead a dying man to salvation. And then they feed, beating even the vultures and the dragonets to the corpse, until they have sucked out its soul."

"Gwythyn's children," the swordsman muttered. "Too close, that was." He frowned. "But the ladies. Not Eupupa. Surely not Eupupa. If these are creatures that can't be seen, then the ladies couldn't have been these invisible ghoul-things." A part of him twitched at the burning memory of those naked, unconditional invitations. "Because I sure as Gelell's goblet could see *them*, bruther."

His mouth tightening, Ehomba dropped his gaze to the gratifyingly solid ground on which they now stood. "So could I, my friend. It was impossible not to see them. That was the Eupupa's intent, to use them to draw such as us into the deepest part of the mirage, where they could set upon us without having to wait for us to die. Where they could suck out our souls even while we still lived." He looked up.

"Those exquisite, sad houris. They were the souls of women who died in the desert. From thirst, from neglect, in childbirth, by falling over a cliff and striking their heads—from any and all means. They were the unlucky ones, whose souls were caught up and stolen by the Eupupa before they could escape spontaneously. Captured, and brought here to be kept in that mirage to serve them that we cannot see." He was gritting his teeth now.

"It is a most unnatural way to not-die, but there is nothing you or I or anyone else can do about it. No wonder they were so frantic for us to take them away. They are souls that want desperately to rest." He shut his eyes. "By what means those like the Eupupa can force a soul to do their bidding I do not know. I do not want to know." Opening his eyes, he turned away from the eastern horizon to look once more to the north.

"Let us leave this place, and try our best to think no more about what we have seen here."

"But wait!" Ehomba did not, and Simna had to hurry to catch up to the herdsman as he resumed walking. "They were all so ravishing, every one of them. No, they were more than ravishing. They were radiant. Surely not all the women who die in the desert are beautiful. Or do the Eupupa choose them that way so they'll make better bait for the unwary—like us?"

Striding along, tireless and exact as always, Ehomba did not answer immediately. When he did, it was with a feeling of disappointment. Not in their narrow escape, but in his companion who had asked the question.

"Simna ibn Sind, my friend. You who claim to know so much about women, and to have known so many of them in person. Did you not know that that is how every woman sees herself—inside?" Lengthening his stride, he pushed on ahead, forcing the pace as if he wanted to put not only their recent experience but also the memory of the experience out of his mind.

Simna considered his companion's words, frowned, shook his head, and caught up to the third member of the party. "Well, that's the first time I've had to try and fight something I couldn't see. It was lucky for us you've seen these Eupupa before."

The litah spoke without turning his massive head. Both jaws, Simna noted for the first time, were stained dark beyond the black. Occasionally the thick tongue flicked out to lick at them.

"I never saw such before."

Simna blinked in surprise. "Then how did you know what to fight? How did you know they were even there?"

The wide, yellow eyes turned to meet the swordsman's. "Don't you ever see anything outside yourself, man? Haven't you ever watched a cat, any cat, suddenly tense and strike at what to you seems to be empty air? We see things, man." Killer eyes flashed. "There's a lot out there, everywhere, that men don't perceive. We do. Some of it is to be ignored, some of it is for play, and some of it"—he snarled under his breath—"some of it is to be killed." With that he lengthened his stride and jogged on ahead.

Left scratching at his chin, Simna watched the tufted, switching tail move out in front of him. "Well I'm glad *I'm* fugging visible, that's all I have to say!" With a shrug he moved to match the herdsman's elevated pace.

Once he thought he felt something brush his face. It was just the wind against his cheek, but he swatted hard at it nonetheless, and looked around, and saw nothing.

Nattering cat, he thought irritably. Filling a man's head with narsty scrawl. Ahead, he thought he could make out a line of trees, the first they had seen in many a night. With the sight of fresh foliage to boost his spirits, he held his head a little higher as he strode onward, and tried to forget all about the dismal events of the past hours.

"Cats and sorcerers," he muttered under his breath. A more morose and melancholy pair of traveling companions he would have had difficulty imagining.

XXVII

Lacking in inner sensitivity he might be, but there was nothing wrong with the swordsman's superb vision. The line of trees he had espied from a significant distance was no mirage.

"At last," Ehomba murmured as they started down a final, gentle slope. Ahead lay a narrow but deep river lined on both sides with small farms and orchards. The leafy crowns Simna had spotted were fruit trees, pungent with blossoms, each verdant upheaval a small galaxy of exploding yellow and white flowers.

The swordsman eyed his friend. "What do you mean, 'at last'? Why should you be so elated by such a sight? I thought you were the dry-country type."

"It is true that I love the land where I live." Dirt slid away beneath the herdsman's sandals. "But that does not mean I cannot love this more. Any man can love a distant destination more than his homeland without forsaking the latter."

"Then why don't you move?" Simna asked him directly. "Why not bring your family, your whole village, up here, where there's plenty of water and good soil for raising crops?"

"Because obliging as this place may be, it is not our home." The southerner spoke as if that settled the matter. "Much as plentiful water and fertile land are to be desired, they do not make a home."

"Then what does?"

"Ancestors. Tradition. A warmth of place that cannot be transplanted like an onion. Certain smells, and sights. The air." He felt of the sack of beach pebbles in his kilt pocket. "The feel of especial places underfoot. The wildlife you live with." He glanced surreptitiously at Ahlitah, who was padding silently alongside. "The wildlife you fight with. In a new place all these things are different, alien, foreign. People are the easiest thing to pick up and move. The others—the others are much more difficult."

Simna shook his head sadly. "I feel sorry for you, bruther. My home is wherever I park my carcass. Preferably a place with good cooking, a soft bed, and a friendly lady. Or a soft lady and a friendly bed."

Ehomba squinted down at him. "Should I feel sorry for you—or should you feel sorry for me?"

"I feel sorry for all three of us." Ahlitah did not look up. "You two, for being clumsy, chattering, two-legged hairless apes, and me for having to put up with you." Turning away, he snorted wearily. "Next time save some other cat's life."

"I will try to remember," the herdsman replied.

They were following a marked path now. No more than a foot wide, it wound like a smashed snake through a leafy field of taro and yam. Yuca bushes shaded the more sun-sensitive young plants.

"Strange." Shading his eyes, Ehomba scanned the numerous fenced plots and the neatly pruned fruit trees they were approaching. "You would think someone would have emerged to challenge us by now. These fields are well tended. Surely there are wild animals here that would feast on these healthy vegetables if the farmers did not keep them away. And the appearance of three strangers in a tillage ought to provoke some kind of reaction. We could be thieves come to steal their crops."

"Yes." With a mixture of curiosity and wariness, Simna studied the luxuriant acreage through which they were traipsing. "If this was my farm and orchard I'd have been out here with arrow notched and ready as soon as anyone showed themselves atop that last ridge we crossed."

"House," Ahlitah interjected curtly. Raising a paw, he pointed.

There were three of them, individual homes sharing a small thorn-bush stockade. The gate was open wide, presenting no obstacle to their entry.

"Hoy!" Simna shouted, putting his hands together around his mouth. "Commander of a legion of legumes, come and greet your guests!" There was no response. With a shrug, the swordsman started for the entrance.

The first house had windows, but the glass was of poor quality and did not allow them to see clearly what lay within. An uneasy Ehomba held back.

"I do not like intruding on another man's privacy."

"What makes you think there's anyone here? You can't violate privacy if there's no one present to claim it." Simna opened the door.

Ahlitah hung back with Ehomba, not out of any respect for the intangible called privacy, but because the interior of human habitations held no interest for him. On the single occasion when he had been obliged to enter one, he had found the interior malodorous and claustrophobic. The occupants, however, had proven a good deal tastier than their surroundings.

Looking more puzzled than ever, the swordsman emerged several moments later. "Empty. More than empty, deserted. There's food in lockers in the pantry, and dishes and clean linen stored neatly in cabinets. Beds are made but haven't been slept in recently." He eyed the surrounding trees with fresh concern. "The people who lived here left not long ago but with no immediate intention of returning. It's my experience that folks don't do that without a compelling reason, and it's usually a disagreeable one."

"Let us try the other houses," Ehomba suggested.

This they did, only to find further evidence of well-planned departure.

"There must be a town somewhere nearby," the herdsman conjectured when they had concluded the brief search. "Perhaps everyone has gone there."

"Hoy, yes." Simna tried to view their eerily silent surroundings with some optimism. "Maybe there's a festival of some kind going on." His expression brightened. "I could do with a little old-fashioned country excitement."

"On the other side of the river, maybe." Ehomba gestured with the point of his spear. "There are more farms, more fruit trees, and beyond that I think I see some hills. If the town is fortified, it would naturally be sited in an area affording the most natural protection."

"Come on then." With a growl, Ahlitah started toward the river. "If we're going to have to swim, I'd just as soon get it over with while the sun's still high enough to dry my pelt."

But they did not have to swim. A perfectly adequate, well-maintained wooden bridge wide enough to accommodate an oxcart spanned the swift, high-banked waterway not far downstream. On the opposite side they encountered more of the tidily deserted habitations, some built of stone as well as wood that boasted several stories. Each showed similar signs of having been conscientiously abandoned by their inhabitants.

"Must be quite a festival." Simna was not yet willing to concede that something untoward had happened to the occupants of the fastidiously tended farms and homesteads.

"I hope not." Padding silently alongside them, the big cat flowed like black oil over the packed earth. "I don't like a lot of noise—unless I'm the one making it."

"Maybe it's a carnival, or a jubilee." Simna put more than his usual strut into his walk as they approached the first of the foothills. "I could do with making a bit of noise myself."

As they entered the gentle, forested hills, the path they had been following widened into a narrow but serviceable road that showed evidence of having recently accommodated many wagon wheels and shoed feet. Before long they found themselves passing numerous transient camps filled with people of all ages and description. Men and women alike wore expressions that seldom varied between exhausted and sullen. Even the children were somber and reserved, watching the passing travelers from the haggard depths of eyes wide with silent hurt.

Old men sat motionless, resting stooped heads in wrinkled palms. Dogs chased wallabies around and beneath wagons and carts piled high with household goods, while cats posed imperiously atop piles of bound linens and towels. Cockatiels and gallahs, parrots and macaws squawked from within cages of wire and wicker, but even their normally boisterous cries seemed muted among their doleful surroundings.

Women cooked food over open fires built of wood taken from the surrounding forest. Ehomba saw no signs of starvation among the bands of wayfarers, or indeed any evidence of physical deprivation whatsoever. Except for their attitudes, all appeared to be in good health.

Some they passed even looked frustrated and angry enough to contemplate assaulting the travelers, but such attitudes underwent a rapid and radical change the instant the would-be aggressors caught sight of the brooding litah. For his part, the great cat ignored the increasingly dense clusters of humans, deigning to exchange glances only with the cats they kept as pets and companions. For their part, the house cats returned his gaze, affirming that each and every one of them knew their place in the hierarchy of felinity without a word, or a hiss, having to be spoken.

"What's going on here?" An increasingly perplexed Simna kept glancing from right to left as they trudged northward past larger and larger concentrations of dour, depressed people. "Where have all these folks come from?" He gestured back down the road they were walking. "Not from the farms along the river. Those houses still contained all their goods and furniture. These people look like they've brought everything they own with them." He scrutinized one face after another as they continued on, trying to divine from their disconsolate expressions what sort of calamity might have befallen them.

"Look at them—exhausted, dazed, like they have nowhere left to go and don't know how they're going to get there. I've seen people like this before. People at the end of their rope. Usually they've been driven from their homes by some natural disaster, or by some marauding hoard. But these—these folk still seem healthy and well fed. By Geesthema, it's not natural. Even the children look as if for the past weeks they've been spoon-fed nothing but hopelessness and despair."

Ehomba concurred. "And it still does not explain what happened to the farmers along the river who deserted their homes and fields." He lifted his gaze to the winding road that led onward into the hills ahead. "Something peculiar is going on here, Simna my friend, and I fear it has nothing to do with a fair or celebration."

"Hoy, bruther, one doesn't have to be a keen reader of men to see that. But what?"

"Perhaps the answer lies over the next hill. Or the last."

They marched on, the butt of Ehomba's spear striking the ground methodically with each of the herdsman's steps, marking their progress like the pendulum of a tall, thin clock. The range of hills was not high, but it was extensive. It took them almost a week to negotiate the entire length of the winding road.

The farther north they traveled, the more families and transients' encampments they encountered, until the hills resembled anthills swarming with displaced farmers and townsfolk. Every time they tried to approach someone to ask the meaning of the unaccountable diaspora, the intended recipient of their questions caught sight of Ahlitah and beat a hasty retreat. Not wishing to panic any of the already obviously frightened migrants and believing it unwise to leave the always hungry litah out of their sight, they continued on, confident that sooner or later they would encounter someone willing to stand and deliver themselves of an explanation.

One, of a sort, manifested itself when they reached the crest of the last hill. The panorama spread out before them was not what they had hoped to descry.

As far as the eye could see, a vast, fertile plan stretched all the way to the northern horizon. Isolated clouds of towering whiteness marched across the sky like floating fortresses, and numerous small rivers and streams filigreed the earth like silver wire. Neatly spaced pockets of construction marked the borders of field and forest, and several towns were visible in lesser or greater detail depending on their distance from the hill.

But no one was tilling the vast patchwork of fields, or working in the towns, or plying the rivers in boats equipped with nets and lines. No pickers worked the orchards, no farm animals roamed the scrupulously fenced pastures. Smoke there was, but it rose not from chimneys but from the burned-out husks of abandoned homes and mills, workshops and granaries. The destruction had been selective and by no means total, as if the devastation had been imposed in a precise and disciplined manner.

In the midst of the robust, healthy pastures and towns there stretched a wall. A hundred feet high, it looked to be made of some yellowish stone. Twenty feet in width, its top was smooth and wide enough to drive wagons along. Or chariots, Simna thought, or cavalry. Armored figures in their hundreds, in their thousands, could be seen running back and forth to position themselves along its length, a length that extended as far to the east and west as they could see.

Nor was the wall straight. Here it curved inward, rippling and twisting, to accommodate the path of a river flowing against its base, there it thrust out sharply to create an arrowlike salient. At quarter-mile intervals, battle towers rose another fifty or sixty feet higher than the rim of the wall itself.

Immediately behind it the travelers could see the brightly colored tents and flying pennons of an army on the march, though at this distance it was impossible to assign an identity to the marchers. The glint of sunlight on armor, however, was very much in evidence. Ahlitah could also make out, marshaled in temporary holding pens, much larger creatures clothed for war.

"Mastodons, I think." The big cat had to squint, as the distance involved was a challenge even to his exceptional vision. "And glyptodonts. Other elephants, and some balucherium as well."

Simna nodded. "Easy enough to see who they're fighting." He gestured toward the base of the hill.

Thousands of figures swarmed over the fields that had been tilled right to the base of the first incline, trampling the crops there, knocking down the neat wooden fences and hedgerows. There were people, of course. No doubt some of them called hastily forth from the first farms the travelers had encountered, called to arms to help defend their country against the invading host.

But there were also dwarves clad in traditional leather and coarse cotton, and arrets, the tall, thin, bark-brown forest people of the west. Among the crowd Ehomba thought he saw a giant or two, massive of brow and heavy of jaw. Unmistakable in their light armor were the chimps and apes, and the smaller monkeys were present in large numbers as well.

Evidently all had shared in the bounty of this land, and now all had gathered to defend it. But the field of battle made no sense, not even to a nonprofessional like the herdsman. On this side the many-varied citizens of the good and fertile country were drawn up in lines of defense, swarming back and forth as if hunting for a weak spot in the enemy-held wall, or for a purpose. But they were crowded in too tightly together, crammed between the wall and the hills.

"I know." Simna was scrutinizing the battlefield intently. "It doesn't look right, does it? Maybe the attackers just took the wall. Maybe it had been built by these people here to defend themselves against an assault from the south, and now they've been pushed back up and over their own defenses."

"I thought of that," the herdsman replied. "But if these people wanted to defend themselves from a southerly invasion, why would they exclude so much of their land? Why would they not build such a wall in the sand hills where we first saw the line of fruit trees, to protect that rich farmland and that country as well? Or at the very least, why not build the wall on this side of that river to the north in order to make use of it as a moat?"

"Don't add up, do it?" The swordsman waved an arm at the field of battle. "Yet here's this great huge long wall, stuck square in the middle of their fields and orchards. And in clear possession of the enemy. Or are these people we've been passing these past days the invaders, and the ones on the wall the defenders of their country?"

Ehomba shook his head. "I do not see it that way, Simna. Were they the defenders, it would not explain why certain farms and homes are burning on their side of the wall. The cultivated lands to the north are the ones that bear the hallmarks of having been invaded and despoiled, not those on this side of the barrier. And these people are the ones whose faces show the blank stare of the displaced."

"I agree. So what's going on here?"

Turning slowly to study the hills, Ehomba scanned the numerous encampments. Below, the assembled fighting forces of all the two-legged tribes in the vicinity were frantically trying to compose themselves for combat. Even from their location at the top of the hill, the travelers could see that chaos commanded more allegiance than order among the disorganized ranks below. Therefore they would have to seek explication elsewhere, among the unarmed and less intractable, whether the individual they settled on wished to prove tractable or not.

"We have to know what is going on," he murmured. "Ahlitah, go and bring back a suitable person."

Massive brows narrowed. "Why me?"

"Because I do not want to waste time arguing with several possibles, and I do not think they will argue with you."

The great cat snarled once before whirling and dashing off toward the nearest encampment. There followed several moments during which Ehomba and Simna occupied themselves trying to make sense of the incongruous situation below before Ahlitah returned with a middle-aged man in tow. Or rather, with the scruff of his well-made embroidered shirt held firmly in the big cat's jaws. The fellow was overweight but otherwise healthy, even prosperous in appearance. Perhaps he had bought himself out of the ongoing strife below.

As Ehomba had predicted, the man had chosen not to argue with the litah.

Disdainfully, the cat parted his jaws and let his prisoner drop. The man immediately prostrated himself before the two travelers. "Please, oh warriors of unknown provenance! I beg of you, spare an ignoble life!" Face pressed to the ground, arms extended before him, the poor man was shaking and trembling so violently Ehomba feared he would destabilize his brains. "I have a condition of the belly that prevents me from participating in the illustrious struggle. I swear by all the seed of my loins that this is so!" Raising his head hesitantly, he stole a glance first at Simna, then at Ehomba. Reaching into a vest pocket, he pulled out a rolled parchment and held it up, quivering, for the herdsman to see.

"Look! A draft of my physician's statement, attesting to my piteous circumstance. Would that it were otherwise, and that I could join our brave citizens and allies in desperate conflict!"

Simna snorted softly. "He's got a condition of the belly, all right. A condition of excess, I'd say."

"Stand up." Ehomba felt very uncomfortable. "Come on, man, get off your knees. Stand up and face us. We are not here to persecute you, and none of us cares in the least about your 'condition' or lack thereof. We need only to ask you some questions."

Uncertain, and unsteady, the man climbed warily to his feet. He glanced nervously at Ahlitah. When he saw that the great cat was eyeing his prominent paunch with more than casual interest, the chosen unfortunate hurriedly looked away.

"Questions? I am but a modest and unassuming merchant of dry goods, and know little beyond my business and my family, who, even as we speak, must be sorely lamenting my enforced absence."

"You can go back to them in a minute," Ehomba assured him impatiently. "The questions we want to ask are not difficult." Peering past the detainee, he pointed with his spear in the direction of the great wall and the roiling surge of opposing forces below.

"There is a war going on here. A big one. For days my friends and I have been passing through hills and little valleys filled with refugees. We have seen fine homes and farms abandoned, perhaps so their owners could join the fight while sending their families to a place of safety."

"There is no place of safety from the Chlengguu," the merchant moaned. Fresh curiosity somewhat muted his fear as he looked from Ehomba to the short swordsman standing at his side. The predatory gaze of the great and terrible litah he avoided altogether.

"Who are you people? Where are you from that you don't know about the war with the Chlengguu?"

Ehomba gestured casually with his spear. "We come from the far south, friend. So you fight the Chlengguu. Never heard of them. Is this a new war, or an old one?"

"The Chlengguu have ceaselessly harassed the people of the Queppa, but by banding together we have always been able to fight them off. For centuries they have been a nuisance, with their raiding and stealing. They would mount and attack, we would pursue and give them a good hiding, and then there would be relative peace for many years until they felt strong enough to attack again. They would try new strategies, new weapons, and each time the farmers and merchants and townspeople of the Queppa would counter these and drive them off." As his head dropped, so did his voice. "Until the Wall."

Ehomba turned to look down in the direction of the line of combat. "It is an impressive wall, but though I am no soldier, it seems to me to be in a strange location. We thought that perhaps it was your wall, and that your enemies had captured it from you."

"Our wall?" The merchant laughed bitterly. "Would that it were so! For if that were the case we would use it to push these murderous Chlengguu into the sea."

Ehomba started slightly. "The sea? We are near the ocean?" Strain as he might to see past the western horizon, he could detect no sign of the Semordria. He was surprised at how his heart ached at the mere mention of it. It had been far too long since he had set eyes on its dancing waves and green depths.

"You mean the Semordria?" the merchant asked. When Ehomba nodded with quiet eagerness the other man could only shake his head. "You really are far from your home, aren't you?" Raising one beringed hand, he pointed to the west. "The Semordria lies a great distance off toward the setting sun. I myself, though a man of modest means and varied interests, have never seen it." His arm swung northward.

"That way lies the Sea of Aboqua, a substantial body of water to be sure, but modest when compared to the unbounded Semordria. Upon its waters ships of many cities and states ply numerous trade routes. I am told that at several locations it enters into and merges with the Semordria, but I myself have never seen these places. I have only heard other merchants speak of them. And I have never heard of a trading vessel with captain and crew brave or foolhardy enough to venture out upon the measureless reaches of the Semordria itself."

Ehomba slumped slightly. "There is something I must do that requires me to cross the Semordria."

The merchant's heavy eyebrows rose. "Cross the Semordria? You are a brave man indeed."

"But if no ship will do that," Simna put in, "how are we supposed to make this crossing? I'm a good swimmer, but no fish."

"From the tales I have heard of the monsters and terrors that swarm in the depths of the Semordria, I believe it a journey even fish would be reluctant to take." The man rubbed his chin whiskers. "But it is rumored that in the rich lands on the far side of the Aboqua there are ports from whence sail ships grander than any that ply the smaller sea. Who knows? You might even find shipmaster and sailors stupid enough to attempt such a passage. Tell me, what do you hope to find on the other side of the Semordria, anyway?"

"Closure," Ehomba told him. "Now, about this Wall. It is a very impressive wall. Behind it I see fields and buildings, some of which have been burned. If it is not yours, then it must be a construction of these Chlengguu. But why build it here, and how did they manage to trap all of you on this side instead of the other, where your homes and villages lie?"

The merchant looked over his shoulder. "My poor family must be in an agony of apprehension at my absence."

Simna fingered the hilt of his sword. "Let 'em agonize a little while longer. Answer the question."

"You really don't know, do you?" The man heaved a deep sigh. "The Wall was not built here." Turning, he pointed to the northwest. "When it first appeared on the outskirts of Mectin Township, no one could believe that the Chlengguu had managed to raise so massive a structure in so short a time. Its true nature was not immediately apparent to the people of the Queppa. That we learned all too soon.

"There was nothing we could do. Our young men and women fought bravely, but the Wall is so high and strong it cannot be breached. The Chlengguu we fought to a standstill, but we could not stop the Wall."

Simna blinked at him, glanced sharply down at the line of battle then back at the merchant. "Are you telling us that these Chlengguu keep moving the Wall forward?" He stared at the unbroken barrier that stretched from far west to distant east. "The whole Wall? That's impossible!"

"Would that it were so, traveler," the other man agreed, "but the Chlengguu do not move the Wall. Each time it advances, it pins us tighter and tighter against the desert lands. That is why you passed so many people, so many refugees. We have nowhere else to go. We are squeezed between the Wall and the desert." He cast a sorrowful gaze downward. "These Relibaria Hills are our last refuge, our final hope. We pray that the Wall cannot surmount them. If it can—" He broke off, momentarily choked. "If it can, then we will be pushed out into the desert, where most of us will surely die, and the fertile lands of the Queppa will belong forever to the Chlengguu."

"I do not understand," Ehomba confessed. "If the Chlengguu do not move the Wall, then how . . . ?"

"See, see!" Gesturing with a trembling hand, the merchant was pointing downward. "Look upon the abomination, and understand!"

Below, activity had increased from the frantic to a frenzy. Scaling ladders were brought forth as the ragtag citizen soldiery of the united Queppa peoples mounted yet another assault on the Wall. Fusillades of arrows flew like hummingbirds but because of the Wall's height were hard-pressed to wreak much havoc among its well-protected defenders. Catapults and siege engines heaved rocks and bales of burning, oil-soaked straw at the crest of the tawny palisade. They were not entirely ineffective. Ehomba saw figures topple from the battlements, to fall spinning and tumbling into the melee of furious fighters below.

From the top of the escarpment the Chlengguu hurled spears and stones and arrows of their own at the attackers below. More ladders were brought up, and mobile siege towers as high as the Wall itself trundled forward. A few Queppa, battling madly, even succeeded in reaching the top of the Wall and pushing back some of its defenders. To Ehomba it looked as if, in one or two places along the line of battle, they might have a chance to overwhelm the Wall's defenders and push them back.

As he and his companions looked on, the Wall began to shiver slightly. At a distance it was difficult to tell if it was really happening. Ehomba rubbed at his eyes, Simna squinted doubtfully, and the singular activity even brought the largely indifferent Ahlitah out of his feline stupor.

There it was again.

"What was that?" Simna muttered uncertainly. "What just happened there?" Reaching out, he grabbed the merchant firmly by the shoulder, sinking his fingers into the soft flesh hard enough to hurt. But the other man just ignored him, staring, his gaze vacant with lost hope.

"There!" Ehomba pointed. "Look there." Alongside him, Ahlitah was on his feet now, growling deep in his throat.

Below, the people of Queppa began to retreat, pulling back their siege engines and all their assembled forces. Atop the Wall, the hard-pressed Chlengguu quickly regained all they had lost. They lined the battlements, jumping up and down, their armor shimmering, yelling and screaming and taunting their fleeing, dispirited quarry. Those Queppa fighters who had taken parts of the Wall were surrounded and butchered, their bodies thrown like so much garbage over the parapets to land among their fleeing comrades.

Then the Wall stood up, all hundred feet and more high of it, all along its considerable impressive length, and took one giant step forward.

XXVIII

Simna tried to believe what he was seeing, shaking his head more than once as if that would make it go away. The hair on Ahlitah's back bristled and his lips curled in a snarl. Ehomba stood between them, holding firmly to his spear, staring at the inconceivable, improbable sight. Nearby, the distraught merchant wrung his hands and wept in silence.

Having advanced one step, the Wall hunkered down. Dust rose from its base as a long, drawn-out *Boooom* echoed across the hills. Atop the battlements, the victorious Chlengguu howled and pranced a while longer. Then, except for the few assigned to the watch, they drew away from the edge, filtering back down stairways on the other side of the barrier to the numerous tented camps that served to house their multitudes. Soon campfires could be seen smoking among the ranked canopies, inviting the advancing night. The abundant serpentine coils of smoke gave the land the aspect of a vast plantation for snakes.

In his mind Ehomba replayed the impossible spectacle he had just witnessed. All along its length the Wall had risen and sprouted hooves. Dark gray, bristle-haired, cloven hooves, with gigantic toes and glistening, untrimmed nails. Hooves whose ankles disappeared into the underside of the Wall. In unison, they had risen as much as they were able and stepped forward, in a one-step march of fleeting but irresistible duration. The merchant had been telling the truth. The Chlengguu had not moved the Wall. The Wall had moved itself.

The heavyset man was watching him. "You see what has befallen us. From the first appearance of the Wall we were doomed. The people of the Queppa have been dying a slow death. The Wall is relentless and invincible. We attack, and sometimes we force back the Chlengguu. But then the Wall moves, overwhelming our war engines, dumping and smashing our siege ladders, forcing us always back, back, until now we are trapped here between it and the desert." Helplessly, he spread his hands.

"What can we do? We cannot fight a Wall that moves. If our soldiers try to outflank it, it grows another length, another extension, until our people are stretched so thin they cannot be supplied. Then the Chleng-guu pour down off their Wall and slaughter the flanking party. These hills are our last hope." Once more he peered downward. "The Wall can march. We pray it cannot climb."

Ehomba nodded, then smiled as gently as he could. "Go back to your family, friend. And thank you."

Much relieved, the merchant nodded and turned to go. Then he paused to glance back, frowning. "What will you do now?"

The herdsman had turned away from him and was staring at the terrain below. "To find passage across the Semordria I have to find a ship capable of crossing it. If all that you have said is true, to do that I must cross this Aboqua Sea and reach the lands to the north. So we will keep going north."

"But you can't!" Licking thick lips, the merchant found his attention torn between his nearby encampment and the eccentric travelers. "You'll never get over the Wall, or around it. Your situation is the same as ours, now. You can only go back." His jawline tightened. "At least your home is safely distant to the south, and you know how to survive in the desert. The people of the Queppa do not."

"Nevertheless, we will continue northward." Ehomba turned to regard him. "Go back to your family, friend, and do not worry about us. You do not have enough worry to spare for strangers."

"There is truth in that." The merchant hesitated briefly, then raised a hand in a gesture that was both salute and farewell. "Good fortune to you, seekers of a sudden end. I wish you luck in your foolishness." With that he turned and hurried off as fast as his thick, heavy legs would carry him.

Simna sidled close to his companion. "I've no more desire to turn and go back the way we came than anyone, but he has a point. How do we get over the Wall?" The swordsman nodded toward the imposing barrier. "I count a pair of guards for every thirty feet of parapet and fire baskets or lamps for light every forty. We'll have to try it at night anyway. We wouldn't have a chance in daylight." He nodded at the third member of the group.

"And what about our great black smelly eminence here? Cats can climb well, but a smooth-faced vertical wall is another matter. You and I can go up a scaling rope, if we can borrow or steal one from this dis-heartened mob of defenders, but what about him?"

The dark-maned head turned to face the swordsman. "I'll get up and over. One way or another, I will do it."

"You won't have to." Ehomba was not looking at either of them, but at the Wall.

Simna squinted at him. "Say what?" Then his expression brightened. "Hoy, right! You'll use your alchemical gifts. By Gyuwin, I'd forgotten about that."

"You cannot forget something that was not there to know," Ehomba corrected him. "As I have told you repeatedly, I have no alchemical gifts to use." Lowering his spear, he gestured with the point. "We will go down among the Queppa defenders and find a place to ourselves, one unsuited to fighting. The next time the Wall rises to advance, we will race beneath it to the other side. It needs longer than a moment to take its step—more than enough time for us to run underneath." Lifting his spear, he smiled confidently at Simna.

"It will be easy. The only care we must take is that no one trips and falls. There will not be enough time for the others to help him up."

"Underneath?" Gazing afresh down at the Wall, Simna swallowed, trying to envision hundreds of tons of yellow mass hovering just over his head. He marked his companion's words well. Anyone who tripped and went down during the crossing might not have enough time to rise and scramble to safety. The Wall would descend upon its hundreds of feet, crushing him, smashing him flat as a crêpe.

Ehomba put a hand on his shoulder, bringing him out of his sickly reverie. "Do not worry, my friend. There will be enough time. Remember—as we run to the north, the Wall will be moving one giant step to the south."

"Hoy, that's right." Simna found himself nodding in agreement. "Yes, we can do it."

"Easier than climbing," the litah pointed out, "and no guards to dispose of while making the passage."

"Okay, okay." Simna had grown almost cheerful. "A quick sprint, no fighting, and we're through. And these Chlengguu won't be looking for anyone to do something that daring." A sudden thought made him hesi-tate. "Hoy, if it's so easy and obvious, why haven't these Queppa folk tried it? Ghalastan knows they're desperate enough."

"Any group of soldiers large enough to make a difference in the fight would surely be spotted from the ramparts by the Chlengguu look-outs," Ehomba surmised. "Since they control the Wall, they could simply command it to cut short its advance and relax, thereby smashing any counterattacking force beneath its weight. It may be that the Queppa have already made the attempt and met such results."

"Yeah." Subject as he was to abrupt swings of mood, Simna was suddenly subdued. "Poor bastards. Having to fight every day and move their women and kids at the same time." His face was grim as he stared downward. "If that Wall can come up these hills then they haven't got a chance. And after seeing the size and number of those hooves, I don't see these gentle slopes being any problem for it."

Ehomba's eyes danced. "Why Simna ibn Sind—one would almost think you were ready to stand and fight on behalf of these people."

The swordsman laughed derisively. "There are certain diseases I fear, Etjole. Among them are the chills and fever the mosquito brings, the swelling of the limbs one gets from an infestation of certain worms, the closure of the bowels, the clap, the spotted death, leprosy, and altruism. I count the last among the most deadly." He glared over at his companion. "I don't see *you* volunteering to help these pitiful sods."

"We do not have the time." Looking away, the herdsman once more considered the Wall they were about to attempt. "I have family and friends of my own. One man cannot save the world, or even particularly significant portions of it."

"Hoy, it's thoughts like that that keep us together, bruther." The swordsman glanced at the third member of their party. "I don't suppose you have any thoughts on the matter?"

"*Snzzz* . . . what?" Ahlitah looked up, blinking. "I was catnapping."

"I thought as much. Go back to your rest, maestro of the long tooth. You'll need your strength for running."

Once more the litah dropped his great head onto his forepaws. "I could make the dash ten times back and forth before you arrived on the other side. Look to your own legs, man, and don't worry about me." The yellow eyes closed.

"Get up," Ehomba chided him. "We need to make ready." Poling the ground with the butt of his spear, he started downward, trailed by Simna and a reluctant, yawning Ahlitah.

None of the dispirited Queppa who saw the unusual trio pass did more than glance in their direction. With so much of their land under siege by the Chlengguu, allies from many townships and counties had been thrown together. Men fought alongside apes they had never met before, and monkeys did battle in the shadow of lightly armored chimps. In such conditions, under such circumstances, the presence of one imposing, long-legged feline was not considered extraordinary.

The travelers descended until they were close enough to the base of the Wall to easily make out individual sentries patrolling the parapet. Turning eastward, they walked until they found themselves among an outcropping of jagged rocks. No Queppa soldiers were present. Such rugged, uneven terrain rendered siege engines and scaling ladders useless. Having the spot to themselves, they settled down to eat an evening meal from their limited stores.

Less than a hundred feet away, the base of the wall loomed. It had the appearance of limestone that had been washed or stuccoed with some thick yellow paste. To look at it one would never suspect it harbored within the underside of its substance hundreds of hooves the size of elephants.

Tearing off a mouthful of dried fish from the whitish lump he held in his fist, Simna chewed slowly and stared at the imposing barrier. "We'll have to be damn careful. These rocks will make for treacherous running."

"Only between here and the Wall." Ehomba sat nearby, arms resting on his angular knees, his mouth hardly moving as he masticated his supper. "Beneath it the rocks will have been crushed flat. With luck, it will be like running on a gravel road."

"With luck," a skeptical Simna murmured. "Well, once on the other side we should be fine. Might be an occasional Chlengguu pillaging party to avoid, but that shouldn't present much of a problem. We'll just give them plenty of room."

Nearby, Ahlitah sighed sleepily. "Should be lots of livestock running free. Easy kill, fresh meat." He growled softly in anticipation.

"Stay alert," the herdsman advised him. "We need to be ready to move at the first sign of activity from the Wall."

"Don't worry about me," the big cat assured him. "Just look after your own skinny, inadequate selves."

It was already dark when they heard, not saw, the first indications of movement: a deep-seated grinding and rumbling that emerged from the base of the wall itself, spreading outward as a vibration in the rocks beneath them.

To all outward appearances sound asleep, Ahlitah was first on his feet, awake and alert, tail flicking back and forth in agitation as he glared at the Wall. Ehomba and Simna were not far behind in scrambling erect.

To left and right they heard the yells and screams of the Queppa defenders, and, behind them, up in the hills, the distraught cries of their families and other noncombatants. Once more, showers of arrows rose from the massed defenders while gobbets of blazing brush and oil were flung against the wall. It was all to no avail, but Ehomba suspected the citizen soldiers felt they had to do something, to try. The flaming missiles did no more damage to the Wall than they would have to any stone monument, and up atop the quivering, trembling barrier the Chlengguu despoilers merely hunkered down out of reach and range.

"It's moving," Simna hissed as he stood watching. "Be ready!"

So near, the raising up of the Wall was infinitely more impressive than it had been from the top of the hill. Dirt and bits of weed and brush were carried upward by its bottom edge, a slow vertical heaving of unimaginable mass. Living stone groaned as it ascended on many multiples of hooves to reveal gigantic nails and pads.

The travelers were racing forward well before the Wall had risen to its full stepping height, arrowing down a slight gap in the rocks. Ehomba sprang lithely from one slab of sharp basalt to another, while Simna bounced from stone to stone like a lump of rubber that had been formed into the shape of a man. As for the litah, it leaped nimbly from one outcropping to the next, clearing in an instant spans that mere humans had to traverse painstakingly on foot.

They sprinted beneath the overhanging awe of the Wall and were swallowed beneath its gargantuan mass. Ehomba could sense the volume above him, millions of tons of solid material balanced on pillarlike but still imperfect toes. Barely visible through shadow and darkness, a few lines of brightness ran through the underside of the barrier, though whether they were fractures in the rock or flowing veins he could not tell.

They raced past one of the immense hooves as it rose up and started forward, an action matched by every alternate hoof under the length of the Wall. When they descended in unison, so would the Wall itself, swallowing them up once again together with everything and anything too slow to get out of its way. But by the time those hundreds of cloven hooves had begun their downward step, Ehomba and his companions had already emerged on the far side of the barrier.

Pausing to catch their breath, they stood and watched as it completed its ponderous single-stride advance, descending quietly to ground with a single long, exhausted *Whoooom*. Dust rose again, scattered, and began to settle. It was done. They were through, across, under.

"Nothing to it," quipped Simna. He was, however, showing more perspiration than the short sprint and tepid evening ought to have generated.

"No room for mistakes there." Tilting back his head, the herdsman gazed up at the top of the Wall. No shapes or bodies were to be seen. The Chlengguu were all on the far side, watching for mischief among the Queppa. No need for them to guard their impenetrable rear. "Let us go."

Turning, they headed north, traveling at an easy trot. No one came forth to question their presence or challenge their progress.

They found an abandoned farm and, without any sense of guilt, made themselves at home in the comfortable surroundings presently denied to the rightful owner. Discovering a still-intact and unpillaged pen of domesticated razorbacks, Ahlitah quickly and effortlessly supplied a feast not only for himself but for his companions. With so many structures still smoldering throughout the length and breadth of the Queppa lands, Ehomba conceded a fire to Simna, who refused to eat his pork uncooked.

There were fine, soft beds in the house, and linen. While the delighted swordsman guilelessly availed himself of the former, Ehomba discovered he could not go to sleep on anything so yielding. He found peace by wrapping himself in a blanket on the wooden floor and trying not to think of the fate of the thousands being squeezed between the Wall and the eternal sands of the south. Thousands for whom such pleasures as a simple good night's rest were denied.

XXIX

Morning was full of mist, as if the sun had been surprised in its bath and risen too quickly, spilling a blanket of saturated sunlight upon the world.

It induced the travelers to linger longer in their appropriated beds, a condition with which the always sleepy Ahlitah was wholly in accord. When Ehomba finally awoke and ascertained the true position of the fog-obscured daystar, he found himself unsettled in mind.

"What's wrong now, wizard of worries?" Sitting up in the elegant, carved bed, a well-rested Simna ibn Sind stretched and then scratched unashamedly at his groin. "We did our running, and all went well. Why don't you try relaxing for a change? Who knows? You might even find the sensation agreeable."

Quietly agitated, the herdsman was staring out a many-paned window at the farm's mist-swathed environs. "I will rest when we are out of this ill-starred country and safe aboard a ship bound for the far side of the Aboqua. Not before." He looked back. "Get up and cover your ass. We should be away from here."

"All right, all right." Grumbling, the swordsman slid his legs out from beneath the heavy wefted bed sheets and began fumbling with his attire. "But not before breakfast. Who knows when we may again have a chance to eat like this? And for free."

"Very well." Ehomba was reluctant, but understanding. "After breakfast."

While most of the dairy products that had not been looted from the forsaken farm stank of spoilage, there remained a substantial quantity of dried and smoked meats. Another section of the walk-in larder was filled from floor to ceiling with jars of preserved fruits and vegetables. Rummaging through the stores, Simna found a couple of loaves of bread decorated by only a few spots of opportunistic mold.

"We should fill our packs." He bit enthusiastically into a mouthful of meat and bread.

"This is not our food." Though uncomfortable at rifling another man's pantry, Ehomba consoled himself with the realization that if they did not eat the bread and other perishables, they would go either to the Chlengguu or to waste.

"Hoy, that's right—leave it for the despoilers. Misplaced good intentions have been the death of many a man, bruther. But not me!" Daring the herdsman to take exception, he began stuffing strips of dried meat and small jars of olives and pickles into his pack. Ehomba simply turned away.

When at last all was in readiness they stepped out into the fog. If anything, the herdsman thought, it had grown thicker since they had arisen. It would be difficult to tell north from any other direction. But he was not about to linger in the homestead until the mist lifted. If they could see any patrolling Chlengguu clearly, then the Chlengguu could see them. Better to take their chances under cover of the low-hanging vapors.

He was only a few yards from the house, turning in the direction where he imagined north to lie, when a thunderous roar shattered the tenuous silence. Whirling, he saw only the last flash of motion as the heavy net landed atop Ahlitah. The great cat bellowed furiously, claws ripping at the material, powerful jaws snapping, but to no avail. Whoever had designed the ambush had made their preparations well: The mesh was made of metal, woven into finger-thick cords like rope. Ahlitah could dent but not tear it.

Chlengguu seemed to come from everywhere: back of the farmhouse, behind bushes, over fence rails, everywhere but straight up out of the ground. Dozens more dropped from the roof to clutch frantically at the fringes of the net, for while the litah was unable to break it, his convulsions were sending panicked Chlengguu flying in all directions. It took forty of them finally to pin down the net and the outraged, wild-eyed feline within.

No nets came flying at Ehomba and Simna. Instead, they found themselves overwhelmed by another half hundred of the forceful Wall masters. The herdsman had hardly begun to lower his spear and Simna to draw his sword when rough hands fell upon them, wrenching their weapons out of their hands and reach. Hobbles were brought forth, and their hands were bound behind their backs. Thoroughly trussed and tethered, they were shoved rudely forward as their captors barked incomprehensible commands at them in the exotic Chlengguu tongue.

"I hope you enjoyed your breakfast," Ehomba muttered as they were marched away from the farmhouse and into the fog.

"That I did, bruther." Exhibiting considerable aplomb in the face of a less than sanguine situation, the swordsman studied their captors. "They're not especially big, but the little buggers are fast." He smiled amiably at the Chlengguu warrior striding along next to him. "Ugly, too." Unable to understand, the soldier marched along stiffly, looking neither to left nor right and certainly not at the grimacing captive.

Behind the herdsman, dozens of warriors bore the frustrated, spitting Ahlitah aloft. So tightly wrapped and rolled in the steel net was the litah that he was unable to shift his limbs. Nor if they had any sense at all would his captors allow him the slightest range of movement. If so much as a single set of claws slipped free, Ehomba knew they would find their way into one of their abductors' necks. Always cautious, the Chlengguu were taking no chances with the biggest and most powerful of their prisoners.

They were excessively thin, the herdsman saw. Slim enough that he looked bulky beside them, and Simna positively squat. They had narrow, sharply slanted eyes that were set almost vertically in their faces, long hooked noses, and small mouths. The two canines protruded very slightly down over the lower lip. Their ears were thin and pointed as well, and the narrow skulls showed no hair beneath their tight-fitting, embossed helmets. Many of these were decorated with long quills and spines appropriated, no doubt involuntarily, from sundry unknown animals.

Coupled with the narrowness of their skulls and faces, the slight natural downward curve of their jawlines gave them a permanently sour facial cast. In hue their skin shaded from dark beige to umber heavily tinged with yellow, as if they were all suffering from jaundice. Fingernails were long, thin, and painted silver. Their finely tooled leather jackets, leggings, and boots were engraved with diverse scenes of mass unpleasantness. The great majority of these were also tinted silver, but Ehomba saw gold, bronze, and bright red bobbing among the argent sea as well.

Most carried two or three tempered lances no thicker than his thumb. A finely honed sickle hung from each waist—a particularly nasty weapon in close-quarter combat. A few of the more discriminating soldiers favored slim-handled spike-studded maces over the more delicate lances.

"I wonder what they have in mind for us?"

"By Gnospeth's teeth, not wining and dining, I'll venture." Simna continued to make faces at his guards, who resolutely ignored him.

"Though there's some dancing houris I wouldn't mind introducing them to. Where's the soul-sucking Eupupa when you need them?"

They were marched on in silence for more than an hour before the mist finally began to lift. Tents began to materialize around them. From time to time Chlengguu soldiers busy attending to their bivouac glanced up to examine the prisoners. Those that made the effort to do so generally ignored the two men in favor of the trussed and bound black litah.

Probably they think we are ordinary Queppa prisoners, Ehomba decided. Simna and I look not so very different from the poor people whose land they are stealing.

With sinking heart, he saw a familiar sight looming up in front of them. The Wall. They had lost all the distance they had gained during their flight of the night before.

They were paraded past several large and elaborately decorated tents until the officer in charge halted outside one that was a veritable villa of cloth and canvas. Multiple standards of red and gold flew from its poles. Ehomba was sickened to see the flayed skins of human bodies alternating with the silken pennants, the grisly trophies snapping noisomely in the wind.

The periphery of the ornate shelter was embellished with threads drawn from precious metals. Two unusually large Chlengguu flanked the twin support posts of an imposing rain flap. Silk drapery provided privacy to those within. Each pole, the herdsman noted expressionlessly, was grounded in the bleached skull of a great ape.

One of the few among their captors who was not clad in silver leather paused to speak to the guards. Conversation was brief, whereupon a bony hand jammed hard into Ehomba's back, sending him stumbling forward. He heard Simna curse behind him as his companion was subjected to similar indelicate treatment. As for Ahlitah, the cat had been quiet for some time. Biding it, the herdsman decided.

If the outside of the tent had been designed to impress, the interior was calculated to overwhelm. Peaks of fabric soared overhead. Sewn into the material, fine jewels simulated the constellations of the night sky. There was richly carved furniture whose lines reflected the slenderness of its owners: tables, chairs, lounges, comfortable but not luxurious. The tent was located in an arena of war. While impressive, its furnishings were anything but dysfunctional.

A quartet of aged Chlengguu seated at an oval table looked on with interest as the prisoners were marched inside. Customarily slight of build, these withered specimens looked positively skeletal. But their sharp, inquisitive eyes belied their physical appearance. They muttered and mumbled among themselves while making cryptic gestures in the direction of the prisoners.

Ahlitah's cortege did not depart until the big cat had been securely staked to the floor. Without even room in which to struggle, the muscular black specter lay still, with only the steady, infuriated heaving of his chest to show that he was alert and unharmed except in dignity.

Three Chlengguu rose from a table groaning under the weight of food, drink, maps, and assorted alien accouterments whose functions the provincial Ehomba did not recognize. One of them was female, though the extraordinary lankiness of the Chlengguu form made it difficult to sex them at first glance. Spidery fingers resting on all but nonexistent hips, the nearest of the trio cocked his head sideways to peer up into Ehomba's face. The sharply angled eyes were unsettling. The herdsman had encountered eyes vertical and eyes horizontal, eyes round and eyes oval, but never before had he gazed back into angular oculi that were anything like those of the Chlengguu.

"*Sirash coza mehroosh?*"

Ehomba kept his face blank. "I do not understand you."

The Chlengguu noble tested the same phrase on the silent Simna, who to his credit had sense enough to keep his extensive farrago of ready retorts locked away in a corner of his brain where they would, hopefully for the duration of the foreseeable future, not get him killed.

Retracing his steps to confront the much taller herdsman the noble asked, in the common voice of men, "Who are you and where do you come from?" His voice was as soft and prickly as hot grease. Gesturing at Simna, he added, "This one could be Queppa, but you—you are different. You have the look about you of someplace else."

"We are both from the south," Ehomba replied. "As is our pet." Behind him he thought he heard the litah stir, but he did not turn to look. From the noble's manner he surmised that turning away from him while he was engaged in his interrogation might be construed as an unforgivable insult. Judging from their extravagant surroundings and the carriage and posture of their interrogators, he and his companions would have to be careful not to give even the slightest offense.

"The south." Daintily, the noble tapped the tip of a painted fingernail against one excessively long canine. "Why should I believe you?"

"Why should we lie?" Ehomba imperceptibly shifted his weight from one foot to the other, an instinctive herdsman's adjustment. "The Queppa hate the south. Who of them would claim to come from where you are driving them?"

The corners of the nobleman's tiny mouth twitched slightly upwards.

"If you are not Queppa, how do you know what they hate or where we are driving them?"

"They told us." Ehomba chanced a nod in the direction of his homeland. "Coming up from the south, we had to pass through them to get here."

"You had to pass through more than the stupid Queppa to get here." The female fairly spat the accusation. "The only way from south to north is over the Wall. That is not possible."

"We did not go over the Wall," Ehomba corrected her. "We came under it."

This claim set the quartet of oldsters to arguing agitatedly over their table. It also prompted the third member of the interrogating trio to speak up. "No one is half-witted enough to try digging under the Wall."

"Who said anything about digging?" Simna was smirking now, virtually strutting in place. "We just waited for it to make ready to step, and when it rose up, we ran under."

The initial questioner dropped his finger from his lips. "Such a thing is possible, of course." He nodded once, curtly. "Very well. I, Setsealer Agrath, accept your explanation. You are courageous half-wits."

"This is not our fight," Ehomba told him somberly. "I personally have no quarrel with the Chlengguu and no affection for the Queppa. This lasting strife is your own. Let us go."

Turning slightly away, Agrath chose a long, thin knife, very much an oversized stiletto, from the assortment of cutlery lying on the table behind him. "Why should we?"

"I have business in the west."

"The west?" Agrath snickered slightly to his associates. "I thought you told us your destination lies to the north."

"I have to go north," Ehomba informed him, patient as he would have been with a child, "in order to find a ship willing to take me west."

"Across the Semordria?" The Chlengg did not laugh so much as hiss breathily. "Now you try my intelligence."

"It's true." Simna jerked his head sharply in his friend's direction. "He's deranged, he is."

"Yet you follow him?"

The swordsman dropped his gaze and his voice. "What can I say? I have perverse tastes. Who can explain it?"

"Who indeed? When we are finished here we will remand you to the custody of specialists whose work is famed even among the Chlengguu. Perhaps they will get the real explanation out of you."

"Hoy, now wait a minute, you—"

The mace that descended struck only a glancing blow to the back of the swordsman's skull or he surely would have died on the spot. As it was, he only crumpled to the carpeted floor, where he lay motionless and bleeding. Ehomba glanced wordlessly in the direction of his friend's unmoving body, then returned his attention to the three Chlengguu nobles. They were watching him expectantly.

"You are not angry at this treatment meted out to your friend?"

Ehomba's voice was entirely unchanged. "Of what use would it be? You want to test us. You might as well have struck me to provoke him. It makes no difference."

"None whatsoever," Agrath agreed, "except that you are standing and he is unconscious." The noble shrugged. "As you say, it could as easily have been done the other way. But I am more curious about you than him. Contrariety is a welcome diversion from the boredom of our inexorable advance."

"We were told it was not always so."

"No." The other male's voice darkened. "Before the Wall it was very different. Now"—he did not grin so much as sneer—"after the Wall, it will be more different still."

"I really don't care whether our specialists work on you or not." Agrath ran the edge of the stiletto along his elongated palm, drawing a thin line of his own blood. His expression never changed. "But I do so enjoy the occasional uncommon curiosity." Removing the blade from his skin, he flicked the point to indicate something behind Ehomba.

Moments later, two soldiers came forward. They were carrying the weapons confiscated from the travelers. These they placed on the already crowded table. After genuflecting twice to the nobles, they carefully backed away and rejoined their comrades.

While the skeletal oldsters continued to bicker and squabble in the background, the nobles proceeded to inspect the outwardly unimpressive weapons. The woman hefted Ehomba's spear, sniffed contemptuously, and dumped it back on the table. Agrath picked up the tooth-studded bone sword, having to use both hands to finesse the weight, and whipped it back and forth a few times. One swipe passed very close to the herdsman's face, but Ehomba did not flinch. If his captors were struck by his stoicism, none of them remarked upon it.

"Bone and teeth." Agrath was singularly unimpressed. "A suitable device for a primitive tribesman."

Sliding the pale white weapon back into its goatskin sheath, Agrath then drew the sky-metal blade from its protective covering. His angled eyes could not widen, but he nodded appreciatively. As he had with its weighty predecessor, he required the use of both strong but thin wrists to support the weapon parallel to the floor. Maintaining this grip, he swung it slowly back and forth. Diffuse sunlight filtering through the fine material of the tent glinted off the exotically forged iron.

"This is more like it." Bringing the flat side of the blade up to his face, he eyed the peculiar lines etched into the metal. "Whoever worked this design into the blade is a master armorer."

"The design was not worked," Ehomba told him. "The lines are inherent in the metal, but must be brought out by dipping the finished blade in acid."

The noble's face squinched up tight as a snake trying to slip into a too-small hole in pursuit of prey. "Nonsense. No such metal shows such lines naturally." Using both hands, he held the sword high, admiring the play of light on the internal crystalline structure. "Perhaps when we have conquered the south I will bring this marvelous armorer into my own service." Lowering the point abruptly, he swung it around until it was dimpling the reawakened Simna's chest. The swordsman tensed, but held his ground.

"Tell me, southerner. How sharp is the edge? How strong the alloy? What could one do with such a blade?"

Ehomba deliberately avoided his companion's face lest the look frozen there cause him to hurry his response. "It can cut through any bone, even that of an elephant or mastodon. The point will penetrate most armors, be they metal or fabric. Striking it with a flint will make a quick fire. And," he concluded, "if held high enough for long enough, I am told by the old women of the Naumkib that it will draw down the moon."

XXX

The softly convulsed modulated exhalation that passed for laughter among the Chlengguu filled the tent. "Does he take us for idiots?" the other male declared sharply. "Or does he think to play with our minds and thereby somehow deflect his unavoidable fate?"

"If he says it's so, then you'd better watch out." Simna struggled with his restraints. "He's a mighty sorcerer."

Plainly amused, Agrath turned back to the stolid herdsman. "Well, southerner? Does your friend speak true? Are you a 'mighty sorcerer'?"

"Note his clothing," opined the female disdainfully. "He doesn't even look like a mighty breeder of rabbits."

Keeping an eye on Ehomba, Agrath raised the sword high, as high as he could manage, aiming the point at the ceiling. Straining with the effort it required, he let go with one palm and maintained the difficult pose, balancing the weapon in a one-handed grip. A couple of the guards commented approvingly.

"There!" The wicked slash of a mouth parted to reveal white teeth. "What now, southerner?" Still holding the blade aloft, he turned toward the command tent's entrance. "It is early enough and the sky clear enough that I can still see a bit of the moon. Though it is more difficult to tell during the day, it looks unchanged to me, and certainly unmoved. Behgron! Please be so good as to check on the position of the moon for me."

One of the officers among the company that had brought in the three prisoners executed a quick, sharp half bow, whirled, and darted outside. His voice came back to those inside clear and crisp.

"It looks the same to me, Your Overlordship. The same color, and it surely has not moved."

"There now." Still holding the weapon aloft, greatly pleased with himself, Agrath eyed his tallest prisoner coldly. "What have you say to that, 'sorcerer'?"

"*I* did not say that it would bring down the moon," Ehomba responded humbly. "I repeat only what the old women of the village have told me."

The Chlengguu noble gave a curt nod. "Well then, it would appear that we have proof that the old women of your village are a bunch of prating, ignorant whores." He waited for the herdsman to say something, but Ehomba kept silent.

"Your pardon, Overlordship." It was the voice of the officer who had gone to stand just outside the entrance to the tent.

"Yes, what is it?" Agrath snapped off the response impatiently. The officer was interrupting his fun.

"It is true that the moon is unchanged, noble Agrath—but there is something else."

"Something else?" The Chlengg's expression twisted uncertainly. "What 'something else'? Explain yourself, soldier."

"I can't, Overlordship. Perhaps you should come and see for yourself."

"We'll do that, and if there is no good reason for this interruption . . ." He left the promise of unpleasantness hanging in the air.

Accompanied by Ehomba and the groaning, recently awakened Simna, the three Chlengguu nobles strode to the entrance of the tent. The senior officer Behgron proceeded to indicate a point in the sky. An irritated Agrath followed the line formed by the slim arm.

"What ails you? I see nothing."

"There, Overlordship." The officer pointed again. "To the left and below the curve of the moon."

"I see a bright star." His anger was growing. "You called us out here for that? As the sun rises it will soon be gone."

"Watch the star, noble Agrath. It's not fading with the rising sun. It is getting bigger."

"Don't be a *noukin*! Stars do not—"

The female noble stepped forward, her head tilted back, her narrow, slanted gaze inclined upward. "Behgron is right. Look at it!"

Not only was the glowing spot in the sky growing steadily larger even as they stared in its direction, but a small streak of light had begun to appear in its wake, like the feathery tail of the splendid white macaw.

"The sword!" Taking a step away from Agrath, the other male

pointed a shaky finger in the direction of the weapon. Natural physiological constraints aside, it was possible that his eyes did widen slightly. *"Look at the sword."*

An ethereal blue-black light now bathed the weapon, engulfing it in an unearthly halo. This put forth no heat. In fact, if anything, the startled Agrath found the sword suddenly ice cold to the touch. Dropping it as quickly as if he had found himself clutching a cobra, he retreated backwards, pressing up against a knot of nervous, wide-eyed guards.

As soon as the blade struck the ground it sprang upward. As everyone present watched in awe and amazement, it rose slowly until it was hovering at chest level above the ground. Still interred in the stunning steely effulgence, it adjusted its position slightly until the sharp terminus was pointing directly at the dilating orb overhead.

By now that fierce ghostly globe had swollen to dominate the sky, having grown larger even than the sun. The tail that trailed behind it was a streak of stark incandescence against the cobalt blue of the heavens. Among the assembled Chlengguu, troops and nobles alike, the first traces of panic had begun to surface.

"What is this, southerner?" Droplets of brown sweat had begun to bead on the noble Agrath's forehead. "I can still see the rim of the moon, so that is not the moon. What is happening?"

Squinting at the sky, Ehomba contemplated the onrushing orb. "I do not know," he informed his interrogator candidly. "I am only a simple herdsman." Lowering his gaze deferentially, he turned back to gaze down at the now highly agitated Chlengg. "To know the answer you would have to ask the prating, ignorant whores of the Naumkib."

The atmosphere was infused with a dull thunder. Unlike ordinary thunder, it did not announce itself and then steal away into the clouds in a series of gradually diminishing echoes. Despite the efforts of their officers to maintain discipline, a number of the guards had broken ranks and were running wildly in several directions. A number of their superiors looked as if they wanted to follow them.

Overhead, the steady thunder had become a screaming, a piercing shrillness that sounded as if the sky itself was coming apart. Hovering in midair, the sky-metal blade continued to emit the same spectral shine, a deep blue light that was almost black. As he eyed it interestedly, Ehomba found himself wondering how something could glow black.

Alarm was now endemic among the Chlengguu. Not only were the guards panicking in the face of the collapsing firmament, so was the rest of the army. Kicked aside in the mad rush to escape, cook fires latched on to tents. Soon, flames from numerous blazes were licking at the sky as if eager to greet their falling sibling. Soldiers clutched and clawed at one another in mad panic, and their massed screaming nearly rose above that of the descending colossus.

Watching the flawlessly organized bivouac plunge into madness and chaos, Ehomba wondered what the reaction was among the Queppa. Powerless to stop what Agrath had set in motion, he could only hope the thousands of refugees were managing their hysteria better than their tormentors.

"Do something!" A trembling Agrath had finally sunk to the level of his terrorized troops. "Turn it from us, make it go away!"

"Free me," Ehomba ordered him.

"Yes, yes, immediately!" With his own gold damascened sickle the noble cut the herdsman's bonds. As he stepped back, his terrified, tapering face was drawn inexorably to the lunatic sky. "Now do something!"

"I will." As mounting hysteria raged around him, Ehomba calmly walked over, stretched out one hand, and reached through the dark aurora to take hold of the radiant sword. The haft was cold, colder than he had ever felt it, but it seemed to warm a little at his touch. Or it might just have been the air itself, which was growing very warm indeed as the onrushing monolith approached the Earth.

Gripping the sword tightly in his fist, he turned around to face the shaken, fearful Agrath. The noble's two companions had vanished back into the tent, as though the sheer magnificence of its decoration might somehow impress the fiery plunging immensity and save them from destruction. Putting his left hand below his right, the herdsman drew back the blade and brought it around in a single swift, sweeping arc.

The expression on Agrath's face did not change even as his head was neatly severed from his shoulders and sent flying toward the entrance to the tent. It bounced a couple of times before coming to rest in the dirt. To their credit, a couple of the guards overcame their panic long enough to draw their weapons and rush toward Ehomba. Pirouetting as nimbly as if he were the lead dancer in a traditional Naumkib ceremony, the herdsman showed them the sword. That was enough. The pair promptly joined their comrades in hysterical flight.

Simna was hopping backwards toward his friend. "Cut me loose, bruther! We've got to get out of here." Lowering the blade, Ehomba swiftly sliced through the swordsman's restraints. "By Golontai's gonads, that's icy!" He rubbed at his emancipated wrists. "How do you hold on to it?"

Ehomba was running back into the tent. "In the winter, the nights in my country can get very cold. A man still has to stand watch over his herd."

"Cold, is it? Hoy, but you've sure given these pinch-faced bastards a chill!" Grinning wolfishly, Simna followed him into the tent.

If not for the naked fear rampant on their faces, the demeanor of the two nobles huddled and trembling beneath one of the carved tables would have been comical. On the opposite side of the tent, the four elder Chlengguu sat with eyes closed, lips moving silently as they recited whatever personal mantras they felt would best prepare them for Death. Nearby, Ahlitah fought futilely against the steel net.

"Lie still!" Ehomba barked as he brought the sword down. Simna looked on respectfully as the blade sliced through segment after segment of the tough metal mesh.

Once his front paws were free, the great black predator was able to push hard enough to snap numerous links and lengths of chain and give the herdsman some help. With Ehomba working his way down to the cat's hind legs, Ahlitah was soon free. He stretched magnificently, fighting to loosen cramped muscles.

"No time for that!" Simna yelled as he recovered the rest of their weapons from the table. The Chlengguu cowering beneath made no move to stop him. "We've got to get away from here. The sky is falling!"

"What is the hairless ape prattling about?" Ahlitah followed the herdsman as they hurried out of the tent.

"You will see," Ehomba assured the litah. And as soon as they were outside, he did.

The piece of sky was close enough now for the scrambling travelers to see that only its nucleus was solid. The remainder of the globe was composed of gases and vapors that were boiling off its surface and streaming back behind to form the now immense but nebulous tail. Actually, the solid portion of the sphere was not very large at all. They did not have time to ascertain exactly how big it might be because it was very near and coming toward them very fast.

It shrieked over their heads, passing just behind them, and hit with a sound like a million banshees all sobbing at once.

"Get down!" Even as he was shouting the warning to his friends, Ehomba was diving into a cramped irrigation ditch. Simna and even Ahlitah imitated his headlong leap without question. He felt the overheated mass of the big cat slam up against him.

Then the sky erupted. Howling winds tore at his body and clothing but largely shrieked past overhead. Out of one eye he could see tents and Chlengguu caught up by the detonation being scattered like toys in every direction. Many of the invaders were screaming, though they could not be heard over the force of the concussion.

As rapidly as it struck, the great wind passed. Rising tentatively from their providential if muddy refuge, Ehomba looked back the way they had come. All around them was desolation. The Chlengguu bivouac, much of the assembled army itself, its murderous equipment and lodgings, trees and surrounding vegetation, had been blown away or in many instances humbled beyond recognition.

Rising from the ditch, the travelers gathered themselves as they gazed southward. An enormous hole had been blasted in the Wall where the falling piece of sky had struck. Thousands of moaning, whimpering Chlengguu soldiers still clung to the untouched portions of the Wall that stretched away unbroken to east and west. The barrier was quivering, trembling slightly from the force and extent of the great wound it had incurred.

Then, to the accompaniment of hundreds of hopeless screams from as many hoarse and hysterical throats, the mortally injured Wall toppled slowly forward and fell, perishing with a reverberant crash and ensuing upheaval of dust, dirt, and Death. Dozens upon dozens of gigantic, gleaming hooves protruded from its upturned underside, stationary and unmoving. Among the cloud of debris that was raised by its collapse was a cloud. Not a dark cloud, but a cloud of darkness. This quickly dissipated into the sky, the wind whisking it northward. A tight-lipped Ehomba followed it with his eyes until it was lost from view.

As the echo of the Wall's fall faded, a new sound could be heard: the cries of thousands of displaced Queppa as they gathered themselves to swarm down upon the dazed and demoralized Chlengguu who had survived. Battle quickly became butchery. Ehomba turned away, disinterested in the outcome. As he had tried to tell representatives of both sides, theirs was not his fight. But no one had listened to him.

Taking a deep breath, carefully stepping over a pair of Chlengguu corpses that had been twisted out of all recognition, he accepted his spear and bone sword from Simna and prepared to resume the trek northward.

The swordsman paced him effortlessly while Ahlitah hung back slightly, pausing repeatedly to groom his ruffled and mussed black fur.

"Please now, bruther," Simna queried respectfully, "tell me once more how much the sorcerer you are not."

The herdsman looked down at his more than slightly skeptical companion. "Nothing has changed, my friend. I am the same man, boasting the same lack of skills beyond a knowledge of cattle and sheep, desert and ocean." Reaching back over his shoulder, he touched the hilt of the sky-metal sword where it rested once more in its scabbard. "The blade did all this, not I. Another made the blade, and others presided over its final forging. If you must have an explanation, talk to Otjihanja the Smithy or the old women of the Naumkib. Not I."

"But you knew what it could do." Simna was nothing if not persistent. "You ran for cover as soon as you could."

Ehomba nodded. "I knew, because I was told by those who know. Not because I carry with me any great store of necromantic knowledge. We were lucky."

"Lucky." Searching his friend's face for hint of cool concealment or calculated mendacity, the swordsman found none. Could it be as the herdsman claimed?

"Well, whatever the explanation, we're alive, and that's what matters." He put a little spring into his step. "Time enough later for clarifications." Shading his eyes with one hand, he squinted at the rubble they were approaching. From a distance, it appeared to be the ruin of a substantial building, perhaps a modest Queppa fortress. Shreds of Chlengguu banners hung limp from its crushed battlements. Shielded by the outer walls, the inner keep appeared to be relatively intact. Nothing moved on the damaged parapet, on the wind-scoured ground outside, or within.

"Let's have a look," he urged his tall companion.

"Why?" Ehomba's gaze narrowed slightly. "We still must reach the Aboqua and find passage north."

Concentrating on the small fortress, Simna muttered distantly, "The Chlengguu had to have a headquarters safely distant from the field of battle. Even with the Wall to protect them, that would be just common military sense." He nodded at the ruins. "Given the number of banners hanging from its stones, this looks like it might have been it."

"So?" Ehomba commented disinterestedly.

Simna smiled up at him. "Please allow me a minute, my laconic master of new lambs. I just want to have a quick look around."

The herdsman sighed tolerantly. "Very well. Otherwise I will hear about it for days."

"Yes you will. Come on." Increasing his pace, he raced on ahead.

Ahlitah watched him break into a sprint. "What ails the ape?"

"I do not know." Ehomba lengthened his stride. It would not do to let Simna out of his sight. The overeager swordsman might stumble into a nest of surviving invaders ready and frustrated enough to take out their anger on the first non-Chlengg who came their way. "But I can guess."

XXXI

The swordsman was not to be found in the vacant courtyard of the fortress. Nor was he in the deserted stables, or the unpretentious, high-ceilinged entry hall. Everywhere was evidence of hasty departure on the part of the Chlengguu who had been stationed in the sturdy stone structure. With every uncontested breeze, scattered scrolls and abandoned papers scooted across the floor like whispering, bleached vermin. Goblets and cups of indeterminate liquid posed forlornly on tables and in alcoves, waiting for drinkers who would never come. Erratic spills stained the floor. Gaps in the rafters showed where a few banners had been ripped from their braces and carried off by the fleeing soldiers.

They found Simna in a back room lying on a bed of gold. The room was small and showed signs of having been partially looted, but enough riches remained to satisfy even the most avaricious. There was some silver extant, and platinum presentation disks, and several chests of jeweled pins and medals. The swordsman lay on his back atop the pile, arms spread wide to encompass as much of the hoard as possible. His eyes were closed and a look of bliss reposed on his face as snugly as a perfumed hot towel.

Ahlitah took one glance at the heaping knoll of inedible metal, sniffed, and padded off in search of something valuable. Ehomba stepped through the open doorway, noting as he did so the broken lock and seal, and knelt to examine a handful of the coins. They were six-sided and stamped with an assortment of profiles and adornments. All of the sharply minted faces were Chlengguu.

"What was that you've been trying to tell me about no treasure?" As he slid down the front of the flaxen gradient, gold bunched up beneath the swordsman's undergarments. He did not find the sensation unpleasant.

Straightening, Ehomba surveyed the accumulation. "All Chlengguu coin and manufacture. This room in this fortress must have been used as the army's treasury. The troops were paid directly from this stockpile."

"And now there is no army." Simna smiled beatifically. "So it's ours." Lifting a fistful of coins, he let the gold trickle out between his fingers and spill across his stomach.

"Yours." Turning away, the herdsman prepared to head off in search of the litah.

"Hoy, bruther! Wait a moment." As Simna sat up, gold tumbled from his arms and chest. Coins bounced musically off the hard floor or ran away and hid against the base of the thick stone walls. "What do you mean, it's mine? Share and share alike, by Gloriskan!"

Pausing, Ehomba looked back at his friend. "I do not want any of it, Simna. It is all yours. I have all I can do to carry wood and water and weapons and a few essentials. Even a little gold is heavy when one has a long ways to walk."

"Not to me it ain't." Hoisting a handful, the swordsman tossed it into the air for the sheer pleasure of watching it catch the light as it fell. "To me it weighs next to nothing. In fact, the more I have to carry, the lighter my step becomes."

"If it makes you happy, you should enjoy it." Ehomba smiled goodnaturedly. "There is little enough happiness in the world. I am sure you will be able to find Queppa who will be delighted to help you take charge of your good fortune." He eyed the pile appraisingly. "I do not know a great deal about gold or money, but I think there is enough there to keep you in comfort for the rest of your life. Not enough to buy a kingdom, perhaps, but nearly anything else." He started through the door.

"Hoy, what's your hurry?"

The herdsman smiled back at him. "I am on a journey that leads to a destination, remember? I hope to reach the shores of the Aboqua in a few days. Be well, my good friend, and have a long and contented life." With that he strode out into the corridor and headed back in the direction of the main hall in search of the litah.

Simna ibn Sind sat contemplating more gold than he had ever believed could be found in one place. Lifting back the lid of one of the small metal-banded wooden chests that floated like carracks among the coins, he let his gaze linger on its contents: military decorations and awards wrought in the semibarbaric and florid style of the Chlengguu. There were formal lapel pins of fine filigreed gold inlaid with emeralds and sapphires, tsavorites and pearls; medals prominent with ivory and amber cameos of unknown nobles; satin ribbons from which hung intricate scenes etched into the faces of rare crystals by master engravers. Each worth a pocket fortune, and all his. The riches of a lifetime.

Rising abruptly, jaw set, he flung the chest aside, causing its contents to spill in an instant of sparkling evanescence across the pile's front slope. He found his companions at the entrance to the main hall, preparing to depart.

"Oh no you don't!" he shouted at Ehomba. Pausing in the act of adjusting the straps of his backpack, the herdsman looked back curiously.

The swordsman stomped up to the taller southerner and got right in his face. "Think you're all too clever, don't you?"

Expression innocent of guile, Ehomba regarded his friend. "Simna, I do not know what you mean."

"Like Grestel's choice you don't!" He gestured angrily back the way he had come. "Thinking you can buy me off with a pittance like that!"

"Pittance? My friend, from what little I know about gold, I would think what you have here enough for any man."

"Leave him to his counting." Ahlitah growled impatiently. "We should make some distance before nightfall."

Simna shot the big cat a look. "You keep out of this, masticator of minor mammals." Not even deigning to respond, the litah sighed and settled down on his belly to wait out the rest of the confrontation. When humans were arguing, it was all one could do. "That's what you want me to think, isn't it?" the swordsman told Ehomba accusingly. "That this is enough. First you tried to convince me you weren't after treasure, and now you're doing your best to use this trifle to bribe me to stay behind. Well, it's not going to work."

Ehomba smiled and shook his head slowly. "My friend, nothing of the sort ever—"

Simna would not let him finish. Instead, he raised a hand and waved it in the herdsman's face. "No, no—don't try to deny it!" A broad grin on his face, he began walking toward the exit. "You may as well forget the whole idea, Etjole. You're not rid of me that easily. I'm sticking to you like a father to his daughter in a naval port until we find the *real* treasure!" With that he marched imperiously through the portal, forcing himself not to look back in the direction of the storeroom and its glittering riches.

Lifting his mane, Ahlitah yawned conspicuously. "Can we go now?"

Shaking his head, the quietly exasperated herdsman followed in the swordsman's wake. "Sometimes, my feline friend, I think I understand sheep better than humans."

Unwinding itself from the floor, the great ebony cat padded along close beside him. "That's because sheep are more sensible than humans. Now, for real intelligence and common sense, you need to talk to a cat."

They emerged into the courtyard. No longer having to compete with a fiery, angry visitor from beyond, the sun shone placidly down on the ravaged expanse of the Queppa lands.

"So then tell me," the herdsman inquired as they began to catch up to the boldly striding Simna, "how does sleeping nineteen or twenty hours a day really affect the quality of your life?"

Predator's eyes swung around to meet his own. "You ask a lot of questions, Etjole Ehomba."

The herdsman smiled agreeably. "It is my nature."

It was farther to the Aboqua than Ehomba had hoped, but not as far as he feared. Keeping to a major north-south trade route that followed a convenient canyon through the range of coastal mountains, they soon found themselves sharing the way with a people who called themselves Maliin. They had fine homes and were not much for farming, tending to concentrate in numerous bustling towns and villages. Reports of the invasion of the Queppa had suffused their daily lives with apprehension and dread, so they were much relieved to hear that the cold, cruel Chlengguu had once again been defeated.

As the bearers of such good tidings, Ehomba and his friends were received with good cheer wherever they stopped. Eager for the latest news from the interior and relieved that it was, for the most part, all good, enthusiastic townsfolk took pleasure in tending to the needs of the quaint trio of pilgrims. Anointed a herald by the grateful populace, Ahlitah had to suffer the attentions of giggling, delighted children. They pulled his tail and buried themselves in his mane. Ehomba was gratified to see the great cat handle it with dignity and forbearance, even if he did spend many moments grinding his teeth in exasperation at the attention.

"I know you would rather eat them," he whispered to the litah during a private moment, "but a guest who devoured the offspring of his hosts would not continue to be regarded with favor. Restrain yourself a while longer, until we can find ourselves a ship."

The litah's tongue lolled as he stared unblinkingly at a pair of particularly plump six-year-olds. Saliva trickled from one corner of his open mouth. This did not unsettle their hosts, who thought the big cat was merely cooling himself.

"Find one fast, man, and tell our friends to keep the meat coming, or as surely as blood runs red I am liable to forget myself."

It was therefore for an assortment of reasons that Ehomba was re-

lieved when, employing some of Simna's Chlengguu gold, they finally
were able to book passage aboard a single-masted, square-rigged merchantman departing for the northern shores of the Aboqua. While more
than a few members of the crew were leery about having so large and
ferocious a feline running loose onboard, they took heart when his
"keepers" demonstrated their control over it.

"Is this really necessary?" Reposing on the open deck with his forepaws crossed and jaws parted wide, a mildly annoyed Ahlitah held a pose
while Ehomba placed his head deep into the cat's cavernous, gaping
mouth. Behind him, sailors whistled and cheered their approval and
admiration. The herdsman withdrew himself and the cat slowly shut his
jaws.

"That should be enough to reassure them you are tame," Ehomba
said under his breath.

The litah's eyes widened slightly. "Tame, am I? They'd better hope
this vessel's supplies are adequate or they're liable to see how 'tame' I
really am." Looking to his right, he inhaled deeply. "I've heard about the
sea but never expected to see it. It smells like certain shallow lakes in
late summer. All brine and brittle."

"The voyage will not be long, as such journeys go, and I think you
will enjoy it." Ehomba ruffled the big cat's mane. "The captain assures
me there will be fresh fish for the duration of our crossing."

Half closing his eyes, the litah placed his head down on his crossed
paws. "Then I'll be content. I quite like fish." Within moments, he was
snoring softly.

"Make sail there!" the first mate was shouting from his post alongside the helmsman. "Let go your main braces! Pulleys and haul. Ware
the jetty cleats!"

Simna joined the southerner forward, where the truncated bowsprit
thrust boldly out over the water. All around them, men were busy preparing to depart the tidy, compact harbor, with its freshly swept streets
and innumerable pots and boxes of flowers.

"Been some time since I've sailed across anything wider than a
lake." He nodded northward. "Onward to treasure and glory, hoy?"

"To the fulfillment of my obligation," Ehomba countered evenly.

"Aye, right, whatever." Grinning expansively, the swordsman
clapped his friend on his narrow back. For the first time in many weeks
they were without the burden of packs and weapons, these having been
placed in their private cabin belowdecks.

"It was good of the townspeople to recommend us to this ship's
master for passage." The sea here was calmer, warmer, less fractious

than the one that washed the beaches below his village, the herdsman reflected.

"Hoy, I never saw so many relieved faces as when we told them of the Chlengguu's overthrow. I think they were grateful enough to buy us a boat, had we but asked them for one."

"This is better." Crossing his arms, Ehomba bent forward to lean on the wooden railing. "I am no sailor."

"Naturally not." Edging close and lowering his voice to a whisper, Simna gave his rangy friend a conspiratorial nudge. "Of course, with your powers you could have commanded a ship to sail itself, right?"

Ehomba sighed wearily. "When will you get it through your head, Simna, that I am nothing more than a humble herder of chewers of cud?"

"Oh, I don't know." Turning away, the swordsman also directed his gaze to the open sea that lay before them. "Maybe when I'm in your company and Corruption doesn't falter, great winds don't perish at your hand, and your sword doesn't call down a shard of heaven to scatter and confuse our enemies."

"All that was accomplished through the knowledge and work of others. I was only a means of conveyance. We have been damned lucky."

"Right. And I am a monk, one much versed in disguise." He chuckled affably. "I'll give you one thing, though, Etjole Ehomba. You're one of the most skilled liars I've ever met. Not the best, by any means, but the most persistent."

"Oh, very well," the herdsman snapped, "believe what you will."

"That's the spirit!" Simna's face was full of admiration. "Stick to your story no matter what." He nodded forward. "It may help us on the other side."

"You have never been to these northern lands?"

"More questions." It was the swordsman's turn to shake his head tiredly. "No, not to these." He jerked a thumb back in the direction of the friendly seaport whose citizens had been so accommodating. "Among the Maliin, those who've made the crossing say that the northern lands are nothing like here, or where we've come from. They say that the level of civilization and enlightenment is such that they're embarrassed to visit there. It makes me wonder what these northern eminencies will think of us. I've been around, but you'll be out of your depth, and the cat will be little more than a novelty."

"I will manage." Ehomba wished he felt more confident. Villages and hamlets he was familiar and comfortable with, but a proper city was something entirely different. No matter. He had no choice. They had to go north to find a ship large and capable enough to cross the Semordria.

The Aboqua chose to be kind as they set out. There were waves, but they were curious rather than threatening. There was movement, but it was calming to the spirit instead of disturbing to the digestion. Flying fish exploded from the water in front of the ship's onrushing prow, shooting away like silver darts to port and starboard before splashing and sinking anew into the welcoming whitecaps. Gulls harassed the stern, taking their ease on the mainspar and railings as they nagged the cook for scraps.

As paid passengers, the travelers were mostly left to themselves, though when Ahlitah would come on deck to nap in the sun the more courageous among the crew would make a game of tiptoeing near for a better look. It was a matter of some merriment among the mariners to see who could creep the closest. There was betting, and a fair amount of money changed hands until Ahlitah, irked at having his naps continually interrupted by the seamen's chatter, finally favored one of the brave sailors with a nip on the leg. That put an end to the encroachment, though for the rest of the voyage the seaman involved wore the bite marks like a medal of honor.

They were several days out when the sky began to darken.

XXXll

Initially, the captain found nothing amiss with the sudden change in the weather. Although the Aboqua was a comparatively benign body of water, it was no stranger to the sudden storms that could affect any sizable sea.

The usual precautions were taken. The mainsail was reefed, hatches were battened down, the pumps were made ready, and all hands were sounded to stations. After being apprised of the situation and the possible dangers, passengers were left to their own devices. Ehomba and his companions could remain belowdecks, relatively dry and warm, or they could wander about above to experience the as yet undetermined vagaries of the weather. All that was asked of them was that they stay out of the way of working seamen.

The nearer the storm drew, the stranger became its aspect. Neither lightning nor thunder announced its impending arrival. Even more astoundingly, there was no wind. Though black as night, the approaching clouds did not writhe and roil. They simply came closer and closer, blotting out first the horizon and then the sky, like the unrolling of some vast, cumbrous black blanket.

Every man stood ready at his station. They were an experienced crew that had run safely before many storms, some mere rain squalls, others of impressive dimensions. But not a sailor aboard could recall ever encountering anything like this.

The dark clouds swept over the ship, enveloping it in a heavy, damp gloom. And still there was no wind. It was as if the storm entire consisted only of the eye of a hurricane, the ferocity of the tempest having absented itself elsewhere.

Uneasy now, the heretofore self-assured and confident mariners nervously eyed the baneful murk that had engulfed them. Where was the driving rain, the strobing lightning, the crashing seas that were the harbingers of any honorable storm? The ship drifted forward on calm seas, her stays barely rattling, her helm responding to the lightest of touches.

First they noticed the smell: a faint, fetid stink that portended no good. It was not the distinctive odor of rotting fish or seaweed. One mate declared that it reminded him of the ancient sewers of the abandoned city of Vra-Thet, whose people had been dead for thousands of years but whose decrepit essence still lingered in its multifarious catacombed depths. Another contended that the stench must have been carried hence on the wind from some great far-off battle in which tens of thousands had perished.

Ahlitah, whose sense of smell was infinitely more sensitive than that of any man aboard, wrinkled his nose so tightly it threatened to curl up and hide beneath his upper lip.

"What is it, cat?" Simna warily eyed the darkness that had swallowed the ship.

"Don't know. Decay, putrefaction, rot. But of what I can't tell."

The swordsman turned to the tall southerner, who was staring out across the bow, one hand holding on to a trembling stay fashioned of finely corded rope.

"How about it, Etjole? As a herder of cattle you should be intimately acquainted with stinks. Any ideas?" The other man did not look back. "Etjole?" Taking a step forward, Simna grabbed his friend by the arm.

"What?" Blinking, Ehomba looked back at his companions. "I am sorry, Simna. Yes, I know what it is."

"Then tell us," Ahlitah prompted him. "I'm not familiar with the smells of the sea, but I know storms, and this reeks like no storm I have ever encountered."

The herdsman's mouth was set in a thin, tight line. "That is because this is not a storm."

Cat and swordsman exchanged a glance. "It's clouds, Etjole," Simna avowed gently. "Racing black clouds usually herald the coming of a storm."

"These are not clouds, either. They are the substance of what has engulfed this ship."

Simna ibn Sind did not like the sound of that. Especially Ehomba's use of the word "engulfed." "Then if not a storm, what?"

Tilting back his head slightly, the herdsman looked upward, scanning the sky from side to side like someone standing at the bottom of a deep well searching for a ray of light. Having overheard, several sailors had left their posts and were hovering nearby, watching the rangy foreigner intently.

"It has been following me for a long time, gathering strength. I first saw it when I helped the People of the Trees defeat the slelves."

Simna's expression twisted in confusion. "The what?"

"It was before you and I met. You may have seen this also, friend Simna, when we fought Corruption. It gyred through the winds that helped to propel the Dunawake, and its essence was everywhere in the shattered lands of the Queppa. Especially in the Wall." He was silent for a moment as he considered the lowering sky. "Ever since the time when I was with the People of the Trees it has been tracking me, waiting for the right moment."

"The right moment?" Staring at the sky, Simna tried to peer through the raven clouds, to see something else where to the naked eye there appeared to be only arching blackness. "The right moment for what?"

Ehomba was as somber and serious as the swordsman had ever seen him. "To swallow."

That conjured up an image even less palatable than the one that had been induced by the herdsman's use of the word "engulfed." "You mean this whatever-it-is is going to try and eat us?"

"It already has." With unshakable calm, Ehomba studied the ominous dark. "We are inside it now. But it has not begun to swallow. It must be stopped before it can."

"Hoy, right, I am in agreement with you there, bruther." Wide-eyed but undaunted, the swordsman beheld their surroundings anew. Had anything changed since the black clouds had first enveloped them? Yes, everything had grown even darker, black as the inside of a chunk of coal. And it was pressing tight upon them, congealing like oil, a cloying, oleaginous mass that was acquiring more weight and substance than was natural for an honest cloud even as they spoke.

A sailor struck out at a limb of murk as it threatened to crawl up his arm. At the blow the gloom broke apart, but the pieces hung in the air, ebony wisps floating in a sable duskiness. Around the ship, a deathless night was descending, threatening to overwhelm and suffocate everyone on board. Sailors brushed at themselves, and cursed in frustration, but their efforts were proving increasingly futile. It was like trying to fight a cloud, a shadow, and that shadow was growing stronger by the minute. Stronger, and all-consuming.

Simna flailed at the deepening gloom as if assailed by giant, ephemeral black bugs. It was midmorning, but not a splinter of sunshine penetrated the ambient obscurity that had enveloped them. Ahlitah snapped at the lazily coiling lengths of deeper blackness that curled around his muscular form like indigo snakes. They broke apart, re-formed, and drew strength and sustenance from the deepening shadow all around them.

"What is it?" Like the rapidly panicking crew, Simna was brushing and slapping furiously at the terrifying blackness. "By Gidan's eyeteeth, what is it?"

"Eromakadi." Ignoring the suffocating blackness that swirled around him and threatened to invade his ears, his eyes, his mouth, Ehomba held tight to the rigging. "Eater of light. It consumes the light around us as well as the light that is life that emanates from us."

"From us?" Next to the swordsman, the litah was tiring as he struggled to do battle against something without substance. His jaws were still mighty, his teeth still sharp, but it is hard to take much of a bite out of an evanescence.

"Our thoughts, our souls, the way we project our animate being into the world. Life is light, Simna, and the eromakadi cannot stand light. Sometimes they are weak and scattered, sometimes potent and powerful. The eromakadi are why bad things happen to good people. Their allies are pestilence and war, bigotry and ignorance. A tiny eromakadi will flock to a contemptuous sneer, a larger one to a gang beating, a great and more powerful one still to a politician's lies. This one has grown especially focused."

Much of what his friend declaimed made no sense to Simna. It was babble and gibberish of the most impenetrable philosophical kind. But whatever it was, the darkness closing tight around them was real enough. He had never been afraid before because his fears had always assumed physical shape and form. Anything that would respond to a sword could be dealt with. But this—it was like trying to fight air.

As he spun about and flailed madly against the insistent, encroaching gloom, he saw Ehomba climb up onto the bowsprit and stand facing the silently boiling blackness, alone. As the swordsman looked on, his lanky friend methodically removed his clothing and let it fall to the deck behind him. Naked, a lean and slender scarecrow of a man who looked even slimmer devoid of his simple raiment, the herdsman braced himself against a pair of stays and spread his arms wide as if invoking the sky.

The frantic crew ignored him. Those among them who saw what was happening thought he had gone mad, and not a few expected to join the tall passenger in madness at any moment. Because the final blackness was closing in tight around them, suffocating sight and sound and thought, if not yet heaving, straining lungs. Could a man be suffocated while still breathing?

Etjole Ehomba stood alone on the bowsprit, detached from the rest of humanity. Stood there by himself, and inhaled.

His chest expanded. Simna could hear it, even above the cries and wails of the raving crew. The sound was that of an ordinary man inhaling deeply, but what happened next was anything but ordinary.

Tiny wisps of blackness began to drift backward, and not of their own volition. They vanished into Ehomba's wide-open mouth, sucked down, away, and out of sight. More voluminous coils of gloom followed, straining to sustain their position but unable to resist. They too disappeared into the innards of the herdsman. And all the while Ehomba continued to inhale, not pausing to breathe normally, his chest distended in a steady, unvarying inhalation.

For the first time since the ship had been overtaken by the darkness, wind assailed its mast and spars and deck. Gusts arrived forcefully from over the bow, but also from abeam and from athwart the stern. It howled down out of the sky, and up from the supporting surrounding waters.

Ehomba never paused, never faltered. He inhaled, and inhaled, and in so doing sucked up that all-encompassing gloom and shadow as if it were essence of cinnamon and myrrh, drawing it all down into him, into somewhere within himself that Simna could not begin to imagine. And still the herdsman did not stop to breathe. Clinging exhaustedly to the rail for support, Simna looked on and wondered at the southerner's stamina. How long could he maintain the suction, keep up the pace? Would what he inhaled fill him up until he exploded, or was it after all nothing more than evil air, a malignant atmosphere that in actual gist amounted to no more than a desolate burp?

Light appeared above the ship: healthful, heartening, natural sunshine. The crew saw it, felt it fall upon them, and set up a ragged cheer. And still Ehomba continued his unnatural insufflation, until the last of the blackness had vanished, drawn deep down within himself. Only then did he close his mouth, give a slight shiver, slump, and fall backwards, limp as a child's cheap ragdoll, onto the hard deck.

Simna was at his side in an instant, and Ahlitah as well, the big cat looming anxiously over the fallen herdsman. Solicitous members of the crew crowded close, wanting to help, until an angry Simna ordered them to stand back and give the fallen herdsman some air.

Putting a hand beneath his friend's head, Simna raised it gently. "Come on, Etjole—breathe! Open your mouth and breathe. Drink in the fresh air of the sea and clear your lungs of that murderous blight." He jiggled the head slightly. "Breathe, damn you!"

The herdsman's eyelids fluttered like small moths on a chill morning. Then his head jerked upward as he coughed, not once but several times. A tiny puff of black vapor squeezed out from between his lips. No bigger than a cotton ball, it drifted upward until it finally dissipated beneath the pellucid blue of the cloud-flecked sky. Simna followed it with his eyes until he was sure it was gone.

Inhaling sharply, exhaling slowly and wearily, Ehomba opened his eyes. When they met Simna's, and Ahlitah's, he smiled. "My friends." Looking around, he frowned to himself. "Why am I lying here like this? Help me up."

A plethora of willing, eager hands made themselves available to exalt the herdsman. Standing by himself, he took stock of his surroundings, then walked forward to where he had dropped his clothes and began to dress himself. When that was done he crossed his arms and leaned forward against the railing, resuming the position he had favored before.

Vigorously discussing among themselves everything that had transpired, the crew returned to their duties. The captain had many questions, but courteously restrained his curiosity. No doubt the remarkable southerner needed some time to himself. Queries about what had happened, however burning, could wait until later.

Simna operated under no such restraints. He was at Ehomba's side as soon as the herdsman had finished dressing. "For the last time, my friend—tell me you are not a sorcerer."

The herdsman glanced sideways at him and smiled. "It will not be the last time, Simna, but I will say it again anyway. I am not."

"Fine. Good. I accept it." The swordsman let his arms dangle over the railing. Dolphins ran before the ship's prow, energized by its presence, glorying in the pressure wave it pushed before it. "All you have to do is explain to me what just happened. I remember you mentioning this thing, this eromakadi, once before. It was when we were about to confront the Dunawake." He struggled to remember. "You said then that nothing could slay it except an eromakasi."

Ehomba hardly heard him. He was thinking of the warm, dry, clean homeland that now lay far to the south. Of a small and unprepossessing but accommodating house, of the music of children's voices at play, and of the woman who was his wife. The remembrances warmed him from within, and made him feel better about continuing to live. Made him feel that he had greater reason, and sweeter purpose, for being.

"I told you the truth, my friend. The eromakadi are eaters of light. They cannot be killed—except by an eromakasi, an eater of darkness." Turning his head sideways, he peered direct and deep into the swordsman's eyes.

"I am a simple herder of cattle and sheep, Simna ibn Sind—and I am also eromakasi. A man can be both." He returned his unblinking gaze to the sea ahead, and to the shore that could not yet be seen but that he knew was there. "That does not make of me a necromancer."

By his side Simna was silent for some time, until the ship's bell rang three times to announce the serving of the midday meal. "Perhaps it does not, Etjole, but you can't deny that it makes you something more than an ordinary man."

Removing his arms from the rail, Ehomba straightened. "Not something more, friend Simna. Not something more."

"Well then, bruther—something other. No, don't try to explain it to me. Not now." The swordsman grinned broadly. "Some days you talk like the most ignorant backcountry bumpkin I ever met, and other times I can't make up or down of your manner of speaking, much less what you're actually saying. Are you genius or imbecile? Idiot simpleton or sorcerer supreme? For the life of me, I can't decide."

His tall friend smiled gently. "Perhaps I am a genius imbecile. Or idiot adept."

Simna ibn Sind shook his head slowly as he rested a comradely hand on his companion's shoulder, having to reach high to do so. "Time enough yet to descry the truth. Doesn't matter one way or the other so long as there's treasure in it. Now come, and let's have something to eat. I'll wager you could use a drink."

Pushing out his chin, Ehomba rubbed appraisingly at his neck. "To tell you the truth, my throat *is* a little sore."

So it was that Ehomba the Catechist and his ill-matched companions came safely to the great harbor city of Lybondai, which lies on the silver coast of the kingdom of Premmois, beneath the perpetually snow-capped Mountains of Nerimab-meleh. There they discovered that in so worldly and cosmopolitan a community not even an Ahlitah was cause for much comment, and their presence among thousands of other travelers from all over the known world went largely unremarked.

All this was consoling to Etjole Ehomba, who was very tired. But being interested in everything, and everything in which he presently found himself being subsumed in newness, he found that he was able to lift his spirits by the asking of questions, a habit too deeply ingrained in him and too much a part of him to break even in unfamiliar surroundings.

Exasperated by his companion's continual querying of every other individual they encountered, Simna finally blurted, "Etjole, must you know everything?"

"Yes," his friend responded without hesitation.

"Must there be an answer to everything?"

The herdsman looked at him as guilelessly and openly as it was possible for one person to look at another. "Of course there must be, Simna. To everything. Otherwise, why would I be here? Or you, or Ahlitah, or anyone else? Why would I be looking to find a Visioness Themaryl, or chancing the wrath of this Hymneth the Possessed? Why would—"

"I'm sorry I asked." Ignoring the bustle and noise of the tavern in which they were presently tarrying, the swordsman buried his face in the simple ceramic goblet before him. "Shut up and finish your drink." At their feet, curled up tight beneath the table, Ahlitah stretched, extended enormous curved claws, yawned, and slipped indifferently back to sleep.

Into
the
Thinking
Kingdoms

For my niece, Alexandra Rachel Carroll

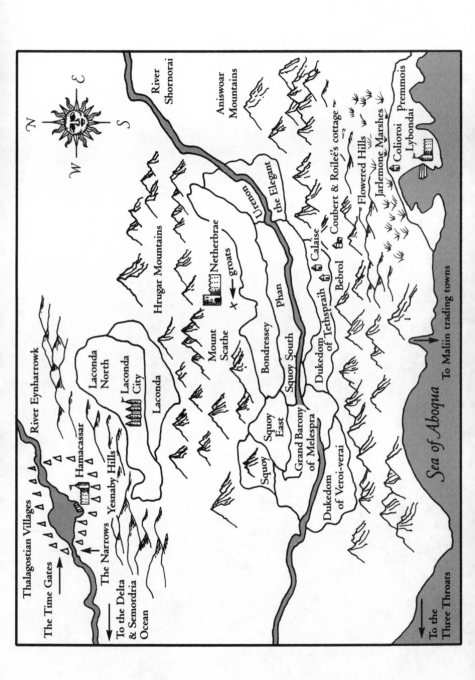

1

The most powerful man in the world couldn't sleep.

At least Hymneth the Possessed thought of himself as the most powerful man in the world, and since those few who might have contemplated disputing him were no longer alive, he felt comfortable with having appropriated the title to himself. And if not the most powerful man, then he was certainly the most powerful mage. Granted that there might be a handful of imprudent individuals foolhardy enough to stand before him as men and women, there were none who dared confront him in the realm of the arcane and necromantic. There *he* was the Master of masters, and all who dabbled in the black arts must pay him homage, or suffer his whims at their peril.

Yet despite the knowing of this, and the sum of all his knowing, he could not sleep.

Rising from his bed, a graven cathedral to Morpheus that had taken the ten finest wood-carvers in the land six years to render from select pieces of cobal, redwood, cherry, walnut, and purpleheart, Hymneth walked slowly to the vaulted window that looked out upon his kingdom. The rich and populous reach of Ehl-Larimar stretched out before him, from the rolling green hills at the base of his mountaintop fortress retreat to the distant, sun-washed shores of the boundless ocean called Aurel. Every home and farm, every shop and industry within that field of view acknowledged *him* as supreme over all other earthly authorities. He tried to submerge his soul in the warmth and security of that understanding, to let it wash over and burnish him like a shower of liquid pleasure. But he could not.

He couldn't shake the accursed dream that had kept him awake.

Worse than the loss of sleep was his inability to recall the details. Nebulous, hazy images of other beings had tormented his rest. Awake, he found that he was unable to remember them with any degree of resolution. His inability to identify them meant it was impossible to deal with their condition or take steps to prevent their return. He was convinced that some of the likenesses had been human, others not. Why they should disturb him so he could not say. Unable to distinguish them from any other wraiths, he could not formulate a means for dealing with them directly. The situation was more than merely irritating. Priding himself as he did on the precision with which he conducted all his dealings, the persisting inexactitude of the dream was disquieting.

He would go out, he decided. Out among his people. Receiving their obeisance, grandly deigning to acknowledge their fealty, always made him feel better. Walking to the center of the grandiose but impeccably decorated bedroom, he stood in the center of the floor, raised his arms, and recited one of several thousand small yet potent litanies he knew by heart.

Light materialized that was solid, as opposed to the feeble sunbeams that entered through the tall window. Taking the form of small yellow fingers that were detached from hands, it set about dressing him. He preferred light to the hands of human servitors. The feathery touch of commandeered glow would not pinch him, or forget to do up a button, or scratch against his neck. It would never choose the wrong undergarments or lose track of a valuable pin or necklace. And light would never try to stick a poisoned dagger into his back, twisting it fiercely, slicing through nerve and muscle until rich red Hymneth blood gushed forth over the polished tile of the floor, staining the bedposts and ruining the invaluable rugs fashioned from the flayed coats of rare, dead animals.

So what if the digits of congealed yellow light reminded his attendants not of agile, proficient fingers but coveys of sallow, diseased worms writhing and twisting as they coiled and probed about his person? Servants' flights of torpid imagination did not concern him.

While the silken undergarments caressed his body, the luxurious outer raiment transformed him into a figure of magnificence fit to do sartorial battle with the emperor birds-of-paradise. The horned helmet of chased steel and the red-and-purple cloak contributed mightily to the plenary image of irresistible power and majesty. Seven feet tall fully dressed, he was ready to go out among his people and seek the balm of their benison.

The pair of griffins who lived out their lives chained to the outside of his bedroom door snapped to attention as he emerged, their topaz cat eyes flashing. He paused a moment to pet first one, then the other.

Watchdogs of his slumber, they would rip to pieces anyone he did not escort or beckon into the inner sanctum in person. They could not be bribed or frightened away, and it would take a small army to overpower them. As he departed, they settled back down on their haunches, seemingly returning to rest but in reality preternaturally alert and awake as always.

Peregriff was waiting for him in the antechamber, seated at his desk. After a quick glance at the two pig-sized black clouds that trailed behind the sorcerer, he rose from behind his scrolls and papers.

"Good morning, Lord."

"No it is not." Hymneth halted on the other side of the desk. "I have not been sleeping well."

"I am sorry to hear that, Lord." Behind the ruddy cheeks and neatly trimmed white beard, the eyes of the old soldier were blue damascened steel. Nearly six and a half feet tall and two hundred and twenty pounds of still solid muscle, Peregriff could take up the saber and deal with a dozen men half his age. Only Hymneth he feared, knowing that the Possessed could take his life with a few well-chosen words and the flick of one chain-mailed wrist. So the ex-general served, and made himself be content.

"Strange dreams, Peregriff. Indistinct oddities and peculiar perturbations."

"Perhaps a sleeping potion, Lord?"

Hymneth shook his head peevishily. "I've tried that. This particular dream is not amenable to the usual elixirs. Something convoluted is going on." Straightening, he took a deep breath and, as he exhaled, the air in the room shuddered. "I'm going out today. See to the preparations."

The soldier of soldiers nodded once. "Immediately, Lord." He turned to comply.

"Oh, and Peregriff?"

"Yes, Lord?"

"How do you sleep lately?"

The soldier considered carefully before replying. "Reasonably well, Lord."

"I prefer that you did not. My misery might benefit from company."

"Certainly, Lord. I will begin by not sleeping well tonight."

Behind the helmet, Hymneth smiled contentedly. "Good. I can always count on you to make me feel better, Peregriff."

"That is my service, Lord." The soldier departed to make ready his master's means for going out among his people.

Hymneth took pleasure in a leisurely descent from the heights of the fortress, using the stairs. Sometimes he would descend on a pillar of fire, or a chute of polished silver. It was good to keep in practice. But the body also needed exercise, he knew.

As he descended, he passed many hallways and side passages. Attendants and servants and guards stopped whatever they were doing to acknowledge his presence. Most smiled; a few did not. Several noted the presence of the noisome, coagulated black vapors that tagged along at their master's heels, and they trembled. Passing one particular portal that led to a separate tower, he paused to look upward. The *woman* was up there, secluded in the small paradise he had made for her. A word from her would have seen him on his way exalted. That was not to be, he knew. Not yet. But he had measureless reserves of confidence, and more patience than even those closest to him suspected. The words would come, and the smiles, and the embraces. All in good time, of which he had a fullness.

He could have forced her. A few words, a pinch of powders, a few drops of potion in her evening wine and her resistance would be forgotten, as frail and fractured as certain tortured tracts of land to the east. But that would be a subjugation, not a triumph. Having everything, he wanted more. Mere bodies equally magnificent he could acquire with gold or spell. A heart was a much more difficult thing to win. He sought a covenant, not a conquest.

With a last look of longing at the portal, he resumed his descent. Passing through the grand hall with its imposing pendent banners of purple and crimson, its mounted heads of sabertooths and dragons, arctic bears and tropical thylacines, he turned left just before the imposing entryway and made his way to the smaller door that was nearer the stables.

Outside, the sun was shining brightly, as it usually was in Ehl-Larimar. Several stable attendants were concluding their grooming of his chariot team: four matched red stallions with golden manes. The chariot itself was large enough to accommodate his cumbersome frame in addition to that of a charioteer. Peregriff was waiting on the platform, reins in hand. He had donned his gilded armor and looked quite splendid in his own right, though he was both overshone and overshadowed by the towering figure of the caped necromancer.

The scarlet stallions bucked restlessly in harness, eager for a run. Hymneth found that he was feeling better already. He climbed into the chariot alongside his master of house and horse.

"Let's go, Peregriff. We will do the population the honor of viewing my magnificence. I feel—I feel like bestowing a boon or two today. I may not even kill anyone."

"Your magnanimity is truly legendary, Lord." The old soldier chucked the reins. "Gi'up!"

Snorting and whinnying, the team broke forward, speeding down the curved roadway that led up to and fronted the fortress. Through the massive portico in the outer wall they raced, sending dust and gravel flying from their hooves. These were inlaid with cut spessartine and pyrope. Catching the sunlight, the faceted insets gave the team the appearance of running on burning embers.

Down the mountainside they flew, Peregriff using the whip only to direct them, Hymneth the Possessed exhilarating in the wild ride. Down through the foothills, through groves of orange and olive and almond, past small country shops and farmhouses, and into the outskirts of the sprawling country metropolis of wondrous, unrivaled Ehl-Larimar.

Looking back, he found that he could see the fortress clearly. It dominated the crest of the highest mountain overlooking the fertile lands below. But the direction in which they were traveling prohibited him from seeing one part of the fortress complex, one particular tower. In that obscured spire languished the only unfulfilled part of himself, the single absent element of his perfection. It bothered him that he could not see it as the chariot raced onward.

Inability to sleep, inadequate angle of vision. Two bad things in one morning. Troubled but willing to be refreshed, he turned away from the receding view of his sanctuary and back toward the wild rush of flying manes and approaching streets.

Manipulating the team masterfully, Peregriff shouted to his liege. "Where would you like to go, Lord?"

"Toward the ocean, I think." The warlock brooded on the possibilities. "It always does me good to visit the shore. The ocean is the only thing in my kingdom that's almost as powerful as me."

Without a word, the soldier cracked the long whip over the team. Instantly, they swerved to their right, taking a different road and nearly running down a flock of domesticated moas in the process. Mindful of the increased pace, the twin ebon miasmas that always trailed behind the necromancer clung closer to his heels. When a brightly hued sparrow took momentary refuge from the wind on the back of the chariot, they promptly pounced on the intruder. Moments later, only a few feathers emerged from one of the silken, inky black clouds to indicate that the sparrow had ever been.

They sped past farmers riding wagons laden with goods intended for market, raced around slow, big-wheeled carts piled high with firewood or rough-milled lumber. Iron workers peered out from beneath the soot and spark of their smithies while nursing mothers took time to glance up from their infants and nod as forcefully as they were able.

Through the sprawling municipality they flew, the chariot a blazing vision of carmine magnificence illuminating the lives of wealthy and indigent alike, until at last they arrived at the harbor. Hymneth directed his charioteer to head out onto one of the major breakwaters whose rocky surface had been rendered smooth through the application of coralline cement. Fishermen repairing nets and young boys and girls helping with the gutting of catch scrambled their way clear of the approaching, twinkling hooves. Buckets and baskets of smelly sustenance rolled wildly as they were kicked aside. In the chariot's wake, their relieved owners scrambled to recover the piscine fruits of their labors.

Within the harbor, tall-masted clippers and squat merchantmen vied for quay space with svelte coastal river traders and poky, utilitarian barges. Activity never ceased where the rest of Ehl-Larimar met the sea. Gulls, cormorants, and diving dragonets harried stoic pelicans, jabbing and poking at the swollen jaw pouches of the latter in hopes of stealing their catch. Except for the inescapable stink of fish, Hymneth always enjoyed visiting the far end of the long stone breakwater. It allowed him to look back at a significant part of his kingdom.

There the great city spread southward, terminating finally in the gigantic wall of Motops. Two thousand years ago it had been raised by the peoples of the central valleys and plains to protect them from the bloodthirsty incursions of the barbarians who dwelled in the far south. Ehl-Larimar had long since spread southward beyond its stony shadow, but the wall remained, too massive to ignore, too labor-intensive to tear down.

Northward the city marched into increasingly higher hills, fragrant with oak and cedar, lush with vineyards and citrus groves. To the east the soaring ramparts of the Curridgian Mountains separated the city from the rest of the kingdom, a natural barrier to invaders as well as ancient commerce.

Under his rule the kingdom had prospered. Distant dominions paid Ehl-Larimar homage, ever fearful of incurring the wrath of its liege and master. And now, after years of searching and inquiry, the most beautiful woman in the world was his. Well, not quite yet his, he self-confessed. But he was supremely confident that time would break down her resistance, and worthy entreaty overcome her distaste.

Unlike the commercially oriented, who employed boats and crews to ply the fecund waters offshore beyond Ehl-Larimar's fringing reefs, solitary fisherfolk often settled themselves along the breakwater and at its terminus, casting their lines into the blue-green sea in hopes of reeling in the evening's supper or, failing that, some low-cost recreation. A number were doing so even as he stood watching from the chariot. All had risen at his approach and genuflected to acknowledge his arrival. All—save one.

A lesser ruler would have ignored the oversight. A weaker man would have dismissed it. Hymneth the Possessed was neither.

Alighting from the chariot, he bade his general remain behind to maintain control of the still feisty stallions. Trailing purple and splendor, his regal cape flowing behind him, he strode over to the north side of the breakwater to confront the neglectful. Peregriff waited and watched, his face impassive.

Other fisherfolk edged away from his approach, clutching their children close to them as they tried their best to make their individual withdrawals inconspicuous. The last thing any of them wanted to do was attract his attention. That was natural, he knew. It was understandable that simple folk such as they should be intimidated and even a little frightened by the grandeur of his presence. He preferred it that way. It made the business of day-to-day governing much simpler.

Which was why he was taking the time to query the one individual among them who had not responded to his arrival with an appropriate gesture of obeisance.

The stubble-cheeked man was clad in long coveralls of some tough, rough-sewn cotton fabric. His long-sleeved shirt was greasy at the wrists with fish blood and oil. He sat on a portion of the breakwater facing the sea, long pole in hand, two small metal buckets at his side. One held bait, the other fish. The bait bucket was the fuller of the two. By his side sat a tousle-haired boy of perhaps six, simply dressed and holding a smaller pole. He kept sneaking looks at the commanding figure that now towered silently behind him and his father. The expressionless fisherman ignored them both.

"I see by your pails that the fish are as disrespectful of you as you are of me."

The man did not flinch. " 'Tis a slow morning, and we had a late start."

No honorific, the necromancer mused. No title, no "Good morning, Lord." By his slow yet skillful manipulation of the pole, Hymneth determined that the fellow was not blind. His reply had already marked him as not deaf.

"You know me."

The man gave the rod a little twitch, the better to jog the bait for the benefit of any watching fish. "Everyone knows who you are."

Still no praise, no proper acknowledgment! What was happening here? It made no sense. Hymneth was fully aware that others were watching. Surreptitiously, covertly as they could manage, but watching still. He would not have turned and walked away had he, fisherman, and child been on the far side of the moon, but the presence of others made it imperative that he not do so.

"You do not properly acknowledge me."

The man seemed to bend a little lower over his pole, but his voice remained strong. "I would prefer to be given a choice in who I acknowledge. Without any such choice, the actual execution of it seems superfluous."

An educated bumpkin, Hymneth reflected. All the more important then, to add to the body of his edification. "You might be more careful in your choice of metaphors. The use of certain words might inspire others, such as myself, to employ them in another context."

For the first time, the fisherman looked up and back. He did not flinch at the sight of the horned helmet, or the glowing eyes that glowered down at him. "I'm not afraid of you, Hymneth the Possessed. A man can only live so long anyway, and there are too many times when I find myself thinking that it would be better to die in a state of freedom than to continue to exist without it."

"Without freedom?" The wizard waved effusively. "Here you sit on these public stones, on this beautiful day, with your son at your side, engaging in a pursuit that most of your fellow citizens would consider a veritable vacation, and you complain of a lack of freedom?"

"You know what I'm talking about." The fellow's tone was positively surly, Hymneth decided appraisingly. "Ultimately, nothing can be done without your approval, or that of your appointed lackeys like the stone-faced old soldier who waits silently in your chariot. You rule ultimately, tolerating no dissent, no discussion. Throughout the length and breadth of all Ehl-Larimar nothing can be done without your knowledge. You spy on everyone, or have it done for you."

"Knowledge is a necessary prerequisite of good governance, my man."

"Ignoring the will of the people is not." Again the pole was jiggled, the long, thin wisp of a line punctuating the surface with small black twitches.

"It's a dangerous thing for people to have too much will." Stepping closer, Hymneth knelt directly behind the man so that he could feel the warm breath of the Possessed on his own dirty, exposed neck. "It makes them restless, and upsets everyone's digestion. Much better simply to live and enjoy each day as it comes, and leave the matter of willing to another."

"Like you." Still the man did not flinch, or pull away. "Go ahead—do your worst. It can't be any worse than the rest of my luck this morning."

"My worst? You really do think ill of me, don't you? If you were more worldly, my man, you'd know that I'm not such a bad sort, as absolute rulers go. I have no intention of doing anything to you." The front of the helmet turned slightly to the right. "Fine boy you have there." Reaching out a mailed hand, Hymneth ruffled the child's hair. The expression on the face of the six-year-old was of one torn between uncertain admiration and absolute terror.

For the first time, the fisherman's granite resolution appeared to falter ever so slightly. "Leave the boy alone. Deal with me if you must."

"Deal with you? But my man, I *am* dealing with you." Reaching into a pocket, the necromancer removed a small stoppered glass vial. It was half full of an oily black liquid. "I will not trouble you with the name of this elixir. I *will* tell you that if I were to sprinkle a couple of drops of it onto this fine stalwart young lad's hip, it would shrivel up his legs like the last overlooked stalks of summer wheat. They would become brittle, like the stems of dried flowers. Walking would cause the bones to splinter and shatter, causing excruciating pain no doctor or country alchemist could treat. Then they would heal, slowly and agonizingly, until the next time he took a wrong step, and then they would break again. And again and again, over and over, the pain as bad or worse with each new fracture, healing and breaking, breaking and healing, no matter how careful the young fellow strove to be, until by adulthood, if he survived the pain that long, both legs had become a mass of deformed, misshapen bony freaks useless for walking or any other purpose except the giving of agony."

His helmeted face was very close to the fisherman's ear now, and his commanding voice had dropped to a whisper. The man's face was twitching now, and several tears rolled down his stubbled cheek.

"Don't do that. Please don't do that."

"Ah." Within the helmet, a smile creased the steel shrouded face of Hymneth the Possessed. "Please don't do that—what?"

"Please . . ." The fisherman's head fell forward and his eyes squeezed tight shut. "Please don't do that—Lord."

"Good. Very good." Reaching over, the warlock ran a mail-enclosed forefinger along the young boy's cheek. The little lad was quivering now, manfully not crying but obviously wanting to, shivering at the touch of the cold metal. "That wasn't so difficult, was it? I'm leaving you now. Remember this encounter with pride. It's not every day that Hymneth the Possessed stoops to converse with one of his people. And be sure to respect my departure appropriately." The silky voice darkened ever so slightly. "You don't want me to come back and talk to you again."

Straightening to his full, commanding height, he returned to the chariot and stepped aboard. "Let's go, Peregriff. For some reason the ocean doesn't hold its usual cheer for me this morning."

"It's the woman, Lord. The Visioness. She preys on your thoughts. But her misgivings will pass."

"I know. But it's hard to be patient."

Peregriff ventured an old soldier's smile. "The time spent in extended contemplation will make the eventual resolution all the more agreeable, Lord."

"Yes. Yes, that's true." The sorcerer put a hand on the older man's arm. "You always know the right thing to say to comfort me, Peregriff."

The white-maned head dipped deferentially. "I try, Lord."

"Back to the fortress! We'll have a good meal, and deal with the turgid matters of state. Let's away from the stench of this place, and these people."

"Yes, Lord." Peregriff rattled the reins and the magnificent mounts responded, turning the chariot neatly in the limited space available. As it turned, Hymneth glanced in the direction of the breakwater's edge. The people there were standing, poles set aside, hats in hand and heads bowed reverentially. The head of one particular man was set especially low, as was that of his son. Both were trembling slightly. Seeing this, Hymneth let his gaze linger on them for longer than was necessary, even though he knew it was petty of him to find enjoyment in such trivial exercises of power.

Then Peregriff chucked the reins forcefully, shouted a command, and the chariot leaped forward, racing down the breakwater back toward the harbor, the city, and the stern cliffs of the Curridgians. Food awaited, and drink, and contemplation of the as yet unattained comeliness of his special guest.

Something darted out in front of the chariot, scrambling frantically to avoid the pounding, approaching hooves of the scarlet stallions. A black cat, skittering across the chariot's path.

"Look out," the necromancer yelled, "don't hit it!"

Even though it brought them dangerously close to the edge of the breakwater, Peregriff obediently and expertly utilized the reins to angle the galloping chargers slightly to the right. Spared, the unprepossessing cat vanished into the rocks. Looking back sharply, Hymneth tried to locate it, but could not.

Having guided the striding stallions back to the middle of the breakwater, his chief attendant was looking at him uncertainly. "Lord, it was only a mangy stray cat. No loss if it were killed."

"No—no loss." Hymneth found himself frowning. What had that singular moment been about? For just an instant, something had burrowed into and infected his state of mind, causing him to act in a manner not only unbecoming but atypical. Whom had he been panicked for—the cat, or himself? It was very peculiar.

Two inexplicable incidents in little more than as many minutes. First the fisherman, then the cat. It was turning out to be an idiosyncratic morning. One that, for reasons unknown and despite Peregriff's best efforts to cheer him, saw him finally reach the fortress still unsettled in mind and more ill at ease than he had been in years.

11

As a conduit for goods from the interior and imports from the exotic south and east, Lybondai provided refuge on a daily basis to a goodly number of extraordinary sights. But even in a port city as worldly and cosmopolitan as the pearl of the southern coast, the somber sight of a jet-black, five-hundred-pound cat with the legs of an overmuscled feline sprinter and the teeth and mane of a fully mature lion padding through the harborfront marketplace succeeded in turning heads.

"What makes you think they're all staring at you?" Drawing himself up to his full, if limited, height, Simna ibn Sind strode along importantly over the well-worn diamond-shaped paving stones.

Ahlitah the black litah snorted softly.

"There are a thousand and one humans milling around us and I can scent thousands more. There are cats, too, the largest of which would provide me with less than an afternoon snack. You don't need a kingdom to rule and pay you homage, Simna. You do that tirelessly yourself."

Glancing upward, the swordsman saw two young women leaning out of a window to follow their progress. When he grinned and waved up at them, they drew back within the painted walls, giggling and covering their mouths.

"There, you see! They were looking at me."

"No," the big cat replied. "They were laughing at you. Me, they were looking at. Rather admiringly, if I do say so."

"Be silent, the both of you." Etjole Ehomba cast a disapproving look back at his garrulous companions. "We will try making inquiries at this harbor pilot's shack first, and if we have no luck there we will move on to the ships themselves."

Hope segued quickly into disappointment. At least the harbor pilots were understanding of their request and sympathetic to their situation. But they were no more encouraging than the ship mates and masters. Among the latter, the kindest were those who brusquely ordered the visitors off their ships. Sadly, they were outnumbered by colleagues who laughed openly in the faces of the supplicants. These were fewer than they might have been, for those who caught sight of Ahlitah lurking behind the two humans wisely decided it might be impolitic to make fun of the inquiry, no matter how outrageous its content.

The last captain to whom they presented the request Ehomba mistook for one of the lesser mates. He was a strapping redhead, freckled of face and taut of sinew, with a broad chest on which curly hairs posed like tiny frozen flames and a mustache that would have been the envy of an emperor tamarin. But when questioned, his bluff good humor and kindly nature proved no substitute for reality.

Letting go of the line he had been holding, the young shipmaster rested hands on hips as he confronted Ehomba. As he preferred to do at such moments, Simna remained in the background. By now the swordsman was thoroughly bored with the endlessly negative responses to their inquiries, which had taken most of the day, and predictive of the response they were likely to receive. In this the young Captain did not disappoint him.

"Take passage across the Semordria? Are ye daft?" A soft growl caused him to glance behind the tall, dark southerner to see the slit-eyed mass of muscle and claw lying prone on the deck behind him. He immediately softened his tone, if not his opinion. "No one sails across the Semordria. At least no ship that I be aware of."

"Are you afraid?" Simna piped up. It was late, and he no longer much cared if he happened to offend some local mariner stinking of fish oil and barnacle scrapings.

The young Captain bristled but, perhaps mindful of the lolling but very much alert Ahlitah, swallowed his instinctive response like a spoonful of sour medicine. "I fear only what is unknown, and no one knows the reaches of the Semordria. Some say that the stories of lands far to the west are nothing more than that: the imaginative ramblings of besotted seamen and inventive minstrels. From the crews of the few ships that venture out one of the Three Throats of the Aboqua to sail up and down the legendary western coasts come tales of creatures monstrous enough to swallow whole ships, and of underwater terrors most foul." He turned back to his work.

"I command this ship at the behest of my two uncles. They have given it unto my care, and as such I have responsibilities to discharge to them. Even if I were so inclined, or sufficiently crazy, I would not contemplate such an undertaking. Best you not do so, either."

"I can understand what you say about a responsibility to others." Ehomba spoke quietly, having heard the same narrative from the captains of more than two dozen other vessels. "I am traveling under similar conditions." His gaze drifted southward. Toward home, and as importantly, toward the grave of a noble man of far distant shores whose dying request had implored the herdsman to save a mysterious woman he had called the Visioness Themaryl.

Pulling hard on the line, the Captain spoke without turning to look at them. "Then you'd best get it through your head that the Semordria is not for crossing. Leastwise, not by any ship or captain or crew that sails the Aboqua." And that was the last he would say on the subject.

"Now what?" Simna stretched as they descended the boarding ramp to the wooden quay.

"We find a place to sleep." Already Ehomba was scanning the inns and taverns that fronted the main harbor. "Tomorrow we try once more."

"Hoy, not again!"

A grim-faced Ehomba whirled on his friend. "What would you have me do, Simna? We cannot walk across the Semordria. Nor can we fly."

"Pour drink enough down me, bruther, and I'll show you who can fly!" The swordsman's tone was belligerent.

"Gentlemen, gentlemen—there's no need to argue between yourselves. Not when I'm here to help you."

They turned together, tall herdsman and stocky easterner. His attention having been diverted by a barrel full of bait fish, Ahlitah ignored it all. The three fishermen who had been making use of the barrel lifted their poles from the water and silently and with wide eyes edged out of the cat's way.

Ehomba studied the stranger. "Who are you, that you want to help those you do not know?"

The man stepped forward. "My name is Haramos bin Grue. I was passing by this very spot when I chanced to overhear your conversation with the captain of this ignoble vessel. Of course he refused your request." The stranger eyed the nearby craft dubiously. "I wouldn't trust that bass barge to convey my ass safely from one side of the harbor to the other, much less across the great Semordria." He winked meaningfully. "You need a proper ship, crewed by men who are used to making such a crossing. Not fair-weather amateur sailors such as these." He swung an arm wide, dismissing the entire harbor and every boat docked or riding at anchor with a single wave.

Ehomba considered the individual who was so casual in impugning the professional capabilities of everyone he and his companions had sounded out that day. Pushy, to be sure, but did he know what he was talking about or was he merely being boastful?

It was impossible to tell simply by looking at him. A stump of a man, several inches shorter than Simna ibn Sind but without the swordsman's incident-inspired musculature, bin Grue was nonetheless a solid specimen, from his short arms to the profound gut that, interestingly, did not quiver when he walked. A tart-smelling cigar protruded from one corner of his mouth, around which his very white, very even teeth were clamped as if on a loose coin. His eyes were deep set and his cheeks bantamweight duplicates of his belly. A fringe of wavy white hair crowned his large head, which protruded above the halo of fluff like a whale shoving its snout through old pack ice. Virtually nonexistent, his neck was a ring of squat muscle on which the impressive head sat and swiveled like a fire-throwing turret on a Vendesian warship. He did not speak words so much as saw them up into individual syllables, spitting out one after another like hunks of rough lumber awaiting the attention of some absent master carver.

For all the man's affability and fine clothing, complete to high-strapped sandals, long pants, and puff-sleeved overshirt cut in a wide V down to the middle of his chest, Ehomba was uncertain as to his motives. Still, there was no harm in learning what he might have to offer.

"You know where we might find such a ship?"

"I certainly do. Not here, in this backass dimple on the Premmoisian coast. To find *real* sailors, you need to go north." His eyes glittered with a recollection that might have been his—or bought, or borrowed. "For a ship to take you across the Semordria, you need to go to Hamacassar."

Ehomba glanced over at Simna, who shrugged. "Never heard of the place."

"The journey is long and difficult. Few know of Hamacassar, and even fewer have visited there."

"But you have." Ehomba was watching the shorter man closely.

"No." Not in the least embarrassed by this admission, bin Grue masticated his fuming cigar as he met the herdsman's unblinking stare. "Did you expect me to lie and say that I had?"

"Let's just say that we wouldn't have been shocked." Simna watched the stranger closely, wishing to find promise in that broad face while at the same time warily searching for snakes. Behind him, Ahlitah was making a mess of the bait barrel and its contents. The barrel's owners stood a goodly distance away, looking on helplessly.

"I won't say that I never lie. I'm a businessman, and sometimes it's a

necessary constituent of my vocation. But I'm not lying to you now."
Pulling the cigar from his thick lips, he flicked the ash at its tip aside,
heedless of where it might land, and replaced it between his teeth,
clamping down with a bite of iron that threatened to sever the slowly
smoking brown stalk.

"I can fix it so you make it safely to Hamacassar. From there on,
you're on your own."

"Not up to the journey yourself?" Simna was toying idly with the hilt
of his sword.

"Not me, no. My business is here. Only fools and idiots would attempt such a journey."

"I see." The swordsman's fingers danced faster over the sword hilt.
"And I ask, by Glespthin, which, in your opinion, are we?"

Bin Grue was not in the least intimidated by Simna's suggestive
behavior. "Supply your own definitions. That's not my job. You want to
get across the Semordria? Take my advice and head northwest to Hamacassar. You won't find a ship here, that's for sure."

"We would be glad to accept any advice you can give," Ehomba
assured him politely.

The smile that appeared briefly on the trader's face was as terse as
his manner of speech. "Good! But not here. My guidance is for my
friends and my customers, not for passing noseybodies."

"And again I say," Simna murmured, "which are we?"

"Both, I hope." With a grunt that would have done a warthog proud,
the trader pivoted and beckoned for them to follow.

Simna had more to say, but with Ehomba already striding along in
the other man's wake, he held his questions. Time enough to quiz this
brusque barterer before they found themselves in too deep with someone who might turn out to be all talk and no substance. Simna was ready
to give the man credit for one thing, though: virtuous or prevaricator, he
was one tough son of a bitch. Throughout the course of the conversation
he hadn't flinched once, not even when the swordsman had shown signs
of readiness to draw his weapon and put an end to the discussion on an
abrupt note.

Looking over his shoulder, he called out to the third member of
their party. "Pull your snout out of that rank keg, cat, and catch up!"

Mouth full of bait fish, Ahlitah looked over at him and growled.
Though it was directed at Simna and not them, two of the three fishermen took the imposing rumble as a sign to make a precipitous entry into
the turgid water of the harbor, while the third dropped to his knees and
prayed. Ignoring them, the massive black cat trotted off in pursuit of his
two-legged companions, occasionally pausing briefly to shake first one

paw and then another in a vain attempt to flick away the fishy water that clung to his toes.

As their new guide led them deeper and deeper into the maze of tightly packed buildings that crowded the waterfront, Simna ibn Sind stayed close to his tall, solemn-visaged companion.

"Where's this fat fixer leading us? I don't like narrow alleys and empty walkways and dead-end closes even when I know their names." He eyed uneasily the high stone walls that pressed close on all sides.

"A good question." Ehomba raised his voice. "Where *are* you taking us, Haramos bin Grue?"

The trader looked back and grinned. Ehomba was adept at interpreting expressions, and bin Grue's seemed genuine enough, if tight. He smiled like a man having difficulty moving his bowels.

"You look tired, and hungry. I thought we'd discuss our business over some food and drink." He turned to his left, into a constricted close, and halted. "Be of good cheer. We're here."

They found themselves waiting while their guide pushed repeatedly on a shuttered door. It was a bland slab of wood, devoid of ornamentation, wholly utilitarian and in no way suggestive that gustatory delights might lie beyond. Dust spilled from around the eaves and it groaned in protest as it was forced inward.

Simna whispered tautly. "Doesn't look like a real popular place. In fact, it doesn't look like any sort of place at all."

"Perhaps the dreary exterior is a camouflage of some sort." Ehomba remained hopeful. "The inside may be a revelation."

It was, but not in the sense the herdsman hoped. Trailing bin Grue, they found themselves in a large, dusty warehouse. The center of the high-ceilinged structure was empty, its floor of pegged, heavily scored wood planks. A rotting pile of hoary crates occupied a far corner while several still intact casks boasting unimaginably aged contents were stacked against the opposite wall. Sunlight fought with varying degrees of success to penetrate the cracked veneer of grime and sea salt that partially opaqued the narrow, oblong upper windows. Responding to their entry, a small, distant shape sprang for cover. Ahlitah leaped after the rat, which, used to dodging and doing occasional battle with stray house cats, expired of heart failure at the sight of the pouncing black-maned behemoth. Settling himself down in a patch of feeble sunlight, the master of the open veldt crunched contentedly on the obscure but zestful morsel.

Simna kept one hand on the hilt of his sword. The warehouse was quiet, deserted, and isolated—the perfect place for an ambush. Ehomba was his usual serene self, too slopping over with inner contentment to realize when he was in grave danger, the swordsman was convinced.

"I'm looking for grog and all I see is rat piss," he snapped at their guide. "Where's this fine tavern you promised us?" He was all but ready to draw his sword and put an end to the bold but perjuring jabberer.

"Right here." Reaching into a pocket of his billowing shirt, the trader withdrew a small box. Both Ehomba and Simna came closer for a better look. The box was fashioned of some light-colored wood, perhaps lignum vitae. All six sides were inscribed with cryptic symbols whose meanings were a mystery to the two travelers.

Grimacing suggestively, bin Grue moved to the center of the open floor, held the box carefully at eye height, and dropped it. Perhaps he also mumbled some words, or spat softly on the wood, or did something unseen with his hands. The box fell, bounced once, twice—and suddenly righted itself, shivering like a rabbit transfixed by the gaze of a hungry quoll.

Retreating from the quivering cube, bin Grue advised his companions to do the same. "Give it room to breathe," he told them. Without understanding what was happening, they both stepped back. Even Ahlitah looked up from the remnants of his rat, the tiny bit of remaining skeleton gleaming whitely from between his enormous front paws.

The box popped open, its sides unfolding smoothly. These in turn unfolded again, multiplying with astonishing, accelerating speed. Light shot upward from the newly hatched sides, which melded together to form a floor. As the travelers watched in amazement and bin Grue stood with hands on hips nodding approvingly, the expanding box sides threw up other shapes. A bar rose from nothingness, complete to back wall decorated with mirrors and lascivious paintings. Tables appeared, and jars and jugs and mugs and tankards atop them. There was bright light that bounded from mirrors, and music from a trio of musicians only one of whom was human, and laughter, and shouting. Most remarkably of all, patrons appeared, arising out of the exponentially multiplying box sides. They took shape and form, hands lifting drinks and food to mouths. Some were drunk, some convivial, a few argumentative. Most laughed and guffawed as if they were having the categorical good time.

A final box side unfolded a large cockroach, which immediately scurried for cover beneath the bar. Bin Grue frowned at it. "Been meaning to get rid of that. There's such a thing as too much atmosphere." Striding purposefully to an empty table, he bade them join him.

More than a little dazed, they did so. Simna had removed his hand from the vicinity of his sword hilt. He continued to regard the trader warily, but with new respect. "So you're not just some wandering merchant. You're a powerful wizard. Well, don't get any ideas." He gestured at Ehomba. "So's my lean and lanky friend here."

"Is he?" Bin Grue grunted speculatively. "Well, he needn't worry about me trying to cast any spells while he's around. I'm no sorcerer, swordsman. Just a trader of goods and services, like I told you."

"But the box, all this . . . ?" Simna stared admiringly at the busy tavern that now filled the formerly empty warehouse.

The trader nodded. "Fine piece of work, isn't it? Hard to find this kind of craftsmanship anymore these days. I told you that I'm no wizard, and I meant it. But I do business with anyone and everyone. My specialty is the rare and exotic. Inventory sometimes brings me in contact with those who practice magic." He peered steadfastly at Ehomba. "If you're truly a sorcerer, as your friend claims, then you'll know that even the greatest of necromancers can't always conjure up what they need. That's where someone like myself steps in." He indicated a small stain on the floor. A square stain, the color of polished lignum vitae. "I acquired the tavern box from an elderly witch woman of Tarsis. She offered me three models: ordinary, with additional gold, or the deluxe. I chose the deluxe."

"What was the difference?" a curious Ehomba asked.

Sitting forward in his chair, bin Grue hefted a tankard that, miraculously, was already full. When he drank, it was full bore and without delicacy. Beer dribbled from his heavy lips and he was quick to wipe the errant droplets away. In his drinking habits as with his manner of speaking he was foursquare and blunt, but no slob.

"The ordinary boxes contain only the tavern. No accessories." He took another swallow. "I like the atmosphere the patrons add."

Simna was watching people eat and drink and make merry all around them. "Are they real? Or only phantasms? Could I put my hand through one of them?"

Bin Grue chuckled. "Can you put your hand through the chair you're sitting on? I wouldn't try it. An ignominious fate, to be thrown out of a nonexistent tavern by artificial habitués." His eyes gleamed and his voice darkened slightly. "Besides, if you get in a fight with any of them you're liable to find yourself sucked down into the box when it shrinks back in upon itself. The spell only holds for a finite amount of time."

"Then we had better get down to talking." Sampling the liquid in the tall metal goblet before him, Ehomba found it to his taste. He sipped courteously.

Simna labored under no such restraint. Slugging down the contents of his tankard, he called for more. The tavern maid who refilled his drinking container topped it off with a saucy smile, and did not object when he drew her close for a kiss.

"Hoy, this is my kind of necromancy!" With drink in hand, the swordsman saluted their host approvingly.

"But you must be hungry as well." Turning, bin Grue clapped his hands. From an unseen kitchen in an unimaginable fragment of the plenum, a quartet of waiters appeared, marching deliberately toward the table carrying platters piled high with all manner of well-sauced and piquant foodstuffs. The last one was stacked high with long slabs of raw meat. This was set before an approving Ahlitah, who fell to devouring them with unrestrained feline gusto.

"Eat!" their host admonished them as he chomped down enthusiastically on a leg of broasted unicorn.

"I've got to hand it to you." Simna's words were muffled by the meat in his mouth. "I've seen travelers use magic to conjure up food. But a whole tavern, complete to back kitchen and bar and celebrating customers?" He waved an unidentifiable drumstick in his friend's direction. "What I wouldn't have given to have had that little box with us when we were crossing the desert!"

"A remarkable piece of enchantment." Ehomba made the confession even as he continued to put away copious quantities of food.

They ate and drank for what seemed like hours, until even the redoubtable Simna ibn Sind could eat no more. As he slumped in his chair, his engorged belly gave him the appearance of a pregnant jackal. Proportionately distended, the great black feline lay on his side on the floor, sound asleep.

Only Ehomba, to bin Grue's unalloyed amazement, continued to eat, steadily and without obvious harm to his digestion.

"Where do you put it?" the wide-eyed trader wondered. "Your stomach is only a little enlarged."

Around a mouthful of steamed vegetables, the herdsman replied contentedly. "Growing up in a dry, poor country, one learns never to turn down food when it is offered, and trains the body to accept quite a lot on those rare occasions when large quantities are present."

"Don't believe a word of it—oohhhhh." Moaning, Simna tried to encompass his immensely augmented gut with both hands, and failed. He became briefly alert when Ehomba removed a small vial from his pack. "There, you see! It's only through the use of sorcery that he's able to eat like this! Tell him, bruther. Tell him what alchemy of reduction is contained in that tiny container you've been secretly sipping from."

"I will." So saying, Ehomba tilted the vial over the top of his overflowing plate. Small white particles fell from its perforated stopper. "Sea salt. Not only does it remind me of home, but I always like a bit of extra seasoning on my food."

Disappointed by this revelation that was not, Simna groaned and fell back in his chair. A hand came down to rest gently on his shoulder. Looking up, he saw the smiling face and other components of the sultry barmaid who had been attending to their liquid requirements.

"Dance with a lonely lady, soldier?"

"Dance?" Simna mumbled. "Dance—sure." Struggling to his feet, he did his best to sweep her up in his arms as they staggered together out onto the small empty section of floor opposite the tootling musicians. It was difficult to tell who was holding up whom. As the trader had promised, the swordsman found to his wonder and delight that his hands did not go through her.

And all the while, to the heavyset merchant's protracted incredulity, Ehomba continued to eat. "I have never seen three men consume as much as you," bin Grue marveled openly. "I am also mindful of something your friend said earlier. Are you truly a sorcerer?"

"Not at all. A simple herder of cattle and sheep, from the far south. Nothing more. Tell me now, Haramos bin Grue—how are you going to help us reach this far-distant Hamacassar?"

"It will be difficult for you, but not impossible. First you must . . . Etjole Ehomba, are you feeling unwell?"

It was not so much that the herdsman was feeling unwell as he was unsteady. Though he did not feel in the least filled up, and still retained much of his extraordinary appetite, he found that his vision had begun to blur. The laughter of the preboxed tavern patrons seemed to reverberate in his ears instead of simply sounding, and the light from the mirrors behind the bar to grow hazy. Outlines became indistinct, and even the formidable bin Grue acquired a certain fuzziness around the edges of his blocky, smooth-domed skull. He was speaking, talking to the herdsman, but his words had suddenly become as indistinct as his face, on which individual features now seemed to float freely, nose switching places with mouth, lips reinforcing eyebrows.

Ehomba's gaze fell to his elegant, slim goblet. The liquor within was light in color and afire with small bubbles that tickled the palate. Perhaps it was the bubbles, a new experience for him. Active and intriguing, they could also serve to divert a man's attention from the actual taste of the nectar. It struck him suddenly that there was something in the current flagon of wine that could not trace its ancestry to any honorable grape.

Striving to look up, he found that he could not even lift his head. The trader had been nothing if not subtle. His blunt and forthright manner had fooled the herdsman into believing their host was not one to exercise patience in any matter. It was to his credit, then, that he had managed to disguise this component of his personality so successfully. Having plied them with ample food and fine drink of inestimable purity, he had similarly bided his time.

Ehomba tried to mumble something, but his lips and tongue were working no better than his eyes. As darkness began to descend, shutting out the bright lights of the mirrors and the now mocking laughter of the reconstituted tavern patrons, he thought he saw bin Grue rise and beckon. Not to his guests, or to any of the discorporal crowd, but to a number of large and ready men who were entering through the single, dusty doorway that opened onto the obscure close beyond.

Then his vision blanked altogether, leaving only his digestion functioning actively, and his stomach the only organ still capable of making noise.

111

It was still light out when sensibility returned to him. Having been gifted with an impressive headache, he found himself sitting up on the dry, bare floor of the deserted warehouse. Of preboxed, unfolded tavern and jovial customers there was no sign. Nor was the owner of the remarkable cube anywhere to be seen. That was hardly an unexpected development, the herdsman mused dourly.

Rising, he staggered slightly until he could confirm his balance. His belongings lay nearby, undisturbed by intruders real or imagined. No doubt one such as Haramos bin Grue regarded such poor possessions as unworthy of his attention, more bother than they would be worth in the marketplace. Or perhaps his avaricious nature had been wholly engaged with more promising matters.

Ahlitah was gone. There was no sign of the big cat, not on the floor where he had been lying nor back among the few crates and corners. Standing in silence, alone in a shaft of sunlight, Ehomba concentrated hard on recovering fragments of memory like scavenged tatters of old rags.

The men whom he recalled entering the warehouse just before he had blacked out had been carrying something between them. What was it? Shutting his eyes tightly, he fought to remember. Snakes? No—ropes. Ropes and chains. Not to rig a ship, he decided. Ehomba had never seen a cat like Ahlitah until he had rescued it from the angry spiraling wind. Half lion, half cheetah, his four-legged companion was unique. Haramos bin Grue was a self-confessed dealer in the unique.

Realizing where the cat must be, the herdsman went in search of his one other traveling companion.

He found him in a far corner, immobilized in the midst of an attempt to carry out an impossible act of physical congress with a beer keg. Half awake, half boiled, he was mumbling under his breath, a besotted smile on his face.

"Ah, Melinda, sweet Melinda. Melinda of the succulent . . ."

Ehomba kicked the keg hard. It rolled over, sending its human companion tumbling. Finding himself suddenly on his back, Simna ibn Sind blinked and tried to stand. One hand fumbled for the sword slung at his side. The fingers kept missing, grabbing at empty air.

"What—? Who dares—? Oh, by Gwasik—my head!"

"Get up." Reaching down, Ehomba extended a hand. Glum-faced and thoroughly abashed, the swordsman accepted the offer.

"Not so hard!" he shouted. "Don't pull so hard!"

Standing behind him, Ehomba held his friend erect with both arms under those of his companion's. It took a moment or two before the stocky swordsman shook himself free. "I'm all right, Etjole. I'm okay." He brushed repeatedly at his eyes, as if by so doing he could wipe away the film of indistinctness that lingered there. "By Ghophot—we were drugged!"

"Very effectively, too." The herdsman was looking toward the door. It hung dangling from one hinge, ready to break free at the slightest touch. Doped or not, Ahlitah had evidently not been taken without a fight. "They have stolen away with our friend."

"What, the cat? Who's taken him?" Simna stumbled slightly but did not fall.

"Our friend Haramos bin Grue. Our would-be guide. With the aid of others, whom he had waiting until the proper moment. But he did not lie to us. He never said anything about abducting our companion." He regarded the nearly demolished door thoughtfully. "The black litah would be worth a great deal to a collector of rare animals. Visitors to the village have mentioned that in larger, more prosperous towns such individuals are not uncommon. I imagine there would be many such in a city as large and sophisticated as Lybondai."

"Well, let's go!" Trying to draw his sword, Simna staggered in the general direction of the doorway. "Let's get after them!"

Reaching out, Ehomba put a hand on his friend's shoulder to restrain him. "Why should we do that?" he declared softly.

Simna gazed blankly up at his stolid, unassuming companion. As always, there was not the slightest suggestion of artifice in the herdsman's tone or expression. "What do you mean, 'why should we do that'? The cat is our friend, our ally. He's saved us more than once."

The herdsman barely nodded. "It was his choice, a burden he decided to take on himself. If we three were starving, he would eat first you and then me."

"Under similar circumstances, I'd eat him, though I'm not very fond of cat. Too stringy. But this situation isn't that situation."

"He is an acquaintance. I like him. But not enough to risk my life and the failure of my journey to burrow into a den of thieves to rescue him. Maybe you do not understand, Simna, but he would."

"Would he, now? Would that we could ask him that question to his flat, furry face. Stay if you must—I'm going after him." The swordsman turned and stumbled, albeit gallantly, toward the doorway.

"What about your pledge to me?"

Simna peered back over his shoulder. "It will be fulfilled—after I've rescued Ahlitah."

"You will fail."

"Has that been written? Who are you to interpret the pages of Fate before they've been turned? Do you think no one is capable of heroics except in your company?"

"Look at you! You can barely walk." Was that an inkling of hesitation in the herdsman's voice? Simna continued to weave an uncertain path toward the door.

"I'm better with a sword falling down drunk than any three warriors stone-cold sober." He paused at the dangling door, frowning. "Didn't this used to have a knob?"

"It does not matter." With a sigh, Ehomba moved to rejoin his companion. "Give it a push and it will most likely fall off that last hinge."

"Oh." Simna did so and was rewarded with a crash as the creaking barrier fell to the floor. "So maybe there are certain pages of Fate you *can* decipher."

"Fate had nothing to do with it." The herdsman strode past him. "Right now I can see straight and you cannot. Come on."

"Right!" Simna ibn Sind drew himself up. "Uh—where are we going?"

"To try and free the cat, if he has indeed been taken by the venal bin Grue. I do not mind leaving him behind, and I do not mind leaving you behind, but if you get yourself killed on account of my reluctance, I would have to carry that with me forever. My soul bears enough encumbrances without having to pile your stupid death on top of them."

"Ah, you don't fool me, Etjole Ehomba." A wide grin split the swordsman's face. "You were just looking for an excuse, a rationalization, to go after the litah."

The herdsman did not reply. He was already out the door and heading for the waterfront.

Despite his boasts of commercial achievement, or perhaps because of them, they were unable to find anyone who had heard of Haramos bin Grue. Repeated questioning of touts, travelers, seamen and servants, merchants and mongers produced blank stares, or bemused head shakes, or indifference. Sometimes the latter was mixed with contempt for the questioners. Ehomba's simple garb and Simna's unindentured status sank them beneath the notice of the city's privileged and elite. Those who replied to their polite inquiries were usually not in a position to know, and those who might be often did not condescend to respond.

"This isn't getting us anywhere." Simna was still determined, but discouragement was settling into his voice like a bad cold.

"Maybe we are going about it wrong." Ehomba was gazing out to sea, a distant look in his eyes as he stared unblinkingly at the southern horizon. A ship corrupted his vision and he blinked. "Perhaps instead of asking individuals on the street, we should seek out one who can look by other means."

"A seer?" Simna eyed his friend uncertainly. "But aren't you a seer, long bruther? Can't you do the far-looking?"

"If I could, do you think I would be discussing the matter now? When will you accept, Simna, that I am nothing more than what I say?"

"When prodigious abnormalities stop occurring in your company. But I accept that you cannot seer." The swordsman turned to drink in the surging mass of humanity and other creatures who filled the waterfront with unceasing activity. "If these insipid folk cannot tell us where to find bin Grue, then maybe they can tell us where to find someone who can."

They were directed to a tiny shopfront set in a stone building lined with narrow shuttered doorways, like vertical shingles. There was no name above the portal, which was embellished with many words written in scripts alien to Ehomba. The more worldly Simna recognized bits of two different languages, and by combining those words he knew from each, he was able to divine some meaning, like reconstituting juice from concentrate.

" 'Moleshohn the All-Knowing,' " he translated for his companion. " 'Comprehender of Worlds and Provider of Sage Mandates.' " He sniffed. "Let's see what he has to offer."

"How will we compensate him for his services?" Ehomba wondered.

The swordsman sighed. "After paying for our passage across the Aboqua I still have some Chlengguu gold left. More than enough to satisfy some substandard waterfront wise man, anyway."

The door was not latched, and a small bell rang as they entered. The unpretentious front room contained a dusty clutter of incunabula, a table piled high with old books of dubious extraction, and a great deal of spoiling food and stale clothing. It did not look promising.

The individual who emerged from a back room popped out to greet them like a badger winkling its way free of a too-small burrow. Moleshohn the All-Knowing's appearance reflected far more prosperity than did his environment. Short and slim, he had a narrow face, bright ferret-eyes, a goatee that appeared to have been grafted onto his pointed chin from a much larger man, flowing gray hair, and more rapid hand movements than a professional shuffler of cards. The air in the modest room was stagnant until he entered. His ceaseless, highly animated waving stirred both it and innumerable dust particles into torpid motion.

"Welcome, welcome, progenitors of a thousand benevolences! What can I do for you?" He did not so much sit as throw himself into the chair behind the table. Ehomba thought the worried wood would collapse from the impact, but the seat and back held. "You need a cheating lover found?" The seer smirked knowingly at Simna. "You seek gainful employment in Lybondai? You want to know the best inn, or where to find the sauciest wenches? The nature of mankind troubles you, or you have acquired some small but embarrassing disease that requires treatment?"

"We have lost something." Ehomba did not take a seat. Given a choice, herdsmen often preferred to stand. There was only one other chair in the room anyway, and Simna had already requisitioned it.

"Do say, do say." As he spoke, Moleshohn was rapidly tapping the tips of his fingers against one another.

"To digress for just a second," a curious Simna responded, "but what *is* the nature of mankind?"

"Confused, my friend." The seer extended an open palm. "That will be one half a gold Xarus, please."

"We are not through." Ehomba frowned at his companion, who shrugged helplessly.

"I always wanted to know that."

"I am no oracle, Simna, and I could have answered that question for you." Looking back at their host, the herdsman explained their purpose and their need.

"I see, I see." Moleshohn's fingers tapped a lot faster now that he had something of substance to consider. "Very large, is it, with the legs of a different sort of great feline altogether?"

Ehomba nodded. "That, and it can speak the general language of men."

"A remarkable animal, to be sure, to be sure. And you say it was taken from you, abducted, by this Haramos bin Grue?"

"He's a slick bastard," Simna informed the seer. "But this all happened only yesterday, so we don't think he can have gone far. Not with Ahlitah as unwilling freight."

"I would think both would still be in the city." Ehomba seemed mildly indifferent to the proceedings, but Simna knew his friend better. "It would take time to find the proper buyer for something like the litah. Nor would a trader as clever as bin Grue accept the first offer to come along. He will seek to get the best price for his acquisition."

"Gentlemen, gentlemen, you are in luck." The diminutive diviner was beaming. "You have come to the right man. Not only am I familiar with the name of Haramos bin Grue, but for a small fee I can have this feline re-abducted and returned to you! Your lives will not be put at risk. There are many men of daring and greed in this city who can be induced to participate in such an enterprise for a pittance. If you will but wait here, relaxing with my books and objects of interest, I will arrange for everything." He rose from his seat. "Your purloined friend shall be returned to you this very night!"

"As Gouyoustos is my witness," declared Simna, "I applaud your initiative, All-Knowing One!" His expression darkened slightly and his voice fell. "What exactly will this 'enterprise' cost us?"

The All-Knowing named a figure, which struck the swordsman as pretty much all-draining. But if the seer could deliver on his promise, it would save them both danger and difficulty. Moleshohn sealed the pact by assenting to accept half payment now, so that he could hire the necessary individuals, and the rest upon safe return of Ahlitah.

It was agreed. They would remain in the cramped but cozy shop until their host returned with their four-legged friend.

"You are not afraid of this bin Grue?" Ehomba put the question to Moleshohn as he was about to depart.

"I know his reputation. Because of . . . certain goods . . . that he deals in, he is known to be more than a mere trader." The oracle winked twice. "But I am the All-Knowing, and as such, I know how to deal with men like him. Do not fear for me, Cosigner of a Solemn Bargain. I can take care of myself." He opened the door, his fingers rapping excitably on the jamb. "I will be back before the turn of midnight with your companion, and for the rest of my money." He shut the door resoundingly behind him. Moleshohn the All-Knowing did everything resoundingly.

The two travelers were left to their own resources, perusing their host's collections by the soft light of well-fueled oil lamps. Somewhat to Simna's surprise, Ehomba revealed that he could read, though his learning was restricted to only the general language of men. Simna could boast of a knowledge of many tongues, though his fluency was frequently restricted to those words not usually to be found in the scholarly tomes of which their host was fond.

In this manner they passed a fair many hours, during which time the sun surrendered the day to the moon, and the noise of the waterfront, though never passing away completely, was much reduced from that of the busy day.

"I wonder if it is after midnight." Ehomba looked up from the book of many pictures he was perusing. "It feels so."

"There's a clock on that shelf over there." Simna pointed. "Can't you see by its face that it's after midnight?"

"A clock?" Closing the book, Ehomba rose to have a look at the strange device. "So that is what this is. I wondered."

Simna gaped at him. "You mean you've never seen a clock before?"

"No, never." Standing before the shelf, Ehomba gazed in fascination at the softly ticking mechanism. "What is a 'clock'?"

"A device for the telling of time." The swordsman studied his friend in disbelief. "It's a peculiar sort of sorcerer you are, that doesn't know the functioning of a clock. How do you tell time?"

"By the sun and the stars." The herdsman was leaning toward the shelf, his nose nearly touching the carved wooden hands that told the hour and the minute. "This is a wonderful thing."

"Hoy, sure." A disappointed Simna found himself wondering if, perhaps, just perhaps, in spite of all they had seen and survived, Etjole Ehomba was in truth little more than what he claimed to be: a humble herder of food animals.

There was a noise at the door and both men turned to regard it expectantly. "Moleshohn!" Simna blurted. "About time. We were beginning to get a trifle concerned about—"

The door burst inward, thrown aside by a brace of Khorog. They were a large, beefy folk, with warty, unkind faces, who were much in demand in the municipalities and kingdoms of the Aboqua's northern shore as mercenaries and bodyguards. They could also, it was abundantly and immediately evident, be employed for less noble purposes. Clad in light chain armor with heavy solid shoulder- and breastplates, they wielded weapons of little refinement, weighty war axes and ponderous maces being the manglers of choice.

Simna had his sword out and had leaped atop the table in a trice. "No wonder Moleshohn the Deceiver wasn't afraid of bin Grue! He's sold us out!" As he flailed madly with his sword, using his superior position to slow the first rush of assailants and keep them momentarily at bay, he shouted frantically. "Do something, bruther! Slaughter them where they stand! They'll be too many through that door and all over us in a moment!"

In the surprise and confusion of the initial assault, Ehomba reached behind his back to grab for the sword of sky metal. Instead, his hand wrapped around his long spear. With no time in which to adjust for the mistake and with grunting, murderous Khorog swarming through the open door, he was forced to thrust with the weapon at hand instead of the one of choice. This despite knowing that the consequences could be as deadly for the spear holder as for those on the receiving end of its inherent inimical qualities.

He knew that the cramped chamber was too small to contain the spirit of the spearpoint, but he had no time in which to consider another action. The grunting, homicidal Khorog were right on top of them. What burst forth from the tooth that tipped the end of his spear expanded not simply to dominate the room, but to fill it.

"Out the back way, quickly!" He could only shout and hope that the swordsman could respond rapidly enough as the dead spirit of the tyrannosaur ballooned to occupy the entire room. The massive, switching tail barely missed him as he grabbed for his backpack and dove through the rear portal.

Those Khorog who were not crushed instantly beneath the weight of the reconstituted carnivore suffocated themselves as they tried to squeeze back through the narrow front door. More were slain, devoured by the rampaging demon as, seeking space to move about and breathe, it burst through the storefront and the outer wall of the building. Its terrible roars and bellows resounded across the waterfront, sending hitherto placid pedestrians running for their lives or plunging into the harbor to escape. Surviving Khorog scattered in all directions, throwing down their cumbersome weapons in their haste to flee. The tyrannosaur's spirit pursued them, snapping at would-be assassins and blameless citizens alike.

Simna had just avoided being stepped on and smashed to a pulp. Only his familiarity with his friend's unexpected stratagems had enabled him to react with a minimum of shock and flee before it was too late. Now he let himself be led, following the herdsman as they stumbled out into the alley behind the shop and hurried back toward the harborfront.

"Wait a minute!" he yelled breathlessly, "why are we going this way? The monster you let loose is out there!"

"I know." Ehomba's tone was as equable as ever, but the swordsman thought he might have detected just a hint of suppressed passion. "But I am hoping there may also be a smaller one slinking about."

Sure enough, they found Moleshohn lying in a small pinnace tied to the main quay, cowering beneath loose canvas as he sought to hide from both the raging prehistoric spirit and the surviving angry Khorog. When the canvas was pulled back to expose his startled face, the All-Knowing appeared something less than omnipotent.

Simna shoved the point of his sword against the seer's throat until he was forced to lean back over the side of the small sailing craft. Eyes wide, their erstwhile host found himself hanging inches from the dark water. Both hands clung to the rail to keep him from tumbling over into the depths, the fingers tapping out a panicked ostinato on the smooth wood.

Teeth clenched, Simna ibn Sind pushed harder with the sword. "I'll give you a choice, oracle. That's more than you gave us. Tell us where to find Haramos bin Grue, and I'll only cut your face instead of your throat!"

"I don't—" the failed prophet began, but Ehomba, looming behind the tense swordsman, silenced the incipient protest with his eyes.

"You betrayed us to him. I should have at least suspected, but I am used to dealings among the people of my country, where souls and manhood are not bartered for gold. Being the All-Knowing, you knew where he was, and what he would pay to be rid of us. Being the All-Knowing, you know that I speak the truth when I tell you that if you do not reveal his whereabouts to us within your next heart's breath, it will be your last."

Simna's sword drew blood from the slim, wrinkled throat.

"Yes, yes, I'll tell you, I'll tell you!" So loudly and hard were the smaller man's fingertips rapping nervously on the gunwale of the pinnace that they had begun to bleed. "He—he has a place of business on Zintois Street. The house is behind. Are you going to kill me?"

Simna grinned wolfishly. "You mean you're the All-Knowing and you don't have the answer to that? Maybe you should change your title to the Maybe-Guessing."

Leaning forward, Ehomba put a hand on the swordsman's shoulder. "Let it go, Simna. If we are going to make the effort to free Ahlitah, we should hurry."

Breathing hard, his friend hesitated. "There is the small matter of the money we paid. In good faith for information, not betrayal." Palm up, he extended a demanding hand.

A trembling Moleshohn fumbled with a hidden pocket. Straightening, he passed the swordsman a fistful of coin. Counting it while Ehomba waited impatiently, Simna had a few choice final words for their betrayer. "If you're lying to us, or have given us the wrong address, we'll find you. My friend is a great sorcerer, a *true* sorcerer. Not a cheap storefront fake like yourself!"

Moleshohn managed to summon a sufficient reserve of inner

strength to protest feebly, "I am not cheap!" before the swordsman fetched him a solid blow to the forehead with the hilt of his sword. The All-Knowing became the Wholly Unconscious and fell back onto the floor of the boat. Tossing the canvas over the body, Simna followed Ehomba back onto the quay. His blade made short work of the hawser that secured the pinnace to the dock. Nodding with satisfaction, he watched as the little boat began to drift slowly out into the harbor.

"When he wakes beneath that heavy cover, maybe he'll think he's dead. A good fright is the least the old scoundrel deserves."

"Come." In the distance, the sounds of destruction and screaming were beginning to fade. The spirit of the tooth could only stalk the earth for a finite amount of time. Meanwhile, a few small fires had erupted in the wake of the two-legged monster's rampage. These would keep the locals occupied for a while, and the few surviving Khorog were in no condition to respond to questions. Content that they faced no pursuit, the two travelers hurried from the scene of confusion.

Zintois Street was situated away from the waterfront and deeper within the city proper. Neatly paved with cobblestones, it wound its way up a small hill, providing those fortunate enough to have their businesses located near the crest with a pleasant view of the harbor and the surrounding city. The storefronts here were large and impressive, bespeaking a wider commercial success than what had been achieved by the lowlier waterfront merchants.

The house of Haramos bin Grue clung like a he-crab to its mate, rising behind and above the street-facing offices. A high stone wall encircled and protected the compound. Its parapet was lined with large shards of broken glass, as beautiful as they were deadly, spiked into the rounded mortar. On the walls and within the compound, as well as on the dark street itself, all was quiet.

"I see no signs of life." Ehomba frowned slightly. "Do not the wealthy folk of these foreign lands set someone to keep watch over their homes and possessions?"

Crouching as he ran, Simna was edging along the wall toward the front door. "If someone is powerful enough, or ruthless enough, their reputation can act as adequate protection. It's cheaper, and can be just as effective. That seems to be the case with our friend bin Grue."

Stretching to his full height, Ehomba tried to see over the wall. "I would expect the merchant to keep a property as valuable and difficult to manage as the litah somewhere in the back of his establishment, out of sight and hearing of random visitors."

Simna nodded agreement. "I don't like going in through the front door, but it might prove the easiest way. If ordinary thieves are afraid to enter, it may be protected by nothing more than a simple lock."

The herdsman looked down at his friend. "Are there such things as simple locks?"

Simna grinned knowingly. "To someone who has made the acquaintance of many, yes."

True to his word, the swordsman made short work of the keyed entrance while Ehomba kept watch on the street. No one was abroad in the much-esteemed neighborhood at that late hour save a few stray cats. Two of these lingered to enjoy Ehomba's earnest attention, waltzing back and forth beneath his soothing palm as he stroked their backs and smoothed out their tails as if they were candle wicks.

"Will you stop that?" whispered Simna urgently as he finished with the lock.

"Why?" Ehomba wondered innocently. "I cannot help you in your work. I *can* help these cats."

"Well, you're wasting your energy. They'll never be able to help *you.*"

Rising, the herdsman moved closer to the door. "You do not know that, my friend. You never know when something you meet may be able to do you a service. Better to show respect to all Nature's creations."

"I'll remind you of that if we ever find ourselves lost in a cloud of mosquitoes." At his gentle but firm push, the door gave inward, squeaking slightly. "There. We're in."

Ehomba followed him through the doorway. "Do you usually find yourself breaking into other people's property?"

"No. Usually I find myself breaking out." Simna squinted as they advanced inward. "Shit!" He jerked back sharply, then relaxed. Something small and fast skittered away into the shadows. "Just a rat."

There was barely enough light to allow them to find their way between high desks and wooden cabinets. A back door led to a small storeroom that was piled high with exotic goods. It smelled wonderfully of fragrant spices and packages of incense, of fine silks and cloths brought from the far corners of the world. There were jars of aromatic liquids and wooden crates bound with hammered brass and copper. Clearly Haramos bin Grue was no dealer in baskets of fish or wagonloads of vegetables. If his tastes reflected his clientele, he would be likely to have powerful friends.

All the more reason, Ehomba knew, to conclude their business and depart as quickly as possible.

They found the big cat at the very back of the inner storeroom, slumped on his side in a cage walled with steel bars that crisscrossed in a herringbone pattern. In the dim light Simna tiptoed forward to whisper urgently at the sleeping feline.

"Ahlitah! It's Etjole and Simna, come to rescue you. Get up, cat! This is no time to nap."

Silent as a shadow, Ehomba peered past him. "He is not sleeping. He has been drugged. It is what I would do if I had to try and keep something like a black litah under control."

Searching for a way in, the swordsman located a half-height door at one end of the cage. It was secured with the largest padlock he had ever seen, a veritable iron monster the size of a melon. Its dimensions did not trouble him. The fact that it took three keys to unlock it did.

"Can you solve it?" Ehomba had never seen such a thing. The Naumkib had no need of such devices.

"I don't know." Simna had his face pressed right up against the heavy appliance, trying to peer within. "The biggest problem is that the multiple locks are most likely sequenced. If I solve the wrong set of tumblers first, it could cause the others to freeze up. Then we'll never get it open."

"You have to try. Which one feels like the first?"

Employing the same small knife he had used to pick the lock on the front door, the swordsman sweated over the three keyholes, trying to decide where to begin.

"Trust your instincts," Ehomba advised him.

"I would, if I were dealing with three women instead of three locks. Metal gives you no clues." Taking a deep breath, he prepared to ease the tip of the small blade into the middle keyhole. "Might as well try here as anywhere else."

"A good choice. Your friend is right, swordsman. You have excellent instincts."

Whirling, they found themselves confronted by a wide-awake Haramos bin Grue. The trader was standing before an open portal where none had appeared to exist. He had gained entrance to the store-room via a secret door set in a blank wall, a not uncommon conceit of suspicious merchants. In one hand he held a small lamp that threw a halo of light around him. That their nocturnal visit had caught him by surprise was proven by the fact that he stood there in his elegant one-piece sleeping gown. The fingers of his left hand were curled tightly around some small object. On his right shoulder, chittering away as madly as any pet parrot, was the scruffy, naked-tailed rat Simna had nearly tripped over in the outer offices.

As Simna continued to fumble with the lock, a solemn-faced

Ehomba turned to step between him and the trader. Oblivious to the strained confrontation, the black litah slept on.

"We have come for our friend," the herdsman explained quietly.

"Have you now?" Bin Grue was not smiling. "In the middle of the night, by breaking into my rooms?"

"A thief has no claim on the protection of the law."

Now the merchant did smile, a slight parting of the lips that was devoid of humor. "I thought you were an expert on cow dung. Now I see that you are secretly a philosopher."

"What I am does not matter. Unlock the enclosure and let our companion go."

"The exceptional cat is my property. I already have three potential buyers bidding against one another for the rights to it. Their agitation as they frantically drive up the price is wonderful to behold. Naturally you must understand I could not give him back to you now." He gestured with the lamp, making the only source of real light in the room dance according to his whim. "Why so much concern over the fate of a mere animal? So it speaks the language of men. A good horse is more valuable, and I have yet to encounter one that can speak even a single word."

"Do not be so quick to judge value until you have talked to the horse," the herdsman replied calmly. "I was not so concerned for the litah as you think. In fact, as my friend can attest, I would have left him to his fate but for one thing."

Bin Grue was listening intently. "What one thing?"

In the uneasy shadows Ehomba's dark eyes might have glittered ever so slightly with a light that was not a reflection of the trader's lamp. "You tried to have us killed."

Bin Grue did his best to shrug off the accusation. "That was Moleshohn's doing."

"Some men are easier to take the measure of than others. The All-Knowing would not have taken that step without your direction, or at least your approval."

"I deny having given it, and having denied it, I offer my apology if you insist on believing otherwise." He smiled broadly, encouragingly. "Come now, herdsman. Why should we let something that reeks mightily and sprays indiscriminately come between us? Allow me to bribe you. I will cut you a fair piece of the action. Why not? There will be plenty to satisfy all. Consent with me, and I promise that you both will leave Lybondai with new clothing, sturdy mounts, and money in your pockets. What say you?"

"I say—that these clothes suit me fine, and that I will not shake the hand of one who acceded in trying to have me murdered." Behind him,

Simna's fingers flew over iron as the agitated swordsman tried to work faster. But the bloated padlock was proving as obstinate as a teenage daughter refused permission to attend the annual Fair of Crisola the Procreant.

On the trader's shoulder, the watchrat crouched low, digging its tiny claws into the material of bin Grue's sleeping gown. The merchant's smile vanished. "I'm sorry to hear that, lover of sheep dags. It means that I will be forced to finish what the helpful but lamentably ineffectual Moleshohn was unable to do." Extending his left arm, he opened his fingers to show what he was holding.

Ehomba eyed it emotionlessly. Behind him, Simna ibn Sind looked up from his so far futile efforts. His eyes widened slightly, then narrowed. Initially wary, he quickly now found himself more perplexed than fearful.

It was another box.

IV

What are you going to do with that?" The swordsman's tone reflected his uncertainty and confusion. "Tavern us to death?"

A second thin, humorless smile split the trader's no-nonsense visage. His jaws worked redundantly, grinding on an invisible cigar. "Did you think I had only one box, night thief? I have a box full of boxes. Not all are home to the benign." Casually, as if utterly indifferent to the consequences of his action, he tossed the box in their direction. Ehomba took a step back as it struck the floor between them.

And began, exactly as the portable tavern bin Grue had brought to light previously before them, to unfold.

No mirrors flashed the light of delectation from behind a bar attended by indulgent countermen. No lithe-limbed maids danced between tables bearing pitchers and goblets of imported libations. There was no cadre of good-natured celebrants to welcome the travelers into their company.

That did not mean that the box was empty.

As the box continued to open and its unfolding sides to multiply, a towering figure rose from its center. It wore heavy iron armor and had shoulders like a buffalo. The massive skull hung low on the chest, and mordant eyes blazed deep within the cold-forged helmet. A spike-studded club rested on one shoulder, and its thighs were as big around as Simna ibn Sind's entire body.

"Brorunous the Destroyer." Bin Grue announced the apparition's arrival with a contented grunt.

A second figure emerged from the softly pulsing, inch-high platform generated by the ever-expanding box. Eight feet tall and thin as a whip, it leaned forward so that its elongated arms touched the floor. Resembling a cross between a spider monkey and an assortment of cutthroats Simna had once known, it held a pair of throwing knives in each hand and drooled like an idiot. A demented, homicidal idiot.

Bin Grue spoke again. "Yoloth-tott, Cardinal Assassin to Emperor Cing the Third of Umur."

Other figures began to appear, massive of limb, effusive of arms, and maniacal of mien. They crowded together in the defiled space limned by the ichorous phosphorescence that spilled from the dilating box. Haramos bin Grue had a name for each one, though he did not call them out as if reciting a register of old friends. His tone was unimpassioned and impersonal, the same he might have used to itemize any inventory.

The result was a pageant of perversion, a bringing together of slavering, marching evil not to be found at any one time in any one place anywhere in the world.

"Behold," he proclaimed flatly when the final apparition had been called forth and the box had unfolded its last. "No greater aggregation of murderers, butchers, and psychopaths is to be found anywhere. All gathered together for your consideration. They act only at the bidding of the master of the box that contains them, and I can tell you from previous experience that their extended suppression in a much-confined space does nothing to improve their already misanthropic temperament. At such times when they are freed from that confinement, as they are now, they're eager to express their sentiments."

Simna ibn Sind had drawn his sword. No coward, he was ready to stand and fight. But, looking at the awful assemblage of accumulated annihilation arrayed before them, he could not help but be less than sanguine about their prospects.

Still, there was something the cold-blooded merchant did not know.

"The sky-metal sword!" he whispered tensely to his tall, phlegmatic companion. "Use the sword! Draw down the wind from the heavens and blow these hard-featured horrors away!"

"In so confined a space that could be dangerous to all of us." Ehomba eyed the assembled grinning, grunting, expectant specters thoughtfully. His unruffled demeanor was beginning to unnerve the trader.

"Look upon the fate that has unfolded before you, herdsman. I have but to give the word and they will rend you from head to foot. They'll rip out your organs and feast on them raw. Have you no fear? Or are you too ignorant to know when death is staring you in the face?"

Ignoring the conglomeration of anticipative vileness, Ehomba reached slowly over his back. Not for either of the two swords slung there, but for something small concealed within his pack. Nor did he thrust forward his walking stickspear with the dark, enchanted fossil tooth that was lashed to its tip. While the merchant watched curiously to see what he was about and Simna ibn Sind hovered anxiously by his side, the herdsman uncurled his fingers to reveal . . .

"A piece of string?" Ibn Sind's lower jaw dropped.

Ehomba nodded once. "Yes. Though my people would say twine, and not string."

Haramos bin Grue sighed regretfully. "It all makes sense now. You have the fearlessness of the mad. Only the completely crazy can be truly brave, because they really never comprehend the dangers before them." He started to turn away. "That won't stop me from having you killed, of course." He proceeded to wave his hand in a certain way, and finished by snapping his fingers three times.

Spriest of all the cunning executioners, the mass murderer Lohem En-Qaun leaped forward, all four eyes ablaze, eager to be the first to draw blood. Matching the leaping wraith's agility, Simna raised his sword preparatory to fending off the attack. As he did so, Ehomba brought his right arm down and up, flinging his short length of twine at the bounding assailant.

A light enveloped the strand, an eerie radiance that seemed to course along its individual fibers. It was not a fiery glow, not in any way especially dazzling or brilliant. The thin cord simply metamorphosed into a kind of coruscating brownness that transcended its lowly origins.

Like a snake emerging from its hole, it lengthened and grew. It whipped around Lohem En-Qaun and snapped all four of his arms to his sides, pinning them to multiple ribs and freezing the would-be slayer in his tracks. Bin Grue gaped, but wore the mask of disbelief for only a moment. He was a hardened man, was the merchant, and in his time had seen much that had toughened him against surprise.

"Kill them." Raising a hand that did not shake, he pointed straight at the two intruders. "Kill them now!"

Unintimidated by their compeer's consternation, the rest of the murderous throng rushed forward—only to be met by the darting, writhing, sinuous length of twine. It caught the ankles of Brorunous the Destroyer and brought the hulking body crashing to the floor, as if binding a mountain. Singing through the night air, loops of glowing strands enveloped and secured Yoloth the Assassin, preventing him from wielding so much as a single knife or throwing star. It fettered the hands and constrained the claws and locked the feet and shuttered the jaws of a dozen of the most vile, proficient killers who had ever lived, and bound them all up together in a single howling, raving mass of impotent destruction.

And then, having done this, it looped and twisted and coiled and curled until it had squeezed them right back down into a strangely imprinted and inscribed box small enough to fit in the palm of a man's hand. Around the box was fitted, snugly and with no room to slip a querulous finger beneath, the original length of string Etjole Ehomba had removed from his pack. No insult was intended, no dry humor contrived, but the little bow with which the binding was finished was far more suggestive than any knot could have been.

Haramos bin Grue was gone. Having finally acknowledged the reality of what he was seeing, he had fled through the back door before the graceful compacting of his terrors could be completed. Simna approached the box and, with gathering boldness, picked it up. Marveling at the simple, six-sided wonder, he rolled it over in his fingers, glanced sharply back at his friend.

"Is it harmless now?"

Ehomba had walked over to the sturdy cage and was gazing at the black, furry mass within. Ahlitah had slept through it all. "So long as you're careful not to loosen the bow." Swinging his pack around, he began to search its depths.

Keeping his fingers well away from the simple twine that secured the box, the swordsman looked around until he found a tall amphora full of fine olive oil. Removing the lid, he dropped the box inside and watched as it slowly sank out of sight in the viscous, aromatic liquid. It would not be among the first places the merchant would think to search. Satisfied, he replaced the cover and moved to rejoin his friend.

As he did so, he kept glancing worriedly at the rear door through which the trader had disappeared. "I know bin Grue's type. He won't give up something this important to him, even in the face of superior sorcery. We've got to get out of here."

Ehomba glared at him and the swordsman was taken aback. The herdsman rarely showed much emotion. "You talked me into this. We are not leaving here without what we came for."

"By Gittam's eyelashes, that's fine with me, Etjole—but we'd best hurry." He indicated the massive padlock. "I can try my hand at that again, but the risk remains the same. Or is there some alchemy you can use on it?"

"I know no alchemy."

"Right," the swordsman retorted sardonically. "You only know twine."

"That was not my doing. In the village there is a man called Akanauk. He is—simple. Here." He tapped the side of his head. "The Naumkib are a tolerant folk, and he is left to himself, to be himself.

When he needs food, it is given to him. Sleeping in a house makes him cry out in the night and wake the children, so some of us built him a platform high up in one of the village's few trees. He climbs up there at night and there he lies and gurgles happily, like a baby.

"Akanauk does not farm, or help in the watching of the herds, or gather shellfish on the shore." As he studied the cage and its single heavily drugged occupant, Ehomba again touched finger to temple. "He does not have the ability to do so. What he does is sit by himself and make things. Simple things. A necklace of colored beach pebbles like those I carry with me in my pocket, or a crown of mint leaves, or armlets of woven palm frond, or lengths of strong cord."

Still watching the back door, Simna indicated that he understood. "So the village simpleton gave you a piece of his homemade string and you took it just to please him, and to remind you of home."

"No," the herdsman replied blandly. "I took it because a traveler never knows when he might need a piece of cord to tie something up."

"Gellsteng knows it's so. Now, use your wizardry to pick this lock so we can get out of here. Even as we speak, that slug bin Grue may be raising arms against us."

"I cannot do anything with that lock. I do not have your skill with such things. And I am no wizard, Simna. You should know that by now."

"Hoy, the evidence is all around me." His gaze narrowed as his friend revealed a small bottle cupped in one hand. It was very tiny. Even when full, the swordsman estimated it could hold no more than a few drops.

The sound of running feet, striking distant stone like gathering rain, made him turn sharply. "If you're going to do anything, you'd better do it quickly. They're coming."

Kneeling by the side of the cage, Ehomba put an arm between the bars and held the little bottle as close to the anesthetized Ahlitah's head as possible. Laying his spear carefully by his side, he reached through the close-set bars with his other hand.

"You might want to step back a little," he advised his companion.

Sword once more in hand, Simna was trying to watch the back door and the cage at the same time. "Why?" he asked pointedly. "Is some djinn going to burst from the phial? Are you going to use a special acid to dissolve away the bars?"

"Nothing like that." The herdsman carefully loosened the bottle's minuscule stopper. When it was almost free, he placed the thumb of his left hand against it and removed his right hand from the cage. This he used for the prosaic and decidedly unsorceral purpose of pinching his nostrils together.

Feet came pounding down unseen steps and the voices of alert, angry men could be heard shouting. "Hurry!" the swordsman admonished his companion. Even as he sounded a final warning he was backing away. Not from the door, nor from the cage, but from that tiny, undistinguished phial of cheap trade glass. Anything that made Etjole Ehomba want to hold his nose suggested strongly that others in the vicinity should be prepared to beat a hasty retreat.

As the back door was flung wide to reveal the stocky figure of Haramos bin Grue backed by a bevy of armed servants and soldiers, the herdsman's thumb flicked the loosened stopper free. Simna saw nothing, but most perfumes are invisible to the eye. What wafted from the interior of the tiny bottle, however, must have been somewhat stronger than attar of roses or essence of myrrh.

As bin Grue's disciples poured in, Ahlitah's nostrils flared wide enough to accommodate a pair of ripened mangoes. Startlingly yellow eyes burst open, a snort louder and higher than that of a breaching whale rolled through the storeroom, and the big cat leaped straight up until its black-maned head banged against the top of the cage. Startled by this sight, the first men into the chamber were brought up short.

The trader harried them onward. "It's only a cat safely secured in a cage. Where is your manhood? Get them!" He thrust an accusing hand at the pair of intruders.

With an invigorated roar that must have been heard aboard sailing ships well out to sea, the black litah whirled within the trap, parted its mighty jaws, and bit down on both latch and attached padlock. Caught within that single massive bite, the lock exploded, sending bits of tumbler and spring and pin flying in multiple directions. As Simna warded off blows from two assailants simultaneously and Ehomba blocked a lance thrust with his spear, the litah pressed its huge skull against the door of its cage and snapped it open.

"Get them, quickly—kill them both!" bin Grue was shouting with mounting concern.

His servitors were no longer listening. No amount of guaranteed remuneration or personal loyalty could compel any man to face the raging quarter-ton Ahlitah. Freed from its stoned slumber, the cat was not only ablaze with a desire for revenge, he was hungry.

Bin Grue was courageous and even fearless, but he was not stupid. Beating a retreat back through the doorway, he vowed to regain possession of the emancipated feline and extract a measure of retribution from its liberators. Between the energized roars of the litah and the screams of men trying to get out of its way, the merchant's audacious affiances went unheard.

The storeroom emptied in less than a minute. The litah would have settled down to eat, but Ehomba was at its side, fingers tugging on the thick mane. "We need to leave. The man who abducted you is no coward. He will try again."

"Let him," snapped Ahlitah, one massive forepaw resting on the back of an unfortunate fighter who had been too slow in fleeing. "I'll deal with any humans who come back."

"We don't want trouble with the city authorities." Breathing hard and still watching the back door, Simna stood on the cat's other side. "If I were bin Grue, that would be my next step. Try to inveigle the local law into helping by telling them that there's a dangerous, crazed animal on the loose in a populated area. A threat to the general citizenry."

"I'm no threat to anyone but that muck master."

"You know that, and I know that, and Etjole knows it too, but it's been my experience that nervous humans tend to throw arrows and other sharp objects at large carnivores long before they'll sit down to discuss events calmly and rationally with them."

"Simna is right." Straightening, Ehomba prepared to depart, spear in hand. He had restoppered the diminutive phial and replaced it in his pack. "We need to go."

Still the furious predator hesitated. Then it turned and, with a parting snarl, followed the two men toward the front doorway. But not before pausing several times along the way to spray the interior of the storeroom with essence of large male cat, thereby ruining for good a succession of exceptionally rare and valuable commodities.

No one was waiting for them out in the street and there was no confrontation as they raced not back toward the waterfront, but in the general direction of the rolling, heavily forested hills that marked the landlocked side of the city.

"Bin Grue's people probably haven't stopped running." Simna jogged effortlessly alongside his taller friend.

Ehomba ran with the supple, relaxed lope of one used to covering long, lonely distances by himself. "If we are lucky. What you told Ahlitah makes sense to me, too, but I think it may take the merchant some time to convince the authorities that there is real urgency to the matter." The herdsman glanced at the sky. "It is still several hours to sunrise. At this hour he may have trouble finding anyone to listen to him, sympathetic *or* skeptical."

Simna nodded agreement. "Tell me, bruther—if it wasn't sorcery, what *did* you use to rouse our four-legged friend from his trance? I've never seen anything, man or beast, released so quickly from the bonds of heavy sedation."

"It was a potion made for me by old Meruba. To wake a man unconscious from injury, so that he may have a chance to walk away from a
place of danger."

"Ah," commented the swordsman knowingly. "Some kind of smelling salts."

The herdsman looked down at him. "No salts, my friend. In the
sheltered river valleys of my country there is an animal we call the oris. It
is the size of a mature, healthy pig, has four short horns and long black
fur that it drags upon the ground. Three red stripes run from its head
along its back and down to the tip of its tail. The female defends itself
against those like Ahlitah that eat meat by spraying from glands above its
hind parts a scent that is God's own musk. This is the same stink it uses
to attract males of its kind, but it will also attract any other warm-
blooded male animal in the vicinity. It can only hope that a male of its
own kind reaches it first. When employed as a defense, it works by
altering the intention of any male meat-eater that threatens attack, and
by confusing any female predator."

"I see." Simna grinned as he ran. "So the perfume of this oris is
irresistible to any male, and you roused our four-legged friend by letting
him have a whiff of the stuff." He found himself eyeing the herdsman's
pack. "When we again find ourselves in more accommodating surroundings, I might ask you to let me have a quick sniff. Just out of curiosity's
sake, you understand," he added hastily.

"You do not want to do that."

"Why not?" The swordsman nodded in the direction of the black
litah, who was leading the way through darkened city streets. "He handled it without trouble."

"The capacity of his nose is many times yours, or ours. But that is
not the problem."

"Hoy? Then what is?"

"Meruba's bottle holds only a couple of drops, but they are not
drops of oris musk. They are drops concentrated from musk taken from
the glands of fifty oris."

"Oh." Simna frowned uncertainly. "That's bad?"

Ehomba looked down at him. As usual, the herdsman was not smiling. "If need be, you will attack yourself."

Simna ibn Sind considered this. He contemplated it from several
angles, eventually coming to the conclusion that he fervently disliked
every one of them.

"That's nasty," he finally confessed to his friend.

"Indeed it is."

Again the swordsman indicated the big cat, pacing along in front of them. "Greater capacity or not, our swarthy friend seems to be managing the aftereffects with no difficulty."

"So far," Ehomba agreed. "Still, with oris musk one can never be too careful." He met Simna's eye as they ran, racing to reach the outskirts of sleepy Lybondai before sunrise. "Why do you think I am making sure to run *behind* the litah?"

V

Everywhere they paused for breath they asked if anyone had news of one Haramos bin Grue, but the people who lived on the outskirts of the great port city had little to do with sailors and traders and those who haunted the waterfront. These craftsfolk survived beneath the notice of the wealthier merchants and traders who dominated the commerce of the south coast of Premmois. At least the wily merchant had not lied about Hamacassar: those they questioned confirmed that it was indeed a real place, and the port most likely to harbor ships and men willing to dare a crossing of the vast Semordria.

In the hilly suburb of Colioroi they did find several local greengrocers who had heard of bin Grue. He was known to them only by reputation, as an influential trafficker in specialty goods whose wealth placed him somewhere in the upper third of the merchant class, but who was by no means as celebrated or affluent or powerful as the famed Bouleshias family or Vinmar the Profuse.

Given the choice, Ahlitah would have scoured the city in search of the man who had briefly reduced him to the status of merchandise. "He not only stole my freedom, he pocketed my dignity and put a price on it." Yellow eyes gleamed as the big cat's words were subsumed in snarl. "I want to eat him. I want to hear his bones break between my teeth and feel the warm flow of his blood running down my throat."

"Maybe another time." Marking step and hour with his walking stickspear, Ehomba led the way along the narrow road that wound through the low forested hills. With each stride the milling masses of Lybondai fell farther behind, and distant, fabled Hamacassar came a step nearer. "First I must fulfill my obligation."

The black cat paced him, the top of its mane even with the tall herdsman's face. "What of my dignity?"

It was always a shock when Ehomba lost his composure. Usually soft-spoken to the point of occasional inaudibility, it was doubly startling on those rare occasions when he did raise his voice. He whirled sharply on the litah.

"To Hell with your dignity! I am unlucky enough to be beholden to a dead man. That is a real thing, not an abstraction of self." He tapped his sternum. "Do you think you are the only one with such worries? The only creature with personal concerns?" Making a grand gesture with his free hand, he took in the sloping seacoast valley behind them and the glistening blue sea against which it snuggled like a sleeping dog by its master's side.

"My wife, my mate, lies uncounted leagues to the south, and my two children, and my friends, and none of them know at this moment if I live or am food for worms. That is a real thing, too. I would just as soon not be here as fervently as you!" Aware that he was shouting, he lowered his voice. "When we reached the southern shore of the Aboqua I was happy, because I thought we could find a ship in the trading towns of the Maliin to carry us across the Semordria. When we reached this place I was happy, because I thought the same thing." His attention shifted back to the path ahead.

"Now I find that we must once again travel an uncertain distance overland to this place called Hamacassar before that will be possible. And who knows what we will find when we get there? More frightened seamen, more reluctant captains? Will we have to cross the river where this city lies and keep marching, keep walking, because in spite of what we have been told its ships, too, will not dare the ocean reaches? I do not want to have to walk across the top of the world."

They strode on in silence for a while, ignoring the stares of farmers tending to their crops or children with sticks herding pigs and fowl, armadillos and small hoofed things with fluttering trunks and feathery tails.

Having inititated the silence, it was Ahlitah who broke it. "You have a mate and cubs. I have nothing but my dignity. So it is more important to me than to you."

Ehomba pondered the feline reply, then nodded slowly. "You are right. I was being selfish. Forgive me."

"Not necessary," rumbled the big cat. "The impulse to selfishness is a natural impulse, one we are all heir to." The great black-maned head turned to look at him. "I wish you would lose your temper more often. It would make you more catlike."

"I am not sure I want to be more catlike. I—" The herdsman broke off. On his other side and slightly behind him, Simna ibn Sind was struggling to suppress his laughter. "What are you sniggering about?"

"You. You're discussing philosophy with a cat." The swordsman was grinning broadly.

Ehomba did not smile back. "What could be more natural? Cats are by their very nature deeply philosophical."

The litah nodded agreement. "When we're not sleeping or killing something."

"You mistake babble for profundity." Raising an arm, Simna pointed. "Better to concentrate on how we're going to get through that."

Just ahead, the hills gave way to broad, flat marshland of interminable width. It extended as far to east and west as they could see. On the northern horizon, a second range of hills lifted rounded knolls toward the sky, but they were quite distant.

Rushes and reeds rose in profusion from the marsh, and throngs of songbirds darted from tree to occasional tree like clouds of iridescent midges. Wading birds stalked subsurface prey while flightless, toothed cousins darted and dove through the murky water. Water dragonets with webbed feet and vestigial wings competed for food with their feathered relatives. Ehomba could see miniature jets of flame spurt from hidden hunting sites as the leathery blue and green predators brought down large insect prey.

That there was plenty of that to go around he did not doubt. The nearer they drew to the water's edge, the more they found themselves executing the informal marshland salute, which consisted of waving a hand back and forth in front of their faces with ever-increasing frequency. Against the irritating insects Ahlitah could only blink rapidly and attempt to defend his rear with rapid switches of his tufted tail.

Simna was first to the water. He knelt and stirred it with a hand. Decaying vegetation bunched up against the shore, its steady decomposition creating a rich soup for those small creatures that dwelled within. Rising, he shook drops from his fingers.

"It's shallow here, but that doesn't mean we can count on walking all the way across." He nodded toward the distant hills, partially obscured behind a rose-hued pastel haze. "Better to paddle."

"Another boat." Ehomba sighed. "It seems we are always to be looking for boats."

They found one with surprising ease, but in addition to paddles, storage lockers, rudder, and a small anchor, it came equipped with an admonition. The orangutan who rented it to them wore a tattered shirt, short pants, and a rag of a mariner's cap. As he advised them, he was continually reigniting the small-bowled, long-stemmed pipe that was clamped between his substantial lips.

"This is a one-way trip for us." A reluctant Simna was counting out some of the last of his Chlengguu gold. "How will we get your boat back to you?"

"Oh, I ain't worried about that, I ain't." In the haze-diffused sunlight, the blond in the reddish gold hair gleamed more golden than usual. "You'll be bringin' it back yourselves, you see." He sat in the rocking chair on the porch outside his small wooden shack and bobbed contentedly back and forth.

Swordsman and herdsman exchanged a look. Indifferent to matters of commerce, the black litah sat by the water's edge and amused himself catching shallow-loving minnows with casual flicks of one paw.

"Why would we be doing that?" Simna asked him straightforwardly.

Removing the attenuated pipe from his mouth, the orang gestured at the marsh with a long finger. "Because you'll never get across, that's why. You can try, but sooner or later you'll have to turn back."

Simna bristled at the ape's conviction but held his temper. "You don't know us, friend. I am an adventurer and swordsman of some note, my tall friend here is an eminent wizard, and that cat that plays so quietly by your little pier can, when roused, be terrible to behold. We have come a long way through many difficulties. No reed-choked, smelly slough is going to stop us."

"It won't be the fen that turns you back," the orang informed him. "It'll be the horses."

"Horses?" Ehomba made a face. "What is a horse?"

"By Gleronto's green gaze!" Simna gaped at his friend. "You don't know what a horse is?"

Ehomba eyed him impassively. "I have never seen one."

The swordsman did not try to disguise his disbelief. "Tall at the shoulder, like a big antelope. Leaner than a buffalo. Like a zebra, only without stripes."

"Ah! That I can envision." Confident once more, the herdsman turned his attention back to their host. "Why should a few horses keep us from crossing the marsh?"

The old ape squinted, staring past them at the concealing reeds and enshrouding bullrushes. "Because they're mad, that's why."

"Mad?" Turning his head to his right, Simna spat, just missing the porch. "What are they mad at?"

With his softly smoking pipe, the orang made stabbing gestures at the swordsman. "Not angry-mad. Insane-mad. Crazy as loons. Deranged, the whole great gallumphing lot of 'em." He stuck the pipe back in his mouth and puffed a little harder. "Always been that way, always will be. They're why nobody can get across the marsh. Have to follow the coast for weeks in either direction to get around, it, but can't get across. Horses. Lunatics on four legs. And a couple of 'em have eight." He nodded meaningfully, seconding his own wisdom.

"That's impossible." Simna found himself starting to wonder about their hirsute host's sanity.

"It's more than impossible, no-lips. It's crazy." The orange-haired ape fluttered an indifferent hand at the endless reach of rush and reed. "But you three go on. You'll see. You've got my little flat-bottom there. Paddle and pole to your hearts' content. Who knows? Maybe you'll get lucky. Maybe you'll be the first to make it across. But me, I don't think so. Them horses are thorough, and they've got big ears."

For the moment, Ehomba chose to accept the old man of the forest's narrative as truth. As a youth he had learned not to disparage even the most outrageous tale, lest it turn out, to his embarrassment and detriment, to be true. As they had already learned on their journey, the world was full to overflowing with the unexpected. Perhaps it was even home to insane horses.

"I do not understand. Sane or otherwise, why should a herd of horses care whether anyone crosses this marshland or not?"

Thick lips concaved in a simian smile. "Why ask me? I'm only a semiretired fisherman. If you want to know, ask the horses."

"We will." Rising from his crouch, Ehomba turned and stepped off the porch. "Let us go, Simna."

"Hoy." Favoring the ape with a last look of skepticism, the swordsman pivoted to follow his friend.

The boat wasn't much, but the edge of the marsh was not the grand harbor of Lybondai. It was all they had been able to find. There had been other fisherfolk, with other boats, but none willing to rent their craft to the travelers. Without exception all had declined sans an explanation. Now the reason for their reluctance was clear. They were afraid of losing their craft to the horses.

With its flat, sturdy bottom and simple low wooden sides, the boat more nearly resembled a loose plank with seats. There was a rudder, which helped them to locate the stern, and the prow was undercut to allow the occupants to propel it over obstructing water plants. There were no paddles, only poles.

"Shallow all the way across, then." Simna hefted one of the tough, unyielding wooden shafts.

"So it would seem." Ehomba had selected a slightly longer rod and was similarly sampling its heft.

"Sadly," declared Ahlitah as he hopped lithely into the unlovely craft, "I have no hands, and can therefore not help." Curling up in the center of the floor, he promptly went to sleep.

"Cats." Shaking his head, the swordsman eyed the litah with digust. "First cats and now, it would seem, maybe horses." Placing one end of his pole in the water, he strained as he and Ehomba shoved hard against the sodden shore. "I don't like animals that much. Except when they're well done, and served up in a proper sauce."

"Then you and the litah have something in common," the herdsman pointed out. "He feels the same way about people."

The marshland might have been a paradise if not for the mosquitoes and black flies and no-see-ums. To his companions' surprise, Simna voiced little in the way of complaint. When a curious Ehomba finally inquired as to the reason for his uncharacteristic stoicism, the swordsman explained that based on the insect life they had encountered on shore, he had expected it to be much worse out in the middle of the slough.

"Birds and frogs." Ehomba's pole rose and dipped steadily, rhythmically, as he ignored the rushes and reeds that brushed against his arms and torso. "They keep the population of small biting things down." He watched as a pair of lilac-breasted rollers went bulleting through the bushes off to their left. "If not for such as them, we would have no blood left by the time we reached the other side of this quagmire."

Simna nodded, then frowned as he glanced down at the litah dozing peacefully in the middle of the boat. "For once I envy you your black fur."

A single tawny eye popped open halfway. "Don't. It's hot, and I still get bitten on both ends if not in between."

Ehomba tilted back his head to watch a flock of a hundred or more turquoise flamingos glide past overhead, their coloration rendering them almost invisible against the sky. Unlike much of what he was seeing and hearing, they were a familiar bird. They acquired their brilliant sky hue, he knew, as a consequence of eating the bright blue shrimp that thrived in warm, shallow lakes.

Disturbed by their passing, a covey of will-o'-the-wisps broke cover and drifted off in all directions, their ghostly white phosphorescence difficult to track in the bright light of day. A herd of sitatunga went splashing past, their splayed feet allowing the downsized antelope to walk on a surface of lily pads, flowering hyacinth, and other water plants. Capybara gamboled in the tall grass, and the guttural honking of hippos, like a convocation of fat men enjoying a good joke, reverberated in the distance.

Yellow-and-gray-spotted coats dripping, giant ground sloths shuffled lugubriously through the water, their long prehensile tongues curling around and snapping off the succulent buds of flowering plants. Web-footed wombats competed for living space with families of pink-nosed nutria. The marshland was a fertile and thriving place, catalyzed with life large and small.

But no horses, mentally unbalanced or otherwise. Not yet.

"Maybe old Red-hair was right *and* wrong." Simna poled a little faster, forcing Ehomba to increase his own efforts to keep up. "Maybe there are a few crazy horses living in here, but they can't be everywhere at once. In a swamp this big they could easily overlook us." He paused briefly to wipe perspiration from his brow. The interior of the marshland was not particularly hot, but the humidity was as bad as one would expect.

"It is possible." The herdsman was scanning their immediate sur-roundings. All around the boat there was motion, and noise, and small splashings, but no sign of the equine impediment the ape had warned them against. "If this morass is as extensive as he said, then we certainly have a chance to slip across unnoticed. It is not as if we represent the forerunners of a noisy, invading army."

"That's right." The farther they traveled without confrontation, the more confident Simna allowed himself to feel. "There's just the three of us in this little boat. It has no profile to speak of, and neither do we."

"We will try to find some land to camp on tonight. If not, we will have to sleep in the boat."

Simna grimaced. "Better a hard dry bed than a soft wet one. I know—in my time I've had to sleep in both."

It was not exactly a rocky pinnacle thrusting its head above the surrounding reeds, but the accumulation of dirt had small trees with trunks of real wood growing from it and soil dry enough to suit the swordsman. Ehomba was especially appreciative of the discovery. The damp climate was harder on him than on his companions, since of them all he hailed from the driest country. But he was a very adaptable man, and rarely gave voice to his complaints.

As was to be expected, all manner of marsh dwellers sought out the unique opportunities created by dry land, whose highest point rose less than a foot above the water. Birds nested in every one of the small-boled trees, and water-loving lizards and terrapins came ashore to lay their eggs. Boomerang-headed diplocauls kept their young close to shore for protection while on the far side of the little island juvenile black caimans and phytosaurs slumbered on, indifferent to their bipedal mammalian visitors.

Night brought with it a cacophony of insect and amphibian songs, far fewer mosquitoes than feared, and still no horses.

"There are meat-eaters here." Simna lay on his back on the sandy soil, listening to the nocturnal symphony and watching the stars through the clouds that had begun to gather above the marsh. "We haven't seen any really big ones, but with this much game there would have to be some around."

"You'd think so." Nearby, the black litah dug his bloodied muzzle deep into the still warm belly of the young water buffalo he had killed. Its eyes were closed, its fins stilled. "Easy meat."

"That is one thing about Ahlitah." Ehomba rested nearby, his hands forming a pillow beneath his braided blond hair. "He sleeps lightly and would wake us if any danger came near."

"Hoy, I'm not worried about being trampled in my sleep. Bitten maybe, but not trampled." Simna turned away from his friend, onto his side, struggling to find the most comfortable position. "I'm even beginning to think that our only concern here might be the tall tales of one crazy old ape, instead of crazy horses."

"He did not seem to me to be mad. A little senile perhaps, but not mad."

"I don't care, so long as we make it safely through this stinking slough." A sharp report punctuated the smaller man's words as he slapped at a marauding hungry bug. His swordsman's instincts and reactions served him well: His clothes were already covered with the splattered trophies of his many mini conquests.

Their slumber was not disturbed, and they slept better than they had any right to expect. Save for the unavoidable bites of night-flying insects that prudently waited until Simna was unconscious before striking, they emerged unscathed from their fine rest.

Rising last, the swordsman stretched and yawned. For sheer degree of fetidness, his untreated morning breath matched any odor rising from the surrounding bog. That was soon mended by a leisurely breakfast of dried meat, fruit, and tepid tea.

Throughout the meal Ehomba repeatedly scanned the reed-wracked horizons, occasionally urging his friends to hurry. Ahlitah was naturally slow to wake, while Simna was clearly relishing the opportunity to dine on dry land.

"Those wise old women and men of your tribe seem to have filled your pack with all manner of useful potions and powders." The swordsman gestured with a strip of dried beef. "Didn't they give you anything to make you relax?"

Ehomba's black eyes tried to penetrate the froth of surrounding vegetation. "I do not think any such elixir exists. If it did, I promise you I would take it." He glanced back at his friend. "I know I worry too much, Simna. And when I am not worrying about things I should be worrying about, I find myself worrying about things I should not be worrying about."

"Hoy now, that makes you a bit of a worrier, wouldn't you say?" The swordsman tore off a strip of dark brown, white-edged, fibrous protein.

"Yes," the herdsman agreed. "Or perhaps I am just exceedingly conscientious."

"I know another word for that." His friend gestured with the remaining piece of jerked meat. "It's 'fool.' "

"That may be." Ehomba did not dispute the other man's definition. "Certainly it is one reason why I am here, patiently tolerating your prattle and the grunts of that cat, instead of at home lying with my wife and listening to the laughter of my children."

Simna's words rattled around a mouthful of meat that required more mastication than most. "Just confirms what I said. Geeprax knows it's true." A look of mild curiosity swept down his face as he folded the last of the jerky into his mouth. "What's up? You see something?" Immediately he rose to peer anxiously in the direction in which his tall companion was staring.

"No." The litah spoke without looking up from its kill. But it began to eat a little faster. "Heard something."

"The cat is right." Wishing he were taller still, Ehomba was straining to see off to the west. Nothing unusual crossed his field of vision. But several large wading birds tucked their long legs beneath them and unfurled imposing wings as they took to the saturated sky. "I cannot see anything, but I can hear it."

Simna had always believed he possessed senses far sharper than those of the average man, and in this he was in fact correct. But as he had learned over the past weeks, he was blind and deaf when compared to both his human and feline companions. It was all that time spent herding cattle, Ehomba had explained to him. Alone in the wilderness, one's senses naturally sharpened. Simna had listened to the explanation, and had nodded understanding, because it made sense. But it did not explain everything. Nothing that he had heard or seen since they had first met quite explained everything about Etjole Ehomba.

With a grunt of contentment, the satiated Ahlitah rose from the neatly butchered remnants of his kill and began to clean himself, massive paws taking the place of towels, saliva substituting for soap and water. Ignoring him, Ehomba continued to stare stolidly westward.

"I still don't hear anything." Simna strained to listen, knowing that with his shorter stature there was no way he would see something before the beanpole of a herdsman did. "By Gyiemot, what are you two hearing, anyway?"

"Splashing," Ehomba informed him quietly.

"Splashing? In an endless marsh? Now there's a revelation. I certainly wouldn't have expected to hear anything like that." As usual, his sarcasm had no effect on the southerner.

"Feet," Ehomba told him somberly. "Many feet."

The swordsman tensed slightly. Looking around, he made certain he knew the location of his sword, removed and set aside during the night. "Hoy. Feet. How many feet?"

The fine-featured herdsman glanced down at him, his voice unchanged. Sometimes Simna found himself wondering if it would change if its master suddenly found himself confronted with the end of the world. He decided that it would not.

"Thousands."

Nodding somberly, Simna ibn Sind turned and bent to pick up his sword.

VI

The pulsing, living wave came at them out of the west, inclining slightly to the north of the island. For a brief moment Ehomba and Simna thought it might pass them in its inexorable surge eastward. Then it began to turn, to curl in their direction, and they knew it was they that the wave sought, and that it would not rush on past.

Its leading edge was uneven, not the regular, predictable curl of a sea wave but a broken, churning froth. The reason behind the raggedness soon became apparent. It was not a wave at all, but water thrown up from beneath thousands of hooves. The horses were driving the water before them, the flying spume like panicked insects fleeing a fire.

The two men and one cat stood their ground. It was an easy decision to make because they had no other choice. The island on which they had spent the night was the only ground on which to stand, and despite their most vigorous poling, the sturdy but unhydrodynamic flat-bottomed boat would have been hard pressed to outrun a determined turtle, much less a stampeding herd. So they stood and watched, and waited.

Potential for trampling aside, it was a magnificent sight. For Ehomba, who had never before seen a horse, the beauty and grace of the massed animals was a revelation. He had not expected that such a variety of size and color might be found within a single fundamental body type. Simna's description had been accurate—within its limitations. These horses *were* much like zebras, but whereas the herdsman knew only three different kinds of zebras, the vast herd thundering toward them exhibited as many varieties as could be conjured from a drawn-out-dream.

Simna was equally impressed, but for different reasons. "I've never seen so many kinds. Most of them are unknown to me."

Ehomba looked over at his friend as they stood side by side on the sodden shore, their sandaled feet sinking slightly into the mushy sand. "I thought you said that you knew this animal."

"A few breeds and colors, yes, but I've never seen anything like this." He indicated the approaching mob. "I have a feeling no one's ever seen anything like this—not the barbarians of the Coh Plateau, who practically live on horseback, or the cavalry masters of the Murengo Kings, who account the residents of their gilded stables their most precious possessions. A man with a good rope, experience, and strong tack could take some prizes here."

"I think you speak of capture and domestication in the wrong place." Ahlitah had finally risen from his drowsing to consider the approaching herd. "These grazers stink of wildness."

Simna sniffed. "You see them as just food."

"No. Not these." The big cat's eyes narrowed as he assessed the onrushing torrent of strong legs and long necks. "Ordinarily, in the midst of such a dense gathering I could make a quick and easy kill and settle down to eat, but these grass-eaters smell of panic and desperation. Crazed grazers don't act normally. They'd be likely to turn on me and trample. Give me sane prey any day."

"Then they *are* mad." Ehomba leaned on his spear and contemplated the massed ranks of animals, which had finally begun to slow as they neared the little island. "I wonder why? They look healthy enough."

"Look at their eyes," Ahlitah advised. "They should be set forward, and staring. Too many roll, as if they're loose in their sockets." Stretching front and then back, he drew himself up to his full height. "Crazy or not, I don't think they'll rush me. No one wants to be the first to die. Stay close, and watch out for their front hooves."

Splashing through the shallows, the front ranks of the equine regiment approached the island and its three occupants. Round, piercing eyes stared, but not all were focused on the intruders. Just as the litah professed, many spun wildly and uncontrollably, staring at nothing, gazing at everything, enfolding visions that were denied to the tense but curious travelers. Several stallions sniffed of the boat where it had been pulled up on shore and tied by a single small line to a tree. One bite of heavy teeth could sever the cord. Or the weight of massed bodies could trample the craft to splinters, marooning them on the island. If the herd chose to do so, Ehomba knew, nothing could prevent them.

Simna's thoughts were exploring similar territory. "Whatever they do, don't try to stop them. They're obviously on edge and unbalanced enough as it is. We don't want to do anything to set them off."

"I do not set anyone off," the herdsman replied quietly. "It is not in my nature. But with the insane, who knows what may be considered a provocation?"

"Steady," Ahlitah advised them. "I've confronted panicked herds before. It's important to hold your ground. Flee, and they'll run you over."

An uneasy silence settled over the standoff, enveloping visitors and herd alike. Even the waterbirds and insects in the immediate vicinity of the island were subdued. Perspiration glistened on the faces of the two men while the litah fought down the urge to pant. Meanwhile, the horses watched quietly. A few lowered their mouths to sample the water plants near their feet that had not been trampled into the mud. Others shook their heads and necks, tossing manes and sending water flying. Neighbors pawed uncertainly at the shallows.

Straining, Ehomba tried to see over their backs, to ascertain the size of the herd. He could not. Graceful necks and elegant heads stretched as far as he could see in all directions. Certainly there were thousands of them. How many thousands he could not have said. If something startled them, if they all chose to rush forward in a frenzy, he and his friends would go down beneath those pounding hooves as helplessly and fatally as mice.

Simna was whispering names at him. Breeds and types in unanticipated profusion. Palomino and bay, chestnut and grizzle, calico and sorrel, roan and dapple-gray rainbowed alongside pintos and Appaloosas. Massive Percherons and shires shaded diminutive but tough ponies while tarpans snorted at the hindquarters of wild-eyed mustangs, and Thoroughbreds held themselves aloof and proud.

There were breeds so exotic and strange even the well-traveled Simna had not a clue to their origins. Despite their outlandish appearance, under the skin every one of them was all horse. There were unicorns pure of color and mottled, with horns ranging in hue from metallic gold to deep green. Eight-legged sleipnirs jostled for space with black mares whose eyes were absent of pupil. Mesohippuses pushed against anchitheriums as hipparions and hippidons nuzzled one another nervously.

"Surely there are not so many kinds in the country you come from," Ehomba whispered to his friend.

The swordsman was overwhelmed by the diversity spread out before him. "Etjole, I don't think there are so many kinds in *any* country. Or maybe in all countries. I think we are seeing not only all the horses that are, but all that ever were. For some reason they have been trapped here, and gone mad."

"You know, Simna, I do not think they look deranged so much as they do frustrated."

"It won't matter if something spooks them and they bolt in our direction. Their frustration will kill us as surely as any insanity." He spared a glance for the sky. Except for a few wandering streaks of white, it was cloudless. No danger to the herd from thunder, then.

But the animals, magnificent and alert, would not leave.

"Let's try something," the swordsman suggested.

Ehomba indicated his willingness. "You know these animals better than I."

"I wonder." Turning, Simna started across the island, careful to make no sudden movements. Along the way, he picked up his sword and pack. Ehomba duplicated his actions while Ahlitah trailed along behind.

The herdsman glanced back. "They are not following."

"No. Now, let's see what happens if we turn north." He proceeded to do so.

The percussive sloshing of water behind them heralded movement on the part of the herd. When the travelers reached the eastern edge of the island and found themselves once more facing the distant, haze-obscured hills, they found that the herd had shifted its position just enough to block their way once again.

Having verified what they had been told, Simna was nodding to himself. "The ape was right. They won't let anyone pass. We can go east or west, or back, but not across the bog."

"We have to cross the marshlands." Ehomba watched the horses watching him. "I have been too long away from home already and we do not know how far it is to this Hamacassar. I do not want to spend months bypassing this place, especially when we are halfway across already."

Simna grooved the wet sand with his foot. "Maybe you should ask them why they won't let anyone through."

The herdsman nodded once. "Yes. Maybe I should." He started forward.

"Hoy! I didn't mean that literally, long bruther."

Swordsman and Ahlitah tensed as the tall southerner strode forward until he was standing ankle deep in the warm water. Among those animals nearest him, one or two glanced sharply in his direction. Most ignored him, or continued to roll their eyes.

"*Can* he talk to them?" The black litah's claws dug into the moist, unfeeling earth.

"I don't see how. Before today he claimed he'd never even seen one." Simna stared at his friend's back. "But I've learned not to underestimate our cattle-loving companion. He seems simple—until he does something extraordinary." The swordsman gestured at the pack that rode high on narrow shoulders. "Maybe some village elder made him a potion that lets him talk to other beasts."

But Ehomba did not reach for his pack. Instead, he stood straight and tall in the shallow water, one hand firmly clutching his spear. Properly wielded, Simna knew that spear could spread panic and terror. Such a reaction would be counterproductive with all of them standing exposed in the path of an unstoppable stampede.

Raising his left hand, palm facing the herd, Ehomba spoke in clear, curious tones in the language of men. "We were told you would not let anyone cross the marshland. We were told that this is because you are deranged. I see wildness before me, and great beauty, but no madness. Only frustration, and its cousin, concealed rage."

At the piercing tones of the herdsman's voice several of the horses stirred nervously, and Simna made ready to run even though there was nowhere to run to. But the herd's composure held. There was, however, no response to Ehomba's words.

Anyone else would have turned and left, defeated by the massed silence. Not Ehomba. Already he carried too many unanswered questions in his head. It was stuffed full, so much so that he felt he could not abide another addition. So in the face of imminent death, he tried again.

"If you will not let us pass, then at least tell us why. I believe you are not mad. I would like to leave knowing that you are also not stupid."

Again there was no response. Not of the verbal kind. But a new class of horse stepped forward, shouldering its way between a sturdy Morgan and a deerlike eohippus. Its coat was a gleaming metallic white, its outrageous belly-length mane like thin strips of hammered silver. In the muted sunlight it looked more like the effort of a master lapidary than a living creature, something forged and drawn and pounded out and sculpted. It was alive, though.

"I am an Argentus." It spoke in the dulcet tones of a cultured soprano. "A breed that is not yet." Eyes sweet and sorrowful focused on the entranced Simna.

What a mount that would make, the swordsman was thinking, on which to canter into frolicsome Sabad or Vyorala-on-the-Baque! Delighted maidens would spill from their windows like wine. Regretfully, he knew the spectacular courser was not for riding. As the equine itself had proclaimed, it did not yet exist. Somehow he was not surprised. Not so extraordinary, he mused, to find the impossible among the demented. He was moved to comment.

"Horses cannot talk," he declared conclusively, defying the evidence of his senses.

The directness and acumen of the animal's stare was disconcerting. Simna was left with the uneasy feeling that not only was this creature intelligent, it was more intelligent than himself.

"These my cousins cannot." The great wealth of mane flowed like silver wine as the speaker gestured with his perfect head. "But I am from tomorrow, where many animals can. So I must speak for all. You were right, man. Here are representatives of all the horses that are, all that ever were—and all that will be. To a certain point in time, anyway." Displaying common cause with its diverse kin, it pawed at the water and the mud underfoot with hooves like solid silver. "I know of none that come after me."

Etjole Ehomba was too focused to be dazzled, too uncomplicated to be awed, either by sight or by confession. "Why will you not let anyone cross the marshland?"

"Because we are angry. Not insane, as other humans who come and affront us claim. Not maddened. We act, just as you see, from frustration." Again the magnificent head shook, sending waves of silver rippling sinuously. "In our running, which is what we do best, each of us has come to find him- or herself trapped in this place. Whether it is something in the heavy, humid air, or in the lukewarm waters, or something else, I do not know. I know only that, run hard and fast as we might, we cannot break free of the grip of this fey fen. It holds us here, turning us individually or as a herd, whenever we try to run free.

"We are in no danger." It glanced briefly and unafraid at the watching, unblinking Ahlitah. "There are predators, but we hold together and none no matter how hungry will chance an attack on so great a gathering. There is more than enough to eat, plentiful in variety and nourishment." It smiled slightly, the one facial cast horses with their expressive lips can effect even better than humans. "And of course, there is plenty of water. But we cannot escape the marshes. Past and present and future, we are all trapped here.

"In our collective anger and frustration, we long ago vowed that for so long as we cannot cross out from this place, none shall cross through. It is a way of expressing our solidarity, our herd-self. Our horseness. You, too, will have to turn around and go back."

"Be reasonable." Feeling a little less endangered, a little bolder, Simna waded out into the water to stand beside his friend. "We mean you no harm, and we're not responsible for your situation here."

"I would be reasonable," declared the Argentus earnestly, "but before I can be reasonable I must be horse. Solidarity is the essence of the herd."

"All of you have at one time or another passed this way, and all of you became trapped here. You say that what you do best is run, yet you cannot run free of this dank, clinging slough." Ehomba's chin rested in his free hand. Watching him, Simna was certain he could actually hear the herdsman think. "It must be wearying to have to run always in water. Perhaps if you had a better, firmer surface you could run easier, run faster." Looking up from his meditation, he locked eyes with the empathetic Argentus. "You might even find a way to run out of this marsh."

"Unfounded speculation is the progenitor of disappointment," the horse that not yet was murmured dolefully.

"I agree, but without speculation there is no consequence."

Simna's spirits soared as he saw Ehomba silently swing his unprepossessing pack off his shoulders. "Now tell me, Sorcerer-not, what wonder are you intending to pluck from that raggedy bag? A rainbow bridge to span the marshland? A roll of string that will uncoil to become a road?" He looked on eagerly. Feigning disinterest, Ahlitah could not keep himself from similarly glancing over to see what the unassuming herdsman was up to.

"I command nothing like that." As he searched the pack's interior, Ehomba gave his hopeful friend a disapproving look. "You expect too much of a few simple villagers."

"If I do," Simna responded without taking his eyes off the paradoxical pack, "it's because I have seen firsthand what the efforts of a few simple villagers have wrought."

"Then you may be disappointed." The herdsman finally withdrew his hand from the depths of the pack. "All I have is this." He held up a tiny, yellow-brown, five-armed starfish no more than a couple of inches across.

Simna's expression darkened uncertainly. "It looks like a starfish."

"That is what it is. A memory from the shores of my home. The little sack of pebbles in my pocket I packed myself, but before I left I did not see everything my family and friends packed for me. I came across this many days ago."

"It's—a starfish." Leaning forward, Simna sniffed slightly. "Still smells of tidepool and surge." He was quite baffled. "Of what use is it except to remind you of the ocean? Are you going to wave it beneath that stallion's nose in the hopes it will drive him mad for salt water, and he will break free of whatever mysterious bond holds him here and lead the entire herd to the shores of the nearest sea?"

"What a wild notion." Ehomba contemplated the tiny, slim-limbed echinoderm. Its splayed arms did not cover his palm. "Something like that is quite impossible. I am surprised, Simna. I thought you were a rational person and not one to give consideration to such bizarre fancies."

"Hoy! Me? Now *I'm* the one with the bizarre fancies?" Mightily affronted, he stabbed an accusing finger at the inconsequential sand dweller. "Then what do you propose to do with that scrap of insignificant sea life? Give it to the tomorrow horse to eat in hopes it will make him think of the sea?"

"Now you are being truly silly," Ehomba chided him. "Starfish are not edible." Whereupon he turned to his left, drew back his arm, and hurled the tiny five-armed invertebrate as far as he could.

A mystified Simna watched it fly, its minuscule arms spinning around the central knot of its hard, dry body. Ahlitah tracked it too, and the Argentus traced its path through the oppressive humidity with an air of superior detachment. The starfish descended in a smooth arc and struck the sluggish water with a tiny plop. It promptly sank out of sight.

Simna stared. Ahlitah stared. The Argentus looked away. And then, it looked back.

Something was happening to the marsh where the starfish had vanished.

A cool boiling began to roil the surface. In the absence of geothermal activity, something else was causing the fen water to bubble and froth. The herd stirred and a flurry of whinnies punctuated the air like a chorus of woodwinds embarking on some mad composer's allegro equus.

Simna edged closer to the nearest tree. Slight of diameter as it was, it still offered the best protection on the island. "Watch out, bruther. If they break and panic . . ."

But there was no stampede. A shriller, sharper neighing rose above the mixed chorale. Responding to the recognizably superior among themselves, the herd looked to the Argentus for direction. It trotted back and forth between the front ranks and the island shore, calming its nervous precursors. Together with the travelers, the massed animals held their ground, and watched, and listened.

The frothing, fermenting water where the starfish had sunk turned cloudy, then dark with mud. The seething subsurface disturbance began to spread, not in widening concentric circles as might have been expected, but in perfectly straight lines. Five of them, shooting outward from an effervescent nexus, each aligning itself with an arm of the no-longer-visible starfish. As the streaks of bubbling mud rushed away from their source, they expanded until each was five, ten, then twenty feet wide. One raced right past the island, passing between the herd and the sand.

As quickly as it had begun, the boiling and bubbling began to recede.

It left behind a residue of uplifted muck and marsh bottom. With the recession of activity, this began to congeal and solidify, leaving behind a wide, solid pathway. Five of them, each corresponding to an arm of the starfish. They rose only an inch or two above the surface of the water. Ehomba hoped it would be enough.

"You have been running too long in water." He indicated the improbable dirt roads. "Try running on that. You might even see a way to run back to where you belong."

Tentatively, the Argentus stepped up onto the raised causeway. Ehomba held his breath, but the stiffened mud did not collapse beneath the horse's weight, did not slump and separate back into a slurry of soil and water. Experimentally, the Argentus turned a slow circle. It pawed at the surface with a front hoof. When finally it turned back to face the travelers, Ehomba could see that it was crying silently.

"I did not know horses could cry," he observed.

"I can talk. Why should I not be able to cry? I don't know how to thank you. We don't know how to thank you."

"Do not give thanks yet," Ehomba warned it. "You are still here, in the middle of these marshes. First see if the paths let you go free. When you are no longer here, then you can thank me." The herdsman smiled. "However far away you may be, I will hear you."

"I believe that you will." Turning, the Argentus reared back on its hind legs and pawed the air, a sharply whinnying shaft of silver standing on hooves like bullion, mane shining in the hazy sunshine. Thousands of ears pricked forward to listen. Once more the herd began to stir, but it was a different furor than before, the agitation that arises from expectation instead of apprehension.

Hesitantly at first, then with increasing boldness, small groups began to break away from the main body. The paints and the heavy horses led the way down one of the five temporary roads. Trotting soon gave way to an energetic canter, and then to a joyous, exuberant, massed gallop. The thunder of thousands of hooves shook the marsh, making the water-logged surface of the island tremble with the rumble of the herd's departure.

Hipparions and eohippuses led the hairier dawn horses off in another direction, choosing a different road, as indeed they must. Their run led them not only out of the imprisoning marshes, but out of the present context. In this world some of them would remain, but in all others they would find themselves running back through time as well as meadow and field.

Eight-legged sleipnirs and narwhal-horned unicorns churned newly made dust from still a third path. Winged horses shadowed their run, gliding low and easy above the path to freedom. All manner and variety of imaginary and imagined siblings filled out this most remarkable gathering of all. There were horses with glowing red eyes and fire breathing from their nostrils, horses with armored skin, and horses the size of hippos. Several of these supported the merhorses, who with their webbed front feet and piscine hind ends could not gallop in company with their cousins.

Two more roads still lay open and unused. Trotting forward, the Argentus came right up to the travelers. The thunder raised by the partitioned herd in its flight to freedom was already beginning to fade. A silvery muzzle nuzzled Ehomba's face and neck. Even so close, Simna was unable to tell if the animal's skin was fashioned of flesh or the most finely wrought silver imaginable.

Ehomba put a hand on the horse's snout and rubbed gently. Zebras responded to a similar touch and the Argentus was no different. Superior it might be, perhaps even more intelligent than the humans, but it reacted with a pleased snuffle and snort nonetheless.

Then it backed off, turned, and climbed up onto one of the two roads not yet taken. With a last flurry of flashing mane and sterling tail, it trotted off down the empty roadway—alone.

Birdsong returned hesitantly to the marsh, then in full avian cry. The hidden mutterings and querulous cheeps of the bog again filled the now still air. From a nearby copse of high reeds a covey of green herons unfolded grandly into the sky. The marshland was returning to normal.

In the distance in several directions, the dust raised by thousands of departing hooves was beginning to settle. The edges of the roads were already starting to crumble, the momentarily consolidated marsh bottom slowly ebbing under the patient infusion of water from beneath and both sides. Shouldering his pack, Ehomba started forward.

"Hurry up. We need to make use of the road while it is still walkable."

Uncertain in mind but knowing better than to linger when the herdsman said to move, Simna grabbed his own pack and splashed through the shallows after his friend. Ahlitah followed at a leisurely pace.

The swordsman glanced back at the island. "What about the boat?"

Ehomba had crossed the road the Argentus had taken. That path was not for them. It led to the future, and he had business in the present. He splashed energetically through the shallows toward the next road. Simna trailed behind, working to catch up. The litah kept pace effortlessly, save for when it paused to shake water from one submerged foot or the other.

"If we hurry and make time before the road comes apart completely, we will not need the boat," Ehomba informed his companion. "It means that we may have to run for a while, but we should be able to get out of these lowlands before evening." As he climbed up onto the second road-bed he glanced back in the direction of the island. "I hope the old ape finds his boat. As soon as people discover that the way through the marshland is no longer blocked by mad horses, they will begin exploring. I have a feeling he will be among the first to do so." He started north-ward along the dry, flat surface. "I do not feel bad about not returning it. More important matters draw us onward, and in any case, you overpaid him significantly."

"I thought you didn't pay attention to such things." Simna trotted along fluidly next to his friend, marsh water trailing down his lower legs to drain out between his toes. As they ran, both sides of the road contin-ued to crumble slowly but steadily into the turbid water. Ahlitah would run on ahead, then sit down to lick and dry his feet as the two humans passed him, then rise up and pass them in turn once again. He perse-vered with this procedure until his feet and lower legs were once more dry enough to pacify his vanity.

"Five roads arose from the five arms of the starfish," Simna was murmuring aloud. "One for the horses of now, one for the horses of the imagination, one for those that live both in the past and the present, and one for the horses of the future."

"And this fifth road, not for horses, but for us," Ehomba finished for him.

The swordsman nodded. "What if you had been carrying only a four-armed starfish?"

Ehomba glanced down at him as he ran. "Then we would be back in that unadorned, slow boat, leaning hard on poles and hoping that the herd left nothing behind that would keep us from traveling in this direc-tion. But this is better."

"Yes," agreed Simna, running easily along the center of the disinte-grating roadway, "this is better. Tell me something—how does a non-sorcerer raise five roads from the middle of a waterlogged marsh with the aid only of a dried-out starfish?"

"It was not I." Ehomba shifted his grip on his spear, making sure to carry it parallel to the ground.

"Hoy, I know that. It's never you." The swordsman smiled sardoni-cally.

"Meruba gave me the starfish. She knows more about the little bays that dimple our coast than anyone else in the village. Many are the days I have seen her wading farther out than even bold fishermen would dare go. She always seemed to know just where to put her feet. She told me that if ever I found myself lost in water with no place certain to stand, to use the starfish and it would help me."

Simna saw that the failing roadbed led toward the nearest of the low, rounded hills that comprised the northern reaches of the Jarlemone Marshes. He hoped the solid dirt underfoot would last until they reached it. The rate of erosion seemed to be increasing.

"What magic do you think trapped all those horses here in the first place?" Simna asked him.

"Who can say? It might have been no more than confusion. Confusion is a great constrictor, ensnaring people as well as animals in its grasp. Once let loose, it feeds upon itself, growing stronger with each uncertainty that it accrues to its bloating body. It makes a tough, invisible barrier that once raised is hard to break through." He shrugged. "Or it might have been a curse, though who could curse creatures so beautiful? Or an act of Nature."

"Not any Nature I know." Simna's sandals pad-padded rhythmically against the crumbling but still supportive surface underfoot.

"There are many Natures, Simna. Most people look at the world and see only one, the one that affects them at that particular moment. But there are many. To see them one has to look deeper. You should spend more time in the country and less in town. Then you would get to see the many Natures."

"I have enough trouble coping with the one, hoy. And I happen to like towns and cities. They have taverns, and inns, and comradeship, and indoor plumbing, and screens to keep out annoying flying things." He looked over at his friend, loping along lithe as an antelope beside him. "Not everyone is enamored of a life of standing on one leg in the wilderness acting as servant to a bunch of dumb cattle."

Ehomba smiled gently. "The Naumkib serve the cattle and the cattle serve us. As do the sheep, and the chickens and pigs. We are happy with the arrangement. It is enough for us."

"A thousand blessings on you and your simple village and simple people and simple lifestyle. Me, I aspire to something more than that."

"I hope you find it, Simna. You are a good person, and I hope that you do."

"Oh, I'll find it, all right! All I have to do is stick to you like a tick on a dog until we get to the treasure. You really don't think I believe all this twaddle about devoted cattle-herding and wanting to live always in houses made of rock and whalebone and thatch, do you?"

"I thought once that you might. You have shown me many times how wrong I was to think that."

"By Ghocuun, that's right! So don't think to slough me off like an old shirt with tales of how much you delight in cleaning up daggy sheep or sick cows. You're a man, just as I am, and you want what all men do."

"And what would that be, Simna?"

"Wealth and power, of course. The treasure of Damura-sese, if it is to be had. Whatever treasure you seek if the lost city really is nothing more than a legend."

"Of course. Do not worry, Simna. I will not try to discourage you. You are too perceptive for me."

"Hoy, that's for sure." Confident in his insight, the swordsman kept a stride or two ahead of the tall southerner, just to show that he could do so whenever he wished.

The hills were drawing near, but beneath their feet the roadway was crumbling ever more rapidly as the marsh sought to reclaim that which had been temporarily raised up from its murky depths. From a width of twenty feet and more the causeway had shrunk to a path less than a yard wide. Down this the travelers ran in single file, increasing their pace. Simna led the way, followed by Ehomba, with Ahlitah effortlessly bringing up the rear. From a yard in width the path shrank by a third, and then a half, until it seemed only a matter of time until they found themselves leaping from one last dry mound to the next.

But they never had to wade. Before the last of the road ceased to exist completely they were standing on dry, grassy land that sloped gently upwards. Turning to look back as they caught their breath, they saw the last stretches of starfish road dissipate, dissolving back into the surrounding waters like a bar of chocolate left too long out in the sun. Exhausted from their run, they settled down on the welcoming green grass and sought in their packs for something to eat.

Before them, the Jarlemone Marshes spread out in all directions, flat and reed-choked, bustling with life both above and below the still waters—but empty of horse.

"This would be a fine place to make a home," Ehomba commented conversationally. "Good grazing for animals, enough of a rise to provide a view yet not subject to landslips, plenty of birds to catch and fish to net."

Simna was biting into a dried apple. "Wait until the people of Lybondai find out that the crazy horses are gone and they can cross the marshland at will. I give this place six months until it looks just like the city suburbs."

The herdsman frowned. "An unpretty picture. The grass will be gone with the quiet."

The swordsman waved the apple at his friend. "Not everyone is like the Naumkib, Etjole. Not everyone finds delight in emptiness and solitude. Most people like to be around other people. When they're not, they get nervous, and lonely."

Resting his chin on his crossed arms, the tall southerner leaned forward. "How strange. When I am around large groups of people, I find myself more lonely than ever. But when I am out in the open spaces, with the wind and the trees and the streams and the rocks for company, I am not lonely at all."

"But you miss your family," Simna reminded him.

"Yes. I miss my family." Rising abruptly, he picked up his pack. "And while very pleasant, sitting here is not bringing me any closer to them."

"Hoy, wait a minute!" Simna scrambled to gather up his own belongings. "I haven't finished my apple yet!"

A short distance away, the litah snorted softly. He had caught a fish and was using his claws to dismember it delicately. Now he was forced to swallow his catch whole. That was fine for his stomach, but not for his attitude. He would have enjoyed lingering over the tasty prize. But the taller human was on the move again. The cat would be glad when Ehomba finished what he had started. This vow of feline fealty was taking them ever farther from the litah's beloved veldt.

Still, a promise was a promise. With a sigh, he rose from the edge of the marsh and padded off after the retreating humans, growling resignedly under his breath.

VII

The War of the Flowers

No one knew exactly when the battle for the valley had begun. The origins of the conflict were lost in the mists of time, flowers being very interested in mist but considerably less so in chronology.

Blessed with growing conditions that were only rarely less than perfect, the blossoming plants had thrived on the hilltops and hillsides. For reasons unknown, the soil that so willingly nourished florescence proved inhospitable to the larger woody plants. Trees and bushes never became established. Most of the errant seeds that were dropped by birds or bats or dragonites never germinated. Those that did quickly found themselves shouldered aside by the vigorous perennials. Blossoms and leaves expanded in the sun, stealing the light and suffocating any hopeful treelets before they could reach the status of sapling. Layers of accumulated ancient nutrients and just the right amount of vital trace minerals ensured perpetual flowering, and every year rain fell when and where necessary: enough to slake but not to wash soil from tender roots.

Damaging hail and wind were unknown. The climate varied lazily between balmy and temperate, never searing hot or killing cold. There were no frosts and no droughts. Grazing animals did not visit the hills, and those insects that were not overtly beneficial were tolerated. These never swarmed in damaging numbers, never achieved the status of a plague. Bees and wasps, birds and beetles and bats took their turn attending to the matter of pollination. And the flowers throve, layering the gentle hills with exorbitant splashes of stunning color, as if some Titan of aesthetic bent had taken a giant's brush and palette to the rolling terrain.

In all this kingdom of flowers only one tract did not bloom. In its very center lay a broad, shallow valley where so much moisture accumulated that the soil became a veritable sponge, too loose and uncompacted to support normal root growth. Long ago the little valley had become a bog, which is a swamp without attitude. In its waterlogged reaches grew ferns and liverworts, but none of the noble blooms. A patrician rose would not have been caught out with blight in such surroundings, and gladioli and snapdragon recoiled from the stench of decomposing vegetation and insects. So tenancy of the valley was left to the flowers' poor cousins, the epiworts and fungi.

Centuries passed, and the flowers were content. On the beneficent hills nothing changed. The summer rains came and were replaced by the winter rains. The sun shifted its arc across the sky but was never less than accommodating. Blossoms opened and closed, petals fell and were replaced, and the empire of color was not challenged.

But while the hills stayed untouched and inviolate, change began to come to the valley. Imperceptible at first, it did not attract notice until the ferns began to die. Soon even the tough fungi started to disappear, vanishing from the shady places and decaying hollows as if abducted. Perhaps some sort of subterranean drain had opened beneath the valley, siphoning off the surplus water that had for so long accumulated there. Or maybe subtle earth movements had compacted the saturated soil so that it no longer held unnecessary rainfall as effortlessly.

The valley was drying up. No, not up—out. It was becoming exactly like the hills that surrounded it. With one exception: Because of all the plant matter that over the centuries had decayed and accumulated in the soggy depression, the soil that resulted was incredibly rich, improbably productive, supremely nourishing. Forever restricted to their ancestral ranges by untenable sandy soils marking their far boundaries, the many varieties of flowering plants that blanketed the hills suddenly found themselves presented with a new phenomenon—room for expansion. This they proceeded to do, sending out shoots and roots and dropping seed at an accelerated rate.

In doing so, they eventually and inevitably bumped up against other flowers from other hillsides attempting to assert their right to the recently reclaimed land. Something new had arrived in the land of the flowers. Something foreign and hitherto unknown.

Competition.

No species needed to move into the valley to survive. No variety or hybrid was in danger of extinction. But the attractions of the enriched soil and open space would not be ignored. Like drugs, they drew every plant in the vicinity forward. New flowers expanded in ecstasy under the stimulus of untapped nutrients and brazen sunshine. And then, they began to crowd one another.

In the past this could not happen. Every flower knew its ancestral space and kept to it, every root acknowledged the primacy of its neighbor. But the novelty of newly opened land had not come with rules. Roots made contact, recoiled uncertainly, and then thrust outward afresh, seeing no reason why they should not. Rootlets began to push against one another, and then to twist, and to attempt to strangle. Above the surface, stems fought to be the first to put forth leaves to catch the life-giving sunlight, and then to blossom and attract insects.

Strife led to adaptation. Flowers grew faster, stronger, taller. Roots became more active, more prehensile, as they did battle for control beneath the surface. Alliances were struck among species. Bold but defenseless camas and fuchsia sought the protection of thorned roses. Verbena and tulip huddled close to poisonous oleander.

Continuous and unrelenting competition led to rapid mutation as first one variety and then another fought for dominance of the fertile valley. Not to be outdone or intimidated by the roses, rhododendron grew thorns of its own. Poppies sprouted tendrils that curled like snakes, coiling around the stems of other flowers and tightening until they cut through the defenseless plant matter. Zinnias developed the ability to raise up on their roots and move, albeit slowly, across the surface, avoiding the skirmishing roots below. Peonies and gladioli seeped caustic liquids from their petals to burn any competing flower that grew too near.

Larkspurs and marigolds put forth leaves with knifelike edges that twitched like green Samurai if another plant came close. Hibiscus and frangipani and other tropicals tried to dominate the senses of pollinating insects by escalating their emissions, thereby denying those life-continuing services to less aromatic growths. Raffelesia flailed at sprouting stems with already massive red and green leaves. Across the length and breadth of the valley the conflict raged, for the most part invisible, insensible, and so slowly that anyone passing through would not have seen or thought anything amiss. This did not matter, since no one was ever present to observe and decide if what was happening in the valley constituted normality or an aberration.

That is, until the three travelers arrived.

They paused for a long time at the top of the southernmost hill. Standing there, they gazed endlessly northward, as if there was something unique or unusual about the sight. As if the millions of flowers spread out before them in blazing profusion were something remarkable and not simply the product of centuries of placid, steady growth.

A silent rush spread throughout the hills as this unprecedented arrival was noted. From the flowers immediately proximate to the visitors there was an initial exhalation of apprehension. This vanished the instant it became apparent that the visitors were not grazers and that young shoots and new blossoms were in no danger of being consumed.

As the visitors resumed their northward march, a number of plants were stepped upon. This was inevitable, given that the flowers grew so closely together that there was no open space between them. But most were resilient enough to spring back, and those that were not provided gaps in which new seedlings would be able to germinate. The flowers did not complain. They bloomed, and tracked the progress of the wonderfully mobile visitors.

Despite the glaring differences between them, the travelers excited no feelings of animosity among the plants. Just like flowers, the three were of different color, shape, and size, showing that normal variation existed even among alien intruders. Similarly, they were crowned by rounded, blossomlike structures atop long stems, and a pair of attenuated forms like leaves protruded from these stems. Only their roots were unusual, giving them more motility than even the most mobile flowers. But taken as a whole, they were not so very different at all.

And they were moving straight for the valley that had long ago become a silent zone of horticultural conflict.

There they paused again. The sun was setting and, like all other growing things, they clearly needed to reduce their activity to coincide with the absence of sunlight. Prior to closing their petals and curling up their leaf-extensions for the night, they utilized wonderfully flexible stem-parts to remove objects from their dorsal sides. From within these they withdrew small bits of dead plant and animal matter, which they proceeded to ingest. The flowers were neither surprised nor appalled. There had long been pitcher plants and flytraps within their midst. In their method of taking nourishment the visitors were being nothing less than plantlike.

Strenuous competition had given a number of the flowers in the valley the ability to function after dark. They did this by storing extra fuel during the day for use after sunset. As soon as the visitors had gone quiescent, just like any normal plant during nighttime, these growths began to stir.

Tendrils of modified columbine and amaryllis twitched, arose, and slowly crept forward. They made contact with the motionless visitor shapes and delicately began to explore their trunks, feeling of roots and blossom-caps with the feathery extensions at their tips. One slumbering form raised a leaf-stem and with astonishing speed slapped at the tendril tip that was traveling gently across its bloom. The runner recoiled, bruised but otherwise undamaged.

The mass of the visitors was astonishing. They seemed to be almost as dense as trees, which the flowers knew from legend, before they had come to dominate the surrounding hills completely. Like plants, the now recumbent stems were composed mostly of water. Colorwise, they were for the most part undistinguished, a sure sign of primitiveness.

Then the probing tendrils made a shocking discovery. There was no indication anywhere within the stout bodies of the presence of chlorophyll! Among those flowers not entirely enveloped in the torpor of night a hasty reassessment was deemed in order. If not plants, what could the visitors be? Superficially, they were nothing like fungi. But fungi could assume many peculiar forms. And if not flower, fungi, or tree, then what? They were much too cumbersome to be insects, or birds.

It was proposed that they might be some monstrous exotic variety of wingless bat. While they seemed to have more in common with plants than bats, there were undeniable similarities. Bats had dense bodies, and were warm to the touch. That was fine for two of the creatures, but the third was completely different, not only from the average flower, but from its companions. It was a great puzzlement.

Identification and classification could wait. As the columbine and amaryllis withdrew their probing tentacles in opposite directions, all sides knew what had to be done. With the coming of the dawn, each would attempt to persuade the visitors to ally themselves with one faction or another. There could be no neutrality in the battle for control of the valley. If they were plants, or even distant relations, they would understand. Understanding, they would be able to make decisions.

And while each of the several blocs desired to make allies of the travelers, none were overwhelmed with concern. Except for their exceptional mobility and unusual mass, none of the three appeared to have any especially useful ability to contribute to the conflict. They boasted no thorns, exhibited no cutting leaves, gave no indication of containing potentially useful toxins. Their large but narrow stems could not steal the shade from a significant number of blossoms, and their drab coloration was hardly a threat to draw pollinators away from even the most unprepossessing common daisy.

Still, in the fight for the valley any ally was welcome. The travelers' exceptional motility held the most promise, though what use a bloc of confederated flowers could make of it remained to be seen. Further evaluation would have to await the return of the sun.

Like any blossoming growth, the visitors' stems strengthened and their leaves unfolded as the first light appeared over the horizon. Extending their leaf pedicels to their fullest extent, the travelers straightened from their resting positions and became fully vertical to greet the sun. One even held its ground for long moments, its bloom fully opened to take in the life-giving light. This action only reaffirmed the visitors' kinship to the brilliant fields of color that surrounded them. Of one thing the flowers were now certain: Whatever they might be, the travelers were no fungi.

But they were too mobile, too free-ranging to be flowers. Some strange combination of batlike creature and plant, perhaps. As the flowers warmed and strengthened under the effects of the rising sun, they considered how best to proceed.

It was the phlox that moved first. Coiled tendrils extended, hesitantly at first, then with increasing determination, to curl around the lower limbs of two of the visitors. At first the newcomers simply shrugged them off, but as the several became dozens and the dozens became hundreds, they reacted more vigorously, emitting loud sounds on frequencies very different from those of bats.

When they backed away, tearing at the clutching tendrils, the orchids saw their chance. In their multitudinous variety, orchids had acquired a great command of chemistry. Operating on the theory that the desirable visitors had more in common with bats than flowers, they generated in one concerted push a single vast exhalation of nectar. The sticky, sweet liquid coated the startled visitors, rendering them flush with stimulation, but they did not react gratefully. Instead of throwing themselves into alliance with the orchids and their collaborators, they began wiping at themselves with their leaves. It was much the sort of reaction a plant might have, since one growth had no need of another's nectar. Perhaps they were not so batlike after all.

The azaleas and honeysuckle continued to hold to that theory. To their way of thinking, the orchids' analysis was correct but not their execution. Considering the mobility of the travelers, more aggressive action was in order. So they gathered themselves and put forth not nectar, but scent. Always strong smelling, they modified their bouquet based on what they knew of the senses of bats and batlike creatures.

The unified emission had the desired effect. Engulfed by the cloud of fragrance, all three of the travelers began to move more slowly. Two of them started to sway unsteadily, and one collapsed. The flowers on which it fell struggled to support it. Working together, they began to move the motionless form up and away from the contested area of the dried bog, hundreds of stems and thousands of petals toiling to shift the considerable weight.

Alarmed, competing verbena and marigolds tried to hold the remaining travelers back, to drag them to their side. Sharpened leaves were thrust forth, threatening to cut at the visitors' stems if they attempted to follow their captured companion. Other leaves covered with tiny, siliceous needles loaded with concentrated alkaloid poisons attempted to set up a barrier between the two larger visitors and the one being slowly but steadily carried uphill by triumphant morning glory and primrose. In the center of the disputed terrain, poisonous poinsettia battled numbing opium poppies for primacy.

That was when the tallest, but by no means the largest, of the three travelers proved once and for all that it and its companions were not flowers. After first steadying its larger companion, it removed a separate stem from its back and attached it to one of its pedicels. As the traveler rotated, this extended pedicel began to swing in great arcs, even though there was no wind. Its augmented, elongated leaf edge was sharper than any thorn.

Flowers went flying as the silvery leaf slashed through stems. Cutting a path through hopeful friend and convicted antagonist growths alike, showing no preference for one blossom over another, the traveler slashed and hacked indiscriminately until it had reached its companion. Advancing on its long, motile double stems, it traveled far faster than the victorious blooms could move the motionless body of the downed visitor.

The astonishingly durable leaf cut a path all around the recumbent individual. Then the taller visitor bent double and, in a display of strength and agility no flower could match, lifted the motionless one up onto its shoulders. Turning, it began to retrace its steps. Hopeful growths tried to trap its stems with their own while tendrils and strong roots sought to ensnare it and bring it down, but that single sharp leaf kept swinging and slashing. Against its irresistible edge not even the toughest root could endure.

Continuing to mow down all before it, the traveler crossed the contested area and rejoined the third member of the group. Though still swaying unsteadily on multiple stems, this largest of the three continued to stand against the combined efforts of every blossom in its immediate vicinity. When the recharged azaleas and honeysuckle tried their vaporous attack a second time, the visitors placed the tips of their leaves over the front part of their blooms, with the result that the effect of the previously overpowering effluvia was not repeated.

Together, the three began to make their way northward across the hills. Millions of alerted flowers waited to contest their passage, but there was little they could do against the devastating power of the silver leaf. In addition, the largest member of the party was now once more fully alert and sensible. It swung its own leaf-ends back and forth, tearing great gouges out of the earth, shredding blossoms and leaves, stems and roots, with equal indifference.

In the immediate vicinity of their flight the devastation was shocking.

Whole communities of blooms were destroyed. But the demise of a few thousand flowers was as nothing to the ocean of color that covered the hills. It would take only one growing season for the despoiled route to be fully regenerated, and new seeds would welcome the gift of open space in which to germinate.

Eventually, each family of flowers gave up the idea of enlisting the travelers in the fight for control of the dried bogland. Instead of trying to restrain the visitors, they inclined their stems out of the way, allowing the remarkable but dangerous specimens free and unfettered passage through the hills. As the ripple of understanding passed through endless fields of brilliant color, a path opened before the travelers. At first they were reluctant to put up their murderous leaves and continued to hack and cut at every blossom within reach. But their suspicion soon ebbed, and they marched on without doing any more damage, increasing their pace as they did so.

Behind them, in the expansive hollow once occupied by the bog, violets wrestled with hollyhocks, and periwinkles took sly cuts at the stems of forceful daffodils. The war for the new soil went on, the adventure of the intruders already forgotten. Once, a small would-be sapling sprang from the dirt to reach for the sun. It might have been a sycamore, or perhaps a poplar. No one would ever know, because a knot of active foxglove and buttercup sprang upon it and smothered it. Deprived of light, it withered and died.

No tree was permitted to grow on the lush, fecund hills. No mushroom poked its cap above the surface, no toadstool had a chance to spread its spores across the fertile soil. From hill to dale, crest to crevice, there were only the flowers. They throve madly, creating a canvas of color unmatched anywhere, and waited for the next visitors. Perhaps others would be more amenable to persuasion, or more flowerlike in their aspect.

It was truly the most beautiful place imaginable. But for one not a flower, a chancy place to linger and smell the roses.

VIII

They did not stop until that evening, when they had ascended to heights where only a few wildflowers grew. Unlike the millions that covered the hills from which they had fled, these were most emphatically nonaggressive.

Ehomba laid Simna down at the base of a large tree with far-spreading limbs and deeply grooved bark so dark it was almost black. A small stream meandered nearby, heading for the flower hills and the distant sea. In another tree a pair of crows argued for the sheer raucous delight of hearing themselves caw.

Ahlitah stood nearby, shaking his head as he stumbled nowhere in particular on unsteady legs, trying to shake off the effects of the insidious perfume. He had handled the effects better than the swordsman, but if Ehomba had not apprised him of what was happening and helped to hurry him out of the hills, he too would surely have succumbed to the second cloud of invisible perfume.

Simna must have taken the brunt of the first discharge, Ehomba felt. A blissful look had come over the swordsman's face and he had gone down as if beneath the half dozen houris he spoke of so frequently and fondly. Then the flowers, the impossible, unreal, fantastic flowers, had actually picked him up and started to carry him off to some unimaginable destination of their own. The herdsman had drawn the sky-metal sword and gone grimly to work, trying not to think of the beauty he was destroying as he cut a path to liberate his friend. The blossoms he was shredding were not indifferent, he had told himself. Their agenda was not friendly. The intervention of active thorns and sharp-edged leaves and other inimical vegetation had been proof enough of that. His lower legs were covered with scratches and small puncture wounds.

The litah had fared better. Unable to penetrate his fur, small, sharp objects caused him no difficulty. Unsteady as he was, he had still been able to clear away large patches of flowers with great swings of his huge paws. Now he tottered about in circles, shaking his head, his great mane tossing violently as he fought to clear the effects of the concentrated fragrance from his senses.

Electing to conserve the safe town water that filled the carrying bag in his pack, Ehomba walked to the stream and returned with a double handful of cool liquid. He let it trickle slowly through his long fingers, directly over the swordsman's face. Simna blinked, sputtered, and sat up. Or tried to. Ehomba had to help him. Woozy as a sailor in from a long voyage and just concluding a three-day drunk, the swordsman wiped at his face and tried to focus on the figure crouching concernedly before him.

"Etjole? What happened?" Simna looked around as if seeing the grass-covered hills, the grove of trees, and his friends for the first time. To his left, the big cat fell over on its side, growled irritably, and climbed to its feet again. "What's wrong with kitty?"

"The same thing that is wrong with you, only to a lesser extent."

"Wrong with me?" The swordsman looked puzzled. He started to stand, immediately listed severely to starboard, and promptly sat down again. "Hoy!" Placing a hand on either side of his head, he sat very still while rubbing his temples. "I remember smelling something so sweet and wonderful it can't be described." He looked up suddenly. "The flowers!"

"Yes, the flowers." Ehomba looked back toward the south, toward the resplendent hills from which they had fled. "For some reason they wanted to keep us there. I cannot imagine why. Who can know how a flower thinks?" He turned back to his friend. "They tried to hold us back with little vines and roots and sharp leaves. When that did not work, they tried to smother us with delight. I caught very little of the perfume. Ahlitah received more. You were all but suffocated." He held a hand up before the other man's face. "How many fingers am I holding up?"

"Five. That's four too many." The swordsman coughed lightly. "First horses and now flowers. Give me the reeking warrens of a city with its cutthroats and thieves and honest, straightforward assassins any day. Those I know how to deal with. But flowers?" Lowering his palms from the sides of his head, he took several deep breaths. "I'll never again be able to feel the same way about picking a bouquet for a favorite lady."

"I am glad that you are feeling better."

"So am I, though I don't ever before remember being knocked unconscious quite so pleasantly." He rose, only slightly shaky. Nearby, the litah was exercising and testing its recovered reflexes by leaping high in playful attempts to knock the agitated crows out of their tree.

"By Gielaraith, wait a minute. If I was unconscious and the cat indisposed, how did I get out of those hills?"

"I carried you." Ehomba was scanning the northern horizon. Ahead, the terrain continued to climb, but gently. No ragged escarpments, no jagged peaks appeared to block their way northward.

The swordsman's gaze narrowed. "The aroma didn't affect you?"

"I told you—you and Ahlitah received a stronger dose than I did. Besides, my sense of smell is much weaker than either of yours." Looking back down, he smiled. "Many years of herding cattle and sheep, of living close to them every day, have dulled my nose to anything very distilled."

"Hoy—the preserving power of heavy stink." With a grunt, Simna straightened his pack on his back. "I'm used to my assailants smelling like six-month-old bed linen, not attar of camellia."

"In a new and strange land one must be prepared to deal with anything." Ehomba started northward. The grass was low and patchy, the ground firm and supportive. Able to hike in any direction they preferred, they did not need to follow a particular path. Behind them, the litah gave up its game of leap and strike, conceding victory to the exhausted crows. "Old forms may no longer be valid. Seeming friends may be masked by lies, and conspicuous enemies nothing more than upright individuals in disguise."

Having shaken off the last lingering effects of the potent perfume, the swordsman strode along strongly beside him. "Hoy, that's not a problem a man has in a dark alley."

Ehomba took in their clean, bracing environs with a sweep of his free hand. "I would rather find myself in surroundings like this facing adversaries unknown than in some crowded, noisy city where one has to deal with people all the time."

"Then we make a good team, long bruther. I'll take care of the people, and you deal with the flowers. And damned if I don't think I'll have the easier time of it."

They slept that night in a grove of smaller trees, welcoming in their silence and lack of activity. They were indisputably trees and nothing more, as was the grass that grew thickly at their bases and the occasional weed flower that added a dab of color to the campsite. The stars shone unblinkingly overhead in a cool, pellucid sky, and they enjoyed the best night's sleep they had had since before embarking on their crossing of the Aboqua.

At least Simna ibn Sind and Ahlitah did. Ehomba found his slumber unexpectedly disturbed.

She was very tall, the vision was, though not so tall as the herdsman. Her skin had the texture of new ivory and the sheen of the finest silk. Large eyes of sapphire blue framed by high cheekbones gazed down at him, and her hair was a talus of black diamonds. Beneath a gown of crimson lace she was naked, and her body was as supplely inviting as a down-filled bed on a cold winter's night.

Her lips parted, and the very act of separation was an invitation to passion. They moved, but no sounds emerged. Yet in the absence of words he felt that she was calling out to him, her arms spread wide in supplication. With her eyes and her posture, her limbs and the striking shape beneath the gown, he was convinced that she was promising him anything, anything, if he would but redeem her from her current plight.

Discomfited by her consummate union of lubricity and innocent appeal, he stirred uneasily in his sleep, tossing about on the cushioning grass. Her hands reached out to him, the long, lissome fingers drawing down his cheek to her lips, then his neck, his chest. She smiled enticingly, and it was as if the stars themselves had invited him to waltz in their hot and august company. He felt himself embraced, and the heat rose in his body like steam trapped within a kettle.

Then he became aware of another, a horned presence looming ominously above the both of them. It too was incapable of speech, though much was conveyed by glaring eyes and clenching teeth. Eyes downcast, the vision of the Visioness pulled back from him, drawn away by an awful unseen strength. In her place threatened the helmeted figure. It blotted out the light, and what it did not obscure, a pair of keening dark clouds that crept along at its heels enveloped and devoured.

"Etjole. Etjole!"

The hideous figure was shaking him now, thrusting him violently back and forth, and he was helpless to stop it. Shaking and—no, it was not the horned and helmeted one. That was a beast inhabiting his dream. The hands on his shoulders were solid, and real, and belonged entirely to the realm of wakefulness.

He opened his eyes to find a concerned Simna gazing down at him. It was still night, still dark out. Unable to stay long in one place, the stars had moved. But the grove of trees was unchanged, undisturbed by hideous intrusion. Nearby, the great humped mass of the black litah lay on its side, snoring softly.

The swordsman sat back on his heels. "Hoy, I don't know what dream you were having, but don't share it with me."

Ehomba raised up on one elbow and considered his memories. "The first part was good. I am ashamed to admit it, but it was good."

"Ah!" In the darkness the worldly swordsman grinned knowingly. "A woman, then. Your wife?"

Ehomba did not meet his gaze. "No. It was not Mirhanja."

A gratified Simna slapped one knee to punctuate his satisfaction. "By Geuvar, you are human, then. Tell me what she was like." His voice dripped eagerness.

Ehomba eyed him distastefully. "I would rather not. I am not happy with my reaction."

"It was only a dream, bruther!" The swordsman was chuckling at his stolid companion's obvious discomfiture. "Wedded or not, a man cannot be acclaimed guilty for enjoying his sleep. A dream is not a prosecutable offense—no matter what women think."

"It is not that. It was not just any woman, Simna. It was her."

"Hoy—then there was significance to it." The swordsman's smile was replaced by a look of grave concern. "What did you learn from it?"

"Nothing, except that she may somehow know that we are coming to try and help her. That, and the realization that she is more ravishing than even the image we saw above the fire that night on the veldt."

"So beautiful," Simna murmured, a far-off look in his eye. "Too beautiful for simple mortals like you and I, methinks." His grin returned, its lubriciousness muted. "That doesn't mean we can't look, at least in dreams. But that wasn't her you were seeing there at the last. You were moaning and rolling about."

"Hymneth the Possessed. It had to be, I think." Ehomba had lain back down, staring up at the stars, his head resting on the cup formed by his linked fingers. "As before, his face was hidden. I wonder if he is hideous to look upon in person."

"With luck we'll never find out." Returning to his own bedroll, the swordsman slipped back beneath the blanket. Having climbed beyond the hills into the gentle mountains, they were now high above sea level, and along with fresh air and quilted silence the night brought with it a creeping chill.

Ehomba lay still for a long time, listening to the quick, sharp calls of nocturnal birds and the muffled voices of inquiring insects. He was both eager and afraid of returning to the dream. But when he finally drifted off, it was into that restful and rejuvenating region where nothing stirred—not even the vaporous images of imagination.

The next day they continued to ascend, but at such a gentle incline and over such accommodating gradients that the increasing altitude imposed no burden on them and did not slow their progress. They saw small herds of moose and sivatherium, camelops and wapiti. Ahlitah made a fine swift kill of a young bull bison, and they feasted luxuriantly.

Small tarns glittered like pendants of peridot and aquamarine at the foot of pure white snowpacks, casting reflections that shone like inverse cameos among the bare gray granites. At this altitude trees were stunted, whipped and twisted like taffy by relentless winter winds. Diminutive wildflowers burst forth in knots of blue and lavender, corn red and old butter yellow. None of them attempted to trip, seduce, or otherwise restrain the impassive hikers in their midst. Small rodents and marsupials dove for cover among the rock piles whenever the marchers approached, and Ahlitah amused himself by stalking them, pouncing, and then magnanimously letting the less-than-bite-size snacks scamper free.

They had already begun to descend from the heights when they encountered the sheep. Simna pronounced them to be quite ordinary sheep, but to the man from the far south they were strikingly different from the animals he had grown up with. Their fleece was thick and billowy where that of the Naumkib's herds tended to be straight and stringy. Their narrowing faces were black or dirty white instead of brown and yellow. And their feet were smaller, to the point of being dainty. These were coddled animals, he decided, not one of which would survive for a week in the wilds of the dry country inland from the village. Yet they remained, indisputably, sheep.

At the strangers' approach they showed they were not as helpless as they looked. Amid much distraught baaing and bleating, they hastened to form a circle; lambs in the middle, ewes facing determinedly outward, young rams spacing themselves efficiently along the outermost rim.

One old ram, obviously the herd dominant and leader, lowered his head and pawed angrily at the ground. Bleating furiously, he took several challenging pronks in the direction of the newcomers. At this point Ahlitah, who had been dawdling behind his human companions, trotted forward to rejoin them. Espying and taking nonchalant note of the ram's challenge, he vouchsafed to give forth a midrange snarl, whereupon the suddenly paralyzed ram froze at the end of an advancing pronk, stood tottering on all fours for an instant or two, and proceeded to keel over onto one side in a dead faint, all four legs locked sideways and straight, parallel to the ground.

"Easy meat," the litah commented idly as they strolled past the trembling herd.

"Mind your manners," Ehomba chided his four-legged companion. "You cannot be hungry. Not after that half an animal you just devoured."

"You're right; I'm not hungry. But I've run too many hot mornings in pursuit of prey that eventually escaped ever to ignore something that looks like roast on a stick." The maned head gestured scornfully in the direction of the herd, and thin, hoofed legs quaked at the casual nod. "These things are domesticated. They are become the vassals of human appetite."

"You can say that again. I love mutton." Simna was eyeing several plump members of the herd more covetously than the big cat.

Ehomba sighed. Belying his stocky frame, the swordsman's appetites were outsized in every way. "If not the shepherd, we may encounter the landholder. Perhaps we can bargain for some chops, if you must have some."

Walking on, they stumbled not on the landowner but upon his dwelling, a modest and unimpressive structure of stone walls and thatched roof. There was a well out front, and a small garden fenced to keep out the wild vermin as well as sheep and goats. Smoke rose unhurriedly from the stone chimney, and flowering wisteria vined its way up the walls and around the door and the single window. Several young lambs grazed in a stone paddock back of the main building. At the travelers' approach, an old dog lifted its head to check them out. Broad bands of white streaked her long black fur. Apparently satisfied, it laid its lower jaw back down on its paws. It did not bark, not even at the sight and smell of the litah.

"Quiet, tidy little place," Simna declared grudgingly. "Simple lodgings for simple folk."

"Even simple folk may have useful information to give." Tilting back his head, the herdsman squinted at the sky. "And there are clouds gathering. If we are polite, and pleasant, perhaps the owner will let us stay the night." Trying to see inside, Ehomba bent low and shaded his eyes with one hand. "When traveling in a strange land, any known direction is welcome." Advancing on the half-open swinging door, the lower half of which was latched, he raised his voice. Impressively, the dog continued to disregard them.

"Hello! Is anyone at home? We see your smoke."

"It's not my smoke, no. It belongs to the fire. But you may come in anyhow, all of you."

Ehomba led the way into the cottage, which was very neat and clean. Among the Naumkib, it would have been accounted a palace. Sturdy chairs surrounded a table. Both were decorated with carvings and fine scrollwork. An iron pot hung from a swing-out cooking bar in the large fireplace, and there was a sink with a hand pump on the far side of the room. Facing a stone fireplace off to the right were larger, upholstered chairs and a sitting couch. Bookshelves filled with well-thumbed tomes lined the walls, and hanging oil-filled lamps were in place to provide light throughout the evening hours. To the left, a door led to rooms unseen, and a short ladder leaning against one wall hinted at the presence of a copious attic. The cottage's lone occupant was working at the sink, wet up to his elbows. He turned to smile at them as they entered.

"Mind your head, stranger. I don't get many visitors, and few your size. Now, I'll be with you in a moment. I'm just finishing up these dishes."

The owner was plainly dressed in ankle-length pants and matching shirt of dark brown. Both were devoid of decoration. The simple elegance and efficiency of the furnishings suggested that they had not been made by the cottage's occupant, but were the product of other craftsmen and had been bought and brought to this place by wagon or other means of transport. If true, it meant that the owner's isolation was deceptive. He was here by choice rather than out of necessity, and had the resources to pay for more than basic needs.

Not that there was any overt reference to wealth to be seen anywhere within the cottage, unless one so considered the many books. But even a poor man could accumulate a decent library through careful purchasing, especially if it was accomplished over a matter of decades. And their diminutive host certainly had, if not obvious wealth, many years to his credit. His beard and hair were entirely gray, full but neatly trimmed, and despite the blush in his pale cheeks he was clearly an individual of considerable maturity.

"Just have a seat, over there, by the fire," he instructed them as he ran a rag across the face of a ceramic plate. "I should have attended to these earlier, but there were new lambs in need of docking, and I thought it better to take care of them first."

"Yes," Ehomba agreed. He watched Simna flop like a rag doll into one of the big overstuffed chairs and then carefully imitated the swordsman's actions. He was not used to such comfort. In the village, beds were stuffed but chairs were straight-backed and hard. "Better to see to that as quickly as possible or they are liable to become fly-blown."

Putting the plate in a drying rack, the owner turned in surprise. "You are a sheep man, then?"

Simna rolled his eyes. "Oh no." Near his feet, Ahlitah wound three times around himself before, satisfied, he lay down in front of the fire.

"Sheep, yes, and cattle. Mostly cattle."

"I have never been a man for cattle." Taking an intricately carved pipe from its stand, the homeowner ambled over to the stone hearth. Selecting a narrow taper from a small box affixed to the rockwork, he stuck it into the flames until it acquired one of its own, then touched the flickering tip to the bowl of the pipe. While he drew on the contents, he spoke around each puff. "Too rambunctious for me, and a bit much for one man to handle. Even with Roileé to help."

"Roileé?" The herdsman searched the room for signs of another resident.

"My dog." The owner smiled delightfully around the stem of his pipe. "She's getting on, and she's lost a step or two, but she's still the best sheepdog in these mountains. I am Lamidy Coubert, and I think you are not from the Thinking Kingdoms."

"How can you tell?" Simna chuckled softly.

Coubert laughed along with the swordsman. Removing the pipe from his mouth, he gestured with its bowl. "Well for one thing, no one I have heard of, not even lords and noblemen, travels with a house cat of quite such imposing dimensions. Much less one that speaks." Seeing Ehomba's expression, he added, "I heard all three of you talking outside as you approached the cottage. And your manner of dress, my friend, is also strikingly new to me." He frowned slightly as he turned to Simna. "Your attire I can almost place."

"You live alone here, Lamidy Coubert?" Ehomba asked him.

"Yes. Except for Roileé, of course."

"Yet you allow us, three strangers, freely into your home. Two well armed, and the third a meat-eater of great size and strength. And you are not afraid?"

Coubert coughed lightly, checked his pipe. "If your intentions were malicious I could not have stopped you. So I might as well greet you." His smile returned. "Besides, I have lived a long time now by myself. Here on the edge of civilization I get few visitors. So I try to treasure those I do."

"I hate to disillusion you, old man, but this isn't the edge of civilization. South of here lies the port of Lybondai and a host of other coastal cities." Simna's throat was calling for refreshment but he decided to hold off a while longer to see if their host offered before he made the request. "And beyond that, the sea of Aboqua, and the cities and cultures of the south. Myself, I'm from far to the east, and I can tell you, we're goddamn civilized out that way."

"I am sure." The oldster was courteously contrite. "I meant no insult. It is simply the view that is generally held in the Thinking Kingdoms, and therefore one with which I am familiar, though I do not hold to it myself." He gestured expansively. "Obviously, you three are as civilized as any people."

"Two." On the thick oval carpet before the crackling fireplace, Ahlitah spoke without lifting his head from his paws.

"Yes, well."

"Where are the Thinking Kingdoms?" Ehomba inquired softly. Beyond the door and window, evening was stealing stealthily over the land. The muffled baaing of sheep was interrupted by the occasional booming of muted thunder. He could not tell which way the gathering storm was moving. With each strobing flash of unseen lightning the walls of the cottage seemed to grow stronger, and to tighten around them all like a finely made, heavy coat. A chill entered via the still open upper half of the double door. Feeling it, Coubert moved to shut the remaining barrier against the rising wind.

"The Thinking Kingdoms are all the lands to the north of here," their host explained as he returned to stand near the fireplace, slightly to one side of the sputtering, popping blaze itself. "There is Bondressey, and the Dukedom of Veroi-verai. Farther to the north one may enter the Grand Barony of Melespra, which is bordered by Squoy East and Squoy South. East of the Grand Barony lies the river port of Urenon the Elegant, and downstream from it the province of Phan that is ruled by the enlightened Count Tyrahnar Cresthelmare.

"Those are only a few of the most notable kingdoms immediately to the north of here. There are many more, to east and west and to the north of Phan."

"And all these tribes—these kingdoms," Ehomba corrected himself. "They are at peace? I ask because we must travel farther north still."

"There are always disputes and altercations, bickerings and controversies." Coubert turned philosophical. "It is the nature of sovereigns to debate. But war is rare in the Thinking Kingdoms. Each ruler prides himself on his or her intelligence and learning. Altercations are most likely to be settled through reasoned discussion, sometimes by greatly respected teams of logicians."

Simna indicated the pack and sword he had removed and placed near his feet. "Everybody's different, Gulyulo says. Where I come from, we talk a lot while we're arguing, but it's usually loud, unreasoning, and in words of one syllable."

"I can believe that." Coubert turned back to Ehomba. "And you, my tall friend? How are disputations settled in your country?"

"The Naumkib are too small and too few to enjoy the luxury of infighting. We are too busy surviving to waste time and energy on individual quarrels."

"Yet despite this claimed pacificity you carry not one but three large and unusual weapons," the observant sheepherder pointed out sagely.

"It was thought I should be as well equipped as possible for this journey. Not every creature, much less every human, that one meets in strange lands is ready or willing to sit down and peacefully work out disagreements."

"Hoy, you can say that again! Especially the ones that want to eat you." Simna started to curl his legs up on the chair beneath his backside, then thought better of it. Not that he was shy, but his feet had not been washed in days, and though he would never admit to it, he was slightly intimidated by the unexpected tidiness of their surroundings.

"Whither are you bound, then?" their host inquired. "To which of the Thinking Kingdoms?" Reflected firelight danced in his pale green eyes.

"To none of them, based on what you have told us." Ehomba felt himself growing sleepy. It had been a long day's march, the welcoming warmth of the fire was seeping inexorably into his tired muscles, and the plushness of the couch on which his lanky frame reposed was intoxicating. "We have to cross the Semordria, and to do that we have learned that we must go to Hamacassar to find a ship."

"Hamacassar!" For the first time since their arrival, the little man looked startled. "So far! And yet just a prelude to a greater journey still. I am impressed. You are great travelers."

"You bet your chin hairs we are." Simna nodded in the herdsman's direction. "And my friend there, he's a grand and powerful wizard. He claims to be doing this only to help some lady, but I know he's really after a great treasure." Looking smug, the swordsman crossed his arms over his chest and compromised with his legs by laying them across a small serving table.

The sheepherder nodded slowly as he digested this information before turning back to Ehomba. "Is what your friend says true? Are you a wizard?"

"Not only not a wizard," the southerner protested, "but not grand or powerful, either. I was well prepared for this journey by the good people of my village, that is all." He threw Simna a dirty look, but the swordsman ignored him. "Some people get an idea into their heads and no matter what you do, you cannot get it away from them. They bury it as deeply as a dog does a favorite bit of offal."

"Oh, don't I know that!" Puffing on his pipe, Lamidy Coubert chuckled under his breath. "A person's mind is a hard thing to change, it is. Living up here by myself like this, I'm often the butt of jokes from the people of Cailase village, where I buy those things I can't make myself. Or I am looked upon with suspicion and uncertainty by those few visitors who do manage to make it this far into the mountains." He manifested a kindly grin. "But after they meet me, their concerns usually disappear quite rapidly. I'm not what even the most fearful would call a threatening figure." He gestured with one hand at the surrounding room.

"As you can see, I don't even keep any weapons here."

Ehomba nodded, then eyed the old man with interest. "Where I live there are many predators. They are very fond of sheep as well as cattle. We have to watch over our herds every minute, or the meat-eaters would take the chance to snatch a lamb or calf. So we need our weapons. You have no predators here?"

"Oh yes, of course. Dire wolves and pumas, small smilodons and the occasional hungry griffin. But Roileé generally keeps them off, and if they're persistent, whether out of deep hunger or ignorance or real stubbornness, I can usually make enough noise and fuss to drive them away."

"That old dog would face down a griffin?" Simna was disbelieving. "She hardly looks steady enough to make it to the nearest ridge top."

"Roileé may have lost a step or two, but she still has her bark, and she can still bite. I haven't lost a lamb to a predator in twelve years."

The swordsman grunted. "Hoy, it just goes to show. Appearances can be deceiving for people. I guess it can be the same for dogs." He scrunched deeper into the obliging back of the chair. "I don't suppose you've got anything to drink? We've been a long time walking with nothing but water to sustain us."

"Of course, of course!" For the second time Coubert looked startled. "My manners—I am getting old." Thunder rumbled in the distance, and not as far off as before. The storm was definitely moving in the direction of the solidly built little cottage.

From an ice-chilled cabinet their elderly host brought out wine, and from a chest small metal goblets. Simna was disappointed in the limited capacity of the drinking utensils, but relaxed after their host set the bottle on the table and did not comment when refills were poured.

"You must tell me." Coubert had taken a seat on the hearth just to the left of the fire. "What are the sheep like in your country? Are they the same as mine, or very different?"

Emitting a soft moan of despair, Simna poured himself a third glass of the excellent spirits and tried to shutter his ears as well as his mouth. Ehomba took up the question energetically, and the two men embarked on a discussion of sheep and sheep-raising, with an occasional aside to accommodate the dissimilar nature of cattle, that required the addition of several logs to the fire. Despite the steady cannonade of approaching heavy weather, Ahlitah was already submerged deep in cat sleep. With his abnormally long legs fully extended to front and rear, his paws nearly touched opposite walls of the cottage. With the assistance of more wine,

Simna ibn Sind soon followed the imposing feline into similar latitudes of slumber.

Coubert's hospitality extended to his offering his guest the only bed. Ehomba would not hear of it.

"Besides," he told the oldster, "it has been my experience that the beds of more civilized people are too soft for me, and I would probably not sleep well in it. Better for me to remain here with my friends." He pushed down on the cushion that was supporting him. "If this couch is also too soft, I assure you I will be very comfortable here on the floor, beside your excellent fire." He glanced significantly upwards. "I think that tonight a strong roof will be the most important aid to sleep."

"I think you're right, my friend." With a kindly smile, their host tapped the bowl of his pipe against the stone mantel, knocking the contents into the fireplace. "Actually, it's been pretty dry hereabouts lately. We could use a good rain." Thunder echoed through the surrounding vales in counterpoint to his comment. "From the sound of it, we're about to have some. I hope you sleep well, Etjole."

"Thank you, Lamidy."

After the old man had retired to the room behind the kitchen, closing the door gently behind him, Ehomba struggled to negotiate with the couch for reconciliation of his long frame. It took some twisting and turning, and his legs still dangled off the far end, but the final position he settled on was not an impossible one, and he felt he would be able to sleep. The soothing fire was a great help, and the profundo purring of the black litah a suitable if not entirely exact substitution for the soothing susurration of the small waves that curled and broke rhythmically on the shore beneath the village.

He awoke to the peal of thunder and the flash of lightning. It revealed a world transformed into brief glimpses of stark black and white. Color returned only when the shocked purple faded from his sight, allowing him to see once again by the light of the dying fire. Ahlitah now reposed on his back with all four legs in the air, his massive skull lolling to one side, leaving him looking for all the world like a contented, spoiled tabby. That was one thing about cats, Ehomba knew: No matter how much they were scaled up in size, they all retained their essential, inherent catness.

Simna lay slumped in the chair, quite unconscious and smelling strongly of the fruit of the vine. The earth could have opened beneath the cottage and the swordsman would have slept until he hit bottom.

A second rumble rattled the room, leaving the herdsman more awake than ever. Rain tiptoed on the thatch and spilled in a succession of channeled bells off the roof to strike the compacted ground outside.

Sleeping in the awkward position had left him with a cramp in his thighs. Grimacing, he swung his legs off the arm of the couch and onto the floor. He would walk off the cramp and then try to go back to sleep in a different position.

In the dwindling firelight he paced back and forth between the couch and the kitchen, feeling the sensation return to his legs. It was on one such turn that he happened to glance out a window precisely when distant lightning flared. What he saw, or thought he saw, momentarily frozen in the stark dazzle, gave him pause.

An uncertain frown on his face, he walked to the door and unlatched the top half. Cool, wet wind greeted him and blowing rain assailed his bare skin. He blinked it away, trying to penetrate the darkness. His eyes were sharp, his night vision acute, but he was no owl. Another flash of light, a boom of thunder close at hand, and his eyes finally confirmed what he had seen through the window a moment before. There could be no question about it.

Yapping and barking excitedly with the strength of a much younger animal, darting back and forth with impossible swiftness, leaping higher into the air than any impala, Lamidy Coubert's dog was herding the lightning.

IX

Wonderment writ large on his face, Ehomba stood in the half-open doorway, watching the implausible. It was enthralling to see the little long-haired dog cut off a bolt before it struck the ground, turning it with a stentorian yelp, cutting back and forth in front of the shimmering flash until it was penned back among the rocks with several others. They hovered there, flickering wildly, apparently unable to decide whether to strike the ground beneath them or recoil back up into the clouds. Like cornered livestock, they were waiting for directions from the supernal sheepdog.

A fresh bolt attempted to slash at one of the garden fence posts. Anticipating its arrival, the dog flashed through the air faster than even Ehomba's trained eye could follow. With a clashing of its jaws it snapped at the descending tip of the thunderbolt, sending it whipping sideways to slam harmlessly into an open, empty patch of ground.

Tongue lolling, eyes bright and alert, the dog stood stolidly next to the garden awaiting the next lashing from the heavens. Then something made her turn, and she saw Ehomba standing in the doorway, staring. Sneezing once, she shook her head dog-style and trotted over to the pen of boulders to yap boisterously at the lightning trapped within. With a great concerted crash and roll the cornered bolts were sucked back up into the roiling clouds from whence they had come, to crackle and threaten no more.

Satisfied, the old dog pivoted and came loping back toward the house. Halting beneath the overhanging lip of the thatched roof, she shook violently, sending water flying in every direction. Her long fur fluffed out, but only partway. It would take more than a shake or two to dry out that thick mop of black and white. Slurping up her tongue, she considered the tall stranger watching her from the other side of the door.

"Well," she exclaimed in words of perfect inflection, "are you going to let me in so I can dry off, or do you mean to make me stand out here until I catch my death of cold?"

"No." Taking a step back, Ehomba opened the lower half of the door. "I would not want that."

She trotted past him and headed straight for the fire. Seeing that the somnolent Ahlitah occupied nearly all of the space before the glowing embers, she sighed and managed to find an unoccupied bit of floor between the big cat's mountainous shoulder muscles and the hearth. There she lay down, breathing easily, and closed her eyes in a picture of fine canine contentment.

Ehomba shut and latched both the upper and lower halves of the door against the wind and rain before walking over to sit down on the hearth opposite the sheepdog. "I have seen dogs work cattle, and I have seen them work antelope. I have even seen them work camels. But never before have I seen one work lightning."

Roileé wiped at her left eye with one paw before replying. "Lamidy has always been a good man, kind and caring. But he is getting old faster than I, and he cannot play as easily or as often as he used to. When I get bored, I have to find ways to entertain myself." She nodded in the direction of the door. "Herding the lightning keeps my reflexes sharp."

"I would think that any dog that can herd lightning could handle even a large flock of sheep on one leg."

"Tut! Lightning is fast; sheep are tricky and, when they want to be, deliberately deceptive. As a herdsman yourself, you should know that."

"I spend most of my time with cattle. Cattle are not tricky."

"No, you are right. Cattle are quite predictable."

"And while we are talking," Ehomba suggested, "I would be very interested to know how it is that you came to be able to talk."

Roileé shook her head and began licking the damp backs of her paws. "Many animals can talk. They just choose not to do so in the presence of humans, who think it a unique faculty of their own. Your striking feline companion talks. He does not want to, though. It is a curse to him."

"A curse?"

"Yes. All he wants to do is kill, and eat, and sleep, and make love, and lie in the sun in a quiet place. That is why he keeps his talking brief. It is not because he is rude; only impatient with an ability he would just as soon not have."

"You assume much in a very short time."

"I assume nothing, Etjole Ehomba. I know."

"Even a dog that can speak does not know everything."

"That is true." The long muzzle bobbed in a canine nod. "But I know a great deal. More than most dogs. You see, I am a witch."

"Ah, now I understand." Ehomba nodded solemnly. "You are a woman who was, through some hex or misfortune, been turned into a dog."

"No, you do *not* understand. It is nothing like that. I was born a dog, I have always been a dog, and I will die a dog. I have never been, nor would I ever want to be, human. Some dogs do nothing all their lives but proffer companionship. Others work. I am a sheepdog. But I am also a witch, taught by witches when I was a puppy." She nodded in the direction of the bedroom door. "For many years I have kept company with Lamidy. I could have done worse. He is a kind and understanding man who knows what I am and is untroubled by the knowledge. It is good for a dog to have a human around. Good for the soul, and to have someone to change a water dish."

"Well, witch Roileé, it is good to know you."

"And I you." Limpid, intelligent dog eyes met his. "You are an unusual man, Etjole Ehomba."

The tall southerner shrugged. "Just a simple herdsman."

"Herdsman perhaps. Simple, I am not so sure. Where are you bound?"

He told her, as he had told people before her, and when he was through she was whimpering querulously.

"It all sounds very noble and self-sacrificing."

"Not at all," he argued. "It is what any virtuous man would do."

"You impute to your fellow humans a greater dignity than they deserve. I like you, Etjole Ehomba. I would help you if I could, but I am bound by the oath that binds together dog and man to remain here with my Lamidy."

"Maybe you can help anyway." Ehomba considered whether he wanted to make the request. And, more significantly, whether he wanted it fulfilled. In the end, he decided that knowledge of a woeful kind was an improvement over no knowledge at all. All enlightenment was good. Or at least, so claimed Asab and the other people of importance. "Can you tell me what lies ahead for my friends and me? We know little of the lands that await us."

The dog exhaled sharply. "Why should I know anything about that?"

"I did not say that you did," the herdsman replied quietly. On the other side of the cat-a-mountain, Simna made gargling pig noises in his sleep. Behind Ehomba, the withering fire continued to cast warmth from its bones. "I asked if you could find out."

Canine eyes searched his fine, honest face. "You are an interesting man, Etjole Ehomba. I can herd the lightning, but I think maybe you could shear it."

He smiled. "Even if such a thing were possible, which it is not, what would one do with clippings from the lightning?"

"I don't know. Feed it to a machine, perhaps." Coming to a decision, she rose, stretched her front feet out before her and thrust her hips high in the air, yawned, and beckoned for him to follow.

She stopped in the cozy room's farthest corner, facing a two-foot-high handmade wooden box with a forward-slanting lid. On the front of the lid someone had used a large-bladed knife to engrave a pair of crossed bones with a dog heart above and singular paw print below. "Open it."

For the barest instant, Ehomba hesitated. His mother and father and aunts and uncles and the elders of the village had often told the children stories of warlocks and witches, of sorcerers and sorceresses who could turn themselves into eagles, or frogs, into oryx or into great saber-toothed cats. He had grown up hearing tales of necromancers who could become like trees to listen silently and spy on people, and of others capable of turning themselves into barracuda to bite off the legs of unwary gatherers of shellfish. There were rumors of hermits who at night became blood-supping bats, and of scarecrowlike women who could become wind. Others were said to be able to slip out of their skins, much as one would shed a shirt or kilt. Some grew long fangs and claws and their eyes were said to be like small glowing moons of fire.

But he had never heard of a witch among the animals themselves, who had not at some time been human. He told her so.

"Do you think only humans have their conjurers and seers? Animals have their own magic, which we share but rarely with your kind. Most of it you would not understand. Some of it would not even seem like magic to you. We see things differently, hear things differently, taste and smell and feel things differently. Why should our alchemy also not be different?" Eyes the color of molten amber stared back up at him. "If you want my help, Etjole Ehomba, you must open the box."

Still he hesitated. A backward glance showed that his companions slept on. There was no sign of movement from the direction of the cottage's single bedroom. "Does Coubert know?"

"Of course he knows." Her muzzle brushed the back of his hand, her wet nose momentarily damp against his dry skin. "No one can live with a witch and not know what she is. Human or dog, cat or mouse, we are all the same. Some things you cannot hide forever even from the ones you love."

"And he has no magic powers of his own?"

"None whatsoever," she assured him. "But he is good to me. I have clean water every day, and I do not have to kill my own food." For the barest instant, her eyes blazed with something that ran deeper than dogness. "We are comfortable here, the two of us, and if a right woman or strong husky were to come along, neither of us would resent the other's pairing. We complement one another in too many ways." She gestured with her black nose. "The box."

His long, strong fingers continued to hover over the lid. "What is in it?"

"Dog magic."

Lifting the cover and resting it back against the wall, he peered inside. No crystal globe or golden tuning fork greeted his gaze. No bottles of powdered arcanity or pin-pierced dolls stared back up at him. There was not much at all in the bin, and what there was would not have intrigued a disgruntled thief for more than a second.

Some old bones, more than a little rancid and well chewed; a long strip of thick old leather, also heavily gnawed; a ball of solid rubber from which most of the color and design had long since been eroded; a stick of some highly polished pale yellow wood covered with bite marks; and a few pieces of aromatic root tugged from a reluctant earth comprised the bin's entire contents.

"My treasures," murmured Roileé. "Take them out and lay them before the fire."

Ehomba did so, taking a seat on the hearth when he had finished. As he looked on, the dog witch used her paws to align them in a particular way: bones here, stick crossed there, ball in position, leather strip curled just so, roots positioned properly to frame them all. With her nose, she nudged and pushed, making final adjustments. When all was in readiness, she lay down on her belly, tilted back her head, and began to moan and whimper softly. Neither Simna nor Ahlitah moved in their sleep, but from outside the cottage there came distant answering howls as wolves and other canids found their slumber disturbed. Ehomba felt something stir deep inside him, emotions primal and hoary, that spoke fervently of the ancient link between dog and man.

Roileé's soft whimpering and moaning was not constant, but varied in ways he had never before heard from a dog. It was not language as he knew it, but something more basic and yet within its own special parameters equally complex. It bespoke wisdom denied to men, the intimate knowings of creatures that moved on four legs instead of two. It reeked of smells he could never know, and an acuity of hearing beyond the human pale. With these skills and senses other knowings were possible, and Roileé was a master of all these.

Within the incandescent depths of the fire something snapped, sending a glowing ember flying. It arced over the hearth to land amid the pile of gatherings. A tiny puff of smoke rose where it had settled among the leather and bones. The puff expanded, became a cloud obscuring the bright eyes of the old sheepdog, and then Ehomba too found himself engulfed.

He had always been a fast runner, but now he seemed to flow effortlessly over the ground as fast as a low-flying eagle. Trees and rocks and bushes and flowers flew past him, the flowers at shoulder level, the trees immense impossible towers that seemed to support the sky. Every sense was heightened to a degree he would not have thought possible, so that distant sights and smells and sounds threatened to overwhelm his brain's ability to process them.

A subtle but distinct odor caused him to swerve to his left. Immediately, the musk sharpened, and seconds later a covey of startled quail exploded from the bush in which they had been hiding. He snapped at them, more out of an instinct to play than a desire to kill, for he was not hungry. Advancing on a small stream, he slaked his slight thirst, and was amazed by the distinctiveness of each swallow, at the chill of the water against his throat and the discrete flavors discernible within something seemingly as bland as the water itself.

A distant rumble caused him to lift his head from the stream, water trickling from his muzzle. Turning in the direction of the sound, ears pricked, he listened intently for a moment. When the rumble came again, he trotted eagerly in its direction, ears erect and alert, nose held high.

As he neared the source of the sound, a new smell filled his incredibly sensitive nostrils. It was acrid and distinct and he knew without having to think that he had smelled it before. But so intent was he on tracking the sound that he put off giving a name to it.

A dark shape, sleek and muscular, materialized from a thick copse of brush nearby. Startled by the unexpected appearance, he bristled and bared his teeth. Recognition quickly allayed any concern. Though far larger and stronger, the shape was familiar. Astonished at the incongruity, both parties stared at one another for a long moment. Then they turned together and, without speaking a word between them, sped off side by side, tracking the source of the sound.

It appeared so abruptly neither of them had a chance to change course, or retreat. Looming over the trees before them, it advanced like soup rising to a fast boil. Devoid of color and nasty of countenance, it swamped the trees, turning bark to black and presenting death as a shower of green needles. Ehomba and his companion turned and tried to flee, but it was too late. The dire emptiness swallowed them both. Most of the sharpened senses he had become heir to vanished: the keen sight, the splendid hearing, the acute taste. Only smell remained, and was rapidly overwhelmed. The acrid, dry, lifeless stink of the eromakadi filled his nostrils, seared his throat, and threatened to inundate his lungs, causing them to swell until they burst. . . .

He blinked, and coughed, but not loudly or harshly. He was back in the main room of the cottage. A few flames still leaped hesitantly from the pile of glowing clinkers that was all that remained of the once blazing fire. In his chair, Simna ibn Sind slept the sleep of spirituous stupefaction. But the litah no longer stretched across the floor from wall to wall. He had curled himself into a tight ball of black fur and was twitching and moaning in his sleep.

"It will pass."

Looking down, Ehomba saw that the sheepdog was watching the larger animal. Turning her head, her warm brown eyes met his. "The big cat was in your dream. Sometimes that will happen. Dreams are like smoke. If there happens to be more than one in the same sleep space, sometimes they will merge and flow together. I don't think that was the kind of dream the cat is used to, but when he wakes he may well not remember any of it." The witch eyes stared. "You remember, though."

"Yes, I remember," the herdsman admitted. "But I do not know what it means."

"You asked me if I could help you see what lies ahead of you. I did as you asked. I was with you and you with me, watching, perceiving, trying to understand." Rising and walking forward, she lifted a paw and placed it on his bare thigh.

"You are doomed to unremitting misery, your quest to failure, the rest of your life to cold emptiness. Unless you end this now. Go home, back to your village and back to your family. Before it is too late. Before you die." Her paw slipped off his leg.

Ehomba looked away, feeling the warmth of the fire against his back, and considered the dog's words. They were words he had heard before, in a town far, far to the south, from someone else. Another female, but not a dog. Another seeress, but one who walked on two legs instead of four. They were very different, Roileé and Rael, and yet they had spoken to him the same words. It was not encouraging.

"I cannot go back. Not until I have fulfilled a dying man's promise. I took that upon myself willingly, and no matter how many prophets and diviners repeat to me the same death mantra I will follow this through to its end."

"From what I just saw and felt, its end will be your end." This pronouncement she delivered in a matter-of-fact manner and without emotion.

"That remains to be seen. It is your interpretation, and that of one other. Events will convince me, not divinations."

"I can only do what you asked me to do."

He smiled gently. "I know, and I thank you for that." Automatically, he reached out and patted her on the head. If he had thought about it he might not have done so, but he need not have worried. Instead of upbraiding him for his temerity, she moved nearer and pressed her muzzle and head against his comforting palm.

"There are some things," she explained, "for which even witchcraft cannot substitute. A kind and comforting hand is one."

"I understand." Sitting there on the hearth, he continued to pet her. "There are many times since I left the village that I could have used such a touch myself."

"You are a good man, Etjole Ehomba." Her head pushed insistently against his soothing palm and she panted easily in the reflected heat of the fire. "The world is a poorer place whenever a good man dies."

"Or a good dog," he added graciously.

"Or a good dog."

"Do not worry. I have no intention of dying."

"Then do not disregard what I have just told you. Try to overcome it. Make me out to be a liar."

He grinned. "I will do my best. Now, tell me something I can use. What lies to the north of here, below these mountains? Coubert spoke of many small kingdoms."

"He spoke accurately." She turned her head up to him but did not move away from his hand. "Lamidy is a learned man, but there are many in the towns and cities to the north who could put his erudition to shame. Not all of them are kind and decent," she warned the herdsman. "You may have to match wits with more than one. I have looked inside your mind, but only a little. I don't know if you're up to it."

"I will manage." He spoke reassuringly if not with complete confidence. "I have always managed. Learning does not frighten me."

"That's good. What of your companions?"

Ehomba eyed his sleeping fellow travelers. "The litah is smarter than anyone thinks but prefers not to show it. No one will expect anything more scholarly from a big cat than a roar or loud meow anyway. As for Simna ibn Sind, his smarts are of a kind not to be found in books and

scrolls, and a valuable complement to my own poor insight in such areas."

The she-dog sniffed. "I don't know if that will be enough to get you
safely through places like Melespra or Phan. When you are uncertain,
look to the night sky, to the left of the moon. There is a certain star there
that may help to guide you safely through moments of uncertainty."

"What star is that?"

"The dog star, of course," she told him. "It is there if you need it, for
serious travelers to follow. That is all I can do for you."

Ehomba nodded appreciatively. "It will have to be enough." Rising,
he yawned sleepily. "The dream was as tiring as it was interesting. I think
I had better get some rest, or tomorrow my friends will lecture me endlessly on my neglect. You must be tired, too."

The witch dog stretched first her front end, then her rear, and also
yawned, her tongue quivering with the effort. "Yes. Magic is always ex-
hausting."

"As must be herding lightning," he reminded her as he sought somehow to compact his lanky frame enough for the couch to accommodate
it.

"No." Head snuggled up against tail, she curled up in front of the
fire. "That was fun."

In the morning Coubert made breakfast for them, providing eggs and
lamb chops and bread, along with a complete haunch of mutton for the
grudgingly grateful Ahlitah. When Ehomba protested at this largesse,
the sheepherder only smiled.

"I have plenty of food. It must be something in these mountains.
The air, or the water, or the forage, but my sheep do better than anyone
else's. They grow fatter, and produce thicker wool, and drop more
lambs."

"You are fortunate," Ehomba told him even as he glanced in the
direction of a certain dog. But Roileé did not react, busy gnawing methodically on a scrungy femur.

"You'll hit Bebrol first," Coubert was telling them. On the other side
of the table, Simna was devouring all that was set before him. "It is the
southernmost town in the Dukedom of Tethspraih. A small province, but
a proud one. North of Tethspraih lies Phan, an altogether more wealthy
and cosmopolitan sort of place. You three will stand out in Tethspraih,
but not so much in Phan and the larger kingdoms. If you want to make
time you should keep to yourselves as much as possible."

"We always do." His mouth full of mutton, the swordsman had difficulty speaking.

"How far from Phan to Hamacassar?" Ehomba ate delicately but steadily.

Coubert sat back in his chair, fork in one hand, and pondered, his lower lip pushing out past the upper edge of his beard. "Hard for me to say. I've never been that far north. Never even met anyone who has." His smile returned. "You'll be able to get more accurate information in Phan. More tea?"

"No, no thank you." Simna wiped at his greasy lips with the back of his forearm. "Your fount of generosity filled me with enough liquid last night. Now I need to fill my gut with solid stuff to sop it up." He punctuated his confession by shoving a sizable chunk of brown bread into his mouth.

"At least let me top off your supplies. I don't know what resources you have."

Food muffled Simna's grunted response. "Hoy! Spent most of our resources, we have."

"You have been too kind to us already," Ehomba told him, ignoring the swordsman's bugging eyes and frantic semaphoring.

"Please allow me to help. It's my pleasure. I have so much, and your journey is of noble intent." Pushing back his chair, he placed his linen napkin on the table and rose. "Besides, Roileé seems to like you, and over the years I've come to trust her judgment. Strange how sometimes a dog can be more perceptive than a person."

"Passing strange," agreed Ehomba. From her place prone on the floor, the witch dog winked at him. No one else saw it, as was intended.

They departed the cottage with their packs stuffed full of jerked mutton and their water bags filled to overflowing. Though Coubert offered to supply one, Ahlitah refused to wear a pack. It was enough, he growled, that he was compelled to suffer the company of men. To expect him to adopt, however temporarily, their constricting accoutrements was too much. He would remain free physically if not otherwise.

Coubert stood in the doorway of his home and waved until they passed out of sight. His dog sat at his feet, saluting their departure with several joyful yips and barks.

"Nice dog, that one," Simna was moved to comment as he hitched his heavy pack higher on his shoulders. "Getting on in years, but still good company."

"More than you know." As always, Ehomba's gaze was focused forward, scanning the lay of the land ahead of them. "She was a witch."

"Hoy? By Gyerboh, I never would have guessed!" The swordsman looked back the way they had come, but the little cottage had already disappeared from view, swallowed up by rolling boulders and brush and the gentle incline they were now descending. "How could you tell?"

"She told me. And showed me some things. In a dream."

Ahlitah looked around sharply. "So that was not a dream within a dream. Thought it might have been you there with me, but couldn't be sure." The big cat shook its head and the great black mane flowed and rippled. "Don't remember much of it. What were you doing in my dream, man?"

"I thought you were in mine. Not that it matters."

Simna's bewilderment underlined his words. "What the Ghoska are you two babbling about?"

"Nothing. Nothing real." Ehomba stepped over a wandering rivulet, doing his best to avoid crushing the tiny flowers that fought for life on its far side. "It is all gone, like smoke."

The swordsman snorted derisively, a common reaction when Ehomba or the cat spoke of things he did not understand. After a while he exclaimed, "So she was a witch, was she? I've known bitches who thought they were witches, but this is the first one who fully qualifies on both counts."

"She was righteous, and helpful." The herdsman did not tell his friend that Roileé had recapitulated the virulent prediction that had first been read to him in distant Kora Keri.

"A man can't ask any more of a bitch, be she witch or otherwise." Pleased with that proclamation of itinerant swordsman sagacity, Simna took the lead. "It'll be great to be back among civilized society again, where a man can find decent food and drink wherever he turns. And perhaps even a little entertainment." His eyes flashed.

"As you yourself pointed out to Coubert, our assets are much reduced. We need to conserve them for necessities, my friend."

"Hoy, bruther, I can see that you and I need to achieve a consensus on just what constitutes a necessity."

They discussed the matter of their meager remaining resources as they walked. When it came to the laying out of specifics, the litah sided with Simna, the only difference being that while the big cat sympathized with and understood the swordsman's baser needs, he himself had no use for any human medium of exchange, being accustomed as he was to taking what he required when he needed it, and slaughtering the rest.

X

Because the mountains that formed the southern boundary of the Thinking Kingdoms sloped so gently from their heights, the travelers did not encounter the grand, sweeping panorama that might have been expected. Instead, they came upon the first outlying pastures and villages of Tethspraih unexpectedly and without drama.

Unlike the farms they had seen south of the Aboqua, these were not patches of forest or desert reclaimed for planting. Neat hedgerows and stone walls demarcated fields that had been planted and harvested for hundreds of years. Venerable irrigation canals carried water to faultlessly straight furrows. There were fields of wheat and rye as well as vegetables and ground-hugging fruits, orchards as tidily pruned as flower beds, vineyards clean enough to sleep in. Sturdier trees hung heavy with nut crops, and melons lined the ridges of water-filled ditches like bumps on a lizard's hide. Flocks of songbirds and small parrots filled the trees with color and the air with song. All were intoxicated with pigment, a golden parrot sporting a bright emerald crest being the most prevalent. A small flock of these opalescent birds performed aerial acrobatics above the heads of the travelers as they advanced, as if greeting them with avian sign language.

Flowers brightened the fronts of even the smallest houses, and the weed-free dirt roads soon gave way to sophisticated stone paving. They passed through small clusters of homes and craft shops that had not quite matured into villages, and then into the first real towns. Wherever they went they excited stares and gossip among the well-dressed populace, due in large part to the inability of even the most supercilious residents to ignore the hulking presence of Ahlitah on their spotless streets. But Ehomba and Simna drew their fair share of stares as well, thanks to their exotic costume and barbaric aspect.

"I don't like being the object of everyone's interest." The swordsman strode along insolently, oblivious to the giggling of the women and the disapproving glares of the men. "This would be a hard place for us to hide—if we needed to hide."

"I fear we will just have to resign ourselves to being conspicuous." The worn butt of Ehomba's spear clacked against the stone of the sidewalk every time he took a stride forward. "This is a much more cosseted country than any we have passed through previously. I do not mind them looking down on us, or thinking we are uncivilized savages, so long as they leave us free to go on our way."

"We don't need food. Our good friend the sheepherder saw to that." The swordsman was peering hopefully at storefronts and into windows of real glass. "But I could use something stronger than tea to drink. It was an easy hike but a long one out of those mountains."

Ehomba sighed resignedly. "You always need something to drink."

His friend shrugged. "Can I help it if I have thin blood?"

"I think a thin constitution is more like it." From his greater height, the southerner searched the street on which they found themselves. "But a tavern is a good place to find information. And that, friend Coubert did not supply in great quantities." Lowering the tip of his spear, he gestured at a likely-looking establishment. Birds nested in the eaves above the entrance, suggesting either that they were inured to noise and violence or that it was a well-behaved place.

The nattily dressed owner took a stance directly opposite the door as soon as he saw what had entered. His disapproving scowl vanished the instant Ahlitah's eye caught his, and he seemed to shrink several inches. While he did not invite them in, neither did he find it expedient to bar their way. Mindful of the fuss their foreign presence had roused, Ehomba and his companions settled themselves in the most isolated booth in the place, thereby relieving the perspiring owner of one major concern, if not exactly endearing themselves to him.

Gold from Simna's rapidly dwindling Chlennguu hoard turned out to be as welcome in Tethspraih as anywhere else, and drink was duly if coolly brought. The tired travelers drank, and watched the comings and goings of patrons, admiring the cut of their fine clothing. Silk and satin were much in evidence, and this was only a modest municipality and not one of the Thinking Kingdom's great cities. Its citizens smelled of wealth and prosperity. And yet, beneath the superficial veneer of general happiness, Ehomba sensed overtones of discontent, of pockets of gloom scattered among the comfortable like measles on a beautiful girl's countenance.

Thoughtfully, he turned back to the mug set before him. Its contents were refined, and warmed his belly. A bright-eyed Simna was already on his second.

"By Goilen-ghosen, Etjole, will you never put away that long face?" The swordsman waved at their impeccable, almost elegant, surroundings. "There's no danger here, no threat. We're not out in the hinterlands of nowhere now, dealing with mad horses and all-consuming black clouds. Can't you relax?"

"I will relax when this journey is done and I am back home with my friends and family."

"Hoy, what a melancholy, brooding traveling companion you are. Might as well be roaming with an undertaker."

"That is not fair," Ehomba protested. "I enjoy a good laugh as much as the next person. And have done so, in your presence."

"Yeah, yeah, so you have. I'm not saying you don't have a sense of humor. It's your general attitude that sours the air around you."

"Then maybe you should point your nose in a different direction!" Seeing that other patrons were staring at them, he lowered his voice. "It is just that when I am not talking, I am always thinking."

Simna was smiling at a distant woman, who was gracefully clad in a flowing dress with fine lace trim. She smiled back, seemed abruptly to remember herself, and turned haughtily away—but not before sneaking another surreptitious glance in the swordsman's direction. He flashed her another grin.

"Then that's your curse, Etjole. Myself, when I'm not talking, I'm not thinking. It's a very restful way to live and lets a man sink into the world instead of having it dumped on his shoulders. You should try it sometime." He took a hearty swallow from the mug before him.

"I have," Ehomba replied disconsolately. "It does not seem to work for me."

Simna nodded understandingly. "Actually, we should both envy him." He gestured with the mug at the black litah. The heavily muscled predator was lying with its spine against the back wall, eyes closed, sound asleep. "Cats now, they not only know how to relax, they've made an art of it."

Abruptly, the laughter and bubbling conversation that filled the tavern died. Through the main doorway, a knot of men had entered as one. The owner, who had been prepared to challenge Ehomba and his friends, did not even attempt to bar their entry. Instead, he moved hastily aside, bowing his head several times out of fearful respect. As soon as they had identified the intruders, the rest of the apprehensive patrons resumed their conversations, keeping their voices unnaturally low.

The men and women wore uniforms of loose-fitting yellow and white, with high-puffed front-lidded caps and yellow leather boots. They carried rapiers and flintlock pistols, whose function the more worldly Simna had to explain to the astonished Ehomba. He had never encountered firearms before, though itinerant traders who occasionally made forays into Naumkib country spoke of seeing such things in the southern cities of Askaskos and Wallab.

The leader of the intruders was a big, burly individual with a profound mustache and close-cropped red hair. As he led his people deeper into the tavern, Ehomba was surprised to see that two of the uniforms were worn by grim-faced older women.

They finally halted before the travelers' table. Hands rested as inconspicuously as possible close to pistol butts and sword hilts. "You!" the leader declared.

"Us?" Simna responded querulously.

"Yes. You are under arrest and are to come with us immediately."

"Under arrest?" An openly confused Simna frowned. "By Gobula, what for? Who are you?"

Muted laughter rose from the uniformed intruders at this blatant confession of ignorance. Their leader, however, hushed them sternly. He did not smile.

"You are obviously strangers here, so it is not surprising you do not know. We are the Servitors of the Guardians of Right Thinking, and you are under arrest for improper contemplations."

"Improper contemplations?" Ehomba's face contorted. "What is that?"

"Thinking not in alignment or kind with the approved general mode of thinking decreed for Tethspraih," the mind cop informed him importantly.

"Well," murmured Ehomba, "since we just arrived in your country, there is no way we could know what constitutes approved thinking and what does not, now could we? I have never heard of such a thing."

"Hoy, that's true," Simna concurred self-righteously. "How can you arrest us for violating some ordinance we know nothing about?"

"I am only following orders. I was told to bring you to the rectory." His fingers hovered close to his sword, and those behind him tensed. On the far side of the tavern, two couples departed in haste without paying their bill. The owner, a petrified expression on his face, did not go after them.

Simna's jaw tightened and his own hand started to shift, but Ehomba raised a hand to forestall him. "Of course we will go with you."

The swordsman gaped at him. "We will?"

"We do not want any trouble. And I would like to know who has been reading our thoughts, and how."

"Well, I wouldn't."

"Then stay." Ehomba waked Ahlitah, whose unexpected and suddenly looming presence swiftly wiped the complacent smiles from the faces of the police contingent. After whispering an explanation to the big cat, it nodded once and ambled out from behind the table. The police drew back farther, but at a sign from their leader kept their weapons holstered and sheathed.

"I'm glad you've decided to cooperate." The officer nodded in the big cat's direction and invoked a grateful smile. "Very glad."

"We have just arrived here and we do not want to make any trouble." Ehomba started toward the door. "Let us go to this rectory and see what is wanted of us."

Simna hesitated, growled something nasty under his breath, then picked up his own pack and followed, falling in beside his friend. "You better know what you're doing," he whispered as the police escorted them out onto the street and turned left. "I don't like jails."

The herdsman barely glanced in his companion's direction. He was much more interested in their new surroundings and in the people who were staring back at him than in the swordsman's complaints. The citizens of the Dukedom were wholly human; no other simians here. No intelligent apes and orangs, chimps or bonobos. To his way of thinking it rendered the otherwise imposing town a poorer place.

Striding along importantly in the forefront, the police official led them through the streets, past stores and restaurants, apartments and workshops, until they crossed a neatly paved square to halt outside the towering wooden door of a large stone structure. It was decorated with finely sculpted portraits of men and women holding all manner of articles upon which writing had been incised. There were tablets and scrolls, bare slabs of rock, and thickly bound books. The graven expressions of the statues bespoke ancient wisdom and the accumulation of centuries of knowledge.

Other signatures of learning festooned the building: chemical apparatus and tools whose function was unknown to Ehomba, mathematical signs and symbols, human figures raising bridges and towers and other structures—all indicating a reverence for knowledge and erudition. For the endemic songbirds and parrots the multiplicity of sculptures provided a nesting ground that verged on the paradisiacal.

Simna was openly mystified. "This doesn't have the look or feel of any jail I ever spent time in."

"You are especially knowledgeable in that area?" Ehomba inquired dryly.

"Hoy, sure!" the swordsman replied cheerfully. "Just part of my extensive résumé of experience."

The herdsman grunted as the door was opened wide by an acolyte clad in a simple white robe emblazoned with mathematical symbols. "We may need to draw on it. Though prior to this journey I had spent little time in towns, I am pretty sure that a police escort is not sent forth to escort people anywhere other than to a jail."

It did not look much like a lockup, however. Simna continued to offer unsolicited comments on their surroundings as they were marched inside. There were no cells, no bars, no downcast prisoners shuffling about in irons. The interior was a fair spiritual and aesthetic reflection of the exterior, with uncowled monks busy at desks and laboratory tables, delving deep into books or arguing animatedly about this or that matter of science.

They were taken to a large chamber that was more like a comfortable living room than a theater of interrogation and directed to seat themselves opposite an empty, curved table. A trio of monks, two men and one woman all of serious mien and middle age, marched in. As soon as they took their chairs, the police official stepped forward and saluted by pressing his open palm to his forehead and then pulling it quickly away in a broad, sweeping gesture.

"Here are the ones you sent us to bring, Exalted Savant."

Simna leaned over to whisper to his friend. "Hoy, let me guess. These are the right high and mighty Guardians of Right Thinking. If you ask me, they look a little bent. I like the gold embroidery on those white robes, though."

"You like anything gold," Ehomba snapped.

The swordsman weighed his friend's comment. "Not always. When I was a stripling I remember a certain aunt whose mouth was full of gold teeth. Whenever she bent to kiss me I would cry. I thought her teeth were solid metal, like little gold swords, and that she was going to eat me up."

"Be quiet," the herdsman admonished him, "and maybe we can get out of here without any fuss if we satisfy them as to our purpose in being in their country." Behind him and slightly to his right, Ahlitah sat on his haunches and busied himself cleaning his face, utterly indifferent to however the humans, friends and strangers alike, might elect to proceed.

"Welcome to Tethspraih." The man in the middle folded his hands on the table before him and smiled. His expression was, as best as Ehomba could tell, genuine.

"Funny sort of way you've got of welcoming strangers," Simna retorted promptly. Ehomba gave him a sharp nudge in the ribs.

The woman was instantly concerned. "Were you wounded while being brought here? Are you in pain? Or are you suffering from injuries incurred while coming down from the Aniswoar Mountains?"

"We are unhurt." Ehomba eyed her curiously. "How did you know we came from those mountains? We could as easily have entered your land from the east, or the west."

Simna commented sarcastically. "I know how, long bruther. A little birdie told them."

The monk seated on the left, with a pleasant round face and twinkling eyes, sat a little straighter. "That's right! That's exactly right." Lowering his voice, he murmured to his associates. "They have been talking to citizens."

"No," insisted the man in the middle. "I think he is just perceptive."

"Funny." The woman was staring at Simna. "He doesn't look perceptive."

Ehomba hastened to draw the conversation away from his companion. "We were told that we were brought here because our thinking was 'not in alignment' with the kind of thinking you have decreed for this country. I never heard of such a thing. How can you decree what people can think?"

"Not 'what,'" the woman corrected him. "'How.' It's the way people think that we are concerned with. What they think about is not our concern."

"Absolutely not," added the man on the far end. "That would constitute an inexcusable invasion of privacy."

Ehomba was unconvinced. "And telling people how to think does not?"

"Not at all." The beaming monk in the center unfolded his hands and placed them flat on the table. The subdued light in the chamber made the gold symbols on his robe dance and sparkle. "It leads to a thriving and prosperous society. Wouldn't you agree that what you've seen of Tethspraih is flourishing, that the people are as healthy and attractive as their surroundings?"

"I would," the herdsman conceded. Not only had these people allowed him and Simna to keep their weapons during the interrogation, but the litah had also been permitted to accompany them into this inner sanctum. This suggested great confidence. But in what? The armed servitors who had escorted him and his friends were stationed outside the chamber. Insofar as he could tell, not one of the monks carried so much as a dagger. What could they do to defend themselves if, for example, someone like Simna lost his temper and leaped at them with sword drawn? Sitting behind their table, they appeared quite indifferent to any danger the armed strangers might pose. Ehomba was simultaneously impressed and wary, and curious to know why.

"All right." The swordsman sighed. "Tell us what we have to do to get out of here. If it's a fine, we'll try to come up with the money to pay it."

"Oh no. Fining you would be a useless gesture characteristic of primitive extortionate regimes." The woman was smiling at him once again. "We might as well put a knife to your ribs in the middle of the street. We'd never think of doing such a thing."

"No indeed," the middle monk added. "We are not an agency of punishment, fiduciary or physical."

Simna relaxed a little. "Hoy, that's good to hear."

"Then what do you want of us?" Unlike his friend, Ehomba did not relax. "Why have we been brought here?"

"Why, so you can be helped, of course." The smiles of the three were brighter than ever.

At this pronouncement the swordsman lost his composure. "What do you mean, 'helped'?"

The monk on the end gazed across at him with infinite compassion. "To think appropriately, of course."

Simna ibn Sind did not like the sound of that. He did not like the sound of it one bit. "Thanks, but I've been thinking for myself for nigh on thirty-one years now, and I'm comfortable with the process just as it is. Set in my ways, you might say."

"Oh, that's all right," the monk assured him. "It's a consideration common to many improper thinkers, and one easily corrected. Don't worry—we'll take care of it for you."

"By Gambrala, do I have to spell it out for you? I don't want 'it' taken care of!"

Ehomba put a calming hand on his companion's shoulder. A by now highly agitated Simna shook it off, but out of consideration for his friend held back the stream of words his tongue was preparing to launch.

"Why do you care how we think?" The herdsman addressed the panel in a voice calm with respect and genuine interest. "We come from other lands and are just passing through your country. With luck we will be beyond the borders of Tethspraih and inside Phan in a few days. Then our way of thinking will no longer concern you."

The woman was shaking her head slowly. "If we allowed that to happen we would be derelict in our duty to our fellow man. All of us would have to do penance."

"If you treat every visitor this way I'd think you wouldn't have much trade with your neighbors." Simna had calmed down—a little.

"Some of our neighbors are amenable to persuasion," the monk on the end informed them. "With others we have treaties that, regrettably, prohibit us from exposing them to the satisfactions that come with decreed thinking. But we have no such treaty with you."

"And because of that," the man in the center added, "we have a wonderful opportunity to spread right thinking to countries whose names we may not even know! Because when you return to your homelands it will be as disciples for the Tethspraih way of life."

"I got news for you," Simna retorted. "The only way of life I'm a disciple for is the Simna ibn Sind way of life. It's pretty popular in its own right, and while I'm real fond of it myself, I'd no more run around trying to inflict it on someone else than I would try to make them eat my favorite pudding."

"We can fix that." The man on the end wore a big smile that thoroughly belied the implied threat behind his words.

"No one said anything to us about such things when we entered your country," Ehomba told them. "If they had, we would have avoided Tethspraih, and gone around its borders."

"The sheepherder should have told you." The woman shook her head sadly. "What a waste of a fine mind. The majority of his thinking is improper."

When he had first met Lamidy Coubert, Ehomba had been unable to understand why such a gregarious and congenial individual would choose a life of isolation in the high mountains. Now he knew. Perhaps Roileé had helped him to escape. But the average citizen of Tethspraih had no bitch witch to assist him or her in flight. Prosperous and successful they might be, but they were trapped here. Or perhaps, he corrected himself, their bodies were free, and only their minds were ensnared.

"I do not know what you mean by proper or improper thinking," he told them. "I know only that my friend Simna thinks the way he thinks, and I think the way I think, and Ahlitah thinks the way he thinks—and that is how we will continue to think."

"We are not concerned about the great cat," the woman replied. "Such beasts are creatures of instinct and not reason." At these words the litah paused momentarily in cleaning its face, then resumed licking and brushing. It seemed content to let Ehomba deal with the controversy.

"But you and your friend will be brought into the fold. And you will be the happier for it."

"I'm already happy enough," an angry Simna retorted. "And I'll stomp anyone who says different!" His fingers grasped the hilt of his sword.

Despite this openly hostile gesture, none of the three monks behind the table reacted apprehensively. From what Ehomba could see, they did not even tense. Where was their protection? he found himself wondering. How were they able to remain completely unruffled in the face of an implied challenge from an obviously agitated, intemperate personality like Simna?

Despite their intransigent words, he was still hoping to avoid a confrontation. With that in mind, he again tried to divert their attention from the combative swordsman. "I do not understand. How did you know how we were thinking when we entered your country? Something must have told you or you would not have been able to send your servitors, your police, to that tavern to find us."

"Your friend already knows, and explained it." The monk in the middle sat back slightly in his chair and smiled deprecatingly. "A little bird told us."

Turning toward the door, he snapped his fingers twice. Simna tensed, expecting the armed servitors to enter. Instead, a young white-clad acolyte appeared. His robe was emblazoned with only two golden symbols. In the wire cage he carried, two small golden parrots were chattering and chirping contentedly. Ehomba remembered seeing their like among the flocks of songbirds that had announced their arrival in Tethspraih. And they had been common in the eaves above the tavern, and in the streets of the town, and among the stone sculptures that festooned the rectory.

They looked like ordinary birds, more spectacularly plumaged than some, less active than others. No more, no less.

After placing the cage on the table, the acolyte bowed respectfully to his superiors and backed out the way he had come. As he passed through the door, Ehomba noted that at least some of the armed servitors remained stationed in the hall outside. While impressive, the monks' confidence was evidently not absolute.

The middle speaker placed an affectionate hand on the top of the cage. "These are Spraithian cockatells. They are very good mimics. Most parrots and other members of their related families can listen to human speech and recite it back. Cockatells are able to do the same with thoughts."

"So that's how you spy on your people." Simna's lips were tight. "We saw the damn little shitters everywhere. How can someone's thoughts be

their own if there's a bird on every windowsill, in every branch, on the
fence post outside each house, soaking up what and how they're thinking? And of course, you people have 'em trained like pigeons, so that
after soaking up enough thoughts they come flying back here, where you
can milk them of other folks' privacy."

"You make it sound like a forced intrusion," the woman responded
disapprovingly. "No one is harmed, no one senses the cockatells at work,
and peace and prosperity reign throughout the land." Reaching into a
pocket of her robe, she removed something and stuck it between the bars
of the cage. The vivacious, feathered pair immediately descended from
the perch where they had been chattering to nibble eagerly at the proffered gift. "In addition, they are playful, attractive birds."

"I didn't see anyone playing with 'em," Simna responded. "And why
do I have this gut feeling they're not real popular as pets?"

"Do not blame the birds." Ehomba gently admonished his friend. "It
is not their fault they have been put to such a use. I doubt they have any
notion of what they are involved in." He watched the pair use their sharp
beaks to shell and then spit out the husks of tiny seeds. "As the savants
say, they are only mimics. They listen, and repeat, but do not understand."

"You couldn't find better spies," Simna growled. His outrage at the
invasion of his innermost privacy was complete, but out of deference to
his friend his sword stayed in its scabbard.

"So from what you have learned from some birds you have decided
that our manner of thinking is wrong, and that you have the right to
change it. Even if we are happy with the way we think and do not want it
changed." The herdsman met each of the savants' eyes in turn.

"You will thank us when we are done." The woman was beaming
again. "You," she declared, directing her words to the quietly fuming
Simna, "will become a much more pleasant and less belligerent person,
one who is kind to others and supportive of extended contemplation."

"By Gouzpoul, don't count on it." The swordsman's fingers tightened on the hilt of his weapon.

"And you," she continued as she turned slightly to face Ehomba,
"will become a teacher, devoting your life to the spreading of the way of
proper thinking among uncivilized peoples."

"It sounds like an admirable calling," Ehomba told her. "Unfortunately, I already have one. There are cattle to be supervised, and chores
to be done. The Naumkib must give over all their waking hours to surviving. I have no time to devote to the profession of wandering teacher. You
need to find another."

"You are the first of your people to visit Tethspraih." The monk seated at the other end of the table was speaking forcefully. "As such, you must be the one to carry our teachings to your land. It is a great honor."

"Yes," added the middle savant. "Besides, you have no choice. You do not have to waste time and energy arguing about it because the decision has been made for you." He smiled encouragingly, reassuringly. "That is the job of savants. To make the right choices for others. We prevent many headaches before they happen."

"Then why are you giving me one now?" Simna ibn Sind had listened to just about enough. Avoiding Ehomba's attempt to restrain him, the swordsman took a bold step forward and drew his blade. Sensing his thoughts, the pair of cockatells stopped eating and fell back to the far side of their cage. They remained huddled together there, their shimmering golden feathers quivering slightly as they were forced to listen to and absorb the blast of unfettered aggression from the swordsman's mind.

Showing that they were indeed human, the savants reacted to Simna's provocation by losing their seemingly everlasting smiles. But no one leaped from their chair or tried to flee. Nor did anyone raise a warning cry to the servitors stationed outside.

Instead, the monk in the center reached quickly beneath the table and brought out a most curious-looking device. The length of a man's arm, it had a handle and a long tubular body that was fluted and flared at the end like an open flower. One finger curled around a small curve of metal set into the underside of the apparatus. Attached to the top was a small bottle or canister. This was fashioned of an opaque substance and Ehomba could not see what it contained.

Resting the wooden handle against his shoulder, the savant pointed the flowerlike end of the device directly at Simna. Exposed blade hanging at his side, the swordsman's gaze narrowed as he stared down the barrel of the awkward contrivance. Not knowing what it did, he was unsure how to deal with the threat its wielder's posture implicitly implied.

"Simna," the herdsman told his friend warningly, "that's enough! Stay where you are!"

The monk at the far end of the table spoke somberly. "It does not matter. Advance or retreat, the end will be the same." His smile returned, though in muted form. "And you will be the better for it."

"The better for it?" Simna glared furiously at the man, utterly frustrated by the unshakable composure of the smugly complacent trio seated behind the table. "I'll be the better for *this*!" Raising the shining blade over his head, he took another step forward. Ehomba shouted a warning and Ahlitah crouched, instantly alert.

The monk aiming the device did not hesitate as he pulled the trigger and fired.

XI

The litah snarled warningly but held his ground. Ehomba instinctively drew back. As for Simna, he ducked sharply, frowned, and then straightened anew. To all outward appearances he was entirely unharmed.

The cloud of powder that puffed from the muzzle of the strange device was primarily pink with deeper overtones of cerise. It enveloped the swordsman for the briefest of moments before dissipating in the still air of the chamber. Simna sniffed once, twice, and then laughed out loud.

"A decent little fragrance. Delicate, not too strong. Reminds me of a girl I spent some time with in a town on the western edge of the Abrangian Steppes."

"Good." The monk lowered the contraption but did not set it aside. "I'm glad it brings back fond memories for you."

"Very fond." Simna grinned wolfishly at the savant. "Fonder than you'll ever know."

"That may very well be true. You are obviously a man of extensive appetites. Mine, I am not ashamed to confess, are more modest. In that respect I envy you, though I cannot say that my envy translates into admiration." He indicated the swordsman's upraised weapon. His two associates were watching closely. "What, may I ask, were you planning to do with that impressive-looking piece of steel?"

Simna looked down at the sword in his hand. "This? Why, I was going to . . . I was going to . . ."

His words trailed away along with his anger. He stared stupidly at the weapon, as if he had once known its purpose but had forgotten, like someone who finds a long-lost piece of clothing in an old drawer and cannot remember how it is to be worn. Slowly, he lowered the blade. His expression brightened when he remembered the scabbard that hung from his belt. Sheathing the metal, he looked back at the trio of inquisitors and smiled.

"There! I guess that's what I was going to do with it." The smile plastered on his face resembled that of several of the lesser sculptures that decorated the exterior of the rectory: bemused, but not vacuous. "I hope we're not giving you good people any trouble?"

"No," the woman told him confidently, "no trouble at all. It's nice to see you right thinking. A lot less painful, isn't it?"

"It sure is." But even as Simna spoke, his lips seemed to be doing battle with his jawline. Small veins pulsed in his forehead and neck, and perspiration broke out on his forehead even though it was quite cool in the darkened chamber. Everything about his expression and posture indicated a man at war with himself—and losing. One hand trembled visibly as it attempted to clutch the hilt of the now sheathed sword. The fingers would twitch convulsively forward and miss, twitch and miss, as if their owner was afflicted with any one of several neuromuscular infirmities.

It was dispiriting to watch Simna take a step toward the table. One leg worked well enough, but the other hung back, obviously reluctant, as if fastened to the floor by metal bolts. The paralyzed grin on the swordsman's face hinted at internal mental as well as physical conflict.

"Better," the monk in the middle declared tersely even as he raised the singular device and pointed it in Ehomba's direction. "As your friend can tell you, this won't hurt a bit. A few weekly treatments and your thinking will be right as rain."

"Yes," agreed the man on his left. "Then you can choose freely whether to return to your homeland, or remain here in beautiful Tethspraih, or continue on your way. Whichever you do, it will be as a contemporary, right-thinking person, with none of the irritating emotional and intellectual baggage that so cripples the bulk of humanity."

"I like my intellectual baggage," Ehomba responded. "It is what makes me an individual."

"So do unfortunately inherent human tendencies to commit murder and mayhem." The woman succored him with an angelic smile. "But they do not contribute to the improvement of the person."

Ehomba tried to duck, to twist out of the way, but it was far more difficult to avoid a cloud than a spear thrust. As the pallid vapor enveloped him he tried not to inhale, only to find that it was not necessary to breathe in the powder directly to experience its effects. The delicate fragrance was an ancillary effect of the substance, not an indicator of its efficacy. It sank in through his eyes, his lips, the skin of his exposed arms and ankles and neck, from where it penetrated to the core of his being. While his feet remained firmly on the floor, he felt his mind beginning to drift, to float. Ahead lay a pillowed rosy cloud, beckoning to him with pastel tendrils while masking his view of the three savants. He was aware that they were continuing to observe him closely. If only he would let himself relax and fully embrace the mist, a great deal of the inner torment and uncertainty that had plagued him throughout his life would vanish, dispersed as painlessly and effectively as vinegar would kill a scorpion's sting.

He fought back. He conjured up stark images of Mirhanja and the children that were faithful down to the smallest detail. He recalled the time he had been fishing in the stream the village used as its source of fresh water, and had stepped on a spiny crawfish. The remembrance of that pain pushed back the insistent vapor, but only for a moment. He recalled the specifics of discussions he had engaged in with the village elders, and arguments he'd had with his wife, and the day they had celebrated his mother's eightieth birthday and it had rained on everyone and everything. He reviewed the minutiae of his journey to this time and place, assigning each an emotion and a day.

He did everything he could think of to keep his thoughts his own— even if they were not "right."

"He's fighting it." Through the brume of befuddlement that threatened to overwhelm him he heard the woman's voice. She still sounded confident, but not quite as confident as previously.

"His channels of thought are more deeply worn and solidly set than those of his companion." This from the monk seated at the other end of the table. "Give him another dose."

"So soon?" The senior of the trio sounded uncertain.

"We don't want to lose him to irresolution." The other man's tone was kindly but firm. "It won't hurt him. He's strong. At worst it may cost him some old memories. A small price to pay for a lifetime of proper thinking."

Benumbed within the fog of right thinking, Ehomba heard what they planned for him, and panicked. What memories might he lose if subjected to another dose of the corrective dust? A day hunting with his father? Favorite stories his aunt Ulanha had told him? Remembrances of swimming with friends in the clear water pool at the base of the little waterfall in the hills behind the village?

Or would his losses be more recent? The number of cattle he was owed from the communal herd? Or perhaps the knowledge of how to treat a leg wound, or bind up a broken bone. Or the wonderful philosophical conversations he had engaged in with Gomo, the old leader of the southern monkey troop.

What if he forgot his name? Or who he was? Or what he was?

The only thing that seemed to fight off the soporific effects of the powder was strong thinking in his accustomed manner. Behind him, Ahlitah had finally roused himself from his slumber. He could hear the big cat growling, but softly and uncertainly. Seeing his friends standing unbound or otherwise unrestrained, freely confronting the three unarmed humans seated behind the table, the cat was not even sure anything was amiss. When it came to the realization that all was not as well as it seemed, it would be too late for it to help. And a burst of thought-corrective powder from the big-mouthed apparatus might render its feline mind incapable of intelligent thought altogether.

No matter how persuasive or compelling the effects, Ehomba had to fight it off—for the sake of his friends as well as himself. The inimical darkness he knew how to combat, but the sweet-smelling pink powder was far more treacherous. It did not threaten death or dismemberment, only a different way of thinking. But the way a man thought determined who and what he was, the herdsman knew. Change that and you forever change the individual behind the thoughts.

Desperately, he struggled to keep rigid, uncompromising images at the forefront of his thinking. Cloying and insistent, the subtle aroma of the powder suffused his nostrils, his lungs, the essence of himself. It ate at his thought processes like acid distilled from orchids.

No! he shouted to himself. *I am Etjole Ehomba, and I think thusly, and not thatly. Leave my mind alone and let my friends and me go!*

"Definitely needs another dose." The woman's expression reflected her compassion and certitude. "Give in to the way of right thinking, traveler! Let yourself relax—don't fight it. From the bottom of my being I promise that you will be a happier and better man for it."

"A happier and better man perhaps." On the other side of the fog that had enveloped him he believed he heard his voice responding. "But I will not be the same man."

The senior of the trio sighed regretfully. "I would rather not do this. I hate to see anyone lose memories, no matter how insignificant."

"It is for the greater good," the savant on his left pointed out. "Society's as well as his."

"I know." After performing a quick check of the small canister attached to the top of the contrivance, the monk raised the metal tube and for a second time aimed it in Ehomba's direction.

The herdsman was frantic. The pink haze was no longer advancing on his thoughts, but neither had it gone away. It hovered before him like a fog bank awaiting a ship being thrust forward by the current, waiting to swallow him up, to reduce his individual way of thinking to the mental equivalent of zero visibility. Reinforced by a second burst from the long-barreled device, its effects would doubtless prove overwhelming.

Ehomba cogitated as hard as he could. Concentrated on bringing to the forefront of his thoughts the most powerful, most convincing images he could call up. Not right-thinking notions, perhaps, but those of which he was most soundly and resolutely convinced. He envisioned Mirhanja, and the village. He contemplated the stark but beautiful countryside of his homeland, the hunting and herding trails that crossed its hills and ravines. He conjured up the faces of his friends and relatives.

Taking careful aim, the well-meaning monk triggered the powder shooter. Thought-paralyzing pinkness blossomed in the herdsman's direction. When it surrounded him he knew he would be the same, but different. Identical in appearance, altered within. He concentrated furiously on the pain of his own birthing, of the lightning strike that had killed an old childhood friend, of the way he and the other men and women of the village had spent all of a night debating how to deal with a visiting hunter who had availed himself of the Naumkib's hospitality, only to be discovered attacking one of the young women. Strong thoughts all, couched in his own unique, individual manner of thinking. From the mouth of the device the salmon-hued haze approached as if in slow motion, like bleached blood.

He thought of the sea.

Behind him, the litah yelped. Another time, the herdsman might have remarked on the unusual sound. He had heard the big cat snarl, and growl, and snore, and even purr in its sleep, but he had never heard it yelp. It would not have mattered if Ahlitah had suddenly burst into traditional village song, so hard was Ehomba fighting to concentrate on his way of thinking. Had he identified it, that which had made the cat yelp would have surprised him even more than the uncharacteristic feline expression itself.

Ahlitah cried out because his feet were suddenly and most unexpectedly standing ankle deep in water. Cold, dark water that smelled powerfully of drifting kelp and strong salts. Nearby, Simna ibn Sind blinked and found himself frowning at something he could not quite put a finger on. Something was not right and, try as he might, he couldn't identify it.

Behind the table, the three savants gaped at the water that had materialized around their feet. Where it was coming from they could not imagine. It seemed to well forth from the solid floor, oozing upward via the cracks between the stones, replacing vanished mortar. Oblivious to what was happening around him, Ehomba continued to concentrate on the oldest, most distinctive entity in his copious store of memories, one he could reproduce with the least amount of effort. He thought of how the sea tasted when sips of it accidentally forced their way past his lips while he was swimming, of the cool, invigorating feel of its liquid self against his bare skin, of the spicy saltiness that tickled his palate and the burning shock whenever any entered his nose. He remembered how its far, flat horizons provided the only real edge to the world, recalled the look of specific creatures that swam sinuously through its depths, saw in his mind's eye the humble magnificence of the abandoned skeletons of creatures large and small that each morning found cast up on its beaches like the wares of a wise old merchant neatly set out for inspection and approval.

And as he remembered, and thought, the sea continued to fill the interrogation chamber, the water level rising with preternatural, impossible speed. It covered him to his knees, reached his hips. Behind him, the agitated litah rumbled and splashed. Having risen from their chairs, the three stunned savants were backing away from the travelers and wading dazedly toward the door. All around Ehomba, pink powder drifted down to the water and was absorbed, dispersing within the rising dark green depths like ground tea leaves in a boiling kettle.

The monks shouted and the door was pulled aside—only to reveal two of the armed servitors slipping and floundering in water up to their waists. The deluge from nowhere was as prominent in the hallway outside the room as it was within, offering neither safety nor dry environs for the fleeing savants.

Half standing, half floating next to Ehomba, Simna ibn Sind shook his head sharply, blinked, and seemed to see his newly saturated surroundings for the first time. Wading with difficulty through water that was now up to his chest, he grabbed the herdsman's arm and pulled violently.

"Etjole! Hoy, bruther, you can turn off the spigot now! Our happy mentors have fled." The swordsman nervously eyed the rising waters. "Best we get away from this stagnant seminary while the awaying's good."

Ehomba seemed not to hear his friend. Cursing under his breath, Simna directed the disoriented Ahlitah to join them. By dint of much hasty pushing and shoving, they managed to position the unresponsive herdsman facedown across the big cat's broad back. In this manner, with their lanky companion wallowing so deep in thought he was unable to rise above his thinking, they walked and waded and swam out of the room.

Emerging from the hallway into the rectory's central inner hall, they kicked their way into a scene of complete chaos. Frantic monks were struggling madly to keep irreplaceable scrolls and tomes above the rising water, which was rapidly climbing toward the second floor. Foaming waves broke against banisters and railings, and thoroughly bewildered fish leaped and flopped in the troughs.

"The main entrance!" Simna shouted as he plunged headlong into the agitated combers and whitecaps. "Swim for the main entrance!"

Though water was able to escape from the few open first-floor windows, these were already submerged and proved themselves unequal to the task of coping with the rising flood. Monks and acolytes bobbed helplessly in the waves. Off to the rear of the hall, above the now sunken master fireplace, a miniature squall was brewing. Looking down into the water, Simna thought he saw something sleek and muscular pass beneath his body. Behind and to the right of him, a flailing servitor, having divested himself of his weapons and armor, suddenly threw both hands in the air. Shrieking, he disappeared beneath the chop, dragged down by something that should not have been living so many hundreds of leagues from the sea, should not have been swimming free and unfettered in the center of the rectory of right thinking.

Following close behind the swordsman, the black litah paddled strongly through the salt-flecked rollers. Turning onto his back while still making for the almost entirely submerged main door, Simna yelled to his limp friend.

"Enough, bruther! You've made your point, whatever it was. Turn it off, make it stop!"

Words drifted back to him, across the water and through the black mane. It was definitely Ehomba's voice, but muted, not as if from sleep but from concentration. Concentration that had led not only to a realization more profound than the herdsman could have envisioned, but to one from which he seemed unable to liberate himself.

"Cannot . . . must think only . . . of the sea. Keep thinking . . . straight. Keep thinking . . . myself."

"No, not anymore!" The swordsman spat out a mouthful of salt water. It tasted exactly like the sea, even down to the tiny fragments of sandy grit that peppered his tongue. "You've done enough!" Around them the residents of the rectory screamed and cried out, kicked and flailed as they fought to keep their heads above water. Not all were good swimmers. At that moment the hall and the rest of the structure were filled not with right thinking or wrong thinking, but only with thoughts of survival.

"Ow! By Gelujan, what . . . ?" Turning in the water, Simna saw that he had bumped his head against the heavy wooden double door that sealed the main entrance to the rectory. Only a small portion of it remained above the rising waters. Opening it was out of the question. Not only would it have to be opened inward, against the tremendous pressure of the water, but the twin iron handles now lay many feet below his rapidly bicycling legs.

Something gripped his shoulder and he let out a small yelp of his own as he whirled around to confront it. When he saw that it was only Ehomba, awakened at last from his daze, he did not know whether to cry out with relief or deal his revived friend a sharp blow to the face. In any event, the uneasy waters in which they found themselves floating would have made it impossible to take accurate aim.

"What now, humble herdsman? Can you make the water go away?"

"Hardly," Ehomba replied in a voice only slightly louder than his usual soft monotone. "Because I do not know how I made it come here." Treading water, he scanned their surroundings. "We might find a second-story window to swim through, but that would mean spilling out onto the streets below and risking a dangerous drop." He glanced down at his submerged feet. "How long can you hold your breath?"

"Hold my . . . ?" Simna pondered the question and its implications. "You're thinking of diving to the bottom and swimming out one of the first-floor windows?"

The herdsman shook his head. For someone who spent so much of his life tending to land animals, the swordsman mused, Ehomba bobbed in the water as comfortably and effortlessly as a cork.

"No. We might not locate one in time, or we might find ourselves caught up and trapped among the heavy furniture or side passageways below. We must go out the front way." He indicated the upper reaches of the two-story-high main door. "Through this."

"Hoy? How much of your mind did you leave in that little room, bruther? Or are your thoughts still tainted by that virulent pinkness?"

Ehomba did not reply. Instead, he turned in the water to face the methodically paddling feline. "Can you do it?"

The big cat considered briefly, then nodded. With his great mane plastered like black seaweed to his skull and neck, he managed the difficult feat of looking only slightly less lordly even though sopping wet. Wordlessly, he dipped his head and dove, the thick black tuft at the end of his tail pointing the way downward like an arrow aimed in reverse. Ehomba followed, arching his back and spearing beneath the surface like a sounding porpoise. With a last mumbled curse Simna ibn Sind pinched his nose shut and initiated a far less elegant and accomplished descent.

The ocean water itself was clean and unsullied, but since only limited light penetrated the rectory, underwater viewing of any kind was difficult. Visibility was limited to a few feet. Still, while Simna's stinging eyes could not locate Ehomba, they had no trouble picking out the massive, hulking shape of the litah. As he held his position, his cheeks bulging and the pack on his back threatening to float off his shoulders, the big cat sank the massive curving claws on its forefeet into the secondary human-sized entry door that was imbedded in the much larger, formal gateway. Then it did the same with its hind feet—and began to kick and claw.

Though working underwater reduced the litah's purchase and slowed its kicks, shredded wood quickly began to fill the gloom around them, drifting away and up toward the surface. A burst of daylight suddenly pierced the damp gloom, then another, and another. Simna felt unseen suction beginning to pull him forward. Kicking hard and pushing with his hands, he held his submerged position. His heart and lungs pounded against his chest, threatening to burst. He couldn't even try to harangue Ehomba into performing some of the magic the herdsman insisted he had not mastered. If something didn't happen very soon, the swordsman knew his straining, aching lungs were going to force him back to the constricted, wave-tossed surface.

Something did.

Beneath the constant attack of Ahlitah's claws, the waterlogged wood of the secondary door not only gave way but collapsed completely. Simna felt himself sucked irresistibly forward. Flailing madly with hands and feet, he tried to maintain some semblance of control over his speedy exodus—to no avail. His right arm struck the doorjamb as he was wrenched through and a dull pain raced up his shoulder.

Then he was coughing and sputtering in bright sunlight as he bobbed to the surface. After making sure that his sword and pack had come through with him, he looked around for his companions.

Ehomba was rising and falling in the current like a long uprooted log. He waved and shouted back to Simna. The swordsman, he noted, was far more agile and confident on land than he was in the water, even though the torrent was slowing as it spread out on the rectory square. Just ahead of him, Ahlitah was already scrabbling for a foothold on the paving stones.

Behind them, seawater continued to gush from the shattered doorway as if from an open faucet. Furniture, pieces of coving ripped from floors, sodden carpets, utensils, and the occasional gasping acolyte broke through the otherwise smooth surface of the flood. Screaming filled the air as stunned, startled citizens scrambled to escape the clutches of the saltwater river. Those who failed to move fast enough found themselves knocked off their feet and ignominiously swept down the street.

Dragging themselves clear of the main flow, the travelers reassembled behind a walled mansion. As Ehomba and Simna checked their packs, they were drenched all over again when the litah chose that moment to shake itself vigorously. After a few choice words from the swordsman, they resumed their inspection.

"Everything I own is soaked." Grousing, he held up a package of dried mutton. "Ruined."

Ehomba was sorting through his own possessions. "We are not in the desert anymore. There will be places to buy food." Rising, he looked around. "We need to find a source of fresh water and rinse everything out. If we do it quickly enough, some of the jerky should survive."

"That's the last time I listen to you where officialdom is concerned." The swordsman's pack squished wetly as he slung it over his shoulders. "Next time we put up a fight instead of going quietly." As they started down the deserted street, he looked back the way they had come. The torrent of salt water continued to gush unabated from the bowels of the rectory. "Sure is a lot of water. When will it stop?"

"I do not know. I thought of the sea to try and keep my thinking to myself, and you see what followed. I do not know how it happened, or why, or how I did what I did." He looked over at his companion. "Not knowing how I started it, I have no idea how to stop it. I am not thinking of the sea now, yet the water still flows." Behind them, cries and the sounds of frantic splashing continued to fill the square around the rectory.

Finding an unsullied public fountain, they removed everything from their packs and rinsed it all in the cool, clear fresh water to remove the salt. That task concluded, they did the same for their weapons to prevent the metal blades from corroding. Few citizens were about, most having locked themselves in their homes or places of business to hide from the intemperate sorcery. Everyone else had run to the rectory square to gawk at the new wonder. Gifted with this temporary solitude and shielded from casual view by Ahlitah's bulk, the two men removed their clothes and washed them as well.

"I feel as if I shall never be dry again." The disgruntled swordsman struggled to drag his newly drenched shirt down over his head and shoulders.

As Ehomba worked with his kilt he squinted up at the sky. "It is a warm day and the sun is still high. If we keep to the open places we should dry quickly enough."

"Hoy, we'll keep to the open places, all right!" Picking up his sword, Simna slid it carefully back into its sodden sheath. "I'm not setting foot in another building until we're clear of this benighted country. Imagine trying to control not what people think but the way they think. By Gwiswil, it's outrageous!"

"Yes," Ehomba agreed as they started up the deserted street. "It is fortunate that the savants have to confront the unconverted in person. Think how frightful it would be if they had some sorcerous means of placing themselves before many people simultaneously. Of putting themselves into each citizen's home or place of business and talking to many hundreds of subjects at once, and then using their magic to convince them to all think similarly."

Simna nodded somberly. "That would truly be the blackest of the black arts, bruther. We are fortunate to come from countries where such insidious fantasies are not contemplated."

His tall companion indicated agreement. "If the sheepherder's description of the boundaries hereabouts was correct, we should be out of Tethspraih before midnight and thus beyond the reach of the guardians of right thinking."

"Can't be soon enough for me." Simna lengthened his stride. "My way of thinking may be skewed, or conflicted, or sometimes contradictory, but by Ghev, it's *my* way of thinking."

"It is part of what makes you who and what you are." Ehomba strode on, the bottom of his spear click-clacking on the pavement. "Myself, I cannot imagine thinking any differently than I do, than I always have."

"Personally, I think the guardians had the right concept but the wrong specifics."

Both men turned to the litah in surprise. Water continued to drip from the big cat's saturated fur. "What are you saying?" Ehomba asked it.

"The problem is not that men think wrongly. It's that they think too much. This leads inevitably to too much talking." Ahlitah left the import of his words hanging in the air.

"Is the big pussy saying that we talk too much?" Simna retorted. "Is that what he's saying? That we just babble on and on, with no reason and for no particular purpose, to hear ourselves jabber? Is that what he's saying? Hoy, if that's how he feels, maybe we should just shut up and never speak to him again. Maybe that's what he'd like, for us not to say another word and—"

Raising his free hand so that the palm faced the swordsman, Ehomba replied softly as they began to leave the urban center of Tethspraih behind. "I am not saying that I agree with him entirely, Simna, but perhaps it would be good if we measured out our words with a little more care and forethought."

"So most of it is waste? Most of what we say has no meaning, or makes no sense, or is of no use to anyone just because he thinks so? Our words are just so much noise hanging in the air, containing no more sense than the songs of the birds or the buzz of bees? What we speak is—"

"Simna, my friend—be silent. For a little while, anyway." Ehomba smiled encouragingly at the smaller man.

"Then you do agree with him?" The irascible swordsman would not let the matter drop. "You think we do talk too much, about nothing of substance?"

"Sorry, my friend." Smiling apologetically, Ehomba pointed with his free hand to the side of his head. "My ears are still full of water, and I cannot hear you properly."

Simna had a ready reply, but decided to set it aside. Was the cursed cat smiling also? That was absurd. Cats could not smile. Yawn, snarl, tense—but not smile. Storing his rejoinder in an empty corner of his memory, he traipsed on in silence, knowing that he could summon it forth for delivery at a later time. He never did, of course.

Both Ahlitah and Ehomba were counting on it.

XII

The country ruled over by the enlightened Count Tyrahnar Cresthelmare proved as welcoming and hospitable as Tethspraih had been treacherous. They were passed through the border gate by curious but cheerful guards, who assured the blunt, inquisitive Simna that in Phan not only would no one try to change his way of thinking, no one would give a damn what he thought.

Never absent for very long in the worst of times, the spring returned to the swordsman's step and the glint to his eye as they accepted a ride into Phan City from a farmer with a wagonload of hay. The city itself put even prosperous Tethspraih to shame. Not only were the buildings more impressive and the people more elegantly attired, but there was a definite and distinctive sense of style about the modest metropolis that exceeded anything the wide-eyed Ehomba had ever seen. The more worldly Simna, of course, was less impressed.

"Nice little burg." He was leaning back with his hands behind his head and using Ahlitah's chest for a pillow. Rocked to sleep by the wagon's motion, the big cat did not object. "Nothing like Creemac Carille, or Boh-yen, or Vloslo-on-the-Drenem, but it does have a certain dash." He inhaled deeply, a contented expression on his face. "First sign of an upscale community, long bruther: The air doesn't stink."

"I wonder if all these little kingdoms the sheepherder told us about are as prosperous as Tethspraih and Phan?" Ehomba was admiring the graceful people of many hues and their fine clothing. Here and there he even spotted an occasional ape, suggesting that the Phanese could boast of more cosmopolitan commercial connections than the more insular inhabitants of Tethspraih. Despite the ornate and even florid local manner of dressing, he was not made self-conscious by his own poor shirt, kilt, and sandals. It would never have occurred to Etjole Ehomba to be embarrassed by such a thing. While the Naumkib admired and even aspired to pleasing attire and personal decoration, not one of them would ever think of judging another person according to his or her appearance.

"Off ye go, boys." The hay farmer called back to them from his bench seat up front. "And be sure and see to it that great toothy black monster gets off with ye!"

Digging his fingers deep into Ahlitah's thick mane, Ehomba shook the cat several times until it blinked sleepy eyes at him. Rumbling deep in his throat, the litah took its own good time stretching, yawning, and stepping down from the back of the wagon. The farmer was not about to rush the operation and, for that matter, neither was the herdsman. No matter how friendly and affectionate when awake, a cat half asleep was always potentially dangerous.

Taking note of the oversized feline, a few stylishly outfitted pedestrians spent time staring in his direction. But no one panicked, or looked down their nose at the tired, sweaty travelers, or whispered snide comments under their breath. Ehomba's excellent hearing told him this was so, and in response to his query, Ahlitah confirmed it.

"This seems to be an unusually cultivated clustering of humans," the big cat commented. "One even remarked on how handsome and imposing was I."

"Evidently all their intelligence has gone into design." Hands on hips, Simna stood in the center of the street surveying their surroundings. A middle-aged man on horseback came trotting past and barely glanced in their direction. While the swordsman admired his flowing green cape, Ehomba noted with interest the schematics of the leather and brass tack, and Ahlitah lowered his gaze and growled deep in his throat at the nearness of so much easy meat. Luckily for the rider's ride, his mount did not meet the big cat's eyes.

"We need to find some sort of general trading house or store where we can replenish our supplies." Reaching around to pat his pack, Simna grinned affably. "One thing about gold: Not much hurts it. Not even seawater."

"I thought your purse was drained." Ehomba eyed his friend uncertainly.

The swordsman was not in the least embarrassed. "I didn't tell you everything, Etjole. I was keeping some in reserve, for myself. But"—he shrugged resignedly—"where I go so goes my belly, and right now it's more empty than my purse. I imagine it's the same with you."

Ehomba gestured diffidently. "I can go a long time without food."

"Hoy, but why should you?" Simna put a comradely arm around the tall man's shoulders. "Take food when and where you can, says I. By the look of this place, whatever we purchase here will be fresh and of good quality. Who knows what the next port of call may bring? To a general store for victuals and then, onward to Hamacassar!"

Ehomba followed his friend across the street. "Why Simna, you sound almost enthusiastic."

The swordsman responded to the observation with a hearty smile. "It's my way of concealing desperate impatience. But I'm not really worried, because I know that the treasure that lies at the end of this quest will be well worth all the time and effort and hardships."

Ehomba thought of Roileé the witch dog's prediction, which echoed Rael the Beautiful's prediction. "I hope so, friend Simna."

Citizens gave them directions to a high-ceilinged establishment several blocks distant. Immediately upon entering it, Simna knew they had been guided to the right place. Larger goods were stacked in the center of the wooden-plank floor, while on either side shelves and compartments filled with smaller articles rose to a height of nearly two stories. Like bees probing flowers for honey, young boys on rolling ladders slid back and forth along these walls, picking out requested items in response to sharply barked orders from busy attendants below. At the far end of the single long room was a small bar fronting a handful of tables and chairs at which habitual denizens of the store's depths sat chatting, drinking, and smoking.

Polite customers made room for the travelers to pass. Or perhaps they were simply getting out of the litah's way. As it always did in the presence of so many humans, the big cat kept its massive head down and eyes mostly averted. This premeditated posture of specious submission went a long way toward alleviating the concerns of old men, and women with young children in tow.

While Simna shopped, Ehomba pestered the clerks with question after question. So much of what he saw on the shelves was new and wonderful to him. There were small mechanical devices of intricate design, and brightly dyed fabrics and household items. Much of the prepackaged food was outside his experience, and an exasperated Simna was obliged on repeated occasions to explain the nature of foreign imports and exoticisms.

When they had accomplished what they had come for, and finalized their purchases, a dour Simna held the last of the Chlengguu gold in one hand and counted the pieces that remained to them. "I'd thought not to retire on this, but to at least make myself comfortable for a while. Now it seems there won't even be enough to last out our journey."

"Be of good cheer, friend Simna." Ehomba put a comforting hand on his friend's arm. "Gold is only as good as the purpose it serves."

"I can think of a few I'd like to have served." The swordsman exhaled tiredly. "We have enough for a drink or two, anyway." He nodded at the patient Ahlitah. "Even the cat can have a drink."

"A pan of water will suffice, thank you." His fur having finally dried out, the litah had regained his last absent iota of dignity. Content, he made himself regally comfortable in a rear corner, much to the relief of the regular patrons of the limited drinking area.

Taking seats in finely made chairs of wicker and cloth, the two travelers luxuriated in the comfort of drinks with actual ice. This striking and unexpected phenomenon so intrigued Ehomba that he insisted they linger over their refreshment. Those seated in their immediate vicinity proved willing listeners to their tales of travels in far-off lands. Expanding in his element, Simna proceeded to embroider the truth and fill in the gaps with extemporaneous invention. Whenever the swordsman would unload a particularly egregious fiction on the audience of rapt listeners, Ehomba would throw him a disapproving frown. These his loquacious companion would studiously ignore. Meanwhile, snug in his corner, Ahlitah slumbered on.

In this manner, plied with cold drinks by an eager and attentive audience, they passed not only the rest of the afternoon but a good portion of the early evening. Eventually though, it appeared that even Simna ibn Sind's fertile narrative was beginning to pale as their once fervent fans began to drift away and out of the store in ones and twos, taking their day's purchases with them.

At last it was pitch dark outside, and their audience had been reduced to two: a pair of husky, bearded manual laborers of approximately the same age as the travelers themselves. Their manner of departure, however, was as unforeseen as it was abrupt.

Catching sight of the blackened street just visible through the distant main entrance, the slightly smaller of the two rose suddenly. His eyes were wide as he clutched at his still seated companion's shoulder.

"Nadoun! Look outside!"

The other man's jaw dropped. He whirled to glare at the man behind the compact bar. That worthy spoke solemnly as he finished putting up the last of his glassware.

"That's right. Ye lads best get a move on or you'll have to make your way home—after."

"Why did ye not warn us?" The first man's tone was strained and accusatory.

This time the proprietor looked up from his work. "Ye be grown men. I am a tradesman, not a baby-sitter."

Were it not for the terrified expressions on their faces, it would have been comical to watch the two men fight frantically to don their fine evening jackets and flee the general store. The shorter of the two flung a handful of money at the proprietor, not bothering either to count it or wait for his change.

Smacking his lips, Simna set his goblet down on the table in front of him and inquired casually of the shopkeeper as he knelt to pick the scattered coins off the floor, "What was that all about?"

The heavyset merchant sported a florid black mustache that curled upwards at the ends. It contrasted starkly with his gleaming pate, which was as devoid of hair as a ceramic mixing bowl. Perhaps in compensation, his eyebrows were ferocious.

"You don't know?" Straightening, he let the fruits of his coin gathering tumble into the commodious front pocket of his rough cotton apron. "You really don't, do ye?"

"It would appear not." Ehomba toyed with the rim of his own drinking utensil. "Could you shed some illumination on our ignorance for us?"

Shaking his head in disbelief, the proprietor came out from behind the bar and approached their table. His expression was thoroughly disapproving. As near as Ehomba could tell, they were alone in the establishment with the owner. All other customers and employees had long since departed.

With a thick finger their reluctant host indicated the wooden clock placed high on a small shelf. "D'ye know what that portends?"

Unfamiliar with mechanical clocks, Ehomba kept silent. But Simna nodded once, brusquely. "It 'portends' that it's twenty minutes to midnight. So?"

The merchant looked past them, toward the main entrance, and his tone softened slightly. "Midnight is the witching hour."

"Depends where you happen to be." Kicking back in his chair, the swordsman put his feet up on the table and crossed them at the ankles. "In Vwalta, the capital of Drelestan, it's the drinks-all-around hour. In Poulemata it's the time-for-bed hour."

"Well here," the proprietor observed sharply, "it be the witching hour."

"For a good part of the evening those two men were relaxed and enjoying themselves in our company," Ehomba pointed out. "When they realized the time they became frantic." He turned in his chair to look outside. On the silent, night-shrouded street, nothing moved. "What happens at this witching hour? Do witches suddenly appear?"

"Nothing so straightforward, friend." Quietly annoyed, the owner glanced meaningfully at Simna's sandaled feet where they reposed on the table. The swordsman responded with a good-natured smile and left his feet where they were. "If it were only a matter of the occasional witch, no one would care, and there would be no need for the Covenant."

"What is this Covenant?" An unpleasant, tingling sensation made Ehomba feel that they were going to have to leave their comfortable surroundings in a hurry. He made sure that his pack and weapons were close at hand.

Leaning back against the bar, the proprietor crossed his arms over his lower chest, above his protuberant belly, and regarded them sorrowfully. "Ye have never been to Phan before, have ye, or heard of it in your travelings?"

The herdsman shook his head. "This is our first time in this part of the world." Off in his corner, Ahlitah snored on, blissfully indifferent to the prattlings of men.

Their host sighed deeply. "Long, long ago, the province of Phan was known as the Haunted Land. Though it was, and is, surrounded by fertile countries populated by happy people, Phan itself was shunned except for those daring travelers who passed through it on the river Shornorai, which flows through its northern districts. Even they were not safe from attack."

"From attack?" Simna's eyes were slightly glazed, a consequence of downing all the free drinks that had been contributed by their now vanished audience. "By whom?"

Hirsute brows drawing together, the owner regarded him sternly. "Not by whom, friend. By *what*. It is a well-known fact that Phan has always provided a home to the dregs and rabble of the Otherworlds, to the noisome trash that is too debased and depraved to find asylum in those regions where such creatures normally dwell." He looked down at his arms and apron. "All spirits and entities need a place to abide, even the most wicked and corrupt. Phan was that place. They congregated here, making this fine land uninhabitable, preying upon and tormenting any daring enough to try and homestead its fruitful plains and lush river valleys."

"Obviously, something happened to change that," Ehomba observed. Simna was listening more closely now, drawn not only to the

proprietor's story but to the growing feeling that it just might have something to do with the hysterical egression of their last two listeners.

The owner nodded. "Led by Yaw Cresthelmare the Immutable, distant and greatest ancestor of the present Count Tyrahnar the Enlightened and founder of the dynasty of Phan, a great gathering of opportun-
ists and migrants resolved to test the limits of the befouled occupiers of
this land. The momentous battle that ensued raged for years. Many died,
but were replaced by hopeful pilgrims from elsewhere. The debased and
profane suffered far fewer casualties, for the dead are hard to kill, but
neither could they drive the determined Yaw and his followers from
Phan. Whenever they wiped out a cluster of pitiful, newly established
huts or a wagon full of would-be immigrants, a new squatter's camp
would spring up elsewhere."

Ehomba indicated the fine, well-stocked store in which they sat. "Yet
here we sit, in the midst of much comfort, and in passing through your
land we saw no sign of the kind of devastation to which you allude."

"As I be saying, this all took place long ago." Uncrossing his arms,
the owner moved back behind the bar. "Neither side could wholly defeat
the other. The degraded had the resources of all the dark crafts at their
disposal, but they could not wreak havoc and destruction everywhere at
once. The followers of Yaw had on their side numbers and persistence.
Eventually, by mutual agreement, an accommodation was reached." He
shook his head at the audacity of it. "Yaw Cresthelmare was a great man.
Imagine, if you will, sitting down to negotiate with goblins and apparitions and demons so vile they are not even welcome in Hell."

Ehomba looked thoughtful. "And the result, it was this Covenant
you speak of?"

"Yes. The Inhuman tried everything to trick Yaw, but it was not for
nothing that he was christened the Immutable, and that Phan and its
neighbors are called the Thinking Kingdoms. The terms of the Covenant
were set solid as the stone that underlies Phan itself, and bolted directly
to it. The debased could not breach the terms, nor even bend them."

"These terms . . . ?" A now fully attentive Simna left the question
hanging.

Elaboration was not needed. "The day was given to the followers of
Yaw, made theirs in which to live and love, to cultivate and populate the
land of Phan as they should see fit. In return, the corrupted and disem-
bodied and their ilk were given the deepest part of the night, to roam
freely wherever they might choose from midnight 'til dawn, free from
insult, attack, or exorcism by the humans who had so forcefully settled
among them."

Simna laughed uneasily as he eyed the now suggestive darkness that ruled the street beyond the still unbarred door. "I'd think that would make for some unsettled sleeping."

"Not so." The proprietor smiled thinly. "The impure keep to their compact." He nodded in the direction of the entrance. "If you will look down as you travel through Phan, you will see that the entrance to every building is circumscribed by a strip of pure copper the width of a man's thumb. This the specters of the night will not cross. It is so established in the Covenant. Behind that copper line, in any building, one is safe not only in body but in dreams. Step outside that line between midnight and dawn and . . ." He shuddered slightly, as if a quick, sharp blast of cold air had just passed over his body and through his soul.

A no longer smiling Simna set his goblet aside and brooded on the import of the proprietor's words. "You're fair game."

"Just so," the owner conceded. "And now ye must be moving along."

"What!" The swordsman did not remove his feet from the table so much as yank them off. "After what you just told us you mean to throw us out into the night?"

"I do." The owner's response was firm. "I accord ye no greater hospitality than I did that pair that left moments ago, and in haste. Now you know the reason for their flight. This is a general store, not an inn." He glanced significantly at the clock, whose soft wooden ticks had grown much louder in the room. "You have time yet. There is a boardinghouse around the corner, only a block distant. It is a modest establishment, but clean and reasonable. The owners are good friends of mine, and not unused to greeting apprehensive patrons caught out celebrating too late to make it back to their homes. A spirited dash of but a few seconds will see you safely there. The street is empty and clear."

"By Gobolloba, let's get out of here!" The swordsman scrambled to slip his arms through the straps of his pack, not forgetting his sword, nor to drain the last drops of liquid gratification from his goblet.

Rising from his chair, Ehomba moved quickly but without panic to rouse Ahlitah from his feline slumber. The big cat was slow to awaken. As Ehomba knelt by its side and spoke softly, Simna fairly danced with impatience in front of their table, his eyes flicking rapidly and repeatedly from his companions to the brooding darkness outside.

"For Gudgeon's sake, will you hurry! Spit in his ear, already! Kick him in the balls. Get him *up!*" Unwilling to kick the litah himself, the swordsman had to be content with flailing at the floor.

Rising on all four powerful, attenuated legs, the big cat stretched and yawned languorously while Simna could only look on and grind his teeth helplessly.

"*If* your hairy majesty would be so kind as to join us in departing," he finally snapped, "it would behoove us to get the hell out of here."

The litah yawned again as he began padding toward the exit. "Ehomba explained things to me."

"Then why aren't you moving faster?" Knowing it would only provoke a delaying confrontation, the swordsman refrained from whacking the cat across its backside with the flat of his blade.

It was Ehomba who responded. "The street appears deserted, and it is not yet midnight, but it is a wise man who checks the ground outside his house before running wildly into the night."

"Hoy, all right. But let's not delay." Simna's sharp eyes were already scanning what he could see of the street to north and south as they approached the doorway.

"You worry needlessly." The proprietor was trailing behind them. A brass ring heavy with keys hung from one hand. "The dead are very punctual."

As they reached the portal, Ehomba looked down. Sure enough, a copper strip gleamed metallically beneath his feet. Inlaid in and bolted to the thick planking, it shone with the light of regular polishing. He stepped over it.

Nothing happened. The night was still and the coolness a relief from the heat of the day. In both directions, neatly shuttered shops looked out on the silent street. Flowers bloomed in window boxes, their blossoms shut against the cold until the next coming of the sun. Someone had washed and swept not only the sidewalks but the road itself. All was orderly, well groomed, and deserted.

Simna and Ahlitah crossed the threshold behind the herdsman. To prove that his words had meaning, the proprietor followed them outside onto the small covered porch that fronted the store. He showed no fear, and Simna allowed himself to relax a little as their erstwhile host pointed.

"Five storefronts that way and ye will find yourselves at the corner. Turn right. The boardinghouse will be the fourth door on your left. Knock firmly lest ye not be heard. And a good night t'ye."

Stepping back inside, he shut the door behind them. Looking through the glass, Ehomba could see him rotating a large brass key in the lock.

"What are we standing here like stupefied goats for? We only have a couple of minutes." Without waiting for his friends, Simna broke into a sprint. Ehomba and Ahlitah followed, running from need but not desperation.

They made it to the corner, but did not turn it.

"What was that?" Ehomba came to an abrupt stop.

"What was what?" Breathing as quietly as possible, Simna halted a few feet in front of the herdsman. "I didn't hear anything. Hoy, what are you looking for?"

Ehomba was peering into the depths of a dark close between two silent, darkened buildings. Simna would not have thought it an activity worth pursuing at the best of times, which the present most emphatically was not. As he looked on in disbelief, the tall southerner stepped into the shadows that were even darker than the surrounding night. With the time beginning to weigh heavily on him and knowing it would not wait or slow its pace for any man, the swordsman moved to place a forceful hand on his companion's arm.

"What do you think you're doing, bruther? I've been late to funerals, and late to appointments, and late to meet with friends on a fine summer's night, but I don't want to be late to the door of this boardinghouse. Come on! Whatever piece of trash has piqued your inexplicable interest will still be there in the morning." Behind them the litah waited quietly, contemplating the abandoned street.

"No," Ehomba replied in his usual soft but unshakable tone, "I do not think that it will."

Within the hidden depths of the close, something moaned. The hackles on the swordsman's neck bristled at the sound. Tight-lipped, he tried to drag his friend back onto the sidewalk. Ehomba resisted.

The moan came again, and while Simna did not relax, some of the fearful tension oozed out of him. It was manifestly a human throat that had produced that muffled lamentation, and not some gibbering perversion set loose from the nether regions of unimaginable perdition.

"Here." The dim outline of the herdsman could be seen picking its way through the rubble. "Over this way."

Muttering under his breath, the swordsman lurched forward, cursing as he stumbled over discarded containers, rotting foodstuffs, and equally pungent but less mentionable offal.

The figure Ehomba was trying to help to its feet was slight to the point of emaciation. It was a man; a very little man indeed, barely four feet tall. It was hard to judge because despite the herdsman's strong supportive arm, the figure's legs seemed to have trouble working. They exhibited a distinct tendency to wander off by themselves, as if possessed of their own individual itineraries. Understandably, this caused some small difficulty to the rest of the attached body.

Once Simna got his arm beneath the man's other shoulder, the two travelers were able to walk the hapless figure out of the close. He weighed very little. Back out on the sidewalk, they set him down, leaning him up against a wall. The swordsman wiped distastefully at his arm. The frail figure was rank as a wallowing boar and the stink attached to him displayed an unwholesome tendency to rub off on anyone making contact with it. Glancing in the humans' direction, Ahlitah wrinkled his nose in disgust.

"Who are you?" Somehow ignoring the stench, Ehomba knelt to place his own face close to that of the barely breathing little man. "We would like to help you. Do you know what time it is?" He nodded toward the dark, empty street. "You cannot stay here, like this."

"Glad to hear you say it, bruther." Apprehensive and impatient, Simna stood nearby, his keen gaze anxiously patrolling the roadway. "Can we go now? Please?"

"Not until we help this poor unfortunate. If necessary, we will bring him with us." The herdsman looked up at his companion. "I will not abandon him to the kind of fate the shopkeeper told us skulks through this city late at night."

"All right, fine! There isn't time to argue. Let's get him back on his feet, then." Simna bent to help the vagrant rise once more, only to draw back just in time as the figure forestalled its incipient deliverance by spewing the contents of his stomach all over the sidewalk.

"By Gieirwall, what a foulness!" Turning his back on the slumping frame, Simna inhaled deeply of fresh night air. Ehomba held his ground, though he was careful to keep out of the line of fire.

Slight as he was, the pitiful fellow had very little left in his stomach to regurgitate. That did not stop him from puking for another minute or so. In counterpoint to his rasping dry heaves, bells rang out solemnly the length and breadth of the city, simultaneously announcing and decrying the arrival of midnight.

"That's torn it," the swordsman muttered. "We've got to get out of here. Now." Bending low but keeping his face turned as much away from the fellow as possible, he spoke in words harsh and distinct. "Did you hear that, whoever you are? It's midnight, and if all we were told is true, the defiled can now freely roam the streets in accordance with your damned Covenant. It is time, friend, to move your bony ass. Why Ehomba wants to save it I don't know. If it was up to me, I'd leave you here, pickings for whatever shambles along."

Rheumy yellow eyes turned to meet the swordsman's. A shaky smile materialized on the bewhiskered, unwholesome face. Pressing one unsteady finger to the side of the tapering, twice-broken nose, the figure replied in a boozy cackle.

"Knucker knows, Knucker does!" Upon delivering himself of this proclamation, he blew yellow-green snot in the direction of the swords-man's sandals.

Simna hopped deftly aside. "Hoy, watch what you're doing, you pu-trefying little relic! Who the Gwerwhon do you think you are?" To Ehomba he added, "He's stinking rotten drunk. By the look and sound and smell of him, he's been that way for some time."

Bracing his scrawny back against the wall, the man rose to an ap-proximation of a standing position. "Didn't you hear what I said? Don't you know who I am?"

"No," Simna growled as he tried to listen and watch both ends of the stygian street at the same time. "Who are you, you walking pile of fossil-ized spew?"

Frowning uncertainly, the man drew himself more or less up to his full, unimpressive height. "I am Knucker. Knucker the Knower." The precarious smile essayed a tentative reappearance. "I know everything." He focused on Ehomba. "Ask me a question. Go on, ask me a question. Anything."

"Maybe later." Gently gripping the fluttering leaf of a man by his shoulder, the herdsman managed to get him turned up the street. "My friend is right. We have to go now."

"Sure, why not?" Knucker the Knower was nothing if not agreeable. "Come on, ask me something. Anything."

Irritated and wary in equal measure, Simna kept pace with Ehomba. "What's the name of my maiden aunt on my mother's side?"

"Vherilza," Knucker replied without hesitation. "And her sisters are Prilly and Choxu."

The swordsman blinked, the potential invisible terrors of the night momentarily forgotten. "How?—by Grenrack's beard, that's right. He's right." Gripping the emaciated figure by one skinny arm, the swordsman thrust his face close to that of the sad figure. "How did you know that?"

"Knucker knows." Once more the man pressed his finger to the side of his nose, but when a worried Simna drew back, the tottering drunkard only sniggered anew. "Knucker knows everything. Go on, ask me an-other." Like a thirsty supplicant in search of rain, he spread shaky arms wide. "I know *everything*!"

Together, Ehomba and Simna half dragged, half carried the lightly built frame around the corner. Up the street they could see a single light burning through the darkness: the identifying, welcoming emblem of the boardinghouse. Simna redoubled his efforts.

"Come on, Mister Know-it-all. Only a little ways farther to go and then you can explain yourself."

"What's to explain?" Head wobbling on his neck as if at any moment it might fall off, Knucker turned to the smaller of his three saviors. "I know everything. Nothing more, nothing less. What part of that don't you understand, you insipid little conscript in the army of the avaricious?"

Gritting his teeth, Simna ignored the insult and concentrated on dragging the feeble corpus up the side street. Trying to keep their charge awake and alert for another couple of moments, Ehomba ventured another question.

"How long before we reach that boardinghouse up the street?"

"I'm not the right one to ask that question."

Simna let out a derisive snort. "I thought you knew everything."

"So I do, but I ain't the one that's going to delay your arriving. Maybe you better ask it."

"Ask him?" Searching both ends of the street, Simna saw nothing. "I don't see anything."

"Not himsh—'it,' " the Knower corrected him, slurring his words.

The swordsman was about to fetch the incoherent drunk a blow to the side of the head when something immensely large and vital appeared directly in their path. Behind him, Ahlitah snarled sharply. The apparition that had materialized to block their path wore no clothes, no shoes—and, more frighteningly, no face.

XIII

Unmoving and silent in the middle of the deserted street, they stared at the phantasm. Despite its lack of a countenance, it conveyed the unmistakable impression of staring back. Ehomba leaned over slightly to whisper to the swaying, shaky enigma who called himself Knucker.

"Okay, you know everything. What is that?"

Lachrymose eyes fought to focus on the forbidding specter. As before, the drunkard did not hesitate. "A vohwn. Having no face of its own, it envies those that do." He tapped the side of his nose with his middle finger. "Be careful: It will try to take yours."

Simna drew his sword. "Well, he can't have this one. I need it." Behind him, Ahlitah tensed and hunted for an opening.

Pulling the sky-metal blade from the scabbard on his back, Ehomba closed ranks with his friend. "And I mine. Mirhanja would still recognize me if I returned home without a face, but how would she look deep into my eyes if they were taken away?" He held his sword out in front of him, the moonlight glinting off the sharply angled etchings in the singular steel.

The vohwn looked at the double display of sharp-edged weaponry, though what it looked with no one could say, and laughed from the vacancy where its mouth might have been had it enjoyed a mouth. It was a sly suspiration, a sound that played beguilingly around the outer ear without ever really intruding, yet they heard it anyway, a laugh that froze only random drops of blood within their veins.

A phantasmal hand, skeletal and blue, reached toward them. Simna ducked. Ehomba held his ground and swung. The sky-metal sword moaned as it cleaved air and wrist. Like an emancipated moth, the severed hand of the vohwn went drifting off into the night, possessed of a life of its own. The specter cried out elegiacally and drew back its arm. As the empty face stared down into the severed wrist, it promptly grew another hand.

The herdsman hissed at the swaying, unsteady Knucker. "How do we get around it?"

"Well," the drunk responded thoughtfully, "you could make a break to your left and cross the street, but then you'd run into the borboressbs."

Glancing in the indicated direction, Ehomba and Simna saw a dark slit of an alley give birth to a dozen or so pony-sized homunculi. They had cloven hooves and walked with a permanent crouch. Bright red skin was subdued somewhat by the feeble moonlight. Goatlike tails switched back and forth and bristle-black hair covered their bodies in isolated, unwholesome patches. Their faces were blunt and plump, distorted by mouths full of sharp snaggle teeth that ran from ear to ear. When they gaped, it looked as if their skulls were split horizontally in half. Each had a single horn of varying length growing from the center of its forehead, and they were armed with curving, scythelike short swords fashioned of metal as bloodred as their exposed flesh.

They had been gabbling in an unknown tongue until they caught sight of the travelers. Now their unfathomable discourse was transmuted into an ominous muttering as they turned toward Ehomba and his companions. The presence of the towering vohwn did nothing to dissuade their advance.

Knucker spat something lumpy and brown onto the street and wiped his mouth with the back of his hand. "Beware the borboressbs. They like to pluck out a man's veins while he's still alive and slurp them down for a snack."

Ehomba tried to count the advancing freaks while keeping a watchful eye on the vohwn. It was still busy regrowing its hand, and had not moved from its position in the middle of the street.

"What about the other way?"

Knucker squinted and struggled to focus. "Well, you might have done that a minute or so ago, but it's too late now." He nodded to no one in particular. "Grenks."

Slithering down the sidewalk came a trio of four-legged blobs that blocked the way from street to structure with a splotchy mass of pulsating pustulance. They looked like animals that had been fashioned from tied-together balloons. Big as buffalo, they loped along on barrel-like legs that bounced them lightly off the ground. They had no feet and no hands. Everything about them was rounded and pulpy. Behind them they left triple trails of ichorous lump-filled slime whose stench reached the travelers even from a distance. It lay where it dripped for long moments before evaporating.

The repulsive, malformed heads were all pop eyes and gaping mouths, the latter limned with greasy, saclike lips. They had no teeth, but from the depths of those revolting maws a single tentacle-like tongue writhed and coiled like a snake carefully examining the world from the depths of its lair. Possessed of a sincere single-minded stupidity, they humped forward indifferent to the presence of the advancing borboressbs and the immovable shade of the vohwn.

"Use your magic!" Confronted by so many numerous and disparate horrors, Simna drew as close as possible to his tall friend as he could without compromising the arc of their weapons. "Call down the wind from the stars!"

"You think it is so easy?" Ehomba gripped his blade firmly. "Such things take time and are not always responsive. Drawing a sword is simple; persuading it to do anything besides cut and slice is not." He was already starting to retreat. "I am trying."

"Hoy, you have to try harder. No, try faster."

"Be quiet and let me concentrate!"

Ahlitah leaped forward, his thunderous snarl echoing off the surrounding structures. The size and presence of the big cat caused the borboressbs to begin to spread out so as to encircle the travelers. Perhaps because it had no face with which to look upon the litah, the vohwn was not intimidated. And the comical carnivorous masses of the grenks came sliming on, oblivious to everything before them.

As they retreated, Ehomba grabbed the stuporous Knucker by the shoulder and pulled him along. Either unaware of or indifferent to the danger confronting them, the besotted little wreck of a man tottered unresistingly backwards in the herdsman's firm grasp.

"What should we do?" The tall southerner gave the drunk a good shaking. "Tell us what to do. How do we get away from these foulnesses?"

Turning bleary eyes to the herdsman, Knucker replied in quavering tones. "You can't. The borboressbs are too agile, the vohwn will be wherever you see, and the grenks never give up until they've been sated. Fight one and the others will fall on you from behind. You're outnumbered, stranger. You're dead." He coughed weakly.

"He doesn't know everything," Simna declared grimly. "We're not dead yet."

"You need help," the frail drunk mumbled.

"Hoy, you don't have to be all-knowing to see that. I have a feeling we can't expect much from these happy, civilized Phanese." Simna scanned the surrounding buildings. A few lights gleamed behind shuttered windows, but none had been flung open to allow the inhabitants to observe what was taking place in the quiet street outside their homes. In the morning, no doubt, a jolly and competent cleaning crew would scrub the pavement clean of any loitering unpleasantness. Children would run hoops and chase each other across bloodstains that would fade with soap and rain and time, and no one would hazard a breach of etiquette by troubling to inquire what had happened.

Its hand regrown, the vohwn moaned and drifted forward. The nearest borboressbs gave it a wide berth. Too ignorant and persistent to recognize a possible danger to themselves and anxious for prey, the grenks oozed closer.

A wisp of cold wind sparked from the tip of the sky-metal blade.

"Hurry up!" Simna eyed the borboressbs nearest him. Four more had already scuttled behind him and were beginning to close in, holding their curved weapons above their loathsome heads like egg teeth extracted from some Ur-snake.

Reaching up and around, Knucker the Knower wrapped fingers sticky with phlegm and puke around the carved figurine that hung from the cord around Ehomba's neck, and yanked. Startled, the herdsman responded angrily.

"Give that back! It will not buy you more than a drink or two."

"Give it back?" Holding it up to his eyes, the little man struggled with difficulty to concentrate on the graven image he had purloined. "Sure, I'll give it back. Here." Drawing back his arm, he somehow managed a shaky throw.

The figurine soared past Ehomba's outstretched fingers to land in front of a pair of borboressbs. It bounced a couple of times before rolling to a halt. One of the cloven-footed abnormalities gave it a passing glance, then stepped on it, grinding it into the pavement. A repellent snaggle-toothed grin split the repulsive face from side to side.

It vanished as the borboressb rose straight up into the air, did a complete head-over-hoof flip, and landed hard on its back. It lay stunned and unmoving.

In place of the carving stood a tall, erect figure limned in pale white flame. Its statuesque shape barely blurred by a coil of tight-fitting crimson and brown fabric, it carried a shield of mastodon hide in one hand and a slim wooden club in the other. The club was thickly studded with the three-sided thorns of the pyre bush. In all his life Ehomba had never seen a pyre bush. It was a part of Naumkib lore, more legend than shrub. But he recognized the thorns instantly, from the tales he had been told as a child. Mirhanja had never seen a pyre bush either, but she could describe one in detail to Daki and Nelecha while reciting bedtime stories. Any Naumkib mother knew what a pyre bush looked like, even if she had never seen one herself.

Momentarily startled, the angry borboressbs turned to confront the intruder in their midst. Two sliced viciously with the scythe-swords they carried. The blows glanced harmlessly off the shield of the new apparition. Swinging the club, it struck the nearest borboressb on one shoulder. Instantly, flames engulfed the horrid creature as fire exploded from its arm. Wailing wildly, it raced away up the street, trailing flame and smoke.

Two more borboressbs jumped the figure. One fell flopping to the pavement, its neck broken by a swinging blow from the edge of the shield. The other caught the tip of the club in its mouth. For a second its eyes grew wide. Then its head exploded in a ball of flame. Gathering themselves, the rest of the enraged aberrations prepared to attack the club-wielding shape simultaneously.

Their coordinated assault was disrupted by the ferocious black mass that landed in their midst. Emitting a ground-shaking roar, Ahlitah sent one borboressb flying with a single swipe of one huge paw. An instant later, it bit off the head of a second.

Seeing their chance, Ehomba and Simna rushed the grenks. Repeated blows from their weapons sliced away huge chunks of quivering, jellylike flesh without halting the creatures' progress. They had no bones and, for all the two furiously flailing men could tell, no blood and no nervous systems. A tentacle-tongue lashed around Simna's sword arm, only to be severed by a downward stroke of the herdsman's blade. The amputated organ lay coiling and writhing on the ground like a worm driven to the surface by a heavy downpour.

Hewing and hacking methodically and without pause, they reduced the trio of obstinate but sluggish grenks to tremulous heaps of coagulated muck that littered the street and sidewalk. Even then, individual lumps of legless tissue tried to hump and slime their way in the travelers' direction.

Having sent the remaining borboressbs fleeing, some with scorched tails and burned limbs and with the raging Ahlitah in literally hot pursuit, the phantasm that had issued from the figurine turned its attention to the looming shade of the vohwn. The incorporeal specter twisted and coiled itself around the new arrival, encircling it with its own ghostly corpus. The faceless perversion began to contract, tightening its own self securely about the figure.

Undaunted, the tall newcomer swung the club lightly but firmly. A pair of pyre thorns made contact with the constricting miasma. An expression of uncertainty, a surprised moan, emanated from the spiraling vohwn. With a soft, empyreal hiss, it saw itself sucked up by the thorns, until only a last wisp of noxious vapor remained to show where it had once writhed. Wetting two fingers by touching them to its lips, the figure reached down and pinched the final bit of vohwn out of existence. A single last, sharp hiss marked its ultimate passing.

Covered in loose lumps of quivering, gelatinous grenk and breathing hard, Ehomba and Simna turned to face the tall, lithe figure that had emerged from the shards of the herdsman's petite carving. Holding firmly to shield and club, it came slowly toward them. Devoid of external assistance and support, Knucker the Knower's legs finally gave out. His bony butt landed hard on the pavement. There he sat, hunched over, rocking back and forth and mumbling to himself, staring down at nothing in particular.

Still edged in pale white flame, the figure halted before the two panting men. And smiled. Ehomba hesitated, uncertain, staring hard, reluctant to trust the interpretation his brain insisted on applying to the information his eyes were conveying.

"Fhastal?"

"Hello, Etjole Ehomba." And the magnificent smile widened.

It *was* Fhastal. But not the wise, wrinkled, hobbling old woman he had known since he was a child. Standing before him was a figure of towering feminine power, unforced sensuality, and burgeoning knowledge. Simna looked on in admiring silence.

"I do not understand," the herdsman said simply.

Placing one end of her shield on the ground, Fhastal leaned the club up against it and rested her folded hands atop both. "The little figure of me was carved not when I was a child or when I was as you know me, Etjole, but when I was like this. So when the seal was broken, I came to you not as I am, but as I was." She chuckled softly. "Was I not something uncommon when I was young?"

"By Gospoed's galloping gonads, I'll vouch for that!" Despite Ehomba's frown of disapproval, the swordsman made not even a veiled attempt to lower his gaze.

Without knowing quite why, the herdsman found himself twitching uncomfortably beneath her white-flamed, uncompromising gaze. Yet it was the same look, only slightly moderated by venerable age, that he had seen in her eyes on the day he had set off from the village. But that was Fhastal: spry, learned, and occasionally coarse, still as fond as anyone of a crude joke or good laugh despite her crippled physique and enfeebled senses.

There was nothing of frailty or failing about the body that stood straight and lithe before him now. But the white flame in which she was circumscribed was growing dimmer even as she spoke.

She glanced briefly down at herself. "Yes, this part of me is withering. From here on I can only be with you in heart and spirit, Etjole Ehomba. A comforting memory at best. Would that it could be otherwise." Raising her arms up and to the sides, she executed a leonine stretch. Observing the swordsman's reaction, Ehomba feared the smaller man's heart would fail him.

"You saved us," he professed simply.

Picking up shield and club, she advanced until she was standing within inches of him. The pale flame that emanated from her body exuded no heat. Her kiss, however, was as full of fire as the pyre thorns.

"Ah, Etjole!" she husked as she stepped back from him. "What a most excellent man you have grown up to be, and what a lucky woman is Mirhanja." Her expression turned serious. "You have a long ways still to travel."

He nodded. "I have been told twice now that if I continue on I will be killed. What can you tell me?"

The exquisite face shifted from side to side. "Nothing, Etjole Ehomba. I can tell you nothing. I am the Fhastal of my youth, and that young woman fought hard to learn what was around her. I had neither the time nor the ability to look ahead. Even now, that is a gift that is denied to me." Turning slightly, she gestured in the direction of the cringing, rocking figure. Having returned from its slaughter, the black litah stood watch over the helpless human shape. "Why not ask him? He knows everything."

Simna made a rude noise. "Knucker the drunker? He knows a lot, I'll give him that much. But everything? Not even the greatest of wizards knows everything. And that disgusting little snot's no wizard."

"No, he isn't," Fhastal the younger agreed. "But I think it barely possible that he may very well know everything, just as he says. The trouble is, knowing everything does not make one perfect. And just as he is no wizard, neither is he perfect." The last vestiges of flickering white flame had nearly vanished from her body, for the first time isolating her supple, graceful form sharply against the frame of night.

Reaching up to his neck, Ehomba grasped the torn strip of cord from which the figurine had hung. It had been with him ever since he had left the land of the Naumkib, a small, cool companion against his bare skin, a familiar weight to remind him of home. Now it was gone.

"I will miss you, Fhastal. Until I return home."

"I hope I'll still be alive by the time you get back. I would like to learn how this turns out for you."

"You should have told me about the carving's power." He spoke in a tone that was chiding but also affectionate.

"I did, Etjole Ehomba, I did!" She was laughing at him now, and for a brief moment the all-encompassing white flame seemed to dance higher, like a live thing summoned fleetingly back to life. "Did I not tell you when last we spoke that you were speaking to the image and that the figurine was the real me? That by your wearing it I would be able to travel with you?"

Now it was his turn to smile as he remembered, fondly. "So you did, Fhastal. I listened to your words but did not hear."

She wagged a finger at him and the simple gesture caused him to experience a start of recognition. When chiding children and their elders alike, as she did frequently and every day, aged Fhastal, real Fhastal, the chuckling, easygoing old Fhastal of the village, wagged her finger in exactly the same way.

"You see clearly and far, Etjole Ehomba, but there are times when you need to listen better!"

"I will remember," he assured her solemnly, speaking as an unruly child would to a doting parent.

"See that you do."

Simna stepped boldly forward. "Hoy, don't I rate a farewell kiss as well?"

The tall figure gazed speculatively down at the eager swordsman. "I think not, friend of Etjole's. You are too quick with the hands that wield that fine sword and, modest maid that I am, I have only enchantment and fire to protect me." Reaching out, she playfully tousled his hair. "Perhaps in another life." With those words, the last of the ethereal enveloping flame flickered out.

"Fhastal, wait!" Ehomba stepped forward, into the space where she had been. No pale efflorescence, no lingering glow, marked her final passage. There was only a faint warmth in the air, a smell of natural perfume, and the teasing tail end of a dissipating, girlish laugh.

"For us." There in the dark and deserted street far from home he stood and murmured to the sky. "She gave the last of her youth to save us. It was embodied in that figurine that she gave me for protection." Turning, he confronted Simna. The swordsman was still staring at the space the beauteous phantasm had vacated, savoring an already dwindling memory. "She could have enjoyed those moments in the company of old friends back in the village, or among those equal to her in experience and learning. But she gave it to us."

"Hoy, and a wondrous thing to behold it was," Simna readily agreed. "Knowledge and fighting ability and a sense of humor all in one woman. Not to mention those—"

Ehomba cut him off. "Show some respect, Simna."

"I would love to, bruther. Hoy, would I give a month of my life to show that woman some respect!"

"That was a vision of her as a youth. Nowadays she is old, and wrinkled, and bent."

The swordsman nodded somberly. "But still beautiful, I'd wager."

"Yes. Still beautiful." Taking a deep breath, he turned toward Ahlitah and the big cat's mewling, unhealthy charge. "She told us to ask questions of Knucker. We should follow her advice."

"Hoy." Simna walked alongside his friend. "Just so long as we keep in mind that no matter how much he knows, he doesn't know everything." The swordsman sniffed. "I don't care what she said. Nobody knows *everything*. Especially a broken-down ruin of a human being like that."

While a disgusted Simna stood nearby and the litah preened blood and bits of dismembered gut from his fur, Ehomba crouched before the gently swaying form of the man they had rescued from the close. A firm push from one finger would have been enough to knock Knucker over.

"How are you doing, my friend?"

The rocking stopped. Bloodshot eyes looked up and blinked like broken shutters. "Fine, fine! Why shouldn't I be?"

Ehomba glanced up at his companions. Ahlitah was ignoring everything while he concentrated on matters of individual feline hygiene. Simna snorted derisively and turned away. The herdsman looked back at the pathetic figure cowering before him.

"You did not see what happened?"

Knucker made an effort to peer around the kneeling form of the tall southerner. The effort would have caused him to keel over had not Ehomba reached out to steady him.

"Something's happened?" Wispy brows drew together. "Who are you, anyway? And why are you standing out here at night in the middle of the street?" He blinked again. "Why am *I* out here at night in the middle of the street?"

"We found you lying moaning in a close." Ehomba was gentle and patient. "It was after midnight and so we . . ."

Fear snapped Knucker's eyes wide open. "After midnight?" Looking around wildly, he tried to rise and failed, having to rely on Ehomba's strong arm to steady him once again. "We've got to get off the street, find shelter! The—"

"We know, we know." The herdsman shifted his supportive hand from the little man's waist to his upper arm. "I think it will be all right for a while, and there is a boardinghouse close by. Come." Rising, he helped Knucker erect.

"You don't understand," the drunkard was babbling apprehensively. "After midnight, there are things abroad in Phan. Bad things. They come out of the darkness and—"

Ignoring the coating of filth that helped to keep the man warm, Ehomba put a steadying arm around the scrawny back. "But we do understand, friend Knucker. We do understand. Thanks to you."

"To me?" Total confusion washed over the grimy, unshaven face. "What did I do? Who are you people?" As Ehomba gently shepherded him toward the unwinking, welcoming light of the boardinghouse and Ahlitah and Simna fanned out to either side to keep watch for trouble, they made their way up the empty but bloodied avenue. "And what am I doing out at night in the middle of the street?"

Off to Ehomba's right, Simna scanned the shadows for signs of potential trouble. But the side streets and alleyways were as quiet as they were dark, innocent in the light of his patrolling vision. As he strode purposefully forward, he shook his head and chuckled harshly. "Knows everything. Sure he does. Sure. Giliwitil knows he doesn't even know where he is!"

XIV

The sleepy-eyed proprietor of the boardinghouse woke up fast when he got a good look at the supplicants who had come knocking at his door. No ex-mercenary backed by a wall full of weapons, no towering muscular warrior nor even especially bold in his personal life, he was nonetheless a man of some determination and, within the limited bounds of his comparatively commonplace profession, courage.

"Come in, quickly!" Holding the door aside, he hastily scanned the street behind the nocturnal visitants.

Ehomba and his friends piled in, the herdsman and Simna supporting the intermittently driveling Knucker between them. Glancing downward as they stumbled through the portal, the tall southerner took note of the thick band of polished copper that gleamed beneath the doorjamb. Out of sight within the night and hugging the front wall of the boardinghouse, Ahlitah had remained unseen by the proprietor. Now the big cat trotted up the steps in the wake of his companions. The owner's eyes grew wide.

"You"—he gulped as he pressed his back against the wall to make room for the massive feline to pass—"you can't bring that thing in here!"

Lambent yellow orbs swung around to regard the stubby little man haughtily. "Who are you calling a 'thing'?"

Startled, the landlord ceased trying to sidle desperately sideways up the hall. "It talks."

"Yes," Ahlitah replied dryly, "it talks." Jaws that were capable of crushing furniture hovered a few feet from the terrified owner's perspiring face. The litah's breath was warm on the man's skin. "Don't you have a house cat?"

"N-n-no," the proprietor stammered weakly.

"Well you do now." Turning away, Ahlitah followed his companions deeper into the building. His broad, padded paws made less noise on the thick throw rugs and wooden planking than did his far less weighty human friends.

The owner trailed behind, anxious to query his visitors but fearful of pressing too close to the big cat. At the same time he dared not raise his voice lest he wake sleeping patrons and precipitate a panic. So he compromised by whispering as loudly as he could.

"Is it a room you want, or just a temporary refuge?" An intense desire to be rid of these eccentric vagabonds and the carnivore that accompanied them fought against his inherent good nature. At the same time he tried to place a distinctive and most disagreeable smell that did not, surprisingly, come from the big cat.

Ehomba looked wordlessly at his friend. With a sigh, Simna checked his remaining gold, knowing even as he did so that there was very little left. Still, if any of it was magicked, it might have reproduced while resting in his purse. A quick check revealed that the gold was still plain, ordinary gold. What remained was no more and no less than what he had seen there the last time.

"Hoy," he exclaimed frostily as he let Knucker's fetid arm slide off his shoulder, "we wouldn't have had to go through all that if not for this maundering sot. It's time for him to contribute to his own stinking survival." Taking a deep breath before he did so, the swordsman put his face close to the drunkard's. "Look here, you. Have you got any money?"

Bleary eyes struggled to focus. "What?"

Making a face, Simna momentarily turned away from the blast of liquorish vapors. "Money. Gold, convertibles, currency of the realm, legal tender. Have you got any?" When Knucker did not reply, the swordsman reached down and began going through the man's pockets. Another time, Ehomba might have objected. But their financial condition was parlous, and any group of village elders gathered to pass judgment on the situation would have agreed that the fellow owed them something for saving his life.

Simna's burrowing produced a handful of dirty coins. Recognizing them, the wavering Knucker tried to protest. "No—not my drinking money!" With one hand he made a grab for the metal disks, only to miss them and the swordsman by a wide margin. Unable to focus clearly, he could not properly judge the proximity of objects, even if the most prominent of those objects was one of his reluctant saviors.

Simna confronted the landlord. "It's a room we want. You wouldn't put a man back out on these streets in the middle of the night, would you?"

Hesitantly, the proprietor accepted the money, counting out only enough to pay for a single night's stay. "You'll, um, be gone in the morning?"

The swordsman's reply was brusque. "We're not hanging around to sample the delights of greater Phan, if that's what you mean."

"We are not tourists," Ehomba added, stating the obvious. He continued to support Knucker by himself while Simna dealt with the landlord. The effort did not exhaust the herdsman. He was used to carrying young calves around, and the small man weighed very little.

The landlord sighed and nodded. "Very well. Come with me." Edging around the litah's bulk, he started up a set of wide wooden stairs. Having settled business, Simna moved to assist Ehomba with his limp burden.

"We appreciate you extending your hospitality to us at this late hour." As they climbed, Ehomba admired the wallpaper and the small pictures that decorated the stairwell.

"You should," the landlord grumbled. While leading the way, he sorted through a large iron ring heavy with keys.

"I—I need a drink," Knucker mumbled.

Looking back, the proprietor gave him a disapproving look. "There is no liquor in this house."

Vacant eyes struggled to meet the owner's. "Yes there is. There are two bottles in a secret drawer in the bottom of your desk. One of brandy, another of whiskey. You hide them there from your wife."

As stunned as if he had walked face-first into a lamppost, the landlord stopped on a landing where the stairs took a leftward turn. "How—how did you know that? Are you a wizard?" He gaped at Simna. "Is this sorry specimen of humanity a wizard?"

"Nope." The swordsman nodded at Ehomba. "He's the wizard. This one here, he's just a dipso who knows everything."

"He can't know everything," the proprietor protested.

A line of slightly yellowish drool dribbling from the scabby right corner of his mouth, Knucker cackled softly. "Your wife knows where the drawer is. Why do you think each time you go there that there's always a little less in the bottles than you remember?" The landlord's lower jaw fell farther. "She also knows that you're tumbling the downstairs maid."

A look of tentative satisfaction came over the stocky landlord's face. "Ha! You may be some kind of besotted seer who can see certain things, but you can't see everything! I know my wife. If she knew that, she would have confronted me with it."

Turning away from the men supporting him, Knucker coughed once. "Not in this instance. Because, you see, she is tumbling the downstairs maid also. It's a matter of mutual tumbling, actually."

The proprietor looked stricken. "By all the deities, you may not know everything, but you know too much!" Turning away angrily, he resumed the ascent. "No more, tell me no more!"

As they struggled up the stairs, Simna leaned closer to the man he was helping to support. "So the lady of the house and a servant are having a twiddle, hoy?" An inquisitive leer stole across his face. "If you know that, you must know all the details."

Turning to him, Knucker tried to stand a little straighter as he was half carried, half dragged upward. "I may be many things, sir, but at least I am not degenerate."

"Hoy. There lies the difference between us, bruther. I admit to what I am."

"A drink." The little man licked his lips and smacked his tongue against his palate, sending out the universal signal of need common to all his kind. "I've got to have something to drink."

"We will try to get you some nice tea as soon as we are settled," Ehomba told him reassuringly. A look of horror came over Knucker's face.

The landlord had stopped outside a door. "I have only one room vacant, and it is far too small for your party. But this one here is a spacious chamber and you will be quite comfortable within—if I can persuade the current occupant to move." He put his finger to his lips as he gently inserted the key in the lock and opened the door. "The gentleman is presently within, but I will offer him a discount and a free breakfast, and I think if I explain the situation to him calmly and rationally he may be willing to accept alternate quarters for the night."

As soon as the door was open, Ahlitah pushed past the assembled humans. "I'll explain the situation to him."

"No!" As the proprietor reached out to grab and try to restrain the big cat, a small but loud voice shrieked warningly within his head, "What do you think you are *doing*?" Ordinary common sense immediately overwhelming his stalwart sense of managerial duty, he hastily drew back his hand.

Silently padding across the floor, the black litah approached the large bed and the single sleeping shape within. Reaching up, he rested a forepaw on the figure's shoulder.

"Mmph—wha . . . ?" The sleeper's eyes flickered. Then they opened wide. Real wide.

Ahlitah leaned close and spoke softly. "Go away."

Wide awake, the naked sleeper gathered sheets and blanket around him and flew off the bed in the direction of the door. "I'm gone," he responded. And he was, not even pausing to complain to the landlord. The stubby owner did not try to stop or slow him. He could not have done so in any event.

"I expect I'll find him downstairs, in my office." He sighed again. "He'll probably want a refund." Stepping into the room, he brought out a striker and lit the two oil lamps within, one on the wall by the doorway and another that sat on a small writing table. "There is another, smaller bed in the second sleeping room. Through that door, there." He pointed. "Please try to keep quiet. It's very late, and everyone else in the house is asleep."

Ehomba assured him that they would prepare for slumber as noiselessly as possible. Having curled up next to the unlit fireplace, the litah was already halfway unconscious.

"Come," the tired herdsman directed his friend. "We will put this fellow into the other bed."

"How come he gets a bed?" Simna protested as they hauled their mumbling cargo toward the other room. "Why not just dump him right here? He doesn't make a very good man. He might make a serviceable doorstop."

Ehomba eyed his companion sternly. "It was his money that paid for these lodgings."

"Hoy, right—but he won't remember that in the morning." He uttered a subdued expletive. "I know, I know. Do what's right. But it pains me, it does."

"There is no need for you to pout," the herdsman chided him. "You may have the large bed. I can tell by the look of it that it is too soft for me." He nodded back the way they had come. "There is a couch, and thick carpets on the floor. I will be fine."

"I wasn't worried about you, long bruther." But the swordsman's tone belied his attempt at callousness.

Together they stripped Knucker of his ragged, profoundly stained clothing. Undressed, he looked even more pitiful than when clothed.

"I wonder when he last ate?" Ehomba murmured as he examined the emaciated torso.

Simna grunted as he tossed short, tattered boots into a corner. "You mean when last he chewed something. This lush has been drinking his meals for some time."

"Perhaps we can get something solid into him in the morning," the herdsman speculated.

Pausing in the process of undressing, Simna looked up curiously. "Why do you care? He's a total stranger and, whether he knows everything or simply less than that, not a particularly admirable one. There are candidates more deserving of your concern."

"No doubt," Ehomba agreed, "but they are not here. He is." He studied the mumbling, self-engrossed figure thoughtfully. "Tell me something, Knucker."

"What?" Looking up, the exhausted little man they had saved from the demons of the night locked eyes with his rescuer. "Who are you?"

As they laid the drunk down on the clean sheets, Simna ventured a coarse observation on the ingratitude of the inebriated.

When a man stands all day doing nothing but watching cattle and sheep crop grass, he learns patience. "It does not matter," Ehomba told him. Bending over the bed, he murmured, "Knucker, what is the meaning of life?"

Their charge was already half asleep. His lips moved and Ehomba leaned close. He stood like that, inclined over the bed and its single diminutive occupant, a look of intense preoccupation on his long, handsome face. After a moment he nodded, and straightened.

"I thought so." His tone suggested quiet satisfaction.

Simna waited. When nothing further was forthcoming, he blurted sharply, "Well?"

The herdsman looked across the bed at his companion. Knucker was sleeping soundly now and, as far as Ehomba could tell, without difficulty. "Well what?"

"Bruther, don't play the coy with me. What *is* the meaning of life?"

"Someday I will tell you." The herdsman started around the foot of the bed, heading for the main room.

"Someday? What do you mean 'someday'?" Simna followed him, leaving the little man in darkness and silence.

In the main room Ehomba contemplated the couch. After first removing his pack and weapons, he began to arrange himself on the thickly carpeted floor. "When you have grown up." Stretching out flat on his back, he closed his eyes and crossed his hands over his lower chest.

"Grown up? Listen to me, master of mewling lambs, I'm not one to take kindly to a comment like that!"

One eye winked open to regard the irate swordsman. "Take it any way you like, but keep your voice down. If we make too much noise and wake the other tenants, the landlord is likely to throw us back out into the street."

"Hoy, him? That soft little self-important innkeeper couldn't throw Knucker out in the street, and that with him completely unconscious."

"Then if you won't be silent for his sake, be quiet for mine," Ehomba grumbled irritably. "And get some rest yourself. It is not long until sunrise, and I would prefer to spend as few nights as possible in this country that is proper and civilized only during the day and dreadful and deadly after dark." With that he rolled over, turning his back to the swordsman.

"When I have grown up, is it?" Growling under his breath, Simna divested himself of pack, sword, and raiment and slipped beneath the sheets of the spacious bed. It was still warm from the recent accelerated departure of its former occupant. That did not trouble Simna ibn Sind, who had slept on mattresses swarming with insomniac rats.

He fell asleep still angry, and dreamed of falling into a bottomless well filled with unending buckets of jewels and precious metals. It would have been a good dream, should have been a good dream, except for one pesky vexation.

Ehomba was there also, kneeling at the edge of the well looking down at the swordsman as the latter tossed coins and gems about like colored candy. The herdsman was not laughing derisively, nor was he heaping calumny upon Simna for indulging wholeheartedly in his base desires. All the impassive, compassionate herdsman was doing was smiling.

In his sleep, Simna ibn Sind tossed and muttered, unconsciously infuriated without knowing why.

Breakfast was served in the room by household staff. Sitting up naked in the big bed, the swordsman favored the pretty servant who brought their food with a come-hither grin. Greatly to his chagrin, she ignored him completely. He did not let her rejection prey upon him. He never did. Anyway, it made good sense. Since they were ensconced upstairs, she was most likely not the downstairs maid.

"Not bad," he told his companions as he masticated fresh rolls with jam and butter, aepyornis egg, bacon, and fruit. As was his nature, he had completely forgotten the brief but heated disputation with Ehomba of the night before.

In his corner, Ahlitah chewed fastidiously on a large leg of raw ox that the landlord had managed to scrounge from the kitchen. Ehomba sat on the floor with his back against the couch as he ate. In between bites and conversing with Simna, he cast occasional glances in the direction of the rear bedroom. The maid had delivered food to its occupant, but whether that worthy was even awake, much less dining, he did not know. As soon as he finished his own food, he would look in on the man they had rescued.

"You are right, Simna. Everything is quite good." The herdsman set a nearly empty glass of milk aside. "You should thank Knucker. He paid for this."

"Thank him?" Sitting up in the bed, the swordsman grunted. "We saved his miserable life at the risk of our own. He should be the one thanking us. But of course, he can't do that, because it would take too much of the worthless wretch's liquefied brain to string two words together."

"On the contrary, not only can I string two words together, I can tie them in assorted semantic knots if the need should arise."

Simultaneously, Ehomba and Simna looked toward the back-bedroom door. Only an indifferent Ahlitah did not glance up from his food. What the two men saw there came close to stunning them both into silence.

Knucker the Knower stood in the portal, but it was not the Knucker they knew. How he had bathed using only the pitcher and basin in the tiny inner bathroom they did not know, but bathe he had. Somehow he had even managed to clean up his clothing along with his body. A knife or razor had been used to remove the ugly stubble from his face. For all they knew, it might also have been the tool of choice utilized to dislodge the significant growth of unidentifiable greenish material from his teeth, which gleamed more or less whitely as he smiled at his saviors.

"I remember everything now." Stepping into the room, he staggered slightly before bracing himself with one hand against the doorjamb. A rapidly steadying finger pointed. "You—you're Etjole Ehomba. I heard him"—and he indicated the staring swordsman—"call out your name. And you, you are Slumva—no, Simna. Simna ibn Sind."

Setting aside the last vestiges of his breakfast, the swordsman slid out of the bed and began to dress, slowly and without taking his eyes off the little man for more than a moment. The litah glanced up briefly before returning to the bone he was crunching in order to get at the marrow within. Smashed or sober, to the big cat humans were all largely the same.

Slipping into his shirt, Simna nodded admiringly at the figure standing unaided by the doorway. "Never would have believed it. I've got to hand it to you, little bruther: You've gone and pulled yourself up out of the mire. Not many men could do such a thing in a single night. Especially not men as far gone as you were when we dragged you out of that close."

"I remember that, too. It's all coming clear to me now." Taking careful but increasingly confident steps, he walked up to Ehomba and grasped the herdsman's arms gratefully. "I don't know how to thank you. Once you've fallen as far as I did, you become so dazed and blind you can no longer find the way back up. For that you need help. You two have given me that gift."

"Genden's encomiums on you, Knucker." Having finished dressing, Simna sat down on the edge of the bed and resumed eating. "I take back what I said about you last night. But you probably don't remember much of that."

"On the contrary, I remember all of it. I have an exceedingly good memory—when it's functioning."

"Then you don't mind that we picked your pocket to pay for this room and food?" The unrepentant swordsman bit down into a final muffin.

"Not at all. I'd only have squandered the money on spirituous intoxicants. Far better it be used for sustenance and shelter. I owe you more, much more, than a night's rest."

His words muffled by muffin, Simna gestured at the other man with the crumbly residue. "Hoy, I'll second that!"

"And I would like to repay you further." Knucker smiled apologetically. "Unfortunately, all the money I had in the world was in my pocket. As you can imagine, I have had more than a little difficulty obtaining any kind of paying work lately."

"How did you come by that money, then?" Ehomba asked him.

Their guest lowered his gaze. "I would do anything for a drink, or for a few coins to purchase it. Please don't make me repeat the details. My condition was degrading enough. How far I debased myself to achieve that state of utter wretchedness need not concern you." Determination in his voice, he lifted his eyes. "I will repay you for your kindness by guiding you safely out of Phan by the quickest and easiest route. I do not know where you are headed from here."

"North by northwest," the herdsman told him simply.

Eagerness shining from his freshly scrubbed face, the little man nodded vigorously. "You will first have to pass through Bondressey. I know that country well and can greatly expedite your passage. I have even been to the foot of Mount Scathe, in the Hrugar Mountains, and can guide you at least that far." He looked anxiously from one man to the other. "What say you?"

Simna shrugged and jerked a thumb in the herdsman's direction. "This be the sorcerer's party. I'm just hanging around, kind of like unplanned baggage."

Knucker's eyes widened slightly as he turned to gaze at Ehomba. "Are you really a sorcerer?"

"No," the herdsman replied tersely. He threw a sour look in Simna's direction, but the herdsman had returned his full attention to the remaining ruins of his morning meal. "I am a keeper of cattle and sheep." A sudden thought made him frown. "But you already know what I am. You know everything."

The little man looked baffled. "Me? Know everything? What are you talking about? I know only myself, and the places I have been, and the bits and pieces of a normal life. How would I know whether you are a sorcerer or not?"

Simna was nodding slowly. "Exactly what I've been saying all along."

Ehomba's gaze narrowed as he stared hard at the speaker. If Knucker was, for whatever unknown reasons of his own, playing out a game behind a mask of feigned ignorance, he was performing like a professional. His expression as he returned the herdsman's gaze was all innocence and sincerity.

"What," he asked the other man slowly, "is the meaning of life?"

Struck dumb by this searching profundity, Knucker looked to Simna for assistance or an explanation. Neither was forthcoming. The little man turned back to Ehomba. "Do you expect me to answer that?"

"You did last night. And very well, too."

Knucker could only stand and shake his head in disbelief. "If I did, then I remember nothing of what was said."

"Name my two aunts," Simna challenged him. He was enjoying Ehomba's discomfiture.

This time their guest essayed a tiny, nervous laugh. "How could I do that? I know nothing of your family. I didn't even know you had aunts, or their number. Far less do I know their names." His brow wrinkled. "But I do remember something."

"Ah," Ehomba murmured expectantly. Simna looked uncertain.

"I remember that others have put such questions to me when I was in another of my rare periods of extended sobriety. I could not answer their questions either, and was bewildered that they would ask such things of me. I was amazed to think that they would believe anyone could answer such queries."

"Anyone indeed," Simna exclaimed, once more on top of the proverbial analytical heap.

"I think I understand." The herdsman rose from the couch against which he was sitting. "When you are clean and sober like this, you remember the normal things that go to make up a life. When you are drunk, you forget them—but know everything else. Truly, what a strange and capricious gift."

"If what you say is true, then it is not a gift but a curse," Knucker responded tightly. "Why can I not retain even a little of this knowing when I am rational enough to make use of it?"

"That I do not know." Ehomba began to check his pack. It was time to go. "But this I do know: From what we saw of you last night, you are far, far better off ignorant and sober than intoxicated and all-knowing." He smiled encouragingly. "In consequence of your having raised yourself up, we will allow you to guide us through Bondressey and as far as the Hrugar Mountains. Any help that speeds our journey is most welcome."

"Gryeorg knows that's true." Simna was shoving the last of the breakfast bread into his pack. "The sooner we reach the end, the quicker I'll have my hands on my share of the treasure."

"Treasure?" Once more, the little man looked mystified.

Ehomba pulled his pack up onto his shoulders and set about adjusting the straps. "My good friend Simna is brave and clever, but prone to delusion. In addition to believing that I am some sort of sorcerer, he is convinced that among other things I seek a great treasure. In truth, it exists only in his mind's eye."

"That's me." Simna made the announcement cheerfully as he ambled around the bed while fussing with his pack. Passing Knucker, he leaned close to whisper urgently. "He says I'm clever, and that I am. Clever enough to see through the denials he's forever prattling to me and everyone we meet. Don't you doubt it, bruther—he's a wizard on the trail of treasure. And I aim to get my share." He nudged the little man in his all-too-prominent ribs. "Who knows? If you play your 'predictions' right and can convince him to let you stick with us, you might come in for a share yourself."

"But I can't make any predictions unless I'm moribund drunk, and when I'm that badly under I don't know what I'm saying, much less what I'm hearing." He drew himself up to his full, if unassuming, height. "Besides, I'm through with drinking myself into stupefaction! Better an ordinary man sober than a seer stinking of debasement."

"A wise choice." Ehomba was straightforwardly encouraging. "That decision will make your company as welcome as your experience of the territory that lies ahead of us. It will be good to have a knowledgeable guide along, and not to have to ask one stranger after another which road is the safest to take, which route the easiest."

"I'll do everything I can," the reborn Knucker assured him. Less confidently, he turned to the black litah. Remaining bone snapped explosively beneath the big cat's powerful jaws. "I will even do all that is in my power to help you, most remarkable of all predators."

Languorously indifferent, Ahlitah turned his head to scrutinize the wavering speaker. "I despise you, you know."

"I—I'm sorry, great maned one. What have I done to so offend you?"

"Nothing." The cat returned to the last of its chomping. "I despise the other two as well. I despise all humans. You are weak, and unattractive, and conflicted within. Not only that, the most robust of your males can make love only a few times a day." He sniffed contemptuously through his whiskers. "Whereas the lion in me can—"

"Hoy, hoy," Simna interrupted, "enough! We've heard all that boasting. But can you make a sword, or tie a fishing line?"

Supercilious brows aimed at the swordsman. Thick black lips drew back to reveal gleaming teeth, and claws longer than a man's fingers sprang from their place of concealment within a massive forepaw. Alarmed, the timorous Knucker drew back.

"Here are my swords," the litah growled, "and here my fishing line."

"Stop it, you two." When he wanted to, Ehomba could growl smartly himself. "It is time to go."

"Hoy," the swordsman agreed. "Let's be away from here while my belly's still full and my temperament under control." He started toward the door.

Rising from his corner, Ahlitah padded after him, brushing against the apprehensive Knucker without so much as glancing in the little man's direction. As he passed Ehomba, however, the ebon hulk snarled softly.

"One day I will have to kill that insufferable windbag. Then I will butcher him like a fat young kudu and eat him, starting with his tongue."

"That is between you and Simna." Ehomba was blissfully indifferent. "But mindful of your promise to me, you will not do so until I have finished what I have come all this way to accomplish."

The great maned head turned to face the herdsman. So close were they that Ehomba could feel the litah's breath on his skin. It was pungent with the bone of dead ox. "You are more fortunate than you know, man, that among cats the code of honor is stronger than it is among humans."

Ehomba nodded his head ever so slightly. "I envy your character as much as your staying power."

The litah grunted its satisfaction. "At least you, Etjole Ehomba, recognize that which is greater than you, and respect that which you yourself cannot achieve."

"Oh, I did not mean that," the tall southerner responded frankly.

"By staying power, I meant your determination to remain with me." So saying, he followed the swordsman out the open door.

Ahlitah hesitated, pondering hard on the herdsman's words. Left behind, the little man looked on curiously. He had seen many things, but never before had he seen a cat pondering hard. Then the big carnivore emitted a series of short, pithy yowls, which, if Knucker had not known better, he might well have mistaken for laughter.

XV

The Parable of the Glass Golem

The four strangers paused to watch the ransacking of the house. Several soldiers broke away from their work to report the presence of the large black carnivore among the group of onlookers, but when neither it nor its presumed masters showed any sign of interfering, Proctor Cuween Bisgrath ordered them back to work.

They were an odd bunch, he decided as he studied them from his seat on the back of Rune, his favorite horse. Three men of radically different size, aspect, and color traveling in the company of the biggest and most peculiar-looking feline he had ever seen. Idly, he wondered if they would be worth interrogating, perhaps with an eye toward charging them a "fine" for traveling through Bondressey without a permit. No permits were necessary, but it was very likely they did not know that, and would pay to avoid trouble.

Contrarily, the wealthiest of them looked unconscionably poor, and it might not be worth his time to try to extract from them what few coins they might have in their possession. Furthermore, if the great predator accompanying them proved high-strung, he might lose a man or two in the process of making an arrest, and with little or no gain to hope for in return.

No, better to let the scruffy vagabonds continue on their way, hopefully right out of Bondressey. They were heading northwest. If they kept to that course they would cross the border in a few days, and good riddance. The mere presence on the streets of such uncouth vagrants was an offense to the kingdom's aesthetics.

"You there!" Pushing down on Rune's stirrups, he stood up in the saddle. "Make sure to check thoroughly the attic and any basement, and the walls for hidden compartments! Miscreants such as these often conceal their valuables in such places."

"Yes, Proctor!" came an acknowledging shout from the officer in charge. Sword drawn, he reentered the building. Household goods were already piling up on the front walkway as soldiers ferried them out from within.

Master and mistress of the handsome abode came stumbling out of the imposing entrance. Despite its size, no servants were in evidence. Their absence suggested that the owners took care of all the general maintenance themselves. That insinuated that they were dedicated workers. Bisgrath was gratified. Taking from the poor and the lazy was unprofitable.

"Please, sir, leave us something!" The master of the house looked older than his years, his face and posture reflecting an unpretentious life devoted to hard work. "All that we have has gone into our home!"

Rune stirred slightly and Bisgrath used the reins to steady his mount. "Ungrateful miscreant! Be glad I am leaving you the house. You know the penalty for failure to pay taxes in a timely and responsible manner. Fortunately for you, I am today in a generous and forgiving mood. Otherwise I would order your insignificant lodgings razed to the ground."

The man stepped back, his gaze glazed by hurt. Stumbling blankly about, he could only turn to watch the emptying of his home. After a moment, he fell to his knees, still staring.

Bisgrath magnanimously allowed the woman to clutch at his left leg and continue to plead for clemency. Not because he had any intention of listening to her, or because that was a quality normally ascribed to him, but because he found her pleasant to look upon. After a while, though, her uncontrolled sobbing began to grate on his patience. Putting a booted foot against her chest, he shoved hard and sent her sprawling. Another time he might have stalked her with Rune, using the horse's hooves as threats and making her crawl. But he was too busy directing the plundering of the household. Someone had to make certain that nothing was overlooked and that the spoils were properly loaded onto the waiting wagons. One for the kingdom, and the one with the heavy canvas covers for him. Astute as he was in matters fiscal, he knew better than to rely on official compensation to sustain his status.

For example, this particular family was not actually in arrears in matters of taxation. Only a simple subtle manipulation of certain texts had made it appear so. By choosing his untutored victims at random, he avoided the attention of his superiors, who were anywise gratified by his

uncanny ability to root out the disobedient among the kingdom's otherwise virtuous citizens.

Overlooked in the turmoil and confusion was a sandy-haired little
girl of seven or eight years. While her parents entreated futilely with
Proctor Bisgrath, she walked wide-eyed away from the house proper.
Intent on their ransacking, the industrious soldiers ignored her. In the
course of her aimless wandering, she found herself confronting an immense black face dominated by huge tawny eyes that seemed to glow
from within. Lips parted to reveal canines longer than her hand. A
tongue emerged to lick speculatively at her arm. It was rough and raspy
as a file and she stepped away sharply.

"Ahlitah!" a man's voice yelled sharply.

The tongue withdrew and the enormous cat looked back and
growled irritably. "Just tasting." With a shake of its magnificent mane it
resumed its pacing.

The place where the tongue had licked her began to burn slightly.
Ignoring the chaos behind her, instinctively shutting out the cries of her
mother, she began to cry.

A man was kneeling beside her. While the mild pain produced by
the big cat's tongue remained, so strange and fascinating was the face
now inclining toward her that her tears stopped. She stared at him, and
when he smiled back it instantly made her feel better. Not better enough
to smile, but sufficient to put a halt to the crying.

"I cannot tell you not to feel bad," he told her. "Do you understand
what I mean by that?" She nodded slowly, wiping at her eyes with the
back of one hand as the man looked past her. Her mother and father had
always told her not to talk to strangers, but somehow she knew that this
oddly dressed man represented no threat.

"My friends and I have a long ways yet to travel, so we cannot stop
to help you or your family. And anyway, this is none of our business." He
had a leather bag or something on his back. Pulling it around in front of
him, he fumbled around inside until he found what he was looking for.
"But since they are taking everything, I want to give you something. It is
a little dolly. It was given to me by a very wise old lady named Meruba. I
know that she would want you to take it."

Opening his fingers, he revealed a tiny doll lying in his palm. Small
enough to fit in her hand, it was carved from a black material that she
did not recognize.

"It's very nice. Thank you, sir."

Reaching forward, he used very long fingers to brush hair out of her
eyes. "You are welcome, child." He started to rise.

"What's it made of? I've never seen anything like it before."

"It is a kind of glass, but not the glass that is made by people. This kind comes from deep within the earth. Sometimes we find it lying about on the ground where I come from. It takes a good edge and makes fine knives and spearpoints. But your dolly is all smooth and polished. It will not cut you."

One of his companions shouted something to him. They had moved on past the house and were waiting for him to catch up. "I have to go now," he told her. "My friends are calling me." He paused a moment, then added, "Tell your mommy and daddy to go to whoever is in charge of bad things like this. If they will do that, I have a feeling they might be able to get some of their things back."

"Yes sir. I will, sir." The girl clutched the diminutive black doll to her chest. The volcanic glass was slick and cold and slightly waxy-feeling to the touch.

The tall, kindly stranger rejoined his companions and they were soon gone from sight. She concentrated on the doll, cooing and murmuring to it. So she did not see her father rise from his knees to charge Proctor Bisgrath angrily, or see the blood fly from his head as an alert soldier caught him a heavy blow from behind with the solid wooden shaft of his pike. She did not see or hear her screaming mother throw herself atop the crumpled, unconscious form, or hear the soldiers laugh as they roughly pulled her away in the direction of the rosebushes that had been her pride and joy.

Ignoring his minions' harmless frolic, Bisgrath continued to supervise the plundering until even he was convinced there was nothing more to strip from the dwelling. Content with the day's work and not a little tired, he ordered the wagons formed up. Obedient soldiers fell into lines on either side of the booty, flanking the two carry-alls. At the Proctor's directive, they began to move out. The larger wagon would be escorted triumphantly back to the city hall. Its smaller sibling would find itself diverted down a little-used side street, eventually to come to rest in the impressive enclosed courtyard of the majestic mansion of Cuween Bisgrath, Proctor General of Bondressey.

Tugging on the reins, the Proctor turned to follow the procession. A shimmer of light caught his eye and made him pause. Curious, he turned back and trotted over to the source of the gleam. It lay in the open palm of a little girl.

Leaning down from the saddle, he smiled unctuously and gestured at the object. "What have you there, child?"

She replied without looking up at him. "I'm not talking to you. You hurt my mommy and daddy."

"Tut now, child. I am only doing my job."

"You're a bad man."

"Perhaps, but I'm good at it. So that makes me a good bad man."
Behind him, the wagons were trundling off in the direction of the central
city.

Frowning, she looked up at him. "That doesn't make any sense."

"Yes it does. You'll understand when you're older. My, but you're a
pretty little thing. Maybe I'll come and visit you later."

"No!" she responded emphatically.

"You have your father's spirit—but I won't hold that against you."
He leaned a little farther out of the saddle. "May I see that little toy,
please? Where did you get it?"

She turned to point. "A nice man gave it to me. He was funny-
looking."

Bisgrath followed her outstretched arm, but there was no sign of the
untidy foreigners. They had disappeared northward. "An exotic artifact.
Perhaps from very far away. How interesting. The carving is very well
done. I have quite a collection of art myself, and I have never seen
anything exactly like it." He extended his hand. "Let me see it."

"No." Clutching the dolly in both hands, she pulled away from his
reaching fingers.

Pouting, he withdrew his hand. "I just want to look at it. If you let
me look at it, I'll give you back some of the things the soldiers took."

Hesitantly, she unfolded her fingers and looked long and hard at the
carving. Then she reached out and up and handed it to him. He turned it
over in his fingers, admiring the exquisite detail and the play of light over
the lustrous black surface.

"It's more accomplished than I thought. Thank you, child." Jerking
on Rune's reins, he turned to go.

Behind him, the girl started screaming. "Give it back! You promised,
you promised!"

"Something else you'll understand when you're older," he called
back to her. He slipped the fine carving into a jacket pocket, wishing the
girl's mother would take charge of her spawn and shut her up. He disliked screaming. But the mother was in no condition to help her child or
anyone else.

He parted with the main body of soldiers after congratulating them
on a morning's work well done, and not before slipping a little something
extra into the palm of the officer in charge. Leaving them to make their
way into the city with the larger of the two booty-laden wagons, he
turned to escort the other down a different road entirely.

Capable hands were waiting to unload, as stone-faced servants responded to his return. None smiled at his success, none offered a cheery

greeting as he dismounted and climbed the steps that led into the great hall. Those who worked for the Proctor did not smile in his presence lest their expression be misinterpreted. By keeping his staff intimidated, Bisgrath felt he insured their loyalty. It was harder to steal from a master you feared than from one you thought of as harmless.

Lunch awaited and, much to the relief of the kitchen staff and servers, was pronounced satisfactory by the Proctor. As he left the dining room, Bisgrath mentally totaled the profit he would accrue from the morning's exertions. A good day's work all around, he decided.

Entering the library, he pondered a number of possible sites for the exotic carving. There were several empty alcoves that would serve to highlight its luster, and a place on the main reading table already crowded with fine lapidary work. In the end he decided to stand his newest acquisition on the inlaid reading table by his favorite chair, where he could admire it frequently until, as he always did, he grew bored by it and sought a fresh replacement.

Putting on his reading glasses and settling himself into the chair, he selected one of several massive ledgers from a low table nearby and opened it on his lap. Since things had gone so smoothly this morning, he had all afternoon in which to ferret out the next subject for persecution. Or rather, he mused as he smiled inwardly, the next blatant violator of the Kingdom of Bondressey's far too lenient tax laws. Afternoon light pouring through the high, beveled glass windows allowed him to read the fine scrawl without strain.

In this pleasant and relaxed fashion he passed the better part of an hour, using a pen to put a damning mark beside the names of half a dozen potential miscreants. Feeling a slight weight against his right arm, he brushed at it casually—only to have his fingers make contact with something hard and unyielding.

Glancing impassively to his right, he found himself staring down at the diminutive glass figurine. Somehow it had fallen against his arm. He frowned, but only momentarily. There was no wind in the room, so it must have been placed at an angle on the end table and fallen over against him. His thoughts focused on the ledger, he absently picked it up and set it back down in the middle of the table, and forgot about it.

Until, several minutes later, he again felt the weight against his arm.

Frowning this time, he picked up the carving and placed it, not in the middle, but on the far side of the end table. Mildly irritated with himself, he settled back into the chair and resumed reading. In minutes he had once more forgotten all about the figurine.

In the silence of the library, where no servant would dare to disturb him, a soft tap-tapping caused him to look up from his malevolent perusal. Following the sound to its source, he turned to his right. His eyes widened and air momentarily paused in its passage through his throat.

Blank of eye, black of body, the carving was tottering on slow obsidian feet across the tabletop toward him.

Leaping from the chair, the ledger falling heavily to the floor at his feet, he gaped at the tiny apparition. It promptly changed its direction to a new heading to reflect his rising.

"What manner of foreign necromancy is this?" There was no one in the library to hear him and the figurine, of course, did not reply. Nor did it pause in its advance.

"Preposterous manifestation, what are you?" Tightening his lips, he reached out and grabbed the carving. A chill ran through him as he felt it moving in his hand. Searching the room, he quickly found what he was looking for.

Into the gilt silver box went the ensorcelled figurine. A turn of the key, the click of the latch, and it was secured. Slipping the key into a pocket, a contented Bisgrath returned to his chair. "I'll attend to you later. I count among my acquaintances many knowledgeable practitioners of the arcane arts. They'll investigate the spell that motivates you, and we'll fast put a stop to this unsanctioned meandering."

Satisfied, he resumed his seat and, a bit more intently than usual, continued with his reading. Another hour passed, at which point he decided it was time to call a servant to bring some drink. He rose from the chair.

There seemed to be a weight on his thigh. Looking down, he saw the figurine clinging with tiny but powerful hands to the leg of his pants as it worked its way steadily upwards. And this time, each minute, a perfectly carved eye was glowing a vivid intense yellow.

With a cry he grabbed the carving and wrenched it free of his leg. Without thinking, he drew back his arm and threw the suddenly hideous little manikin as far and as hard as he could. It slammed into one of the tall windows that lined the library's west wall. Even before it did so, he found himself wincing. Fine leaded glass was immoderately expensive.

But the windows were thick and well made, and this one did not crack. Neither did the carving bounce away. As he stared, it adhered to the transparency and, beneath his incredulous gaze, began to diffuse into it, glass melting into glass. The figurine grew smaller and smaller as a black stain spread across the center of the window. It continued to disperse and disseminate until it had disappeared completely.

Realizing that he was breathing hard enough to make his lungs ache, Bisgrath forced himself to calm down. Approaching the window, he reached up to feel gingerly of the place where the carving had struck.

There was no sign that anything was amiss. The thick glass was not chipped, and even up close there was no sign of the corrupt foreign blackness that had appeared to diffuse within the material.

Quite astonishing, he thought. He would have to inquire of learned acquaintances as to the meaning of the episode. Meanwhile, there was work to be done. But first, something to drink.

Using a pull cord to summon a servant, he once more returned to his chair and to his malicious scrutiny of the ledger's contents. Finding several more prospective victims helped to relax him and set his mind at ease. When the servant knocked, he barked an irritable "Enter!" without looking up from his work. The choosing of unwitting innocents to savage never failed to raise his spirits.

Entering silently, the servitor approached with tray in hand—only to signal his entrance with an abrupt metallic crash that caused Bisgrath to look up sharply. "What the blazes do—" He halted in mid-accusation. The servant was not looking at him. An expression of utter terror was imprinted on his face. The silver tray lay forgotten at his feet, the contents of the pitcher it had held having spilled out across the immaculate hardwood floor.

Puzzled, Bisgrath turned to follow the man's gaze, whereupon he whipped off the reading glasses and flung them aside, unable to believe the evidence of his own eyes.

Peering out at him from the window and occupying most of its height was an outline of the black glass carving, its eyes burning like oil lamps on a particularly dark and chill night.

With a stuttering scream, the servant fled the room. Rising and backing slowly away from the window, Bisgrath fumbled along the wall for the weapons that were mounted there. Arranged in a decorative semicircle, they included a great number of killing devices more suitable for use by common infantry than a cultivated gentleman like himself. That did not stop him from wrenching a short, heavy war ax from its holding clips.

Uttering a cry of defiance, he charged the window. The inhuman fiery gaze seemed to follow him as he rushed across the room. It went out when he slammed the ax into the glass, bringing more than half of it down in a shower of crystalline fragments.

Panting heavily, the ax clutched convulsively in both hands, he backed away. Birdsong filtered in from outside and a cool Bondresseyean breeze blew unbidden into the library. The tall black image had vanished. *Help,* he thought fearfully; *I need a magician here to tell me what is going on.* He knew several names and would send servitors to summon them immediately—yes, immediately. He turned for the doorway. As he did so, out of the corner of an eye he caught sight of a discrepancy.

The carving had reappeared, its eyes burning as fiercely as ever, in another of the tall library windows. And this time it was not a flat, picturelike image, but a mass formed in glistening, solid relief, its thick arms reaching out, outward into the room. Ten feet tall, the dreadful apparition was composed entirely of black volcanic glass, as if it had drawn strength and substance from the leaded glass of the window itself.

Screaming wildly, Cuween Bisgrath hurled the war ax at the glossy, brutish homunculus that was slowly emerging from the thick pane of the window. It shattered noisily, sending shards both transparent and black flying in all directions. Stumbling from the room, the Proctor General tore up the stairs that led to the second floor and to his private quarters. He was going mad, he decided. None of this was actually happening. He didn't need magicians; he needed a doctor.

He shouted for his servants, but none responded. Having heard from the servitor who had entered the library and subsequently bolted and seen the look on his face, they had one and all fled the mansion. They had found something they were more afraid of than the Proctor's wrath.

Staggering into his bedroom, Bisgrath slammed the door behind him and threw every one of the heavy bolts. Designed to withstand a full-scale assault by a company of armed soldiers or hopeful assassins, its unrelenting solidity helped to reassure him. Breathing a little easier, he made his way to the splendid bathroom. Spacious enough to accommodate six bathers, the marble tub beckoned. He strode purposefully past, knowing that he had to find a physician to diagnose whatever ailment was causing him to experience such profoundly disturbing hallucinations. He would make a cursory attempt to clean himself up and then ride himself to the offices of a particularly well-known practitioner who specialized in unusual afflictions. And when he returned, treated and well, the shrieks of delinquent servants would make themselves heard all the way to the border with Squoy.

Cold, lightly minted water splashed on his face from the magnificent enameled basin refreshed him instantly. Reaching for a cloth, he wiped droplets clear, enjoying the reinvigorating tingle they left on his skin. Raising his gaze to the filigree-edged mirror, he tried to understand what had happened to him, and how.

Bare inches away, incandescent yellow eyes set in an impassive black mask of a face peered menacingly back at him, burning hotter than ever.

Choking on his own fear, he reeled away from the accusing, threatening face in the mirror that belonged not to him but to some emotionless brute. His fumbling fingers contracted spasmodically around the first thing they touched. Drawing back his arm, he tried to throw the iridescent drinking goblet as hard as he could at the silently taunting mirror.

The effort nearly caused him to fall. Looking down at his hand, he saw that the goblet had a hold on his wrist and would not let go. Or rather, the fiend that was emerging from the rainbow-hued glass would not.

Screaming, spinning wildly, he smashed the goblet against the marbled wall. Glass went flying in multicolored splinters, the light from a thousand fragments momentarily illuminating the bathroom with a full spectrum of brilliance and fear. It obliterated the dark demon that had been emerging from the hand-blown glass goblet, but not the one in the mirror. Blood bubbled from a dozen tiny cuts on his hand and face. Ignoring them, he backed out of the bathroom and slammed the door as hard as he could.

Articulating the wordless dirge of the living unhuman, two more hulking representations of the carving were seeping out of the bedroom windows, their jet-black bodies massive and irresistible. Leaping across the bed to the safety of the bedroom door, Proctor Bisgrath frantically drew back one security bolt after another. Before fleeing into the outer hall, he picked up a heavy iron doorstop and threw it at the nearest of the advancing homunculi. The metal struck the figure with a loud crack. Half the face shattered and crumbled away without slowing the inexorable advance of the black glass manikin in the least.

His howls and screams echoing through the empty, great house, Bisgrath flew back down the stairs. For one seeking escape, it was an ill-advised choice. From every window and mirror, from every frosted-glass cabinet and graceful chalice, the indefatigable progeny of the obsidian carving lurched and tottered toward him, heavy arms outstretched, fingers curled like black flesh hooks. In every one of them, pitiless eyes burned soullessly.

There was no way out, he saw. But maybe, just maybe, there was a way in. He had not risen to the position of Proctor General for all the kingdom of Bondressey through dint of slow wit and ponderous thinking. Whirling, he rushed back into the library.

The four monstrous forms that lumbered out of the remaining unbroken windows were each large and heavy enough to crush an entire patrol beneath their bulk. But, relentless as they were, their movements were not the swiftest. Ducking beneath the whooshing sweep of a grasping arm, he darted along the back wall until he reached a bookcase filled with innocuous tomes on the art of gardening. Moaning like a chorus of doom, the four huge figures turned to follow. A menagerie of smaller cousins poured in through the door that led to the great hall.

Pulling out a specific book that was not a book, Bisgrath held his breath as the heavy bookcase that was not a bookcase rotated silently on a concealed pivot. Ducking into the secret room beyond, he leaned hard on a lever set in the wall that was a match to the nonbook outside. The monstrosities were remorseless, but he had seen nothing to suggest that they were in any wise clever.

Since no windows opened onto the secret reading room, he found himself fumbling in the dark. But no windows meant no glass. There were no drinking utensils, no mirrors. He should be safe in the stone-wall chamber, for a little while at least. Feeling along the edge of the reading table, he located the large candlestick standing there. Using tapers stored in a box near the base, he ran his fingers up the length of the candle to the wick. Striking one taper, he lit the cylinder of beeswax and then another on the other side of the table. Warm, safe light suffused the room. Faintly, he could hear the assembling horde keening and moaning horribly on the other side of the bookcase door. Fists of heavy black glass began to pound rhythmically against the barrier, like distant drums. The pivoting gateway held, but for how long it would continue to do so he could not be sure.

Pulling priceless volumes off the wall, he finally found the one he was searching for and carried it to the table. It was bound in fraying old leather and weighed as much as a small saddle. If he could not send word to a magician, then he would make his own magic. He had done so on a limited basis in the past, and he would do so again now. Always more dilettante than pupil, he wished now that he had paid more attention to such studies. But why bother to learn the intricacies of the mystic arts when one could always hire a professional to do the job better?

As the pounding outside increased, he was encouraged by the continued stability of the doorway. Working the index, which was an entire book unto itself, he finally found the item he was looking for. By the steady, reassuring illumination of the twin candles he flipped through the heavy weight of pages until his fingers stopped them at the appropriate chapter.

There it was: a simple recitation for banishing spirits that might arise up out of statues. Leaning over the open book and squinting in the flickering light, he saw that the spell was deemed effective on sculpture rendered in any medium: stone, metal, wood, bone, shell—and glass.

Turning to the thudding portal, he raised a clenched fist and bellowed defiance. "Pound away, brood of foreign devils! In another moment you'll all be dead and gone, extinguished, like steam off a hot stove! Nothing and no one besieges Cuween Bisgrath in his own house!"

Turning back to the book, he bent low over the relevant paragraphs.

Though writ small, they appeared elemental and shorn of unpronounce-able terms. To make sure he committed no potentially hazardous errors in the reciting of the formula, he reached automatically for the pair of reading glasses that were always kept safe in the single pull-out drawer beneath the reading table.

And made the mistake of putting them on.

XVI

"Hoy, bruther, what did you give to that poor little thing, anyway?"

"Nothing much." Ehomba strode along easily as they climbed into the first foothills. "It was a little doll, a carving that had been given to me by one of the women of the village." He glanced over to where the emancipated Knucker was stopping to inspect every flower they passed, as if seeing and sniffing each one for the first time. "When you are going away on a long journey, people give you peculiar odds and ends, in the hope that this or that frippery might at some time prove useful. I saw no particular use for the carving, and thought that since the girl appeared to be losing everything she owned, she might enjoy the comfort of a doll, however small and hard."

The swordsman took a playful swipe at the tuft on the end of Ahlitah's switching tail. Looking back, the big cat's eyes narrowed. With great dignity, it loped on ahead, effortlessly outdistancing its human companions.

"Maybe you have got kids of your own, bruther, but your woman must have done the raising. No girl that age is going to cuddle up to a piece of black rock."

"It was not rock." Ehomba stepped carefully over a patch of small, bright blue flowers.

"Whatever." The swordsman shook his head sadly. "You're always the one in such a hurry, Etjole. If you waste time to pause and jabber with children unfortunate in their choice of parents you'll never get to where you're going."

"Yes, I suppose you are right, Simna. There was nothing we could do for her family without making ourselves the targets of those soldiers, and she will probably throw the figurine away at the first opportunity."

"Don't take it to heart, bruther." The swordsman gave his tall friend a condoling slap on the back. "People are always thinking they can make a difference in some stranger's life, and invariably they end up making things worse." Raising his voice, he called out to their new companion.

"Hoy, Knuckerman! There's footpaths all over this place. You're supposed to be guiding us. Stop snorting those stinking weeds and show us the right one."

Bright-eyed and alert, the little man straightened and nodded. "Your animal is still moving forward on the correct line. Keep following him. If he makes a wrong turn I'll let you know. Don't worry."

"Why should I worry?" Simna murmured aloud. "We're following the lead of the man who knows everything. Or used to. I wonder: If we got a drink or two into him—not enough to destabilize him, mind— would he stay sober enough to understand the question and still be able to know the answer?"

As they walked, Ehomba dutifully considered the proposition. "I do not think so. I believe that with Knucker and his knowing it is all one way or all the other. There is no middle ground."

Simna showed his disappointment. "Too bad."

"But he is happier this way. And healthier, with a new outlook on the future. Look at him."

"Hoy, hoy. Clean and sober but useless. A fine trade-off, that." The swordsman strained to see over the next hill. They were entering dense forest, fragrant with towering pine and spruce. "Didn't he say something about an interesting town not far ahead?"

Ehomba nodded. "Netherbrae." The herdsman surveyed the steeply ascending hills. "Two days' journey from here and well outside the borders of Bondressey."

"Good." Simna increased his pace. "I could do with some surroundings that were interesting instead of civilized."

"Cannot a place be both?"

"Hoy, but given a choice, I much prefer the former over the latter. Ow!"

Reaching up, the swordsman felt the back of his head. The source of the slight but sharp pain was immediately apparent: A sizeable pinecone that had fallen from a considerable height was still rolling to a stop near his feet. Ehomba's gentle grin at his friend's discomfort vanished when a similar missile struck him on the shoulder. Together, the two men peered warily up into the trees. As they did, another cone landed several feet away.

Simna took consolation from his tall friend's ignorance. The herds-man had never seen seeds like these before. There were no towering evergreens in the land of the Naumkib.

"Such trees drop their cones all the time," the swordsman explained. "We just happened to be walking in the wrong place at the wrong time." As he finished, another cone struck Ahlitah on his hindquarters. The big cat whirled sharply and smacked the offending seed pod twenty feet before it could roll off his backside and hit the ground. His dignity was more injured than his hip.

"Your location had nothing to do with it." Knucker had rejoined his new friends, but instead of on them his gaze was focused on the inter-locking branches overhead. "We're being targeted."

Ehomba's excellent eyesight could discern no movement in the tree-tops except for the occasional bird or dragonet. One pair of mated azure dragonets was busy enlarging a prospective nesting hole high up in the otherwise solid bole of a giant spruce. Each would inspect the cavity, lean forward and blast it with a tiny, precisely aligned tongue of flame from its open mouth, then sit back and wait for the fire to burn itself out. The pair was already through the bark and into solid wood. Several days of such careful work would leave them with a fire-hardened black cavity in which to raise their young.

The herdsman kept an eye on them as he and his friends continued to make their way through the cool, enclosing woods. Both dragonets were fully occupied with the task of excavating their nesting hole, and neither paid the least attention to the party of three men and one cat tromping through the forest litter. Certainly they did not pause to kick pinecones at the figures far below.

"I do not see anything throwing these cones at us," Ehomba de-clared. Even as he concluded the observation, two more cones landed close by his feet, just missing him. His eyes instantly darted upward, but there was no sign of movement in any of the branches immediately over-head.

A smiling Knucker tapped the side of his nose with a long finger. This time, nothing came out. "We must be under attack by groats." He scanned the treetops. "Troops of them are common in these woods. They don't like visitors."

As a particularly heavy cone plummeted to strike him a glancing blow on the left foot, Simna loudly offered to trade his blade for a good bow and a quiver full of arrows.

"It wouldn't do you any good," Knucker assured him.

"Why not?" More insulted than injured by the cone, the swordsman spoke without taking his eyes from the branches overhead. "I'm a pretty good hand with a bow. What are these groats, anyway?"

"Small furry creatures that live in the treetops in forests like these." Holding his hands out in front of him, Knucker aligned the open palms about three feet apart. "They have long tails and feet that can grip branches as strongly as hands, in the manner of monkeys, but their faces are like those of insects, hard and with strangely patterned eyes."

Ehomba hopped clear of a falling cone nearly the size of his head that he was fortunate to spot on the way down. It hit the ground with a weighty thump that held the potential for serious injury. As the bombardment continued and the first small cones gave way to far larger woody projectiles, the situation began to deteriorate from merely bothersome to potentially serious.

"I have good eyes and I have been looking for a long time," the herdsman replied, "and still I see nothing like what you describe."

Knucker's expression turned serious. "That's because the fur of the groat is invisible. You have to look for their eyes, which is the only part of them that reflects light."

Searching for three-foot-long furry creatures ambling through the treetops was one thing. Hunting only for isolated eyes was far more difficult. A cone that could have knocked a man unconscious struck Ahlitah squarely on his head, provoking a roar that shook the needles of the surrounding trees. It did not intimidate the unseen groats, who continued to rain cones down on the hapless intruders at an ever-increasing rate.

More cones suggested the presence of more groats. While this made the travelers' situation more perilous, it also improved the opportunities for detecting the elusive creatures. Moments after he executed an elegant if forced little dance that enabled him to dodge half a dozen falling cones, Simna stabbed an arm skyward.

"There! By that big branch thrusting to the east from this tree next to us. There's one!" Reflexively, he fingered the hilt of his sword. The large compound eyes of the otherwise invisible arboreal tormentor glistened in the afternoon light. No accusatory chattering came from the creature or from any of its companions. The barrage of cones was being carried out in complete silence.

Simna was not silent, however. Ill equipped to deal with an attack from above, he was reduced to screaming imprecations at their unseen adversaries. Unsurprisingly, this had no effect on the volume of cones being dropped upon him and his friends.

By this time they had broken into a run. Their progress was made difficult because they had to keep more or less to the trail as located by

Knucker while avoiding not only the falling cones but also the dense mass of trees. Straining to pick out eye reflections in the branches overhead, Ehomba struck one smaller tree a glancing blow with his shoulder. While trying to determine the extent of the resultant bruise, he was hit by two smaller cones launched from above. Gritting his teeth, he pulled himself away from the tree trunk and ran on.

"These groats!" he yelled at Knucker, who was having a hard time keeping up with the pace. "What would they do if they killed us? Eat us?"

"Oh no," the wheezing little man assured him. "They'd just make sure we were dead and then go away. They only want their forest back. As I said, they don't like visitors."

"Can't they tell that we're trying to leave as fast as we can?" Raising a hand over his head, the swordsman warded off a cluster of small cones. Despite their moderate size, they still stung when hurled from a considerable height.

"They probably can't." Knucker was gasping for air now. It was clear to Ehomba that their new companion would not be able to keep up for much longer. Something had to be done. But what? How did one fight an opponent beyond reach and impossible to see except for its eyes?

Simna thought he had the solution. "Do something, Etjole! Blast them out of the treetops, turn them into newts, call up a spell that will bring them crashing down from the branches like stones!"

"How many times do I have to tell you, Simna—I am not a sorcerer! I can make some use only of what wiser ones have given to me." Looking up, he dodged to the right just in time to avoid a pinecone as big as a beer tankard, and almost as heavy.

"Hoy, then use the sky-metal sword! Call up the wind from between the stars and blow them clear out of the woods!"

"I do not think that would be wise. The wind that rushes between the stars is not a thing to be trifled with. You do not bring it down to earth every time you have a problem." While running, he waved at the imposing, surrounding trees. "I could try to bring down the wind, but once summoned it cannot be easily controlled. It could bring down every tree in this forest along with the groats. Better to endure a pounding by seed pods than by falling trees."

"In your pack." Simna was tired of running. He wanted to stand and fight, but doubted their assailants would oblige him. Even if they did, it would be hard to do battle with three-foot-long invisibilities. "There's always something in that pack of yours! A magic amulet, or a powder to make smoke to hide us, or another figurine like the one that summoned Fhastal the younger."

"Fhastal's sword would be of no more use to us here than our own." The herdsman looked for a place to halt that offered some concealment from the arboreal barrage. "And I have no magic pills or conjurer's tricks. But I do have an idea."

"Glewen knows I'd rather have an amulet," Simna yelled back, "but at this point I'll settle for an idea. If it's a righteous one."

There were no caves in which to hide, no buildings in which to take refuge, but they did find a lightning-scarred tree whose base had been blasted into a V-shaped hollow. In this they all took refuge from the steady rain of spiky projectiles. Glittering eyes gathered in the branches overhead as the peripatetic yet silent groats continued to pelt this temporary sanctuary with cones.

Slipping his pack off his back, Ehomba dug through its depths until he found what he was looking for. Simna crowded uncomfortably close. The tree hollow was barely large enough to accommodate the three men. With the addition of the litah's substantial bulk it was difficult to breathe, much less move about.

Removing his searching hand, the herdsman displayed a slim, irregularly shaped, palm-sized slab that was dull gray metal on one side and highly polished glass on the other. The reflective surface was badly scratched and the metal pitted and dented. It looked like a broken piece of mirror.

"What is it?" The swordsman was openly dubious. "It looks like a mirror."

Ehomba nodded. "A piece of an old mirror. An heirloom from Likulu's family."

"That's all?" Simna stared uncomprehendingly at his tall companion. "Just a mirror? What would you be carrying a mirror around for? I haven't noticed that you've been paying special attention to your appearance." Expectation crept into his voice. "It's more than a mirror, isn't it? It has some kind of unique properties to help you vanquish your enemies?"

"No," Ehomba replied flatly, "it is only a mirror. A device for letting people see themselves as they are."

"Then what good is it?" A large cone slammed into the ground close enough to the swordsman's right foot to cause him to try to jerk it farther back into the hollow. But there was no more room. And the groats, seeing that their quarry was trapped, were growing bolder, descending to lower and lower branches the better to improve their aim. Twinkling compound eyes of bright blue and green began to cluster together. Above and below them, plucked pinecones appeared to float in midair.

"The sun is still high, and very bright." Holding the mirror firmly in one hand, Ehomba prepared to step out from beneath the protection of the tree hollow. "Their eyes are large. If I can bounce the sunlight into them and blind one or two, the others might panic and run." He glanced briefly over at his friend. "This is what I carry it for—to reflect the sun. In my country if one encounters trouble it is the best way to signal for help across long distances."

"I'd rather have bows and arrows." Leaning ever so slightly forward, Simna tried to locate the nearest of their tree-loving tormentors. "But if you think it's worth a try . . ."

The herdsman did not wait for Simna's opinion. Stepping out into the open, he located two pairs of drifting eyes and angled the piece of mirror so that it would shine directly in their faces. Sunlight shafting down between the trees struck the glass and bounced upward, dancing around the groats' heads. It was a difficult and tricky business. The active groats rarely stayed in one place long enough to catch the full glare from the mirror.

What happened next was unexpected. Knucker looked on in fascination, but Simna was not surprised. He had come to expect the unexpected in the herdsman's company.

Catching sight in the mirror not of the reflected sunshine but of themselves, first one, then two, then a dozen of the invisible cone throwers came sliding and climbing down from the branches to gather as if mesmerized around the mirror. Soon the entire troop was clustered before Ehomba, gazing enthralled into the scuffed, reflective glass. It was an unnerving sight: two dozen or more sets of compound eyes adrift above the forest floor. Up close, the travelers saw that the groats' invisible fur did not render them perfectly transparent. Where one of them moved slowly, there was a shimmering in the air that reminded Ehomba of waves of heat rising from the desert floor.

Behind him, Simna was drawing his sword. His tone reflected his homicidal expression. Squeezing out of the hollow in the tree, the black litah was right beside him.

"That's it, bruther. Keep them hypnotized just a moment longer, until I can get in among them." He swung his weapon experimentally. "All I've got to do is aim for the eyes. Packed together like you have them, I'm bound to get a couple with each blow."

"No," Ehomba warned him. "Keep back. For another minute or two, anyway. They are not hypnotized. It is—something else."

The swordsman hesitated. Ahlitah halted also, growling uncertainly deep in his throat. "I don't follow you, bruther. We may not get another chance like this."

He was about to add something more when the groat nearest the mirror suddenly let out a startled, high-pitched squeal, the first sound they had heard one of their invisible assailants utter. Leaping straight up into the air, it promptly turned and fled. Crowding close to fill the space vacated by their rapidly retreating cousin, two more pairs of eyes abruptly sprang backwards. Unseen lips emitted panicked screeches as the entire band scrambled to flee.

It was all over in a matter of moments. One second the groats were there, clustering around the palm-sized fragment of mirror, and the next they were gone, fleeing eyeballs escaping in all directions into the safety of the deep woods.

Grateful if bewildered, Simna slowly sheathed his sword. A hesitant Knucker finally emerged from the protection of the scarred tree. Finding a suitable patch of sunlight, Ahlitah began to preen himself.

"By Goroka's coffee, what happened?" He looked to his friend. "You didn't blind them all. I don't think you blinded any of them."

"I do not think so either." A greatly relieved Ehomba turned to face his baffled friends. "The only thing I can think of is that they saw themselves in the mirror—for the first time. Since they are invisible to us, and to the litah, they must always have been invisible to themselves." Slowly, he held up the reflective shard. "A good mirror shows everything as it is. It must have shown them what they looked like under their invisible fur."

Stupefaction gave way to laughter as Simna roared with amusement. "And by Guquot's baggage, they must not have liked what they saw!" Wiping tears from his eyes, the swordsman sauntered over to rejoin his tall friend. "I guess not all mirrors are glazed equal." He reached for the fragment. "Here, let me have a look."

To the swordsman's surprise, Ehomba pulled the mirror out of his reach. "Are you sure, friend Simna?"

The shorter man frowned impatiently. "Sure? Sure about what?"

"That you really want to see yourself as you are." The herdsman's tone was as earnest as ever. But then, Simna reflected, it was usually so. Reaching out quickly, he snatched the scrap of polished glass from his companion's fingers.

"A mirror's just a mirror," he muttered. "Besides, I already know what I look like."

"Then why do you want to look again?" Ehomba asked quietly. But the swordsman seemed not to hear him.

Grinning confidently, Simna turned the mirror in his palm and held it up to his face at arm's length, striking a mockingly noble pose as he did so. It was clear he intended to make light of the enterprise. What resulted was coldly mirthless.

As he stared, the sardonic grin gradually faded from his face. Its place was taken by a sense of solemnity his companions had never before associated with the high-spirited, lighthearted swordsman. It aged him visibly, drawing down the corners of his eyes and setting his mouth into a narrow, tight line devoid of animation or amusement. He seemed to be looking not into the mirror, nor even at his own reflection, but at something much deeper and of far greater import.

What that was none of them knew. Before they could ask, or steal a look at the image in the mirror, Simna lowered it to his side. He had entered a state of deep contemplation that was as shadowed as it was unexpected.

"Simna?" Inclining his head a little closer to his friend, Ehomba tried to peer into the smaller man's downcast eyes. "Simna my friend, are you all right?"

"What?" With an effort, the gravely preoccupied swordsman pulled himself back from the profoundly meditative region into which he had sunk. He raised troubled eyes to his concerned companion. "It's okay, bruther. I am okay."

"What did you see?" Crowding close, Knucker gazed in fascination down at the shard of polished glass and metal dangling from the swordsman's fingers.

"See?" Struggling to resuscitate his affable, easygoing self, he tossed the mirror into the air, watched it tumble end over end a couple of times, and made a nimble catch of the awkward oblong shape with one hand. "I saw myself, of course. What else would you see in a mirror besides yourself?"

"Here, let me have a look." The little man extended eager fingers.

Manifesting an indifference he did not feel, Simna handed it over. Knucker quickly raised it to his face and peered expectantly into the glass.

Knucker the Knower stared sadly back at him. It was him, to be sure, but not the him that stood on the trail, straight and sure, clear of eye and scrubbed of skin. The face that peered hauntingly out of the mirror was that of the Knucker Ehomba and his companions had found besotted and soiled in a squalid close, lying barely conscious in his own filth. Yellowed phlegm trickled from a corner of the half-open mouth, the face was smeared with accumulated grime and muck, and the disheveled hair was tightly matted enough to repel investigative vermin. It was the face of a man condemned to a short and miserable life of continued drunkenness and destitution.

He resisted the image and everything it said about him, quickly passing the mirror back to the swordsman. "Something's wrong. That isn't

me there. That isn't myself as I am. That's a reflection of me as I was."
He turned angrily on Ehomba. "Why did you show that to me? Why?"

"I did not show it to you." The herdsman's voice was level and
unchanged. "You asked to look into it, and demanded it from Simna.
Remember?"

"Well, it's wrong, all wrong." A disgruntled Knucker turned away
from both of them.

"It could be," Ehomba admitted. "You would have to ask Likulu
about that. Myself, I brought it along to use for signaling, not to serve as
an ordinary mirror."

"Hoy, whatever it be, it sure ain't no ordinary mirror, bruther."
Simna gripped the rectangle of battered material securely. But he did
not look into it again.

Behind him, a loud chuff signified to the presence of the litah. "I'd
like to have a look. I've only seen my reflection in still waters."

"Hoy, that's a fine idea!" His characteristic vivacity returning, the
swordsman gladly presented the reflective face of the mirror to the big
cat, winking at his companions as he did so. He couldn't wait to see what
kind of effect it had on the majestic and insufferably arrogant feline.

"There." He strove to position the mirror to ensure that Ahlitah had
the best view possible of his own reflection. "Is that all right? Can you
see yourself clearly?"

Luminous, tawny eyes narrowed slightly as they gazed into the glass.
"Yes, that's fine." The litah nodded slowly. "That is about how it should
be."

Simna's expectant "Watch this!" grin soon gave way to a look of
uncertainty. Frowning, he directed the hesitant Knucker to come and
hold the mirror. As soon as the smaller man had a good grip on the
rectangle, the swordsman walked around to stand alongside the big cat,
pressing close to the massive, musky mass so that he too could get a good
look at the predator's reflection. Because of the slight angle, his view was
not as good as the litah's, but it was sufficient to show the likeness in the
mirror.

A proud and imperious countenance gleamed back at him, the black
litah powerfully reflected in all its mature vigor and resplendent virility.
So resplendent, in fact, that the image in the mirror not only sported a
pale golden halo, but cast sparks from its extremities, from the tips of its
ears and the end of its nose as well as from elsewhere. The black mane
had been transformed into a glistening, rippling aurora of ochroid indigo
that framed the rest of the regal visage in a magnificent effulgence.

With a soft snort, Ahlitah turned way from the mirror, unimpressed.
"Yes, that's about right."

The redness that bloomed on the swordsman's cheeks had nothing to do with a surfeit of sunshine. "It can't be!" Whirling around to confront Ehomba, he shook the fragment of scored, metal-backed glass in the herdsman's face. "Knucker's right! There's something wrong here. This unnatural mirror is possessed by an evil spirit. One that delights in laughing at us."

Ehomba did his best to accommodate his companion's concern. "You may be right, Simna. But do not come to me looking for explanations. I told you: It was a gift, one of many, hastily thrust upon me prior to my leaving the village. To me, it is just a mirror. A piece of polished glass that reflects things as they are—though what other properties it may possess I do not know. To understand more, you would have to—"

"Ask Likcold, or whatever her name is—I know." Frustrated, the swordsman started to return the mirror to its owner—and hesitated. "Hoy, bruther, why don't you have a look?" He gestured behind him. "Everyone else gazed into the glass. Why not you?"

Ehomba smiled amicably. "I already know what I look like, Simna."

"You do, do you?" The smaller man's gaze narrowed, and there was a glint in his eye. "That's what I thought. That's what we all thought." He held the mirror up to his friend's expressionless face. "Go on then, Etjole. Have a look. Or can it be that as a mighty sorcerer, your true reflection might be just a little different from what anyone would expect?"

The herdsman paused a moment before replying. "Oh, give it here. We are wasting time with this." Taking the mirror, he held it beneath his face and peered downward. "What a surprise, Simna. I see me."

"Hoy, but which you?" Stepping over to his friend's side, the shorter man struggled to see the herdsman's reflection. "Here, lower it a bit and let me have a look."

"And me also." An inquisitive Knucker hurried to join them.

Ehomba tilted the mirror slightly downward. Immediately, his two companions let out comparable yelps and looked away, rubbing at their eyes. Wiping with the heel of one hand at the tears that streamed down his face, Simna snapped at his friend.

"Would you mind not including the sun with your reflection?"

"Sorry." Stepping into the shade, the herdsman repositioned the mirror for his curious friends. Pressing close, Simna and Knucker gazed expectantly into the glass. The reflection of Etjole Ehomba smiled half-heartedly back at them.

"Give me that!" Jerking the mirror from the herdsman's fingers, Simna aligned it himself. After adjusting it several times and viewing the resultant reflection from a number of different angles, he finally handed it back to its owner, uncertain whether to be disappointed or relieved.

"Hoy, it's you all right. Nothing but you. Just you."

"What did you expect, Simna?" As he spoke, Ehomba fastidiously returned the mirror to its place in his pack.

"Something else, bruther. Something besides your reflection. Something other than normal." He shrugged. "But it was just you. Might as well have been looking into a mirror in an inn." Sighing deeply, he put his hands on his hips and stared up the narrow trail that wound through the forest. "How much farther to this Neitheray?"

"Netherbrae," Knucker corrected him. "Another day, perhaps two. I know the way, but I have only been there once myself, and that was in passing long ago."

Gathering himself, the swordsman started forward. "Let's get after it, then." He glanced up into the branches. Dragonets could rain fire down on a man, and birds other things, but these he did not mind. It was the groats he had no desire to meet up with again, and where one troop lived, another could follow.

Ehomba and Knucker trailed the swordsman's lead. Rising from his sitting position, Ahlitah brought up the rear. As he padded along in the humans' wake, he focused great yellow eyes on the herdsman's back. He did not say anything, nor did he intend to say anything, about what he had seen. The less he was compelled to converse with men, the better he liked it. But being intelligent, he was curious. For now he would keep that curiosity to himself. Doubtless an explanation would be forthcoming sometime in the future, either by design or by accident.

When the two smaller men had first looked into the mirror held by the man from the south, they had been momentarily blinded by reflected light. Nothing unusual about that.

Except that at the time, the sun had been in front of the herdsman, and not behind him.

XVII

Simna was anticipating a fairly typical isolated mountain village, with pigs and heptodons, chickens and raphusids running loose on rutted, muddy streets, children wailing, laundry hanging from unshuttered windows, and the pervasive stink of waste both human and animal. Given such low expectations, it was not surprising that when it finally came into view through the surrounding trees, the reality of Netherbrae gave a boost to his spirits as well as to his tired legs.

They were all relieved. The previous day had seen them climbing steadily up a trail become increasingly steep. Though it was not mentioned, each of them found the possibility of a night's sleep in a real bed quietly exhilarating.

"What an appealing little place." His fingers locked in the straps of his backpack, Simna ibn Sind's step had become positively jaunty as he gave Knucker a friendly nudge. "I admit I was a bit worried about what we might find, but if anything you understated its charm." He lowered his voice slightly. "I wonder if the local ladies are as attractive as their surroundings?"

As the travelers entered the unfenced, unguarded hamlet, people looked up from their work to smile and wave. Used to encountering the occasional traveler in their mountain hideaway, they were not wary of the three men and their imposing feline companion. Their unforced greetings were, if anything, effusive.

As Knucker led them deeper into the thoughtfully laid-out community, Ehomba admired the wonderful homes and shops. None rose higher than a single story, though many boasted sharply raked roofs that accommodated spacious lofts. Every exposed beam and post, board and railing had been carved with care and attention. Crossbeams terminated in the beaked heads of forest birds. More animals than the herdsman could count leaped and browsed and slumbered and inclined graceful wooden necks to sip from pools of richly grained carved water.

There were wooden flowers in profusion, gaily painted to approximate their natural tints. The shutters that flanked open, glass-free windows were inscribed with mountain scenes, and the fences that enclosed neat yards and gardens were comprised of pickets of every imaginable style and size. Small stone wells were topped with sheltering roofs of all possible shapes, from round to octagonal.

Each shop or storefront was engraved with scenes that depicted the profession they housed. The entrance to the village cobbler's was lined with oversized wooden shoes in several styles and varieties. A smithy boasted the unique distinction of displaying assorted iron and other metal objects carved in wood. Wooden rolls and muffins, pies and cookies outside the bakery looked fresh enough to eat. Not merely the flowers, but a great many of the other sculptures had been painted with as much skill as they had been carved.

The undersized streets that separated the storybook buildings were hard-packed earth, but the travelers kicked up no dust as they walked. The reason for this became apparent when they encountered a cluster of women bending to pick up any forest debris while pushing heavy horsehair brushes along in front of them.

"I admire their cleanliness." Simna smiled and bowed gallantly as they passed the street sweepers. Several of the women smiled and curtsied in return. "But sweeping the dirt's a bit much."

"I recall another town we passed through that was obsessed with cleanliness." Ehomba's expression was unflappable as ever, but he was keeping a careful watch on the buildings they passed. "Do you remember? We had problems there."

"Hoy, but this is only a little village. I wouldn't expect to find the same kind of trouble here."

The herdsman was unable to relax. "I do not like things that are too perfect."

"Fine." Bending over, Simna spat on the herdsman's foot. "There. Something that's not perfect. Feel better now?"

Glancing down, the tall southerner ignored the trickle of saliva. "I have been drooled on by many animals. Spittle does not make something imperfect."

The swordsman shook his head sadly. "I hope your wife and kids are more spirited than you, Etjole, or it's a dull, dead family life you lead for certain."

Ehomba turned to his friend. "I am told by others that Mirhanja is among the liveliest and most engaging of women. Certainly she seems so to me."

"Or maybe it's just in comparison to you, bruther. In your company, a rock would appear the essence of merrymaking."

"You are not the first to assert that if I have any faults, a sometimes overriding seriousness might be among them."

"Might be?" The herdsman chortled in disbelief. "Hoy, long bruther, and the moon might be far away, the oceans deep, and women fickle. Yes, you might tend to the sedate just a trifle. But that's all right— we don't hold it against you." He looked around at the others. "Do we, friends?"

"Not I," professed Knucker quickly.

"I find you all infantile and silly in the extreme." Ahlitah avowed this with utter seriousness. "Among humans, the most thoughtful strive long and hard to attain the exalted level of perfect twit."

"That's profound," Simna retorted, "coming from one who proclaims the location of his home by pissing all around it."

"Look, there's the inn!" Knucker made the announcement hastily and a bit too loudly. Swordsman and litah glared at one another for a long moment, whereupon the disputation was set aside by mutual unspoken consent, as had been dozens of similar arguments.

Splendid as had been the decorations they had beheld throughout the town, those fronting the inn put all their carved predecessors to shame. It was still only a single-story structure, but the upper loft or attic was proportionately larger in scale, allowing for a number of rooms to be located above the main floor. Not only forest creatures but inanimate inventions of the wood-carvers' fancy stared out from the wide, handsomely milled entrance. There were oaken arabesques and pine flutings, rain clouds of spruce overhanging redwood mountains, and much, much more.

Following Knucker up the steps, they found themselves in an anteroom empty but for a plump, rosy-cheeked woman in her midthirties. She was using a fine-whisked broom to tidy the highly polished hardwood floor. Strain though he might, Ehomba could not see that there was anything to sweep. To his eyes the floor appeared immaculate.

"Welcome, visitors!" She smiled expansively. "Welcome to Netherbrae. I hope that you will find our rooms comfortable, our linens sweetsmelling, and our food and drink to your liking."

"I'm sure we will," Simna assured her. "I take it you can accommodate four of us?"

"Oh yes, certainly!" Leaning her broom against a wall that was no less spotless than the floor, she clasped her hands together and nodded hospitably. "It is a slow time of year for us and we are glad to have your trade. You should know that there will be a townsparty here tonight. Naturally, as guests, you are invited."

"A party!" The swordsman nodded approvingly. "I don't remember the last time I was at a party." He grinned teasingly at Ehomba. "It certainly wasn't in *your* company." Turning back to their congenial and proper hostess, he added, "We'd be delighted to attend."

Her smile flickered, but only for an instant. "I must have misunderstood. You said that there were four of you? But I see only three."

Turning slightly, Ehomba nodded in the direction of the litah. Having entered late, the big cat had settled down onto its belly, its front legs stretched out in front of it. "Three men, and one feline."

Their hostess's smile did not waver, but a new and unexpectedly biting sternness crept into her voice. "Surely you don't expect that great black thing to join you in your room?"

"Ahlitah is one with us," Ehomba explained. "Why can he not stay? He is intelligent, and can speak as well as any man."

"That is not so." The black cat spoke without lifting his head. "I can speak better."

It required a visible effort, but their hostess managed to maintain her smile. "It is a filthy animal!"

All of a sudden the paint that highlighted the skillful wood carvings outside seemed to dim slightly, the perfectly trimmed rows of flowers to reveal one or two weeds. Seeing the herdsman's jawline tighten uncharacteristically, Simna stepped quickly forward.

"Of course it is, m'dear, and we quite understand. My tall friend here"—he jerked a thumb in Ehomba's direction—"comes from a land far to the south, where shepherds often stay out in the fields with their herds and flocks for days on end. So he's used to being with animals and finds it only natural to sleep in their company. Furthermore, he's unfamiliar with towns. Might I ask, lady, if there is anyplace where our cat could find shelter?"

Much mollified, the proprietress nodded to her right. "There are stables around back. At the moment they're unoccupied, so that monstrous great creature won't have any mounts to disturb. There's water out there, and plenty of straw, and it will keep some of the chill away. It gets cold up here in the Hrugars."

"I'm sure that'll be okay." Grinning tensely, the swordsman turned to look at the nonchalant Ahlitah. "Won't it?"

The big cat's face twitched slightly. It might have been a shrug. "I'd as soon not smell humans."

"And I will stay with him." Ehomba was no longer smiling at their hostess. "I know you have your policies. Please do not concern yourself on my account. I prefer a hard bed to a soft one in any case, as my companions can tell you."

"Fine, good!" Muttering softly, Simna turned away from him. "I suppose you expect me to show solidarity by joining you in sharing the delights of the barn?"

"Not at all," Ehomba told him. "You should enjoy your comforts where you can find them."

"That's good to hear, because that's exactly what I'm going to do." The swordsman was insistent. "After that climb out of Bondressey I want to soak in a hot tub, and lie between clean sheets, and awaken warm and rested."

"As well you should." Ehomba looked past him and inquired politely, "Around the back of the inn, you said?" Arms folded, the hostess nodded sternly.

"Sleep well," Simna told him sarcastically. "Knucker and me here—we're sure going to. Aren't we, friend?"

"I hope so," the little man ventured uncertainly.

"Right! Come on, then." Putting an arm around the hesitant Knucker, the swordsman started past the proprietress and up the hall. "If you would show us to our room, m'dear?"

"Gladly." Favoring Ehomba with a last disapproving look, she turned and took the lead from the two smaller men.

"Out, back, and around." Pivoting, Ehomba led the way back out through the entrance. The litah rose and followed.

"You don't have to do this, you know," the big cat told him as they trooped down the front steps and turned to their right.

"I know that."

"I'm not asking you to keep me company. I enjoy my solitude."

"I know that also. I meant what I said about town beds being too soft. Straw will be better for me."

"Suit yourself. It makes no difference to me." Ahlitah was silent until they reached the stable. It was as sturdy and well made as every other building they had encountered in the village—even if it was intended only for the housing of filthy animals. "What about this 'towns-party' tonight?"

"The woman's sharp reaction to you may have been an anomaly, but I think it would be better to take no chances. If these people will not allow filthy animals to stay in their inn, I have a strong feeling that they will not embrace them at their social gatherings."

Entering the stables, the litah began to hunt for a suitable resting place to spend the night. "You are probably right, Etjole Ehomba. I wonder how they feel about entertaining filthy humans?"

"From the woman's tone of voice I think she was referring only to matters of personal hygiene when she used the word 'filthy.' My fear is that bounded emotions may run deeper and nastier than that."

Poking his head into an empty stall, Ahlitah grunted. "Wouldn't surprise me. I'll stay here and catch up on some sleep." He snorted and shook his head, the great black mane swishing back and forth like a gigantic dust mop. "I have been behind on my sleep ever since we left the veldt." Satisfied, he looked up curiously. "Are you going?"

"I have to. Not because I particularly want to, although in spite of their prejudice this is an interesting place, but because I feel it necessary to keep an eye on Simna. When he is not careful of what he says, his mouth can get him into trouble."

"He and I almost have something in common, then. I like to put trouble in my mouth." He emitted a silky growl. "Here's a good place."

Together, they flopped down on the thick pile of hay. It was a recent threshing, still soft and pliable, with a good view of both the front and back entrances to the stables. There Ehomba would rest until suppertime. After that would come the townsparty, which he, as traveler and guest, would attend. So long as he was there to keep Simna's mouth full of food, he knew, the swordsman was unlikely to cause problems.

Taken in the inn's tavern, the evening meal was excellent, as artistically and competently prepared and presented as the building in which it was served. Nor were the three travelers the only ones eating there. Locals began to trickle in with the setting of the sun, finding their way through Netherbrae's immaculate streets with the aid of small, elegantly repoussé tin lanterns. Soon the tavern was alive with laughter and earnest conversation. Men discussed the opening of a new patch of forest to logging, for the village supplied many wood products to Bondressey and Squoy. Women talked children and household tasks, and both genders indulged in much good-natured gossiping.

As the three travelers sat at one of the long communal benches, they spoke mostly among themselves. But as the evening wore on and the tavern became more crowded, the jocularity more general, and the banter more boisterous, they inevitably found themselves drawn into conversation with the locals. Certainly Simna was. Knucker was a hesitant talker, and Ehomba could be downright noncommunicative.

Leaning out of his chair, the swordsman inquired casually of one burly native seated nearby, "So you cut a lot of trees, do you?"

"Why not?" The man's hands were thick and callused from a lifetime of heavy physical labor. "We have lots of trees, and the Bondresseyeans pay well for our timber. Besides, a two-man cross-cut saw makes awfully quick work of carrots, so we might as well use them to cut trees." His companions roared and Simna deigned to smile graciously at the spirited outpouring of bucolic humor.

"Any lady loggers among you?" He grinned hopefully.

The laughter around him died instantly. Grave expressions took the place of the easy affability that had prevailed. "That would be an abomination. No Netherbraen, man or woman, would stand for it."

"Hoy," murmured Simna contritely, "it was just a question. Remember, my friends and I are strangers here."

"That's true . . . yes, that's so . . ." Gradually the group regained its smiles and humor. "A lady logger—talk like that could get a man condemned."

"Condemned?" Ehomba joined the dialogue. "Condemned by whom?"

"Why, by Tragg, of course." The locals looked at one another and shook their heads in mutual commiseration at the visitors' ignorance. "Tragg is the God of wandering forest paths. Whoever follows His way and His teachings will live a long and happy life here in the Hrugar Mountains. So it has always been for the citizens of Netherbrae."

"This is what your priests tell you?" Subsequent to his initial faux pas, Simna tried to couch his comments in the least offensive manner possible.

"Priests?" The men exchanged a glance and, to the swordsman's relief, burst out laughing once again. "We have no priests!"

"We know the truth of what Tragg tells us," avowed another, "because it has always been the truth. We don't need priests to tell us these things. We are as much a part of the Thinking Kingdoms as Melespra or Urenon the Elegant."

"Yes. The only difference is that we choose to live in simpler surroundings." The villager nearest Simna gestured expansively. "No need here for estates or castles. Our homes we decorate with humble wood, enhanced and beautified by our own hands. All of this Tragg tells us."

"Does he also tell you that animals are filthy creatures?" Ehomba asked the question before Simna could catch the gist of it and stop him.

The swordsman was needlessly concerned. Another of the villagers answered freely and without hesitation. "Of course! Whenever we are unsure about anything, we put our faith in the teachings of Tragg and they tell us what to do."

"And these teachings," Ehomba inquired, "they are never wrong?"

"Never," declared several of the men and two of the women in concert.

"But I thought you said that Netherbrae was as one with the Thinking Kingdoms. If you rely on the teachings of Tragg to tell you what to do, then that means you are not thinking about what to do. You are substituting belief for thought."

Leaning close to his friend, Simna whispered urgently, "I've been around a lot, bruther, and based on my experience and travels, I'm telling you it'd be best to drop this line of conversation right now."

"Why?" Ehomba countered innocently. "These are thinking people, inhabitants of one of the Thinking Kingdoms. People who think are not bothered by questions." Raising his voice, he inquired loudly, "Are you?"

"Not at all, friend, not at all!" declared the villager seated across the table from the herdsman. "Belief does not replace thought. It complements it." Grinning broadly, he added, "We think about what we believe in."

"And we believe what we think." Having had a good deal to drink, the woman who concluded the tenet broke out giggling. Her friend quickly joined in, and once again merriment was general around the table.

Ehomba started to say something else, but this time Simna was in his face before the words had time to emerge. "Hoy, bruther, if you've no concern for your own well-being, then have a care for mine, would you? No more of this. A change of subject to something innocuous is in order."

"I—oh, very well." Observing the strain in the swordsman's expression, Ehomba decided to forgo the questions that were piling up inside him—for now. He replaced his intended words with the contents of the ceramic tumbler that had been set out before him.

Someone was speaking from atop a chair near the rear entrance. Ehomba recognized him as the general manager of the inn. Not the owner—that was a title reserved for the husband of the woman they had first met. The speaker had a prominent belly and cleverly coifed mustache that wrapped around much of his jowly face. A logger he was not.

"Friends, visitors! You've seen it before, watched it and wondered, and now tonight, we once more bring it before you to embellish your enjoyment of the evening and the solidarity of our precious community." Pivoting carefully on the slightly shaky chair, he gestured grandly toward the back door. It was particularly wide and tall, with an interesting arched lintel. A sense of anticipation blanketed the crowd. By mutual silent agreement all conversation was muted.

"I give you," the general manager proclaimed, "the nightmare!"

Cheers and whoops of expectation rose from the crowd, an atavistic howl that rattled the walls of the tavern. By dint of their early arrival and fortuitous seating, Ehomba and his companions had an unobstructed view of the arched doorway. Now they looked on in silence as the doors were flung wide.

Though the cage rolled easily on four thick wheels, it still took the combined exertions of four strong men to pull and push it into the tavern. The spokes of the wheels, the hubs, and the cage itself were decorated with etchings of mystic signs and mysterious figures. Even the bars and the massive padlock were made of wood, lovingly polished to reveal a fine, dark grain. Despite the height of the arched double doorway, the top of the cage barely cleared the twenty-foot-high opening.

Standing inside the cage and gripping two of the bars was a ten-foot-tall something.

It was as massive as it was tall, and Ehomba estimated its weight as equal to that of any three large men. It was hard to tell for sure because the creature was covered entirely in long, thick strands of dark gray hair streaked with black. The skull was more human than simian, and the black eyes that glared out from beneath massive, bony brows were full of rage. The nose was not as flat as an ape's, but not as forwardly pronounced as a human's. Through the waving, gesticulating arms of the crowd the herdsman thought he could make out five fingers on each hand and as many toes on each foot.

Not an ape, then, but not a member of the family of man, either. Something in between, or an offshoot unknown to the people of Naumkib. The more it roared and rattled the tree-sized wooden bars of its rolling cage, the more the crowd jeered and hooted.

Yelling an unimaginative and slightly obscene insult, someone in the throng stood up and threw the remnants of a warm meat pie at the cage. Passing through the bars, it struck the nightmare just above its right eye. Wincing, it turned to roar at its assailant. The laughter this induced caused food to come flying from all directions: pies, half-finished legs of meat, vegetables, gnawed rolls greasy with butter. At first the creature withstood the barrage and continued to bellow defiance at its captors. But gradually its roars and howls died down. Assaulted by food and taunts from every direction, it eventually retreated to the middle of its cage. There it sat, hunched over and no longer trying to deflect the edible missiles, doing its best to ignore the onslaught.

"Make it get up and bellow again!" someone yelled laughingly.

"Somebody get a long stick and poke it!" suggested another.

Ultimately the mob grew bored. Evidently this was not the first time they had amused themselves at the pitiful creature's expense. Ignoring the cage and its lone occupant in their midst, they returned to their banqueting, trading jokes and gossip and casual conversation as if nothing out of the ordinary had transpired. Simna and Knucker slipped back into the easy camaraderie tendered by the citizens of Netherbrae more comfortably than did Ehomba.

"That's a beast and a half." The swordsman tore into a hunk of fresh, heavily seeded bread. "Where'd you capture it?"

A woman seated across and slightly down the table from him replied. Not because it was her place, but because all the men within range of the swordsman's question had their mouths full of food.

"It was taken in the forest far from here, where the Hrugar Mountains begin to climb toward the sky." She sipped daintily at her tumbler. "Not far from the lowest slopes of Mount Scathe. It took two parties of men to bring it down with ropes, and three to haul it back to Netherbrae on a makeshift sled."

"An impressive feat." Ehomba spoke quietly, as always. "What was it doing?"

She blinked at him, her eyes still lively but her tone momentarily confused. "Doing?"

"When it was captured. Who was it attacking, or threatening?"

The husky man seated next to her cleared his throat and replied before she could respond. "It wasn't attacking or threatening anyone, friend. I know—I was there." He grinned proudly. "I was one of the woodcutters who brought it down. Such strength! It fought us like a mad thing, which of course is what it is. A savage, unclean beast."

Ehomba considered. "But surely the forest is full of animals. Why take this one from where it was living and bring it all the way back to Netherbrae?"

"Because it's not useful." Another man spoke up. "The wapiti and the rabbit, the birds and the rodents, are all useful, all nutritious." With a piece of pork he gestured in the direction of the now silent cage. The slice of meat flapped loosely in his hand. "Just by looking at this thing you can tell it's no good to eat."

The herdsman nodded understandingly. "Then why go to the trouble of bringing it all the way back here?"

Several of the diners exchanged looks of incomprehension. "Why, because its presence was defiling our forest!" another woman declared. Her explanation was seconded by numerous murmurs from those seated nearby.

The oldest man at the table spoke up. "The teachings of Tragg tell us that the forest and everything in it belongs to us, the people of Netherbrae. We have followed those teachings and they have been good to us. Tragg is much pleased. The trees are ours to cut down, the nuts and berries ours to gather, the animals ours to eat. Anything not of use must be given a use, or eliminated." A chorus of exuberant "Aye!"s rose from his fellow citizens.

"You have seen how clean our community is. That is because we are careful to get rid of everything that is not useful."

"Very interesting," Ehomba admitted. "What about us?"

Next to him Simna paused in midbite. Knucker's eyes began to dart and his fingers to fidget. But the silence that enveloped their table lasted barely a second or two before the old man responded.

"Visitors bring stories of other lands, new knowledge, and amusing tales. These things are useful. We look forward to them because we do not travel ourselves." Looking around the table, he grinned and nodded. "Why should we? Who would ever want to leave Netherbrae?"

This time assent was not only general but loud, amounting to cheering more than mere agreement. Ehomba thought some of it might have been a little forced, but in the general melee of good humor it was hard to tell for certain.

"If the beast is of no use, why do you keep him around?"

"Of no use?" Rising from his seat, a slim young man hefted a small bowl of table scraps. "Watch this!" Drawing back his arm, he threw it at the cage. It described a graceful arc before striking the massive, hairy back right between the shoulders and bouncing off. The cowed creature shuffled forward an inch or so, looking neither up nor around.

Sitting down, the young man laughed heartily. His companions at the table laughed with him.

"It amuses us." The words of the woman who had first spoken broke through the general jocularity. "By letting children throw things at it, their fear of the beasts that inhabit the deep forest is lessened. And in this we feel we are truly heeding the word of Tragg, and not straying from the example he long ago set for us Himself."

Someone passed the herdsman a plate full of fat pulled from various meats. "Here, friend. Wouldn't you like to have a go yourself?"

A softly smiling Ehomba declined politely. "Your offer is generous, and in the deep spirit of friendship we have already come to admire here in Netherbrae, but since I am not a true follower of Tragg and am sadly ignorant of so much of his teaching, I feel it would be presumptuous of me to participate in one of his ceremonies. Better not to waste it."

"Who said anything about wasting it?" To the accompaniment of encouraging hoots and hollers, one of the other women seated at the table rose and threw the plate. Her arm was not as strong or her aim as accurate as that of the young man who had preceded her. To much good-natured merriment, the plate fell short and clanged off the floor of the cage. But she was applauded for her effort.

His face an unreadable mask, Ehomba rose from the bench. "We do not know how to thank you enough for this wonderful evening, and for the hospitality all of you have shown us. But we are tired from our long walk today, and must be on our way tomorrow. So I think we will turn in."

"Tired?" Raising his recently refilled tumbler, a gleeful Simna saluted their new friends and surroundings. "Who's tired?"

Glaring down, the herdsman put a hand on his companion's shoulder. A surprisingly heavy hand. "Tomorrow we must start across the Hrugar Mountains. We will need our rest."

"Hoy, bruther, and I'll get mine." The terse-voiced swordsman brusquely shook off the long-fingered hand. "I'm your friend and confidant, Etjole. Not one of your village adolescents."

Next to him, a determined Knucker raised his own drinking utensil. "I'm not tired, either. I can't remember the last night I had such a good time!" Hesitantly, he sipped from his cup. When no one objected, he sipped harder.

"Same here." Simna smiled up at the dour-faced herdsman. "You're so concerned, bruther, use some of your sorceral skills. Sleep for the three of us!"

"Perhaps I will." Disappointed in his companions, Ehomba rose and headed for the entrance to the tavern that led to the inn's outer office and the front door, leaving his friends to their elective dissolution.

Across the table, two men leaned forward, inquisitive uncertainty on their faces. "Is your traveling companion truly a sorcerer?"

Simna took a slug from his tumbler, ignoring the fact that Knucker was once more imbibing steadily. Furthermore, the little man gave no indication of stopping or slowing down. But the swordsman was feeling too content to notice, or to object.

"I'm convinced of it, but if so he's the strangest one imaginable. Insists he's nothing but a herder of cattle and sheep, refuses to use magic even to save his own life. Depends on alchemy he insists arises not from any skills of his own, but from that bequeathed to him by old women and such of his village." The swordsman looked in the direction of the main portal but Ehomba had already disappeared, on his way to rejoin the fourth member of their party in the stables around back.

"I've seen much of the world in my travelings and met many strange folk, but by Giskret's Loom, he's for surely the most peculiar and mysterious of the lot." Silent for a moment after concluding his explanation, he shrugged and downed the contents of his tumbler. Accompanied by smiles and laughter, it was quickly refilled.

"He didn't look like much of a sorcerer to me," declared one of the men.

"You'd far sooner convince me that someone that odd-looking dotes on the droppings of cows!" quipped another. General jollity followed this jest.

Simna knew the not-so-veiled insult to his friend should have bothered him. But he was having too good a time, and the middling attractive woman at the far end of the table was eyeing him with more than casual curiosity. So he thrust the abrasive comment aside and smiled back at her. He'd always been good at ignoring that which distressed him, especially when it came at the ultimate expense of others.

Alongside him, a happy Knucker held out his tumbler to be refilled. Within that sturdy container many things could be drowned—including promises made.

XVIII

Nothing moved in the dark depths of the tavern. The still air stank of stale beer and spilled wine, but it was not silent. Gruntings and snortings that would have been at home in any sty rose from the dozen or so intoxicated bodies that lay sprawled on the floor and, in one case, across a table from which plates and other dinner debris had been solicitously removed. All of the unconscious were male. For a woman to have been left in such circumstances would have gone against the teachings of Tragg. Under the Traggian codex, men and women had clearly defined roles. Public inebriation was not an option available to representatives of the female gender.

When the managers of the inn had finally called a halt to the communal townsparty, the majority of revelers had contentedly tottered or been carried off to their homes. Only the most severe celebrants were left behind to sleep off the aftereffects of the festivities safely. As for the managers themselves, they and their assistants had long since finished cleaning up what they could and had retired to their own rooms.

Amidst the general silence and intermittent snoring, one figure moved. It did not rise from the floor or tables, but instead entered through the front portal. This was not locked and stood open to the outside. No one locked their doors in Netherbrae. There was no need for anyone to do so. The adherents of Traggism had complete faith in one another. They had to; otherwise the entire system would collapse upon the fragility of its own moral underpinnings.

Picking his way among the tables and benches, Ehomba occasionally had to step over or around a somnolent villager. Making less noise than a moth, he approached the motionless cage. It remained where it had been left, in the middle of the tavern, its sole occupant squatting in the center of the caged floor, hunched over and still. Piles of food dimpled the interior and clung stubbornly to the wooden bars.

The herdsman halted a few feet from the rear of the wheeled cage. For several moments he simply stood there, contemplating the massive, hirsute back of the imprisoned creature. Then he said, in a soft but carrying whisper, "Hello."

The nightmare did not move, did not react.

"I am sorry for the way you were treated. It was a saddening display. It is at such times that I feel closer to the apes. There are people whose sense of self-worth is so poor that the only way they can feel better is to degrade and humiliate something else. Preferably something that cannot fight back. I just wanted to tell you that before I left here, so that you would know there are human beings who do not think that way." His encouraging smile was a splash of whiteness in the dim light. "It is too bad you cannot understand what I am saying, but I wanted to say it anyway. I had to say it." His business in Netherbrae concluded, he turned to leave.

A voice, deep and hesitant, halted him in the darkness. "I can understand."

Turning back to the cage, Ehomba walked rapidly but silently around to the other side. From beneath the jutting escarpment of bone that was the creature's brow, dark eyes peered out at the herdsman. One finger traced tiny, idle circles in the pile of slowly decaying food that littered the floor of the cage.

"I had a feeling. I was not sure, but the feeling was there." The herdsman nodded ever so slightly. "It was something in your eyes."

A soft grunt emerged from between the bars. "You not from this place."

"No." Taking a chance, trusting his instincts, Ehomba moved a little closer to the enclosure. "I am from the south. Farther to the south than you can probably imagine."

"I from north. Not so far north."

"We were told how you came to be here." With little else to offer the caged creature, the herdsman proffered another smile. "I did not enjoy the telling of it, just as I do not enjoy seeing anyone being forced to endure such conditions. But there was nothing I could do. My friends and I are strangers here. We are few; the villagers are many."

"Understand." The terse reply was devoid of accusation.

"I am a shepherd of cattle and sheep. My name is Etjole Ehomba."

"I am Hunkapa Aub."

Fresh silence ensued. After several moments of shared contemplation, the herdsman looked up. "Would you like to get out of that cage, Hunkapa Aub?"

Large, sensitive eyes opened a little wider. The hunch in the creature's back straightened slightly. "Hunkapa like." Then the humanoid expression fell once again. "Cage locked."

"Where is the key?"

"No good." The great hairy skull shook slowly from side to side. "Village teacher got."

Ehomba chewed his lower lip as he considered the situation. "It does not matter. I have something with me that I think can open the lock."

The creature that called itself Hunkapa Aub did not dare to show any enthusiasm, but he could not keep it entirely out of his voice. "A tool?" When the herdsman nodded once, the hulking arthropoid rose slightly and approached the bars. "Ehomba go get tool!"

By way of reply the herdsman turned and made his way back out of the tavern as silently as he had entered. In the ensuing interval, the caged creature sat unmoving, its eyes never leaving the doorway through which the visiting human had vanished.

Hope was high beneath all that thick gray hair when Ehomba returned. He was not alone. A muscular jet-black shape was with him, gliding wraithlike across the floor despite its bulk. Together, they approached the rear of the cage. Hunkapa turned to scrutinize the herdsman's companion. Dark eyes met yellow ones. Silent understanding was exchanged.

With a comradely hand Ehomba brushed the bushy black mane. "My tool. Ahlitah, meet Hunkapa Aub."

The big cat's growl was barely audible. "Charmed. Can we get out of here now?"

Extending an arm, the herdsman pointed. "Lock."

Padding forward, the litah contemplated the heavy clasp. It was made of ironwood, umber with black streaks. Opening its massive jaws, the cat bit down hard and chewed. The crunching sound of wood being pulverized resounded through the room. It was not a particularly alarming sound. Nevertheless, Ehomba wished there was less of it.

A few querulous grunts rose from the scattered bodies, but none rose to seek the source of the gnawing. Several moments of concerted feline orthodontic activity resulted in a pile of sawdust and splinters accumulating on the floor. Stepping back, Ahlitah spat out bits and pieces of ironwood. All that was left of the lock was a curved section of latch that Ehomba promptly removed. Lifting the arm that barred the cage door, he retreated to stand alongside the impatient Ahlitah.

Tentatively, Hunkapa Aub reached out with one huge hand and pushed. The barred wooden door swung wide. Lumbering silently forward, he checked first to the right and then to the left, his hands holding on to either side of the opening. Then he stepped down onto the tavern floor. His arms were proportionately longer than his legs, but his knuckles did not quite scrape the ground. How much of him was ape, how much man, and how much something else, Ehomba was not prepared to say. But there was no mistaking the meaning of the tears that welled up in the erstwhile nightmare's eyes.

"No time for that." With a soft snarl, Ahlitah started back toward the entrance. "I'll take him to the stable and we'll wait for you there. You'll be wanting to go upstairs and drag those two worthless humans you insist on calling your friends out of bed."

"I will be quick," Ehomba assured the big cat.

Marking the room numbers as he made his way down the narrow passage, Ehomba halted outside number five. As was customary in Netherbrae, the door was not locked. Lifting the latch as quietly as he could, he pushed open the door and stepped inside. The room was in total darkness, the curtains having been pulled across the window.

A sharp blade nicked his throat and a hand clutched at his left wrist, pulling it back behind him.

"It's too late for maid service and too early for breakfast, so what the Gojorworn are . . . ?" The fingers around his unresisting wrist relaxed and the knife blade was withdrawn. "Etjole?"

Turning in the darkness, Ehomba saw the subdued glint of moonlight on metal as the swordsman resheathed his knife. "Having trouble sleeping, Simna?"

"I always sleep light, long bruther. Especially in a strange bed. That way I feel more confident about waking up in the morning." Weapon secured, the shorter man stepped away from the wall. "You jested that I might be having trouble sleeping. I might ask you the same question."

"Get your clothes on and your things together. We are leaving."

"What, now? In the middle of the night? After that meal?" To underline his feelings the swordsman belched meaningfully. The sound echoed around the room.

"Yes, now. After that meal. Ahlitah is waiting for us in the stables—with another. His name is Hunkapa Aub."

Grumbling pointedly, Simna began slipping into his clothes. "You pick up companions in the oddest times and places, bruther. Where's this one from?"

"From a cage."

"Hoy, from a—" In the darkness of the room the swordsman's voice came to a halt as sharply as his movements. When he spoke again, it was with a measure of uncertainty as well as disbelief. "You broke that oversized lump of animated fur out of its box?"

"He is more than that. Hunkapa Aub is intelligent. Not very intelligent, perhaps, but no mindless animal, either."

"Bruther, no matter where we go you seem to have this wonderful knack for endearing yourself to the locals. I wish you'd learn to repress it." Darkness blocked the faint light from the single curtained window as the swordsman slipped upraised arms through a shirt. "When they discover their favorite subject for culinary target practice has gone missing they're very likely to connect it to this late-night leave-taking of ours."

"Let them," Ehomba replied curtly. "I have little use for people like this, who would treat any animal the way they have, much less an intelligent creature like Hunkapa Aub."

Simna stepped into his pants. "Maybe they don't know that he's intelligent."

"He talks." Anger boiled in the herdsman's tone as he looked past his friend. "Where is Knucker?"

"Knucker?" In the dusky predawn Simna quickly assembled his belongings. "You know, bruther, I don't believe the little fella ever came upstairs. Near as I can recall, when I left the townsparty traveling two steps forward, one step back, he was still drinking and carousing with the locals."

"Are you ready yet?"

"Coming, coming!" the swordsman hissed as he struggled to don his pack. "Ghobrone knows you're an impatient man. You'd think it was this Visioness Themaryl who was waiting for you downstairs."

"If only she was." Ehomba's tone turned from curt to wistful. "I could make an end to this, and start back home."

They found Knucker not far from where the three of them had originally been seated, sprawled on the floor with limbs flopped loosely about him. The stench of alcohol rose from his gaping, open mouth and his once clean attire was soiled with food, liquor, and coagulated vomit. His face was thick with grime, as if he had done some serious foreheadfirst pushing along the floor.

"Giela," Simna muttered. "What a mess!"

Kneeling by the little man's side, Ehomba searched until he found a wooden serving bowl. Tossing out the last of its rapidly hardening contents, he inverted it and placed it beneath Knucker's greasy hair. It was not a soft pillow, but it would have to do. This accomplished, he set about trying to rouse the other man from his stupor.

Simna looked on for a while before disappearing, only to return moments later with a jug three-quarters full. Watering Knucker's face as if it were a particularly parched houseplant, he kept tilting the jug until the contents were entirely gone. The last splashes did the trick, and the little man came around, sputtering slightly.

"What—who's there?" Espying the basics of a friendly face in the darkness, he smiled beatifically. "Oh, it's you, Etjole Ehomba. Welcome back to the party." Frowning abruptly, he tried to sit up and failed. "Why is it so quiet?"

Disgust permeated the herdsman's whispered reply. "You are drunk again, Knucker."

"What, me? No, Ehomba, not me! I had a little to drink, surely. It was a party. But I am not drunk."

The herdsman was implacable. "You told us many times that if we helped you, you would not let this happen to you again."

"Nothing's happened to me. I'm still me."

"Are you?" Staring down at the prostrate, flaccid form, Ehomba chose his next words carefully. "What are the names of my children?"

"Daki and Nelecha." A wan smile creased the grubby face. "I know everything, remember?"

"Only when you are drunk." Rising, the herdsman turned and started past Simna. "Paradox is the fool at the court of Fate."

Simna reached out to restrain him. "Hoy, Etjole, we can't just leave him here like this."

In the dark room, hard green eyes gazed unblinkingly back at the swordsman's. "Everyone chooses what to do with their life, Simna. I chose to honor a dying man's request. You chose to accompany me." He glanced down at the frail figure on the floor. Knucker had begun to sing softly to himself. "He chooses this. It is time to go."

"No, wait. Wait just a second." Bending anxiously over the chanting intoxicant, Simna grabbed one unwashed hand and tugged firmly. "Come on, Knucker. You've got to get up. We're leaving."

Watery eyes tried to focus on the swordsman's. "Your father abandoned your mother when you were nine. You have no sisters or brothers and you have always held this against your mother, who died six years ago. You have one false tooth." Raising his head from the floor, the little man turned to grin at the silent, stolid Ehomba. "There are 1,865,466,345,993,429 grains of sand on the beach directly below your village. That's to the waterline with the tide in. Tomorrow it will be different." Letting go of the dirty hand, Simna straightened slowly.

"The axis of the universe is tilted fourteen point three-seven degrees to the plane of its ecliptic. Matter has twenty-eight basic component parts, which cannot be further subdivided. A horkle is a grank. Three pretty women in a room together suck up more energy than they give off." He began to giggle softly. "Why a bee when it stings? If you mix sugar cane and roses with the right seeds, you get raspberries that smell as good as they taste. King Ephour of Noul-ud-Sheraym will die at eight-twenty in the evening of a moa bone stuck in his throat. I know everything."

A grim-faced Simna was watching Ehomba carefully. Finally the herdsman bent low over the prone body and forestalled the little man's litany of answers with an actual question.

"Tell me one thing, Knucker."

"One thing?" The giggling grew louder, until it turned into a cough. "I'll tell you anything!"

Eyes that could pick out a potential herd predator lurking at a great distance bored into the other man's. "Can you stop drinking whenever you want to?"

Several choking coughs brought up the answer. "Yes. Whenever I want to."

Ehomba straightened. "That is what I needed to know." Without another word, he stepped around the querulous Simna and started for the door. With a last glance down at the giggling, coughing Knucker, the swordsman hurried to catch up to his friend.

"Ahlitah and Hunkapa will be growing anxious. We will pick up my pack and leave this place." As they reached the open entrance to the inn, Ehomba nodded in the direction of the still dusky horizon. "With luck and effort we will put good distance between ourselves and Netherbrae before its citizens connect Hunkapa's disappearance with our departure."

A troubled Simna kept looking back in the direction of the tavern. "But he answered your question! You said yourself that he told you what you needed to know."

"That is so." Exiting the inn, they started down the entryway steps. "You were right all along, Simna ibn Sind. When he is drunk he believes that he knows everything. And it is true that when he is drunk he knows a great deal. Perhaps more than anyone else who has ever lived. But he does not know everything." Exiting the building, they turned rightward and strode briskly toward the stables. "His answer to my question proves that there is at least one thing he does not know."

Anxiously watching the shadows for signs of early-rising Netherbrae-ans, the swordsman wondered aloud, "What's that, bruther?"

Ehomba's tone never varied. "Himself."

XIX

Simna quickly recovered from the shock of hearing their new companion hold up his end of a conversation, albeit with a severely limited vocabulary. As Ehomba had hoped, they succeeded in putting many miles between themselves and the picture-perfect village of Netherbrae before the sun began to show over the surrounding treetops. Exhausted from what had become a predawn run, they settled down in the shade of a towering gingko tree. Even Ahlitah was tired from having not only to hurry, but also to spend much of the time scrambling uphill.

While his companions rested down and had something to eat, Ehomba stood looking back the way they had come. It was impossible to see very far in the dense deciduous forest, so closely packed were the big trees, but as near as he was able to tell, there was no sign of pursuit from Netherbrae. Nor could he hear any rustling of leaf litter or the breaking of more than the occasional branch.

"How's it look, bruther?" Simna ibn Sind glanced up from his unappetizing but nourishing breakfast of dried meat and fruit.

"Nothing. No noise, either. And the forest creatures are chattering and chirping normally. That says to me that nothing is disturbing their morning activities, as would be the case if there was even a small party of pursuers nearby." He turned back to his friends. "Perhaps they do not think Hunkapa worth pursuing."

"Or too dangerous," Simna suggested. "Or maybe there's a convenient proscription in the teachings of Tragg against hunting down and trying to recapture a prisoner who's already escaped." After gulping from his water bag, he splashed a little on his face. In these high mountains, with sparkling streams all around, there was no need to conserve. "There's just one problem."

"What is that?" Ehomba asked patiently.

The swordsman gestured toward the lofty peaks that broke the northern horizon. "Knucker was our guide. How the Garamam are we going to find our way through to this Hamacassar? Without a guide we could wander around in these forests and mountains for years."

Ehomba did not appear to be overly concerned. "Knucker needs to find himself before he goes looking for someplace like Hamacassar. Easier to find a city than oneself." He nodded at the beckoning peaks. "All we have to do is continue on a northward track and eventually we will come out of these mountains. Then we can ask directions of local people to the city."

"That's all well and good, bruther. But scrambling over a couple of snow-capped peaks takes a lot more time than walking along a well-known trail. We could try following a river, but first we have to find one that flows northward instead of south, and then hope it doesn't turn away to west or east, or loop back on itself. A guide would probably cut weeks or months off our walking and save us from having to negotiate some rough country." He stoppered his water bag. "I've been lost in mountains like these before and, let me tell you, I'd rather take a whipping from a dozen amazons."

"You would rather take a whipping from a dozen amazons even if you were not lost," the herdsman retorted. "All we can do is do our best. Between the two of us I am confident we will not find ourselves wandering about aimlessly for very long."

"Hunkapa see Hamacassar."

"What's that?" Startled, Simna looked up from the last of his dried biscuit. Ehomba too had turned to stare at the newest member of the group. Dozing against a great arching root, the black litah ignored them all.

Ehomba proceeded to question their hulking companion. Seated, Hunkapa Aub was nearly at eye level with the tall southerner. "Hunkapa see Hamacassar," he repeated convincingly.

"You mean you've been in the port city?" Simna didn't know whether to laugh or sneer. Though the shaggy brute was slow, he was not entirely dumb. The swordsman decided to do neither. "How did you find it? Accommodations to your liking?"

"Not visit Hamacassar." Hunkapa Aub spoke slowly and carefully so as to keep both his simple words and even simpler thoughts straight, in his own mind as well as in those of his new friends. "I see." An enormous hairy arm rose and pointed. "From slopes of Scathe Mountain. First mountains go down. Then flat places where men grow foods. Beyond that, way beyond, is river Eynharrmawk—Eynharrowk. On this side Eynharrowk is city Hamacassar." Reaching up, he touched one thick finger to an ear almost entirely obscured by dark gray hair. "See river, go Hamacassar."

Ehomba pondered the creature's words silently. Simna was not as reticent to comment. "Hoy, that were quite a speech, Aub. Why should we believe the least of it?"

"Why would he lie?" Tapping a finger against his lips, Ehomba studied the guileless, open-hearted brute.

"He's not lying." Both men turned to look at the supine Ahlitah. The big cat had rolled over and was lying on its spine with all four feet in the air, scratching itself against the rough-edged woody debris that littered the forest floor.

"How do you know?" Simna's disdain was plain to see.

Concluding its scratching, the litah tumbled contentedly onto its side. "I can smell it. Certain things have strong smells. Females in heat, fresh scat, week-old kills, false promises, and outright lies." He sneezed resoundingly. "The new beast may be slow and ignorant, but he is not a liar. Not in this matter, at least."

Dropping his hand from his lips, Ehomba tried to see into the depths of Hunkapa Aub's being. He was unable to penetrate very far. There was a veil over the creature's soul. Aware that Simna was watching the both of them expectantly, he tried to reassure them all with another question.

"You say that you have seen Hamacassar but have not been there. Have you ever been out of the Hrugar Mountains?"

"No. But been to edge. Stop there." He shook his head and shag went flying in all directions. "Don't like. Humans say and do bad things to Hunkapa Aub."

"But you know the way through the high mountains and down into the foothills on the other side?"

The brute rose sharply to tower over Ehomba. Simna and Ahlitah both tensed—but the hulking creature was only showing his eagerness and enthusiasm. "Hunkapa know! You want Hunkapa take you?"

"We want very much." Ehomba smiled reassuringly.

"Hunkapa not like people cities, but—you save Hunkapa from cage. Hunkapa owe you. So—Start now!" Without another word, their humongous friend turned and headed off in the direction of Mount Scathe, eating up distance with inhumanly long strides.

"Hoy, wait a minute there!" Simna struggled to get his kit together. Ahlitah was already padding off in the brute's wake, with Ehomba not far behind. It took the swordsman some awkward running to catch up to the rest of them.

He hoped they would not run into any free-living, isolated mountain dwellers like old Coubert. Not with Hunkapa Aub and the black litah in the lead. Simna did not want to be responsible for inducing heart failure in some poor, unsuspecting hermit.

Like all high mountain ranges everywhere, the peaks of the Hrugars were loftier than they appeared from a distance. Towering over them all was Mount Scathe, a ragged, soaring complex of crags whose uppermost pinnacle clawed at any cloud passing below sixteen thousand feet. Gashed by deep valleys through which angry, rushing streams commuted to the lowlands, they presented a formidable barrier to anyone advancing from the south.

True to his word, Hunkapa Aub seemed to know exactly where he was going. When Simna complained about having to scramble up a particularly difficult incline, Aub remarked in his own subdued, laconic fashion that the slopes to either side of their ascent were far more difficult. When Ehomba wondered one afternoon why the river valley they were following was curving back southward, their shaggy companion implored him to be patient. Sure enough, by evening the stream and its valley had turned north once again.

They climbed until the air grew thin in their lungs, hardly fit for breathing. In this rarefied clime Ehomba and Simna moved more slowly, and the black litah padded on with head down instead of held high. But their guide was in his element. In the chill, dilute air he seemed to stand taller. His stride became more fluid. His confidence expanded even as his companions began to suffer from second thoughts.

Wearing every piece of clothing he had brought with him and as a consequence looking not unlike one of the unfortunates who haunted the back alleys of Bondressey, Simna kept slapping his hands against his sides to keep warm.

"Are you sure this is the way, o bushy one? We've been walking for many days now."

Hunkapa looked back at the swordsman, who was huffing and puffing to keep up. Actually, Simna welcomed the fast pace. It helped to keep his body temperature elevated. "Right way, Simna. *Only* way." A thick, woolly arm rose to indicate the soaring rock walls that hemmed them in on both sides. "Go up that way, or over there, and you die. Hunkapa okay, but not you, not Etjole." A guileless grin split the bewhiskered face. "You not got hair enough."

"I not got a lot of things," replied the swordsman peevishly. "Right now, patience happens to be one of them."

Though equally as cold and uncomfortable as his shorter companion, Ehomba did not manifest his discomfort as visibly or as vocally. "The mountains lie between where we were and where we are going, Simna. I am as sorry as you that there is no easier way. But we are making good progress." He turned to their pathfinder. "We *are* making good progress, yes?"

"Oh very good, very good!" Back in his beloved mountains, their great, lumbering guide was full of high spirits. His enthusiasm was infectious, and some of it could not help but be imparted to his companions. This lasted for another couple of days.

Then it began to snow.

Only once before had Ehomba seen it snow, during a hunting journey to the far distant mountains that lay to the northeast of his home. It had taken many days to get there, during the coldest time of the year. He remembered marveling at the wet white splotches that fell from the air and melted in his hand, remembered the soft, silent beauty of the sky turning from blue to gray and then to white. It was an experience that had stayed with him all his life.

That snow had melted quickly upon striking the warm ground. This snow remained, to be greeted by that which had preceded it. Instead of melting, it accumulated in piles. In places it reached higher than a man's head, just like drifting sand in the desert. That was what the big, fluffy patches were, he decided. Cold white dunes, rising on the mountain slopes all around them.

Familiar with snow and all its chill, damp manifestations from his homeland and many wanderings, Simna was less than overwhelmed with wonder. What he was, was uncomfortable and increasingly nervous.

"What are you gaping at, Etjole?" Shivering, he did his best to match his stride to that of the tall southerner. "If we don't start down from this place pretty quickly we could freeze to death up here."

"I was just admiring the beauty of it," the herdsman replied. "The land of the Naumkib is all earth colors: yellow and orange, gray and brown. To be surrounded by white is an entirely new sensation for me."

"Is dying a new sensation for you?" Simna indicated their guide, striding along blissfully in front of them. "This is his country. What if he decides to abandon us up here some night, or in the middle of a storm like this? We'd never find our way out. Treasure's no good to a man frozen stiff as an icicle."

"Then think of the treasure, friend Simna. Maybe thinking of it will warm you."

The swordsman's eyes widened slightly. "Then there is a treasure?"

"Oh yes. Greater than any an ordinary king or emperor can dream of. Mountains of gold in all its many manifestations, natural and crystalline, refined and fashioned. Gold as bullion and jewelry, gold that was coined by forgotten ancients, gold so pure you can work it with your bare hands. And the jewels! Such treasures of the earth, in every cut and color imaginable. There is silver too, and platinum in bricks piled high, and precious coral in shades of pink and red and black. More treasure than one man could count in a hundred lifetimes, let alone spend."

Simna eyed his friend reprovingly. "And all this time you've been denying its existence to me. I knew it, I knew it!" One hand clenched into a triumphant fist. "Why tell me now, in this place?"

"As I said. To warm you."

"Well, it's done that." Straightening slightly, the swordsman forcefully kicked his way through the steadily accumulating snow. "Let it blizzard if it wants to! Nothing's going to stop us now. I will not allow it." Tilting back his head, he shouted at the sky. "Do you hear me, clouds? I, Simna ibn Sind, will not permit it!"

By the following morning, with the snow still falling, his energy had flagged. In this the swordsman knew he need not be ashamed, because none of his companions were doing well. Lowlanders all, the unrelenting cold had begun to pick at their remaining reserves of strength, stealing their body heat like vultures biting off mouth-sized bits of flesh from a fresh corpse.

Seated around the morning fire they had managed to build in a snow cave, the two men and one litah huddled as close to the flickering flames as they could without actually catching themselves or their clothing on fire. Seemingly immune to the cold, their good-natured guide had left the cave early to go in search of wood for the blaze. Locating sufficient tinder dry enough to burn had taken him several hours. By the time he had finally returned, it was snowing harder than ever.

"This is not good." Rubbing his long fingers together over the flames, Ehomba spoke solemnly to the hulking form that blocked the entrance hole. Hunkapa Aub was shutting off some of the wind and cold from outside with his own body. "How much farther? How long before we can start down out of the mountains?"

Overhanging brows drew together. "Still several days, Etjole. Hunkapa see this hard for you. I can carry, but only one at a time."

"Our legs are not the problem, Hunkapa." The herdsman fed one of the last dry branches to the little blaze. "It is too cold for us. Our bodies are not used to this kind of weather. And the snow makes it much worse. The wetness freezes our skin when it touches, and blocks out the sun."

"Start down soon." The massive shape shifted its back to seal the entrance to the snow cave more tightly.

"Several days is not soon, Hunkapa. Not in these conditions." Ehomba cast his gaze upward. "If the snow would stop and the sun would come out, then maybe."

Simna shivered beneath his thin clothing. "Bruther, I swear by Gaufremar I'm not sure anymore what you are: sorcerer or steer herder. Maybe both, maybe neither. This cold makes it hard for a man to think straight, so I'm not even sure of what I'm saying right now." He lifted anxious eyes to his friend. "But if ever there was a time for magic, it's come. The rug that walks says it's several days before we can start down? I'm telling you here and now I don't think I can take another morning of this. My skin feels like frozen parchment, my eyes are going blind from staring into this damnable whiteness, and I'm reaching the point where I can't feel my legs anymore. My hips force them forward and when I look down I see that I'm still standing. That's the only way I know that I haven't fallen."

"Simna is right." Everyone turned to look at Ahlitah. The great cat was huddled in a ball alongside the fire. A force of nature, all ebony muscle and fang, even he had exhausted his strength. "Something has to change. We can't go on in this."

It was a momentous moment: the first time since they had begun journeying together that the litah and the swordsman had ever agreed on anything. More than any eloquence or deed it underscored the serious-ness of the situation. Both looked to their nominal leader, to the lanky herdsman who sat cross-legged before the inevitably diminishing fire. Ehomba stared into the fading flames for a long time. There was no more wood.

Finally he raised his eyes and looked first at Ahlitah, then at the shivering swordsman. "You know, I am cold too."

Reaching behind him, he dragged his pack to his side. Brushing snow from the flap that Mirhanja had embroidered and beaded herself, he began to search within. Simna leaned forward eagerly, expectantly. Ever since he had joined company with the herdsman, wonderful things had emerged from that pack. Simple things that in Ehomba's skilled, knowing hands had proven to be much more than they first appeared. What would the enigmatic herdsman bring forth this time?

A flute.

Lightly carved of ivory-colored bone, it had eight small holes for fingering and was no bigger around than the herdsman's thumb. Licking his lips to moisten them slightly, Ehomba put the narrow end to his mouth and began to play.

A lilting, sprightly tune, Simna thought as he listened. Foreign but not unfathomable. The herdsman played well, though not skillfully enough to secure a place in the private orchestra of any truly discerning nobleman. Next to him, the litah's tail began to twitch, back and forth, back and forth in time to the music. Hunkapa Aub closed his eyes and rocked slowly from side to side, his immense shoulders rubbing snow from the roof of the temporary shelter.

It went on for some time as the fire died in front of them. Finally Ehomba lowered the instrument from his lips and smiled thoughtfully. "Well?"

Simna blinked uncertainly. "Well what?"

"Did you like it?"

"Pretty-pretty!" was their guide's enthusiastic comment. Ahlitah let out a snort that was less haughty than usual—a compliment of sorts. But Simna could only stare.

"What do you mean, did I like it? What difference does it make whether I liked it or not?" His voice rose to a shout. "By Gilgolosh, Etjole, we're dying here! I want to see some serious sortilege, not listen to a concert!"

Ehomba did not shed his smile. "Did it make you want to dance?"

The swordsman was so angry he might actually have taken a swing at his friend. What madness was this? That was it, he decided. The terrible, killing cold had manifested itself differently in each of them. With Ehomba, it had finally revealed its insidious self in the form of a hitherto hidden dementia.

"Me dance!" Hunkapa Aub was still rocking slightly from side to side, remembering the music. "Etjole play more!"

"If you like." Bringing the slim flute back to his lips, the herdsman launched into another tune, this one more lively than its predecessor. Simna would have reached out and snatched the accursed instrument from his companion's fingers, but his own hands were too cold.

Rocking to the music, Hunkapa Aub backed out of the opening and into the snow where he could gambol unconfined. Picking up his pack, Ehomba followed him. Ahlitah was not far behind. Muttering to himself, an irate Simna remained in the snow cave until the last vestige of the dissipating campfire vanished in its own smoke. Then he donned his pack and, with great reluctance, crawled outside to rejoin the others.

Halfway out of the cave he stopped, staring. When he finally emerged it was in silence and with eyes wide, gaping at the sky, the ground, and the surrounding mountains. The air was still icy cold, and it was still snowing as hard as ever.

But the snow was dancing.

Not metaphorically, not as the component of some ethereal poetic allusion, but for real.

Across from the entrance to the snow cave two triple helixes of ice crystals were twirling about one another, rippling and weaving as sinuously as a sextet of bleached snakes. The twirling embrace conveyed snow from the sky to the ground in loose, relaxed stripings of white. Nearby, the powdery stuff fell in sheets. That is to say, not heavily, but in actual sheets—layer upon layer of frosty rectangular shapes that sifted down from unseen clouds with alternating layers of clear air between them. As they descended they fluttered from side to side like square birds.

Individual flakes darted in multiple directions, as careful to avoid colliding with one another as a billion choreographed dancers. Miniature snowballs bounced through the air while hundreds of snowflakes combined to form many-pointed flakes hundreds of times larger. The instant they reached some unknown critical mass they fell with a thump into the fresh banks that lined the sides of the icy stream that ran through the narrow valley, leaving behind temporary holes in the snow that assumed the shape of a thousand dissimilar stars.

Snow fell in squares and spheres, in octahedrons and dodecahedrons. Möbius strips of snow turned inward upon themselves and vanished, while shafts of snow winkled their white way through the centers of snowflake toroids. And in between the snow there was light: sunlight pouring down pure and uninterrupted from above. It warmed his face, his hands, his clothes, and sucked the paralyzing chill from his bones.

All of it—shapes and swirls, giant compacted snowballs and individual flakes—danced to the music of the thin bone flute that was being wielded by Etjole Ehomba's skillful hands.

"Come on, then," he exclaimed, looking back to where Simna was standing and staring open-mouthed at the all-engulfing world of white wonder. "Let us make time. I cannot play forever, you know." He smiled, that warm, knowing, ambiguous smile the swordsman had come to know so well. "As you have been so correctly and ceaselessly pointing out for past these many days, it is cold here. If my lips grow numb, I will not be able to play."

As if to underline the seriousness of the herdsman's observation, the minute he had stopped playing the blizzard had settled in once more around them, the falling snow distributed evenly and unremarkably from the sky, and the sun once more wholly obscured.

"You should know better by now than to listen to me, bruther. Keep playing, keep playing!" Simna struggled through the drifts to catch up to his friend.

Turning northward, Ehomba again set mouthpiece to lips and blew. His limber fingers danced atop the flute, rhythmically covering and exposing the holes incised there. The euphony that filled the air anew was light, almost jaunty in expression. It tickled the storm, and the snow responded. As before, a plethora of shapes and suggestions took hold of the weather, buckling and contorting it into a thousand delightful shapes, all of it composed of nothing more animate than frozen water.

As they trekked on, the herdsman continued to sculpt the storm with his music. The shapes it took were endlessly fascinating, full of charm and whimsy and play. But delightful as they were to look upon, Ehomba's companions valued the sun that shafted down between them far more. After a little while Simna found that he was able to remove his outer coverings and hold them up to dry. Ahlitah paced and shook, paced and shook, until even the tips of his mane had regained their optimal fluffiness.

As for Hunkapa Aub, he danced and spun and twirled with as much joy as the snow, his fur-framed expression one of soporific bliss. Even so, he was not so distracted that he failed to notice important turnings in the path. Here, he declared, pointing to an especially large slab of granite protruding from the side of the valley, we turn to the left. And here we leave the river for a while to clamber over a field of talus.

As they marched on in ever-increasing comfort but without being able to truly relax, Simna kept a careful watch over his tall friend. Ehomba's words of warning were never very far from the swordsman's mind. How long *could* he keep tootling on that flute? Hiking and playing each demanded endurance and energy, both of which were in short supply among the members of the little expedition. Ehomba was no exception. Like everyone else, he was cold and tired. A lean, deceptive energy kept him going, but he was no immortal. Without food and rest he too would eventually collapse from exhaustion.

Even as the sun continued to slip-slide down between the pillars and spirals of dancing snow, Simna was keenly aware of the massed, heavy clouds overhead. Shorn of inspiring music, the snow they were dropping would meld once more into a dense, clinging blanket from which there might not be any escape. He willed what strength he could to his tall friend, and tried to remember the melodies of folk songs long forgotten in case the herdsman's musical inspiration began to flag.

Ehomba played on all the rest of the morning and into the afternoon. Conscious of their precarious situation, the travelers did not pause for a midday meal, but instead kept walking. They would rest when the herdsman rested. Until then, it was far more important that they keep moving than eat. Their bodies screamed for food to turn into heat, but they ignored the demands of their bellies. Time enough later to feed their faces. Time enough later for everything once they were safely out of the mountains.

Ehomba was starting to miss notes, to falter in the middle of alternate tunes, when a gleeful Hunkapa began hopping about with even more ardor than usual.

Simna muttered his reaction to the litah. "I'd say the simpleton has gone mad, except that it would be hard to tell the difference. What's got into him now?"

"Perhaps he is especially inspired by the tune Ehomba is presently fluting," the big cat replied thoughtfully.

"I'm surprised he can hear it." Simna eyed the herdsman worriedly. "For the last hour or so his playing has grown quieter and quieter. I'm afraid our friend may be running out of wind."

The swordsman was right. Ehomba was almost done, his fingers cramped from fingering the holes atop the flute and his lips numb from blowing into the mouthpiece. But Ahlitah was also correct. Their hirsute pathfinder was indeed singularly inspired, but not by the herdsman's playing. As swordsman and cat closed the distance between themselves and their leaping, gyrating guide, they saw for themselves the reason why. Bellowing joyfully into their cold-benumbed ears, Hunkapa Aub confirmed it.

"Go down!" he was hooting. "Go down now; down, down, down!"

Ahead lay more snow-covered slopes. They were no different from the white-clad terrain the travelers had spent the past difficult days traversing, with one notable exception: all inclined visibly downward. Additionally, the stream they had been following intermittently now visibly picked up speed, tumbling and spilling in a series of crystal-clear cataracts toward some far-distant river, as if the water itself could somehow sense the proximity of gentler climes and more accommodating surroundings.

Cloud and fog continued to eddy around them as they picked up the pace. The downgrade enabled them to increase their speed without any additional exertion while simultaneously taking some of the strain off their weary legs. Falling snow sustained its miraculous waltzing, Ehomba's faltering music inspiring ever newer patterns and designs in the air. The only difference was that now the pirouetting snowflakes began to surrender a gradually increasing percentage of the open sky to the unobstructed sun.

By evening they had descended from alpine hardwood forest to slopes thick with dogwood and bottlebrush, oak and elm. The ground was bare of snow, and flowers once more brightened the earth between trees and bracken. As Ehomba finally lowered the flute from his lips, the last dozen snowflakes trickled down from above. Concluding a miniature ballet in twinkling white, they corkscrewed around one another down past the herdsman's face, and paused in the fragile grip of a passing breeze to bow solemnly in his direction. Then, one by one, they struck the warm, rich soil and melted away into oblivion, leaving behind only tiny snowflake ghosts that each took the form of half a second's lingering moisture.

A solicitous Simna promptly came forward to peer into his friend's face. "How are you, bruther? How do you feel?"

"Myph—mimith . . ." Reaching around back, the herdsman took a long, slow draught from his water bag. After wetting his lips, he smacked them together several times before trying one more time to form a reply.

"My mouth is—sore. But otherwise I am all right, Simna. Thank you for inquiring. I am also very hungry."

"We're all hungry." Looking around, the swordsman located the black litah. The big cat was scratching itself against an obliging tree and purring like an old waterwheel. "Hoy, kitty! What say me and thee go and kill something worth chewing?"

Before Ahlitah could reply, Hunkapa Aub was standing in front of Simna and waving his arms excitedly. "No kill, no hunt!"

"By Gomepoth, why not? Maybe you're not hungry, fur face, but me and my friends are starving. All that walking and fighting that cold has left us as empty as a triplet of grog buckets on a forty-year-old's first wedding night."

"No need." Taking the protesting swordsman by the arm, their guide dragged him forward. Though the muscular, well-conditioned Simna did his best to resist, it was like trying to brake a runaway mountain.

Hunkapa halted at the edge of an unseen, unsuspected overlook. Once he was exposed to the splendid panorama that was spread out before him, Simna stopped struggling. They were quickly joined by Ehomba and Ahlitah.

Below and beyond the last foothills of the northern Hrugars, lush farmland dotted with numerous towns and small rivers spread out before them. The revealed countryside resembled a landlocked river delta. Hundreds of canals linked the natural waterways, from which the setting sun skipped layers of pink and gold and purple. Several larger communities were big enough to qualify as small cities.

In the far distance, just visible as a sparkling thread of silver below the sky, was the majestic main river into which every canal and stream and waterway between the Hrugars and the horizon flowed. Hunkapa Aub pointed and gesticulated exuberantly.

"See, see! Great river Eynharrowk." His trunk of an arm shifted slightly to the west. "Cannot see from here, but over there, that way, on the great river, is Hamacassar."

"At last." Utterly worn out, Simna sank to the ground as his legs gave way beneath him.

"We are not there yet." Tired as he was, Ehomba chose to remain standing, perhaps the better to drink in the view that was as full of promise as it was of beauty. "And do not forget that Hamacassar is only a possible waypoint, a place for us to look for a ship with captain and crew brave enough to dare a crossing of the Semordria."

A pleading expression on his grime-flocked face, Simna ibn Sind looked up at his companion. "Please, Etjole—can't we delight in even one moment of pleasure at having lived through this past week? Will you never allow yourself to relax, not even for an instant?"

"When I am again home with my family, friend Simna, then I will relax." He smiled. "Until then, I anoint you in my stead. You are hereby authorized to relax for me."

Nodding understandingly, the swordsman spread both arms wide and fell back flat on the ground. "I accept the responsibility."

Still smiling, Ehomba moved to stand next to the quietly jubilant Hunkapa Aub. "You do not want us to go hunting because you think we can get food more easily in the towns down below."

Their hulking guide nodded vigorously. "Many places, much food. Not see myself, but come here often and spy on flatland people. Hear them talking, learn about flatlands." He eyed the tall southerner questioningly. "We go down now?"

Ehomba considered the sky. Away from the snow and cold, they might have a chance to reach a community before dark. He was not so concerned for himself, but Simna would clearly benefit from a night spent in civilized settings.

"Yes, Hunkapa. Go down now." He put a hand on one massive, shaggy arm. "And Hunkapa—thank you. We could not have made it through these mountains without your guidance."

It was impossible to tell whether the beast was blushing beneath all that thick hair, but Hunkapa Aub turned away so that Ehomba could not see his face.

"You save me, I help you. Thanks not needed."

Ehomba turned to Simna. "Come on, my friend. We will go down into civilization and find you a bed."

The swordsman groaned piteously. "That means I have to walk again? On these poor feet?"

Their guide immediately moved toward him. "Hunkapa carry."

"No, no, that's not necessary, friend!" The speed with which Simna ascended to his supposedly untenable feet was something to behold.

Together, the four travelers commenced their departure from the lower reaches of the inhospitable Hrugars. As they descended, Ehomba thought to inquire of Hunkapa as to the name of the country they were entering.

"Hunkapa listen to flatlanders talk." He gestured expansively with an imposing arm. "This place all one, called Lifongo. No," he corrected himself quickly, his brows knotting. "Not that." His expression brightened. "Laconda. That it. This place, Laconda."

It was Simna's turn to frown. "Funny. Seems to me I've heard that name mentioned somewhere before, but I can't quite place—" He broke off, staring at Ehomba. The herdsman had stopped in his tracks and was staring, his lips slightly parted, straight ahead. "Hoy, bruther, you all right? You owe someone money here?"

"No, friend Simna. You are correct. You have heard that name before." Turning his head, he met the curious eyes of his companion. "You heard it from me. Laconda is the home of Tarin Beckwith, the noble warrior who died in my arms on the beach below my village." He returned his gaze to the magnificent vista extending before them.

"He cannot ever come home—but now, if fate is willing, perhaps I can return the honor of his memory to his people."

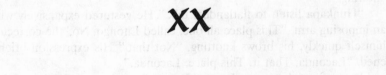

Long before they reached the outskirts of the first town they found themselves in among vast orchards of mango and guava. Planted in even rows and trimmed as neatly as any garden of roses, the trees were heavy with fruit. Eventually the travelers encountered growers and their assistants. Initial cheerful greetings were tempered by fear when the Lacondans caught sight of Hunkapa Aub and the black litah striding along behind the two men, but Ehomba and Simna were quick to reassure the locals that their unusual, and unusually large, friends would do them no harm.

Awed and wide-eyed, the orchardists provided the visitors with instructions on the best way to pass through their country to Laconda North, for it was from there and not Laconda proper that Tarin Beckwith had hailed. Questioning revealed that despite their apparently contented demeanor the people still lived in a permanent state of mourning. Everyone knew the tale of how the perfidious warlock Hymneth the Possessed had come from a far country to steal away the joy of Laconda, the Visioness Themaryl. Of how the finest and most well-born soldiers of both Laconda and Laconda North had sought to effect her return by every means at their disposal, only to return dispirited and defeated, or not to return at all. The warlock Hymneth had taken his prize and vanished, some said across the Semordria itself. A few brave souls from both countries were reputed to have chased him that far. None had ever returned.

"Aren't we going to tell them what you're here for?" Simna kept pace with the tall southerner as they strode along the secondary road of commerce that connected Laconda with its sister state to the north.

People on foot, on horse- or antelope-back, or in wagons goggled at the sight of the two men leading the great cat and the hulking beast.

"There is no need." Ehomba kept his attention on the road ahead. It was dusty, but wide and smooth. After struggling through the Hrugars, walking normally felt like flying. "If we stop to speak to these people they will want to know more. Someone will inform the local authorities. Then they will want to hear our story." He glanced over at his friend. "Every day I am away from my home and family is a day I will never have back. When I am old and lie dying I will remember all these moments, all these days that I did not have with them, and regret every one of them. The fates will not give these days back to me." He returned his gaze to the road. "I want as little as possible to regret. We will explain ourselves in Laconda North. That much I owe to the parents of Tarin Beckwith—if they are still alive."

Not only were they alive, but Count Bewaryn Beckwith still sat on the northern throne. This was told to them by the easygoing border guards who manned the station that marked the boundary between the two Lacondas. The armed men marveled at Hunkapa and shied away from Ahlitah, but let them pass through without hesitation. In fact, they were more than happy to see the back of the peculiar quartet.

It was in Laconda North that the travelers encountered the first fish. Not in the canals or streams that were more numerous in the northern province than in its southern cousin, nor in the many lakes and ponds, but everywhere in the air. They swam through the sky with flicks of their fins and tails, passing with stately grace between trees and buildings. The Lacondans ignored them, paying drifting tuna and trevally, bannerfish and batfish no more mind than they would have stray dogs or cats.

"There's plenty of free-standing water hereabouts in all these canals and ponds, and I feel the humidity in the air," Simna observed as a small school of sardines finned past on their left, "but this is ridiculous!"

"The fish here have learned not only how to breathe air instead of water, but to levitate." Ehomba admired a cluster of moorish idols, black and yellow and white emblems, as they turned off the road to disappear behind a hay barn. "I wonder what they eat?"

His answer was provided by a brace of barracuda that rocketed out from behind a copse of cottonwoods to wreak momentary havoc among a school of rainbow runners. When the silvery torpedoes had finished their work, bits of fish tumbled slowly through the muggy air, sifting to the ground like gray snow. If such occurrences were relatively common, Ehomba knew, the soil hereabouts would be extremely fertile. Having done his turn at tending the village gardens, he knew that nothing was better for fertilizing the soil than fish parts and oil.

Though they did their best, it was impossible to ignore the presence of the airborne fish. The Lacondans they encountered went about their business as if the bizarre phenomenon were a perfectly natural everyday occurrence, as indeed for them it was. Once, they saw a pair of boys laughing and chasing a small school of herring. The boys carried nets of fine, strong mesh attached to long poles. With these they caught not butterflies, but breakfasts.

Ehomba and Simna did not have nets, and Hunkapa Aub was much too slow of hand to grab the darting, agile fish, but they had with them a catching mechanism more effective than any net. With lightning-fast, almost casual swipes of his claws, Ahlitah brought down mackerel and snapper whenever they felt like a meal.

There was no need to look for an inn in which to spend the night. The air of Laconda and Laconda North was warm and moist, allowing them to sleep wherever the terrain took their fancy. This was fortunate, since the swordsman's stock of Chlengguu gold had been exhausted. With food plentiful and freely available, they did not lack for nourishment. It was in this fashion that they made their way, in response to ready directions from farmers and fish-catchers, to the central city. Within a very few days they found themselves standing outside the castle of Count Bewaryn Beckwith, ruler of Laconda North.

It was an impressive sight, a grand palace surrounded by an iron-topped stone wall. Beyond the gate was an expansive, paved parade ground. Elegantly uniformed soldiers stood guard at the gate or trooped past within on fine stallions and unicorns. Beyond lay the palace itself, a three-storied fancy of white limestone and marble. No turrets or battlements were in evidence. The sprawling structure before them served as a home and a seat of governance, not a fortress designed to repel a formal military attack.

"We should announce ourselves." From across the street Simna was conducting a thoughtful appraisal of the layout of the royal residence.

"Yes." Ehomba started forward, the tip of his spear clicking against the paving stones. "The sooner I have done my duty here, the sooner we can move on to Hamacassar."

The guards at the florid wrought-iron gate were dressed in thin coats of blue and gold. They were sleeveless, a sensible adaptation in the warm and humid climate. Long blue pants were tucked into short boots of soft leather, also dyed blue. Each of the four men, two flanking either side of the entrance, was armed with a short sword that hung from a belt of gold leather and a long, ornate pike. They stood at attention, but not immovably so. They became much more active when they saw the unprecedented quartet approaching. To their credit, they kept the pikes erect and made no move to challenge the approaching travelers with weapons poised.

Ehomba walked up to the guard who appeared to be the senior member of the four. The man pushed his gold-trimmed blue cap back on his head and gaped; not at the herdsman, but at the looming mass of Hunkapa Aub.

"Well now, what *do* we have here?"

"A friend from the mountains." Ehomba addressed the man politely but not deferentially. There were only a few individuals in this world whom the herdsman deferred to, and this wide-shouldered gentleman in the blue uniform was not among them.

"The Hrugars, eh?" Another of the guards came forward to join the conversation. He and his colleague exhibited no signs of panic, confident in their position and their weapons. It spoke well of their training, Ehomba decided. "He's dressed for it, anyway. That's a fine heavy coat he's wearing, though I confess I don't recognize the animal it came from."

"It's not—" Ehomba started to say, but Simna stepped in front of his tall companion both physically and vocally.

"And well tailored to him it is, too." Looking back over his shoulder, the swordsman flashed his friend a look that managed to say, wordlessly and all at once, "This is a city, and you're from the country, and I know city folk and their ways better than you ever will." It was enough to prod Ehomba into holding his peace while the enterprising swordsman did the talking.

"We've come a long way to see the Count. Farther than you can imagine."

The guards exchanged a glance. "I don't know," the one who had first spoken opined. "I can imagine quite a distance." Leaning loosely on his pike, he contemplated Simna's semibarbaric attire. "Do you think this is a public hall, where anyone can just walk in and make an appointment?"

"What business have rascals like you with the Count?" Though far from hostile, the second guard was not as amicable as his comrade.

Simna straightened importantly. "We have news of his son, Tarin Beckwith."

It was as if all four guards had been standing on a copper plate suddenly struck by lightning. The two who had said not a word and who did not even appear to have been listening to the conversation whirled and dashed off toward the palace, not even bothering to close the heavy iron gate behind them. As for the pair of casual conversationalists, they no longer gave the appearance of being disinterested in the peculiar quartet of visitors. They gripped their pikes firmly while their expressions indicated that they now held the travelers in an entirely new regard.

"The noble Tarin has not been heard from in many months. How come you lot to know of him?" The senior of the two guards was trying to watch all three of the foreigners simultaneously. For the time being, he ignored the big cat that was snoozing prominently on the pavement.

Simna was forced to defer back to his companion. Noting that his spear was not as long as the sentry's pike, Ehomba once again retold the tale of how he had found Tarin Beckwith and many of his countrymen washed up on the beach below the village of the Naumkib, and of how the young nobleman had expired in his arms. Fully alert now, the guards listened intently, wholly absorbed in the story.

When Ehomba had concluded his tale, the second guard spoke up. "I knew young Beckwith. Not well—I am far below his station—but there were several occasions on which he joined the palace guard on maneuvers. He was a fine person, a true gentleman, who never put on airs and enjoyed a good bawdy joke or a pint of lager. Everyone in Laconda and Laconda North had hoped . . ." The younger man was unable to continue. Evidently the Count's son had been not just liked, but loved, by the populace.

"I am sorry," Ehomba commiserated simply. "There was nothing I could do for him. He was a victim of this warlock who calls himself Hymneth the Possessed."

"Abductor of the fair Themaryl, the Visioness, the greatest glory of the Lacondas." The senior guard sounded wistful. "I never saw her myself, but I've spoken with others who had the privilege. They say that her grace and beauty eclipsed that of the sun itself." His tone darkened. "If what you say is true, then because of this evil magician the Lacondas have lost both her and the noble Tarin." The echo of hastening footsteps made him turn.

A dozen palace sentinels were arriving on the run, led by the two who had formerly been helping to guard the front gate. Badly out of breath, one of these performed an odd salute that the senior among the staff returned with a stiff snap of one hand.

"The Count wishes to see these travelers immediately, without delay!" The messenger gasped for air. "They are to be brought to the main dining chamber, where they will be received by the Count and the Countess themselves!" He looked over at the two men and their odd companions with new respect.

Frowning uncertainly, the senior guard hesitated. "What about the big cat?"

Sucking wind, the messenger nodded sharply. "It is to be conducted to the dining chamber as well. The palace adviser said clearly to bring all four of them."

"As they wish." Turning back to Ehomba, the senior guard smiled encouragingly. "Don't be intimidated by the palace, or by any representatives of the court you find yourselves introduced to. They're a pretty inoffensive bunch. Laconda North is a very serene country. As for the Count, he's been known to bluster a lot, but not to bully. The fact that he wishes to see you himself is a good sign."

"We're not intimidated by anything." Simna swept grandly past the guard station. "We've fought Corruption and Chlengguu, crossed the Hrugars and the Aboqua, brought down pieces of the sky on our enemies, and made the weather dance to our songs. Mere men we do not fear."

The guard forced himself not to laugh. "Just speak soft and true and you will get along well with the Count. He is not fond of braggarts."

"Hoy," declared Simna as he marched importantly down between the double line of soldiers that had formed up to escort them into the palace, "I don't brag. I only tell the truth. Honest ibn Sind, they call me."

As Ehomba passed the friendly, encouraging sentry, he whispered to him in passing. "Please understand, it is not that my friend is being boastful. He talks like this *all* the time."

The parade ground seemed endless as they crossed it under the watchful eyes of the heavily armed escort, but eventually they reached the shade of the nearest building. From there they were ushered inside and down halls decorated with fine tapestries and paintings. Floating fish were everywhere, their movements constrained by fine netting or transparent glass walls. Exotic tropicals in every color and shape and size were employed in the palace as living decorations. Certainly their iridescent, brilliant colors were as attractive as any of the magnificent but static artworks that dominated the walls.

Eventually they reached a high-ceilinged chamber dominated by a U-shaped table large enough to seat a hundred people. At the far end a dozen anxious figures awaited their arrival. Dazzling tropicals swam freely through the air, unconstrained by netting or other barriers. As the room was devoid of windows, there was no need to place internal restrictions on their movement.

The far end of the table had been set with fine china and silver. Platters had hastily been piled high with the best the palace's kitchens had to offer. Simna's mouth began to water, and Ahlitah licked his lips at the sight of so much meat, even if it had been badly damaged by treatment with fire.

A tall, elegant man with a slightly hooked nose and thinning blond hair that was gray only at the temples rose to greet them, unable to wait for the travelers to make the long walk from the main doorway to the far end of the table. Much to Simna's chagrin, he ignored the swordsman and halted directly in front of Ehomba. His voice was very deep and resonant for one so slim.

"They told me you were dressed like barbarians, but I find your costume in its own way as courtly as my own. As for its imperfections of appearance, and yours, they are excused by the difficulties and distance you have had to deal with in your long journey here." Stepping aside, he gestured expansively at the table. "Welcome! Welcome to Laconda North. Rest, eat, drink—and tell me what you know of my son. My only son."

While the two humans were seated close to the head of the table, room was made for Ahlitah and Hunkapa at the far opposite end. Neither the shaggy mountain dweller nor the big cat felt in the least left out of the ensuing conversation. The litah had no interest in the yapping discourse of humans, and Hunkapa Aub would not have been able to follow it clearly anyway.

The food was wonderfully filling and the wine excellent. Trembling servitors even prevailed upon the cat to try a little of the latter, stammering that it was traditional and to refuse to do so would be to insult the hospitality of the house of Beckwith. Ahlitah magnanimously consented to lap up a bowl of the dark purple fluid. The attendants had less difficulty persuading Hunkapa to do likewise.

At the head of the table Ehomba and Simna displayed a deportment more refined than their attire as they enjoyed the best meal they had partaken of in many a day. Ehomba had always been a relaxed eater, and Simna revealed a surprising knowledge of manners more suited to cultivated surroundings than he had hitherto exhibited in their travels together.

"Not much point in trying to use a napkin when there's none to be had," he explained in response to the herdsman's murmured compliment. "Same goes for utensils. Fingers or forks, I'm equally at home with either of 'em." He sipped wine from a silver chalice with the grace and delicacy of a pit bull crocheting lace.

Seated next to the Count was a woman only slightly younger than himself who had spent much of the meal sobbing softly into a succession of silk handkerchiefs as everyone listened closely to Ehomba's story.

When he at last came to the end of the tale of how he had encountered her son, she rose and excused herself from the table.

"My wife," Bewaryn Beckwith explained. "She has done little else these past months save pray for our son's safe return."

"I am sorry I had to be the one to bring you such bad news." Ehomba fingered his nearly empty chalice, gazing at the bas-reliefs on the metal of men pulling fish from the canals and from the sky of Laconda with entirely different kinds of nets. He was suddenly very tired. No doubt the good food and congenial surroundings combined with the exertions expended in crossing the Hrugars were merging within his system to make him sleepy.

"He died as bravely as any man could wish, thinking not of himself or his own wounds but of those being suffered by others. His last words were for the woman."

"The Visioness." Beckwith's long fingers were curled tightly around his own golden drinking container. "To have suffered two such losses in one year is more than any people should be asked to bear. My son"—he swallowed tightly—"my son was as loved by the people of Laconda North as Themaryl was by our cousins to the south. The shock of their disappearance is only now beginning to fade from the body politic."

"I have told you of my intention to try and restore the Visioness to her people in accordance with your son's dying wish. I am sorry there is nothing I can do about him. After his death he was"—the herdsman hesitated, reflecting briefly on how customs differed widely in other lands—"he was given the same treatment my people would have accorded any noble person in his situation." Ehomba rubbed at his eyes. It would be most impolite to fall asleep at so accommodating a table. Someone like the empathetic Beckwith might understand, but they could not count on that.

Still, the need for rest had become overpowering. Looking to his left, he saw that Simna was similarly exhausted. The swordsman was shaking his head and yawning like a man who—well, like a man who had just crossed a goodly portion of the world to get to this point.

As he started to rise preparatory to excusing himself and his companions, Ehomba found that his chair seemed to have acquired the weight and inertia of solid iron. With a determined effort he pushed it back and straightened. Finding himself a little shaky, he put a hand on the table to steady himself.

"I—I am sorry, sir. You must excuse me and my friends. We have been long on the road and have traveled an extreme distance. As a consequence we are very tired." Eyelids like lead threatened to shut down without his approval and he struggled to keep them open. "Is there somewhere we can rest?"

"Hoy, bruther!" Next to him, a sluggish Simna struggled to stand up. Failing, he slumped back in his seat. "There's more at work here than fatigue. Gwoleth knows—Gwoleth knows that . . ." His eyes closed. A second or so later they fluttered open. "Gwoleth be crammed and damned—I should know. As many taverns as I have been in, as many situations . . ." His voice trailed away into incomprehensible mumbling. As Ehomba fought to keep his own eyes focused and alert, the swordsman's head slumped forward on his chest.

Intending to call out to the black litah, he tried to turn, only to find that his body would no longer obey his commands. Tottering in place, he succeeded in resuming his seat. He wanted to apologize to their host, intending to explain further their inexcusable breach of manners, but he found that he was so tired that his mouth and lips no longer worked in concert. An irresistibly lugubrious shade was being drawn down over his eyes, shutting out the light and dragging consciousness down with it. Dimly, he heard someone speaking to the Count.

"That's done it, sir. Fine work. You have them now."

That voice, what remained of Ehomba's cognitive facilities pondered—*where have we heard that voice before?* As awareness slipped painlessly away, he thought he smelled something burning. It too brought back a faint flicker of a memory.

"Murderer!" That accusation was spat in Bewaryn Beckwith's sonorous tone. But whom was he accusing of murder? Someone new who had entered the room?

A hand was on his shoulder, shaking him. In the light, downy haze that had inexorably engulfed him, he hardly felt it. "Murder my son and then brazenly seek my help and hospitality, will you? You'll pay for it, savage. You'll pay for it long and slow and painfully!" As he delivered this pledge the Count's voice was trembling with anger.

Me, Ehomba thought distantly. *He is accusing me of killing his son.* What an absurd, what a grotesque sentiment. If only he could talk, Ehomba would quickly disabuse their host of the feckless fantasy. But his mouth still refused to form words. Where would the Count get such a bizarre notion, anyway?

The other voice came again. It was blunt and the words it rendered terse and to the point.

"Kill them quickly or slowly, sir, it matters not to me. But as we earlier concurred, I claim the sleeping cat for myself and, if you are agreeable, that big ugly brute lying next to it as well."

"Take them if you will." Barely controlled fury now underlay every clipped syllable of the Count's speech. "It is the one who did the actual killing I want. I suppose I'll detain his supporter as well. A man should have company while under torture."

"If you say so, sir. And now, if you'll pardon me, I need to direct the laying of nets on my property."

As the light of wakefulness shrank to a last, intermittent point, Ehomba finally recognized the second voice. It was one he had never expected to hear again, and its presence boded no better for their prospects than did the Count of Laconda North's threatening words.

Haramos bin Grue.

XXI

When consciousness returned it was accompanied by a pounding at the back of the head that would not go away. Wincing, Ehomba fought to keep his eyes open. With every effort his vision grew a little clearer, a little sharper. That did not mean he much liked what he saw.

The dining room with its fine table settings and liveried servants was gone. The travelers had been moved to some kind of reception room, larger but more sparsely furnished. The paintings on the walls were not of reassuring domestic scenes but instead depicted a procession of Lacondan counts and their consorts. There were also landscapes and images of pastoral life, well rendered and patriotically infused. Exquisite tropical fish, those inexplicable living ornaments of Laconda, drifted and swam through the air of the reception hall. Lining the walls, alert and heavily armed blue-clad soldiers stood like silent sculptures.

At one end of the room a double throne of becoming modesty rested on a raised dais. Heavily embroidered banners formed a suitably impressive backdrop to the royal seat while providing some of the opulent trappings of office the chairs themselves lacked. One seat was empty, the other held a brooding Bewaryn Beckwith. Standing next to him was a squat, pug shape from whose thick lips protruded a lightly smoking cigar. No look of triumph scored the merchant's round face. Satisfaction, perhaps. With bin Grue it was only business as usual.

When he noticed the herdsman staring at him, he grunted around the tobacco. "Nobody gets the best of Haramos bin Grue. You should've let me have the cat."

Alongside the herdsman Simna ibn Sind was coming slowly awake.

As he returned to the world of cognizance, he became aware of the strong cords binding his arms behind his back.

"Hoy, what's this?" Blinking, he focused not on the pensive nobleman but on the stubby shape standing next to him. "It's the pig-man!" Futilely, he began to fight against his fetters. "Let me free for a minute. No, half a minute! You don't even have to give me a sword!"

While his friend raged, Ehomba saw that a metal net now secured the glowering black litah behind him. A second similar mesh had been used to bind up Hunkapa Aub while he slept. Whatever drug had been slipped into their wine had done its work efficiently and with admirable subtlety. No wonder the Count's servants had insisted that Ahlitah and Hunkapa partake of the specially treated libation.

Their gear lay piled nearby, his pack and weapons atop Simna's. These might as well have been left on the other side of the Hrugars. He was bound so tightly he could barely move his fingers, let alone his arms and legs. No doubt bin Grue had made sure of that. But he was not sorry for himself. He had faced death many times before. His only regret was that he would not be able to tell Mirhanja and the children good-bye, and that they would never know what had happened to him. Also, it was more than a little discouraging to realize that they were going to die for a lie.

If there was anything more depressing than his own situation, it was the pitiful plight of Hunkapa Aub. The big, easygoing beast was sitting hunched over and silent with his head hung down toward his feet, exactly as Ehomba had first seen him penned back in Netherbrae. After all he had been through, and after having his freedom restored, he was once again destined for life in a cage, to be tormented and jeered at by thoughtless, faceless, uncaring humans. Ehomba was glad he could see only the solid, imposing back and not the creature's countenance.

"What have you to say before I pronounce sentence?"

Turning away from his friends and ignoring Simna's unbounded ranting, Ehomba tried to meet Count Bewaryn Beckwith's stare with as much sincere probity as he could muster. "The individual standing next to you does not deserve to share your presence. He is Haramos bin Grue, a false merchant of Lybondai."

"I know who he is," the Count replied curtly. With one hand he brushed aside a dozen amethyst anthias who were swimming across his line of vision. Fins twitching, they skittered silently out of his way. "He came all the way from the far south to warn me of your coming, and to tell me the truth of what happened to my son."

"The truth is he knows only what I told his employee, an old man with no more scruples than himself." Ehomba tried to shift his position and found that he could move his backside and bound legs in concert, but had no chance of standing up. Speaking from a seated position weakened his words, he knew, if only psychologically. "He has twisted and distorted it for his own ends. Every time he opens his mouth, he feeds you bullshit."

"Not only a murderer and a liar, but coarse." Using only his lips, bin Grue manipulated the smoking cigar from one side of his mouth to the other.

"Hear my friend, great Count!" Evincing impressive reserves of energy, Simna continued to fight futilely with the ropes that bound him even as he spoke. "He tells the truth. And if you don't release us, doom will befall you. My friend is a great and powerful wizard!"

A hand slowly massaging one temple, Beckwith regarded the herdsman coldly. "Is that so? He looks like a common assassin to me, one who can do nothing without stealth and a knife to slip into some innocent's back. But I am willing to be convinced." Eyes blazing, he leaned forward on the throne. "Your friend says you are a powerful magician, southerner. Prove his words. Free yourself." Against the walls, a number of the vigilant soldiers shifted uneasily.

"I am no assassin," Ehomba replied. "Hymneth the Possessed is the murderer of your son."

"A wizard." With a blunt, humorless laugh, Beckwith sat back on his throne.

Simna stopped struggling against his bonds long enough to lean to his left and whisper to his companion. "Come on, Etjole. This be no time for reticence. Show them what you can do. Reveal your powers to them!"

The herdsman nodded in the direction of their collected kit. "What small powers I may access lie in the bottom of my pack, Simna, which I cannot reach. I am sorry. Truly I am."

"Well then, remonstrate with this fool! He's so blinded by the loss of his son that he can't think straight. That's when slime like bin Grue can do their work."

"I will try." Redirecting his words to the dais, he spoke clearly and with the confidence of one who speaks the truth. "Think a moment before condemning us, noble Beckwith. If I were truly your son's killer, why would I come all this way and present myself to your court? What possible reason could I have for undertaking such a long and dangerous journey?"

Beckwith replied without hesitation. "To claim the treasure, of course." He glanced to his right. "Now it will go, as it rightfully should, to my new friend here."

For the first time, Haramos bin Grue smiled. And why not? Not only was he going to reclaim the black litah and acquire an additional attraction in the form of the disconsolate Hunkapa Aub, there was apparently a good deal more at stake.

"I knew it!" Simna burst out. He glared murderously at his tall friend. "There was treasure all along! You've been lying to me—but I never believed you, you sanctimonious southern scion of a promiscuous porker!"

Honestly baffled, Ehomba gaped at his friend. "Simna, I do not know what you are talking about." He nodded as best he was able in Beckwith's direction. "I do not know what *he* is talking about."

"But I do know—now! At last I understand. Oh, you were so subtle, you were, so adept at parrying my questions about 'treasure.' " Turning sharply away from the herdsman, Simna ibn Sind gazed expectantly at the throne. "There's a reward, isn't there? For information about your son. That's the treasure!"

A wary Bewaryn Beckwith nodded slowly. "There has been for months. Knowledge of it was spread far and wide in hopes of securing some information as to Tarin's whereabouts. This good merchant earns it by dint of the invaluable information he has brought me. I am only thankful that he arrived in time to tell me the truth of how things really are, and to inform me of your nefarious intentions." His attention shifted back to Ehomba. "It is clear you not only murdered my son, but intended to claim the reward for bringing us the news of his death. Simple man that I am, I cannot conceive of such incredible arrogance."

"Hoy, I can, noble sir!" Not only was an obviously outraged Simna not finished, he appeared to be just warming up. "For weeks I have been attending to this mumbling, stone-faced charlatan, seeing to his needs, waiting upon his desires, helping to protect him from all manner of difficulties and dangers. I did this of my own free will because in my heart I knew he was after treasure. I could smell it in his words, sense it in the way he stared at the far horizons. And, humbly avaricious fellow that I am, I wanted a piece of that treasure for myself. That was all I was interested in: I admit it. Condemn me for my confession if you will, but give me credit at least for my honesty. I am ashamed to admit that it never bothered me that he killed the man who inspired him to come all this way. Your son, noble sir."

Ehomba's jaw dropped in utter disbelief. "Simna!"

The swordsman sneered at him, " 'Simna'? What is this use of my name to express outrage? Am I now reduced to nothing more than a surprised expletive? 'Simna' yourself, you fakir, you champion of lies, you user of honest men. You fooled everyone, even the cat, but you can't fool me any longer!" Straining against the ropes that enveloped him, he struggled to bow in the direction of the throne. It required considerable flexibility and effort.

"Sire, Count Beckwith, I abjure this deceptive and conniving villain now and for all time! I was wrong to think the treasure that I knew he sought could be come by honestly, but you must see, you have to see, that I could not have suspected otherwise. He is a master of deviousness, which he cleverly masks with a studied attitude of simple affability. Free me, give me back my life, and I will tell you everything! I see now that there never was any treasure in this for me, fool that I was."

Beckwith stared hard at the bound swordsman, the fingers of one hand tap-tapping against the arm of the throne. "Why should I let you go? You have nothing to give me." He nodded in the merchant's direction. "This good gentleman has already told me everything."

"Impossible, sire! He can only have told you what his ancient employee told him. Only I have traveled in this prevaricator's misbegotten company since near the very start of his journey. Only I have been privy to all of his plans and intentions." He lowered his head and his voice. "Besides the murderer himself, only I know the most intimate details of your son's death."

To his credit, bin Grue's expression never changed. "He's lying," the merchant avowed brusquely.

"Lying?" Bewaryn Beckwith eyed the foreign trader thoughtfully. "Lying about what? Are you saying that perhaps this stranger was not responsible for the death of my son?"

"No, sire, of course not. We both know better than that." Ehomba thought bin Grue might have been starting to sweat a little, but he could not be sure. Like the rest of Laconda, it was hot and humid in the reception chamber.

"Then what could he be lying about?" the Count pressed him. "Not his own participation in my son's murder. You told me yourself it was carried out by the tall southerner alone."

"That's true, sire, but—I know a little of this talkative person, and I know that he is not to be trusted."

"I have no intention of trusting him, but if he knows more of my son's death than you, he deserves at least to be heard." Leaning forward, he glared down at the semisupine swordsman. "Speak then, vagrant, and if what you say satisfies me, I may decide to spare your inconsequential life."

Simna shifted awkwardly on the floor. "Your indulgence, sire, but the pain in my arms and legs from these ropes is severe, and distracts my thoughts."

Beckwith sat back in his seat and waved indifferently. "Oh very well—cut him loose."

"Sire," bin Grue protested as two burly soldiers stepped forward to release the swordsman from his bonds, "I don't think that's a good idea."

"What, are you afraid of him, Haramos? I thought it was the assassin who claimed to be a sorcerer."

"No, sire, I'm not afraid of him." The merchant was watching the relieved Simna intently. "I just don't trust him. I don't trust any of them."

"You don't have to trust them, my friend. The hairy brute and the giant cat are well and truly shackled, and these troops you see here are my household guard, the pride of Laconda North." He indicated Simna who, freed from the heavy ropes, was gratefully rubbing circulation back into his wrists and legs. "He is but one man, and not a very big one at that. Calm yourself. Why, despite the differences in our ages I think I could take him in a fair fight myself."

"I suspect that you could, sire." The liberated swordsman was eager to please.

"Flattery is for wiping asses, vagrant, and mine is clean. Now—my son's passing? How did happen? Spare no detail, no matter how repellent."

After a glance at the two brawny guards who flanked him on either side, Simna began. It was an elaborate tale, rich with intrigue and deception. Even the pair of sentinels were drawn into the story, though they never let down their guard. Only bin Grue, who knew the real truth, was not taken in. Unable to object more strenuously without bringing suspicion on himself, he could only watch and wonder at the swordsman's exhibition. From the standpoint of pure theater, the tough-minded merchant had to admit, it was quite a performance.

As for Ehomba, he could only sit in silence and wonder at the swordsman's motivations. While he could understand the opportunistic Simna's desire to employ every means at his disposal to try to save himself, the herdsman would have preferred it did not involve digging a deeper grave for the sole local representative of the Naumkib, who were not present to speak in their own defense.

Simna wove more and more detail into his story, one moment gazing imploringly heavenward, the next pointing a trembling arm in Ehomba's direction. Walking up behind the herdsman, he began beating him about the head and shoulders as he spoke, belaboring the bound southerner with insults and accusations as well as solid, unrelenting blows. Beckwith watched expressionlessly while bin Grue gnawed nervously at his cigar and wondered what the swordsman was going to do for a big finish.

It came soon enough. As he returned to stand between the two heavyset guards, Simna's voice rose to a shout, a climax of indignation and outrage. "Look at him, sitting there! Do you see any remorse written on his face? Do you see any hint, any suggestion of apologia for what he's done? No! That's how he always is. Stone-faced, devoid of expression, unchanging whether picking a man's mind or taking his life. He deserves to die! I would kill him myself for what he's done to me, but I am unarmed." Reaching back, he gave the slightly nearer of the two guards a strong shove in the herdsman's direction.

"Go on, get it done, execute him now! I want to see his blood run! I deserve to see it!" When the guard hesitated, Simna pushed the other one forward, shoving insistently. "Show me his head rolling on the floor."

"Simna ibn Sind, you are a faithless and unprincipled man!" Belying the swordsman's accusations, Ehomba's face contorted in a rictus of anger and betrayal. "You will die a lonely and miserable death that fully reflects your worthless life!"

"Probably," the swordsman retorted, "but not just yet." Whereupon he bolted, quick as a cobra, in the opposite direction. Both guards turned and grabbed for him, but having been shoved several steps forward, the wily Simna had put them just out of reach.

Half-somnolent troops instantly scrambled to block the nearest exits. Others rushed to protect the Count. Startled by all the sudden activity, decorative drifting fish darted confusedly to and fro. Another dozen soldiers rushed the agile swordsman. They lowered or drew their own weapons as the frantic Simna scrabbled madly at his and Ehomba's pile of personal belongings. His fingers wrapping around a sword hilt, he pulled it free and threw it not at the grim-faced, oncoming soldiers, but toward his companion.

"Hoy, bruther! Bring down a piece of the sky on this ungrateful place! Conjure forth the wind that rushes between the stars and blow these knaves through their precious walls! Litter the floor with their skeletons as the star wind tears the flesh from their bones!"

Slipping free of the ropes that had restrained him, which Simna's supple fingers had astutely undone in between beating the herdsman madly about the head and body, Ehomba rose in time to catch the tumbling sword by its haft. There was only one problem with the swordsman's bold and bloodthirsty admonitions.

It was the wrong sword.

Instead of the sharp blade fashioned of gray sky metal, in his haste and confusion Simna had snatched up the herdsman's other sword, the one made of bone lined with serrated, triangular sharks' teeth. A fearsome and efficacious weapon to be sure, but not one that could by any stretch of anyone's imagination bring down so much as an errant rain cloud. It was a thing of the sea, not of the sky.

Having taken up his own sword subsequent to flinging the weapon to Ehomba, the rueful swordsman realized his mistake. "Hoy, I'm sorry, bruther." Sword held in both hands, he was backing away from the advancing semicircle of soldiers. A sword was not of much use against pikes, but he was determined to sell his life as dearly as possible. If naught else, at least he would go down with a weapon in his hand and no shackles on his wrists and ankles. They would die like men and not like mad dogs.

"Nothing to be sorry for, friend Simna." Ehomba held the tooth-lined sword high overhead, its sharpened tip pointed at the tense but unconcerned soldiers. "There are fish everywhere in this place, so what better weapon to fight with than one that owes its edge to the sea?"

"Kill them!" It was the curt voice of Haramos bin Grue, declaiming from behind a line of blue-coated troops. "Kill them now, before he . . . !"

Hidden on his throne, Bewaryn Beckwith could be heard responding querulously, and for the first time, with a hint of suspicion in his voice. "Before he—what, Haramos?"

It was a question Simna ibn Sind was asking silently. Nearby, Ahlitah was awake and roaring, adding to the sense of incipient chaos. Emerging from his gloom, Hunkapa Aub had straightened and was shaking the metal mesh of his netting with terrifying violence.

A blue aurora had enveloped the blade of the sea-bone sword. It was dark as the deep ocean, tinged with green, and smelled of salt. At the sight of it the advancing soldiers halted momentarily. From the dais, their liege's voice urged them on.

"What are you waiting for?" Bewaryn Beckwith bellowed. "They are only two and you are many. Take them! Alive if possible—otherwise if not."

One of the two thickly muscled guards who had been duped by Simna stepped forward, holding his heavy sword threateningly out in front of him. His voice was that of reason, not anger.

"This is senseless. Why disgrace yourselves by spilling blood inside the palace? You should meet your fate with dignity." Holding his blade at the ready, he extended his other hand. "Give up your weapons."

"Look!" one of the men behind him shouted. An uncomfortable susurration rippled through the contracting circle of soldiers.

Something was emerging from the point of the herdsman's sword. Gray on top, white on the bottom, it swelled massively as it expanded away from the bone. It looked like a giant bicolored drop of milk oozing out of nothingness parallel to the floor. As it continued to increase in size it began to grow individual features, like a closed flower sprouting petals. And it just kept getting bigger and bigger.

The ornamental floating fish in the reception hall identified it before any of the soldiers. They vanished through open doors as if propelled by lightning and not fins, evaporating streaks of yellow and orange, red and gold. In one case they literally flew through a squad of blue-clad reinforcements hurrying to the chamber. It was as if they had not fled, but vaporized.

The gray-white mass grew fins of its own, and a great, sickle-like tail. A pair of black eyes manifested themselves. They were jet black and without visible pupils. All of these details were ignored by those in the room as they focused on a single predominant feature: the mouth.

It was enormous, capable of swallowing a person in a single swallow. Multiple rows of gleaming white, triangular teeth lined the interior of that imposing cavity. Their edges were serrated on both sides of the sharp point, like steak knives. The largest was more than three inches long. It was a peerless mouth, unlike anything else in all the undersea kingdom. When viewed from straight on, jaws and teeth combined to form a uniquely terrifying smile.

The great white shark broke free of the tip of the bone sword and drifted toward the assembled soldiers. Several broke and ran, but the rest bravely held their ground, their long pikes extended. A second gray-white teardrop shape was beginning to emerge from the weapon. If anything, it promised to be larger than its predecessor.

One of the soldiers thrust his pike at the looming predator. Extending its jaws beyond its lips, the great white ate it. Left holding a length of useless wood, the soldier sensibly threw it away, turned, and sprinted for the nearest door.

"Hold your ground!" Bewaryn Beckwith commanded from the vicinity of his throne. "Fight back! They are only fish, like the ones you see every day on the streets of the city."

The Count of Laconda North was half right. They were only fish, but they were most assuredly not like the ones the soldiers saw every day. They were not decorative, they were not inoffensive, and they were hungry. And now there were three of them, with a fourth on the way as the fecund sword gave birth yet again.

To their credit, the soldiers responded to the appeal of their liege. They tried to encircle two of the sharks and attack with their long pikes. Several thrusts struck home, and droplets of red shark blood spilled in slow motion to the floor. But the wounds only enraged the sharks. With their great curved tails propelling them explosively through the air, they snapped at whatever happened to come within reach, be it pike, soldier, or unfortunate furniture.

One great white the soldiers probably could have contained. Two and then three forced them into a holding action. When the sixth emerged full grown from Ehomba's sword, the reception hall dissolved into general blood and chaos.

Soldiers broke and fled, pursued by unrelenting carnivorous torpedoes. The fortunate escaped down corridors of panic while their slower, less agile comrades were actively dismembered. It was not long before limbs littered the floor and the fine furnishings and papered walls were splashed with crimson. Convoyed by a close-packed detachment of desperate soldiers, Bewaryn Beckwith, Count of Laconda North, escaped through a secret bolt-hole located behind the throne dais. Many members of his escort were not as lucky.

As for Haramos bin Grue, he attempted to flee along with the Count, only to find himself shoved roughly back into the bloody pandemonium that had enveloped the hall. As his guard kept them separated, Beckwith had just enough time to shout a passing farewell before ducking to safety.

"Not a sorcerer, Haramos? You lied to me about that. Could it be that you lied also about how my son died?"

"No, sire—believe me, I told the truth!" Despite the fact that he was unarmed save for a pair of small concealed knives, the merchant resisted the soldiers. But it was hard to fight with someone when there was a foot of sharp blade and six feet of wooden shaft between you and your opponent. Such was the advantage of the steel-tipped pike.

"That is the murderer, down there! That uncouth, uncivilized southerner. And he is no sorcerer, by his own word! Though I admit to being fooled by the sorceral devices he carries with him."

"You are right about one thing." Beckwith paused as he crouched to pass beneath the low overhang of the escape portal. His guard fought to keep a curious great white away from their Count. "Someone here is being fooled. I wish I had the time to sort it out." He hurried into the concealed passageway. One by one, his soldiers tried to follow him. Many succeeded. Others lost limbs and, in a couple of cases, their heads to the rampaging shark.

Falling back, bin Grue pressed himself against the wall and began to make his way toward the nearest exit, edging steadily away from the royal dais. Before him was being played out an unparalleled spectacle of remorseless carnage. He had nearly reached the door when he made the mistake of bolting. The rapid movement caught the attention of one of the marauding great whites. When he turned, the merchant did not scream in fear but instead cursed violently. His end, therefore, was in keeping with his nature all his life, a reflection of internal toughness and perpetual ire. It made no difference to the shark, which bit him in half.

Out on the floor of the reception hall there were now eight great whites circling slowly in search of additional prey. The once grand chamber had taken on the aspect of an abattoir, with blood, guts, and body parts scattered everywhere. The last live soldier had fled.

Sloshing through the shallow lake of unwillingly vented bodily fluids, Ehomba advanced on his still imprisoned friends. Simna followed, hugging as close to his tall friend as possible without actually slipping into his clothing. He had seen how fast the floating sharks could move and had no intention of separating himself from their procreator even for an instant. Soulless black eyes tracked his movements, but the sharks did not attack. A number had settled to the floor and were feeding, gulping down whole chunks of soldier, uniform and all.

"You are a very canny man." With a free hand the herdsman rubbed his sore face and shoulders. "As soon as the opportunity presents itself, I intend to pay you back for your canniness."

"Hoy, bruther, I had to make it look real, didn't I? I needed to distract them from what I was doing behind your back. Any sleight of hand needs a good diversion to be effective." He grinned. "I was beginning to wonder if you'd ever pick up on what I was trying to do."

"I admit you had me concerned at first. What finally revealed your true intentions was the degree of your pleading. I think I understand you well enough to know that you would go down fighting before you would grovel."

"Depends on the circumstances," the swordsman replied without hesitation. "If the need arose, I could grovel with the best of them." He nodded in the direction of the throne. "But not because of a lie, and never in front of a fat toad like bin Grue." His tone was harsh. "I saw him go down. He won't be putting anybody in a cage ever again."

Ehomba replied somberly. "Not all the methods a man perfects to protect himself work all the time. That is one thing about sharks: They cannot be reasoned with, distracted, or bribed. Stay close to me."

The swordsman did not have to be reminded. The presence of twenty tons or so of floating, fast-moving great white rendered the immediate surroundings decidedly inhospitable.

"Let me guess. You're not working any magic whatsoever. You have no idea how this is happening. You're just making use of the enchanted sword fashioned for you by the village smithy Okidoki."

"Otjihanja," Ehomba corrected him patiently. "That is a silly notion,

Simna. A smithy works only with metals." He hefted the tooth-lined bone shaft. "This sword was made by old Pembarudu, who is a master of fishing. It took him a long time to gather all the teeth from the shore and mount them together on the bone. It is whalebone, of course. A shark has no bones. It is one of the reasons they make such good eating."

Keeping low, Simna ibn Sind made hushing motions with one hand. "Don't speak of such things, Etjole. One of these finny monsters might overhear and get the wrong idea."

The herdsman smiled. "Simna, are you afraid?"

"By Ghogost's gums, you bet I'm afraid, bruther! Any man confronted by such sights who did say he was not would be a liar of bin Grue's class. I'm afraid whenever you pick up a weapon, and I'm afraid whenever you pull some innocent little article out of that pack of yours. Traveling with you, I have learned many things. When to be afraid is one of them." Still smiling, but grimly, he gazed evenly up at his tall companion. "You're not a man to inspire fear, Etjole, but your baggage—that's another matter."

Ehomba did his best to reassure him. "So long as I hold the sword, I command its progeny. See . . ."

Lowering the weapon, he touched the tip to the metal netting in which Ahlitah was imprisoned. Immediately, the nearest shark turned and swam toward it. Snarling, the black cat backed as far away as it could from jaws that were even more massive and powerful than its own.

With a snap, the great white took a mouthful of mesh. Thrashing its head from side to side, it used its teeth like saws. When it backfinned and drew away, it left behind a hole in the net large enough for the litah to push through.

Under Ehomba's direction, two sharks performed a similar favor for the fourth member of their party. Expanding the resultant gap with one shove of his mighty arms, Hunkapa Aub emerged to stand alongside his friends.

"Big fish, bad bite."

Simna nodded. "I would say, rather: bad fish, big bite—but the end is the same." Looking around, he surveyed their tormented surroundings. The reception hall had been the scene of solemn slaughter. "Let's pick up our gear and get out of here. I've had about enough of Laconda—north, south, or any other direction."

"Soldiers chase?" Hunkapa wondered sensibly as they cautiously exited the room.

"I do not think so." Sea-bone sword held out in front of him, Ehomba led the way. Forming two lines of four each, the great whites fell into place on either side of the travelers.

Their measured departure from the lowlands of Laconda created a stir among the populace that laid the groundwork for stories for decades to come. As was common in such matters, with each retelling the participants expanded in size and ferocity. Ehomba became the malignant warlock of the sea, come to wreak havoc among the gentle floating fishes of Laconda. Simna ibn Sind was his gnomic apprentice, wielding a sword impossibly larger than himself. Hunkapa Aub was a giant with burning eyes and long fangs that dripped olive green ichor, while the black litah was a streak of hell-smoke that burned everything it touched.

As for the escort of flying great whites, they were magnified in the storytellers' imaginations until they had become as big as whales, with teeth like fence posts and the temperaments of demons incarnate—as if the reality were not frightening and impressive enough.

Domestic fish scattered like arrows at the approach of the travelers and their silent escort. Unwarned citizens dove for the nearest cover or hastily shuttered windows and barred doors. More than size or teeth, empty black eyes, or swaying tails, the one thing those who observed the passage of the remarkable procession never forgot were the frightful frozen grins that scored the inhuman faces of the great whites.

No one followed them and, needless to say, no one tried to stop them. By the time they reached the northwestern periphery of Laconda North, the border guards, having been informed of what was making its inexorable way in their direction, had long since decided to take early vacation. Marching across the modest, well-made bridge that delineated the frontier, the travelers found themselves in the jumble of lowland forest known as the Yesnaby Hills.

There Ehomba turned and stood alone, eyes shut tight, the sea-bone sword held vertically before him. As Simna and the others looked on, one by one the great whites swam slowly through the humid air to return whence they had come. The sword sucked them back down as if they were minnows disappearing into a bucket.

When the last tail had finned its way out of existence, Ehomba slipped the sword into the empty scabbard on his back and turned to resume their journey. A strong hand reached out to stop him.

"A moment if you please, long bruther."

Ehomba looked down at his friend. "Is something the matter, Simna?" The herdsman looked back in the direction of the deserted border post and the Laconda lowlands. "You are not worried about the Count sending his soldiers to chase us down?"

"Not hardly," the swordsman replied. "I think they're smarter than that. What I'm beginning to wonder is if I am."

"I do not follow your meaning, my friend." Nearby, Hunkapa Aub and Ahlitah were exploring a small cave.

"When you found out where we were, you decided to inform this Beckwith of his son's fate. The result is that he thinks you killed his heir, and that if he is given another chance, he'll kill you."

"I do not think that is the case. The more time he has to ponder what transpired, the more I believe he will come to question the truth of what bin Grue told him."

"Could be, but after what you did to his court he's still not exactly going to be ready to greet you with open arms if you come back this way. What I'm trying to say, Etjole, is that you don't owe anything to a man who wants you dead. So we can concentrate on finding the real treasure and forget all this nonsense about returning some rarefied blue-blooded doxy to her family."

"Not so," Ehomba insisted. At these words, the swordsman's expression fell. "The Visioness Themaryl, whose safe return home I promised Tarin Beckwith to try my best to effect, is a scion of Laconda. Not Laconda North. She is of a noble family other than the Beckwiths. Therefore, whatever they may think of me, now or in the future, it does not affect my pledge." Smiling apologetically, he turned and resumed course on a northwesterly heading. After uttering a few choice words to no one in particular, Simna moved to join him. The two hirsute members of the group hurried to catch up.

"I guess you're right, bruther. You're no sorcerer. You just have learned friends and relations who give you useful things. So you have those to make use of, and the benefit of remarkable coincidence."

"Coincidence?" Ehomba responded absently. At the moment, his attention was devoted to choosing the best route through the hills ahead.

"Hoy. We find ourselves in a country where the fish swim through the air. Not knowing the properties of your other weapon, when I break free I automatically reach for the magical blade whose attributes I am familiar with: the sky-metal sword. But instead I grab the weapon that, it turns out, can give birth to the most monstrous and terrible fish in the sea." Crowding his friend, he tried hard to make the taller man meet his eyes. "Coincidence."

Ehomba shrugged, more to show that he was listening than to evince any especial interest in what his friend was saying. "I could have made use of the sky-metal sword. Or this." Lifting the walking stick-spear off the ground, he shook it slightly. A distant, primeval roar whispered momentarily through the otherwise still air.

"So you could," Simna agreed. "But would they have been as appropriate? The spear would have summoned a demon too large for the room in which we were imprisoned. The sky-metal sword might have brought down the walls and ceiling on top of us."

Now Ehomba looked over at his companion. "Then why did you want me to use it?"

"Because we would have had a better chance of surviving the smashed rumble of a palace than a certain knife in the neck. Of course, once I threw you the sea-bone sword everything worked out for the best."

"I did not know you were going to fool your guards long enough to grab it and throw it to me," the herdsman responded.

"Didn't you?" Simna stared hard, hard at his tall, enigmatic friend. "I often find myself wondering, Etjole, just how much you do know and if this unbounded insistence on an unnatural fondness for livestock is nothing more than a pose to disguise some other, grander self."

Ehomba shook his head slowly, sadly. "I can see, after all that we have been through together, friend Simna, how such sentiments could trouble your thoughts. Be assured yet again that I am Etjole Ehomba, a humble herdsman of the Naumkib." Raising his free hand, he pointed to a nearby tree heavy with unexpected blossoms. "Look at the colors. I have never seen anything like that before. Is it not more like a giant flower than a tree?"

Hoy, you're a shepherd for sure, mused Simna ibn Sind even as he responded to his friend's timely floral observation. In the course of their long journeying together, Ehomba had talked incessantly of cattle and sheep until on more than one occasion the swordsman had been ready to scream. A shepherd and a—what had the southerner called it?—an eromakasi, an itinerant eater of darkness. The question that would not leave the swordsman's mind, however, was, What else exactly, if anything, *was* Etjole Ehomba?

XXII

When finally they crested the last of the Yesnaby Hills and found themselves gazing, improbably and incredibly, down at the great port city of Hamacassar itself, Simna could hardly believe it. To Hunkapa Aub and Ahlitah it was no cause for especial celebration. Despite its legendary status, to them the city was only another human blight upon the land.

As for Ehomba, there was no falling to knees and giving thanks, or lifting of hands and hosannaing of praises to the heavens. Contemplating the fertile lowlands, the smoke that rose from ten thousand chimneys, and the great shimmering slash of the river Eynharrowk against whose southern shore the city sprawled in three directions, he commented simply, "I thought it would be bigger," and started down the last slope.

Their arrival occasioned considerably less panic than it had in land-locked kingdoms like Bondressey and Tethspraih. Reactions were more akin to the response their presence had engendered in Lybondai. Like Hamacassar, the bustling city on the north shore of the Aboqua Sea was a cosmopolitan trading port whose citizens were used to seeing strange travelers from far lands. At first sight, the only difference between the two was that Hamacassar was much larger and situated on the bank of a river instead of the sea itself.

Also absent were the cooling breezes that rendered Lybondai's climate so salubrious. Like the Lacondas, the river plain on which Hamacassar had been built was hot and humid. A similar system of canals and small tributaries connected different parts of the widespread, low-lying metropolis, supplying its citizens with transportation that was cheap and reliable. The design of the homes and commercial buildings they began to pass with increasing frequency was intriguing but unsurprising. As they made their way through the city's somewhat undisciplined outskirts, they encountered nothing that was startling or unrecognizable. Except for the monoliths.

Spaced half a mile apart, these impressive structures loomed over homes and fields like petrified colossi. Each took the form of an acute triangle that had been rounded off at the top. Twenty feet or so wide at the base, they rapidly narrowed to their smooth crests. Ehomba estimated them to be slightly over forty feet in height. Each structure was penetrated by a hole that mimicked its general shape. Seven or eight feet wide, the hole punched through the monolith not far below its apex.

The mysterious constructs marched across the landscape in a broad, sweeping curve, extending as far to the east and west as the travelers could see. They were not guarded, or fenced off from the public. Their smooth, slightly pitted flanks made them impossible for curious children to climb. Nor were they sited on similar plots of land. One rose from the bank of a wide, sluggish stream while the next all but abutted a hay barn and the third flanked the farm road down which the travelers were presently walking. In the absence of significant hills or mountains, they dominated the flat terrain.

Leaving the road, the travelers took a moment to examine one up close. Beneath their fingers the pitted metal was cool and pebbly to the touch.

"I don't recognize the stuff." Simna dragged his nails along the lightly polished surface. "It's not iron or steel. The color suggests bronze, but there's no green anywhere on it. Standing out in the weather like this you'd expect bronze to green fast."

"It would depend on the mix in the alloy." Ehomba gently rapped the dun-colored surface with a closed fist. As near as he could tell it was solid, not hollow. A lot of foundry work for no immediately discernible purpose, he decided. "If it is not an alloy it is no metal I know."

"Nor I." Leaning back, Simna scrutinized the triangular-shaped hole that pierced the upper portion of the construct.

Hunkapa Aub pushed with all his weight against the front of the structure. It did not move, or even quiver. Whoever had placed it here had set it solidly and immovably in the earth.

"What for?"

Ehomba considered. "It could be for anything, Hunkapa. They might be religious symbols. Or some sort of historic boundary markers showing where the old kingdom of Hamacassar's frontier once ended. Or they might be nothing more than part of an elaborate scheme of municipal art."

"Typical human work. Waste of time." Ahlitah was inspecting the stream bank for edible freshwater shellfish.

"We could ask a local. Surely they would know." Wiping his hands against his kilt, Ehomba started back toward the road.

"Hoy, we could," Simna agreed, "if we could get one to stand still long enough. They don't run from the sight of us, but I've yet to see one that didn't hurry to lock him- or herself away if it looked like we might be heading in their direction." Making a face, he indicated their two outsized companions. "Get the cat and the shag beast to hide themselves in a field and you and I might be able to walk up to a farmhouse without the tenants shutting the door in our faces."

Back up on the road, they once more resumed their trek northward. The nearer they got to the river, the more residents of Hamacassar they encountered. These gave the eccentric quartet a wide and wary, if polite, berth.

"There is no need to unsettle any of the locals." Ehomba's staff stirred up a little puff of dust each time it was planted firmly on the hard-packed surface. "I am sure we will learn the meaning of the monoliths in the course of making contacts throughout the city." He strode along eagerly, setting a much more rapid pace than usual.

"Hoy, long bruther, I'm glad you're in a good mood, but remember that not all of us have your beanpole legs."

"Sorry." Ehomba forced himself to slow down. "I did not realize I was walking so fast."

"Walking? You've been on the verge of breaking into a run ever since we came down out of the hills." The swordsman jerked a thumb over his shoulder. "The brute's legs are longer than yours and the cat has four to our two, but I'm not in either class stride-wise. Have a thought for me, Etjole, if no one else."

"It is just that we are so close, Simna." Uncharacteristic excitement bubbled in the herdsman's voice.

"Close to what?" The swordsman's tone was considerably less ebullient. "To maybe, if we're lucky, finding passage on a ship to cross the Semordria, where we then first have to find this Ehl-Larimar?" He made a rude noise, conducting it with an equally rude gesture.

"Considering how far we have traveled and what difficulties we have overcome, I would think that you could show a little optimism, Simna."

"I'm a realist, Etjole." The swordsman kicked a rock out of his path and into the drainage ditch that ran parallel to the slightly elevated roadbed.

"Realism and optimism are not always mutually exclusive, my friend."

"Hoy, that's like saying a beautiful daughter and her suspicious father aren't mutually exclusive." He watched a wagon piled high with parsnips and carrots pass by, rumbling in the opposite direction. The team of matched toxondons that was pulling it ignored the immigrants, but the two men riding on the wagon's seat never took their eyes off Ehomba and his companions.

They did not pass any more of the monoliths. Apparently these existed only in the single line they had encountered on the outskirts of the city. But there were many other architectural wonders to dazzle the eyes of first-time visitors.

Hamacassar boasted the tallest buildings Ehomba had ever seen. Rising eight and nine stories above the widest commercial streets, these had facades that were decorated with fine sculpture and stonework. Many wagons plied the intricate network of avenues and boulevards while flat-bottomed barges and other cargo craft filled the city canals to capacity. These were in turn spanned by hundreds of graceful yet wholly functional bridges that were themselves ornamented with bas-reliefs and metal grillwork. Though curious about the singular foursome, the locals were too busy to linger and stare. The closer they came to the waterfront, the more pervaded the atmosphere became with the bustle and fervor of commerce.

"A prosperous kingdom." Simna made the comment as they worked their way between carts and wagons piled high with ship's supplies, commodities from all along the length of the great river, foodstuffs and crafts, and all manner of trade goods. "These people have grown rich on trade." Slowing as they passed a small bistro, he inhaled deeply of the delicious aromas that wafted from its cool, inviting interior.

Taking him by the arm, Ehomba drew him firmly away from the scene of temptation. The swordsman did not really resist.

"We have no money for such diversions," Ehomba reminded his friend, "unless your pack holds an overlooked piece of Chlengguu gold."

A downcast Simna looked regretful. "Alas, the only portion of that which remains golden is my memory." By way of emphasis he shifted his pack higher on his back. "Another lunch of jerked meat and dried fruit, I fear." Behind him, crowding close, Hunkapa Aub smiled ingenuously.

"Hunkapa like jerky!"

"You would," the swordsman muttered under his breath. As the sun climbed higher in a simmering, hazy sky, the humidity rose accordingly. But not all was the fault of the climate—they were approaching the riverfront.

Ships of all manner and description crowded the quays as lines of nearly naked, sweating stevedores proceeded with their unloading or provisioning. Shouts and curses mingled with the clanking of heavy tackle, the flap of unfurling canvas, the wet slap of lines against wooden piers and metal cleats. All manner of costume was visible in a blur of styles and hues, from intricately batiked turbans to simple loincloths to no-nonsense sailors' attire sewn in solid colors and material too tough for anything equipped with less dentition than a shark to bite through. It was a choice selection of barely organized chaos and confusion made worse by the presence of frolicking children, gawking sightseers, and strolling gentlefolk.

Ehomba was very hopeful.

It proved all but impossible to convince any of the busy workers to pause long enough to answer even a few simple questions. Those who at first try appeared willing evaporated into the teeming crowd the instant they caught sight of the black litah, or Hunkapa Aub, or both. Afraid of the trouble his two nonhuman companions might up-stir in his absence, Ehomba was reluctant to accept Simna's suggestion that he and the swordsman temporarily leave them behind.

Exasperated by his tall friend's caution, the swordsman explained that if they could not part company even for a little while, they would have to query the operators of each craft one by one. While Ehomba concurred, he pointed out that they could begin with the largest, most self-evidently seaworthy craft. It was not necessary to inquire of the master of a two-man rowboat, for example, if he would be willing to try to transport them across the vast, dangerous expanse of the Semordria.

They began with the biggest ship in sight, one docked just to the left of where they were standing. Its first mate greeted them at the railing. After listening politely to their request, the wiry, dark-haired sailor shared a good laugh with those members of his crew who were near enough to participate.

"Didja hear that, lads? The long-faced fellow in the skirt wants us to take 'im and 'is circus across the Semordria!" Leaning over the railing, the mate grinned down at them and stroked his neatly coifed beard. "Would you like to make a stopover on the moon, perhaps? 'Tis not far out of the way, and I am told the seas between here and there are more peaceful."

The muscles in Ehomba's face tightened smartly, but he kept his tone respectful. "I take it that your answer is no?"

A vague sensation that he was being mocked transformed the mate's grin into a glower. "You can take it anyway you want, fellow, so long as you don't bring it aboard my boat." As he turned away he was smiling and laughing again. "Cross the Semordria! Landsmen and foreigners— no matter where a man sails he's never free of 'em."

The response was more or less the same everywhere they tried. Most of the larger, better-equipped vessels plied their trade up and down the great watery swath of the Eynharrowk and its hundreds of navigable tributaries. A whole world of kingdoms and merchants, duchies and dukedoms and independent city-states was tied together by the Eynharrowk and its sibling rivers, Ehomba soon realized. They were the veins and arteries of an immensely extended, living, shifting body whose head lay not at the top, but in the middle. That head was Hamacassar. If they could not secure transportation there, they were unlikely to happen upon it anywhere else.

So they persisted, making their way along the riverfront walk, inquiring even of the owners of boats that seemed too small or too frail to brave the wave-swept reaches of the Semordria. Desperation drove them to thoroughness.

There *were* craft present that from time to time risked the storms and high seas of the ocean, but without exception these clung close to shore whenever they ventured out upon the sea itself, hiding in protected coves and harbors as they plied ancient coastal trade routes. Their crews were brave and their captains resolute, for the profits to be made from ranging so far afield from the Eynharrowk were substantial.

It was at the base of the boarding ramp of one such coastal trader, a smallish but sturdily built vessel, that a third mate supervising the loading of sacks of rice and millet provided their first ray of hope.

"Ayesh, there are ships that cross the Semordria." He spoke around the stem of a scrimshawed pipe that seemed to grow directly from his mouth, like the extended tooth of a narwhal. "More set sail westward than return. But now and again some master mariner reappears laden with wonderful goods and even better stories. Such captains are rare indeed. They never change ships because their owners keep them content. Their crews adore them and are spoiled for use on other vessels. Having sailed under the best, they refuse to haul a line for anyone not as skilled."

Ehomba listened intently, making sure to let the mate finish before asking any more questions. "Where might we find such a ship, with such a crew?"

Squinting at the sky and focusing on a hovering cloud that might or might not contain a portion of the evening's rain, the mate thought carefully before replying.

"Among those of us who sail the Eynharrowk, the *Warebeth* has passed beyond reverence into legend. It is rumored that she has made twelve complete crossings of the Semordria without losing more than the expected number of seamen. I have never heard of her taking passengers, but then it is not the sort of trip most landsmen would consider. Certainly she's large enough to accommodate guests." As he related this information the mate kept nodding to himself, eyes half closed.

"A three-master, solid of keel and sound of beam. If any ship would take landsmen on such an arduous voyage, ayesh, it would be the *Warebeth.*"

"Excellent," declared Ehomba. "Where do we find this craft?"

Removing his pipe, a process that somewhat surprisingly did not require a minor surgical procedure, the mate tapped the bowl gently against the side of a nearby piling. "Sadly, friends, the *Warebeth* left yesterday morning for a two-month journey upriver to the Thalgostian villages. If you're willing to wait for her return, you might have yourselves a ship." He placed the stem of the pipe back between his yellow-brown teeth.

"Two months." Ehomba's expression fell. "Are there no other choices?"

Sea dragonets perched on a nearby piling sang to one another, punctuating their songs with intermittent puffs of smoke. "Ayesh, maybe one." Turning, the mate pointed downriver, his finger tracing the line of the waterfront walk. "Try the out-end of quay thirty-six. If I'm not mistaken, the *Grömsketter* is still there. Captain Stanager Rose on deck, unless there's been a change of command since last I heard of her. She's done the Semordria transit more than once, though how many times I couldn't tell you. Not the wave piercer the *Warebeth* is, but a sound ship nonetheless. Whether she'll take wayfarers or not, much less landsmen, I don't know. But if she's still in port, she's your only other hope."

Ehomba bowed his head and dipped the point of his spear in the mate's direction. "Many thanks to you, sir. We can but try."

"Can but try indeed, bruther." Simna stayed close to the herdsman as they left the pier and began once more to push their way through the dynamic, industrious crowds. Behind them, the broad beam of Hunkapa Aub kept potential pickpockets and busybodies away by sheer force of his hulking presence. Given a space of his own by the crowd, which despite its preoccupations nevertheless kept well clear of the big cat, the black litah amused itself by pausing every so often to inspect pilings and high water for potentially edible harbor dwellers.

It turned out that in his eulogistic description of the *Warebeth* and its accomplishments, the neighborly and helpful mate had underrated the *Grömsketter.* To Ehomba's inexperienced eye it looked like a fine ship, with broad, curving sides and a high helm deck. There was only a single mainmast, but a second smaller foremast looked able to carry a respectable spread of sail between its crest and the bowsprit. Heavy-weather shutters protected the ports, and Simna pointed out that her lines were triple instead of double braided. Even to his eyes, she was rigged for serious weather. Her energetic crew looked competent and healthy.

As he contemplated the craft, the herdsman sought his companion's opinion. "What do you think, Simna?"

"I'm no mariner, Etjole." The swordsman scrutinized the vessel from stem to stern. "Give me something with legs to ride, any day. But I've spent some time on boats, and from what little I know she looks seaworthy enough. Surely no sailor would set out to traverse the Semordria on a craft he wasn't convinced would carry him across and back again."

Ehomba nodded once. Together they walked to the base of the boarding ramp. A few sailors were traveling in both directions along its length, but for the most part the majority of activity was taking place on board.

Putting his free hand alongside his mouth, the herdsman hailed the deck. "Hello! We are travelers seeking to cross the ocean, and were told you might be of service in such a matter!"

A tall, broad-chested seaman stopped coiling the rope he was working with to lean toward them. He was entirely bald except for a topknot of black hair that fell in a single thick braid down his back.

"You want passage across the Semordria?" A tense Ehomba nodded in the affirmative, waiting for the expected laugh of derision.

But the sailor neither laughed nor mocked him. "That's quite a pair you have with you. Are they pets, or tamed for sale?"

The black litah snarled up at the deck. "Come down here, man, and I'll show you who's a pet."

"Bismalath!" the man exclaimed. "A talking cat, and one of such a size and shape as I have never seen. And the other beast, it is also new to me." He beckoned to the travelers. "I am Terious Kemarkh, first mate of the *Grömsketter*. Come aboard, and we will see about this request of yours."

As they started up the ramp, a subdued but still obviously eager Ehomba in the lead, he called across to the mate. "Then you are preparing for a crossing of the Semordria?"

"Ayesh, but it's not up to me to decide whether you can, or should, travel with us." Completing the coil he had been working on when they had first arrived, he let it fall heavily to the deck. "That's a decision for the Captain to make."

Once aboard, the travelers saw that everything they had suspected about the *Grömsketter* continued to hold true. She was solid and well maintained, with no rigging lying loose to trip an unwary sailor and her teak worn smooth and clean. Lines were neatly stowed and all hatches not in use firmly secured.

The mate greeted them with hearty handshakes, electing to wave instead of accepting the affable Aub's extended paw. "A seaman has constant need of the use of his fingers," Terious explained in refusing the handshake. "Come with me."

He led them toward the stern and the raised cabin there. Bidding them wait, he vanished through an open hatchway like a mouse into its hole. Several moments passed, during which the travelers were able to observe the crew. For their part, the mariners were equally curious about their unfamiliar visitors. Several tried to feel of the litah's fur, only to be warned off by intimidating coughs.

Hoping that their host would return before the big cat's patience wore thin and it decided to remove an arm or other available extremity from some member of the crew, Ehomba was relieved when Terious popped back out of the hatchway. His expression was encouraging.

"Though in a surly mood, the Captain has agreed to hear you out. I explained as best I could that you were not from the valley of the Eynharrowk and had obviously traveled a great distance to try and effect this transit. I pointed out that with the *Warebeth* having already sailed, and upriver at that, the *Grömsketter* was your last best hope of crossing the ocean." Stepping out on the deck, he waited alongside them.

Both travelers studied the dark opening. "What sort of man is this Stanager Rose?" Simna asked anxiously.

The first mate's expression did not change. "Wait just a moment and you will see for yourself."

A muttered curse rose from below and a figure started to rise toward the light. An open-necked seaman's blouse was pushed into bright red pants with yellow striping, the legs of which were in turn tucked into boots of durable black stingray leather. A tousled mop of shoulder-length red hair was held away from the face by a wide yellow bandanna. A sextant hung from one hand, and a long dagger was slung through a double loop at the waist. Its haft was impressively jeweled.

Ehomba bowed once again. "We thank you for allowing us on board your ship, Captain, and for deigning to consider our request for transportation."

"Right. That's all it is right now, traveler—a request. But I'll give you a hearing." Steel-blue eyes looked the herdsman up and down, speculating openly. "Terious was right: You are a spectacle all by yourself, tall man. Taken together with your companions, you're unnatural enough to claim a marketplace stage and charge admission just to look at you." A sea-weathered hand reached up and out to come down firmly on Ehomba's shoulder.

"Despite what you may have heard, it can get tiresome out in the middle of the ocean. Even on the Semordria. At such times, new entertainment is always welcome."

"We are not entertainers," Ehomba explained simply.

"Didn't say that you were. But you'll have stories to tell. I can see that just by looking at you." A hand gestured expansively downward. "You two come with me and we'll talk. I'm afraid that, garrulous or not, your woolly companions will have to remain on deck, as they'll never fit through this hatchway."

Nodding, Ehomba turned to explain the situation to Ahlitah and Hunkapa Aub. Doing so left Simna alone with the Captain. He was trying to think of something to say before his tall friend returned, but with the first mate standing nearby it was difficult to come up with just the right words, and he sensed he would have to be careful. From first sight, Stanager Rose had struck him as someone not to be trifled with. However much he wanted to.

Because, sea-weathered or not, the Captain of the *Grömsketter* was one of the most beautiful women he had ever seen.

XXlll

After leading them down to the officers' mess and directing them to their seats, she had drink brought by an attentive mess steward. It was some kind of spiced fruit juice neither Ehomba nor Simna recognized, flavorful but only slightly alcoholic.

"What is this?" Ehomba asked politely.

"Sicharouse. From Calex, across the ocean." She smiled proudly. "Sealed in oak casks, it ferments during the return crossing and is almost ready to drink when it arrives here in Hamacassar. Turned a tidy profit on it more than once, we have." Folding her hands on the heavy ship's table, she stared piercingly at Ehomba. "We leave in two days and I've a ship to prepare for departure. You wish passage across the ocean?"

"We do." As Simna ibn Sind appeared to have been suddenly and uncharacteristically struck dumb, Ehomba found that he had to do all the talking. "We journey to a kingdom called Ehl-Larimar."

Eyes widening slightly, Stanager leaned into the embrace of her high-backed chair. The swordsman found himself envying the wood. "Heard of the place, but never been there. From what I recall, it lies far inland from any seaport. It's certainly not close to Calex." Simna suddenly found his voice: He groaned.

"I understand." Ehomba was unsurprised and unfazed by this information. "Ultimately reaching Ehl-Larimar is our business. But to get there we must first cross the ocean."

She nodded once, curtly. "We have space, and I am willing to take you." Her eyes met Simna's. "Even though it's transparently clear there's not a seaman among you. You and your creatures would have to stay out of the way of my crew. You wouldn't be confined to quarters, mind. I just ask that you be careful where you go, when you go, and what you do when you get there."

"Not long ago we crossed the Aboqua," he told her, "and gave the crew that attended to our needs no cause for complaint."

Turning her head to her left, she spat contemptuously. "The Aboqua! A pond, for children to splash in. I've beaten through storms that were bigger than the Aboqua. But at least you know what saltwater smells like." To Simna's chagrin, she returned her full attention to Ehomba. "What can you pay?"

It was the herdsman's turn to be rendered speechless. In the excitement of searching out and finally finding a ship to carry them, he had completely forgotten that payment for their passage would doubtless be demanded. The oversight was understandable. Among the Naumkib such matters arose but infrequently, when the village received one of its rare visits from a trader making the long trek north from Wallab or Askaskos.

Unable to reply, he turned to his more worldly friend. Simna could only shrug helplessly. "If you're thinking of the Chlengguu gold, it's all gone, bruther. We've spent every last coin. I know what you're thinking, but there's none tucked away in my pack or my shirt. More's the pity. I should have secreted some more away."

Stanager listened silently to the brief byplay. "Do you have anything to trade? Anything of significant value you would be willing to part with?"

The swordsman started to respond, but Ehomba stopped him before the words could leave his mouth. "No! We've risked our lives to save Ahlitah from just such a fate. I will not see him sold to satisfy my own needs."

Simna eyed him sharply. "Not even to get yourself across the Semordria?"

"Not even for that." The herdsman looked back at the Captain. "We have very few possessions, and these we need."

She nodded tersely, her red hair rippling, and started to rise from the table. "Then I wish you good fortune in your difficult endeavors, gentlemen. Now if you will excuse me, I have a long and strenuous voyage ahead of me, and many last-minute preparations to supervise." The audience was at an end.

Ehomba did not panic. It was not an emotion he was heir to. But seeing their best and only hope of crossing the ocean about to walk out the door, he certainly became uncommonly anxious. A sudden thought made him rise halfway from his own chair as he raised his voice.

"Wait! Please, one moment."

An impatient look on her deeply tanned face, Stanager Rose hesitantly resumed her seat. Simna was eyeing his tall friend curiously. The swordsman expected the herdsman to start digging through his pack, but this was not what happened. Instead, Ehomba reached down and fumbled briefly in one of the pockets of his kilt. What he brought out caused Simna's gaze to narrow.

The Captain nodded at the fist-sized cloth sack. "What've you got there, tall man? Gold, silver, trinkets?"

"Pebbles." Ehomba smiled apologetically. "From a beach near my village. I brought them along to remind me of home, and of the sea. Whenever the longing grew too great, I could always reach into my pocket and rub the pebbles against each other, listen to them scrape and clink." He handed the sack to Stanager. "Once when I was much younger a trader came to the village from far to the south, farther away even than Askaskos. A friend of mine was playing jump-rock outside his house with some pebbles like these. Passing by, the trader happened to see and admire them. He offered my friend's family some fine things in exchange. After receiving approval from Asab, the trade was made." He gestured for the Captain to open the sack.

"If they were valuable to a trader who had come all the way from south of Askaskos, maybe they will have some value to you as well." He hesitated. "Though I would be sorry to have to give up my little memory bag."

Stanager was considerate if not hopeful. Taking pity on the lanky foreigner, she pulled the drawstring that closed the neck of the little cloth bag and turned it upside down. The double handful of pebbles promptly spilled out onto the tabletop. Struck by the light that poured in through the ports, the pebbles sparkled brightly. They were rough and sea-tossed, with most of the edges worn off them.

Simna's eyes opened so wide they threatened to pop right out of his head and roll egglike across the table. Like little else, his reaction did not escape the Captain's notice.

"So, Owl-eyes, you think these pebbles are valuable too?"

Recovering quickly, the swordsman looked away and exhaled indifferently. "Hoy, what? Oh, perhaps a little. I know very little about such things. To me they're nothing remarkable, but I believe my friend is right when he says that they might have some value."

"I see." Her gaze flicked sharply from one man to the other. "*Ayesh*, I am no expert on 'pebbles' either, but my supercargo knows a good deal about stones and their value. We will soon learn if these are worth anything—or if you are trying to cozen me with stories." Pushing back in her seat, she yelled toward the open doorway. "Terious! Find old Broch and send him down here!"

They waited in silence, the Captain of the *Grömsketter* in all her stern-faced beauty, Ehomba smiling hopefully, and Simna gazing off into the distance with studied indifference.

"What are you gaping at, little man?" an irritated Stanager finally asked the swordsman.

"Hoy, me? Why nothing, Captain, nothing at all. I believe I was momentarily stunned, is all."

She chuckled softly. "The last man who tried to compliment his way into my berth found himself traveling in the bilges until we reached the town of Harynbrogue. By that time he was so ready to get off the *Grömsketter* he didn't much care what I or anyone else look like. You could smell him making his way into town even after he was well off the ship."

Simna adopted an expression so serious Ehomba had to turn away to smother a laugh. "Why Captain, you wrong me deeply! Such a notion would never cross my mind!" Solemnly, he placed one hand over his heart. "Know that I have taken a vow of celibacy until we have successfully concluded our journey, and that every member of this crew, be they male or female, need have no concerns along such lines when in my presence."

Stanager was still smiling. "I think you are one of the more notable liars I have ever hosted on this ship, but since you will in all likelihood be off it in a few moments, your dubious protestations of innocence do not matter." She turned as a figure darkened the doorway. "Broch, come in."

Weatherbeaten as a spar at the end of its useful life, the supercargo entered on bowed legs. He was even shorter than Simna, and considerably thinner. But the wrinkled, leathery brown skin on his arms covered a lean musculature that resembled braided bullwhips. His fulsome beard was gray with a few remaining streaks of black, and his eyes were sharp and alert.

Stanager gestured at the collection of tumbled pebbles spread out on the mess table. "Tell me, what do you think of these?"

The old man looked, and though it seemed impossible, his eyes grew even wider than had the swordsman's. *"Memoch gharzanz!"* he exclaimed in a language neither Ehomba nor Simna recognized. "Where—where did these come from, Captain?"

She gestured at Ehomba. "These gentlemen together with their two, um, nonhuman companions desire to make the Semordria crossing with us. This is what they offer in payment. Is it sufficient?"

Seating himself at the table, the old mariner removed a small magnifying lens from a pants pocket. It was secured to the interior of the pocket, Ehomba noted, by a strong string. Bending low, he examined several of the pebbles, taking them up one at a time and turning them over between his fingers, making sure the light struck them from different angles. After studying half a dozen of the pebbles, he sat back in his chair and repocketed the glass.

"These are the finest diamonds I have ever seen. Half are flawless, and the other half fine enough to grace the best work of a master jeweler."

"That's for the clear ones," Simna agreed even though he was as surprised as anyone else at the table, "but what kind of stones are the others?"

"They are *all* diamonds," Broch explained. "Clear, yellow, blue, red, green, and pink, diamonds all. Mostly three to four carats, some smaller, a couple as large as six." Swallowing, he eyed the tranquil herdsman intently. "Where did you get these, foreigner?"

"There is a beach near my village."

"Ah." The supercargo nodded sagely. "You picked them out of the gravel on this beach."

"No," Ehomba explained quietly. "I just grabbed up a handful or two and dropped them in my little bag." He indicated the scattering of sparklers that decorated the tabletop. "The whole beach is like this. The pebbles are all the same. Except for the different colors, of course." His smile was almost regretful. "I wish I had known that they were so valuable. I would have brought more."

"More." The old man swallowed hard.

Ehomba shrugged. "Sometimes the waves wash away all the pebbles and leave behind only sand. After a big storm the pebbles may lie as deep on the shore as a man's chest. At such times, when the sun comes out, the beach is very pretty."

"Yes," murmured the supercargo. He looked slightly shell-shocked. "Yes, I would imagine it is." Shaking his head, he turned to the expectant Stanager. "They have enough to book passage, Captain—or to buy the ship many times over. Take them. Give them the finest cabin. If they wish, they may have my own and I will sleep belowdecks with the rest of the crew. Give them anything they want."

"Really," an embarrassed Ehomba demurred, "passage will be quite sufficient. Our two large friends can find room in your hold, among your cargo."

"Done." Reaching across the table, Stanager shook the tall southerner's hand. "You really didn't know these stones were diamonds, or that they were valuable?"

"Oh, they have always been valuable to me," Ehomba conceded. "Feeling of them reminds me of home." He glanced over at the supercargo. "Take your payment, please."

"A *fair* payment," Simna interjected in no-nonsense tones. "We've hidden nothing from you, been completely up-front. As the old man says, we could always buy ourselves a ship."

"Ayesh," agreed Stanager, "but it wouldn't be the *Grömsketter*, and whatever crew you engaged wouldn't be the *Grömsketter*'s crew. Have no fear, foreigner—this is an honorable vessel crewed by honest seamen." She nodded at her supercargo. "Take the payment, Broch."

Licking his lips, the elderly mariner contemplated the riches strewn so casually before him. Finally, after much deliberation, he settled on the second-largest stone, a perfect deep pink diamond of some six carats.

"This one, I think." Hesitating to see if the owners objected, he then quickly plucked the rough gem from the table. "And a few of the smaller." He smiled. "To give the selection a nice play of color." Having made his choices, he handed them to Stanager.

"Thank you, Broch." She deposited them in her empty drinking mug. "Please wait outside for us."

"Thank you, Captain." He turned to leave.

"Just a second." Simna was smiling knowingly. "What about the one that 'accidentally' got caught under your fingernail? Middle finger of the left hand, I believe?"

"What? Oh, this." Feigning confusion, the old man removed a half-carat stone from beneath the offending nail and placed it back on the table. "Sorry. These small stones, you know, are like sand. They can get caught up in anything."

"Sure they can." Simna was still smiling. "Etjole, pack up the rest of your pebbles."

The herdsman scooped the remaining stones into the little cloth sack. Old Broch watched his every move to see if he might overlook any. When it was clear that the herdsman had not, the supercargo sighed regretfully and left.

"Well then." Planting both palms firmly on the table, Stanager pushed back from the table and stood. "Welcome aboard the *Grömsketter*, gentlemen. I'll have Broch show you to your cabin, and we'll see about getting your oversized companions properly settled below. You have two days to enjoy the sights and delights of Hamacassar. Then we set sail downriver for the Semordria, far Calex, and the unknown."

"Thank you, Captain." Ehomba executed his half bow. "Is there anything else we should know before we depart?"

"Yes." Turning her head to look at an expressionless Simna, she declared sweetly, "If this foreign creature doesn't take his hand off my ass I will have Cook mince and dice him and serve him tomorrow morning for breakfast hash."

"Hoy? Oh, sorry." Simna removed the offending hand, eyeing it as if it possessed a mind and will of its own. "I thought that was the chair cushion."

"Think more carefully next time, foreigner, or I will prevent any further confusion by having the errant portion of your anatomy removed."

"I said I was sorry," he protested.

"Your eyes argue with your words." She led the way out of the mess.

Later, as they followed old Broch through a narrow passage, Ehomba leaned down to whisper to his companion. "Are you mad, Simna? Next time she will have you quartered!"

A dreamy lilt tinted the swordsman's voice. "Her beauty would drive a man mad. A little sunburnt, yes. A little hardened by the weather, to be sure. But to see her at ease on a broad bed, divested of mariner's attire, would be worth a couple of those diamonds to me."

"Then I will give you the diamonds, but keep away from her! We have yet to enter the Semordria, much less cross it. I am a good swimmer, but I do not want to have to exercise that skill in the middle of the ocean."

The swordsman was quietly outraged. "You ask me to deny myself, bruther. To go against the very substance of my being, to refute that which comprises a most basic portion of myself, to abjure my very nature." He deliberated briefly. "How many diamonds?"

By the morning of the third day all was in readiness. Standing tall on the helm deck, the old woman who handled the ship's wheel waiting for orders alongside her, Captain Stanager Rose gave the order to let go the fore and aft lines and cast off. With becoming grace, the *Grömsketter* waltzed clear of the quay and slipped out into the gentle current of the lower Eynharrowk. Adjusting sail and helm, she aimed her bow downstream. With only the mainsail set, she began to make use of the current and pick up speed.

Ehomba and Simna had joined the Captain on the stern while Hunkapa Aub lounged near the bow and the black litah slept curled atop a sun-swathed hatch, his long legs drooping lazily over the sides.

"A fine day for a departure." Stanager alternated her gaze between the busy crew, the set sail, and the shore. Only when she was satisfied with the appearance of all three did she devote whatever attention remained to her passengers. "We'll be through the Narrows by midmorning. From there it's easy sailing to the delta and the mouth of the

Eynharrowk." At last she turned to the two men standing next to her, once more focusing on Ehomba to the exclusion of his shorter companion.

"Did you sleep well, herdsman?"

"Very well. I love the water, and the cabin bunks are sturdy enough so that my spine does not feel like it is falling out of my back."

"Good. Later, Cook will begin to amaze you with her invention. We're fortunate to have her. A ship may make do with a poor navigator, feeble sailors, even an indifferent captain, but so long as the food is good there will be few complaints." Her tone darkened. "Enjoy the river while you can, Etjole Ehomba. Where it is smooth the Semordria is wave-tossed, and where it is inoffensive the sea is deadly. Throughout the crossing each one of us must be eternally vigilant. That includes any passengers."

Simna nodded somberly. "As long as one can see the danger, it can be dealt with. Sometimes even made into an ally."

She frowned at him for a moment, then looked away, returning her attention to the view over the bowsprit. "Your presence here is not required. You may relax in your cabin if you wish."

"Thank you," Ehomba responded courteously, "but after so long afoot it is a pleasure to be able to simply look at and enjoy our surroundings."

She shrugged. "As you wish. If you'll excuse me now, I have work to do."

"Mind if I tag along?" Like a debutante donning her most expensive and elegant gown, Simna had put on his widest and most innocent smile. "I haven't been on that many boats. I might learn something."

Her expression was disapproving. "I doubt it, but you've paid well for the run of the ship." She started forward.

"Now then," the swordsman began, "the first thing I want to know is, what areas of the *Grömsketter* are off limits to us?"

Turning away from them, Ehomba moved to the rail and watched as the outskirts of industrious, hardworking Hamacassar slid past. They were on their way at last. Not on the Semordria itself, not yet—but on their way. How much farther they would have to travel to reach Ehl-Larimar once they landed on the ocean's far shore he did not know. But whatever it was, it too would be crossed. Somewhere, he knew that the shade of Tarin Beckwith was watching, and whispering its approval.

The Narrows comprised opposing headlands whose highest point would not have qualified as a proper foothill on either side of the snow-capped Hrugars, but on the otherwise plate-flat floodplain they stood out prominently. Accelerating as it passed through, the vast river's volume was compressed, causing the *Grömsketter* to pick up speed. As they drew near, Ehomba saw that what at first appeared to be trees were in fact more of the extraordinary triangular towers that they had first encountered on the southern outskirts of greater Hamacassar.

With Stanager absent from the helm deck, he wandered over to query the stolid, stocky woman behind the ship's wheel. "Your pardon, Priget, but what are those odd free-standing spires?"

"You don't know?" She had a thick accent that he had been told instantly identified her as coming from far upriver. "They're the time gates. They're what has kept Hamacassar strong and made it the preeminent port of the middle Eynharrowk. Kept it from being attacked and looted for hundreds of years. The Gate Masters' guild watches over them, decides when they are to be used and when kept closed."

Ehomba pondered this as the helmswoman nudged the wheel a quarter degree to port. "What kind of gates did you say they were? Does time gate mean they are very old?"

"No. They are . . . hullo, what's this?" Setting his question aside, she squinted to her left. Moments later Stanager was back on the high stern, Simna trailing behind like an eager puppy.

She ignored both men. "You see the flags, Priget?"

"Yes, Captain. How should we respond?"

Stanager looked conflicted. "The flags are small and still a goodly distance off. Hold your course and we'll see what they do. They may be testing us, or flagging a small boat somewhere close inshore."

"Ayesh, Captain." The helmswoman settled herself firmly behind the wheel.

Sensing that now was not a good time to lay a raft of queries upon the Captain, Ehomba and Simna both held their questions. The *Grömsketter* continued to slip swiftly downriver, using its mainsail more for steering than propulsion in the heightened current.

Following their eyes, Ehomba saw what they were scrutinizing so intently. Near the base of the second triangular monolith on the south bank stood a cluster of reddish buildings dominated by a three-story brick tower. Atop this formidable structure was a mast from which presently flew three large, brightly patterned flags. The designs that were of such evident significance to Captain and helmswoman meant nothing to him, nor to Simna. He also thought he could see several figures waving both arms above their heads.

A hand came down on his shoulder as the swordsman pointed. "See there, Etjole. Something is happening."

Between the towers that stood on opposing headlands a deep blue glow was coalescing. Shot through with thousands of attenuated streaks

of bright yellow and white like captured lightning, the effulgence extended from the crests of the towers down to the surface of the river,
clearing it by less than half a foot. From the depths of the potent luminescence there emanated a dull roar, like an open ocean wave curling
and breaking endlessly back upon itself. The glow flowed swiftly from
tower to tower, as far as the eye could see. Remembering what Priget
had told him of the structures' purpose, Ehomba imagined that the deep
cobalt light must extend to encircle all of greater Hamacassar.

"That's it." Stanager looked resigned. "They're calling us in. Priget,
steer for the inspection docks."

"Ayesh, Captain." The helmswoman promptly spun the wheel. Slowing only slightly, the *Grömsketter* began to turn sharply to port.

"What's happening? Why are we heading in?" Relaxed and talkative
only moments ago, Simna was suddenly nervous.

"Probably only a random check," the Captain assured him. "The
Gate Masters run them on occasion, both to flex their muscles and remind travelers on the river of just who is in charge, and to ascertain the
condition of the time gates." She nodded toward the dense blue radiance. "Those, at least, appear to be functioning flawlessly."

"I do not understand." Simna spoke both for himself and his friends.
"What are these time gates? What is that banded blue glowing?"

Stanager Rose did not smile. "You really are from far away, aren't
you?"

"Captain," the swordsman told her, "all your long and difficult journeys notwithstanding, you have no idea."

She spared him barely a glance before turning back to Ehomba.
"The streaked blue glow is Time itself. The ancient Logicians of Hamacassar long suspected that time traveled in a stream, like the Eynharrowk. So they found the Time that follows the great river and channeled
it. Here Time flows through a canal, much like the hundreds you have
seen crisscrossing the city itself. It runs through the time gates and can
be turned on or shut off by a master gate that lies to the northeast of the
city. When the master gate is opened, Time is allowed to run in a circular
channel all around the border of Hamacassar. Until it is closed and the
time stream shut off, no one can enter or leave the city. No criminal may
flee, no enemy enter." She nodded forward.

"As you can see, it flows as effectively over water as across the land."

"What would happen if you just tried to run it?" Simna was a direct
man, and it was a direct question.

By the Captain's reaction, however, not a well-thought-out one.
"Why, any vessel attempting to sail through would be caught in the
currents of Time and swept away, never to be seen or heard from again. I

don't know what that would be like, because no ship or person who has been caught up in the time flow has ever come back out to speak of the experience." She nodded toward the rapidly approaching outpost. "We'll see what they want and then we'll be on our way again. I'm sure it's nothing of significance, and will likely cost us half an hour at most."

Despite the Captain's reassurances, Ehomba was distressed to see a double line of heavily armed soldiers drawn up on the dock. They carried crossbows and battle swords but wore little armor, impractical in the heat and humidity of the Hamacassarian lowlands. They wore uniforms of streaked emerald green and sandals instead of boots, again in keeping with the practicalities imposed by the climate.

Waiting to greet the *Grömsketter* as it bumped up against the dock were half a dozen men and women of varying age. All wore similar colors, but much finer fabrics. The single togalike garments were belted at the waist with yellow-gold braid, and extended only as far as the knee. Sleeves ended at the elbow. Shading their heads were peculiar tricornered hats that mimicked the design of the time gates. None of the assembled were smiling.

Clinging to the mainmast rigging with one hand and leaning out over the water and the dock as the ship pulled in, Terious hailed the gathering. "Good morning to you, virtuous Gate Masters! Do you wish to board?"

A stern-faced, handsome man in his forties replied. "Only if necessary, *Grömsketter*. We won't keep you long. We're looking for someone."

"A fugitive?" Behind the helm deck railing, Stanager was murmuring aloud to herself. "We've hired three new men and one woman for this crossing. I wonder if all were thoroughly checked?" Leaning over the rail, she shouted down at the Gate Master. "Does this person you seek have a name?"

As she spoke, preoccupied faces turned in her direction. Ehomba and Simna stood close by. Suddenly another of the Gate Masters, an older woman, spoke out sharply.

"No name, only an aura—and there he is!" Raising an arm, she pointed sharply.

Straight at Ehomba.

XXIV

On board the *Grömsketter* all eyes turned to the obviously bemused herdsman. When he did not respond, Stanager again addressed the assembled officials. "This man is a passenger on my ship. Though known to me for only a few days, I have found him to be a responsible and worthy individual. What is it you want with him?"

"That is our business," another man shouted upward. "Turn him over and you may proceed on your way. Refuse, and your vessel will be boarded. Those who comply may depart freely. Those who resist will be killed or taken before the Board of Logicians to have their ultimate fates resolved."

Stepping away from the railing, Stanager turned to stare up at her long-faced passenger. "I don't understand any of this. What do the Gate Masters want with you? What have you done?"

"I tell you honestly, Captain: to my knowledge, nothing." Ehomba was aware that the eyes not only of his friends but of the crew were on him, watching and waiting to see what he would do. "But I cannot allow my own circumstances to put you and your people in danger. You have done nothing."

"By Gorquon's Helmet, neither have we, Etjole!" The right hand of Simna ibn Sind rested firmly on the hilt of his sword. "I'll not see you handed over to an unknown fate. Not after all we've been through together!"

The herdsman smiled fondly at his friend. "What is this, Simna? Loyalty? And without a gold piece in sight?"

"Mock me if you will, long bruther. You wouldn't be the first." The swordsman's face was flush with anger. "Dying in combat with some monstrous beast or battling an attacking army is a worthy death for a man. You deserve better than to rot in some cell accused of Gwinbare knows what imaginary crime."

"No one has said anything about dying or rotting in a cell." Ehomba's voice was calm, his manner composed. "They may only want to talk to me."

"Hoy, but for how long?" Simna gestured sharply in the direction of the assembled soldiers and officials. "They said that once they have you, the rest can sail on. That doesn't sound to me like they plan to let you go anytime soon, and you said yourself we shouldn't wait two months for another ship."

"So you should not." Raising his hands, the herdsman placed them on his friend's shoulders. "I hereby charge you, Simna ibn Sind, with completing my task, with fulfilling my promise to the dying Tarin Beckwith. Stay with the *Grömsketter*. See her across the Semordria, and find your way onward from there."

The swordsman tensed. "What madness is this? What are you saying, Etjole?"

Removing his hands, Ehomba turned back to the railing. "I am getting off the ship." He looked to Stanager. "Captain, as soon as I am on the dock and the Narrows are once more cleared to navigation, set your course downriver and sail on." She eyed him purposefully for a long moment, then nodded once.

A ladder of rope and wood was thrown over the side. Ehomba started toward it, only to be grabbed and held by the swordsman.

"Don't do this, bruther! You have your weapons; I have my sword. There is the black litah and Hunkapa Aub. We can fight them off!" His fingers tightened on the taller man's arm.

Gently, Ehomba disengaged himself from his friend's grasp. "No, Simna. Even if we could, sailors who have no part in this might get hurt, or killed. As could any of us, yourself included. Stay on the ship. Sail on." He smiled warmly. "Think of me as the river carries you to the sea." Turning away, he stepped over the side, straddling the railing preparatory to climbing down the ladder.

"Stop there!" a voice commanded from below. Crossbow bolts were trained on the herdsman. "No weapons. Leave them and the pack on your back on board the ship. You can claim them upon its return."

Removing the sword of sea bone and the sword of sky metal, Ehomba passed them to a stricken Simna. They were joined by the long walking stick-spear. Lastly, the herdsman slipped off his backpack and handed it to a somber-faced Terious. Hunkapa Aub was crying outsized inhuman tears. Ehomba was grateful that the black litah was still asleep.

It might not have been possible to restrain the big cat with words. Had it been awake, the spilling of blood might have proven unavoidable.

Descending the ladder, he jumped the last few feet to the dock, landing with a resonant *thump* on his well-worn sandals. Instantly, he was surrounded by soldiers. With an approving nod, one of the Gate Masters turned and gave a signal to someone in the brick tower. Flags flashed in the direction of the opposing headlands, where other flags responded.

How it was done Ehomba could not tell. The time gates that surmounted the headlands were too far away for him to discern the mechanisms involved. But the shimmering, coruscating blue haze that blocked the Eynharrowk abruptly vanished, though it remained in place everywhere else.

Aboard the *Grömsketter* shouts rang loudly. He could make out the brisk, lively syllables of Stanager's commands and the deeper echoes of Terious and the other mates. Deliberately, the sleek ship pulled away from the dock and turned its bow once more toward the Narrows. Along the railing he could see an openly distraught Simna staring back at him. Behind the swordsman the hulking mass of hair that was Hunkapa Aub stood and waved slowly. He continued to follow them with his eyes until a hand shoved him roughly in the middle of his back.

"Move along, then. There are coaches waiting to take us back to the city."

Turning away from the *Grömsketter,* receding rapidly now that it was edging back out into the main current, Ehomba began the long march to the end of the dock. Gate Masters paralleled him on both sides and were in turn flanked by their stalwart, alert soldiers.

"Maybe now you can tell me what this is all about?" he asked the green-clad official on his left. Like his sisters and brothers, the man's hands were locked together in front of him.

"Certainly. We don't act arbitrarily, you know. There is a reason for this. Your arrival was predicted by the Logicians. Taking their measurements from disturbances in the Aether and the flow of Time, they calculated the cognomen of your aura and its probable path. As you have seen, Hamacassar is a big place, where even a distinctive aura can hide. We almost missed you. That would have been tragic."

Ehomba frowned, openly puzzled. "Why is that?"

The Gate Master looked up at him. "Because according to the Logicians' predictions, if you were allowed to proceed on your chosen course unhindered, the flow of Time would have been substantially altered, and perhaps unfavorably."

"Unfavorable to whom?" In the lexicon of the Naumkib, forthrightness invariably took precedence over tact. Ehomba was no exception.

"It does not matter. Not to you," the official informed him importantly. "Having committed no crime, you are not a prisoner. You are a guest, until your friends return. Or if you prefer, you will be allowed to leave in one month's time, once the *Grömsketter* is well out to sea and beyond reach." The man smiled. His expression was, the herdsman decided, at least half genuine.

They were nearing the end of the dock. "What makes you so certain that if I was permitted to continue on my journey Time would react adversely?"

This time it was the woman on his right who replied. "The Logicians have declared it to be so. And the Logicians are never wrong."

"Time may be a river," Ehomba responded, "but logic is not. At least, not the logic that is discussed by the wise men and women of my village."

"His 'village.'" Two of the Gate Masters strolling in front of him exchanged a snickering laugh.

"This is not a village, foreigner," declared the man on the herdsman's left meaningfully. "This is Hamacassar, whose Board of Logicians is comprised of the finest minds the city and its surrounding provinces can provide."

Ehomba was not intimidated. "Even the finest minds are not infallible. Even the most reasonable and logical people can make mistakes."

"Well, according to them, detaining you is not a mistake. Whereas letting you continue on most surely would be."

The tall southerner glanced back down the dock. In the distance, the sturdy hull of the *Grömsketter* was passing through the Narrows, traveling swiftly westward as the current continued to increase its speed. Turning his attention to the red-brick administration buildings up ahead, he saw several antelope-drawn coaches lined up outside. More soldiers waited there, a mounted escort to convoy him and the Gate Masters back to the city.

"You know," he murmured conversationally, "logic is a funny thing. It can be used to solve many problems, even to predict things that may happen in the future. But it is not so very good at explaining people: who they are, what they are about, why they do the things they do. Sometimes even masters of logic and reason can think too long and too hard about something, until the truth of it becomes lost in a labyrinth of conflicting possibilities."

While the woman on his right pondered his words, the man on his left frowned. "What are you trying to say, foreigner?"

"That anyone, however clever they believe themselves to be, can think too much." Whereupon he lurched heavily to his right, slamming his shoulder into the startled female official and sending her stumbling and crashing into the two soldiers marching close alongside her. In a confusion of weapons and words, all three went toppling together off the end of the dock to land in the shallow water below.

"Stop him! Don't kill him, but stop him!" the senior Gate Master shouted.

With dozens of soldiers in pursuit, Ehomba ran inland. A lifetime of chasing down errant calves and stray lambs allowed him to outdistance all but the most active of his pursuers, not to mention the Gate Masters who trailed huffing and puffing in their wake. Neither group was in any especial hurry. There was nowhere for the herdsman to go. If he entered the water they would quickly chase him down in boats. The headland toward which he was running ended in a low bluff overlooking the river. All other directions were sealed off by the still active time gates, through which the flow of Time continued to ripple and shimmer.

"Stop!" yelled a voice from behind him.

"You can't get away!" shouted another. "There's nowhere to go!"

But there was somewhere to go. Or rather, somewhen.

Taking a deep breath and making an arrow of his clasped hands, Ehomba leaped forward and dove headfirst into the time stream.

Somewhere far around the curve of the world, the most powerful sorcerer alive woke up screaming.

From the hole Ehomba's body made in the channel, Time spewed forth in a gush of unrestrained chronology. Amid shrieks and howls, Gate Masters and soldiers alike were swept up and washed away in the flood of Time, to disappear forever into some otherwhen. The detained deranged foreigner was forgotten in the survivors' haste to close all the time gates and so shut off the flow to the devastating leak.

Once this had finally been accomplished, reluctant soldiers were sent to scour the area where the tall stranger had disappeared. Though not hopeful, the Gate Masters knew they had to try. The Logicians would demand it. As expected, there was no sign or suspicion that the foreigner had ever existed. He was gone forever: vanished, swept away, taken up by the river of Time. With wondering sighs and expressions of regret for those colleagues who had been lost in the short-lived disaster, they set about composing themselves for the journey back into the city. It was an occurrence that occasioned much animated discussion among the survivors.

Caught up by the river of Time, Ehomba kicked and dug hard at the eras that rushed past. Growing up by the sea, he was a naturally strong swimmer. Still, it was hard to tread years, difficult to hold one's breath as

wave after wave of eternity broke over one's mind. But to the determined and well conditioned, not impossible.

He swam on, trying to make timefall as close to the point where he
had entered the river as possible. The current was strong, but he had
expected that and, by his angle of entry, done his best to anticipate it.
Caught up in the flow of Time, he was battered and buffeted by astonishing sights. Animals ancient and fantastical rushed past. Great machines
the likes of which he had never imagined clanked ponderously forward
down unsuspected evolutionary paths, and all manner of men inhabited
times immemorial and impossibly distant.

He was almost out of breath when a faint gleam caught his eye.
Turning in the Time flow, he kicked hard for it. It was one of the blazing
yellow-white streaks he had seen from his own time, viewed now from
the inside out. This in itself was a wonderment to him, for he did not
know that it was possible to see light from the inside out. The current
tore at him, insistent and relentless. He felt himself weakening.

Worse than that, he was running out of Time.

Below the Narrows of Hamacassar the Eynharrowk once more became a
broad, placid highway. Smaller boats traveling in the same direction as
the *Grömsketter* kept closer to either shore, while those beating their way
upstream gave her a wide berth. Small islands dotted with reeds and
cattails had begun to appear, the first outposts of the great delta into
which the torpid river spread before at last entering the ocean. Fishermen had erected modest homes on the larger islets, and spread their nets
from long poles rammed into the shallows.

The *Grömsketter* kept to the main channel. With the widening of the
river, the current had dissipated considerably over the past weeks and
her speed had slowed accordingly. Crewmen and -women palavered
boisterously as they worked the ship, but among her remaining passengers the mood was glum.

Simna was unable to think straight. His friend had charged him with
completing the journey begun in the far south, but how was a common
mercenary like himself to know how to proceed? Ehomba's mystic weapons remained on board, but the swordsman was more leery than hopeful
of figuring out how to make proper use of them. He had no money, the
herdsman having carried off the remaining "beach pebbles" in his
pocket. His one ally was the imposing but simple-minded Hunkapa Aub.
As for the black litah, upon awakening and learning what had transpired,
the big cat had promptly announced his intention to leave the ship at the
first opportunity. As he explained inexorably to Simna, his allegiance had

been to the herdsman personally, not to his cause. With Ehomba gone, the cat considered its obligation at an end.

"Don't you care about what he began?" the swordsman had reproached the litah. "Do you wish all his efforts to go for naught?"

The big cat remained unperturbed. "His efforts are, and were, of no interest to me. It was the person I chose to associate with. I am sorry he is no longer here. For a human, he was a most interesting individual." The moist black tongue emerged to lick and clean around the nostrils. "I always wondered what he would have tasted like."

Simna sneered openly, not caring how the sleek predator might react, finding that he presently cared about so little that it shocked him. "It's all primeval to you, isn't it? Food, sex, sleep. You've acquired nothing in the way of culture from your association with us. Nothing!"

"On the contrary," the litah objected. "I have learned a good deal these past many weeks about humankind. I have learned that its culture is obsessed with food, sex, and sleep. The only difference between us is that you don't do any of it as well."

"By Geenvar's claws, I'll tell you that—"

The discussion was interrupted by a loud cry from the lookout. Posted atop the mainmast, the seaman was pointing and shouting. Fully intending to resume his dialogue with the big cat, Simna glanced curiously in the direction indicated by the mariner. At first he saw nothing. Then the subject of much commotion came into view and he found himself surrounded and carried forward by excited members of the crew. Not that he needed any help.

Etjole Ehomba was standing on the end of a small, handmade pier, waving casually in the *Grömsketter*'s direction. Except for a rip or two in his kilt and shirt, he looked healthy and relaxed.

Unsuspected excitement in her voice, Stanager Rose roared commands. The mainsail was reefed and the sea anchor cast off astern to slow their speed. As she hurriedly explained to Simna, she did not want to risk anchoring and stopping in the event that the soldiers of the Gate Masters were giving chase. This despite the fact that no troops or pursuers of any kind were in evidence. The swordsman did not argue with her. He was of like mind when it came to not taking chances.

One of the ship's lifeboats was quickly put over the side. Commanded by Terious himself, it plucked the waiting Ehomba from the end of the pier and, propelled by six strong oarsmen, returned to the *Grömsketter*. The sea anchor was hauled in, and this time all sails were set.

Ehomba's friends were waiting impatiently to greet him as he climbed back aboard. Attempting to clasp the tall southerner by the arm, Simna was nearly bowled over as Hunkapa Aub rushed past him to envelop the herdsman in an embrace that threatened to suffocate him before he could explain what had happened. From the helm deck, Stanager Rose looked on with pretended disinterest.

When Ehomba finally managed to extricate himself from Hunkapa's smothering grasp, Simna confronted him with the question that had been bothering him ever since they had first caught sight of the herdsman standing alone on the pier.

"I am half convinced that you are what you claim to be, Etjole: nothing more than a humble herder of cattle and sheep." He gestured back toward the section of river that was falling far behind. "However, the other half of me wonders not only how you escaped the Gate Masters and their minions, but how you managed to appear in the middle of the Eynharrowk *ahead* of us. I know you can play the flute and spew forth heavenly winds and white sharks from your weapons, but I didn't know that you could fly."

"I cannot, friend Simna." With a smile and nod in the Captain's direction, the herdsman began to walk forward, seemingly little the worse for his experience. "No more than a bird without wings. But I can swim."

As had happened to him more times than he cared to remember in the herdsman's presence, Simna ibn Sind did not understand.

"Time is harder to tread than water, my friend, but it can be done. We of the Naumkib are taught how to swim at an early age. It is a necessary thing when one lives so near to the sea, and to other great emptinesses." Reaching into a pocket, he began to roll the remaining beach pebbles in the little cloth sack fondly through his fingers. Whereas before he had never paid any attention to the activity, now, each time he heard them grind together, Simna winced.

"I swam hard, my friend, determined never to give up." Ehomba smiled. "Giving up would have meant renouncing my pledge to Tarin Beckwith, and never seeing my home or family again. I vowed that would not happen. After treading Time for a while I tried to swim back out a little ways from where I had entered the river of Time." A shrug rippled his shoulders.

"But the current was powerful. Time is like that, always moving forward, always flowing strongly. So I did not come out where I wanted to." He looked back over his shoulder. "Emerging several weeks before I entered, I found myself on this little island. I built a small shelter of reeds, and the clumsy pier you saw, and caught fish and mussels and clams. And I waited for you. A month after a few minutes ago, the *Grömsketter* came through the Narrows." Reaching out, he put a comradely arm around the swordsman's shoulders. "And now, here you are."

The explanation did nothing to mitigate the look of utter bewilderment that had commandeered the swordsman's countenance. "Wait now, bruther. We just saw you off the ship and in the surly company of those Gate Masters not more than—"

"A few minutes ago. I know." They were approaching the bow. "But I have been waiting for you nearly a month. Time is a river most strange, my friend. Strange as only those who swim in it can know."

"But if you were there, and now you are here . . ." Simna's brows furrowed so deeply they threatened to pinch off his nose.

"Do not ponder on such things too long," Ehomba advised him. "That was the Logicians' problem. Overthinking can snarl the most elegant logic." Raising a hand, he gestured forward. "Ahead lies the great delta of the Eynharrowk. Soon we will leave behind the land for the Semordria. The eternal ocean that I have fished in, swam in, and played in all my life. If the shore is so amazing, what wonders must lie hidden beneath its outer depths?"

"Some that bite, I've no doubt." Inhaling deeply of the still steamy air, the swordsman leaned against the bow rail and gazed westward.

Feeling something bump him firmly from behind, Ehomba turned to see the black litah standing at his back. Typically, he had neither heard nor sensed the big cat's approach.

"So you're back." The long-legged carnivore yawned, revealing a gape that extended from the herdsman's head to his belly. "Pity. I was looking forward to returning home."

"No one is restraining you," Ehomba reminded him.

"Yes someone is. I am." As he addressed Ehomba, yellow cat eyes glared at the herdsman. "Call it a matter of culture. I am stuck with you lot until the next time you try to die."

"Then I will do my best to avoid that, and make an end to this business as quickly as events allow."

The cat nodded impressively, the freshening breeze from off the bow ruffling the magnificent black mane. "We seek the same thing."

"Hoy, not me," Simna protested quickly. "It's the treasure I'm after!" He eyed the herdsman sharply. "Whether it consists of legendary Damura-sese itself or nothing more than 'beach pebbles.' So don't try to deny it, bruther!"

Ehomba sighed resignedly. "Has it ever done me any good to do so?"

"No," the swordsman replied emphatically.

"Very well. The Visioness Themaryl. Treasure. No denials."

Satisfied, Simna went silent. Its freedom once again postponed, the black litah chose a sun-soaked section of deck, curled up into itself, and went back to sleep. Astern, Hunkapa Aub was watching a handful of sailors at dice while struggling to comprehend the intricacies of the game.

Waiting for the sea, Ehomba watched the river and thought of Mirhanja, and his children, and the way the same ocean they were about to enter lapped at the beach below the village. Soon it would be calving season at home, and he knew he would be missed.

Did ever any among the living drive a man so hard and so far as one dead? he found himself wondering.

A
Triumph
of
Souls

For my nephew, Joshua Francis Carroll

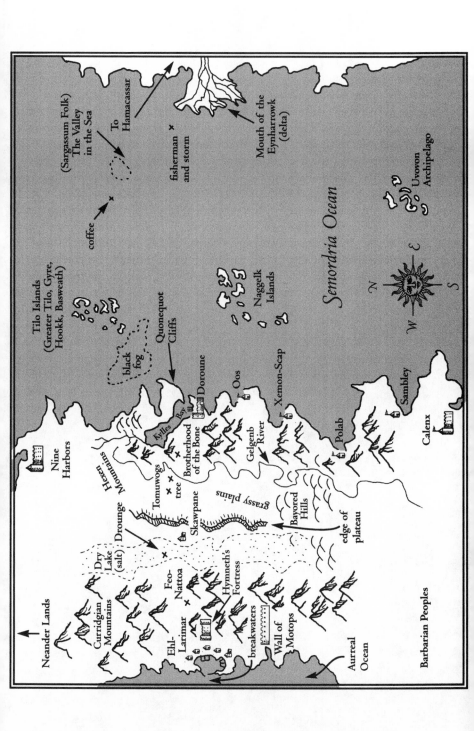

1

He is coming. And he is not alone."

So spake the Worm.

It had started out to be a better day. Waking after a passable night's rest in a less discontented mood than usual, Hymneth the Possessed had chosen to dress in armor and accoutrements that were celebratory instead of intimidating. Gold-trimmed leggings tucked tightly into high boots of dark-crimson embossed leather. Scarlet armor covered him from head to thigh, and rubies so red they were almost black studded the gloves that encased his bare hands. Instead of horns, the high-ridged crimson helmet with its rearward-sweeping feathered crest gave him the appearance of some great and noble raptor diving to Earth.

Eyeing the result in the narrow floor-to-ceiling mirror at the far end of his dressing chamber, he found that he was well pleased with the effect. Today he would inspire only awe among his servitors and subjects, and leave terror in the closet.

At his high-pitched, intricate call, the twin eromakadi ceased their hunting of small bright things beneath the massive bed and came to heel. Intricately filigreed satin cape swirling behind him, he exited the sleeping chamber in a flurry of gold and crimson and made his way downstairs.

As usual, he ate alone, attended only by silent servants desperate to be free of his company but unable to show their true feelings. Their frozen smiles and polite inquiries after his health fooled him for not a minute. Their fear was as plain to hear in their voices as if they had been bound and bleeding in his presence. The slight tremolo at the end of every sentence, the swift darting of eyes whenever they thought he was not looking, the infinitesimal quiver of lower lips: Their emotions were as blatantly obvious to him as bulging eyes and hacking sobs.

He ignored it all, pretending to be taken in by the pitiful subterfuges as they served him. These were the best of the best, the few who could survive in his service without going mad or begging for dismissal. It made no sense. Was he not a kind and even generous master? Other nobles of wealth and power regularly beat their staff. Still others paid only a pittance for services rendered. In contrast to this, he was tolerant of oversights and paid well. And, in addition, there was the prestige that went with working in the house of the master of Ehl-Larimar. He could not understand why his people were not content.

Yes, it was necessary occasionally to discipline a menial for a job overlooked or poorly done. Yes, his methods for doing so were undeniably—well, different. As in everything, he prized efficiency above all. Why it should matter to people if a miscreant was crippled or given the face of a bat or frog instead of simply being broken on the rack or blinded in the traditional manner he could not understand. Was it not better to have the teeth of a rat than none at all? Sometimes he felt he would never understand the reasoning of the common man.

Of the gustatory delights that burdened the dining table he normally would consume only a small amount. The remainder of the pancakes, eggs, meats, breads, jams, butters, fruits, cereals, juices, and cold drinks would be divided among his kitchen staff. He grunted to himself as he ate, passing food and liquid through the lower opening in the crimson helmet. They might tremble too badly to eat in his presence, but he knew that once he was done the food would vanish rapidly into hungry mouths. Which was well enough. Let them serve him. Love he would find elsewhere.

Love he sought, actually, in only one place.

Lifting his gaze to the stairway that entered the dining chamber from the left, he tried to imagine her descending to join him. Did his best to envision the fluid succession of perfect curves and contours concealed by clinging ripples of satin and silk, the hair like ribbons of night draped across bare shoulders that put the finest ivory to shame, and the eyes that were like sapphires. Eyes that he would have given half a world to have focused on him.

He imagined her approaching, not walking but flowing like mercury across the floor, weight shifting sensuously with each step, lips of blood-red brighter than his armor parting slightly as she raised one delicate hand to place it on his shoulder and whisper in the voice that turned men's legs to jelly and set their groins ablaze, "Good morning, My Lord."

Little enough, he agonized inside, to want. Little enough. Yet even now, after all this time, the best he could hope for was that she would not curse him aloud in his presence. She would eat later, he knew. In her room, or after members of the entourage he had assigned to her had assured her he had left to attend to matters of state. He possessed no more of her presence than he did of her passion.

Suddenly the morning no longer seemed so propitious. The food curdled in his mouth. Angrily, he pushed his plate away, and the two servitors attending him twitched visibly. Neither man ran, however. They knew all too well the fate of those who had fled the presence of the Possessed without first being properly dismissed.

Leaning back in the high, sculpted chair of carmine cobal, he rested his armored chin against one massive fist and brooded. After several minutes, the two servants exchanged a glance. The one who had lost the wordless debate took a step forward. His voice was deferential and suffered from only a slight quavering.

"Lord, if you are finished, should we clear away the dishes?"

He waved an indifferent hand. "Yes, yes, take it away. Take it all away!"

Bowing obsequiously and repeatedly, the man and his companion began to remove the masses of food and flatware. Hymneth sulked in his chair, contemplating aspects of life and death to which most living creatures were not privy, until a loud crash penetrated his pondering and brought his head around.

The second servant, a well-built and comely youth of some twenty and four years, was kneeling over the fragments of a shattered enameled tray. Muffins and sweet rolls, breads and breakfast cakes were still rolling away in several directions. From his crouch, he looked up to see the helmeted head staring down at him. The look on his face was one of sheer paralyzed terror.

"L-lord, I'm sorry. I'm so sorry. I—I will pay for it." Hastily, he began sweeping the larger fragments into a pile, not caring if he cut himself on the fractured ceramic.

"Pay for it? It would take six months of your wages, lackey. I wouldn't think of taking that from you. It would be cruel. In the absence of your salary I am sure you have loved ones who would go hungry. Besides, it's only a plate. In this castle there are hundreds of plates."

"Yes—yes, Lord." Some of the terror drained from the man's face. He swept faster, trying to gather up every last shard and white splinter.

"However," Hymneth continued, "while I could care less about a plate, you broke something else. Something much more valuable."

"Something else, Lord?" The attendant looked around helplessly, seeing nothing but broken crockery and spilled baked goods. Next to him, the other servant was already backing away, straining desperately to make himself invisible, discorporeal, nonexistent.

"Yes." The Possessed sat up straighter in his grand chair. "My train of thought. And that I cannot abide." One huge, powerful arm rose slowly.

"No, Lord, please!"

The other attendant turned away and wrapped his arms around his head so he would not be able to see what was coming. A twitch of sickly green leaped from Hymneth's armored hand, writhing and coiling like a giant heartworm. It struck the kneeling servant on the back of his neck. Instantly his entire body arched rearward as if struck by a heavy hammer. With a muffled scream he snapped forward to lie prone on the floor, arms outstretched to both sides, unconscious.

Wearied by this constant need to discipline his staff, Hymneth slumped back into his chair and waved diffidently. "Take him out of here. Then come back and clean up the rest of this mess."

Shaking violently, the other servant slowly removed his hands from around his head and straightened. When he saw the figure of his friend lying on the floor, he screamed. It caught halfway in his throat, broken by the realization that the noise might offend the looming figure seated at the head of the table.

"Well?" the Possessed admonished him tersely. "Get on with it."

"Yes—yes, my Lord." Fighting to control his trembling, the other man reached down and grasped the unconscious servant by his wrists. Slowly, he began to drag the limp body from the room.

"Throw some water on him," Hymneth ordered. "He'll be all right. And maybe from now on he won't drop dishes when I'm thinking."

The other attendant did not reply. The Possessed's meaning was clear. Indeed, it would be much harder for the young servant to drop dishes or anything else. Because he now had four limbs to carry them with: his two arms, and the pair of slick, green, sucker-laden tentacles that had sprouted noisomely from his shoulders.

"And when he comes around, tell him that he's still on full pay!" Hymneth remembered to shout to the rapidly retreating menial.

Am I not the soul of tolerance and understanding? he thought. As always, it was a puzzlement to him why his people did not love him openly, instead of from within the pit of fear.

Dispensing such magnanimity always made him feel better. He had started to rise when Tergamet entered. One of his many advisers, he was subordinate to Peregriff, who was no doubt even now reviewing his Lord's schedule for the day. Tergamet was wise, and the master of a magnificent long beard, but he had a regrettable tendency to tell Hymneth what he thought the Possessed wanted to hear, instead of the truth. Perhaps this was understandable, in light of the warlock's occasional tendency to set ablaze specific portions of the anatomy of the attendants in his vicinity whenever a piece of particularly disagreeable news was conveyed to him. In that respect, he supposed Tergamet was braver than most.

"Yes, what is it?"

"And how is my Lord this morning?" The elderly adviser bowed as low as his aging back would allow.

"Impatient, as always. So don't bother inquiring after my condition. I know that you, as much as everyone else in this benighted pile of stone, would rejoice at the sight of me dead."

Tergamet fluttered a protesting hand. "Oh no, Lord! How can you think to say such a thing to me, one of your most trusted and loyal retainers!"

"I don't trust anyone, old man, and loyalty is a commodity to be bought, like expensive wine and cheap women." His irritation was growing. "What news? Not the harbor pilots again, with this nonsense about Krakens interfering with their work. I've told them how to fight back, and what poisons to use."

"No, Lord. It is not the harbor pilots." Eyes that still saw sharply rose to nearly meet his. "It is the Worm, Lord. It wishes to speak with you."

Hymneth considered, then nodded slowly. At this news, the two small eromakadi that attended his ankles danced excitedly around his legs. Termaget was careful to keep them in view. Simple contact with either one could suck the life out of a man. The Possessed they merely bounced off like agitated spaniels.

"The Worm, you say. What about?"

The senior adviser bowed again and spread his arms wide. "I do not know, my Lord. It will speak only to you."

"And quite properly so. Very good, Termaget. You may go."

"Thank you, Lord." Bowing and scraping, the old man retreated toward the main doorway. As he turned to depart, Hymneth considered whether to let the eromakadi take a playful nip at his heels. Nothing serious; just a week or so out of his remaining years. Days someone like Termaget would probably waste anyway. Hymneth decided against it, knowing that the old fellow probably would not see the humor in the situation.

His cape flowing behind him like blood running down the outside of a chalice, he exited the dining room. Instead of striding toward the audience chamber as he normally did this time of morning, he turned instead to his right in the middle of the main hall. The door there was bolted with a hex and locked with a spell, both of which yielded to the keys of his voice. He did not bother to seal it behind him. It would take a braver man or woman than dwelled in the castle to try the steps that began to descend immediately behind the door. Hex and spell were designed not to keep them out, but to seal something securely within.

Torches flared to life at his approach, the flames bowing briefly in his direction. As Hymneth descended the corkscrewing stairway, one of the eromakadi darted swiftly upward behind him to suck the life out of one torch. The flame screamed, a high-pitched conflagratory shriek, as it died. When Hymneth turned to reproach the black gust of horror, it hid behind its twin like a censured child.

Down the Lord of Ehl-Larimar went, below the sewers that carried water and waste away from the castle, below the dungeons where men and women and children wailed and whimpered in forgotten misery, below even the unshakable foundations of the massive fortress itself. Down until there was nothing left but the raw Earth—and the Pit that had been gouged from its heart.

At this depth nothing could live that basked in the light of the sun. In the perpetual darkness, things that rarely saw the surface burrowed and crept, mewling and cheeping softly to others of their own kind, hoping to avoid the mephitic, malodorous monstrosities armed with teeth and claw that would prey readily on anything that moved. An eerie glow came from the phosphorescent fungi that thrust bulbous, deformed stalks and heads above the surface of the Pit, giving it the appearance of some ghastly, unwholesome garden. In this place even the air seemed dead. All movement took place below the surface, out of sight, out of light.

Until Hymneth arrived, with eromakadi in tow.

Pausing on the last step, the final piece of clean, hewn stone that bordered the Pit, he gazed speculatively down into its depths. His boots, he knew, would require days of scrubbing to make them clean again. As he slowly lifted both arms up and out, his steady, sturdy voice shattered the diseased stillness.

"Alegemakh! Borun val malcuso. Show thyself, and speak!"

For a long moment there was nothing. No sound, no movement except the breathy stirring of the eromakadi. Then soil began to tremble, and shift, disturbed by some movement from below. Clumps of moist loam shuddered and individual particles of dirt bounced and quivered until at last they were thrust aside by something monstrous.

The Worm arose.

It burst forth from the earth, shedding dirt and uprooted fungi from its flanks. Pellucid mucus glistened along the length of its body. A length that no man, not even Hymneth the Possessed, had ever measured. The Worm might be ten feet long, or twenty, or a hundred. Or it might curl and coil all the way through to the other side of the Earth. No one knew. No one would ever know, because attempting the knowing meant death. Of all men, only Hymneth had power enough to meet the Worm in this place, chiseled out of the solid rock halfway between air and earth, and survive.

It lifted above him, shimmering and immense, its great tubular body arching forward like that of a questing serpent. Its upper girth, if not its length, was measurable. From where it emerged from the ground to its head it was as thick around as a good-sized tree. The last eight feet of it tapered to an almost comically small mouth, no bigger around than a barrel. From this darted and fluttered, like the tongue of a snake, a long, wet, flexible organ tipped with four tapering, sharp fangs that pointed forward. It was not a tongue, but a device for piercing the body of prey and sucking out their soft insides. The Worm's diet was varied—it would eat dirt as readily as blood.

Darting away from their master's side, the twin eromakadi began to feast on the light emitted by the bioluminescent fungi. Completely enveloping a helpless mushroom or toadstool, they would hover thus until its light had been consumed before moving on to another, leaving behind a shriveled and dying lump where before there had been life, however humble.

The Worm too pulsed with its own pale, necrotic glow, but they kept clear of that massive, hovering body. Not because they were afraid of it, but because they knew it was there to meet their master. And of all the things in the world, the eromakadi feared only Hymneth the Possessed.

Vestigial eyes no larger than small coins focused on the tall, armored figure waiting on the lowermost of the stone steps. Black as the eternal night in which they dwelled, they had neither pupils nor eyelids. But they recognized the tall figure. Long ago, Worm and man had struck an accord. Hymneth provided the Worm with—food. The Worm, in turn, kept a kind of watch over the realm of the Possessed. It had the ability to sense disturbances in That Which Had Not Yet Happened. The great majority of these it ignored.

But out on the fringes of the future it had detected something. Something active, and advancing, and imbued with might. In keeping with the covenant it had made with the man, it duly remarked upon this commotion.

"He comes. And he is not alone."

Hymneth had lowered his arms. As the eromakadi spread small deaths throughout the chamber, he concentrated on the tapering head of the Worm swaying high above his own. "Who comes, eater of dirt?"

The Worm's voice was a high hollowness. "A master of the necromantic arts. A questioner of all that is unanswered. One who seeks justice wherever he treads. He comes this way from across the Semordria."

"That is not possible. The eastern ocean is not a lake, to be crossed at will by casual travelers. They would have to travel far to the south, pass through the Straits of Duenclask, and then sail north against the current through the waters of the Aurreal."

"A strong boat guided by a bold Captain brings him, and the three who journey by his side."

"Only three?" Hymneth relaxed. This descent to the depths had been unnecessary after all. "That is a small army indeed."

"I render no judgment. I speak only of what I sense."

The Possessed chuckled softly, the crimson helmet reverberating with his laughter. "I will alert the navy to keep watch for any odd vessels entering the harbor. As always, I thank you for your attention, Worm. But in this matter your insight seems to be sorely lacking."

"Sense," the Worm whispered. "Not judgment." It was silent for several moments, its upper length weaving slowly back and forth above the churned surface of the Pit. "They come for the woman."

That piqued Hymneth's interest. "So the young Beckwith was not the last. I thought with putting paid to him and his crew I had seen the last of these misguided aristocrats. They worry me like fleas." He sighed. "Well, in the unlikely event that any of them should reach Ehl-Larimar I will tell Peregriff to alert the castle guards. But I have more confidence in the ocean. Even if they reach these shores my gunboats will stop them before they can cross the outer reefs." He shook his head sadly.

"You would think they would recognize who they were dealing with, and stop shipping their sons off to be slaughtered. The error of false pride. As if running this kingdom didn't make demands enough upon my time."

"Feed me." The immense, looming mass of the Worm swayed hypnotically back and forth, the flickering light of the stairway torches gleaming off its terrible piercing teeth. "I tire of soil. I have done my share. Feed me."

"Yes, yes," Hymneth replied irritably. He had already virtually forgotten all that the Worm had told him. As if a mere four possible invaders were anything to worry about, even if one happened to be a so-called master of the necromantic arts. There was only one dominating master of matters sorcerous and alchemical, and that was Hymneth the Possessed.

As he started back up the stairs he almost hoped these predicted intruders did manage to survive the impossible journey across the ocean. It had been a long time since he had fought a duel, and it would be good to have someone worthy to exercise his powers against. Though he doubted any of these potential assailants would qualify. To the best of his knowledge, there were no worthy masters living on the other side of the Semordria in the Thinking Kingdoms. For all the threat it posed to him, the Worm might as well have kept the information to itself and not disturbed him. He departed disappointed.

"Feed me!" The reverberant moan rose insistently behind him.

Where the stairs began to disappear upward, Hymneth paused to lean over and peer downward. The head of the Worm vacillated below him now. "For information like that you deserve nothing. But I am mindful of the covenant between us. I'm sure Peregriff can find a few condemned, or condemnable, to bring to you. The axman will gain a rest."

"I await." With a wet, sucking sound the Worm began to withdraw into the damp earth. It would lie there, Hymneth knew, with only its head above the surface, until the promised unfortunates were brought. Cast into the Pit, they would be pierced by the creature's mouth parts, their internal organs and muscles and flesh liquefied, and the consequent putrid, gelatinous mush sucked out. No one could complain, Hymneth mused virtuously, that his dungeons suffered from overcrowding.

As he climbed upward, the two eromakadi reluctantly left the last of the surviving fungi to accompany him, impenetrable black clouds that hovered at his heels. Occasionally they would show very small, slanted red eyes, but most of the time they kept themselves as black as pitch. Visitors who knew what they represented were as terrified by their silence as by their shapes.

Hymneth had mounted nearly to the top of the corkscrewing stairwell when a voice, pure and melodious as the golden bells of a benign spirit, called down to him accusingly.

"So this is where you spend your time. In the depths of the Earth, consorting with demons!"

Taken aback by the unexpected intrusion, he tilted his head to peer upward. High above him, a portrait of beauty unsurpassed gazed down. Not even the look of utter disgust on her face could mar the perfection of her countenance.

"My beloved Themaryl, this is business of state! Nothing more. I converse in the depths. I do not consort."

Her face furrowed with loathing. "You smell of things diseased and rotting. I thought—I thought we might talk, so I sought you out. I'm glad that I did, for it gave me the chance to see yet again your true self!" With that she whirled and fled upward, back to her rooms, back to the tower that she had made a prison for herself.

Bad timing, Hymneth thought in an agony of frustration. Of all the mornings and moments to parley with the Worm, of all the hours available to all the days, he had chosen the one time she had relented enough to descend from her steeple. Falling to his knees, he let out a cry of utter despair, knowing even as he did so that it would have no effect on her. Delighting in his anguish, the eromakadi clustered closer, inhaling of the darkness that had suddenly suffused his soul.

Slowly, his clenched fists fell away from the eye slits of his helmet. Someone had told her where he was. Someone had shown her where he was. Admittedly, he had decreed that she be given the run of the castle. But whatever fool had believed that included access to the Pit had, while displaying adherence to the letter of his command, shown excruciatingly bad judgment.

He rose to his feet. With all of Ehl-Larimar to administer and govern, he could not afford to tolerate those who exhibited bad judgment. Especially not those who did so in his own home, his sanctuary. When she had inquired as to his whereabouts, someone had taken her by the hand and guided her to the door that led to the Pit. It was a given. Mere directions would not have allowed her to find the unprepossessing door by herself, much less to enter.

Talk. She had thought they might talk. It had been months since she had said a word to him other than to demand that he return her to her home and people, and today, this morning, she had been ready to talk. A major breakthrough in their relationship shattered like cheap glass. Another setback when he might have hoped, just a little, for progress. And all because of someone's bad judgment.

That night the villagers who lived below the castle, on the slopes of the mountains, put cotton in the ears of their children and laid extra blankets across their beds. They slept in the same rooms with them, sharing their beds or lying on linens spread out on the floor. They made sure all animals were secured tightly in their barns and corrals, paddocks and pens. They did this because of the screaming that drifted down from the castle like black snow.

Up above, the unfortunate were being punished for a lack of good judgment. It went on all through the night. As dawn neared it grew so bad that even the bats fled the vicinity. The children slept, but their parents were not so lucky. One family lost two horses, dead from heart attacks, and another a brace of goats that, maddened by the sounds, broke free of their pens and fled into the forest, never to be seen again.

All told, the slope-dwelling citizens of Ehl-Larimar counted themselves lucky when the sun finally appeared over the mountaintops and the last of the shrieking died in a sudden, violent choking. They proceeded to go about their morning chores and business as if nothing had happened, as if the previous night had been only a bad dream, to be quickly forgotten like any bad dream. The women of the villages, however, found themselves with extra washing. Having spent the night oozing fearful sweat in great profusion, they and their husbands had stained many a nightdress beyond immediate reuse.

High above, government officials and administrators came and went, unaware of the frightfulness that had subsumed the fortress the night before. If they noticed anything out of the ordinary, it was that the castle's retainers moved a little faster than usual, and that they were less inclined to meet the eyes of visitors.

Far below, in the depths of the mountain, where earth met rock and where normal folk did not go, the Worm slept, its midsection swollen and bloated.

11

So still was the morning that the gull feather Simna let fall fell straight down. When it landed on the deck it just lay there, a puff of discarded dirty white that could easily be shifted by a waking woman's sigh. But it did not move.

It was more than an absence of wind. It was as if the air itself had become paralyzed, petrified in place. Though they had seen and experienced many things in their travels, the crew of the *Grömsketter* murmured superstitiously among themselves while anxiously watching the skies for any sign of movement. But the clouds themselves remained exactly where they had appeared at sunup. It was one thing for a ship to be becalmed, quite another for the upper reaches of the sky itself to grow still as death.

The only way they knew for certain that they still lived in the realm of air was because they continued to breathe. It was possible to make a breeze by blowing, as Simna demonstrated when he dropped to all fours and blew hard against the abandoned feather. It scudded a little ways across the deck, twisting and flipping, before it settled once more into a motionless, trancelike state.

Just above the helm deck Stanager Rose stood in the rigging, shading her eyes with one hand as she surveyed the surrounding sea. It was smooth as a mirror, undisturbed by wave or, more importantly, wind. They were two days' sail out from the delta of the Eynharrowk on a due westerly heading, and no longer moving. Nothing was moving. Even the seabirds had deserted them in search of wind to help support their wings. It was uncanny, it was worrisome, and it was hot.

"Never been becalmed like this before," she murmured.

On the deck below, Hunkapa Aub was chatting with Priget, the helmswoman, and trying to learn something about the basics of open-ocean navigation. She had plenty of time to talk to him since the ship's wheel, left unattended, was not moving. Ahlitah lay on the main deck, sleeping in the shade. The utter absence of a breeze was making the morning too hot even for him. Simna ibn Sind had tied a strip of colorful cloth around his forehead to soak up some of the perspiration. Though as unhappy with the unnatural stillness as anyone else aboard, the sight of Stanager Rose clinging to rigging helped to mitigate his unease.

Etjole Ehomba stood just below and to one side of the troubled Captain. Though no mariner, he knew well the moods of the sea, and right now the Semordria was not behaving in a proper maritime fashion. He had experienced still air before, while standing on different beaches in the vicinity of his village, but never anything like this. Heavy, hot, and stagnant, it tempted a man to take a whip to it, as if the very components of the atmosphere themselves had gone to sleep.

Stanager climbed down from the rigging. "The longer we sit here, the more of our supplies we waste. Too much of this and we'll be forced to return to the delta to reprovision."

"We could eat less," Ehomba proposed, "and catch rainwater to supplement the ship's stores."

"If it rains," she replied. "I don't gamble with the lives of my crew. Or my passengers."

"Do you ever gamble?" Simna's forced cheerfulness fooled no one.

"Only when it's a sure thing." Ignoring him as usual, she strained to see past the bow. "May have to try kedging, but in which direction I haven't decided. It would pain me to have to tuck tail and go back to the delta." She squinted upward. All sails were set, and hung loose as dead ghosts from both masts.

"What's this 'kedging'?" Simna wanted to know.

She sighed. "Landsmen. We lower all the small boats and put the anchors in them. They row out as far as the lines will go, then drop anchor. This pulls the ship forward. Raise anchors and repeat, as many times as necessary until a breeze fills the sails. It's hot, hard work. A last resort for desperate sailors."

"I cannot go backward," Ehomba told her. "I have spent too much time already just in going forward."

"Then find me some wind," she declared curtly, "so we can escape these cursed doldrums!"

"The sky-metal sword!" Simna blurted. "Surely even a moment's work with that would bring down enough wind to move the ship."

Stanager frowned. "What is the mad elf blabbering about?"

"Something possible, but dangerous." Reaching back, Ehomba wrapped his fingers around the haft of the sword. Simna looked on expectantly. Among those aboard the *Grömsketter,* only he knew what that enchanted blade of otherworldly metal was capable of in the hands of his tall friend.

Reluctantly, Ehomba released his grip. Simna looked pained.

"Why the hesitation, bruther?"

"It is a chancy thing to consider, Simna, and not something to be attempted in haste. I have to think first how best to go about it. Too little wind is not a problem. But too much wind could shred the sails or even capsize the ship. And what if I thrust it wrongly to the heavens and call down another piece of sky? Here there are no holes in the ground for us to hide in, and nowhere to run."

"That's fine, Etjole." The swordsman made placating motions. "Take your time. Decide how to hold the weapon, which way to point it, what angle to incline the blade against the Earth. Only when you're satisfied that you know what you're doing should you go ahead."

Ehomba eyed his friend speculatively. "And if I'm not satisfied?"

Simna shrugged. "Then we sit. And sweat. And try to think of something else."

A thin smile curled the Captain's delectable upper lip. "I've heard you boasting endlessly to the crew, swordsman. Perhaps we should put you in a small boat behind the *Grömsketter* and let you jabber there all you wish. Maybe that would generate hot air enough to fill the mains'l just enough to get us moving."

He smiled back. "You don't like me very much, do you, Captain?"

"Not very much, no. If you were under my command, I'd have you swabbing decks and bailing bilges all the way to Doroune."

"I wouldn't mind being under your command, Stanager—depending on the commands, of course." He grinned irrepressibly.

She turned away, disgusted. "You are incorrigible!"

"Actually, I'm from a little village near Rakosy. Incorrigible is a bigger town that lies to the northwest."

"Boat ho!"

At the cry, everyone tilted their heads back to look up at the mainmast. The lookout was gesturing slightly to port.

It took the better part of an hour for the small, single-masted craft to drift into view. Stolid and unimpressive, a wholly utilitarian little boat, its aft half was piled high with pilchard and sardine, so much so that it rode lower in the water than otherwise would have been expected. Nets fashioned of strong cord and spotted with cork floats hung from the boom and over the sides. Its lone sail hung as limp from the mast as did those of the *Grömsketter.*

The single occupant was busy hauling in one of the nets, but not too busy to wave at the much larger vessel.

"Ayesh!" the fisherman sang out. "What ship?"

From near the bow, the first mate responded. "Good fishing?" Terious added by way of making conversation.

Grinning through his white-flecked beard, the lone sailor gestured at his catch. "As you see."

"You're not afraid to be out of sight of land, all by yourself?" the mate inquired. Several of the other members of the crew had moved to the railing to watch the discourse. In the detestable stillness, any diversion was a welcome one.

"Not I. Crice is the name, sir, and I am known throughout the delta for my bravery." He indicated his mast and sail. "I know the winds hereabouts better than any man, you see, and am always confident of finding one to carry me home."

Cupping her hands to her mouth, Stanager shouted across to the solitary harvester of the sea. "Ayesh, can you find one for us, good sir? We have been stalled here this past day and a half."

"Sorry." He waved again. "I have the last of my catch to bring in and then I must return home. You know that every ship must find its own wind. Not all have my skill."

Stanager flushed, her cheeks reddening. It was an oblique insult and probably unintended, but it still set the Captain's blood to racing. When it came to seamanship, she took a back seat to no man or woman. This solitary sailor who stank of fish guts and oil was taunting her, albeit gently.

Persistent he might be, even irritating, but Simna knew when to keep his mouth shut. Observing the look on the Captain's beauteous face, he sidled away from her and closer to Ehomba.

"What do you think, long bruther?" He nodded in the direction of the little fishing boat. "Is his an empty boast?"

"I was admiring his catch." Ehomba gestured at the glistening mound that weighed down the boat. "All small fish, all silver of side. Very difficult to see under normal conditions. When looking down into the water from the deck of a boat, it is hard to separate such a school from sunlight. But in these conditions, with the surface absolutely calm and undisturbed by wind, they would stand out much more clearly to a man with a net."

Simna's brows furrowed. "So the man is a good fisherman and brave to boot. What of that?"

"While he has been working and talking I have been studying everything on his boat. Though more than a little windy himself, I think he is no natural master of wind. He does not have the look. But there is no mistaking the confidence he has in his seamanship." Raising his voice, he called out to their visitor.

"Gatherer of fish, that is a most unusual bottle I see resting by your tiller. Though large and well blown it does not appear to hold drink, or anything else. Yet I espy something moving within. What does it contain?"

So startled by this unexpected inquiry was the fisherman that he dropped the net he was hauling in, letting it splash back over the gunwale. Once back in the water its contents, writhing and convulsing, wildly finned their way to freedom.

"It's only a bottle, sir. You have—remarkable eyes."

"From watching over my herd, looking out for predators. What is in the bottle?" Everyone on board the *Grömsketter* was watching Ehomba now. Men and women who had been resting in the shade rose from their places to crowd the railing.

"Nothing, good sir." Ignoring the fact that he had just lost the majority of his most recent catch, the fisherman resumed hauling in the one net that remained hanging over the side. He looked and sounded slightly agitated. "It's just an empty bottle that I carry about with me. For storing caught rainwater."

Simna was staring at his tall friend. Etjole was on to something, had seen something, he knew. But what? Now that the herdsman had singled it out, he too located the large bottle that rested near the tiller of the small boat. It was big enough to hold several gallons, with a bulbous body and a narrow, tapering neck that terminated in an elaborate metallic stopper the color of pewter. Hard as he stared, he could not discern any contents.

Ehomba, however, felt differently. Strongly enough to argue about it.

"I can see movement within the glass. To catch rainwater anyone would use a bottle with a much wider mouth. I know: I have had to do so in dry country on more than one occasion. So what is it, fisherman? Why are you lying to us?"

When the last of the net had been hauled in and piled on the deck of the little craft, its owner took a seat in the stern, resting one arm on the tiller. "You have no weapons that can reach me or you would have shown them by now. So I will tell you, landlord of sharp eyes. The knowledge will do you no good."

Baffled, Stanager had moved to stand close to Simna. "What nonsense is he prattling?" she whispered. "I can make sense neither of what he is saying nor of your friend."

Inclining his head close to hers, the swordsman murmured a reply. "I'm not sure, but Ehomba is a strange man. A good friend, to be sure. Straightforward and dependable. But different from such as you and I. He knows many things. I believe him to be a great sorcerer."

"What, him?" Almost, she laughed aloud. Almost.

"Say then that he is a sometime student of that which would mystify the rest of us. If he says there's something in that bottle, then I believe him, though I can't see it myself." He pointed. "It lies there, by the stern."

"I see it," she admitted, leaning closer. After a moment she shook her head dubiously. "It looks empty to me."

"Hoy, but then why is our trawling friend looking so uneasy, and speaking of weapons? Could it be that the bottle contains something of great value, whose nature he is wary of revealing?" In the course of their intense whispering his arm had slipped around her waist. Intent upon the byplay between herdsman and fisher, she took no notice of it, and thus allowed it to remain in place.

Lifting the bottle by its narrow neck, Crice held it up for all to see. Half the crew saw only a thick-walled container, perfectly blown and devoid of bubbles in the glass, sealed with a peculiarly sculpted pewter stopper. Among the rest there were many who thought they saw movement within the translucent vessel. Given the distance between the two craft, it was difficult to say what, if anything, occupied the bottle's interior. But it was now clear to the most sharp-eyed among the crew that something did.

Whatever it was, Ehomba had been first to espy it. Among them all, he was the only one to have an idea what it might be. Convinced of his invincibility, the fisherman proceeded to confirm the herdsman's suspicions.

"Here's your wind, sailors! You think yourselves masters of the sea and all that's above and below it—but I, Crice, command the air!" He held the glass container a little higher. "Here in this bottle I have all the wind that covers this portion of the sea. Found it at the bottom of a chest in a ruined ship. Must have been a thousand years old, she was, and reeking of magic fantastic and decayed. But the stopper on this bottle was intact, and I, yes I, discovered by myself how to open and close it. I let a little out when I need it and keep the rest shut up when I don't." He gestured at the perfectly flat, motionless water on which both craft floated. "That way I can see the fish I seek as clearly as if looking through a window. When I have enough, I let out just the right amount of wind in precisely the appropriate direction to carry me home."

"No wonder he's not afraid to travel out of sight of land," Simna whispered. His hand tightened a little on the Captain's waist.

"Not if he can control all the wind in this part of the ocean, no." Pressing forward against the railing, Stanager raised her voice. "Ayesh, fisherman, can you not let us have back a little of that wind?"

"Every ship must find its own," he reiterated implacably. "And if I give some to you, that will mean less for my sail. How much do you think a bottle like this can hold, anyway? I found the bottle, I captured the wind, and now it's mine! Seek out your own breezes."

Sitting back down in the stern, he pointed the neck of the bottle toward his mast. Slowly and very carefully, he unscrewed the pewter stopper just a little.

Emerging from the glass alembic, a gust of wind immediately filled his small sail, sending its thrusting curve billowing outward. Seeing this, several sailors on board the *Grömsketter* looked to their own masts, only to see their own sails luffing uselessly against spar and line. Yet to look at the little boat was to see it beginning to accelerate with a freshening breeze astern. Except no breeze advanced from the vicinity of the stern. It had emerged straight from the bottle that the fisherman was now firmly restoppering.

"Etjole, do something!" Simna blurted anxiously. At the same time, Stanager became aware of the arm coiled around her waist and stepped away. Her expression was a mixture of anger and—something else. "If he gets away with all the wind from this part of the sea we could be stuck here for weeks!"

"I know." Ehomba had not taken his eyes from the little boat heavily laden with fish and its contrary master. "I need a stone."

"A stone?" Simna knew better than to question his companion. If Ehomba had declared that he needed a purple pig, the swordsman would have done his best to find one.

Actually, on board a ship the size of the *Grömsketter*, finding the pig might have been the easier task. Of all the lands they had journeyed through together, of all the astounding places they had visited and countries they had traversed, here was the first that was devoid of stones, and here the first time Ehomba had required one.

"Ballast!" the swordsman yelped. "There must be ballast in the hold!"

Stanager was quick to disappoint him. "We carry base metals. Ingots of iron and copper that we can trade with the inhabitants of the towns on the other side of the Semordria. You'll find no rock in the belly of the *Grömsketter.*"

"Well then, there must be at least one stone somewhere on this ship! Firestone in the galley, to protect her wooden walls."

The Captain shook her head sadly. "Firebrick."

"In someone's sea chest, then. A memento of home, a worry stone, anything! If Ehomba says that he needs a stone, that means he needs—" Simna broke off, gaping at his tall friend.

Reaching into a pocket of his kilt, the herdsman had removed the small cotton sack of "beach pebbles" he had carried with him all the way from his home village. As Simna looked on, Ehomba selected the largest remaining, a flawless five-carat diamond of deeper blue hue than the surrounding sea, and shoved the remaining stones back in his pocket.

"No, long bruther." The swordsman gestured frantically. "Not that. We'll find you a rock. There's got to be a rock somewhere on this barge; an ordinary, everyday, commonplace, worthless rock. Whatever it is you're thinking of doing—don't."

The herdsman smiled apologetically at his friend. In his hand he held a stone worth more than the swordsman could hope to earn in a lifetime. In two lifetimes. And somehow, Simna knew his friend was not planning to convert it into ready currency.

"Sorry, my friend. There is no time." Pivoting, he returned his gaze to the little boat, now starting to pick up speed beneath the press of the freed breeze its sail had captured. "Soon he will be out of range."

"I don't care what—" the swordsman halted in midcomplaint. "Out of range? Out of range of what?"

"Rocks," Ehomba explained simply—so simply that it was not an explanation at all, but only another puzzlement. Raising his voice, he directed his words to the retreating fisherman. "Truly you are the master of winds! But you must control them through spells and magicks. No mere bottle that fits in a man's lap can contain more than the air that Nature has already placed inside."

"You think not, do you?" The fisherman turned in his seat, one arm resting easily on the tiller. "You'd be surprised, traveler, what a bottle can hold."

"Not a bottle that small," Ehomba yelled back. "I wager it is not even made of glass, but some marvel of the alchemist's art instead!"

"Oh, it's glass, all right. Alchemist's glass perhaps, but glass incontestably. See?" Holding the bottle aloft and grinning, he tapped the side with a small marlinspike. The smooth, slightly greenish material clinked sharply.

As soon as the fisherman had begun to lift the bottle, Ehomba had placed the blue diamond in his mouth. At first a startled Simna suspected that the herdsman intended to swallow it, though for what purpose or reason he could not imagine. Not knowing what to think, Stanager had simply looked on in silence.

That was when Ehomba began to inhale. Simna ibn Sind had seen his friend inhale like that only once before, when on the Sea of Aboqua he had consumed an entire eromakadi. But there was no darkness here, no ominous roiling haze with luminous red eyes, not even a stray storm cloud. The sky, like the air, was transparent.

The herdsman's chest expanded—and expanded, and swelled, until it seemed certain he would burst. Those members of the crew close enough to see what was happening gawked open-mouthed at the phenomenon of the distending herdsman while Stanager, brave as she was, began to back away from that which she could not explain and did not understand. Hunkapa Aub looked up in dumb fascination while Ahlitah, as usual, slept on, oblivious to what was happening around him.

Just when it seemed that the skin of the herdsman's chest must surely rupture, exploding his internal organs all over the deck and railing, he exhaled. To say explosively would be to do injustice to the sound that emerged from his chest and mouth. It reverberated like gunpowder, echoing across not only the deck but the sea as well. The force of it blew its perpetrator backwards, lifting Ehomba's feet off the deck and sending him crashing into the smaller railing that delimited the fore edge of the helm deck. Hunkapa ran over to make sure the herdsman was all right.

As for Simna, he remained at the railing, realizing that Ehomba had expelled more than just air. There had been one other thing in his mouth, and it was not his tongue that had been violently discharged across the water.

In the little boat, the disdainful fisherman was preparing to tap his bottle a second time with the metal marlinspike to demonstrate the qualities of its composition when the ejected diamond struck it squarely in the middle, shattering the glass and sending green-tinted shards flying in all directions. The fisherman had barely an instant to gape at the ruined container, its neck and stopper still clutched tightly in one hand, before the winds it had held burst to freedom.

All the winds that had swept a section of sea greater than a man could see in any direction, and all of it released at once.

"Etjole, you right still?" The shaggy countenance of Hunkapa Aub was leaning low over his lanky friend. Ehomba sat, dazed but conscious, against the railing.

"I am . . ." he started to reply. Then a sound reached his ears—a rising sound—and he yelled out even as he wrapped his arms tightly around the nearest post. "Grab something and hang on! Everybody grab someth—"

The liberated winds struck the *Grömsketter* amidships, howling like a thousand crazed goblins suddenly released from an asylum for insane spirits as they tore through the masts and rigging. Struck hard enough to cause the sturdy vessel to heel sharply to starboard. For a terrifying moment, in the midst of that awesome roar, Stanager was afraid the ship was going to turn turtle. Her list reached seventy degrees. But as the initial blast began to subside, the ballast in her hold asserted itself. With maddening slowness, she began to roll back onto an even keel.

Clinging to the rigging, her skin and clothing soaked with gale-driven spray, the Captain screamed orders to the crew. Stays were drawn taut, the mainsail boom secured, the wheel steadied. Somehow, the sails held. Working his way aft, Terious Kermarkh silently blessed a succession of unnamed sailmakers. Tough fabric caught the wind and contained it.

But with demented gusts blowing from every direction, the sails kept wrapping themselves around the masts, making it impossible for the ship to maintain a heading, any heading. In the teeth of the disordered, chaotic gale there was no choosing a course.

Terious fought his way to within shouting distance of the helm deck. Standing below, he yelled up to the wheel. "Captain, we've got to get out of this! We're starting to take on water!"

"Keep the fores'l reefed, Mr. Kermarkh! All hands hold to stations!" Maintaining a firm grip on a storm line, her experienced sea legs absorbing the impact of every pitch and roll, she staggered over to where Hunkapa Aub and Simna ibn Sind hovered solicitously over their tall friend. Awakened from his sleep by the sudden, unexpected storm, the black litah stood nearby. The heaving, pitching deck did not concern him, not with four sets of powerful claws at his disposal to dig into the wood.

"Mr. Ehomba, you've taken us from the doldrums to the roaring forties, from not a ghost of a breeze to all the winds of the four corners of the compass. But they've been let loose all together and all at once, and as a consequence blow from all directions unaligned. You got us into this, now you have to get us out, or we'll sit here and spin like a top until we sink!"

Still dazed from the blow to the back of his head, Ehomba accepted the help of his friends to rise. Simna helped him up. Once erect, Hunkapa embraced him in an immovable grasp that held him steady.

Observing the anarchic weather that had enveloped the *Grömsketter,* Ehomba thanked his friends and told Hunkapa to release him. The broad-shouldered man-beast complied reluctantly. All kept a wary watch on the herdsman as he half climbed, half slid down the steps that led to the main deck and disappeared below. Moments later he emerged with the sky-metal sword gripped tightly in one hand.

Simna eyed him uncertainly. Along with everyone else, he had to shout to make himself heard above the howl of clashing winds. "Hoy, long bruther, what do you want with that? We need less wind, not more of it!"

"Not less, Simna." Ehomba wiped perspiration from his eyes and forehead. "What we have is what we need. It only wants some guidance."

Climbing back onto the helm deck, he made his way to the stern railing. There he tried to assume a solid stance, but the pitching and rolling of the ship made it impossible. Without using at least one hand to grip a stay or line, he kept stumbling from side to side, forward or back. Leaning against the railing helped a little, but when the bow of the *Grömsketter* rose sharply, the motion threatened to pitch him over the side.

"This is not working," he declared aloud.

"I can see that, bruther!" Spitting seawater, Simna clung to the railing next to him. "What do you need? What do you want?" Spume-flecked wind shrieked in their ears.

"My feet nailed to the deck, but that could cause problems later." Grimly searching the ship, the herdsman espied the big cat standing foursquare and four-footed to the left of the helm, as stable as the mainmast. "Ahlitah! I need your help!"

"What now?" Grumbling, the cat released its grip on the battered teak and turned. His extended claws held the decking as firmly as crampons on a glacier.

"I need someone to brace me," Ehomba told him. "Can you do it?"

The big cat considered, yellow eyes glowing like lamps in the darkness of the rising storm. When lightning flashed, it was the same color as the master of the veldt's pupils. "It'll be awkward. My forelegs are not arms."

Ehomba pondered, then shouted again. "Hunkapa! Brace yourself against Ahlitah and hold me! Hold me as high up as you can!"

"Yes, Etjole! Hunkapa do!"

The litah set itself immovably against the back railing, the claws of each paw nailing themselves to the deck. Then Hunkapa Aub stepped across the cat's back and straddled him, locking his shaggy ankles beneath the feline belly. With Hunkapa thus anchored to the litah, and Ahlitah fastened firmly to the deck, Hunkapa put huge, hirsute hands around the herdsman's waist and lifted him skyward. The *Grömsketter* rocked in the wind and waves, she rolled and pitched, but on her helm deck the unlikely pyramid of cat, man-beast, and herdsman rode rigid and straight.

Holding the haft of the sky-metal sword in both hands, Ehomba raised the otherworldly blade skyward, lifting it into the storm. When the flat, etched blade began to glow an impossibly deep, spectral blue, Simna immediately sought cover from something that he knew was more powerful than the conflicted storm itself.

A gust struck the pulsating glow—and bounced off, shearing away to the west. A complete concentrated squall bore down on Ehomba, only to find itself shattered into a thousand timid zephyrs. Swinging the great blade, secure in Hunkapa Aub's powerful grasp, Ehomba battled the winds.

No stranger to danger, Stanager crouched close by Simna and looked on in astonishment. "Ayesh, I was wrong to doubt you about your friend: It's a sorcerer he is!"

"Hoy, ask and he'll tell you it's not him but the sword that wreaks the magic. A sword he did not make himself, but that was given to him. No wizard he, he'll tell you again and again. Just a herder of cattle and sheep lucky enough to have learned friends."

She looked at him through the wind and rain. "Then which is he, Simna? What is the truth?"

"The truth?" He considered a moment, then broke out in the irrepressible grin that, when words failed, defined him. "The truth is a riddle wrapped in an enigma—or sometimes in a nice piece of hot flat bread fresh from the oven. That's my friend Etjole."

Stanager Rose was a woman of exceptional beauty and competence—but not a great deal of humor. "In other words, you don't know whether he's actually an eminent alchemist, or just a vector for the sorcery of others."

Simna nodded, rain dripping from his hair and chin. "Just so. But this I do know: I've seen renowned swordsmen battle a dozen skilled opponents at a time, I've seen them fight off beasts armed with fang and claw, I've watched others deflect the attacks of mosquitoes the size of your arm and thorn trees with minds of their own—but this is the first time I've seen anyone use a blade to fence with wind!"

Indeed, Ehomba was not merely parrying the gusts that swirled around him, but doing so in a manner that saw one after another line up aft of the ship. Deflected by the weaving, arcing sword and its attendant indigo aurora, gale after gale was forcefully merged to blow steadily from astern. Gradually the *Grömsketter* stopped sailing in ragged circles and resumed a westerly heading. The storm continued to rage, but now the bulk of it, aligned by blows from Ehomba's blade, raged from directly behind the ship, driving it across the wild Semordria in the direction it had originally been traveling.

Steer the winds as he might, Ehomba could not subdue them, not even with the wondrous sword. Priget once more gained control of the helm, and managed to keep the ship on course, but before the herdsman had been able to get the winds organized and under control the *Grömsketter* had taken a terrible beating.

"We need a respite." Stanager had taken one half of the wheel, opposite her helmswoman. "A blow from the blow." She flung her head to one side and slightly back, flipping sodden red hair out of her face. "An island in whose protected lee we could shelter would be best, but none lie close on our chosen heading." Tilting back her head, she examined the storm-swept sky. "Of course, we are no longer sailing on our original heading. I think we have been blown many leagues northward."

"Put me down, Hunkapa." As the hulking biped obediently complied, Ehomba smiled up at him. "You did well, my hairy friend. Are you all right?"

Through the rain and darkness the bulky figure beamed at him. "Hunkapa like to help. Hunkapa strong!" Long, powerful arms reached up and out, as if to encompass all ocean and sky.

"Strong enough." The herdsman blinked away rain, staring forward. Simna was at his side, trying to follow his friend's line of sight.

"What is it, bruther? What do you see? An island?" His tone was hopeful. Not that he cared overmuch for the condition of the *Grömsketter,* so long as she continued to float, but as a landsman raised on open plains and prairies, he felt himself overdue to stand on something that did not precipitously and unpredictably drop away from beneath his feet.

"No, not an island," Ehomba replied as softly as he could, given the need to be heard above the wind. "Something else." Turning, he addressed the stalwart redhead. "Captain, I think if you head your ship fifteen degrees to port you may find the respite you are looking for!"

Squinting into the squall, she tried to descry what her singular passenger was pointing out. "I don't see anything, Mr. Ehomba."

"Please, call me Etjole. If you do not see anything, then you *are* seeing it."

Her expression contorted and she barked at the tall southerner's companion. "Simna! What nonsense is he talking?"

The swordsman could only shrug. "Sorcerers speak a language unto themselves, but I've learned these past many weeks to heed his advice. If he says to sail toward nothing, I'd be the first man to set my helm for it."

Stanager mulled over this second suggested absurdity in succession. "I see no harm in sailing toward nothing." Her gaze drifted upward.

"The storm holds steady behind us. A little to port or starboard will not strain the stays any more than they already are. Helm to port!" she ordered Priget. Working in concert, the two women forced the wheel over.

It was late afternoon before they arrived at the place Ehomba had espied through the depths of the tempest. It was not, as he had told Simna, an island. Nor was it land of any kind. But it was a place of calm, and rest, in the midst of raging windblown chaos. That did not mean it was a haven for the exhausted crew of the *Grömsketter* and their battered ship. What the herdsman had seen and what they were about to enter into proffered an entirely unnatural and potentially perilous tranquillity. It was a valley.

A valley in the sea.

111

The bowl-shaped depression in the ocean's otherwise unbroken expanse was large enough to hold most of Hamacassar. Through the fulminating winds they could see that the ocean sloped gently down into the glassy green basin on all four sides. Attempting to analyze the impossibility, Stanager would have ordered the *Grömsketter* hard to starboard to avoid it, but there was no time. One moment the ship was thundering westward, driven by gales whipped into line by Ehomba's parrying blade. Then its bow was tilting downward into a trough the likes of which no sailor aboard had ever seen.

The concavity lay not between the crests of two waves, but between four uniquely stable oceanic slopes. Several women and not a few of the men held their breath as the ship's keel began to slide downward at a perilously sharp angle. As she descended she picked up speed, though not a great deal. It was not so very different from sailing upon level waters, save for the fact that a mariner had to guard against sliding along the deck until he fetched up against the bow.

The unrelenting gusts that had been flailing the ship from astern immediately began to moderate in intensity. Pounding squalls became gentle breezes. Ehomba estimated that the floor of the valley lay little more than a hundred feet below the surrounding surface of the ocean proper. Not a great difference, but one sufficient to provide them with a safe haven while the winds liberated from the mysterious bottle blew themselves out overhead.

They could hear those freed siroccos and emancipated mistrals blustering and raging overhead, but they did not blow down into the olivine depression to roil the serene waters. There was no perceptible current; only a gentle lapping of wavelets against the tired sides of the ship.

Climbing down out of the rigging, Stanager confronted her tall, laconic passenger. "For someone who's never been to sea, you seem to know much of its secrets."

Ehomba smiled gently. "I have lived by the shore all my life. The Naumkib learn to swim before they can walk. And there are many in the village who have been farther out on the waters than I. A wise man is a sponge who soaks up the experiences of others."

With an acknowledging grunt, she studied the walls of water that formed the basin. "I would've preferred the lee of an island."

"This was the only refuge I saw," he replied apologetically.

"I'm not complaining, mind." As the *Grömsketter* rocked contentedly in the mild swells, she turned and shouted commands. "Terious! Tell Uppin the carpenter to pick a crew to help him and have him get started on the necessary repairs. Once they've begun, see to the sails and rigging. Choose two men to settle the mess belowdecks!"

"Ayesh, Captain!" Turning, the first mate commenced to issue orders of his own.

Scrutinizing the enclosing green slopes, Stanager remained uneasy. "This valley we've slipped into; will it stay stable? If these walls decide to collapse in upon us, we'll become instant chum."

"When the old people of my village who have the most experience with the sea mention such a place, they speak of it as something that lingers long. I think we will be all right here. How long will it take your people to make the ship right again?"

She deliberated. "The damage is not crippling, but if left unattended to, it would surely have become so. We've a full day's work ahead of us, more likely two."

"Good!" Simna, for one, was not disappointed. Leaning on the rail, he surveyed their implausible surroundings. "I could do with a couple days of knowing where my legs are going to be at all times. Not to mention my belly." He glanced hopefully at the herdsman. "If this phenomenon is as steadfast as you say, bruther, maybe we could lower one of the small boats and do some fishing."

"I do not see why you could not," Ehomba replied encouragingly.

"Why not fish from the *Grömsketter*?" Stanager frowned at him.

"My tackle won't reach the water."

"Tackle?" Her puzzlement deepened in tandem with her frown. "I didn't notice any fishing gear among your baggage."

He winked at her. "You were looking at the wrong baggage." Turning, he yelled down in the direction of the mainmast, where a large black, furry mass lay half asleep, purring sonorously. "Hoy, kitty! Feel like some fresh fish?"

The litah yawned majestically. "I told you not to call me that. But I always feel like fresh fish."

"Then I'll be right down." Passing the Captain, the swordsman arched his eyebrows at her. "That's my tackle."

The sounds of hammering and sawing rose from the main deck where Uppin the carpenter and his commandeered assistants were already hard at work making preparations to carry out the necessary repairs to the ship. Something rose up behind Ehomba and the Captain, shading them from the intermittent sun.

"Hunkapa go fish too?"

"Not this time, my friend." Ehomba smiled sympathetically. "A little enthusiasm on your part goes a long way. I can see you catching a fish and in the excitement of the moment, drenching Simna and Ahlitah all over again." He indicated the bustle of fresh activity that filled the main deck. "Why not see if you can help the crew with their work? I am sure they could use an extra pair of strong hands."

More than human teeth flashed amidst the gray hair. "Good idea, friend Etjole. Hunkapa strong! Hunkapa go and help."

Stanager watched him descend to the main deck in a single, booming hop that disdained use of the stairs. "Sometime you must tell me how you came to gain the allegiance of two such remarkable creatures."

Ehomba grinned. "Simna would be upset that you left him out."

She snorted derisively. "In my time I've had to deal with all too many puffed-up, self-important vagabonds and mercenaries like him. He aspires to far more than he can ever hope to attain."

"Do not underestimate him. He swaggers like a farmyard cock, but he is brave, courageous, and, to a certain degree I have yet to measure accurately, true."

"I know what he is," she retorted sharply. "The question is, what are you, Etjole Ehomba?" One toughened yet surprisingly soft shoulder pushed, perhaps accidentally, perhaps not, against his side.

"What I am, Captain, is a humble herder of cattle and sheep. One with a loving wife and two fine children, whom I do not fail to miss every day of this seemingly eternal journey."

Eyes green as the sea and nearly as deep peered up at him. "Every day?" she inquired meaningfully. When he nodded slowly, she sighed and turned her gaze back to the panorama of sweeping liquid slopes and calm surface. "Ordinarily I have no time for landsmen, not even one who knows as much of the sea as yourself. Terious now; ayesh, there's a man!"

"A fine fellow," Ehomba agreed, perhaps a shade too quickly.

She noticed, and cut her eyes at him. "Do I make you nervous, herdsman?"

He composed his reply carefully, but sincerely. "Captain, until recently I would not have thought it possible for a flower to survive with only seawater to nurture it. Yet it not only survives, but blooms as brightly as any land-based blossom."

She smiled. "That's the difference between you and your friend." She indicated the longboat from which a chortling Simna ibn Sind and lightning-fast Ahlitah were hauling in all manner of edible fish. "I've always preferred the artful to the impertinent." Pushing back from the railing, she faced him squarely. "I have to go and supervise the repair work. I've known many men who, at the drop of a sailmaker's needle, will extol the surpassing virtues of their home port until a listener's ears grow numb. When those same men find themselves far from home in strange and stormy waters, they are grateful when a calm and inviting harbor makes itself known."

He smiled. "Though no mariner, I consider myself an experienced navigator in such matters."

"Then you should know that when in uncharted seas and hoping for a good night's rest it's the smart sailor who seeks a tight berth instead of a loose mooring." With that she brushed past him and descended to the main deck.

Simna's excited whooping and hollering as Ahlitah pulled in one fish after another with great, swift sweeps of his paws drew Ehomba's attention back to the water off the port side. Overhead, the liberated winds were finally starting to dissipate, borne aloft on their own wild energy as they dispersed to the four corners of the world. With its calm green slopes, mild temperature, and gentle breezes, the valley was a wonderfully tranquil space. A man could make a life in such a place, he mused, save for the fact that he would immediately begin to sink and drown. It belonged to the fishes, and to the seaweed that rode its small waves in broad, thick mats, and to the seabirds that from time to time descended raucously to hunt for fry and fingerlings among the lazily drifting greenery.

It reminded him of the beaches below the village, of a home that was distant in space and becoming increasingly distant in time. Glancing to his left as he leaned on the rail, he saw the shape of Stanager Rose stalking back and forth among her crew, barking orders and encouragement. Dangerously distant, he thought as he resolutely returned his attention to his two mismatched companions and their exuberant efforts to mine the piscine realm of its subsurface riches.

True to her estimate, the last repairs to the *Grömsketter* were completed by late afternoon of the following day. Fatigued but elated, Stanager emerged from her cabin and the luxury of a Captain's private sun-heated shower to join her passengers on the helm deck. Below as well as aloft, the reinvigorated crew was making final preparations for departure, as much rejuvenated by the respite from sailing and rough weather as was their ship.

Stanager refused to let the concern that had nagged at her ever since their arrival in the sanctuary dilute her high spirits. "All is in readiness," she told her guests. "We can leave now or on the morrow and resume our course westward. I have ciphered our position. Though we were blown far north into waters I do not know, the necessary adjustments are straightforward enough. We will sail a little more to the south, and still arrive at the trading port of Doroune less than a week later than originally planned. We carry more than enough stores to sustain us through the delay." She contemplated the placid waters.

"There is only one element I cannot account for, and that my experience is not equal to." Raising a hand, she gestured over the railing. It did not matter in which direction she pointed, because their surroundings were identical on all sides. And therefore, so was the problem.

"I have sailed through straits so narrow they would pinch a coal lugger's gut, navigated my way past shelves of coral and rocks so black they could hardly be seen by the lookout. I have taken the *Grömsketter* safely past whirlpools strong enough to suck a lesser vessel down to its doom, and seen to a fire in the galley in the middle of the night. But I have never, ever, had occasion to try to sail uphill." She was watching Ehomba closely.

"This astonishing liquid vale has been a welcome refuge. Now, how do we escape it?"

Ehomba returned her gaze. Nearby, Simna ibn Sind leaned back against the rail and grinned. It always amused him when his tall friend startled the skeptical with one of his unexpected magical revelations. He looked forward with great anticipation to the look of amazement and realization that was soon to come over the Captain's beautiful face.

"I do not know," the herdsman replied frankly.

"What?" Stanager's expression hardly shifted.

Simna's grin widened. "Hoy, he's just toying and teasing with you." He smiled at his companion. "The stiffer they are, the harder it is for them to loosen up and have a laugh. Right, long bruther?"

Ehomba turned to him. "I am telling the truth, Simna. I do not know how we are going to get free of this place and back out onto the upper ocean proper."

"Right, sure!" The swordsman smiled at their hostess. "Would you believe that there was a time when I thought he had no sense of humor? Tell her, Etjole. Tell her now."

"I just did," the herdsman responded quietly. He considered the watery late-afternoon panorama. "I have no idea how one is supposed to sail uphill."

His expression falling, Simna straightened away from the railing. "This isn't funny, bruther."

Ehomba glanced over at him. "Why should it be? As you have said yourself, I have no sense of humor."

Stanager moved nearer. "If you had no notion of how to leave a place like this, why did you guide us into it?"

"Because you insisted you needed a place to rest and repair, and this was the only such shelter I could detect. Attend to the ship first, I thought, and deal with the leaving later."

"Well, the later has arrived, bruther." Simna was no longer smiling. "Time to deal with it."

"I am trying, my friend." He looked hopefully at their Captain. "Have you any ideas?"

Placing her hands on the rail, she regarded the valley in the sea. Soon it would start to grow dark again. "Terious and his people are stout of arm and strong of back, but I don't think even they could kedge uphill." She spared a quick glance for the sails. "We have some wind, but not enough to gain sufficient momentum to push us up one of these enclosing slopes. We might sail partway before sliding back. This is a magical place. Your friend claims you are a magician." Her gaze was steely. "Make some magic, Etjole, or we will surely all grow old together in this place."

"My friend is constantly overrating my abilities. It is a conceit of his."

"There must be a way out!" Simna was, however mildly and gracefully, feeling the gnawing edge of panic. "You speak to dolphins; I've seen you do it. Call them up and make a bargain with them! Have them pull and push us back to the surface above."

"I can speak to the sleek people of the sea, yes," Ehomba admitted, "but I cannot call them up, Simna. And believe me, I have been looking for them. But from where we are now I see neither spout nor fin."

"Then talk to the fishes! I know there are many here, and of diverse kinds. Strike a compact with them."

The herdsman flashed a look of regretful sadness. "Would that I could, my friend. But fish are of a lower order than dolphins, and can speak but few words." Peering out across the sea, he tried to see hope where there was only seaweed and water.

"The sky-metal sword! Call forth a wind strong enough to fill every sail and blow us out of here."

"Now Simna, remember what I have told you. Care must be taken in the use of that blade. If it is used too often and too many times in the same period, the consequences of its employment become dangerously unpredictable. Perhaps in a few weeks it might be safe to try again."

"A few weeks!" Whirling, the swordsman stalked off in search of a sympathetic ear to bend with his complaints. Knowing that the cat would not tolerate his ranting, he settled instead on poor Hunkapa Aub, who would sit and smile patiently through any tirade, no matter how lengthy or pointless.

"What are we going to do?" Stanager had moved to stand close to the herdsman—though not so close as before.

"As I said, I do not know." Ehomba brooded on the matter. "The answer is here. There is always an answer, or there could not be a problem. But I confess I do not see it. Not yet."

She put a hand on his shoulder. A reassuring hand, devoid of secondary meaning. "Look hard then, herdsman. I will look elsewhere, and between us it can be hoped that a solution will be discovered." Turning, she headed toward the main deck.

Left to himself, Ehomba contemplated fish and weed, sea and sky. Somehow the *Grömsketter* had to be pushed or pulled out of the valley and back onto the surface of the ocean proper. If it could not be done by wind or muscle power, then some other way must be found. His eyes fell to where the water lapped gently against the sturdy side of the ship.

If only Simna was right and I could talk to fish, he thought. But those fish he could speak with had little to say, fish not being noted even at their most amenable as being among the most voluble of conversationalists. Yet again it struck him forcefully what a wonderful place the valley would be to live, if only there was a little bit of land.

Of course, in the absence of land there were other things with which the appropriately equipped might endeavor to make a living. There was an abundance of fish, and calm conditions, and seaweeds in abundance.

A fragment of an old tale of Meruba's popped into his head. He struggled to remember the details, to envision all of it, but it hovered frustratingly just out of reach, skipping and skittering away from his most strenuous efforts at recall.

He went to bed with it nagging at him, and the ship still trapped within the haven that had become a prison.

*   *   *

"Put a boat over the side."

The morning had dawned a duplicate of the previous mornings in the valley: calm, sunny, the water stirred by only the gentlest of breezes. Anxiety was now scribed plain on the faces of the crew, for, having completed even unnecessary repairs, they had begun to wonder why they continued to remain in the watery depression, and at the lack of explanation from their Captain and mates.

"Going fishing?" Hovering near the stern rail, Simna ibn Sind eyed his friend glumly.

"In a manner of speaking." The herdsman turned back to Stanager. "What I intend will demand my full attention."

"I'll send Terious to row you. Unless you plan to go far."

"I hope not. You are not coming?"

She gestured behind her. "The *Grömsketter* is my charge. A Captain does not leave her ship in the middle of the ocean unless it is at the invitation of another vessel to visit. But I will watch."

He nodded. "Let us not waste time, then. When the sun rises to the midpoint of the sky, it will be too hot."

"I know. What are you looking for, Etjole?"

"I am not sure. A part of an old wives' tale."

"That's not very encouraging."

He smiled hopefully. "The old wives of the Naumkib are not like any others."

As soon as the boat had been safely lowered, Ehomba followed the first mate aboard. Settling himself in the bow, he instructed the complaisant Terious to row for the thickest, densest mat of seaweed he could find.

"We won't make much progress through that," the mate warned his passenger as he pulled hard and steady on the oars. The boat moved away from the *Grömsketter,* out into the open water of the valley. "And not for very long, either. As soon as we're in among the weed it will be like trying to row through mud."

"Then we will back out and try another place." Ehomba stood in the bow, one foot on the small foreseat, his right arm hanging at his side and the left resting on his knee.

True to the first mate's word, they soon found themselves surrounded by thick green water plants, the little boat struggling to make any additional headway despite Terious's most strenuous efforts.

"This is the best I can do," the mate declared.

"Row us back out, then." Ehomba's sharp, experienced eyes scanned the mass of weed and saw nothing. It stank of salt and the open ocean. "We will try another patch."

They did not have to. A dark, slick shape was rising before them. Decorated with leafy structures that perfectly mimicked the surrounding seaweed, trailing streamers of glossy green the exact same size and shape as kelp roots, it regarded them out of black, pupil-less eyes that were gently bulging ovals lustrous as black star sapphires. The small slit of a mouth was a tiny oval set over where one would expect to find a chin, except there was none; the rest of the face was smooth and shiny as the seaweed it counterfeited. Gills on both sides of the neck revealed themselves only when they rippled to expose momentarily the pink beneath.

"Kalinda uelle Mak!" Terious exclaimed as he briefly lost his grip on the oars. "What in the name of all the ten seas is that!"

"A missing piece of memory," Ehomba told him, not flinching away from the aqueous apparition. "Part of a tale told since childhood to the young people of my village by those of the Naumkib who have been to sea." Manipulating his expression in what he hoped was the appropriate manner, he made a round circle of his mouth and blew softly. "It is a sargassum man."

IV

The initial reaction on board the *Grömsketter* to the sudden eruption of the gilled, beleafed, brown-and-green homunculus directly in front of Ehomba was one of confusion and alarm. His sleep disturbed, Ahlitah stirred reluctantly to wakefulness. Simna and Hunkapa Aub rushed to the railing, and it was the swordsman who broke out into a broad grin and hastened to reassure the crew.

"It's all right! I told you my friend was a wizard. See what he has summoned up out of the sea."

"It didn't look like he called anything up," declared one of the crew from his position in the rigging just above the helm deck. "It looked like they were starting to back clear of the weed and the malformed thing just arose in front of them."

Simna threw the sailor a look of transient anger, then smiled anew at the uncertain Stanager. "No, Etjole called it forth. You'll see. Everyone will see." He returned his attention to the patch of drifting weed where the confrontation was taking place.

I hope, he thought uneasily.

Out on the open water, observing that his lanky passenger had not lost his, Terious regained his composure. "A *what* man?"

Not taking his eyes from the inquisitive dark green humanoid shape that now bobbed effortlessly in front of them, Ehomba endeavored to explain. "Sargassum man. They dwell in the mats of seaweed that float on the surface of all the oceans of the world. I have never seen one before, but they were described to me in stories told by the old people of my village." Glancing back over a shoulder, he regarded the astonished mate curiously.

"Did you not know, Terious, that the world is home to many kinds of men? There are humans, like you and I, and sargassum men, like this fellow here. There are cavemen, and neander men, treemen and sandmen, and many other kinds of men not often encountered but as comfortable in this world as you or I."

The mate shook his head slowly. "I have never heard of or seen any of the kinds of men you speak of, sir."

"Ah well. It may be that living in such a poor, dry land as the Naumkib do, we learn to see things a little more clearly than other peoples. Perhaps it is because there is so little around for us to look at." Turning back to the leafy humanoid shape that waited patiently in the midst of the mass of weed, Ehomba pursed his lips in an odd way and made sputtering noises. To Terious they sounded like the gurgling a child makes when it blows bubbles underwater. After all that he had witnessed during the last several days, the mate was not at all surprised when the outlandish sea creature responded in kind.

"Good day to you, sargassum man." Ehomba hoped he was remembering to make the sounds exactly the way his grandfather had instructed him.

In this he must have been successful, because the green-skinned being replied in kind. "Hello, landsman. You are an interesting color."

"I am not green, if that is what you mean." When Ehomba smiled, the sargassum man made a perfect round O with his lipless mouth. Tongue and gullet were entirely black. "I did not expect to find one of your kind here—but I had hope."

" 'One'?" Lifting a supple, tubular arm that was fringed with kelp-like protrusions, the humanoid made a sweeping gesture. "My entire family is here; my wife and three children, and my uncle and his wife and two children, and an elderly cousin."

Strain his eyes as he might while surveying the surrounding floating weed, Ehomba could see nothing. "They must be far away."

A burbling noise rose from the depths of the sargassum man's throat. It reminded the herdsman of the sound a badly clogged drain might make. "They are right here." Turning slightly to his left, he pointed. Not off into the distance, but down.

Two sargassum children popped their heads out of the water not an arm's length from the boat, giggling like gargling eight-year-olds. They so startled Terious that for the second time he momentarily lost his grip on the oars. Watery laughter trailing behind, the effervescent pair ducked back beneath the weed mat. Though they were blowing bubbles less than a foot below the surface, their natural camouflage made them impossible to see even when Ehomba looked directly at them.

"We like this place," the adult was saying. "It is always calm here. The winds are mild and no landsmen ships with hooks and nets visit the valley." His expression, insofar as it was possible to do so, darkened. "No sharks, either. And this weed patch is thick and healthy and full of good things to eat."

"What do you find to eat in the weed?" The sun was still high, the languorous afternoon warm, and Ehomba was not above making casual conversation. Who knew when the chance to do so with another of these people might arise? Stuffed full of questions as always, he was reluctant to bring up the reason for his coming lest it cut the conversation short.

"The same sort of things a landsman would find in his garden. The weed itself is very tasty, and despite how uniform it appears to most landsmen, there are actually many different kinds of weed. Each has its own spice and flavor. Living in the weed are millions of little creatures; shrimp and small fish, and the larger fish that prey upon the smaller. There are comb jellies and moon jellies in many flavors, seahorses that crunch when you bite into them, and shellfish that have to be sucked out of their homes and down your throat. Oh, there is plenty to eat." Pushing a leafy hand down through the dense mat of green stuff and into the water, he drew forth a juvenile octopus.

"No thank you," Ehomba told him politely.

"What's he doing?" The first mate tried to see around Ehomba. "What are you two talking about?"

The herdsman glanced back. "Food."

"Oh." Terious was not displeased. He quite liked octopus himself. "What does he say about getting us out of here?"

"I am coming to that." With a reluctant sigh, Ehomba remembered that he was not here to discuss the delights of sargassum living, and that on the larger boat behind him waited anxious others silently watching who were depending on him to extricate them from what had become an inopportune situation.

"We think your valley is beautiful," he told the humanoid, "and we would like to stay and visit, but we have business to attend to on the other side of the ocean."

"Landsmen spend too much time attending to business and not enough time living. If you spent more time in the sea you would be happier."

"I could not agree with you more," Ehomba replied. "However, I am a herder of cattle and sheep, and they do not do as well in the ocean as jellyfish and clams."

"I fathom." The sargassum man popped something small and blue into his mouth.

"There is a problem with our leaving. Our ship cannot sail up the walls of your valley. There is not enough wind to make her go fast enough. Not even if we sailed in circles until we got going as fast as we can and then tried. We need help."

The humanoid nodded gravely. What strange thoughts must lie behind those impenetrable black eyes? the herdsman wondered. What sights must they have seen? To someone like himself who so loved the sea, the temptation to wish oneself a similar life was almost irresistible. Not all wishes in life, he reminded himself, could be fulfilled. He knew that despite his yearning, his desire to spend time at sea would have to restrict itself to long swims from shore and endless walks on the beach below the village. Perhaps, he mused, the sargassum man longs to walk on dry lands.

"We can do nothing." The sympathetic humanoid spread leafy arms wide. "We *could* pull your ship out of the valley, but it would take a thousand sargassum men, and there are not that many dwelling within many weeks' journey of this place. Most live farther to the south, where the water is warmer and the seaweed beds more extensive."

"Then there is nothing you can do for us?" Though disappointed, Ehomba was not surprised.

"Nothing. Nothing by ourselves." The humanoid pressed four kelp-like, nailless fingers to his forehead. "Others might well do better."

"Dolphins?" The herdsman's hopes rose. "There are dolphins in the area? I can tell them myself what it is that we need."

"No. No dolphins here. They like clear, open water where they can swim fast and breathe easy. None of their greater cousins are around, either. It is too bad. A few of them could easily pull your boat to safety. But I think I know someone who might be able to help you. This is not a certain thing, landsman. But I like you. You come to learn and not to lecture, without hook or net or line, and, unlike most of your kind, you have learned how to look into the water and see something besides food. I will do what I can." He started to sink back beneath the weed-choked surface.

"Wait!" Ehomba burbled. "When will we know if you can help?"

With only his head remaining above water, the sargassum man gurgled a reply. "When the king comes to you. If he is willing."

Then he was gone.

Leaning over the prow of the longboat, the herdsman peered down into the water. There was a lot of life to see less than a few feet from his nose: tiny crustaceans crawling through the gently bobbing mat, the flash of falling sunlight off the silver sides of small fish, the fine patterns of jellyfish drifting near the surface like abandoned, sodden doilies of fine lace. But no sargassum man. He was gone. Or at least it appeared that he was gone. Like his offspring, he might well be lingering only a few feet away, laughing silently at the blind landsman who had eyes but could not see.

"Take us back to the ship." Ehomba turned away from the water and sat himself down. His back ached from leaning so long over the prow.

Reversing his position on the center seat, the first mate took a firmer grip on the oars and pulled hard to extricate them from the clinging weed. "Well, sir? What did the weed fella say? Will they help us?"

"They cannot. But he promised to speak to one who might, and entreat with him on our behalf."

"One what?" Looking back at his passenger as they pulled free of the weed and into open water, he hauled on one oar and pushed on the other, turning them toward the *Grömsketter.*

"I am not sure. One king, I think."

The first mate's heavy brows drew together. "There are no kings out here."

"There are watery kingdoms just as there are kingdoms of the land, friend Terious. Who are we to say whether these folk have kings of their own, and if so, what their nature might be? We must have help to escape this valley, and if that means treating some creature of the sea as a king, why, I will be the first to bow down before him and beg assistance." His gaze left the mate to travel out across the water, toward the surrounding walls of sloping sea that prevented them from continuing on their way.

"It will not be a king of dolphins, though. Or one of their larger cousins, nor sargassum people. It will be something else."

"How will we know it, then?" Impatient to be back aboard ship, Terious drew hard on the oars, putting his back and full weight into each stroke. "Will it come to us trailing a royal retinue, dressed in rich garment and jewels with a high crown perched upon its head?"

Ehomba shrugged. "I suppose you will know as well as I, my friend. We do not know what it is, but I suspect it will not be wearing clothes or crown. No creature of the sea that I have ever seen or heard tell of does so."

"Nor any that are known to me," the first mate replied as he strained at the oars.

They were right about the clothing, but wrong about the crown.

The sun slipped below the western rim of the valley, its shafting light turning the upper reaches of the slope into a sheet of emerald. Darkness descended on the valley in the sea, on the noble ship bobbing gently in the ripples that were not strong enough to qualify as swells, and on her apprehensive yet expectant crew.

Etjole Ehomba was no less anxious than any of them. With the ship's lamps alight and several secured high up in the rigging to mark the vessel's location to any passing craft—or king—he stood on the main deck and stared out to sea, wondering at the sargassum man's parting words. What dwelled out there that was not porpoise or whale yet was potentially strong enough to free the *Grömsketter* from her obstinate sanctuary? What mysterious acquaintances did the green humanoid intend to converse with on their behalf?

A familiar voice nudged up alongside him. "Hoy, long bruther: We're pondering the same thing, I think." The swordsman's gaze was similarly drawn to the black waters on which the ship rode, and to the unknown depths beneath her keel. What monstrous life-forms swam and fought and died there, down in the unfathomable abyss? Which of them could free the ship and her crew and send both on their way? Sea serpents? Simna had heard many tales of such. The horrid great Kraken, with its clacking beak and tentacles like a pack of pythons? A king, Ehomba said the weed man had told him. But king of what?

"Did you ever stop to consider what lies out there, Simna?" The herdsman spoke without taking his gaze from the water, even though in the hush of night nothing save a few fleeting phosphorescences were visible, minuscule ghosts scuttling across the surface of the sea.

"I'm not you, Etjole. I'm more inclined to ponder on what lies on the far shore, how expensive it is, how attractive, and how much longer I have to spend rattling around inside a wooden hull before I'll be able to investigate it."

Ehomba murmured something inaudible before replying with conviction. "You are right, my friend. You are not me."

"The treasure's to be found in distant Ehl-Larimar, isn't it?" As forthright as henna on a courtesan's cheeks, avariciousness rouged the swordsman's words. "Watched over by Hymneth the Possessed. He's obsessed by this Visioness he's abducted, and so are you, a little bit, but his real concern and yours is the treasure he guards in his castle."

"Simna, I really don't—" Ehomba's reply was cut short by a shout from the third mate. She was standing in the rigging on the starboard side, the opposite side of the ship from the two travelers.

"Ware the gunwales! Something's coming up!"

Everyone not on duty, passengers included, rushed to that side of the ship. With many of the crew already belowdecks either in their hammocks or preparing to retire, it was not immediately swarmed. There was room for each individual to peer over the side without crowding out a neighbor.

At first Ehomba saw nothing, only dark water and the barely perceptible reflection of a slivered moon. Then one of the sailors standing by the boarding ladder that always hung over the side as a precaution, should anyone fall in, shouted and gestured straight downward. What had moments before been apparent only to the mate from her elevated vantage point could now be seen by all as it rose from the depths.

Several members of the usually steadfast crew broke and ran as soon as they caught a glimpse of the apparition, hurling themselves below-decks in hopes of hiding themselves away from the monstrosity. Others thought to find safety higher up in the rigging. That left the main deck clear save for Stanager and the bravest of her company. Terious was not surprised to see that the tall southerner held his ground, but the continued presence of the great black cat, the simple-minded brute, and the husky swordsman led him to comment admiringly on their unity of purpose.

"After what we've seen and been through together these past weeks, my ponytailed friend, there's nothing above or below the waters that can frighten us." Even as he delivered himself of this characteristic burst of bravado, Simna was contemplating making a dash below for his sword, but he held back. For one thing, a smart man could judge the imminence of danger by monitoring the herdsman's posture and expression. Ehomba showed no sign of concern, much less panic. He had not stiffened or drawn back from the apparition that was ascending majestically from the depths. If he felt safe, then it was most likely that all who remained in his vicinity could likewise count themselves reasonably secure.

Also, bolting the scene in search of weaponry would not make much of an impression on Stanager, who stood tense but agreeably disposed to greet whatever was making its way up toward her ship.

The legs emerged first. Long and skeletal white they were, with touches of pink and carmine, as if a ghost had spent an evening making itself up to attend a masked ball. Fearsome barbs and spines protruded from each limb. They were tipped in ebony, legs armed with quill pens that had been dipped in the blackest of inks. Then the body appeared, equipped with an even more conspicuous array of anomalous weaponry. Bulging eyes stared up at the humans that lined the railing. They goggled from the terminus of stalks that weaved slowly from side to side.

Those terrible spines helped first one leg, then another, to secure a grip on the boarding ladder. Turning itself sideways, the visitant from the frigid ocean deep began to make its way upward. Muttering softly and swiftly to their respective chosen deities, two more of the crew fled for the safety and anonymity of their quarters.

From claw-tip to claw-tip, the creature hauling itself up out of the water was no less than twenty feet across. Seaweed clung to extruded spurs and hung from legs and eyestalks. Water dripped from its body while tiny bubbles oozed around the edges of the multipart mouth.

Simna was at once fascinated by and disappointed in the nocturnal caller. "Your weed man was right, bruther. He sent to us a king." The swordsman made a disgusted sound. "A king crab."

"A king crab, yes," Ehomba readily agreed, "but is that all it is?"

His companion frowned. "I don't follow you, Etjole. Not that it's the first time your reasoning has left me blind, deaf, and dumb."

The herdsman continued his line of thinking. "It is a king crab, but is it also a king among crabs? Look at its head."

"Must I?" Even as he objected, the swordsman complied. The longer he stared, the more his frustration gave way to dawning realization. There in the dim glow supplied by the *Grömsketter*'s oil lamps he saw those spines and projections in a new and implausible light. Squint a little, squeeze the eyes tight, and one could almost see those chitonous barbs and protuberances coming together to form, if not an actual crown, at least an approximation of a comparable configuration.

"What now?" he muttered. "Don't tell me, bruther, that you can talk to even so lowly a creature as this? Big as it is, it is still only a crab, a creature that spends all its life grubbing in the muck and ooze at the bottom of the sea."

"You have many good qualities, friend Simna, but you also have an unfortunate tendency to underestimate all manner of living things based upon their lifestyle. I know of men who abide at rarefied heights yet who cannot be trusted to tend to their own children, while others who live in the depths of poverty and homeliness I would charge with the safekeeping of my own wife."

Simna was not so easily rebuked. "Then if I underestimate, you overtrust, my friend."

Ehomba smiled. "Perhaps between us, then, we may make one sensible human being." He turned away as long, clawed legs came clambering over the side of the ship. "You are right to say that I cannot 'talk' to a crab. But there are numerous manners of speaking, Simna, of which the Naumkib know more than many other peoples. It is what comes of living in a lonely country. You learn to make yourself known to whatever inhabits the same land as yourself, however many legs it happens to walk upon."

The prodigious crustacean finally clambered over the railing to settle on the deck with a waterlogged *thunk*. Stalks swiveled bulbous eyes to right and then to left. Behind it, a captivated Stanager Rose spoke to Ehomba without taking her eyes off the visitor.

"If this is what your weedy man meant when he told you he would try to implore a king to come calling on us, then he must have believed you could communicate with it. I certainly can't. I would know how to boil it, but not talk to it. I certainly don't see what other use it can be of to us."

"Nor do I," Ehomba confessed. "But you are right, Captain. The sargassum man must have had a thought in mind or he would not have asked this creature to seek us out. I will try my best to find out what is afoot." As soon as he stepped forward, the huge crab scrabbled sideways to confront him. It was wary, but not afraid. Nor had it reason to be; not with those enormous sharp-spined arms with which to defend itself.

"What is afoot not indeed, but aplenty," Simna murmured to the hulking Hunkapa, who stood open-mouthed behind him. Unsurprisingly, the shaggy mountain did not react to what the swordsman felt was his best sally in some time.

Behind both of them, the black litah stood and stared in silence. From time to time its long tongue would emerge to lick heavy lips. The humans aboard were not alone in their fondness for the taste of crabmeat. The cat restrained the impulses that were surging through it. Ehomba had scolded him before for trying to eat an envoy. It was, the herdsman had pontificated at the time in no uncertain terms, not only bad manners but very poor diplomacy.

But oh, Ahlitah mused, what a meal this visitor would make!

Standing alone before the visitant, aware that those watching viewed it from perspectives as wildly different from one another as from his, Ehomba considered how best to proceed. The type of talking itself was no stranger to him. He had known it since childhood, albeit with a considerably lesser degree of eloquence. He simply did not want to get off on the wrong foot. Offend this noble creature and it would doubtless plunge itself right back into the depths it had risen from. It was not for nothing that its kind were called crabs.

Raising both hands, he began to wiggle several of his fingers in a certain manner. Though when it came to sheer number of limbs his counterpart had him outgunned, not all could be used simultaneously for conversation. Out of the water, at least, several had to be used at all times to support the weighty body.

"Well would you look at that!" Not for the first time Simna was all but struck dumb by an unexpected talent of his lanky companion. This time there was no question that sorcery was not involved. It was, as Ehomba had tried to explain, simply a different kind of speaking. One that made use of hand signs, or in the case of the crab king, foot signs, to express notions, emotions, and ideas.

After several minutes the giant crustacean and the tall human were practically shouting, so rapid and intense had the movements of their respective limbs become. It was certain that much was being said, but what, not a man jack among the crew had a clue. Neither did Simna ibn Sind, or the black litah, and certainly not the utterly engrossed Hunkapa Aub, who had to pause to ponder the meaning of any sentence longer than ten words.

Eventually the frenetic exchange of signs slowed. Bending low, Ehomba extended a hand. It was met by a thorny claw. They did not shake, exactly. The crustacean's armature would not properly allow it. But there was a definite physical meeting, following which those remarkable legs proceeded to carry their owner once more up over the railing and down the side of the ship. Rushing to the rail, those members of the crew who had remained on deck watched as the spiny, starlike shape sank once more beneath the wavelets, swallowed up entire by water the color of blue-black ink.

Direct as always, Stanager was first to question Ehomba. "Are we to make anything of that? Or was it no more than an unlikely dialogue?"

Turning to her, the herdsman smiled. "They are going to try to help us. Not because it is in their nature to do so, or because it would ever happen under ordinary circumstances—but because the sargassum man asked it of them. As fellow creatures of the sea, it seems they have a compact of sorts that is very old, and inviolate. The king was reluctant, but as soon as he saw that I was able to speak with him, his last uncertainties disappeared."

"I'm glad they're going to try to help us," Simna put in. "If not, I'd hate to think we let such a superb meal just walk away."

Ehomba glanced over at his friend. "Odd you should say that, Simna. The king was thinking the same about you. About all of us. His people are quite fond of the taste of man, having dined on numerous occasions on the bodies of sailors drowned at sea. At the bottom of the ocean, it seems, nothing goes to waste."

The swordsman envisioned himself sinking, slowly sinking to the soft sands below, his face turned blue, his eyes bulging in a manner not unlike the crab's. Saw himself settling to the bottom, to be visited not long thereafter by first one small crab, and then another, and another, until dozens of tiny but sharply efficient claws were ripping at his saturated flesh, tearing off bits of meat to be stuffed into alien, insectlike jaws, there to be ground into . . .

"Like I said." Simna swallowed uncomfortably. "I'm glad they're going to try to help us." He blinked. "Hoy, wait a moment. Who are 'they'?"

"The king and his minions, of course. Apparently he commands a substantial empire, even if all of it is hidden well beneath the waves."

"I don't understand." Stanager's expression showed clearly how much she disliked not understanding. "How can they help us to leave this valley?"

"The king did not say." Ehomba looked past her, to the east. "He told me that we should wait here until morning, and then we would all see if the thing was possible."

Her tone was sarcastic. "That we can certainly do! It's not as if we had plans to be anywhere else." Nodding past Terious, she indicated the hopeful, attentive crew. "Set the watch, Mr. Kamarkh. All crew to be sounded to quarters if anything, um, unusual should start to happen." Raising her voice, she addressed the others herself. "All of you, hear me! Get some sleep. With luck"—and she glanced at the studiously noncommittal Ehomba—"tomorrow will find us freed of this place.

"Though how," she murmured as she turned and strode past the herdsman, "I cannot begin to imagine."

V

It was not a perfect morning, but it would do. As was his wont, Ehomba rose with the sun. Normally one to sleep in, even aboard ship, Simna ibn Sind bestirred himself as soon as he sensed his rangy companion was awake. Whatever was going to happen, he was not about to miss it. And if nothing happened, as he half suspected it might, why then he would have a fine excuse for returning early to bed.

Hunkapa Aub was already awake, it being hard for him to sleep long in the cramped space he had been provided in the hold. There was no sign of Ahlitah, there being little that could rouse the big cat from its rest. Hands working against one another behind her back, Stanager Rose nervously paced the helm deck as she stared out to sea. She manifested more anxiety than she intended when Ehomba finally showed himself.

"Anything?" Shading his eyes against the sharpness of the early morning sun, the herdsman scanned the surrounding waters.

"Nothing. Nothing at all, unless you call the presence of a hundred or so flying fish significant. I hope your crab was not keeping you hand-talking so long merely because he valued the opportunity for conversation."

"I do not think so. And he is not my crab, nor the sargassum man's. Whatever happens, he was most definitely his own crab."

A cry came from the lookout. It was indistinct, perhaps because the man was choked with surprise. But his extended arm, if not his foreshortened words, pointed the way.

Rising from the calm surface of the sea beneath the bowsprit was a line of crabs. All manner of crabs. Every type and kind and variety of crab the sailors of the *Grömsketter* had ever seen, as well as a goodly number that were new to them. Ehomba recognized some they did not, and there were many that he had never seen before. There were blue crabs and stone crabs, snow crabs and lady crabs, rock crabs and green crabs. There were tiny sand crabs and fiddler crabs, each sporting a single grotesquely oversized dueling claw. Pea crabs vied for space in the line with hermit crabs, while pelagic crabs shared the water with benthic crabs that were utterly devoid of color and nearly so of eyesight. There were king crabs, too, but of them all were subjects and none visibly a king.

The line they formed was a good two feet wide and stretched across the surface as far as one could see. Stretched all the way across the valley and up the nearest aqueous slope, in fact. Claws linked tightly to claws while spiny legs entwined, the chitonous queue continuing to thicken and grow even as those aboard the trapped vessel gathered to gaze at the astonishing sight.

"Millions." Much as he liked the taste of crab, Simna found he was not hungry. He remembered all too clearly what Ehomba had told him the night before about the crustaceans' traditional taste for the flesh of drowned men. "There must be millions of them!"

"Tens of millions," the herdsman agreed. Beneath the bowsprit the clacking of claws and scrape of shell on shell was almost deafening.

"How does this help us?" In her years at sea Stanager Rose had seen many strange things, but nothing to quite match the crustaceal armada presently assembling beneath the bow of her ship. "What do we do?"

"I know!" Never one to hesitate at venturing expertise in matters where he had none, Simna spoke up enthusiastically. "Etjole's going to magick them so that they carry us on their backs. As soon as enough have congregated, hoy?"

Ehomba eyed his friend dolefully. "There is no magic in this, Simna." Looking past him, he smiled encouragingly at Stanager. "When a hundred million crabs present themselves at the ready, Captain, I think it might be advisable to throw them a line."

"Throw them a . . . ?" For the barest of instants she gazed back uncomprehendingly. Then she turned and barked orders to Terious and the rest of the waiting crew.

The strongest cord on board was made fast around a fore capstan. When the mate was convinced it could be knotted no better, the unsecured end was heaved over the bow. It landed with a convincing splash just to the right of the line of floating crabs.

Immediately, those forming the end of the line nearest the ship swarmed over the rope. At any other time and in any other place they might well have tried to eat it, but not this morning. Sharp claws dug deep into the thick hemp, legs burying themselves into the folds of the triple weave.

"Line going out!" one of the crew monitoring the capstan shouted.

Stanager glanced briefly at Ehomba. He did not react to the warning and continued to lean over the bow watching the frenzied crustaceans. "Let it go," she directed the crew tersely.

The capstan whirred as more and more of the valuable cordage was taken up by the crabs, until at last only the terminal coils securing it to the capstan itself remained. Stretched out beneath the bowsprit, the rest of the line was completely obscured by swarming crabs. As those who managed to crowd into the bow observed, the thick cable was being drawn taut, and tauter still, until the visible portion that was suspended in the air between water and bowsprit twanged from the tension that was being applied to it.

Very slowly but perceptibly, the *Grömsketter* began to move.

"All hands to stations!" Stanager bellowed. Behind her, men and women swarmed into the rigging or to posts on deck. Priget stood like a barrel behind the helm, her eyes aloft as she searched for the first hint of a good stiff breeze.

When the ship reached the base of the oceanic slope there was a collective intake of breath among her crew. Exhaling in concert and producing a noise like a billion tiny bubbles all bursting at once, the line of crabs continued to pull the ship forward. That and the scrape of millions of carapaces rubbing against one another were the only sounds they made.

The elegant sailing vessel's prow rose slowly, slowly. Sailors reached for something to keep themselves from falling backward as the ship began to slide *up* the slope toward the smooth ridge above. At the halfway point someone erupted in an involuntary cheer, only to be quickly hushed by his superstitious fellow seamen. Who knew what might disturb the crabs at their arduous work? If the line broke, if a few hundred thousand claws and legs lost their grasp, then the ship would surely slide right back down into the peaceful but terminal watery valley—perhaps forever.

The rim drew near, nearer—and then it was beneath the *Grömsketter*'s bowsprit. Very gradually the ship ceased ascending and she leveled out. When the stern was once more on an even keel with the bow, several of the most senior mariners could no longer restrain themselves. They began to dance and twirl around one another out of sheer joy. Priget turned the great wheel, adjusting the ship's heading slightly. Wind began to billow her sails. Not strongly, but it was enough. And it was behind them. Picking up speed, the ship began to move away from the valley under her own power.

In front of it, the crabs were scattering, abandoning the line and sinking back down into the depths from which they had been commanded. Seeing this, Stanager ordered the heavy line winched in swiftly lest it back up and wrap around the bow, fouling their advance. She would have thanked the hardworking crustaceans who had joined together to drag them clear of the valley, but how did one thank a crab? She put the question to the most unfathomable of her unique quartet of passengers.

"Do not thank them yet." While, with the exception of the dozing cat, his companions celebrated along with the crew, the herdsman did not. He remained where he had been standing, hard by the bowsprit and staring at the water forward of the ship. "The crabs helped us because their king commanded them to do so. But I do not think they were alone. I do not see how they could have done such a thing by themselves."

"Why not?" Free of the valley and with a fair wind astern, Stanager was in too good a mood to let the solemn-faced traveler mute her high spirits.

"Certainly they were by themselves in their millions strong enough to drag the ship clear, but any line, however mighty, needs an anchor against which to pull." He waved diffidently at the gentle swells through which they were cutting. "What was theirs?"

"Who knows?" She shrugged, much too relieved to be really interested. "The top of an undersea mountain, perhaps, or a shelf of corals."

"Corals would not hold up under the strain. They would break off."

"Well, the submerged mountaintop, then." He really was a man to discourage good cheer, she decided. Not naturally grave, but given to an inherent reluctance to let himself go and have a good time. Simna ibn Sind was incorrigible, but at least he knew how to celebrate a success. Deciding to put the proposition to a small test, she reached down and pinched the stoic herdsman on his stolid behind. Startled, he finally took his eyes off the sea.

"So you are alive after all." She grinned cheerfully. "I was beginning to wonder."

His expression was one of utter confusion, which pleased her perversely. "I—I did not mean to dampen anyone's spirits. I am as gladdened as everyone else that we are safely out of the valley. You have to excuse me. It is simply that as long as I am afflicted with an unanswered question, it is impossible for me to completely relax. I can manage it a little, yes, but not completely."

"I'm surprised that you are able to sleep," she retorted.

Now it was his turn to grin. "Sometimes, so am I."

"Come and have a grog with me." She gestured over the bow. "Doroune lies that way, to the southwest. We'll have you and your friends there soon enough, and from then forward I'll be denied the pleasure of your company. Prove to me that there is some truth in that statement."

His uncertainty returned. "What, that we'll reach the coast soon?"

"No, you great elongated booby." She punched him hard in the thick part of his right arm. "That there's pleasure to be had in your company."

For an instant, inherent hesitation held him back. Then he relaxed into a wide smile. To her surprise, not to mention his own, he put his arm around her. "I do not especially like the taste of seamen's grog, but under the circumstances, it is the taste I think I should seek."

Even those members of the crew assigned to duty high up in the rigging joined in the festivities. Internal lubrication caused a number to sway dangerously at their positions, but by some miracle the deck remained unsplattered. The *Grömsketter* continued to make headway, albeit more slowly than the efficient Stanager Rose would have liked.

The celebration continued unchecked until one lookout, his vision blurred but his mind still vigilant, sang out with an utterly unexpected and shocking declamation.

"*Kraken!* Kraken off the port bow!"

On the main deck, conversing intimately with one of the female members of the crew, Simna ibn Sind heard the cry and sat up like a man stabbed. He had never seen such a thing as the lookout proclaimed, but he knew full well what it was *supposed* to look like. Stumbling only slightly, he abandoned his nascent paramour and staggered forward. Ehomba was already there, staring like a second figurehead out to sea.

"What . . . ?" The swordsman steadied himself as he slammed up against the railing. "What's happening, bruther? I heard the lookout. . . ."

"Hoy," the herdsman murmured, mimicking a favorite exclamation of his friend. "We had our rescue." Turning back to the water, he nodded to the southwest. "Now comes the reckoning."

It arrived with ten immense arms each weighing a ton or more. Pale pink in color, the benthic colossus had surfaced less than a mile from the ship. Now it moved effortlessly closer, making a mockery of the desperate Priget's attempt to steer clear of its cylindrical bulk. A few crabs and barnacles clung to its smooth flanks, while scars revealed the history of titanic battles with sperm whales that had taken place in the depths of the ocean.

In an instant Stanager was beside Ehomba, even as she was beside herself. She could only stare in alarm and astonishment at the abyssal apparition that was making a leisurely approach to her ship. What else could one do when confronted by the sight and reality of the Kraken?

"That is what was at the other end of the hundred million crabs," the herdsman informed her quietly. "That is the only creature strong enough to both grip and anchor them."

"But—what does it want? The crabs have gone, scattered back to their homes."

"They were commanded. This is no crab, and would have to have been asked. I do not know what it wants, but whatever that may be, we had better hope we can supply it. The elders of my village have spoken many times of the Kraken, and I do not recall them commending it for its placid nature." He tried to inject an optimistic note into the litany. "They are a diverse family. Hopefully this one will be amenable to reason."

"Reason? *That?*" She gaped at him.

"The Kraken and their smaller cousins are among the most intelligent creatures in the sea. I thought an experienced mariner like yourself would know that."

"I am a Captain of people," she protested. "I do not converse with squid!"

He turned from her, back to the many-armed monster that was approaching the ship. "Perhaps you should learn."

It swam right up to the bow. There was a sharp bump as the *Grömsketter,* jarred by the contact, shuddered slightly. The Kraken did not try to halt the ship's progress, though it was clearly more than massive enough to do so if it wished. Instead, it swam lazily alongside, paralleling the vessel's advance. One of the two major tentacles rose high out of the water, reaching up to probe curiously at the lookout nest that topped the mainmast. The sailor stationed there crouched down, painfully aware of the inadequacy of his pitiful shelter.

Sidling to the side, Ehomba leaned as far over the railing as he dared and found himself gazing into a luminous, very alert eye. It was quite similar to his own, except that the Kraken's was nearly three feet in diameter. If he was not careful, a man could lose his mind in that eye, he warned himself.

The glistening orb twitched slightly and stared right back at him. Its pupil alone was far larger than Ehomba's eyeball. Behind Ehomba, Stanager and Simna waited breathlessly, knowing that the monster could pluck the herdsman from the deck as effortlessly as they would pinch a bud from a long-stemmed flower.

Ehomba smiled, for all the good that might do, and as he had done with the king of all the crabs, commenced to twist and wriggle his fingers.

The Kraken floated alongside, its tentacles weaving lazy patterns through the air and water, and studied the herdsman's limber gyrations. If so inclined, it was easily large enough to drag the entire ship down into the depths, locked in an unbreakable cephalopodian embrace. Iridescent waves of color, of electric blue and intense yellow, rippled through its skin as it flashed chromatophores at the apprehensive and uncomprehending crew.

Lowering his hands, Ehomba made a single final, sharp gesture with one pair of fingers—and waited. Eyes that were full of unfathomable intelligence regarded him silently. Then the Kraken lifted half a dozen enormous tentacles from the water. Responding, men and women bolted for cover or tried to make certain of their hold on lines and posts. But the monster was not attacking; it was replying.

When those six gigantic limbs had risen from beneath the surface, a powerful urge to flee had surged through Simna ibn Sind. Mindful of Stanager's presence, he had held his position. Besides, there was nowhere to run to. Watching his lanky companion converse with the apparition by means of simple finger movements was akin to observing an infant engaging in casual chat with a mastodon via a confabulation of giggles. Only the possibility that the exchange might turn unpleasant, resulting in the sinking of the ship and the loss of all on board, kept him from smiling at the sight.

When he could stand it no longer, he let loose with the question that was on the verge of driving him and everyone else on board mad. "For Gojokku's sake, bruther—what's it saying? What are you two *talking* about?" He hesitated only briefly. "You *are* talking, aren't you?"

"What?" As if suddenly remembering that he was not alone aboard the *Grömsketter,* Ehomba turned to gaze reassuringly at his companions. "Yes, we are talking. In fact, we are having a most pleasant conversation." Even as he replied to Simna, the herdsman continued to twitch and contort his fingers into patterns that meant nothing to his fellow humans.

"Hoy, then how about letting us in on a bit of it?"

"Yes," agreed an anxious Stanager. "What does it want?"

"Want? Why, it wants what I told Simna any creature in its position would probably want. Payment. For anchoring the hard-shelled multitude that pulled us out of the valley."

Stanager was uneasy. "By all the sea gods and their siblings, what form of 'payment' could such a creature require?" Peering over the side, she observed the powerful, parrot-like beak protruding from the center of the mantle—a beak large and sharp enough to bite through the hull of a ship. "If it's hungry, I'm not sacrificing any of my crew. We have preserved meat aboard, and fresh as well as dry fish. Might it be satisfied with that?"

Turning back to the eye of the Kraken, Ehomba worked his fingers. Once again, immense tentacles semaphored a reply. Wishing to make certain that there was no miscommunication, the herdsman repeated the query and for a second time made scrupulous note of the response.

"Coffee."

"What?" Simna and Stanager blurted simultaneously.

"It says it wants coffee. Not too hot, if you please. Tepid will do fine. With sugar. Lots of sugar."

It was the Captain who replied. "You're joking, landsman. I know it must be you because nothing that looks like that is capable of making jokes."

"On the contrary, though this is the first Kraken to come to my personal acquaintance, I know from experience in the shallow waters below my village that squid have a very highly developed sense of humor. But it is not joking. It wants coffee. I admit that it is a request that puzzles me as well."

"Well, that's something, anyway, if you're as bemused as I am."

"Yes," he admitted. "What exactly is 'coffee'? I gather from the description that it is some kind of food."

While Simna slowly and carefully elucidated to his tall friend the nature of coffee, explaining that it was a warm beverage not unlike tea, Stanager conferred with the ship's cook. They had tea and coffee both. Not being an addict, the Captain had no difficulty with agreeing to sacrifice their store of the darker beverage. Parting with an entire sack of sugar, more than half the ship's supply, was another matter. The alternative, however, was surely more dispiriting still.

"Have you a cauldron?" Ehomba asked her. "Perhaps for rendering out seal blubber?"

"This is not a fishing boat. Cook will use her largest kettle to prepare the brew." Stanager peered past him, to where the Kraken continued to hover like a mariner's worst nightmare hard by the port bow of the *Grömsketter*. "It will have to be big enough."

As matters developed, the iron kettle was more than sufficient to hold the multiple gallons of dark, aromatic liquid. After the sugar was added and stirred in and when it had cooled to a temperature Ehomba thought appropriate, it was presented with some ceremony to the waiting cephalopod.

A tentacle powerful enough to rip a ship's mainmast right out of its footing reached over the railing. The prehensile tip hooked beneath the kettle's sturdy handle. Without spilling a drop, the Kraken lifted the heavy iron over the side. Ehomba's companions rushed to the railing, expecting to see the contents of the kettle vanish down that clacking beak in a single prodigious swallow. Instead, the monster tipped the kettle ever so slightly forward, and sipped. A vast, invertebrate sigh rose from within, and the Kraken seemed to slip a little lower into the sea. As it drank, other tentacles dipped and waved.

"What's it saying, bruther?" An enchanted Simna looked on as his friend strove to communicate with the many-armed visitant.

"It is wondering why it is drinking alone, and why we do not join it."

Stanager replied absently. "It was our entire supply of coffee that went into that kettle."

"Tea will do," Ehomba assured her. "I could do with a cup myself. This has been thirsty work."

"Hoy, and I'll have a cup as well, Captain!" Simna grinned broadly.

"Just remember that I am the master here," she growled back at him, "and not some serving wench put aboard for your amusement." Muttering to herself, she went once again to confer with the cook.

So it was that Etjole Ehomba and Simna ibn Sind came to sit on the railing near the bow of the graceful sailing vessel, their sandaled feet braced against the rigging, delicately sipping tea while the herdsman conversed on matters of wind and weather, tide and current, the nature and flavor of various seafoods, and the vagaries of men who set forth to travel upon the surface of the sea, with as intimidating and alien a beast as ever plied the deep green waters.

In the course of their conversation the Kraken's skin would undergo dramatic shifts not only in color but of pattern. Merely by willing it so, it could generate the most captivating designs and schematics utilizing its own body as a canvas. By the time it was reproducing intensely colorful herringbones and checkerboards, the crew had abandoned its initial fear in favor of spontaneous bursts of applause.

"Just how," Stanager asked Ehomba as she stood nearby sipping her own tea, "does the Kraken develop a taste for something as foreign to the ocean as coffee?"

Putting the reasonable question to the multiple-limbed sea beast, the herdsman received an immediate and unequivocal answer. "It was once dozing on the surface at night when it collided with a merchant ship cruising down the eastern coast that now lies far behind us. Furious and alarmed, it reacted instinctively, and attacked. The merchantman was slow but well laid up, and fully loaded from a trading expedition to the eastern reaches of the Aboqua. Included among its cargo were several tons of coffee. The smell, I am told, was quite powerful.

"Aboard the merchantman was another like myself who speaks the tentacle-claw-finger language of the sea. Attempting to convince their enormous assailant to grant them their lives and allow them to continue on their way, they plied it with every manner of goods on board. Some the Kraken accepted, like a pair of live bullocks. Others it rejected. None carried the weight of persuasion until it tasted the coffee one crewman brought on deck for the agitated Captain. It also ate the crewman, but apparently humans go well with coffee, and so the overall effect was not significantly diminished." Ehomba drained the last of his tea.

"It held the merchantman in its grasp and its galley busily brewing until there was no more coffee to be had from its stores and cargo. Only then, with both its taste and anger assuaged, did it allow the ship to depart. Ever since, whenever a vessel has sailed near, it has risen from the depths in hopes of encountering that dark brown liquid again. Until now, it was always disappointed."

Stanager nodded understandingly. "In every country that I know of, tea and wine are far more common libations than coffee. It is a luxury." She made a face. "One that will now be denied to us for the duration of our journey across the Semordria."

"Better to complete that journey with thirst unslaked than perish with full cup in hand," the herdsman admonished her sagely.

"I agree, but I know of drinkers of this beverage who would not. To them it is not a refreshment, but an obsession." Looking past him, she watched the monster gingerly drain the last drops from the iron kettle. "Who would have thought to count the Kraken among their number. I hope," she added at a sudden afterthought, "that having quenched its fancy it will not now request someone to munch upon. I am fond of every member of my crew, and would not willingly give the least of them over to such a fate."

"The Kraken was angry with the ship that ran into it." Ehomba did his best to reassure her. "It is not angry at us." Long, supple fingers moved rapidly. "On the contrary, it is delighted to have received the best coffee it has ever tasted."

As if to underscore the herdsman's observations, a massive tentacle reached back over the railing to place the empty kettle conscientiously on the deck. Sending a surge against the side of the ship, the Kraken slowly moved away as its tentacles wove a complex pattern in the air. A pattern only one man aboard the *Grömsketter* could unravel.

"We are free to go, with thanks and in friendship."

Nodding tersely, Stanager turned and shouted orders. Shorn of their many-armed source of wonder and entertainment, sailors snapped out of their phantasmagoric reverie and back to work. Sails were made ready, lines drawn taut.

"Several days we lost because of the winds you freed from the old fisherman's bottle, and several more from making repairs and waiting down in the valley in the sea." Achieving only partial success, she tried to keep the irritation and impatience out of her voice as she spoke to her tall passenger. "If the winds are favorable we might make some of it up. If not, the lost time will see certain of our stores sorely thinned."

"Maybe there is a way to regain a little of the time we have lost." Turning back to the rail, Ehomba wagged his fingers energetically at the drifting Kraken. Simna paid little heed, certain that his friend was bidding their exotic erstwhile drinking companion good-bye. In point of fact, the herdsman had something different in mind.

Strikingly different.

Returning to the ship, the immense cephalopod promptly wrapped all ten of its tentacles one after the other around the vessel's sturdy sides. Startled seamen were shaken loose from the lower rigging or knocked off their feet by the repeated impacts. With its arrow-like tail pointing westward and its beak hard up against the prow of the ship, the Kraken held her in an unbreakable titan's grasp.

A gasping Stanager had instantly stopped handing out orders and directives to stumble back to Ehomba's side.

"What's going on? What went wrong?"

"Wrong?" Utterly unperturbed, Ehomba was as calm as the heavens. "Nothing has gone wrong, Captain." He gestured at the mammoth-eyed beast that even as they spoke continued to tighten its grip on the ship. "You expressed a desire to recover some of our lost travel time. I have coaxed our new friend into assisting us in this enterprise. See?" He gestured forward.

Seeing that he was trying to point out something beyond the bow, Stanager moved warily forward and looked down. At the base of the Kraken's mantle, a pale yellow tube had emerged. The translucent organ was pulsing slightly, as if readying itself to perform some unknown function. Having eaten many a squid, Stanager Rose was more than familiar with the organ, but not with its function. This was about to be made clear to her and to the rest of the *Grömsketter*'s crew.

"I suggest you grab something and hold on to it." Looking past her, Ehomba repeated the warning even as he took a firm grip on a nearby stay. "Everyone hold on tight!" Noticing the stocky helmswoman still standing at her post far back on the helm deck, he added as loudly as he could, "You too, Priget!"

"Just a minute." Stanager put a restraining hand on his arm. "If Priget steps down, who's to steer the ship?"

The herdsman nodded once more at the bulbous bulk that now blocked much of the view forward. "I have already given our friend a heading. You see, Captain, I have been watching you these past many days, and have learned much. It is my nature to be curious about everything, including the operation and navigation of a vessel like this." Looking down, he saw the cylindrical yellow organ contract slightly. "Hang on. I am going to." So saying, he turned away from her and made sure his fingers were wrapped tightly around the stays.

"Why?" she snapped. "What's going to hap—"

Impelled forward by the stream of water ejected by the Kraken from its rearward-facing siphon, the great sea beast shot westward across the surface of the sea. Held firm in its tentacular grasp, the *Grömsketter* went with it. Several sailors who had failed to fully heed Ehomba's warning were nearly left behind as the deck was all but yanked out from under them. The term "jet propulsion" was one that was as yet unknown to Stanager Rose and her crew, even as it applied to squid of all sizes and species, but the practical effects of the process were abundantly evident in their astoundingly swift progress across the water.

Her bow lifted largely clear of the surface, ship and squid shot across the sea at a velocity no sailing craft, however well crewed and captained, could ever hope to match. Once she was convinced of the stability of the arrangement, Stanager Rose ordered all sails reefed and pennants and flags broken out and hauled aloft, determined to show the Kraken that it was not the only one that could alter the color and design of its appearance.

How much lost time this astonishing tandem journey recovered Stanager was not prepared to say, though it was evident from her expression when the Kraken, tiring of the game, finally let them go, that it was significant. Flashing a kaleidoscope of colors and patterns at them as it sank beneath the swells, the sea's most intimidating monster disappeared back into the depths from which the king of crabs had originally called it forth.

The lesson of the extraordinary encounter was not lost on the members of the *Grömsketter*'s crew. To wit: Never wag an unknowing finger at a squid, and when crossing those stretches of ocean that are endlessly wide and eternally deep, always carry a sufficiency of coffee.

VI

The Land of the Faceless People

People invariably fight with their neighbors. How often and how seriously is just a matter of degree. It did not start out that way in the Tilo Islands. Originally, it is said, in the days when settlers first arrived, necessity compelled everyone to cooperate. Survival took precedence over the usual petty human squabbles and disputes. Imposing predators lived on several of the islands, notably Greater Tilo and Hookk. Dealing with them was a matter of concern for the entire community.

Eventually, farms spread across all the islands, of which there were six that boasted cultivatable land. Towns were raised, and fishermen set forth in small boats to net the silversides that gathered in substantial numbers in the shallows. A few hearty folk even settled the rock-strewn smaller islets. They could not farm there, but individual gardens were made possible by soil patiently carried boatload by boatload from Greater Tilo, Hookk, and Gyre. And there were always the eggs of nesting seabirds to collect and sell in season.

The settlers of the Tilos prospered. So isolated were the islands that they were never threatened by seafaring raiders. The climate was congenial, with only occasional severe winters and drenching summers. No one much minded, as long as the fields continued to yield significant crops. With the use of guano hauled from the seabird rookeries, the fertility of the land was not only maintained but enhanced. There was even a modest deposit of dragonet guano, which as any farmer knows makes by far the best fertilizer due to the eclectic nature of dragon diet.

How and when the disputes began no one can say. History being a succession of individual memories clouded by lies and personal agendas, it was impossible to ascribe blame. Some insist it all started when a rogue from Greater Tilo stole away the love of a Gyre man's wife. Others believe it had something to do with cheating involving a load of potatoes from Basweath, potatoes being the staple food crop and therefore a matter of some gravity among the Tiloeans. Still others insisted the arguments began when a group of villagers on Middle Tilo took to calling an old woman by the name of Granni Scork a witch.

Disagreements soon gave way to fighting. Shifting alliances between islands and even between individual villages were made and broken. Fights occasionally escalated into full-blown battles. Crops were carried off or destroyed, fishing nets stolen or shredded, young women treated with less than the respect that had formerly been accorded to them. Given the vagaries of weather that seasonally assaulted the islands, these clashes drew much-needed muscle and energy away from the business of growing and gathering food, repairing and building homes and shops, and generally maintaining the seemly level of civilization that the Tiloeans had hitherto enjoyed.

It was at this point (though no one can put a precise date to it) that a fed-up Granni Scork revealed to one and all that she was actually truly indeed a witch, as had been claimed all along but had since been forgotten by neighbors more interested in slaughtering one another than in following up on such hazy accusations. Observing the chaos that was consuming her beloved islands and threatening the very fabric of civilized society there, she resolved to deal with it in her own particular peculiar manner.

Seeing the faces all around her distorted with hate, and suspicion, and fear of one's neighbors, she dealt with the problem in a manner most admirably straightforward. From that point on, she declared, faces would be banned from the islands. Unable to narrow their eyes and draw up their noses and twist their mouths in expressions of animosity and dislike, the people of the Tilos would not be able to provoke reactions among their fellows. It would no longer be possible to flash looks of envy, of loathing, of disgust or dismay.

Of course, the absence of faces also eliminated any expressions of love, or caring, or just casual interest, but that was the price of peace among people too embittered to deal with the situation that had arisen and gotten out of hand in any other way.

At first there was panic, general and profound. But as soon as the initial pandemonium died down and people discovered that they could go on with their lives much as before, it was generally agreed that life was far better without the incessant fighting and conflict. Despite the absence of faces, people found that they were somehow able to perceive their surroundings sufficiently to carry out every activity that was necessary to life. To a certain extent they could still somehow see, hear, and smell. These senses were much muted, but not entirely absent. This impossible contradiction was generally ascribed to the magic of Granni Scork.

As for that redoubtable old lady, she saw to it that her own countenance traveled the same path as those of her neighbors. The loss didn't bother her. She had never particularly liked her face, and had in fact ceased caring for it very much some forty years earlier. When queried about its absence, she readily admitted that she was glad to be rid of the damned thing.

Much to the Tiloeans' surprise, they discovered that many of them agreed with her. One unexpected consequence of the loss of face (so to speak) was that within the society of islanders, all jealousy was eliminated. Without a face, no one could be accounted beautiful on sight or, more importantly, ugly. With everyone possessed of the same flat, blank visage, other qualities came to define a person's worth. Kindness, intelligence, good humor, skill at work replaced the superficialities of beauty when it came to judging another individual. With nothing to covet, covetousness too vanished among the Tiloeans.

Gradually they came not only to resign themselves to their loss of face but to give thanks for it. Fighting not only vanished as a social component of island society, but life among the Tiloeans was better than ever. They returned to the tending of their farms, to their harvests and gathering, and to the cordial neighborly relations that had prevailed when the islands were first settled.

So convinced did they become on the subject that a special corps was designated to make the rounds of all Tiloean buildings. It was their job to remove faces from every piece of art, sculpture, and craftwork in the islands, so that these artifices would appropriately reflect the new look of the inhabitants and the restored peace it had brought them. Only one problem remained.

What to do with all those expunged human facades.

For while Granni Scork had been able to remove them, her skills did not extend to obliterating them entirely. For many months, dislodged eyes, noses, ears and mouths drifted like clouds of fleshy butterflies over the islands, fitfully seeking places to rest. After Granni Scork's death, the now faceless people debated what to do with these persisting flocks of aimless facial components. While they did not want them to threaten the wonderful peace that had settled over the islands, neither could they quite bring themselves to extirpate something that had, after all, until recently comprised an intimate part of their individual selves.

There was much debate on the matter. Friendly debate, since it could not be disrupted by angry expressions among the participants. Eventually it was decided to make a celebration of the business at hand. Fishermen busied themselves weaving more of those ultrafine nets that were used to catch the very smallest fish. An islands-wide party was held, following which there was a great roundup of face parts in which every citizen participated.

With much shouting and yelling and waving of hands and reed screens, the emancipated noses and mouths, eyes and ears were herded together to be caught in the mesh nets. These were then taken to a small but secure central repository that had been built into the mountainside of Greater Tilo, where they were stored in a large locked chamber with no exit. And everyone was satisfied.

People passed on, and when they died their respective facial components perished with them. As part of the ritual attendant on the birth of a new child, that infant's face was ceremonially expunged and evacuated to the repository, there to join hundreds of similar floating bits. Each year a festival was held to commemorate the original gathering of the emancipated faces, with the celebration terminating at the repository in the presence of much good food and drink. For the islanders were still able to eat, passing sustenance through narrow, inexpressive slits in the lower portions of their faces where lips and teeth had once reposed.

Similarly, they could hear through tiny dots in the sides of their heads, and smell through dots in the center, and see, after a fashion, through dots situated higher up. The arrangement was too minimal to be called a face, and each was utterly identical to that of its neighbor. These openings only manifested themselves when they were required. When a person did not need to smell, for example, no dots were present in the center of his or her head.

Occasionally, visitors arrived in boats that pulled up on the shores of the Tilos. They were immediately taken in hand lest they disturb the delicate faceless balance that made life in the islands so agreeable. Their faces were removed and placed in the repository with all the others. After an initial period of anguish and despair (but no screaming, in the absence of mouths), these unwilling immigrants slowly adapted to their new lives, blending in successfully with the original islanders and adding vigor and energy to what otherwise might have become a decadent and inbred stock. Because of this, the Tiloeans actually looked forward to the rare visitations from representatives of the outside world.

There came a day when a much larger vessel than usual arrived in the archipelago, sailing on a westerly heading between Greater Tilo and Hookk. It did not run up onto a beach but instead anchored offshore. This was understandable, the local fisherfolk knew, due to the visitor's size and the water she drew. As was standard procedure in such cases, a formal greeting committee was chosen from among the most respected islanders and given the task of visiting the ship preparatory to welcoming its occupants into Tiloean society.

There was no reason for those on board the visiting vessel to suspect treachery. From experience, the Tiloeans knew that craft that called at the islands were usually in search of replenishments for their stores. So the fishing boats that sailed out to greet the newcomers were loaded down with the best the islands had to offer: marvelously fresh vegetables and fruits, baskets of shelled nuts, racks of filleted fish, and cooked carcasses of the eocardia and isocromys and other strange rodents and rabbitoids that roamed the islands' rocky reaches.

Observing this approaching bounty, those on board the vessel overcame their initial revulsion at the sight of the people without faces. Their queasiness quickly gave way to camaraderie as the Tiloeans boarded the craft and announced their intention to supply the visitors with whatever they might require in the way of food and water. This was not a lie. The islanders thoroughly enjoyed sharing the munificence of their harvest with callers from the outside world. It was a way of introducing them to the good life that Tiloean society had to offer.

Through their subdued senses the islanders wandered about the ship, finding much to admire in its construction and design. As experienced sailors, the crew of such a vessel would find plenty of work on the islands. It was a bit of surprise to find that they came not from the west, as was commonly the case for those who found themselves in the Tilos, but from much farther away, from the distant eastern lands that lay far across the open reaches of the Semordria.

No matter. They would make good citizens one and all, as soon as their initiation was complete. A feast was decreed to celebrate their arrival. It would take place on the deck of the ship that very evening. The Captain proved agreeable to this offer, and her crew positively enthusiastic. In the calm, safe anchorage formed by the two islands, it would be possible to enjoy the promised festivities on a steady deck.

Everything was supplied by the islanders: food, drink, and entertainment. Their excitement was infectious, and they quickly had the crew relaxing and enjoying themselves. And why not? The enthusiasm of the Tiloeans was genuine, reflecting their delight at the imminent prospect of so many new bloodlines from outside joining with their own. Indifferent to all the noise and human activity, Ahlitah promptly abandoned the main deck in search of a quiet place below where he could sleep undisturbed.

Engulfed by such a sea of open and honest conviviality, the sailors let themselves go with an abandon they had not felt since their last days on the mainland. The upper deck of the ship became a scene of riotous exuberance, lit by the lamps hung in the rigging and marred only by the inability of the islanders to laugh in concert with their new friends. For that, real lips and mouths were required.

But the Tiloeans managed to convey their pleasure in other ways that readily communicated themselves to the exhilarated sailors. Among other things, the islanders had become masters of dance. When several of the extremely comely men and women who had come aboard for the celebration proceeded to divest themselves of their attire, a corresponding number of mariners happily joined them in mutual dishabille.

The party went on well into the early hours of morning, by which time nearly all the celebrants had fallen unconscious either through the effects of strong drink or simple contented exhaustion. Nothing was suspected by the crew since the visiting islanders had eaten and drunk of the same victuals as they. Unbeknownst to them, subtle seasonings that affected a person's consciousness had been cooked into all the food. As a consequence, they slept harder than would normally have been the case.

A small flotilla of fishing boats soon surrounded the visitor. From within, islanders ready with ropes and nets boarded the silent ship. The carousing citizens who had partaken of the night's celebration would be returned to their homes to recover from the effects of the soporific seasonings in their own beds. As for the somniferous members of the crew, they were carried one by one into the fishing boats and taken ashore.

Zealous, willing hands affectionately unloaded them onto waiting wagons for the brief journey to the repository. There they were lovingly placed on clean cots, one for each man or woman. When the last had been transferred from the wagons, the priests entered. These were the heirs of Granni Scork, insofar as she had any. They were there to bless the transformation of the sailors from irritable, anxious folk capable of such primitive emotions as rage and envy and mistrust into serene, gracious residents of the Tilos.

When the priests had finished their work, bestowing their benedictions on the new citizens-to-be, they relinquished the repository to a solemn line of villagers carrying ropes and soft leather cuffs. Among them were many fishermen, these being the best and most knowledgeable people when it came to the securing of bindings and knots.

One by one they tied the visitors to their beds. Not to make prisoners of these nascent friends and neighbors, but for their own good. Tradition held that travelers newly deprived of their faces were not always immediately receptive to the painless transformation, and tended to go on wild, mad rampages of despair and self-destruction, injuring themselves and sometimes other unwary Tiloeans. So they would be kept secured until they came, each in his or her own fashion, to accept the inevitability of their new lives.

Earnest attendants maintained a watch until the faces of the visitors began to reflect their new surroundings and the work of the priests. Ears were usually the first to go, followed by nostrils and then the rest. As these rose like newborn moths from the faces of their sleeping owners, they were shooed and herded into the back of the repository and into the great domed chamber where hundreds of other facial elements waited to greet them. One by one, the sleeping countenances of the newcomers were reduced to smooth, featureless blanks.

Commotion filled the room when they began to wake and discover themselves faceless. Instantly, gentling attendants were at the newcomers' sides, soothing them with soft, wordless sounds and reassuring touches. These would be needed in quantity over the next few days, until the panicked sailors began to exhaust themselves or otherwise calm down.

All of the frenzy and hysteria was physical. The newly faceless tried to scream, but in the absence of lips and mouths could utter only terse, noncommittal sounds. They tried to cry; an impossibility in the absence of eyes. Communication with one another and with their new benefactors would have to wait until they were taught the language of soft utterances and signs.

The largest among them, a great hairy creature who was as much beast as man, had required the largest chains on the islands to restrain him. His oversized cot rocked and bounced with his struggles, but strive as he might, he was unable to free himself. The Tiloeans took no chances, and had overbound the shaggy mountain just to be sure. In his frantic, undisciplined exertions he was nearly matched by several of his much smaller shipmates. None succeeded in breaking free, though a number continued to exert themselves well into the later part of the day.

With nightfall came a certain calm as the newly defaced company realized the hopelessness of continuing to struggle. The watch within the outer repository was changed and new islanders (if not new faces) arrived to replace the first attendants. These murmured soothingly to the bound guests, striving to assuage their understandable distress. After all, one does not lose one's face every day. But they would all be the better for it; they would see. Or rather, perceive, seeing in the old sense being one more unnecessary aptitude that had been painlessly excised from their personages.

No lights were lit in the chamber. None were needed, since those within perceived rather than saw, and for perceiving, light was not necessary.

The Tiloeans were much taken with their new residents. Nearly every one was of sound, hearty physical stock. They would constitute a wonderful addition to the general population. Already, eligible young men and women from all the islands were choosing favorites in hopes of striking an acceptable match. There were many to pick from, since every member of the ship's crew had been brought onto Greater Tilo from the fine ship now bobbing unattended at anchor in the little harbor.

But in taking her crew, the islanders had overlooked one who was not.

Something that was not even faintly human stirred in the bowels of the otherwise abandoned vessel. It had retired there in search of some peace and quiet during the raucous festivities of the night before. Perceived as entirely inhuman by the Tiloeans who had scoured the ship from stem to stern in search of slumbering crew, it had been relegated to the category of livestock or ship's pet and subsequently ignored.

Now it stretched, yawned, and slowly made its way upward until it was standing on the main deck. Confusion confounded it. A whole day had obviously passed, yet the detritus of the wanton celebration supplied by the faceless islanders still lay scattered everywhere about the ship. The big cat's heavy brows drew together. This was most unlike the human Captain, who experience had shown not merely favored but demanded a taut, spotless vessel.

Wandering through the quarters of officers, crew, and passengers, the black litah's unease increased as every successive cabin turned out to be as empty as the one before. Padding to the railing, it observed numerous lights onshore, indicating that while life had abandoned the ship, it was present in plenty on the nearby island. Clearly, something was seriously amiss. Not that the cat particularly cared about the individual fates of an assortment of ill-smelling, ill-bred humans, but it was painfully conscious of a still unpaid debt to one of them. Also, despite its exceptional physical abilities, it could not sail the ship by itself. For lack of an opposable thumb, it thought, many things were lost.

It was the possessor, however, of certain compensations, not the least of which was exceptional physical strength and senses that would put those of the most sensitive human to shame. Putting both massive forepaws on the railing, it pushed off the deck and plunged over the side, landing with a surprisingly modest splash in the calm black water. Power-ful legs churning beneath its sleek body, it paddled steadily toward shore.

Arriving safely on a deserted beach south of the main cluster of lights, it shook itself several times. Ignoring an inherent impulse to pause and dry itself further, it contented itself with fluffing out its magnificent black mane before heading north. Trotting along the beach with eyes and ears alert and nose held close to the ground, it inhaled an excess of odors both familiar and exotic. No stranger by now to salt water, it was able to discard quickly hundreds of natural scents as immaterial to its search. When it encountered human spoor it slowed slightly, continuing onward only when it identified the odor as unfamiliar.

When at last it intersected a shallow beach that reeked not only of one but of a number of familiar body odors, it knew it had come to the place where its friends had been brought ashore. There was neither smell nor sight of a struggle, which the cat found most peculiar. Knowing that the human Captain would not have left her ship wholly untended and therefore suspecting foul play, the litah had expected to find evidence of a fight. In the absence of such evidence, it grew, if possible, more wary than ever.

Voices approached and the litah hunkered down behind one of the small boats that had been drawn up onshore. Two figures passed, faceless like those who had come aboard the ship to participate in the human festivities. The litah could have killed them silently and easily, with a single bite to the neck of each. But ignorance made it cautious. Not knowing what it was up against, the big cat held off doing anything that might alert the locals to its presence on their island.

Instead, it waited motionless for the two blank-visaged humans to pass. Dark as the night, it was virtually invisible in the absence of a bright moon, and the strollers did not even look in its direction. When their silhouettes and voices had faded into the distance, the litah left the beach and moved inland.

So recent and strong were the multiple smells of his friends and the crew that he was able to diverge from the actual path whenever it seemed he might pass into the open. Always picking up the scent trail after such momentary digressions, the litah soon found itself concealed within a patch of brush, eyeing the entrance to a single impressive stone structure. A quick circumnavigation of the edifice turned up no traces of his companions. Therefore it was reasonable to assume that they had been taken inside, where the spoor vanished.

Two islanders stood guard at the entrance. At the moment they were chatting with one another, relaxing beneath cloudy but otherwise clem-ent skies. As guards their presence was more ceremonial than necessary.

More than anything, they were there to attend to the needs of those fettered within should any of them become hysterical beyond the bounds of expectation or tradition.

This pair the litah slew. Not because it was unavoidable or because it felt a sudden surge of bloodlust, but because it was the quickest way to ensure their silence for as long as should be necessary. Padding through the unbarred doorway, it entered a corridor awash in darkness. Any human wandering about in such circumstances would have quickly stumbled into walls or tripped and fallen to the floor. The litah's eyesight, however, was infinitely sharper than that of any man.

Those same feline senses enabled it to locate its companions quickly. Faceless they might be, but nothing could disguise their individual odors, especially after a day and a night of struggling frantically against their bonds. Delicately employing bloodied teeth and claw and always keeping an ear alert for the sounds of approaching islanders, the litah freed them one at a time from their restraints.

Freedom brought only minimal joy to men and women who had lost their faces. It was one tall, easily recognizable individual who, exhibiting profounder perception than any of the others, caught hold of the litah's mane and led it not outside but deeper into the structure.

Turning a final corner, they confronted an elderly wise man with an impressive white beard that covered most of his otherwise vacant face. Sensing their presence, he rose from the cross-legged position in which he had been resting to brandish the ceremonial spear he held. Before he could throw it or utter a warning, he fell beneath the litah's huge paw, his neck broken and his upper spine shattered.

Behind him was a heavy wooden door. From the other side of that door arose a constant, relentless hum. It was the kind of noise a hundred subdued beehives might generate. Striding forward, the tall faceless human began to pound on the door. It was braced with double bolts and the bolts themselves secured with large padlocks.

Backing up as far as it could in a straight line, the black litah let out a reverberant roar that shook dust from the walls of the enclosed space and exploded forward. Beneath its onrushing mass, bolts, locks, and door went down together.

Beyond lay a single expansive, domed chamber. Buzzing like a million wasps, hundreds of eyes, ears, noses, and mouths rushed the sudden gap. The intruders, human and cat alike, ducked away from that torrent of fleeing lineaments.

Separating themselves from the choleric mass, six specific features slowed before the tall man. Pausing to ponder the vacant countenance-as-canvas to make certain it was the appropriate blank, they slowly drifted forward to reattach themselves to the smooth skin. The eyes went first, signaling to their fellow facial traits the correctness of the decision. Mouth followed, and then nostrils and ears, until the face of the tall man had been fully restored.

In the outer chamber other bits and pieces of individual countenance were searching out and relocating themselves on the faces from which they had been detached. It seemed impossible that every feature should find its proper owner, and there was some contentious bumping and fussing when, for example, two noses tried to fit on the same face or two ears to occupy the same side of a head. But eventually everything straightened itself out, much as individual seal pups somehow manage to find their mothers amidst tens of thousands of identical-appearing females.

Faces reinstated, the members of the ship's crew vowed to die fighting rather than surrender them again to the pernicious machinations of the islanders. The faceless bodies of the two guards lying athwart the entrance were favorably remarked upon by the escaping sailors. Arming themselves with branches of wood or pieces of stone, they made their way down toward the waterfront where the fishing boats were beached.

As it developed, there was no need to take up arms. The islanders were far too busy trying to fight off their liberated facial traits. Virtually attacking their former owners, the organs that had matured in isolation now instinctively sought to reattach themselves to visages that had never known them.

Tiloeans were seen fleeing their homes in the middle of the evening, swatting and flailing at aggressive noses and ears, their arms swinging wildly to keep persistent eyes from taking up residence in the location of former sockets. Never having known the senses that had been banished since birth, they had no idea how to cope with them. Those islanders whose ears found the right heads were stunned by the loudness a couple of convoluted slabs of flesh could convey. Others kept newly restored eyes shut tight lest they be mentally blinded by the shock of sharply outlined images delivered direct to the brain. Noses brought not satisfaction but nausea, and mouths a mindless, disconsolate wailing that began to spread all across the island—and to other islands, as freed features flocked to owners living there.

With the aid of nets and clubs, the aroused populace tediously began to bring the situation under control. Eyes and ears were rounded up and bagged for return to the domed chamber. Stunned noses fluttered and hopped on the ground, to be recovered and placed in bags by busy, faceless children. A carnival of the grotesque was on view as Tiloeans with one eye and a mouth, or two ears and nothing else, struggled to clean up the mess engendered by the mass release of features.

Nor were the impatient, agitated organs always precise in their deployment. Stumbling along the paths and past the village, the departing crew saw men and women with ears where their eyes ought to have been, noses taking the places reserved for mouths, and individual eyes occupying the high points of faces where nostrils ought to reside. All of which contributed to the general chaos and allowed the sailors to escape unchallenged.

Commandeering several fishing boats, they rowed their way back to the waiting *Grömsketter.* Ignoring the danger inherent in attempting to pass through close-set islands at night, the Captain ordered all sail put on. Not one of the grateful crew challenged her decision. Had she so ordered it, they would have jumped into the water in a body and pushed and kicked the heavy craft with their own hands, so frantic were they to flee that gentle, kindhearted, accursed land.

It was only when they were safely clear of the Tilo Isles and their bizarre inhabitants that the mariners took the time to note that not everything had been put back the way it had formerly been. There was some question as to which eye belonged to whom, and what lips ought rightly to reside above certain chins. This posttraumatic confusion was understandable and was soon sorted out. Personal disappointments aside, it was understood that everyone had recovered his or her rightful features, and that if anyone held any second thoughts on the matter, they were best kept to oneself, since nothing could be done in any event to further alter the current state of affairs.

What lingering discontent existed was quickly swallowed in the wave of euphoria that followed the last peak of the Tilos falling behind the horizon astern. Everyone realized they should be grateful for having had the proper complement of features returned to them. After all, everyone knows it is better to have the wrong nose than no nose at all.

There was one attempt made to honor and praise the black litah for effecting their freedom and the restoration of their countenances, but the big cat forcefully demurred. Such frivolities were time-wasting activities fit for humans, it avowed curtly, and not for nobler species like himself. Besides, it went on to explain, it was by nature already lionized, and had no need of gyrating, genuflecting humans to remind it of that fact.

But despite the cat's insistence, a few brave sailors did manage to slip in a stroke or two when it was not looking, before dashing quickly back to their posts. After a while the litah gave up trying to frighten them off, even going so far as to tolerate their accolades and attention. Once when it was being the recipient of such attention, the lankier of its human companions caught it purring thunderously to itself. Confronted with this embarrassing contradiction, the litah promptly retired below, and thereafter showed itself as little as possible except at mealtimes and when taking the occasional feline constitutional around the deck.

VII

After the remarkable occurrences of the past week it was a relief to passengers and mariners alike to find themselves navigating a calm sea devoid of preternatural spectacles. Except for the flock of web-footed pink and white sea dragonets that glided gracefully past one morning, nothing out of the ordinary presented itself for their perusal. Life aboard ship resumed a normalcy it had not known since the *Grömsketter* had first cleared the mouth of the now distant Eynharrowk delta.

They were still in waters foreign to Stanager Rose and her crew, but sailing on the right course to make landfall somewhere north of the trading town of Doroune. The sometimes gruff Captain seemed pleased with their progress, and voiced aloud the hope that they would encounter no more unaccountable interruptions.

It was a false hope.

Contrary to what landsmen think, there are many kinds of fog. These are as familiar to mariners as the many varieties of wind and rain are to a farmer. There is the fog that sneaks up on a ship, scudding along the surface of the sea until it begins to cling in bits and pieces to its hull, gradually building up until it is heavy enough to creep over the bow and obscure a skipper's vision. There is fog that arrives in thick clumps like gray cotton pulled from some giant's mattress. Some fog drifts down from the sky, settling over ship and crew like a moist towel, while another fog rolls over the ocean in the proverbial bank that is more like a dark gray wall than a line of mist. There are almost as many species of fog as dog and, like dogs, each has its own peculiarities and unique identifying characteristics and habits.

There was nothing striking about the fog that began to assemble itself around the *Grömsketter*. At first. It announced itself as a single patch drifting out of the west, neither especially dense nor dark. Gray and damp, it floated toward the bowsprit and sailed past on the starboard side. Few of the crew paid it any heed. All of them had seen fog before, sailed through it, and come out safely on the other side.

When additional patches showed themselves later in the morning, it occasioned some comment among those on duty. The lookout in particular was concerned, and announced that they appeared to be entering a region of fairly contiguous mist. Stanager Rose directed Terious to make the usual preparations for running through cloud. These consisted of placing additional lookouts in the rigging and reefing some of the canvas. Better to go a little more slowly and be sure of what lay ahead than to charge blindly onward at full speed.

Sensing the ship slowing, her passengers came out on deck, to find themselves greeted by the congealing grayness.

Ehomba commented on the unhurried activity aloft. "You are taking in sail."

"Ayesh." They were standing on the helm deck. Stanager's attention was focused on her crew, not on curious passengers. "When general visibility's cut, a wise seaman doesn't take chances with what can't be seen. Don't want to run into anything." She smiled tersely. "Don't worry. Either this will lift or we'll plow right through it. That's the nature of sea fog."

"Run into what?" Standing at the railing, Simna was peering into the thickening gloom, struggling to penetrate the damp haze. "Another ship?"

"Possible, but most unlikely," she told him. "A floating log could do real damage, but I am more concerned with drifting ice." She squinted skyward, sighting along the mast. "As far north as the liberated winds blew us, we run the risk of encountering one of the great floating mountains of ice that sailors sometimes pass. Run hard into one and we could easily be hulled. I've no wish to be cast adrift, marooned on an island that's steadily melting beneath me."

"I'd melt beneath you."

"What's that?" Her gaze swung sharply from sky to passenger.

Turning and leaning back against the railing, Simna smiled virtuously. "I said that I felt you entreating your crew."

"Oh." Eyes narrowing, she looked away from him and back toward the main deck. "Certainly is thick. I'd hate to wander into another group of islands like the Tilos. No way to navigate unknown straits in this. We'd have to drop anchor and wait for it to lift."

No islands presented themselves, but neither did the fog slide away.

Instead, it continued to thicken, to the point where sailors could only see but a little ways in front of them, and had to do a certain amount of work by feel. It was not the density but the darkness that began to concern Stanager.

Standing by the wheel, she surveyed the brooding layer that had engulfed her ship. "Never seen fog this dark. This thick, ayesh, but never so black. And it seems to be growing worse. But that's not possible. Fog, even the heaviest fog, is gray and not black."

Simna's eyes widened as he remembered another boat crossing. "Eromakadi!"

"What's that?" She blinked at him.

Ehomba interrupted before his companion had a chance to explain. The silent herdsman had been studying the fog for some time now. "No, Simna. It is not what you fear. Bad enough, but not what you fear." Reaching out, he swirled one long-fingered hand through the dank atmosphere. "Not thick enough to cut, but not eromakadi, either. See how I stir it?" He waved his hand back and forth. "Being a live thing, eromakadi would react. This is truly an ocean fog, and of a kind I have seen before, that rolls in off the ocean as easily as it clings to it." He looked over at Stanager, partially obscured by the black fog even though she stood only a few feet away.

"But on land, it does not linger. And a man carrying a lamp through his village does not have to worry about running into floating logs or drifting mountains of ice." He smiled encouragingly. "Only into sleeping dogs and laughing children."

"This is no game." Her expression was grim. "If it gets any thicker or darker, my people won't be able to see well enough to perform their duties." Without being able to see him, she shouted to her first mate, knowing that he was somewhere below on the main deck. "Mr. Kamarkh! Light and set all lamps! And be careful! A burning ship will cut through this fog, but that's not the kind of light I want to see!"

"Ayesh, Captain!" came the mate's stalwart reply.

Moments later, pinpoints of light began to appear throughout the ship: in the rigging, at the ends of spars, atop both masts and along her sides. But so dense and dark had the mist become that they barely shone bright enough to illuminate their immediate surroundings, much less the water through which the *Grömsketter* was cutting.

"This won't do," Stanager muttered. "Lookouts can't see a thing. Even if they did, it'd be too close to avoid. We're going to have to furl all sail and put out the sea anchor until this thins or lifts."

"That will cost us time." Ehomba did not phrase it as a question.

"Ayesh. But I've no choice." She stared at him through the gloom. "I won't risk my ship."

"How long do you think before it clears enough to continue?" Simna asked.

Her response was not encouraging. "Impossible to say. Something this intense, it might be days. Or weeks."

"We do not have weeks," Ehomba observed quietly.

"I know. I hope you gentlemen like fish, because if we're forced to remain here for very long, we're going to be eating a lot of it." She turned away from them to give the necessary orders.

"Wait."

Her gaze swung back to the tall passenger. "Wait for what, herdsman? I respect you for what you've done, but don't try to tell me my business."

"I would not think of it. It is only that I would like to try something." He glanced in his friend's direction. "Simna, would you bring me the sky-metal sword?"

"Would I like to be locked in the Pasha of Har-Houseen's harem for a week?" Elated, the swordsman dashed to the nearest hatch and vanished within as swiftly as a meerkat diving into its burrow.

Stanager eyed her enigmatic passenger warily. "More wind? Should I alert the crew to be ready for some sorceral gale?"

Ehomba sighed heavily. "As I have had to tell my friends repeatedly, there is no sorcery involved. I am only making use of what the wise people of my village have been kind enough to provide me."

"I'm only interested in the consequences, Etjole. Not the source."

"There will be no wind." He smiled to himself. "Simna is a good man and a fine fellow, but sometimes his enthusiasm gets the better of his thinking. The sword of sky metal is not for calling up a casual breeze when one is too hot, or a gust of wind to fill a sail. When loosed to do all that it can, it is an extremely difficult blade to control." He nodded skyward. "It might as easily sink this ship as blow it free. But there are all kinds of winds. Eminent sailor that you are, you know that there are winds within the sea as well as above."

"Winds within the sea?" She frowned. "Are you speaking of controlling the currents?"

"I am not mariner enough to chance such a thing, and the effects of the sword are not so precisely controlled. But I think there is one path I might explore." His smile widened even as his tone grew increasingly speculative. "It is a good thing that I have lived all my life close to the water. One does not have to spend time on a boat to know what wonders lie beneath the waves. Simply walking a beach can also be highly instructive."

He was interrupted by Simna's return. The swordsman held the sky-metal sword carefully in a double-handed grip. Having seen what it could do, he had no wish to find out what might happen if it was accidentally dropped.

"Here you are, bruther!" He passed the sword to its owner. "Now, by Geulrashk, call us up some wind and disperse this muck! Clear the air, Etjole!" Eyes shining, he stepped back.

"I cannot," Ehomba told him. "Too dangerous. A ship is a fragile thing. We already have enough wind. What we need is a way to see clear to making use of it."

"Gojom help me, I don't understand, bruther." It was a sentence Simna ibn Sind had come to use frequently in the presence of his enigmatic friend.

Grasping the hilt of the sword firmly in both hands, Ehomba slowly raised it skyward in front of him, the blade held vertically and as straight as one of the *Grömsketter's* masts. An intense blue glow began to emerge from the metal, pale at first but intensifying rapidly to azure and then indigo. It pushed back the fog instantly—but only for a few yards on either side of the radiant sword.

Expecting something grander, Simna was openly disappointed. As for Stanager, she was quietly grateful for the modest improvement in the clarity of her immediate surroundings. At least the men and women on deck and up in the rigging would be able to see her without straining. Down by the mainmast, a seated Hunkapa Aub saw the blue luminescence and delightedly clapped two massive hands together.

"Pretty light!" he exclaimed in the tone of a delighted child. "Pretty, pretty blueness!"

"It's pleasing to look upon, all right." Simna grunted. "But it's no beacon sufficient to guide this ship."

"No, it is not. Nor is it intended to be. But perhaps like will follow like." Holding the resplendent sword as carefully as if it were a cauldron of boiling oil, Ehomba turned and slowly made his way to the side of the ship, trailing the gently pulsating blue aurora around him.

One of the several emergency boarding ladders that always hung over the side scraped wetly against the stern. Still holding the blade vertically, Ehomba transferred his grip to one hand. With the other, he grasped the uppermost rung of the rope-and-slat ladder and started over the side. It was a delicate balancing act that did not allow the herdsman to relax for a second.

"Hoy, Etjole, what do you think you're doing?" Seeing his friend disappear over the side, Simna rushed to the railing. Leaning over, he watched as Ehomba, carefully balancing the length of refulgent metal in a single-handed grip, made his way down the ladder toward the dark sea below. Only the circle of blue light from the blade made it possible for the swordsman to follow his friend's progress. Without it, the frightful thickness of the mist would have quickly swallowed him up.

"What's going on?" Though intensely curious as to what the tall passenger was about, Stanager would not abandon her position by the helm.

"I don't know." Tensely, the swordsman watched his friend continue his descent. "But I can tell you this much—he's not out for an afternoon's swim."

The bottom of the ladder trailed backward in the dark water. Ehomba reached a rung where his feet were occasionally submerged and stopped there. Still firmly grasping the tough, sea-cured rope with one hand, he abruptly let gravity take hold of the mass of the weapon and swing the point downward. Keeping the fine edge facing forward, he was able to maintain his grip as the blade cut through the water. The deep blue radiance was clearly visible beneath the surface.

Even though the edge sliced easily through the gentle swells, the ocean still tugged and pulled on the sword. Gritting his teeth, Ehomba held on, the hilt locked in his long-fingered grip, the blue glow penetrating deeply into the waters that tried to steal it away from him. Above, Simna and Hunkapa Aub watched from the rail. The swordsman could see that the strain of holding on to the ladder with one hand and the submerged blade with the other was tiring his friend.

"Want me to spell you awhile, bruther?" he called out.

The herdsman's face turned upward. Somehow, he managed to grin. *He'll grin when he's on his deathbed,* Simna mused. *It'll be the last expression he wears.*

"Thank you, friend Simna, but all is well."

"Well as what?" the swordsman retorted. "What is it you hope to do?"

"Light a way through this confusion." With the effort of looking upward putting additional stress on his body, Ehomba lowered his head.

Hunkapa dropped a massive, shaggy arm over the side. "Look, look! More prettinesses!"

Simna squinted. Something was rising from the depths of the ocean. It was not large—no longer than one of the *Grömsketter*'s small boats— but it was lined with lights that flashed bright yellow and pale red. As it loomed nearer the surface he saw that it was a fish—but a fish unlike any finned denizen of the deep he had ever seen before, either in kitchen or in art.

Its body was more than nine feet long and silvery black, but it was no thicker around than a ribbon. A single long fin ran the length of the spine, and two tiny pectoral fins fluttered just beneath and back of glaring eyes the size of dinner plates. Above the head three long spines bobbed and weaved, and each was tipped with a bright yellow light. Prominent in the narrow, gaping mouth were fangs like shards of broken glass.

It was soon apparent that it was not alone.

Drawn by the light of the sword, all manner of wondrous deepwater creatures were rising to the surface. They swam and drifted and hovered about the cerulean halo of the sky-metal sword like moths romancing a candle on a summer's eve. As the abyssal ascension gave rise to this luminescent benthic epiphany, more and more of the crew crowded to the port side to gape. Though somewhat muted by the persistent fog, their reactions were a mixture of awe, wonder, and sheer childlike delight in an exotic and beautiful phenomenon the likes of which none of them had ever encountered before.

Up came a pair of fish like bloated black bladders, one thirty times larger than its companion. Each had a single long, curving appendage like a thin filament fishing line attached to its forehead, from whose tip twitched a lure of irresistible intensity. Their eyes were so small as to be almost invisible, and they burned with the fire of a hundred natural lights. Nearby swarmed a school of a thousand small silvery fish, each flashing a thumb-sized soft blue light from just aft of its eye.

There were jellyfish larger than any the sailors had ever seen, their pulsing bells decorated with blue and green and yellow lights that trailed fifty-foot-long tentacles of unbroken luminescence. Deep-sea sharks swept tails full of sapphire light in steady arcs, like glowing oars in the water, and all manner of toothy fish darted to and fro in balls of intense yellow or green.

But it was when the tiny lanterns of natural luminescence finally arose that the sea around the *Grömsketter* turned from dark to light. There were billions of them, seemingly in as many shapes and sizes, many so small that even sharp-eyed seamen wearing spectacles could barely make them out. Ehomba could. The herdsman's vision was particularly acute.

Then the mid-ocean merfolk arrived, showing oval, slightly protuberant eyes and gills that flashed gold around the edges. They displayed elegant patterns of light along their sides and fins and carried short staffs tipped with transparent crustacean bodies scavenged from the hidden places of the sea. These were filled with glowing krill individually selected for their color and brightness. A number of merfolk rode in shell chariots drawn by man-sized seahorses that glowed brown and were harnessed with kelp and sea-grass strips radiating an intense crimson.

The lightwhals came too. Looking like crosses between oversized dolphins and blind seals, they radiated a ghostly, pellucid purple. There were night penguins that emitted green light only when hunting in dark seas, and merlions whose manes were fringed with pallid lavender. The mournful, watery moans they exchanged with their land-bound cousin Ahlitah resounded regretful and forlorn across the mist-shrouded swells.

There were deep-ocean crabs whose shells boasted imbedded iridescences in lines of intense green spotted with azure, and strange turtles whose carapaces wore diadems of lights like pulsating jewels. Eels slithered and writhed like living lightning, while squid and cuttlefish ranging in size from palm-sized to giants that might have been family of the Kraken itself sent waves of opalescence rippling through their skin. Sea butterflies more colorful than any of their terrestrial counterparts flew beneath the surface on wings tinted emerald and topaz and tourmaline, occasionally emerging from the water in jubilant bursts of dazzling effulgence.

Drawn by the incomparable blue glow emitted by the sky-metal sword, all this great upwelling of light and life swirled around the *Grömsketter*, disturbing neither water nor sky but overwhelming and beating back the darkness imposed by the clinging fog. Whereas before Stanager and her crew could barely see one another clearly enough to avoid running into each other on the deck, now the excess of spectacular natural light illuminated the sea around the ship for nearly half a mile, making not only onboard activity but also navigation possible.

"Terious!" the Captain shouted. "Set the mains'l and the lower fores'ls! Let's punch through this murk before our herdsman's flock grows bored and decides to sink back from whence they came." Her classic profile was aglow with light from the thousands of luminescent deep-sea dwellers that had gathered around the ship.

Simna had not left his position by the rail. "Better to worry not about losing their interest, but about my friend losing the strength in his arm."

It was a procession never to be forgotten by all who saw it: the graceful *Grömsketter*, sails set and making her way southwest, englobed by millions of colored lights worn by as fantastic a profusion of undersea life as could be assembled in one place. Even experienced seamen would have been paralyzed by all that beauty, had they not been so busy.

Stanager Rose kept her crew occupied lest they lose themselves in the embarrassment of natural magnificence.

Thrust back by the luminescence, the fog began to shrivel and disperse, until a single light brighter if not more beautiful than all those assembled began to illuminate the scene from above. Then even the blue intensity of the sword could not sustain the interest of the visitors from the deep. In their tiny millions and larger pairs and trios they began to sink back into the abyss from which they had risen, untold numbers of lights descending and dissipating, until, with a last silent wave of a phosphorescent scepter, one of the deep-sea mermen saluted the ship and turned his glowing chariot ultimately downward.

The sun burned away the last of the fog, enabling the crew to put on still more sail and to flee from that darkling, benighted patch of ocean. Then it was time to bring forth a small quantity of the ship's precious supply of ice, kept sealed in the darkest, coldest depths of her hull. Not to cool her crew, who were certainly sweating heavily enough to deserve it, but to ice down the muscles of one of her passengers. Held in one position for so long, Ehomba's left arm and fingers had become badly cramped. The application of ice wrapped in towels might not equal the recent display of magic, but it was blessedly effective.

While the herdsman sat on the helm deck trying to restore the flow of blood to his aching muscles and tendons, Simna gingerly held the sky-metal sword. As always, the crosshatched lines on the blade fascinated his eye.

"How do you make it work, Etjole, if you are not the sorcerer you keep insisting you're not?"

The herdsman would have shrugged, but his cramped shoulders would not allow it. "Practice, friend Simna. Otjihanja showed me some things, and other elders had suggestions. It is not something to be described. You must *feel* the proper motion, the way the weight of the metal travels through the air and fights the pull of the Earth."

Simna nodded. "You know, it's funny. When I was younger I would have taken that as a challenge, and as a result probably tried something stupid."

"I do not see much that has changed with age." Curled up against the railing that separated the helm deck from the main deck below, the black litah murmured sleepily.

"And I do not take criticism of my profession from a yowling devourer of carrion." When the big cat chose not to respond, Simna turned back to his lanky friend. "Having seen what this remarkable blade can do, I would no more try to make use of it than I would a sculptor's chisel or a musician's lute."

Ehomba smiled softly. "You did, once."

A startled Simna looked sharply at the seated herdsman. "I thought you were asleep!"

Ehomba looked away. "I was."

The swordsman started to reply, discovered that he did not have an adequate response at hand, and decided against it. Instead, he laid the wondrous weapon carefully down alongside his seated friend and pulled the thin blanket a little higher on Ehomba's narrow shoulders. The herdsman had spent far too much time with his hand and part of one arm immersed in the cold water. Sorcerer or not, he was starting to shiver.

"I will be all right." He smiled reassuringly up at his concerned companion. "The ocean below my village is much colder than this, and I have spent many an hour wading and swimming in its waters."

"I don't care," Simna told him. "Any man can catch a chill and die from the complications." He looked out to sea. "Attract like to like, you said. More like light to light. It was a grand sight. I never dreamed quite so many splendid phantasms dwelled in the sea, and all of them lit from within by sorceral glow."

"Not sorceral," Ehomba corrected him. One hand held the edges of the blanket tight against his throat. "The lights you saw were all natural, manufactured from within their own bodies by the creatures themselves. There was nothing of sorcery about it."

The swordsman's forehead furrowed. "How do you know that?"

"Because many such creatures wash up dead on the beaches near my home. Their bodies are flaccid and their lights dimmed, but they still glow for a little while after dying." He nodded toward the clearing sky. "The waters offshore from my village go down very deep. It must be exceedingly dark in the depths, like a perpetual night, for the creatures that live there to need to make their own light."

"A handy property," Simna agreed. "There have been times when I would have liked to have been able to shine a little light from my own body."

The herdsman looked at him strangely. "Everyone does so, Simna. It is just that it is difficult to see. It takes practice to separate it out from the natural light that surrounds us every day."

The shorter man laughed easily. "So you're saying that I glow like those fishy things? Like a jellyfish, maybe?"

"No, not like a jellyfish. The light that people, or at least most people, emit, is something very different. But you do glow, my friend. Less intensely in ways than you would like to believe, and more brightly in other kinds. There are many, many different kinds of light."

"Well, at least I'm not dark." Simna enjoyed the notion, even though he was not sure he understood at all what his cryptic companion was talking about. "How about everyone else?" Turning, he gestured at those nearby, not really expecting the herdsman to respond.

Instead, Ehomba rested his chin on his knees and squinted, pausing once to wipe away a lingering droplet of salt water. "The Captain, she glows only a very few colors, but those colors are as pure and strong as I have ever seen in a person. The helmswoman Priget emits light in fits and bits, like the sparks from a fire. That man working the ropes over there, his lights are few and dim, but far from being absent." The herdsman's gaze roved the open decks.

"The lights of the first mate are also strong and unadulterated, but not nearly of an intensity approaching that of the Captain. Certain shades and tints are completely absent in Ahlitah, but those colors he does manifest are almost overpowering." He sniffed and, lifting a hand from beneath the blanket, rubbed his nose.

Simna's natural reaction to all this was to laugh heartily. But seeing the seriousness with which Ehomba was rendering his appraisals, the swordsman could not quite bring himself to do so. The herdsman was jesting, of course. Having one of his silent, slightly taciturn chuckles at the expense of a friend. People, much less cats like Ahlitah, did not glow. If they did, someone as sharp-eyed as himself would surely have noticed it by now. But he was happy to run with the joke, enjoying the fertility of his laconic companion's imagination. His friend might or might not be the mighty sorcerer Simna supposed him to be, but he was certainly a fine storyteller. The sincerity with which he spun his tall tales only added to their seeming veracity.

"You overlooked someone." He indicated a large, unkempt gray mass resting on the deck like a pile of discarded rugs. "What about Hunkapa Aub?"

Ehomba gazed thoughtfully in the direction of their humble companion. "He is a strange one. I can descry occasional bursts of light from him, but they are very subdued and difficult to catch." He grinned gently. "Maybe it is all that fur. Certain things can block out a person's light. Although I have never before known hair to do it, neither have I ever known anyone covered with quite so much hair." His attention drifted. "I think the rest of the day will be fine. I wonder how far we are from Doroune?"

Simna straightened. "I'll go and ask Stanager."

"Yes," Ehomba commented, "I have noticed that you and the Captain have begun to get along better these past several days."

The swordsman winked conspiratorially. "You've been around me long enough by now to know that I'm a very persistent fellow, long bruther. And not just in the matter of lost treasures to be found." Grinning, he turned and marched off in the direction of the helm, where Stanager Rose was conversing with Priget.

"Be careful," the herdsman called after him.

"Why?" Simna smiled back over his shoulder. "Afraid I might figure out how to see her 'light'?"

"No," Ehomba responded. "Afraid that you might see it. You're all too easily blinded by such things, Simna ibn Sind."

VIII

After so long out of sight of land (the Tilo Islands being a horrific recollection that every man and woman aboard firmly desired to expunge from their memories), the majestic spectacle of the Quonequot Cliffs looming on the western horizon roused a throaty cheer from passengers and crew alike when they finally hove into view. Rising vertically a thousand feet from the waves that broke against their base and plunging to untold depths below the surface, the white-chalk precipices terminated in a massive headland that marked the entrance to Kylles Bay. Beyond and within lay the fabled western trading city of Doroune.

Stealing a moment from her navigational duties, Stanager Rose left the helm in the capable hands of Priget, who had guided the *Grömsketter* into the bay several times before, and walked over to stand alongside the most puzzling passenger she had ever carried. At present, he was gazing thoughtfully over the starboard side, studying the lofty white escarpment as the ship neared land. Dragonets of many sizes and colors glided regally along the cliff faces, where they found safe nesting sites among the sheer walls. In this they were not alone. Ceaseless screeching and cawing and hissing testified to the competition for prime sites among dragonets and puffins, gulls and terns. As Captain and passenger stood side by side at the rail, a formation of great osteodontornids glided by overhead, their twenty-foot wings momentarily blocking out the sun, their tooth-filled beaks intent on tracking a school of small fish shoaling by just beneath the breaking spume.

"What will you do now?" she inquired of the silent herdsman.

He did not turn to look at her, but instead kept this gaze on the immense chalky headland. "As I told you before we set out on this crossing, I am bound by personal covenant to journey to a land called Ehl-Larimar, there to seek out a woman called the Visioness Themaryl, and return her to her family in Laconda. Ehl-Larimar lies to the west of here, so it seems I must keep traveling west." Shifting his attention from the imposing headland, he smiled down at her. "I have already been too long away from home. I hope I do not have to travel so far west that I meet myself coming."

She laughed, caught herself, and choked slightly on the unusual reaction. "That's silly, Etjole. Nobody can meet themselves coming."

With a sigh, he returned his attention to the place where the incoming swells shattered themselves against the white ramparts. "It depends how far west one has to go, and what one means by 'west.' This Doroune, is it as big as Hamacassar?"

She shook her head. "Haven't been that far inland—the crew and I keep pretty much to the harbor because that's where both our business and recreational interests lie. But from all that I've seen and heard on previous trips, it's a much smaller place. Most of the coastal towns we visit and trade with are like that. Transit points for goods from farther inland. They don't get many visitors from across the Semordria." She grinned confidently. "Everyone knows only fools and imbeciles dare attempt the ocean crossing."

Solemnly, he put a hand on her shoulder. "As one fool to another, let me say that it has been an honor to travel on your ship, Captain Rose."

She nodded once, as eloquent an acceptance of the compliment as she could manage. Straightforward praise made her uncomfortable. Easier for her to deal with a storm or a mutinous crew than an unabashed encomium.

"Thanks." They were silent for a while, standing side by side, watching the sea and the birds and the dragonets as Priget and Terious deftly maneuvered the *Grömsketter* around the southern tip of the headland and into Kylles Bay. Heading north once again but this time in calm, sheltered waters, Ehomba soon found he could make out the steeples and peaked roofs of Doroune in the distance.

"Look," she said finally, "I'll be a goodly while sailing down the coast and then back up again, selling off not only our own trade goods but those we pick up along the way. Can't give you exact times and dates because this sort of unscheduled trading isn't done to a timetable. But we'll for sure be calling at Oos, Xemon-scap, Polab, Sambley, and Calenx. Can't say if we'll go farther than that. The weather south of Calenx can turn at the drop of a line." It was her turn to put a hand on his arm.

"If your travels take you to any of those cities, don't depart without asking about us. If—when you've accomplished your quest, you'll be wanting passage home. Can't take you to Ehl-Larimar—don't even know where it is—but we *can* carry you back across the Semordria." This time her grin did not surprise her. "Try and hang on to a few of your pebbles. I like you, Etjole Ehomba. I find much to admire in you. And much that bewilders me. But while I like to think there's much goodness in my heart, that doesn't include free passage."

He nodded understandingly. "A few pebbles. Thoughts of them will keep your supercargo feeling younger than his years."

"Broch's a good fellow. Sharp mind, sound seaman. He's devoted to me, and to the ship, and has made it his mission to see to it that both of us stay afloat. Enjoy your last moments on the *Grömsketter,* Etjole Ehomba. She'll miss you, and so will I." She stepped back from the railing. "There's much of interest to see on the final leg of our approach into Doroune. Now if you'll excuse me, I have some small matters of navigation to attend to below."

He watched her until she disappeared down one of the ladders that led to the main deck. Straight of back and purpose, she was a fine woman. The sea had burnished her like bronze, had knocked off all the rough edges and replaced them with the sharpness of salt and the fire of red coral. Mirhanja would like her, he decided.

High on the white cliffs above, dragonets and seabirds screamed as the ship came around. It would be strange, he thought, to have again beneath his feet a floor that did not roll. Were he not so devoted a herdsman, he had often thought he might have become a sailor.

But such a thing was not possible for a Naumkib. They were a people of their land. If men such as he went off to sea, who would watch over the village and the herds? He inhaled deeply of the fresh, pungent salt air, knowing that it might be some time before he could fill his lungs with it again.

Activity busied the docks of Doroune, but the crowds and freneticism he had encountered in Hamacassar were absent. There was about the people here a sense of purpose, but not desperation. They wanted to make money, but none were dying of the need to do so. It was a simpler place, an easier place, especially for four strangers.

What, he found himself wondering, would Ehl-Larimar be like?

After spending the night on the boat, the following morning Ehomba was more than a little shocked to see Hunkapa Aub carrying Simna ibn Sind down the unloading ramp, with a dour Ahlitah padding behind. From above, Terious and Priget waved good-bye. Of Captain

Stanager Rose there was no sign. He was not surprised. She had made
her farewell to him the previous day.

"Simna, what happened? What is wrong with you?"

"Wrong?" Tired eyelids fluttered and a wan smile flashed across the
swordsman's countenance. "Hoy, nothing's wrong, bruther." With a
shaky hand he gestured toward his feet. "Me legs aren't working right
just now, that's all. A little rest and they'll be fine." Looking away from
his tall friend, he let his eyes roll skyward. "Me, I'm already fine. Very
fine indeed. Except for me lower appendages, thank you." With that he
closed his eyes, and was almost instantly asleep.

Hunkapa bore Simna's limp body effortlessly as they made their way
inland from the docks. Puzzled, Ehomba sought enlightenment from
Aub, even though he felt he was attempting to mine a strata devoid of
that particular ore.

"What happened to him?"

"Don't know." Brows like shredded rags drew together as the big
biped struggled to cogitate. "Friend Simna not much speak today." The
bestial visage brightened. "Simna say he talk navigation with Captain
Rose. Last night."

"Naviga—?" Finding understanding where he had expected to
unearth none, the herdsman concluded the excavation silently. Clearly,
for his friend Simna, whatever else they might stumble into, Doroune
had for him already proven a propitious port of call.

Halting in the middle of a small plaza with a public drinking fountain before them, Ehomba considered the shopfronts that ringed the
circular square. "We need a guide, some information, and instruction."

Still carrying the swordsman, who was by now awake, moaning, and
holding himself, Hunkapa gestured with his great shaggy head. "Ehomba
want go west. Hunkapa guide! That way, west." Next to him, Ahlitah
commented by farting.

Leaning on his spear, the herdsman smiled tolerantly at his oversized companion. "That is very good, Hunkapa. I am glad you know
which way is west. But before we start we should try to learn something
about the country we must pass through."

Eventually a resident brave enough to stop at Ehomba's request
directed them to a large dispatch house where wagons of many sizes and
descriptions were being fitted out with sails. The travelers had already
encountered several of these sturdy, wind-powered vehicles steering
their way around the city. According to the helpful citizen, the dispatch
center was a good place to find not only transportation inland, but also a
guide to convey them there.

Their inquiries met with the same kind of amused skepticism

Ehomba had encountered before. It was a reaction that, on repetition, was beginning to grow tiresome. Was he the only man who believed that to travel from one place to another, no matter how reputedly dangerous or difficult, all that was required was for one to start walking in the requisite direction?

"Lissen, you," stammered the ancient pathfinder who was too bored not to talk to them, "we all every one of us knows where Ehl-Larimar lies." Raising a shaky finger that resembled a strip of rolled saddle leather, he pointed westward. Behind Ehomba, huge hands clapped delightedly together.

"See, Etjole, see! Hunkapa know, Hunkapa guide!"

"Be quiet, Hunkapa," the mildly annoyed herdsman admonished his hulking friend. The matted one fell silent.

"If you all know how to get to Ehl-Larimar, why cannot one of you guide us there?"

"Because the difficulty's not in the knowin', it's in the goin'." Peering behind his questioner, the elderly guide considered the herdsman's blond hair. "Why you braid up your locks like that, man? Seen wimmens do it, but never 'til now a buck."

"It is the style among the men of my village." Uncharacteristically, Ehomba was becoming impatient with this short, skinny sage, who reminded him of chattering macaws. "What is so difficult about the going to Ehl-Larimar that you and all your colleagues refuse to take us?"

Aged eyes that had seen much rolled in their sockets as if loose. "Why, out west there's dangerous wild critters everywhere, some of 'em monstrous big, others with long fangs that drip poison." To emphasize the latter, he protruded his upper jaw far beyond the lower and flapped it to simulate biting motions. "First you have to get through the Hexen Mountains. Then there's the demons what live in the interior, and hostile tribes of things thet ain't always human." He was waving his birdlike arms wildly now, using them to magnify the drama of his own declamations.

"Get past them, and then there's the Tortured Lands, and beyond thet, the Curridgian Mountains with their ice fields and rock slides." Lack of wind finally forced him to call a halt to the hymn of horrors.

"And after that?" Ehomba asked quietly.

"After thet? After thet!" Calming himself with an effort, the senior pathfinder took a deep breath. "Why, after thet is Ehl-Larimar its very self, and beyond there, the Ocean Aurreal."

"Another ocean?" Raising himself up, Simna had his hirsute nurse place him on the ground. On shaky legs, he confronted his lanky friend. "By Guisel's gearing, Etjole, no more long sea voyages! I beg you!"

Ehomba's brows rose slightly. "I thought you enjoyed our sojourn on the sea."

Anxious eyes gazed up at him. "Hoy, long bruther, it wasn't the voyage that leaves me looking like this. It were the arrival."

The herdsman nodded noncommittally. "Somehow I do not think we would face a similar situation on another ocean entirely, but I will certainly keep your concerns in mind. I do not see why it would be necessary for us to take passage on this western ocean anyway, since if it lies to the west of Ehl-Larimar, we should reach our destination before we encounter it." Turning back to the guide, who was by now feeling sorely left out of the verbal byplay, he offered his thanks for the information.

While not one of the available pathfinders could be induced to travel with them, the master of the dispatch center was persuaded to sell them a windwagon and supplies. Ehomba was once more astonished to see in what exalted regard other peoples held the humble colored beach pebbles he had brought with him from the shore just north of the village. While the supply in the little cotton sack was diminished, it was by no means exhausted, suggesting that if the same responses were to be encountered elsewhere, they might be able to pay for their needs the rest of the way to distant Ehl-Larimar without misgiving.

Though with Hunkapa Aub and the black litah aboard, the windwagon was a bit crowded, it held them all, together with their newly purchased supplies. Steering was by means of a straightforward tiller-and-axle arrangement, and manipulation of the single simple square of canvas that provided the wagon's motive power posed no problem for travelers who had just spent weeks aboard a large sailing vessel. To the cheers and jeers of the personnel at the dispatch station (their respective individual reactions being directly related to how much of the visitors' story they had happened to overhear), the four adventurers once more set sail, this time in a craft both smaller and noisier than the graceful and recently departed *Grömsketter.*

A plentitude of roads and wagon tracks led off in all directions from Doroune. By far the greatest number led north or south to the other trading towns and farming communities of the fertile coastal plain. A lesser selection offered access to the western horizon. Choosing the most direct, the travelers soon found themselves clear of the city and its suburbs and among tillage of grain and vegetable. People working in the fields would look up and wave, at least until they caught sight of Hunkapa Aub or the black litah. Unlike the worldly citizens of sophisticated metropolises such as Hamacassar or Lybondai, the peoples living on this side of the Semordria were of a far more insular nature.

So while they were cordial, they tended to keep their distance whenever the wagon pulled up outside an inn or tavern. Though less openly friendly than the inhabitants of distant Netherbrae, they were at the same time more accepting of the ways of others. Soon enough Ehomba and his companions began to receive warnings similar to those that had been voiced by the aged guide in Doroune.

"You might as well turn back now." The blacksmith who had agreed to perform a final check on their wagon spoke meaningfully as he rose and knelt, rose and knelt while moving from one wheel to another.

"Why?" Ehomba shielded his eyes as he gazed westward, to where the track they were following vanished into looming hills densely forested with ancient beech and oak, sycamore and elm. "My companions and I have crossed many high ranges, and this that lies before us does not look either very high or very difficult to scale."

"The Hexens?" The affable blacksmith moved to another wheel. "They're not. Takes a while to get through them, but the road goes all the way across. At least it did last I heard tell of it. Even a child could make the walk."

The herdsman was openly puzzled. "Then what is the danger from these mountains?"

Taking a hammer and chisellike tool from his heavy work apron, their host began to bend back and tighten a bolt that was threatening to work its way loose.

"From the mountains, none." Looking up, he stared hard at the lean and curious visitor. "It's what lives in the Hexens that you have to watch out for. Deep in the inner valleys, where the fog lingers most all the day long and people never go." He shrugged and turned away. "Leastwise, those people that go in and come out again. What happens to the ones who go in and don't come out, well, a man can only guess."

"Hoy, we're not easily frightened," Simna informed him. Nearby, Ahlitah was playing with the blacksmith's brace of brown-and-white kittens, having promised Ehomba not to eat any of them. They assaulted the big cat's mane and tail while he batted gently at them with paws that could bring down a full-grown buffalo with a single blow. "Go ahead and guess."

The blacksmith paused in his work. "You really mean to do this, don't you?"

Simna made a perfunctory gesture in the herdsman's direction. "My friend has a fetish for the west. So that's the way we go. Would it be safer to head north or south and then turn inland toward our destination?"

The blacksmith considered. "I'm no voyager like you." He indicated the sturdy house and shop set just back off the road. "Family man. But settled here, at the foot of the Hexens, I meet many travelers. Go north and you're liable to run into bad weather. But south—head south and then turn west, and you'll skirt the base of the mountains." He turned back to his work. "Of course, there are other dangers to be encountered when traveling in the south."

"How long must we move south before we could turn west again and miss these mountains?" Ehomba was willing to consider reasonable alternatives.

"A month, maybe two, depending on the condition of the roads and the weather. This time of year, traveling weather's best between Oos and Nine Harbors. That's where you are right now, more or less."

The herdsman nodded tersely. "Then we go west from here."

"Why am I not surprised?" Simna's sigh was muted. He knew his tall friend well enough by now to have put money on his response. "You were going to tell us about the dangers we might run into in these Hexens."

"It's not a certain thing," the pensive blacksmith replied. "Many people make the crossing and return safely to the coast. For traders who do so, the rewards are considerable."

"I can imagine, if so many folks are too scared to even attempt it. What happens to those who don't make it back? Bandits?" The swordsman was extrapolating from similar situations that existed on the borders of his own homeland.

The blacksmith was shaking his head. "Bandits people can deal with. Tolls can be met, bribes paid, ransoms raised. Highwaymen would not discourage more people from traveling to the west. It is the Brotherhood of the Bone that terrifies would-be travelers and keeps them at home." Hitherto ringing, his voice had dropped to an edgy whisper.

"Do we have to ask what that might be?"

"Doesn't matter." The blacksmith's tone remained subdued. "I can't talk about it. Not openly, in front of others. You're determined to push on, so I'll just wish you good luck." He indicated the front of his shop, where Ahlitah was toying with the delighted kittens and Hunkapa Aub lay half asleep, sitting up against one side of the entrance, his mouth open wide enough to reveal a gap sufficiently commodious to accommodate both nest- and abode-hunting birds. "You are obviously knowledgeable wayfarers, and you have powerful nonhuman friends of your own. With luck, you'll make it. You might not have any trouble at all." He spread his hands wide and smiled regretfully. "Iron and steel I can forge for you, but not luck."

"You said 'nonhuman,' " Ehomba remarked. "Are the members of this Brotherhood of the Bone not human?"

"Some are, some ain't. I hope you don't have occasion to find out."

Rising, he replaced his tools in his apron and wiped his hands. "Come inside for a cold drink and we'll settle your bill." His expression darkened ever so slightly. "You have money?"

Simna smirked knowingly. "Money enough. Before we left Doroune we took the time to cash a pebble."

In the depths of the mountains it was difficult to remember the admonitions of blacksmith and guide, so congenial were the surroundings. Though the splendid forest crowded the wagon track on both sides, it was not oppressive. Heavy broad-leaf litter covered the ground, making a carpet for deer and elk, broad-shouldered sivatherium, and droopy-horned pelorovis. Squirrels of many species foraged among the ground cover, methodically conveying found foods from the surface to their homes high up in the accommodating trees. Ehomba was particularly taken with one short-tailed gray-and-brown variety that built endless tiny ladders to assist them in reaching the highest branches. Communities of these enterprising rodents traveled safely back and forth between boles by means of tiny carts suspended from thin but strong ropes.

Rabbits scurried about in profusion, providing effortless hunting for Ahlitah and a welcome supplement to their purchased provisions. Since no one had been able to tell them exactly how far it was to Ehl-Larimar, they availed themselves of every opportunity to feast off the land. Stowed food was to be conserved, since it might prove vital to their well-being should they encounter less-productive country.

Acorns and chestnuts could be easily gathered from beneath heavily laden boughs, and small rushing streams were everywhere. Morning and evening mist kept the temperature on the chilly side, but to travelers who had successfully crossed the great Hrugar Range hard by the base of Mount Scathe itself, the occasional discomfort was minor at most.

Birds in their colorful profusion nested in the forks of branches. Their darting songs echoed through the woods. One persistent archeopteryx in particular kept attacking their provisions in hopes of stealing one of the smaller brightly wrapped packages of food. When their attention was diverted it would dive-bomb the wagon, attacking with teeth and claws, until one of the travelers shooed it away. Cawing huffily, it paralleled them for quite a ways, flapping awkwardly from tree to tree until the next opportunity for avian larceny presented itself. Eventually it gave up and fell behind. As poor a flyer as a hoatzin, it could not trail them forever.

After a number of days of easy, relatively comfortable travel interrupted only by the occasional need to get out and pull or push the wagon where there was an absence of wind, Simna had begun to relax. It was a state of being that Hunkapa Aub never exited and Ahlitah pursued with feline determination. Of the four travelers, only Ehomba remained on perpetual alert. This situation the swordsman was content to live with.

Lying against the back of the wagon, hands behind his head, he looked up contentedly as his lanky friend adjusted the single sail. Today's breeze was not strong, but it blew steadily from the east, driving them through the narrow canyon they were currently traversing.

"The people of this coast are really missing something by restricting their settlements to the flatlands east of these mountains." He waved a casual hand at the enclosing forested slopes. "This is wonderful country. Clean, bracing air, lots of small game, no dangerous predators that we've encountered, fertile soil, and some of the best timber I've ever seen. There are trees in here old and strong and big enough to supply lumber for a hundred thousand homes and ten thousand ships the size of the *Grömsketter*."

Intent as ever, Ehomba was watching the forest slide past on either side of the track. Tugging on a line, he trimmed the wagon's single sail slightly. "It may be that this Brotherhood would object. Certainly if they harry individual travelers they would rise up against any organized settlement. Perhaps that is why none exists."

Simna waved diffidently. "Gwouroud knows that's not it, bruther. They're just fearful folk hereabouts. They feed off the tall tales and spook stories of their neighbors. I've been through provinces like that, where everyone is so credulous they're scared to set foot beyond their own village." Closing his eyes, he inhaled deeply of the brisk, unpolluted air, its innate refreshingness enhanced by the extra oxygen being pumped out by the forest.

The wagon hit a rut and bounced, jarring Ahlitah momentarily awake. "Pick your trail with care, man," he rumbled.

"There is only one." Ehomba's response was curt. "And while we have the wind with us, this is no flying machine to soar smoothly over what water has cut." Moments after Ehomba composed his terse rejoinder, the wagon began to slow.

Opening his eyes again, Simna ibn Sind saw that the wind still blew in gusts sufficient to drive the vehicle. It was Ehomba who was bringing them to a gradual halt as he turned the sail sideways to the breeze. Frowning, the swordsman sat up.

"Hoy, bruther, why are we stopping?" A glance at the sky showed that it was too early for the midday meal. It was time for them to be covering as much ground as possible, not pausing to rest or engage in casual contemplation of their surroundings. "This wind is meant to be used."

"So are your eyes." Standing near the rear of the wagon, the herdsman held his long, slim arm out straight, parallel to the ground and pointing to his right, off into the woods.

Blinking, Simna glanced in the indicated direction. So did an insouciant Hunkapa Aub. Curled up near the back of the wagon, the black litah ignored the delay in favor of sleep.

"I don't see anything, bruther." The swordsman's confusion showed itself in his face. "What are you pointing at? What am I supposed to be looking for?"

"In that big elm. A bird." Ehomba sighted along his arm. "I understand your difficulty. It is not very big. About the size of a sparrow."

Simna made a face. "You stopped so we could look at a sparrow?"

"There!" Ehomba's identifying finger shifted slightly to the right. "It just flew into the tree next to it. It is a little closer now. See?" He gestured impatiently with his arm. "Near the outer end of the lowermost large branch, among the leaves."

Realizing that to resume headway meant humoring the herdsman, Simna muttered under his breath. As he adjusted his position slightly in the wagon, he was nearly knocked over by the abrupt shifting of the hairy mass next to him.

"Hunkapa see, Hunkapa see!" Their oversized companion was pointing excitedly, bouncing up and down in the wagon. The stalwart wooden bed creaked dangerously. "Bird without!"

"Without?" Time to put an end to whatever nonsense had afflicted his friends, Simna decided. "Without what?" Straining, he followed the pair of pointing arms and used them to fix his gaze on a particular branch in a certain tree.

He located the bird, and as he did so the small hairs on the back of his neck erected. That was more than the bird could do. It had no hair to stiffen, or feathers either. Nor skin, nor muscle or insides.

Sitting on the branch and preening itself with its naked white beak, the small flying creature ignored all the attention its presence had prompted. Satisfied, it spread proportionate, compact wings and rose from its perch, flying off into the forest, a small white specter comprised of nothing but naked, fleshless bones.

Ehomba had watched many birds in flight, and dragonets, and even certain specialized lizards and frogs, but this was the first time he had ever seen a skeleton fly.

IX

The skeletal sparrow was but the first of many they encountered as they drove deeper into the heart of the Hexens. There were more birds: crows and robins, jays and grosbeaks, neocaths and nuthatches. But they were not alone. It was not long before they found themselves traveling through a dense and dismal section of forest where flesh was scarce and scoured bone dominant.

Skeletal hares hopped among the roots of sheltering trees. Four-footed white skeletons scampered through the branches trailing furless vertebrae like the whiptails of scorpions. Once, a cluster of capybara peered up at the travelers from the shelter of their stream, staring at the wagon from the mindless depths of dark, voided eye sockets. For the travelers, it was unsettling enough to encounter such sights. To see them staring vacantly back was more unnerving still.

Devoid of skin and muscle they might be, but the inhabitants of these woods ran and flew and hopped and jumped with as much energy as their more fully rounded, naturally fleshed-out counterparts. The only other observable difference between them and their tissue-heavy relations was the degree to which they stared at the passing visitors: stared with a degree and intensity that grimly belied their dearth of eyes. If not for the presence of healthy trees and bushes, Simna could well have believed that they had rolled on into the land of the dead.

Studying the forest as they rattled along the increasingly ill-maintained dirt track, bumping over rocks and clumps of uncropped weeds, they watched a misshapen panoply of normal life play itself out among the vegetation. Ehomba pointed out a skeletal badger busily excavating a new burrow with more than adequate claws—but no pads on its feet. A great bull elk trotted past, displaying horns that in its entirely emaciated state seemed certain to make it too top-heavy to stand up, much less run. But it managed to stay erect nonetheless.

Once, a bobcat of bones leaped from concealment to take down a large rabbit. Normally, there is no more piercing and heart-rending sound in the wilderness than the cry of a dying rabbit, but this one could only emit the noise of bare bones rubbing together. Settling down to its meal, the ghostly feline began to gnaw on its victim, pinning it to the ground with limber white paws. Biting and ripping with sharp teeth, it methodically dismembered its prey, cracking open the smaller bones to get at the marrow within.

Tiny skeletal fledglings croaked in nests carefully built by osseous parents. A trio of cassowaries loped across a clearing, their exposed ribs clacking against one another like castanets as they ran. Cumbersome grizzly skeletons grazed in a dense path of wild blackberries. Occasionally one would become entangled as the thorny vines wrapped tightly around ribs or arms. One bear-shape pushed its snout deep into the copse, emerging with it stained blue-black by berry juice. A vine thrust upward through the underside of the jaw to emerge from one eye socket. This vegetal invasion appeared to have no effect on the lumbering ursinoid.

Why a skeleton would need to eat was but one of many questions contemplated by the travelers. As was his nature, Ehomba very much wanted some answers, whereas his companions simply wished to be clear of the blighted chasm as rapidly as possible. Even Ahlitah, who had a particular taste for marrow, sensed the unwholesomeness of the place and expressed his desire to leave it behind.

Abruptly, the wagon made a sharp swerve. "Hoy!" Simna called out as he was thrown off his feet. "Who's steering?" Looking around as soon as he managed to recover his equilibrium, he caught sight of Ehomba taking in the sail. "Etjole, what are you up to, man? Surely you don't mean for us to camp here?"

"Not camp." The herdsman spoke while continuing his work. "But we have to stop for a moment." By way of explanation he nodded forward.

A large tree had fallen across the wagon track, blocking it completely. Thick underbrush on either side prevented them from going around. The toppled trunk would have to be moved, or cut through, or else the wagon would have to be unloaded and hauled across, with their supplies following from hand to hand, one package at a time.

"By Givouvum, what a place for a rest stop!" Grumbling loudly at the inconvenience, the swordsman vaulted over the side of the wagon to inspect the impediment.

"A stop, yes, but from the look of it, no rest." Ehomba was soon standing alongside his friend. Together they pondered how best to proceed, whether to try to remove the log or move themselves across it.

Not one given to much pondering, Hunkapa Aub lumbered over to the top of the tree where it lay among a host of smaller saplings it had smashed in the course of its fall. For a long moment he stood in silence, considering the supine column. Then he bent his knees, gripped the upper stretch of the tree in both huge hands, and with a rolling grunt lifted it off the ground and began to pull it deeper into the woods and off the road. Joining reluctantly in the effort, the black litah put its forehead against the shattered base of the tree. Digging in with all four sets of claws, it pushed while Hunkapa pulled.

It took them less than ten minutes to move the trunk far enough off the track for the wagon to squeeze past. Starting back to their vehicle, Ehomba found himself wondering how much more of the blighted forest they had yet to traverse, and whether they would be out of it by nightfall. Hopefully, they would be far away before darkness fell, provided nothing else materialized to impede their progress.

That feared something else took the form of several dozen figures who emerged from behind the wagon and the brush off to one side. Each skeletal warrior carried a heavy wooden club or spear, save for several who brandished weapons confiscated from unlucky predecessors. A few wore scavenged armor. Ill-fitting helmets of bronze and steel bounced loosely on naked, bony skulls. Feathers and iridescent insect parts protruded from the metal crests, supplying a macabre touch of color to warriors whose appearance was otherwise almost entirely the bleached, chalky white of naked bone. Many of the animate advancing cadavers were missing teeth or limbs.

Worse, they stood between the travelers and their vehicle, in which all their weapons were stored.

However, they were not entirely defenseless. As sepulchral shouts rose from the gaunt, ghastly regiment and weapons were upraised, Hunkapa Aub and Ahlitah took matters into their own hands and charged.

The shaggy man-beast's unearthly howling combined with the big cat's thunderous roars were enough to give even the dead pause. As the skeletal raiders hesitated, the improbable duo tore into them. It was a revelation to Simna to see the ferocity with which the gentle, soft-voiced Hunkapa scattered their attackers. Sword cuts failed to penetrate his thick, hairy coat, and spears he knocked aside with sweeping sideways blows of his massive arms. Grabbing up one clattering, cackling cluster of bones, he dismembered it as easily as the swordsman would a chicken. Ripping another assailant into pieces, Hunkapa threw chunks of bone at its companions, bowling them over with the force of his throws. Skeletons were knocked askew or trampled underfoot.

Eyes blazing, Ahlitah was not relying on his stentorian bellows to scatter the enemy. Powerful, curving claws severed skulls from shoulders while heavy paws shattered vacant rib cages and limbs. The crackle of bones being crunched echoed through the woods every time the litah's powerful jaws locked onto another gaunt figure.

While their two nonhuman companions wreaked havoc among the surprised attackers, Ehomba and Simna made a dash for the windwagon. Ducking beneath a spear thrust, Simna rolled into the legs of his assailant, bringing the startled skeleton down on top of him. Reaching up and around, he locked both hands and forearms around the skull. Much to his surprise, it was warm. Gritting his teeth, he twisted his hands and arms in opposite directions. With a snap, the neck broke and the head came away in his fingers. As the decapitated skull tried to sink its exposed, gleaming teeth into his arm, the sickened swordsman flung it as far as he could.

Ehomba leaped sideways to avoid a sword stroke and brought his right leg around the way Asab had shown him and the other young men of the village when they were of an age to learn about fighting. Its legs taken out from under it, the skeleton went down on its back. As it rolled toward him, flailing energetically but wildly with its sword, the herdsman was able to reach the wagon. Simna joined him seconds later. While Hunkapa Aub defended one side of the vehicle and Ahlitah the other, the two men scrambled for their weapons.

"Send the sharks after them!" Simna shouted as he picked up his own sword. Long knife gripped between its teeth, a skeletal soldier was attempting to scramble over the side of the wagon and into the bed. The swordsman dispatched it with a single blow that cleaved the raider from collarbone to sternum. Cut vertically nearly in half, it fell back, clutching at itself.

"I cannot!" Ehomba fumbled among the supplies. "The magic of the sea-bone sword works only on attackers made of flesh and blood. Sharks will not attack bones. Neither will the spirit of my walking spear."

"Hoy, then take up the sky-metal sword and call down the wind from between the stars to blow them apart!" With a grunt, Simna stabbed a climbing warrior between the ribs. Since his weapon met only air, it did no damage. With a curse, the swordsman drew the weapon back and hacked sideways, beheading his adversary. That stroke had the desired effect.

"Remember, Simna, the sky-metal sword is not a shaman's instrument, to be so casually wielded." The herdsman indicated the surrounding forest. "This place is too confining. If I were to succeed in bringing down the wind it would uproot trees and send them flying in all directions, as likely to do away with us as our attackers." He continued to busy himself in the center of the wagon.

With barely enough time to glance in his friend's direction, Simna finally shouted in exasperation, "By Gokhoul, bruther, what are you doing?"

"Setting sail. Hold them off, my friends, hold them off!"

With the battle-tested Simna shouting orders, he and Hunkapa and the black litah did just that, giving Ehomba time to ready their vehicle. As soon as the sail was up and fully set, he called out to his companions to join him within. Simna was first back aboard, followed by Hunkapa Aub. As the wagon, under full sail, began to pick up speed, Ahlitah ran alongside, dispatching those skeletons that tried to keep pace. Any that drew near found themselves crushed between powerful jaws or knocked asunder by claw-tipped paws.

Only when the last of their jabbering, gesticulating, spear-waving pursuit had fallen too far behind to pose any threat did the big cat rejoin his companions, clearing the space from ground to wagon in a single long, easy leap. Once on board he sat back and began to lick his wounds. They were minor, nothing worse than a few scrapes and the occasional shallow cut.

"It's nothing," he insisted in response to Ehomba's solicitous inquiry. "I've taken worse from wildebeest." As the cat spoke, it groomed its face and mane with moistened paw. "One time I took a blow to the stomach from the spiked tail of a full-grown female glyptodont protecting its young. Now, *that* hurt." Twisting its head around, it began to lick a bloody gash on its right flank. "Made the kill anyway."

"Hoy?" Sword laid out across his knees, Simna was sitting down, his back resting against the interior wall of the wagon. The was no blood on the blade: only the accumulated white stain of powdered bone. "I always wondered what glypto tasted like."

"Like pork." The black litah lifted its head suddenly, ears pricked, listening intently. Seeing this, Simna immediately scrambled to his knees and turned to scan the dense woods through which they were racing.

"What is it? More of them in the trees? They can't hope to run us down. As long as we have wind at our backs and clear road ahead they'll never catch us."

"Footsteps." The litah sat still as a sculpture in obsidian, listening. On the other side of the wagon, an intent Hunkapa Aub was likewise scrutinizing the forest. "Not human. Not human skeletons, that is. Something else."

"Something else, how?" Standing tall in the rear of the wagon, Ehomba steered them expertly down the track and past the most egregious ruts and potholes.

"Heavier," the litah explained bluntly.

They came tearing out of the trees off to the left, the cavalry riding not to the rescue but intent on total destruction. There were too many to count as the windwagon, with full canvas up and traveling at top speed, negotiated one dip and curve after another in the increasingly uneven track.

Baying like a hundred xylophones all playing in concert, skeletal warriors came pounding out of the forest on skeleton mounts, waving their weapons over their bleached skulls as they sought to ride down the fleeing wagon. Naked pelvises sat astride the ivory-colored spines of horses and mules, zebras and okapis, kudu and pronghorn. It was a charge the likes of which even an experienced horseman like Simna ibn Sind had never hoped to see, a charge from Hell.

But even as their mounted assailants bore down on the fleeing travelers, the forest was thinning out around them, giving way to more open country. A grateful Ehomba had more room in which to maneuver. No longer restricted exclusively to the narrow wagon track, he was able to utilize the windwagon not only as a vehicle to effect their escape, but as a weapon.

When a pair of high-riding, mace-swinging skeletal warriors turned their mounts toward the rattling, bouncing wagon, Ehomba adjusted the sail to angle the heavy vehicle not away from but directly toward them. The front end of the wagon slammed into the startled attackers, sending a shower of broken, splintered bone flying over the passengers as their assailants were smashed to bits. Meanwhile, any raider that rode too close risked a blow from Hunkapa Aub's fist, Ahlitah's paws, or Simna ibn Sind's sword. Grimacing ferociously, the swordsman stood up in the unstable wagon bed to taunt their attackers. He still had his sea legs from their weeks on the *Grömsketter,* and this especially allowed him to keep his balance.

"Come on, you offspring of bastard boneheads!" Gleefully, he waved his sword in expert circles. "Here's a tooth longer than any of yours. Come close and see how it bites! What's the matter—afraid of dying?"

"Simna, it is not good to taunt the dead."

The swordsman threw his long-faced friend a wild-eyed glance. "Tend to your tillering, bruther, and leave me to deal with the departed. They should have stayed dead."

Emitting hollow, sinister cries, the remainder of the skeleton cavalry whipped their mounts with whips of slivered bone and closed on the windwagon. Try as they might, they could not surround it in sufficient numbers to overpower its passengers. Every time it looked as if more than two of the attackers might have a chance to leap or climb aboard, Ehomba would steer the vehicle away from their skeletal chargers. Cut down by Simna's flashing sword or pulverized by the strength of Ahlitah or Hunkapa Aub, their numbers were steadily reduced even as their determination was redoubled.

Compared to the horde that had participated in the initial assault, few were left when the windwagon struck the brush-covered gully. It bounced once, flew into the air, struck the hard ground on the far side, and overturned. Ehomba barely had time enough to warn his companions to grab something to hang on to before he was slammed to the ground and thrown from the wagon.

Everyone but Ahlitah lay dazed and unsteady. All cat, the black litah had reacted to the imminent crash by leaping clear of the wagon, twisting his body in midair, and skidding to a stop on all fours. Snarling warningly, it took up a position in front of the overturned wagon bed as the mounted skeletons stumbled down one side of the narrow chasm and up the other.

By the time they reached the site of the crash, the wagon's occupants had recovered their equilibrium and their weapons. With nothing left to steer, Ehomba had picked up the sky-metal sword. While it might not be time to make use of it to call down pieces of the sky or the wind from between the stars, its blade was still sharp and functional. The overturned wagon lay on its side, one wheel still spinning futilely in the air like the kicking hind leg of a dying lizard. With its solid wooden bed against their backs, they readied themselves to deal with the remaining skeletal warriors arrayed against them.

Instead, the mounted skeletons drew up in a line opposite the toppled vehicle. Weapons at the ready, they sat staring with empty eye sockets at the contentious living. Their mounts pawed with skeletal hooves at the ground, snorting through ragged-edged nostrils of varying length.

"What's this, bruther?" Not taking his eyes from their hesitating attackers, Simna whispered to his tall companion. "What are they waiting for?"

"I do not know." Holding the sky-metal sword out in front of him, Ehomba considered the surrounding forest. Though much reduced in density, there were still too many large trees scattered nearby to chance drawing down the wind from the heavens. But if the attackers persisted, he realized that he might have to chance it. Certainly if their assailants were reinforced by others from within the deep woods, he would be left with no choice. Warmed by his hands, the sword quivered expectantly.

The skeleton that dismounted was neither the tallest nor the most stout of those pale white specters that were arrayed against the travelers, but it strode forward with a stiff-jointed dignity none of its demised confederates could match. With plucked feathers streaming from the gilded helmet that rocked atop its bleached skull, it approached the living. Simna's fingers whitened on the haft of his sword and Hunkapa Aub growled deep in his throat. Ahlitah stood almost motionless, his massive chest heaving slowly in and out with his steady breathing, ready to pounce the instant Ehomba gave the word.

Halting barely a spear length away, the skeleton placed one bony arm across its splayed rib cage—and bowed. Then it straightened, steadying the flamboyant helmet on its naked skull, and began to speak in a voice that was deeper than a whisper but not much stronger.

"You fight well." The wind carried away the last syllable of every word and the straining travelers had to listen closely to make out the meaning of each. "You put a great many of the dead to sleep, for which they are eternally grateful."

"Hoy?" Simna smiled tautly. "Come a little closer, Mr. Bones, and I'll gladly assist you in joining them."

The white skull swiveled. Empty sockets peered into the swordsman's living eyes. "That is not to be the way of things, master of a steel tooth."

"Then what is the way of things? Tell us." Without lowering his guard for an instant, Ehomba queried the expired but animate mediator.

Simna muttered knowingly. "Always the questioner, Etjole, even when the one replying is Death itself."

"We are not Death," the skeletal envoy explained softly. "Only dead. The difference is of significance." With a sweep of one white-boned arm, it indicated those mounted warriors waiting patiently behind it. "We are the Brotherhood of the Bone. This forest we claim as ours, a place of quietude and darkness in which to linger after life has given us up but before death claims us forever. Here we dwell but do not exist, occasionally taking out the frustration of being neither or either on those mortals foolish or courageous enough to dare the byways that we haunt." A chalky arm pointed in their direction.

"You are sufficiently brave to pass, but there is a problem."

"A problem?" Simna laughed humorlessly. "You send dozens of

your own to try and slay us where we stand and now you say there is a 'problem'?" He tossed his sword easily back and forth, swapping it from hand to hand. "Come forward, the lot of you, and we'll show you how Simna ibn Sind and the great sorcerer Etjole Ehomba deal with their problems!"

"You might yet escape." The envoy made the confession even as it looked to their overturned wagon. "Yet your vehicle will need time to be put right, something you cannot do while fighting us. Even as we speak, hundreds more of the Brotherhood are riding to our aid, called hither by the sounds of battle and breaking bones. If you flee right now and the wind holds, you might well outdistance them all. But if you are delayed by fighting—" This time it was the envoy's meaning and not his speech that trailed off.

"It's a damned bluff!" Simna wanted very badly to rush forward and separate the taunting skeleton's skull from its shoulders. "Let's finish them!"

Ehomba ignored him, straining to listen, to pierce the distant woods with hearing that was more acute than that of most men. Strive as he might, he knew that there were among his companions ears far more sensitive than his own.

"Ahlitah?"

The big cat sniffed the air even as it listened intently. After a moment, yellow eyes looked in the herdsman's direction. "I think I hear something. It might be the wind—or it might be fleshless feet. Hundreds of them."

"Might be, might not be—what need for speculation?" Simna took a step forward. "By Geewenwan, I say we put an end to this!"

"They are mounted and we are afoot," Ehomba sensibly pointed out. "It is a doable thing, friend Simna, but as the envoy points out, killing even the dead takes time. All of you have come this far because of me. I will not give up your lives for a cause become yours only by accident." Lowering his sword, he approached the envoy.

An alarmed Simna looked on uneasily. "Etjole, I don't know what you're thinking, but don't think it!"

Halting several feet from the skeleton, Ehomba met vacant eyes with his own speculative gaze. "You said something about us being brave enough to let pass, except there was a problem."

The bleached skull nodded slightly. "You have dispatched many from the Brotherhood and sent them on their final path to rest. Those who do so must take the place of at least one who has departed our company. If this is done willingly, then the others may live, and will be allowed to quit our presence still citizens of the world of the living."

Ehomba nodded understandingly. Behind him, Simna was growing rapidly more agitated. The herdsman continued to ignore him. "I have your word on this?"

"Here is my hand on it." Skeletal fingers reached toward him. "What remains of it."

Wrapping his own long, weathered fingers around the bare white bone, Ehomba embraced the warm, smooth grip.

"Which of you will come willingly to the Brotherhood?" The envoy was looking past him. He need not have done so.

"I will."

"What?" Behind him, Simna took a confrontational step forward. "What's all this ungodly mumbling about? Etjole, what have you promised this—this fugitive from an unhallowed grave?"

Rejoining his companions, Ehomba put both hands on the swordsman's shoulders. Inclining his head slightly, he stared hard and evenly into the smaller man's eyes.

"Simna, do you still believe I am a mighty sorcerer?"

"Yes—but you've always denied it. I know your way with words. What trick of sophistry are you playing now?" The swordsman eyed his friend warily.

Dropping his hands from the other man's arms, Ehomba looked up at the hulking, hirsute form of Hunkapa Aub. "What about you? Do you believe in me, my hairy friend?"

"Hunkapa—believe in Etjole." The broad figure replied slowly and solemnly, his response tinged with uncertainty over what was to come.

"And you, Ahlitah? What about you?" The herdsman gazed affectionately at the big cat.

It yawned. "Do what you will. If you die, I go home. If you live, I continue with you. Only one thing I know for sure: I'm sick of the taste of marrow. So do something."

"I will." Turning back to the swordsman, the tall southerner smiled reassuringly. "No matter what happens, no matter what you see here, you must promise to continue the journey westward away from this place. Watch, friend Simna. Watch, and trust me."

"Trust you? Trust you to do what? Etjole . . ."

The swordsman reached for his friend but was unable to restrain him. After placing the sky-metal sword in Hunkapa's hand, a resigned Ehomba walked back to confront the expectant envoy. Halting before the skeletal warrior, the herdsman nodded once. "I am ready."

The envoy made a gesture and started to raise his sword. Ehomba lifted a hand to forestall the first cut. "Hold! I will save you the trouble."

Standing between the living and the dead, the herdsman parted his jaws to form a wide oval—an oval that grew large, and then larger still. It was impossible for any human mouth to open so wide. Even among the mounted skeletons there was a stirring at the sight. Among all the onlookers only Simna ibn Sind and the black litah were not shocked by the gape of the herdsman's expanding maw, for they had seen Ehomba do something similar before.

No human could part its jaws so wide—but Etjole Ehomba was more than human. He was also eromakasi. There was no darkness to eat here, no threatening eromakadi to consume. But that did not prevent him from making use of his remarkable oral abilities. Wider still stretched his jaws and lips.

Then, with a delicacy of step and perfect aplomb, his skeleton emerged from the container of his body, stepping out from within through the accommodating aperture of the herdsman's unnaturally distended mouth.

X

Like a prosperous merchant discarding a favorite dressing gown, Etjole Ehomba's skeleton continued to slip free of his clothing and skin until it stood, white and glistening, before the silent, approving envoy. When the last lingering flesh had been sloughed off, the mounted warriors vented a cadaverous cheer, waving their weapons in the air and reining their assorted skeletal mounts up on their hind legs in celebration.

"No!" Sword upraised, a horrified Simna rushed forward—only to fall hard as something tripped him. Looking down, he saw, staring back at him from amid the pile of attire and skin and muscle that had moments before cloaked his companion in the garb of life, the face of his good friend. Though unnaturally flaccid and flattened in the absence of its usual sturdy frame, it was smiling reassuringly.

"Calm yourself, Simna. Did I not tell you to trust me?"

Shocked, the swordsman scrabbled back on hands and knees. "Etjole, is it you? Are you alive?"

"Alive but limp. As a wet rag, like the saying goes. Lift me up, my friend. I want to see what is happening."

Placing a hesitant arm beneath the flattened head, Simna fought down the queasiness in his gut as he raised the soft, slightly rubbery remnant of his friend and held it where it could face their former assailants. Having turned away from the living, Ehomba's expelled skeleton was following the envoy to the line of waiting skeletal mounts. There the envoy swung himself up onto the bare-boned back of a once noble but now wholly desiccated steed and reached down. Taking the proffered hand, the tall, slim skeleton that had just walked away from its owner leaped up onto the exposed spine.

With a final salute, the grisly members of the Brotherhood turned and, passing in review in double file, trotted away, leaving the living to their own devices. Slack as a sack of beans, Ehomba watched them and a part of him go.

"I hope it can hang on for a while. The Naumkib are not known for their horsemanship."

"It wouldn't matter anyway, bruther." Simna followed the line of mounted skeletons as they disappeared into the trees. "No amount of practice could prepare one for riding saddleless astride bare bone." He looked down at his friend. "Why have you done this?"

"To put them off." The eyes that stared back up at him sank deeply into the limp, unsupported flesh. "Ahlitah was right. I could hear the approaching hundreds also."

"But the sky-metal sword! You could have tried to use it."

"Not in a place like this. We would have died of it," the herdsman replied simply.

"So we would have died." Simna's frustration came pouring out. "Anything's better than living like this!" He ran an open palm down the length of his freshly pliant friend.

The fold of flesh that was Ehomba's mouth smiled. "Did I not ask you to trust me?"

"Hoy, so you did, but to what end? Do you expect us to cross the remaining unknown country that lies between here and Ehl-Larimar with you in this condition? And what if we were to do so, and succeed? How will you fight this Hymneth the Possessed? Am I supposed to stand behind you and work your legs and sword arm like some kind of mad puppeteer? I'll have none of it, I tell you! I consider myself a brave man, but not a fool." His tone turned bitter. "If there is good magic in this, I don't see it."

"You will, my good friend. Lay me down easy. Take up the tiller and lines and sail us out of here."

"Hunkapa!" Simna exclaimed. "Give me a hand and let's right this wagon." As soon as their transport was once again resting upright on all four wheels, the swordsman proceeded to check the axles and undercarriage. Despite the jolt it had received during the hard landing, everything appeared intact. "Here, hold him up so he can see. I have to steer."

"Steer where?" Gently, the shaggy hulk took the limp body of the herdsman in his massive arms, cradling the empty but animate human envelope as easily as he would a child.

"West. Where else?" Settling himself in position, the swordsman tore into ropes and lines, adjusting the sail to catch the wind that, fortuitously, continued to blow from the east. Almost immediately, the wagon began to move. It creaked and groaned in places that previously had been silent, but nothing fell off. Very soon, they were scooting along the increasingly bumpy track at a respectable rate of speed.

They made good progress with no more interruptions. Ahlitah hunted, bringing back rabbits and small antelope to feed not only himself but his companions. For Ehomba there were mashed-up berries and chopped fish. His mouth and teeth still worked, but the lack of any bony support left him unable to chew all but the softest foods. Much to Simna's continued surprise, the herdsman seemed content. He could not walk, but he could pull himself along the ground with his long, lean-muscled arms and kick out with his legs. So long as he did not try to raise up any higher than his arms could push him, he did not appear to be suffering greatly.

The swordsman marveled at his friend's stoicism. Anyone else he had ever known, upon sacrificing their skeleton, would have lapsed into melancholy. Not Ehomba. He was positively buoyant, commending Simna on his steering, Ahlitah on his hunting, and Hunkapa for his help and perpetual good spirits.

"By Gierbourne if I don't think you're a happier man without it," the swordsman finally commented on the fifth day after the fateful final encounter with the representatives of the Brotherhood.

"A skeleton has many uses." Lying in Hunkapa Aub's trunklike arms, Ehomba twisted himself slightly to meet his friend's gaze. "But traveling upright is not always the best way to live. It exposes one to the wind, and to the spears and arrows of enemies. There are advantages, too, to a low profile. Ask any snake."

"I agreed to help a man, not a snake." Grumbling, Simna concentrated on his steering. "Looks like a river up ahead. Big one."

Ehomba had Hunkapa hold him high. "I think the wagon track stops before it reaches the bank. But there are not as many trees on the other side, and the land is more level than what we have just come through. We should be able to make use of this vehicle for a while longer yet."

"Good," the swordsman snapped. "I'm starting to wonder if maybe I haven't done too much walking for too little reward these past several months."

"Why Simna, are you starting to have second thoughts? What about the treasure?" From within sagging pleats of flesh the herdsman smiled at him.

"Hoy, what about the treasure?" The swordsman trimmed a line. "In all this time I've heard nothing about it from you, except when you chose to deny its existence. Now that things have turned troublesome, you tease me with it." He stared hard at the flaccid figure. "When I wax enthusiastic on the subject, you claim it doesn't exist. But if I express skepticism, you lose no opportunity to remind me of it." His expression tightened.

"Don't think to play me the fool, long bruther. If I decide that's what you're about, I'll drop you like a year-old egg and vanish into the bush."

Ehomba managed to shrug, a ripple that ran through his right shoulder like a small wave lapping repeatedly at a sand beach. "You are right, friend Simna. There is no treasure. It is only a trick to keep you with me, to buy your aid. I am ashamed before the elders of my village." A limber, boneless hand fluttered in the swordsman's direction. "Go now. Leave with your dignity still intact. I release you from your vows."

"Don't tempt me, bruther! Don't think that I won't. I'll stop this gut-churning box on wheels right here and get out, and leave you in the care of one too stupid to know better and another who'd as soon eat you for supper as help you!"

"Do it, then. Stop now, Simna, and take your leave while there's still time." Ehomba rarely grew angry, or raised his voice. "Forget about the treasure. It does not exist. It is only a phantom you have raised up in your own mind to justify your continued journeying in my company. Free yourself of it! Abandon the wagon and make your way back to the coast and its welcoming towns. I will not think ill of you for doing so. Only a fool risks his life for an illusion."

"That's right. By Gworjha, you're right!" Pulling in on the lines, the swordsman trimmed the sail. The windwagon slowed to a stop. Behind him, the black litah looked up sleepily.

"What now?" it growled softly.

Hunkapa supplied a ready explanation. "Big river." He looked uncertainly from Ehomba to Simna. "Big argument."

"That's right." Securing the lines, a determined look on his face, the swordsman was gathering up his kit and a limited share of their dwindling supplies. "I'm leaving!"

The big cat was only mildly interested. As always, it found sleep of more interest than the often unaccountable doings of humans. "What for?"

Ehomba elucidated. "Simna has realized that the treasure he sought in my company does not really exist, and he will no longer waste his time seeking it."

"That's right!" The swordsman fumbled with his gear. "Only a fool and an imbecile risks his life for no recompense." Having arranged his kit and stuffed his backpack full, he put one hand on the side of the wagon. Looking back, he glared at the rubbery, limp length of the herdsman gazing back at him from within the cradle of Hunkapa's arms.

"Well?"

"Well what?" Ehomba's demeanor was as pleasant and placid as ever. "I wish you a safe journey back to the coast. One man traveling alone and making little noise should be able to avoid the attentions of the Brotherhood. Perhaps we will meet again someday."

"Hoy, not if the fates are kind to me." The swordsman started to lift himself over the side of the wagon. He had only gone partway when he paused. While he hovered between wagon and ground, the look on his face underwent a slow but profound change.

"*Hoyyyy*—you think you're very clever, don't you, wizard?"

"Clever?" Ehomba considered. "My mother and father thought that I was. Among the herders of my age I am considered tolerably adept."

Simna let himself down, back into the wagon. He was grinning ferociously. "Master of magic you may be, or you may not, but the day will be long indeed when your kind can outwit Simna ibn Sind!"

The flaccid shape looked puzzled. "I do not follow you, my friend."

Even as he spoke, the swordsman was disencumbering himself of pack and weapon. "You're a shrewd fellow, Etjole Ehomba. Far more subtle than most. You almost had me!" He wagged an admonishing finger at the slack outline. "Your language is simple, but you know how to use logic to twist a man's thoughts. You actually had me convinced there was no treasure! Planted the notion anew in my mind until it seemed to be my own. Well, it won't work! I'm a little slow, long bruther, but I'm not like other people. When I get a grip on something, I don't let go until I've shaken all the nourishment out of it. You won't cheat me of my share so easily!" Settling himself at lines and tiller, he prepared to swing the sail around to catch the wind.

"Try all the thought-twisting you wish, but you'll not be rid of me. No one talks Simna ibn Sind out of his share of treasure."

Ehomba sighed, his ribless chest rising and falling less than it would have had it been properly supported from within. "You are certainly a most determined man, friend Simna. Once you get an idea in your head, nothing can take it from you."

"That's right, and don't you forget it, mentor of calves." The swordsman pulled hard on a line.

"Wait!" Ehomba rose up as far as he could in the cradle of Hunkapa's arms.

"What for?" Jawline set, Simna continued to ready the windwagon. "So you can try more of your sorceral tricks and word games to discourage me? I don't think so."

"It is not that. Someone is coming." A shaky, rubbery arm rose to point back in the direction they had come.

Frowning, a reluctant Simna turned to gaze back up the wagon track. "I don't see anything. If you're trying to stall so I'll leave before we cross the river, you're wasting your time, Etjole. Like it or not, I'm coming with you. All the way to Ehl-Larimar."

"From out of the trees, a little to the north. A lone rider. An old friend."

"What 'old friend'?" Exasperated, Simna turned fully on the bench seat. "We have no friends here, and no member of the *Grömsketter*'s crew would leave her to come this far inland. We don't—" He broke off in midsentence as a single figure hove into view. Ehomba was right; it *was* an old friend.

It was the herdsman's skeleton.

Pushing its mount hard, the long, lanky collection of bones kept low, head forward and arms locked around the neck bones of its osseous steed. Legs pounding, the skeletal stallion picked up speed as it struck the slight downslope leading to the edge of the river.

"But how . . . ?" Simna's query trailed away, and he could only turn a look of bafflement on his friend.

From within the folds of flesh that comprised his sunken face, the herdsman smiled back at his companion. "If deprived of the rest of him, a man's skeleton gets lonely."

"You knew it would come back to you," Simna declared accusingly.

"I knew it would try. I hoped it would succeed. I have always had confidence in all of me, my friend." A boneless hand fluttered in the swordsman's direction. "Keep sail up. It will be back among us soon."

"Not soon enough." Rising to his full height and lifting Ehomba effortlessly as he did so, Hunkapa Aub nodded in the direction of the densest part of the forest. "Bones come also."

Instantly, Simna was on his feet and staring along the line of Hunkapa's sight. Sure enough, from among the trees there now poured an entire battalion of the Brotherhood. They came streaming toward the windwagon, some on foot, others riding an even greater assortment of skeletal grotesqueries than the travelers had seen previously, yelling and screaming in their hoarse, ossified whispers while waving all manner of weapons above their bleached skulls.

"Gipebwhen," Simna murmured nervously. "There must be hundreds of 'em!" He looked sharply at his soft friend. "What do we do?"

"Cross the river," Ehomba told him. "Cross it quickly, I should say. Sail, Simna. Fill the sail."

"Hoy, right, sure!" Settling himself back on the seat, the swordsman hastily brought lines and tiller into play. As the single canvas filled with the steady breeze, the high-wheeled wagon once more began to move toward the water.

"Just one thing, bruther." As he spoke, Simna deftly controlled the lines that kept the vehicle's sail properly trimmed. "What do we do when we reach the river? Swim for it? This conveyance is no boat."

"No indeed," the pliant figure of his friend replied, "but save for a few braces and nails it is all wood, light and strong. I am hoping it will float."

The windwagon continued to pick up speed. "And if it doesn't?" an anxious swordsman inquired further.

"Then I will float better than any of you." The eyes that gazed back at the swordsman did not smile.

Howling and moaning, the Brotherhood of the Bone angrily pursued the turncoat skeleton and its fleshy friends. Repeatedly looking back over his shoulder, Simna ibn Sind tried to cajole more speed out of the solid but clunky windwagon. It had been built for durability, not speed. The breeze held behind them, but he found himself wishing for one of the gales they had encountered at sea. Occasionally he inhaled deeply and blew into the sail, more as a gesture of encouragement to the wind than out of any expectation of increasing their velocity, however minutely.

"Come on, hurry!" Holding Ehomba easily in one arm, Hunkapa Aub was using the other to beckon repeatedly at the herdsman's fleeing skeleton. Spears began to fall around the fugitive. One struck its mount, but passed harmlessly through the rib cage without becoming entangled in the bleached white legs.

Then it was racing alongside, barely keeping pace with the steadily accelerating windwagon. With its bony mount exhausted and beginning to fail, Ehomba's insides had no choice but to risk the jump from vertebrae to vehicle. Letting go of the ossified stallion's neck bones, it leaped, arms outstretched—and fell short.

Only to be caught at the wrist by a massive, hairy hand. Thick fingers wrapped around the delicate bones and strained, pulling the skeletal structure bodily into the wagon.

"Set me down," Ehomba directed his massive friend. Obediently, Hunkapa complied.

Having no breath to catch, the skeleton did not hesitate. On hands and knees it crawled over to the limp form of its outer self. With an effort, Ehomba opened his mouth. It was the mouth of an eromakasi, trained to expand sufficiently to swallow darkness of any size. Inserting first a hand, then an entire arm, the wayward skeleton wriggled and wiggled itself back into its fleshy sheath.

Slowly, Ehomba's shape and silhouette filled out, returning to normal. When the last of the animate white bone had disappeared down his gullet, he contracted his greatly distended mouth and sat up. Working his jaws up and down and from side to side to realign his skin with his skull, he twisted and turned as he sat in the bottom of the jouncing, rocking wagon. Finally satisfied, he stood up for the first time in days, and stretched. Simna had not heard so much creaking and groaning and cracking since he had been forced to spend a stomach-churning night alone in their cabin aboard the *Grömsketter.*

Looking over at him, the herdsman smiled contently. "That is better. Much better. Life is easier without a skeleton because there is less strain on the body, but being unable to stand up soon grows tiresome." His smile vanished as he grabbed quickly for the mast and shouted. "Watch out!"

"Hoy?" Simna sat up straight and gripped the tiller and control lines tightly in his fingers. So entranced had he been by his friend's structural renascence that his attention had wandered from their heading. In the interim, they had run out of road.

The windwagon hit the water hard, sending up a fan-shaped shower of water that sprayed higher than the mast. Instantly, the boxy vehicle slowed. Caught by the sluggish current but still powered by the wind out of the east, it began to drift with agonizing slowness across the broad, flat expanse of the unnamed river.

Lying in the rear of the vehicle, the black litah lifted its ebony head and yawned, trying to work up an interest in the proceedings. "They're still coming. Better get a move on."

"We're making as much speed as we can! This is no pinnace." Glancing down, Simna saw water beginning to filter up between the slats, threatening to submerge his sandaled feet. The wagon was caulked against the weather, but it was never the intention of its builders to make it watertight. How long the seals would hold against the pressure of the river its hopeful passengers could only guess.

The army of the Brotherhood reached the bank where the wagon had driven into the languid flow. Many halted there, pulling up and reining in their mounts. Dozens of the more determined dead, driven by anger and fury at the deceitful betrayal of the living and his promised contribution to their ranks, did not. Urging their ashen mounts onward, they plunged headfirst into the current.

"They're still coming!" Frantically, Simna tugged on lines and tiller, trying everything he could think of to augment their sluggish pace.

Himself fully restored, Ehomba quietly contemplated the skeletal spectacle aft. "Easy for the dead to be brave."

"Complimenting them is not likely to save us," the swordsman snapped.

His tall companion smiled over at him. "Keep your hand on the tiller and your mind on the sail, friend Simna. Bravery and intelligence do not always go hand in hand." He turned his attention back to the onrushing skeletal horde. "Oura says that after they have been dead for a while, people tend to lose their mental edge. They may remember well the little things, but the greater picture starts to escape them."

Simna frowned, and despite the herdsman's admonition turned to look at the waters behind them. What he saw raised his spirits far more than any gust or gale.

Charging forward without pause, those members of the Brotherhood of the Bone intent on punishing the retreating living who had dared to take back one of their own struggled out into the current of the wide, deep river. Struggled out—and began to sink. For while the living carry within their bodies the means with which to accomplish natural, unforced flotation, the long dead do not. Bone sinks. Confronted by this inescapable fact, mounts and riders closed no more than a few yards between themselves and the escaping windwagon before, despite their frenzied determination, they began to slip beneath the surface.

The blanched skeletons of once-powerful coursers kicked futilely at the water that dragged them down. Not to their deaths, for they were already dead, but to a river bottom gluey with accumulated mud and decomposing plant matter. Their furious riders sank with them. From a position of safety halfway across the river and slightly downstream, the wagon's passengers watched as a number of their would-be pursuers crawled laboriously out onto the bank they had so recently and precipitously left, there to dry themselves in the sun as they rejoined their more conservative deceased comrades. Not all of them made it back out, some having managed to mire themselves forever in the grip of the shifting, glutinous river bottom.

Simna would have given a cheer, but he was too tired. Besides, he knew he might need his remaining energy for a swim to the far bank. With every gust of wind they drew nearer to that gently sloping haven, but at the same time the wagon continued to take on water.

"Will we make it, do you think?" he asked Ehomba.

The tall herdsman contemplated the dirty backwash swirling around his feet. "I do not know, Simna. I am an expert neither on wagons nor boats. The sides are well made, and will hold. But that will not do us any good if we sink below the surface like our pursuers." He raised his gaze to the sail that continued to billow westward. "If the wind holds . . ." His contemplative murmur trailed off into the sustaining breeze.

Amazingly, when there was nearly a foot of water inside the windwagon, it stopped sinking. The natural buoyancy of the wood that had been used in its construction kept them afloat, though with so much water inboard their progress was greatly reduced. They were no longer sailing so much as drifting with the current.

Before long, the small army of the Brotherhood had vanished from sight as the river took a westward bend. They were very close to the opposite bank now, tantalizingly close, but if they jumped overboard and swam, it meant that their supplies, not to mention themselves, would be drenched. Ehomba elected to try to ride it out, hoping that the combination of current and wind would carry them safely to shore. Simna concurred.

"If it sinks under us, we'll have to swim for it anyway," the swordsman pointed out. "Might as well stay as dry as possible for as long as possible."

Even as he concluded the observation, something jarred the wagon sharply, bringing it to a shuddering halt. Simna grinned cockily. "Nothing like having a request filled on the spot. We just hit a sandbar." Leaving the tiller set, he sloshed to the left side of the wagon and peered over the side. The murky water obscured and distorted everything that lay more than a foot below the surface, but by leaning over, the swordsman was able to make out the broad, dun-colored, slightly curved shape that had brought their aimless odyssey to a halt.

"It's a sandbar, all right," he informed his companions confidently. "Looks like it stretches all the way to shore." Still grinning, he gathered up his sword and backpack. "We can walk from here."

Ehomba hesitated. "Simna, I am not sure. . . ."

"Not sure?" The stocky swordsman hefted his pack higher on his shoulders as he prepared to step over the side. "Not sure of what, Etjole? With those long legs most of you will stay drier than most. Hunkapa's the one to feel sorry for." He nodded in the shaggy hulk's direction. "With all that fur he'll soak up this brown muck like a sponge."

"Hunkapa be okay," their massive companion assured him.

"Hunkapa always okay." After mimicking his ponderous friend's childish tone, Simna pointed out a spar splint floating on the floor of the wagon. "Sandbars are usually firm enough for walking, but I don't want to step onto one made of silt and sink up to my neck. If I'm going to look like an idiot I want company. Hand me that length of good wood, Hunkapa."

Obediently, Aub passed it across. Gripping it firmly in one hand, the swordsman threw a leg over the side of the nearly motionless wagon and thrust the length of lumber downward, anxious to see how far it would slide into the upper reaches of the sandbar. To his surprise and gratification, it didn't sink at all. The gently convex surface was firm, yielding only very slightly to his exploratory prodding.

"There, you see?" He took some pleasure in being able to chide Ehomba. The soft-voiced, solemn-visaged herdsman was right so often it was beginning to grow irksome. "Easy walking. Get your stuff and let's get out of here while we're still afloat."

Leaning around the mast, Hunkapa Aub tried to see into the murky water. "Is strong enough to hold me, Simna?"

"Sure! Here, see for yourself." The swordsman thrust the wooden pole hard into the water.

Taking offense at this latest and most flagrant outrage, the sandbar promptly erupted in Simna's face, drenching him with dun-colored water, decaying plant matter, and smatterings of the snails, freshwater crustaceans, and startled amphibians that had been living on its back. The swordsman was knocked down by the impact. Ehomba nearly went over backwards into the river, catching himself on the tiller only at the last moment, and Hunkapa Aub was knocked to his knees.

Wrenching its head from the mud in which it had been buried, the great eel whipped around to confront its assailant. Normally placid and somnolent during the heat of the day, it could no longer ignore the stabbing annoyance near the center of its spine. Rising from the shallows, it arched skyward for an instant to get its bearings. Tooth-lined jaws parted in the middle of the streamlined green-black head while tiny black eyes struggled to focus. Espying the intruder nearest to its back, it plunged downward, mouth agape. Simna was reciting his last will and testament as rapidly as he could, but he saw that he would not be able to finish it in time.

Something like a gout of black flame exploded past him, rising into the sky to meet the descending fanged skull before it could strike. Instinctively, Simna thrust his sword upward in a parrying gesture, but it never made contact. The enormous eel had been jolted sideways, back into the water. The concussion as it struck rocked the windwagon, once more knocking all three of its occupants off their feet. Three, because one had gone missing.

Clinging to the tiller for support, shaking water from his face and braids, Ehomba hung on as their waterlogged transport rocked in the waves stirred by the stupendous underwater encounter. "Can you see anything? Simna!"

Dazed and drenched, the swordsman fought to get a grip on the rim of the wagon. Clinging leechlike to the rocking sideboard, he struggled to peer over the side. "No!" A small geyser hit him square in the face, forcing him to turn away and spit river water. "Can't see a thing—nothing!"

Squinting through the dirty, flying liquid, the herdsman sputtered, "Ahlitah! Where's Ahlitah?"

Of them all, only Hunkapa Aub, utilizing his prodigious strength, managed to struggle to his feet in the midst of chaos and tempest. "Hunkapa see him!" Sodden hair hanging in triangular, downward-facing points like limp, gray pennants from the underside of his arm, he pointed.

"How . . ." Ehomba spat out another mouthful of water. "How is he looking?"

There followed a pause, which ended when Hunkapa Aub declared, "Hungry."

The highly localized squall subsided almost as abruptly as it had struck. Around the waterlogged windwagon the river once again grew calm. Within, everything that had not been tied down was afloat, bobbing in the water that had bubbled or sloshed in. Not even the inherent buoyancy of the sturdy planking would keep them afloat much longer, Ehomba saw.

In front of the wagon and paddling steadily for shore was the black litah. In its powerful jaws it gripped the broken neck of the great eel. The nightmare head hung severely to one side, the black eyes glazed with death.

"Hunkapa, we must go with Ahlitah," Ehomba told his husky companion. "You are the only one strong enough to pull the wagon."

The massive man-beast regarded the herdsman with limpid, mournful eyes. "Hunkapa would do, Etjole. Only one problem. Hunkapa cannot swim."

"Cannot . . . ?" It was rare indeed for Ehomba to be taken aback. When they had first plunged into the river to escape the pursuing minions of the Brotherhood, all the time they had been sailing and drifting across, even after they had become dangerously waterlogged and had begun to sink, the big brute had not said a word.

Simna was lying with his back against the inner wall of the wagon, his chest heaving, his sword hanging limp in the tepid water. He was still trying to recover from the experience of having been less than a few seconds away from being eaten by his "sandbar." Ehomba pushed past him to peer over the front of the saturated vehicle.

The eel had been lying half-buried in the ooze that stretched out from the nearby bank. Though no sandbar, the mud bank did incline gently shoreward. He and Simna would have to swim for a little bit, but Hunkapa's head should remain above water.

When informed of this, the shaggy biped hesitated. "Don't know, Etjole." He peered warily over the side of the wagon. "Hunkapa afraid."

"You have to try," the herdsman told him. "I think it is shallow enough so that you can walk, but if not, you will have to try to swim. I knew how to swim before I could walk. It is a more natural motion than walking." He started to gather up his kit and spear, securing the two swords to his back.

"If you find yourself in trouble, just watch me." He smiled encouragingly. "We cannot stay here, Hunkapa. This wagon is coming apart. If the current catches it, there is a good chance it will drift out into the deep part of the river. Then there will be no opportunity for you to walk."

He could see the fear on the creature's face. So powerful, and yet so afraid of an element in which Ehomba found himself very much at home. Reaching up, he took one massive paw in his hand.

"Come with me, Hunkapa. We will go in together. Do you understand? We have no choice."

Slowly, the shaggy head nodded. "Hunkapa—Hunkapa understand. Go together. Ehomba look out for his friend." Huge fingers squeezed painfully tight, but the herdsman did not complain. He glanced back over his shoulder.

"You coming, Simna? Or does your love for this vehicle extend to floating downriver with it?" He mustered an ironic smile. "Swim a little ways and your feet might strike a sandbar."

"They might strike something else, too," the swordsman growled ominously. Sheathing his sword and holding his backpack above his head, he slipped both legs over the side of the steadily sinking wagon. With a grimace, he dropped into the cloudy, silt-rich water.

"Together now." Ehomba allowed his hand to be half crushed as he stepped resolutely over the side. River buffeted him as Hunkapa Aub's much greater mass displaced water. The ungainly hulk disappeared— only to reappear seconds later with its head well above the surface. Astonishment and delight beamed from the guileless, hair-covered face.

"Hunkapa not have to swim! Hunkapa's feet on bottom!"

"I hoped it was so." Treading water while struggling to keep his pack dry, the herdsman started to kick for the shore. Against his back, the seabone sword quivered orgasmically at the sensation of being submerged. Anyone else would have found the unexpected vibration unnerving, but Ehomba had anticipated it. What more natural than that the wondrous weapon should react to being placed in the surroundings from whence it had originally evolved?

Suddenly he was out of the water, high and dry, heaved skyward by a robust thrust from below. No gigantic eel bursting from the depths this time, but the hand of Hunkapa Aub, lifting him from beneath. Effortlessly, the herdsman's huge companion placed his angular friend on broad, hirsute shoulders. In this manner Ehomba rode in comparative comfort the rest of the way to the shore. Only his ears suffered, bruised by an unending stream of blistering profanities from the struggling Simna, who, forced to swim, trailed well behind.

XI

As they drew themselves up on the reed-lined, accommodating bank, they scanned the now distant opposite shore for signs of their pursuers. But the Brotherhood of the Bone, unable to cross by swimming or riding, had given up and gone back to the dark, sheltering forest that was their refuge and abode. The weary travelers were safe, if once more afoot.

Taking a seat on the gentle, grassy slope, Ehomba unpacked his gear and spread it out beside him to dry in the sun. Like a high-priced over-stuffed rug liberated from a sultan's palace, Hunkapa Aub sprawled nearby, basking gloriously in the heat of midday. The herdsman watched gravely as the windwagon that had carried them so far and so well slowly drifted off downstream, sinking slowly into the riverine depths.

Nearby, an exhausted Simna finally emerged, dripping, from the water. Stumbling up the bank, he tossed his pack to one side, not caring if it spilled its contents all over the grass. Through no effort of his own, it did not. His sword he slipped back into its scabbard, which he then removed and dumped next to the pack. Swaying slightly, murky water and the occasional tadpole running off him in rivulets, he staggered over to where the black litah lay panting. Its forepaws lay on the crushed throat of the great eel. As the sodden swordsman approached, the magnificently maned cranium swiveled slowly to regard him.

Halting before the cat and its kill, Simna stiffly dipped his head and made a sweeping gesture with one arm. "Look before you leap, my master at arms always told me. I admit it: There are times when I'm forgetful."

The litah replied thoughtfully. "There are times when you're an idiot."

Gritting his teeth, Simna looked off to one side for a long moment. Still breathing hard, he rested one hand on a knee. "You're not making this any easier for me, cat. I came over to thank you for saving my life."

Massive eyebrows rose haughtily. "Saving your life? Did I save your life? Dear me, I suppose I did." Ahlitah turned back to his kill. "If it will make you feel any better, I assure you it was coincidental. It's just that I happen to be very fond of eel." With that, the great head dipped forward and puissant teeth tore into the slick, green-black flesh.

"Hoy, well, thank you anyway, thou maestro of piquant sprays. Simna ibn Sind embraces chance salvation over intentional abstention any day." Stumbling as he turned, he made his unsteady way back to the place on the bank where he had dropped his gear. Behind him, the clear warm air of afternoon was filled with contented crunching sounds.

Exhausted, and mentally as well as physically spent from their exertions of the morning, they made camp in a thick copse of impressive shade trees not far from the river. The woods on the western bank closely resembled those they had passed through on the opposite shore, except that on the western side larger trees were fewer and farther between.

"These woods seem to be thinning out." Seated next to the campfire, Ehomba reached down to give the wooden spit on which their evening meal of freshly caught fish was broiling another turn. "If that turns out to be so, it is a great shame. We could have made good use of the windwagon on open plains."

Lying on the other side of the fire with his head against the pillowing flank of Hunkapa Aub, Simna watched the meal cook. Hungry as he was, the tantalizing aroma that rose from the sizzling fish verged on the sensuous.

"Hoy, long bruther, we've traversed desert and veldt, mountain and marsh on foot before. By Gumitharap's calluses, we'll cross whatever lies before us as well."

Ehomba smiled fondly over the flames at his sometimes trying but ever willing friend. "Optimism becomes you, Simna."

The swordsman looked up and grinned. "Not being dead does wonders for a man's spirits." Lifting his head and glancing to one side, he indicated a slowly heaving dark mass lying off by itself a little ways away from the fire. Having ingested an unholy vast quantity of eel, the black litah was locked in a sleep that mimicked the deceased.

"Kitty there won't own up to it, but he saved my life. I don't buy all that pompous indifference about his just being after a meal. He could catch fish anytime. He knew what he was doing."

"I suspect that you are right, my friend." Rising, the herdsman wiped down the front of his kilt. "I was thinking how nice it would be to have something else to eat with the fish. I think we passed a fruit tree a little ways back, and I know I saw some mushrooms." Picking up his spear, he started away from the fire and into the forest.

"Don't go too far, bruther," Simna exclaimed warningly. "We don't know these woods. There may not be any possessive, ambulatory collections of bones click-clacking about, but unknown nights often hide all sorts of hungry beasties."

Ehomba replied without looking back. "I remember the tree as only being a little ways from camp, Simna. You rest here, and do not let our supper burn."

"No chance of that, famished as I am." Sitting up and away from Hunkapa Aub, who snorted and rubbed his nose briskly in his sleep, the swordsman gave the improvised spit another turn.

With half the moon and all the stars to guide him, the herdsman worked his way back through the woods until the campfire was only a distant flickering among the trees. Convinced that he had already wandered too far, he tried a little more to his left—and there was the tree he had remembered passing. It was a wild orange, its limbs bristling with long thorns. Their presence did not worry him because he had no intention of trying to climb into those protected branches.

Using the ancient but still sharp tooth that tipped his spear, he cut away the ripest of the brightly colored spheres within reach. Each time a severed stem fell, the faintest, most ethereal of roars could be heard. Sometimes the spirit of the tooth could be invoked for purposes other than engendering mass confusion and destruction: gathering oranges, for example.

With the aid of the spear it only took a few minutes to accumulate enough of the juice-heavy fruit to more than sate himself and his friends. He knew that Hunkapa Aub would probably eat Ahlitah's share. To the best of Ehomba's knowledge, large carnivorous cats were not fond of fruit.

Slinging his spear against his back, he made a basket out of the folds of his kilt and filled the resultant concavity with the best of the oranges. Nearby, he located the mushrooms he had passed earlier and added several handfuls of the tasty fungi to his growing accumulation. Satisfied, he started back toward camp.

He was within sight of the fire when something sprang silently from behind one of the trees he was passing to press an incredibly sharp knife tightly against his neck. His hands dropped, sending mushrooms and oranges spilling to the ground, rolling away from his feet. Despite his acute herdsman's senses, he had not seen or heard his assailant. Or smelled it, which was not surprising when its nature became apparent to him. It had no smell.

Old bones generally did not.

"Surprised to see me, swindler of promises?" The voice was breathy, unnatural, and familiar. It belonged to the envoy of the Brotherhood of the Bone.

"Very much so." The edge of the bone knife dimpling his throat was sharp enough to cleave a notion. "From what I saw, I did not think any of you or your brethren could swim the river, or walk across its bottom."

Whispering in his ear, the skeleton smiled. "Who said anything about swimming or walking?"

"Then how did you get across?" With the bony rib cage pressing hard against his back, Ehomba could not reach his spear. His swords lay back in camp, laid out neat and useless alongside his blanket.

"Flew, of course." A spectral chuckle rattled the vacant chest. "Dead dragonets carried me. It was hard for them, but there was no choice. I couldn't use dead birds. When they die, they lose their feathers along with their flesh. But bats and dragonets retain their wing membranes for quite a while. Took a dozen of them to bring me over, and they'll never make it back. Their wings are too frayed, too desiccated. It doesn't matter. They were dead before they took off from the other bank anyway. Dead here, dead there: Location means nothing, and doesn't change anything."

Ehomba stood perfectly still. "That means you are marooned here now as well, and will never be able to rejoin the Brotherhood."

Teeth chattered. "No, but I'll have something better. I'll have their revenge. You promised your bones to us in return for our letting your friends go. Then you called them back. Charlatan." The edge of the knife pressed a little deeper. The herdsman felt a tiny trickle of warmth start to flow down past his collarbone to his chest.

"I did no such thing," he protested softly. "I left you my insides, as was agreed. If they preferred my company to yours, that is no reason to blame me."

"Isn't it? As if you didn't know they would find a way to return to you."

"Actually, I was not sure. I hoped they would. I need my insides. They are of more use to me than to you."

"They won't be, in a moment."

"Bruther, what . . . ?" Holding his sword in a firm, two-handed grip, Simna stepped out of the shadows. The looming mass of Hunkapa Aub stood to one side of him, a softly growling Ahlitah on the other.

"Keep your distance!" the envoy shouted warningly.

"Etjole . . ." Seeing the knife that was gripped in the skeleton's hand, the swordsman measured the distance between them. Too far. "If you cut him . . ." he began.

"What?" The envoy cackled amusedly. "You'll kill me? You're more than a century too late to make that threat hold up, traveler. When I'm through with him, maybe I'll have your bones too. They look to be an interesting set, all squashed down and out as they are."

Simna looked as if he wanted to say something else, but he was interrupted by a loud *crack*, the dry cry of splitting wood. Automatically, everyone's gaze snapped upward into the night. Everyone's, that is, except Ehomba's. The instant the skeletal assassin's attention was diverted, he broke free of the bony grip and threw himself forward and down. Reacting, the envoy of the Brotherhood raised the knife, hewn from the shinbone of a comrade, and was about to strike lethally downward when the enormous broken bough landed on top of him with a reverberating crash.

Bones and splinters went flying in all directions. Rolling away from the impact, Ehomba stared at the branch that had crushed his would-be executioner. The bleached skull was no longer intact or visible, having been pulverized by the considerable weight of falling wood. Leg and arm and rib bones lay scattered everywhere.

His friends were at his side before the dust settled. Hunkapa Aub simply lifted the herdsman bodily and set him on his feet. Feeling of the cut that had been made to his throat, Ehomba knew he would have to wear a bandage there for a few days at least. Had it gone half an inch deeper his life would be gushing out between his fingers. The falling branch had startled the envoy for barely an instant, just long enough to allow his captive to break away.

Now the bones of the murderous, spectral visitant lay strewn across the ground, dispersed and harmless.

Satisfied that their friend and guide was not seriously injured, Hunkapa Aub and the black litah returned to camp. Simna remained to inspect the shattered bough. Having fallen from somewhere halfway up the side of a truly imposing trunk, the branch was greater in diameter than many of the mature trees nearby.

"That's what I call a lucky break," the swordsman commented. "It doesn't look rotten, and I see no evidence of termites or other insects having been at work, so something else must have caused it to fall." He gazed evenly at his tall companion. "Fall just then, and just there. I don't suppose a man who continually denies being a wizard but who can step out of his own skin would have had anything to do with that?"

Having brushed himself off, Ehomba had bent to recover as many of the spilled mushrooms and oranges as he could. Like the envoy, many had been squashed beneath the weight of the broken branch. Whatever he scavenged would have to do. He was not going back into the forest in search of replacements. One nearly fatal fruit-gathering expedition a night was enough.

"As a matter of fact, Simna, I did not. Grateful as I am, it was as much of a surprise to me as to the rest of you."

"Hoy, right, sure." The swordsman wore a peevish expression. "That's what you always say, bruther. You just happened to be standing under that branch, and it just happened to break and fall right on that homicidal stack of bones. No magic, no sorcery. Just coincidence, and nothing more."

Having picked up those oranges and mushrooms that were unbruised, Ehomba glanced over at his companion. "I cannot explain it, Simna. But I know that there are times in a man's life when it is best not to question things too closely." Tilting his head back slightly, he sniffed of the night air. "Something is burning."

"Our supper!" Whirling, Simna broke into a run, but not before looking back over his shoulder as he darted past his friend. "By Gnomost's gneels, if I didn't know better, I'd *swear* I'd seen that tree before. Funny thing, that."

"Yes." Ehomba too spared a last, lingering glance for the immense old oak as he followed his frantic companion back into camp at a more leisurely pace.

The incident was not discussed as they ate, but everyone watched the surrounding woods a little more closely, paid a bit more attention to the distant rustlings and rattlings of the nocturnal forest creatures. The fish was delicious, not badly burned as Simna had feared, but only thoroughly cooked. As Ehomba had surmised, the addition of broiled mushrooms to the meal and wild oranges for dessert was an excellent complement to the main course. Even Ahlitah tried a little of everything, much to the surprise of both his human companions.

"I'm always open to new experiences," he told them as he spit out orange peel. "That's one I won't have to open myself to again. Paugh!" Nothing wrinkles in disgust, Ehomba mused, quite so exhaustively as the face of a displeased cat.

With Hunkapa Aub agreeing to take the first watch, the others retired, the two men to their blankets and the black litah to the mat of leaves and grass he had assembled with his paws. Ehomba drifted off with one hand feeling gingerly of his throat and the strip of cloth that now separated it from the beaded necklaces he wore.

As he slid into sleep, his thoughts drifted into dream—but it was most unlike any normal dream, or even a normal nightmare.

He was running, running hard, but on all fours. Bushes and grass sped past at an astonishing rate of speed. Though he could feel the ground beneath his feet and therefore knew he was not flying, with each prodigious stride he left it below him for an impossibly long time.

Startled by his sudden appearance, something with wide eyes looked up to encounter his gaze. Utterly paralyzed by the unexpected eye contact, it stood frozen for an instant and then flashed by as he raced past. A rabbit, too small and scrawny to bother with. Little more than a mouthful or three, certainly not enough to satiate the voluminous hunger that burned in his belly. He needed, and was after, bigger prey.

When he exploded from the high grass the herd panicked. Though it meant he would have to exert himself a little more to make a kill, he was exhilarated by the fear his appearance had incited. Eland and elk bolted in every direction, eyes rolling with fright, tongues lolling from open mouths. Impala and syndyoceros crashed into one another and bounded away wildly as they sought the safety of the herd that had not yet reformed.

In the confusion Ehomba had an entire minute to single out a victim: more than enough time. Settling on an old bull elk, he accelerated to maximum speed. The elk never had a chance. Ehomba hit it head-on, his open jaws slamming into the hairy throat and locking like a vise. The elk tried to lower its head in order to bring its massive horns to bear on its attacker, but, already caught and held in a death grip, it had no real chance to defend itself.

Blood flowed into and through Ehomba's jaws, exciting every nerve and sensation in his body. Unable to fight, the elk tried to run. His assailant's weight made sustained flight impossible. The prey sank to its knees, then its belly, and finally went limp, suffocated by the tightening of its attacker's jaws.

Ehomba held on for another several minutes until he was sure death had arrived. Then, crouching alongside the body, one paw placed possessively on the carcass, he began to eat. Blood and muscle, organs and bone, all vanished into massive, efficient jaws. Lingering over the kill, he ate intermittently for the rest of the afternoon and on into early evening. Only then did he rise and move away, belly dragging low, back into the high grass. There he found the stream, and drank for long minutes.

Locating a small clearing, he lay down heavily in the shade of a cluster of yellow-blooming hopak trees and began to groom himself. It was impossible to get all the blood off his muzzle no matter how many times he licked a paw and ran it across his face, but he made a start. The rest of the stain would come out later, following repeated washings. Glutted and content, he slumped down on his side and fell into a sleep any passing traveler might easily have mistaken for death. But despite his seeming somnolence, the sound of a snapping twig would be enough to rouse him instantly. In the depth of his deep sleep, one foot kicked out repeatedly.

Wrapped in his blanket beside the campfire, Ehomba's left leg twitched restively.

Ahlitah was dizzy. Not from chasing his tail, which when absolutely convinced no one and nothing else was watching he would occasionally do to relieve unrelenting boredom, but from trying to maintain an alien and utterly unaccustomed posture. With each step he took, no matter how short and cautious, he was convinced, absolutely certain, that he was going to fall over. Yet despite his fear and misgivings, he did not.

By all that ran and crawled and swam and flew, what had happened to his other pair of legs?

And his eyes. And his ears, and his nose! Though he could see adequately, the acuity of vision he usually enjoyed had been replaced by a pale, fuzzy imitation of normal sight. Objects located more than a short distance away were unidentifiable. Anything at a reasonable distance blended invisibly into the landscape or the horizon. Furthermore, it was as if he were gazing through a steady downpour. Colors were washed out or absent entirely. It was horrible: He felt half blinded.

Nothing was audible except that which was in his immediate vicinity. The familiar panoply of distant sounds, the constant susurration of animate life, was entirely absent. It was as if the world had suddenly gone silent. There were noises and the echoes of movement close by, but nothing else. No complaining insects, no scuttling lizards or slithering snakes, no chirping birds. The wing-beats of dragonets no longer whispered in his ears, and the delectable murmur of prey animals cropping grass was sorely wanting.

As for the wonderful universe of scents that normally filled his nostrils, its absence constituted a kind of olfactory blindness that made his severely impacted vision that much worse. It was a struggle, a strain, a surreal effort to smell anything at all. What odors he was able to identify were so homogenized it hardly seemed worth the effort to inhale.

Simply keeping his ridiculous body from falling down demanded a preposterous share of his considerably reduced energy. And yet he was conscious of the fact that, though shorter, it was a much better body than many of those that were in motion around him. Feeling greatly enfeebled and not knowing what else to do, he instinctively sought shelter.

A nearby enclosure seemed to promise privacy if not enlightenment. Given his severely diminished capacity for perceiving the world around him, it was hardly surprising that he should be wrong about this, too. The edifice was not empty.

Ordinarily he would have attacked and killed the pair of two-legged young females that came running toward him. For reasons unknown and inexplicable, he did not. Instead, he allowed them to carry out a mock attack on his person; striking him about the chest and arms, gamboling around his middle, and prattling inanities into his ears. They made muted howling noises. The younger, a lithesome female not long past the cusp of puberty, was only slightly more respectful of his person than her elder. The air of commingled anticipation and affection they projected was oddly unnerving, as if it were forced rather than natural. Their strongest efforts to pull him farther into the enclosure notwithstanding, they struck him as wretchedly weak.

So did the third female figure that appeared from another part of the enclosure to throw both fore and hind legs around him. To his astonishment and disgust, instead of extending her tongue to lick his face by way of greeting, she thrust her tongue deeply into his mouth. So startled was he by this unexpected, unnatural act that he forgot to bite it. She, however, was not averse to nibbling on his ear. At least something about the otherwise inane interaction between himself and the unknown female made sense!

Most unexpectedly, given the extreme distaste and inner turmoil his extraordinary situation had brought about, he felt the heat rising in his loins. Disturbed and bewildered, he did not bother to resist as the female led him to another, darker portion of the enclosure. At least, he thought with relief, she had dismissed her irritating, overly exuberant predecessors.

When he realized what she had in mind, he knew only one way to react. Evidently, this did not displease her. Quite to the contrary. The mechanics of the act as well as its immediate consequences were surprisingly conventional, a touch of familiarity in alien surroundings for which he was grateful. After they both rested awhile, he was prepared to repeat the process. Again, the female had no objection.

By the fourth time, she was regarding him with unabashed awe. By the fifth, with hesitancy. When he ventured to initiate a sixth reiteration with as much enthusiasm as the first, she retreated precipitously from the darkened portion of the enclosure. Her reaction only confused him further. As was typical of his kind, he was prepared to continue for the rest of the day and far on into the night. Clearly she was not.

His head hurt. Agitated and bemused, he stumbled back to the enclosure's entrance. A pair of very large two-legged males were waiting for him there. They bore weapons and grim expressions. Standing behind them, the female with whom he had recently consorted appeared in a state of extreme agitation, pointing and jabbering in his direction. The looks on the faces of the two armed males grew ominous.

If there was one thing he was in no mood to tolerate at that moment, it was the absurd verbalizations and oral circumlocutions of a brace of irritable bipeds. To let them know how he was feeling, he voiced a warning roar. The effect was salutary. The fur stood up on their heads, their eyes grew as big as emu eggs, and they turned and bolted in the opposite direction as fast as their hind legs would carry them, flinging their weapons aside while screaming at the top of their lungs. From other enclosures, startled faces peered out in search of the source of the sound. Feeling much better about things, he strode out of the bordello. Though he had neglected to pay, no one dared to confront him.

Lying well away from the campfire, Ahlitah smacked his lips as he rolled over onto his back.

Simna frowned as he entered the city. The golden towers, the marble archways, the teeming crowds of barkers and bazaaris, the fragrant smells of fine cooking—all were absent. In their place were simple houses of stone and wood and thatch. In lieu of richly garbed horses and moas, dogs and rodent-hunting cats roamed the streets. Where he normally would have expected to see paving stones of granite there was only packed earth.

A few women tracked his progress as he advanced. Some were ancient, others not yet old enough to understand. Those of young and middle age were tall, proud, and comely, with elegant necks and straight backs, full breasts and curving backsides. He grinned at them and a few smiled back, though there was a hesitancy in their expressions that bruised his ego.

Where was he? Was this not the entrance to Vharuphan the Radiant, renowned capital of the Dhashtari Emperors? Where were the great domes of polished green verdite and the fine gilded latticework famed near and far across half a continent? The nearest thing he saw to fine latticework was a sturdily constructed well. As for domes, there was one of brick for firing pottery, and it was not habitable.

As he wandered in a daze something struck him in the legs. Looking down, he saw a young girl clinging to him and beaming delightedly, her sweet innocent features blushing with love. As he struggled weakly to disengage himself from her pythonic embrace, a young man stepped down from the porch of a nearby house and approached. In one hand he carried a spear suitable in size and weight for someone no longer a child but not yet an adult. It was more than toy, less than weapon. Bowing low, he then put a hand on Simna's arm and smiled, revealing a blaze of perfect white teeth.

Stunned and not knowing what else to do or where to go, Simna allowed himself to be led by hand and arm up the steps of the porch and into the house. In a back room an astoundingly handsome woman stood before a stone counter, using knives of differing size and heft to slice and butcher what remained of a human hindquarter. When Simna made gagging sounds, she turned. A conflagration of a smile spread across her face, making her appear more beautiful than ever and somewhat minimizing the effect of the bloodstains that spotted her apron and overblouse. The ensuing kiss she bestowed upon him almost, but not quite, allowed him to overlook the import of the three harrowing words she spoke to him.

"Welcome home—husband."

Simna ibn Sind woke up screaming.

The sounds of his yelling and thrashing about startled his companions to wakefulness. This included Hunkapa Aub, who, having never been relieved of his watch, had fallen asleep where he sat. Around the dying embers of the campfire the forest was silent, and night still held sway over the world.

Ehomba rushed to his friend's side. "Simna, what is wrong? Is there anything I can do?" Nearby, Hunkapa Aub was still trying to shake the sleep webs from his brain while the black litah looked on unblinkingly.

"Anything you can . . . ?" The swordsman looked up at his rangy companion. "Yes, by Guquaquo. If you ever hear me making noises like that in my sleep ever again, wake me instantly." Putting both hands to his head, he stared blankly at the corpse of the campfire. "Hoy, what a nightmare! I—I was domesticated!"

His expression twisting, Ehomba stood up and stepped back. "Is that all?"

Simna fixed the herdsman with a look of utmost seriousness. "Bruther, every man has his own fears. I do not mock yours. Grant me the same courtesy."

Ehomba nodded soberly. "You are right, my friend. I apologize." His expression tightened slightly. "I am curious, for I also had a most peculiar dream. I had four legs and the keenest imaginable senses, and was hunting."

"And I," Ahlitah put in with a reverberating growl, "walked on two legs like humans, and visited a place where intercourse was expected to be paid for with human money."

It was left, unsurprisingly, for Ehomba to sort out what must have taken place.

"I do not know what happened, or how, but it seems that some unknown mechanism has caused our dreams to slip from one individual to the next." He nodded at the swordsman. "You got my dream, Simna." His gaze shifted to the intent big cat. "I dreamed Ahlitah's dream. And he must have suffered through yours."

The swordsman nodded vigorously. "Hoy, that's crazy, but crazy logic is logic still. I certainly . . ." His expression twisted. "Wait a minute. What do you mean, 'suffered'?" He turned sharply to the watching litah. "Did my dream then cause you suffering?"

"Beyond doubt," the big cat replied. "I dare say you would have enjoyed it."

"Cursed unfair," the stocky warrior grumbled. "Every man—and cat—should keep to their own dreaming. Who asked you to snatch mine?"

"Believe me," Ahlitah replied, "if I had been allowed any choice in the matter, I would have opted instead for the dream of the nearest rodent. At least in such a dream I would have had the proper number of legs."

"Hoy, that's no given because—"

Ehomba cut him off. "Hunkapa Aub; you were asleep when Simna's nightmare woke us all. What did you dream?"

Enormous shaggy shoulders heaved, framing a look of utter ingenuousness. "Hunkapa not dream, Etjole. Sleep soundly."

Simna uttered a rude noise. "The slumber of the dumber. In ignorance there is purity."

"We must take care in the future." A thoughtful Ehomba gazed into the last dying embers of the campfire. "It could be dangerous for one to dream too often the dreams of another, be it man or beast."

They sat awhile together, discussing the remarkable occurrence. Eventually, fatigue overcame concern and they retired once more, this time to sleep the sleep of vacuity that refreshes the mind. In the morning they were rejuvenated—and much relieved. In the future they resolved to monitor their own sleep as well as that of one another more closely, the better to prevent a recurrence of the unfortunate slippage of the night before.

They resolved also to eat no more mushrooms gathered from this particular forest, no matter how nourishing or tasty they looked.

XII

Very soon they no longer had to worry about the unknown properties of forest mushrooms of any variety, because those delightful but often mysterious edible fungi soon vanished, along with the last remnants of the forest itself.

They did not lose the trees entirely, but instead of dense woods or even isolated thickets, individual boles grew in isolated hollows or followed the course of the occasional stream. Otherwise, the ground was covered with a tall yellow-green grass that came up to Simna's hips. They had traveled through worse before, but it still would have made for slow going if not for Hunkapa Aub. With his thick coat of hair to protect him from cuts and scratches, he was virtually immune to stickers and sharp-edged grasses. Following him as he plowed a path westward, they made steady progress.

The presence of many small creeks and streams meant they did not have to burden themselves with full bags of water, and the shade their gullies supplied provided a welcome respite at mealtimes and at night. After sundown, tiny covert creatures ringed each campsite with querulous cheeping sounds. Whenever one of the travelers attempted to locate the source of these gentle fanfares, they quickly evaporated into the surrounding grass. Whether animal, insect, or wee folk of the prairie, their true nature remained shrouded in mystery. Whatever they were, Ehomba decided, they were curious but not hostile.

Monstrous bison ranged the grassland, browsers larger than any Simna or Ehomba had ever seen. The travelers gave these hulky dark brown herbivores a wide berth. Ahlitah had to be restrained from testing his skills against such tempting, oversized game.

"There is no need," Ehomba argued with the big cat as they traipsed along in Hunkapa Aub's wake. "There is plenty of smaller game. What would be the point of risking your well-being to bring one of the beasts down?"

"To prove that I could do it." Passionate cat eyes looked up at the herdsman. The litah was panting in the heat of the day, thick black tongue lolling out one side of its mouth. "I know you don't understand. It's a predator thing."

"I understand that if you were to spark a stampede with one of your attacks we could all be killed. There is no shelter around here. I understand that if you go down beneath those great hooves and break a leg or two we would not be able to carry you."

"Man, you waste almost as much time worrying about things as you do wondering about them." Idly, Ahlitah slapped a big paw down on a field mouse that was unwisely attempting to cross behind Hunkapa and ahead of them. As it was not even big enough to chew, the cat swallowed the snack whole. "When it comes to matters mystical, I defer to you. When it comes to the business of killing, you should trust in me."

"Very well then," Ehomba argued. "Suppose you catch one and bring it down. What if it falls on you? I know how strong you are, but these grazers are huge. A dying one would be difficult to handle."

The great maned head nodded slowly. "That is a valid point. Even the most skilled hunter can fall victim to an accident."

"Besides," the herdsman went on, "what would we do with all that meat?"

"Ordinarily, I would live nearby until it was consumed." The litah snorted. "But since we are traveling on a human timetable, something that sensible would be out of the question." He was silent for a while, pacing easily alongside the herdsman. "Perhaps you are right. I'll find something else to kill."

"Thank you," Ehomba told him.

They camped that night in a depression where a small natural dam of rocks and debris had formed a narrow but deep pool. Not only did it provide them with a source of fresh water, but it also offered a chance to bathe and even, to a very limited degree, to swim. In this Ehomba took the lead, demonstrating once again the natural affinity for water that he had demonstrated on more than one occasion. Simna was a fine swimmer, while the black litah contented himself with rolling about in the shallows and following his immersion with a dust wallow. Unable to swim, Hunkapa Aub splashed about near the shore like a happy child.

It was therefore surprising that Ehomba woke not to the smell of damp vegetation or surroundings, but to an odor that was distinctly acrid.

Sitting up and pushing aside his blanket, he tilted his head slightly and sniffed. The sun was just considering the eastern horizon and none of his companions were yet awake. The smell was as familiar as it was distinctive, but from what direction was it coming? Of one thing and one thing only he was certain: Something in their vicinity was ablaze, and it wasn't the extinguished campfire.

Turning his head slowly to his right as he tried to locate the source of the odor, his gaze fell upon the black litah. As was its manner, it had awakened noiselessly. Now it was sitting back on its hindquarters, nose in the air, inhaling silently.

"You smell it also," Ehomba murmured.

The big cat nodded once. "Something burning. What I can't guess yet."

"Can you tell where? Which direction?" Knowing how much more sensitive the big cat was to odors of every kind, Ehomba ceased his own efforts in favor of the litah's.

There was a pause, then Ahlitah lifted a forepaw and pointed northward. "That way. And coming closer, fast."

"Better get everyone up."

While he roused Simna, the black litah prodded Hunkapa Aub to wakefulness. By the time the swordsman was sufficiently conscious to communicate, the sharp, acrid smell of burning vegetation was thick in Ehomba's nostrils.

"Etjole?" Raising himself up on his elbows, Simna blinked once, then wrinkled his features. "Somebody making breakfast?"

Satisfied that his friend was awake, the herdsman straightened and gazed soberly to the north. "I think this grassland is on fire."

It came roaring toward them like a wall, advancing in a solid line from horizon to horizon. Orange flames framed in red fed hungrily on the dry grass. Their superhot crowns licked at the sky, rising fifty feet and more before transmuting themselves into gouts of dense black smoke that obscured the clouds. Fleeing before the blaze was a rampaging menagerie of terrified creatures large and small. Broad-winged raptors and agile dragonets swooped and darted in waves before the flames, feasting on the insects and small game that were being driven from their hiding places by the onrushing conflagration.

Wind drove the fire forward. Where it advanced too rapidly for those in its path to escape, charred corpses littered the smoking, blackened earth in its wake.

"By Gapreth!" Suddenly wide awake, Simna was scrambling to gather up his gear. "The pool! Into the pool!"

"It is not wide enough," Ehomba countered. "The fire is too big. The flames will consume the grass on both sides and merge above the surface. They will suck the air from above the water, burn the lungs and suffocate anyone who is not fish or frog." Even as he spoke, the towering flames had advanced another ten feet nearer to the campsite. "Downstream! If we can find a pool too broad for the flames to overreach we will be safe."

Carrying everything, they fled from the onrushing blaze. Ahlitah flew effortlessly over rocks and gullies that slowed less nimble companions. Burdened by packs, lesser individuals than Ehomba and Simna would have fallen fatally behind. Hunkapa Aub was not graceful, but his expansive stride compensated for his occasional ungainliness.

As they fled, the stream continued to flow strongly alongside them, holding out the promise of a hoped-for refuge somewhere up ahead. When the ground showed signs of sloping slightly upward, Ehomba took heart. The slight alteration in terrain strongly suggested that the water that was now flowing downhill beside them would soon have to come to rest in a large, still body.

It was the tallest of the travelers who sang out moments later. "Hunkapa see water!"

"Another pond?" a gasping Simna inquired. He was panting hard not so much from running as from the rising temperature. In spite of their exertions, the wall of flame was gaining on them, and the fire gave no indication of tiring.

"No pond, Simna." The shaggy biped stumbled, caught himself, and loped on. "Hunkapa see lake!"

Unless their hirsute companion's definition of a lake was radically different from their own, Ehomba knew they would soon reach a place of safety. Seemingly intent on proving that good news came in bunches, like grapes, the wind chose that moment to drop to almost nothing. The grass fire continued to burn behind them, but it was no longer racing south at high speed.

"Watch yourselves." The composed warning came from Ahlitah. "We're not alone. There are animals up ahead. Big animals."

"Of course there are," Simna wheezed. "Probably seeking safety in the lake just like we are."

"No." The big cat sounded puzzled. "Actually, they're coming this way."

That made no sense, Ehomba reflected as he ran, covering the uneven ground with long, supple strides. His swords bounced against his back. Why would any creature deliberately be heading toward the fire, even if the wind had fallen?

As he topped a slight rise he saw them for himself, an irregular line of golden brown shapes arrayed between the fleeing travelers and the looming silvery sheen of the prairie lake. Its calm, expansive waters beckoned, promising relief from the heat and refuge from the raging blaze.

The beasts initially espied by the black litah boasted dark stripes along their lower flanks and each of their six legs. They had short, nobby tails and oddly flattened skulls like the heads of digging spades. The slightly protuberant eyes that gazed out at the world from the upper corners of the weirdly triangular skulls were covered with transparent membranes that glistened in the sun. Double rows of sharp incisors were visible in the long, flattened jaws. From the summit of the skull projected a single bizarre horn that curved forward and up.

They were built like grazers, Ehomba saw; heavy of body, thick of fur, and short of leg. But their teeth were designed for biting and chewing flesh, not grass or other plant matter. Yet among the dozens of incisors he could see not a single canine tooth or tusk. Such teeth were suitable for biting off and slicing up large chunks of meat, but not for killing. This singular orthodontic arrangement marked them as scavengers. So did their stumpy legs, with which they could never hope to run down even the smallest of healthy herbivores.

As for what they scavenged, that was abundantly clear. At least two of the sturdy, stockily built creatures could be seen chewing on the charred, blackened remains of less fortunate animals that had been mortally injured by the fire. Apparently these extraordinary beasts tracked the advancing flames much as the opportunistic raptors hunted in front of them. Since they plainly could not move very fast and would be unable to outrun any blaze, he decided, they must be exceptionally sensitive to the smallest shifts in the fire's or wind's direction.

Moments later, evidence was given to show that he was only partially correct. The bizarre hexapods did indeed feed upon those unfortunate creatures who had been caught and killed by the flames. But the striped carnivores were not scavengers: They were hunters. They did not follow behind the grass inferno or measure its progress from in front.

They caused it.

Even as he and his companions ceased running and slowed to a stop, the true function of the curious "horns" that projected from the center of each of the beasts' foreheads made itself known. They were not horns at all, but hollow structures formed of hardened keratin. From these organic nozzles the slow-moving carnivores expressed streams of liquid that caused the long, dry grass to ignite on contact. Flames erupted between the fleeing travelers and the lake as the line of beasts began to set fire to everything in their path.

And the wind was rising again.

Enclosed by raging wildfire, the only place in the vicinity that promised any safety was the stream. Barely a few feet wide and not as deep, it offered only temporary shelter at best to Ehomba and Simna. Hunkapa Aub and Ahlitah were far too bulky to be able to conceal themselves beneath the rushing waters.

Had they made an immediate charge, they might have succeeded in bursting through the oncoming flames with only minor burns. Already, that option was denied them. Like the grassland behind, the fresh growth ahead was now fully engulfed.

With the flames advancing and the heat rising from the merely uncomfortable to the unbearable, they clustered together. Trapped within his thick, shaggy coat, Hunkapa Aub was suffering terribly and on the verge of passing out. They had to do something quickly.

Head inclined forward, Ehomba was searching the tops of the grasses intently. An agitated Simna watched him, wondering what he was doing when they should be picking a direction in which to make a run for it.

"Bruther, there's nothing there but grass!" Above the roar of the approaching flames he gestured sharply to his left. "I say we try back to the west. The stream should delay the fire for a minute or two!" Instead of responding, the herdsman maintained his intent exploration of the wind-whipped yellow-green blades. "Etjole! We're out of time! What are you looking for?"

His lanky friend replied without looking up from his search. "Tomuwog burrows! They are our only chance."

"*What* burrows?" Sweat streaming down his face and neck to stain his shirt, the swordsman blinked as his companion continued what appeared to be an aimless examination of the grass. Why, he wasn't even directing his attention groundward, where one's gaze would be expected to be focused if he was hunting for some kind of den.

It made no sense. Never mind that Simna had never heard of a tomuwog and had no idea what such a creature might look like. Even if it dug a burrow large enough for a human to crawl into, anything large enough to accommodate Hunkapa Aub or the black litah would have to be a veritable cave, harder to avoid seeing than not. And they had passed no such opening in the earth in the course of their flight. With the constricting blaze crackling all around, he turned a slow circle. There were a few small holes in the ground, the largest of which would prove a tight squeeze for a corpulent mouse. Anyone trying to burrow away from the flames would need not only a physical refuge, but one large enough to sustain a sizable air pocket.

"Bruther, this is crazy!" Spreading his hands wide, he implored his companion. "We have to make a break for it! Otherwise we'll . . ."

Ehomba disappeared. Not instantly, as if he had evaporated in the rising heat or vanished into some sorceral otherwhere, but gradually. It happened right in front of the swordsman's disbelieving eyes. One moment the tall southerner had been standing before him, scanning the tops of the blowing grass. Then he started to go away. First his long spear, prodding and probing. Then the hand and arm holding it, followed by the rest of him, until all had been erased from view.

Simna was not the only one startled by the herdsman's unexpected and inexplicable disappearance. Hunkapa Aub walked all around the area where Ehomba had vanished, and Ahlitah paced the spot sniffing like a huge black dog.

The flames were closing in, narrowing the circle of unburned grass and breathable air. Simna started to cough, choking on the ashes from the carbonizing vegetation and the air that had begun to sear his lungs. Surely Ehomba hadn't abandoned them for some mystical refuge only he could access? The swordsman had to admit that such a development was not beyond the bounds of possibility. How often had Ehomba spoken of the need first and foremost to fulfill his perceived responsibility to the deceased scion of distant Laconda? How many times had he made it clear, to Simna as freely as to total strangers, that the resolution of that journey took precedence over everything else?

A sweating Simna ibn Sind scanned his surroundings. Encircled by leaping flames, with the earth itself seemingly beginning to incinerate around him, he saw nowhere to run, no place to hide. This was not a good place to die, out in open country witnessed only by insects and rodents, his body about to become food for indolent meat-eaters that under normal circumstances he could run circles around. From the time he had been old enough to understand the significance of life and the finality of death he had planned to depart this plane of existence in a blaze of glory that would be immortalized in ballad and song. Now it seemed he was to expire simply in a blaze, as something else's dinner. Where were the cheers, the shouts to admire him as mind and body shriveled and dissolved? The circumstances were ignominious to a fault.

On the verge of passing out from the encroaching heat, Hunkapa Aub had fallen to his knees. Panting like a runaway bellows, the black litah sat back on his haunches, waiting for the end.

Then a hand appeared out of nowhere, beckoning. It was followed by a familiar face. "Hurry! There is little time."

"We don't need you to tell us that, bruther!" Without stopping to realize that Ehomba was beckoning to him from within a circle of nothingness, Simna stumbled toward the gesturing hand.

It grabbed hold of his own and pulled. Almost immediately, the unbearable heat disappeared. The swordsman found himself standing in a corridor of coolness. Mere feet away now, the fire continued to rage. But he could no longer feel it.

Mouth slightly agape in wonder, he extended tentative fingers toward the blaze. They halted inches from the nearest tongue of flame. Pushing experimentally, he found that there was a slight give to the invisible surface that kept him separated from instant incineration, as if he were pressing against transparent rubber. There was no noise. Whatever was protecting him from the flames also shut out all sound from beyond.

Turning, he reached out in the opposite direction. The corridor in which he was standing was no more than six feet wide, in places a little less. As he stared in amazement, the flames seemed to burn right through to continue their march of fiery destruction on the other side. Within the miraculous passageway everything was a calm, cool blue-green: the soaring but silent flames, the scorched earth they left in their wake, the bodies of small animals too slow to flee, even his own clothing and flesh.

Looking back the way he had come, he saw that Ehomba too had acquired a soft tinting of pastel blue-green. So had Hunkapa Aub, who had followed the swordsman to safety. Reflecting his own coloring, Ahlitah was a dark shade of green. Among them all, Simna was the lightest in color.

Walking back toward his friend, he found that he could begin to feel the heat from the fire again. Pivoting, he discovered that as soon as he took a few steps in the opposite direction, the threatening warmth dissipated. Hunkapa Aub joined him to make more room near Ehomba.

"Where are we?" the swordsman heard himself wondering aloud. He did not expect an explanation from the hulking Hunkapa, much less a reasonable one.

A hairy hand reached out to stroke the resilient, transparent wall. "Somewhere else." It was as sensible an answer as Simna could have hoped to receive.

As soon as the black litah had been brought to safety, Ehomba squeezed past them to take the lead again. Gesturing for them to follow, he led the way through the last of the fire, heading west once again. Behind, the line of pyro predators began to root among the charred rubble for well-done meals.

The blue-green corridor was not straight. It changed direction several times, winding through unburned brush and grass, down gullies, and up over small hills. After an hour of this, Simna was moved to comment.

"It's not for me to question how you saved us, bruther, but we're well away from that range fire and the creatures that keep it going. Why can't we just step back out into the real world?" Behind him, Hunkapa Aub was having to advance bent double. The ceiling of the passageway was not much higher than the corridor was wide.

"You can try," Ehomba informed him without looking back, "but I do not think you will have much luck."

Taking this as a challenge, the swordsman pushed against the pellucid barrier. Beyond, unburned brush pressed right up against it, and a pair of small yellow and black birds were courting only inches from his questing fingers. Ordinarily, they would have fled in panic, chirping wildly. But they did not seem to see or smell him and did not react to his near presence at all.

He pushed harder, then leaned all his weight against the boundary.

"Here. Let me try." Stepping up beside him, the black litah lifted a paw to expose five-inch-long talons, pointed like knives and sharp as razors. Claw and dig as he might, they made absolutely no impact on the wall. The litah could not even leave scratches. It was the same with the dark blue-green floor underfoot.

Having stood patiently by while his friends satisfied their curiosity, Ehomba now turned and once again headed off westward. A thoughtful, somewhat chastened Simna followed. He was not upset or uneasy: only curious.

It was delightfully cool within the corridor, with even the sun having acquired a blue-green tinge. The surface underfoot was smoother than the ground outside but not slippery: ideal for running. Only the absence of water concerned him. Their water bags were more than half full, but despite the containers he toted on his back, Ahlitah needed to carry drink for Hunkapa Aub as well. That portable source would begin to run out in less than a couple of weeks.

In response to his query, Ehomba assured him that he had no intention of keeping to the corridor for anywhere near that length of time. His sole intention in disappearing into it was to find a means of escape and a temporary refuge from the fire.

"What is this place, bruther?" Within the passageway, voices acquired a deeper cast, reverberant and slightly echoing.

"I told you when I was looking for one." The herdsman angled to his right. "Careful, there is a bend here. We are in a tomuwog burrow."

"Hoy, this is a burrow?" Looking to right and left, Simna could see clearly in every direction. The only difference from what he would have accounted as normal was that everything he saw was tinted varying degrees of blue-green. "By Geletharpa, what is a tomuwog? I've never heard of such a creature, much less seen one."

"You will not see one," Ehomba told him. "Unless you know how to look for them. They are difficult to track, even for the Naumkib. I am considered one of the best trackers in my tribe. There is no reason to hunt them, since they make poor eating. But in times of difficulty, their burrows can provide a place to hide. We were lucky." He started to slow. "Ah, this is what I was looking for. We can rest here awhile."

A baffled Simna slowed his own pace to a walk. Try as he might, he could discern no difference in their surroundings, and said so.

As he took a seat and began to unburden himself of his weapons and pack, Ehomba smiled patiently. "Stretch out your hands. Walk around a little."

The swordsman proceeded to do so. To his surprise, he discovered that they had entered a blue-green chamber some twenty feet in diameter. The ceiling had also expanded, allowing poor Hunkapa Aub to straighten up at last. He stretched gratefully.

Simna found himself drawn to a seven-foot-wide zone of glistening aquamarine-tinted light. It formed a translucent mound that reached perhaps a fourth of the way to the ceiling. Extending a hand, he found that his fingers passed completely through the phenomenon, as would be expected of something that was composed entirely of colored light.

"What's this? Some distortion in the corridor?"

"Not at all." Taking his ease, Ehomba was unpacking some dried fruit from his pack. "That is a tomuwog nest." When the swordsman drew his hand back sharply, his lanky friend laughed softly. "Do not worry. It is empty. It is the wrong time of the year."

While Hunkapa Aub sighed heavily and stretched out on the floor, trying to work the accumulated cricks and contractions out of his neck and back, the black litah explored the far side of the enclosure. Realizing that he was hungry too, Simna rejoined his friend. Outside, beyond the walls of the enchanted chamber, blue-green antelope were methodically cropping blue-green grass, entirely oblivious to the presence of the four travelers conversing and eating not more than a few feet away.

"These tomuwogs," the swordsman began, "what do they look like?"

"Not much." Ehomba gnawed contentedly on dried pears and apples. "The tomuwog live in the spaces between colors." Mouth half full, he gestured with his food. "That's where we are. In one of the spaces between blue and green."

"Excuse me, bruther? That doesn't make any sense. There is no space between colors." The swordsman's brow furrowed as he struggled with a concept for which he had no reference points. "There's blue, and then there's green. Where and when they meet, they melt together." He made clapping motions with his hands. "There's no 'space' between them."

"Ordinarily there is not," Ehomba readily agreed. "Except where the tomuwog dig their burrows. It is just a tiny space, so small you and I cannot see it. Cats can." He nodded to where the litah was still exploring the far reaches of the chamber, poking his head into bulges and side corridors. "Ask Ahlitah about it sometime."

"But this is not a tiny space we have been running through, and are sitting in now," Simna pointed out.

"Quite true. That is because it has been enlarged by one or more tomuwog to make a burrow." He gestured with his free hand. "As I have already told you, this is one of their nesting chambers. Tomuwog burrows are hard to see and harder to find, as you would expect of something that only occupies the space between colors. I was hunting for one while the fire was closing in around us. As I said, we were lucky to find it." Finishing the pear, he started on a dehydrated peach.

"The walls of their burrows are very tough. They would have to be, or people would stumble into and break through them all the time."

"And we've passed these things before?" Simna made stirring motions in the air with one downward-pointing finger.

"Of course. They are not common, but are widespread. I remember a particularly large burrow from the mountains near Netherbrae, and one in the desert where we encountered the mirage of the houris. And there were a number of others."

"By Guoit, why didn't you ever point one out to me, bruther?"

Ehomba shrugged. "There was no need to. You would not have enjoyed entering them anyway. Most were warm burrows."

The swordsman's expression twisted. "There are different kinds of burrows?"

"Certainly. It depends which colors the tomuwogs are burrowing between. If red and yellow, which are hot colors and seem to be more common, then the burrow will be warm, or even scalding. If the blue is separated by black instead of green, then conditions inside the burrow can be extremely cold." He smiled appreciatively. "Blue-green is best, though it is still a little warm for running. A darker blue, more indigo, would have made for an even more comfortable refuge."

Simna sat shaking his head in amazement and disbelief. "To think that such wonders exist all around us, in every time and place, and want only the knowing of them to be seen and utilized."

"Oh, there is much more, my friend. Much more." The herdsman bit into a large, crunchy piece of preserved apple. "The world is awash in marvels that most men never see. Usually it is because they are too busy, too hurried, to look. Looking takes time. One does not become a good tracker overnight."

Simna nodded slowly. "Or a good hand with a sword. In the learning of that, I bled a lot. It took me many years, many curses, and many cuts before I became proficient."

"As does the accumulation of any worthwhile knowledge," Ehomba agreed.

Tilting and turning his head, Simna took in more of the remarkable chamber. "The corridor we came through was not large for a person, but pretty big for a burrowing animal. These tomuwogs must be of good size."

"See for yourself." Putting the remainder of his food down slowly and carefully, Ehomba nodded to his right. "Here comes one now."

Xlll

Simna paused with food halfway to his mouth. Sensing the approach of the burrow's owner, the black litah growled a warning as it moved off to one side. Eyes shining, Hunkapa Aub put both hands together and murmured delightedly.

"Pretty, pretty."

The adult tomuwog was bigger than any of the travelers, but it was only partially there. A glittering, roughly cylindrical shape, it entered the nesting chamber on noiseless feet of aquamarine light. One moment it stood out in sharp relief, the next it was reduced to a drifting cloud composed of splintered sapphires. With each step, portions of its supple, streamlined body slipped in and out of sight. Half solid, half illusion, it inspected them warily out of eyes that were pale blue mother-of-pearl.

It had a short tail that struck blue-green sparks from the air as it flicked nervously from side to side, and a narrow snout of a face that glittered as if faceted. Huge sparkling pads front and rear resembled flippers more than feet. The edges of these appendages caught the ambient light and bounced it back in clipped, prismatic jolts to the retinas of onlookers. The shimmering claws had to be sharp, Simna reflected, to slice a path between two colors.

Filtered blue-green light danced off the creature's flanks, so bright that from time to time the entranced intruders were forced to turn their faces away from so much brilliance and blink away tears. Simna found himself wondering what a tomuwog that inhabited the space between red and orange might look like, or between purple and red. Certainly they would be no less colorful than the singular slow-moving one before them.

That the tomuwog was aware of their presence there could be no doubt. Twinkling eyes examined each of them in turn. Upset at their presence but apparently convinced they posed no immediate threat, it proceeded to haul itself over to the glittering, glimmering nest and settle itself atop the pile of carefully scavenged color.

Resuming eating, but slowly so as not to startle the placid creature, Simna leaned over to whisper to the herdsman. "Where do they come from, bruther? Eggs?"

"I am not sure." Observing the remarkable beast, Ehomba wore a satisfied smile. "I believe they lay light. This light then matures according to the predominating colors within which it is brought up, and becomes a full-grown tomuwog. As I have said, they are shy creatures and difficult to see. They almost never wander outside their burrows."

A sudden thought caused the swordsman to put down the remainder of his food. "Hoy, what do they eat? Doesn't look like it has any teeth."

"That is a real mystery, Simna." In contrast to his hesitant companion, Ehomba had no trouble finishing his food. "No one has ever seen a tomuwog eating. I would not think there was much to eat between blue and green, but if my elders had not explained it to me I would not have thought there was much space there, either. Perhaps they forage on little bits of wandering moonlight, or the motes we see dancing in a shaft of afternoon sunshine. Since no one knows what they eat *with*, it is understandable that nobody knows what they eat." Seeing the look on his friend's face, he added, "Whatever it is, I do not think that people are a part of its diet."

"Hoy, I certainly don't see any blue-green teeth." Cautiously, the swordsman resumed feeding.

They were soon finished with their meal. When Ehomba decided they had rested long enough, he led his companions out of the chamber. Choosing a corridor that led west, they left the tomuwog sitting serenely on its twinkling nest. It made no move to interfere with their departure. From the time it had arrived until the moment they departed, it had uttered not a sound.

The passageway provided a smooth-floored, controlled-climate means of making progress. As they jogged along, they passed other herds of grazing animals, and flocks of birds large and small. As far as these active inhabitants of the prairie were concerned, the travelers were invisible. And so long as they kept to the tomuwog tunnel, they effectively were.

The extent of the corridor did not surprise Ehomba. Tomuwogs, he explained to his friends, dug very elaborate, very complex systems of burrows that boasted but few entrances. After a number of days, however, he decided it was time to sacrifice concealment and convenience for the world that lay beyond the tunneled realm of blue and green. For one thing, the corridor was devoid of anything except cool air and blue-green light. They would soon need to find food and fresh water.

Simna fingered the transparent, unyielding wall that enclosed them. "So how do we get out, bruther? Cut ourselves a hole?"

"Only a tomuwog can do that, Simna." As they trotted down the corridor, the herdsman was scanning the ceiling. "We must find a natural entrance."

"You said there weren't many."

Ehomba nodded. "That is so. It is why I want to find one before our food or water begins to run any lower." With his spear, he gestured behind them. "I would hate to have to retrace our steps all the way back to the place where the firemakers nearly entrapped us."

Simna grunted his agreement and thought little more of it. But by the evening of the following day he was starting to grow concerned. The thought of starving to death in plain view of rolling fields of edible plants and herds of plentiful game, pinned like an ornamental butterfly between layers of blue and green, was singularly unappealing.

It was therefore with considerable relief, and not a little confusion, that he slowed to a halt behind Ehomba. The herdsman had raised a hand and was staring off to his left. Squinting in the same direction, Simna could see nothing. Or rather, nothing that differed from the rest of their surroundings.

"There is our exit." Though he did not manifest it outwardly, Ehomba was greatly relieved. Entrances and exits to tomuwog burrows were even more scattered than he had led Simna and the others to believe. Knowing that if he appeared worried it would have weighed heavily on them, he had maintained an air of quiet confidence ever since they had left the nesting chamber. He had also eschewed mentioning that tomuwog burrows were subject to a variety of external strains and pressures, and therefore prone to collapse. What would happen to anyone who found him- or herself caught in a tomuwog cave-in he could not imagine, except to be certain it would not be pleasant.

"I don't see anything," Simna murmured.

"There's nothing there." The black litah snorted.

"Exactly." Ehomba started forward, toward something only he could see. Or rather, toward nothing only he could see.

When Simna emerged from the burrow, the return of multihued light together with the sounds and smells of the world outside threatened to overwhelm his senses. Hunkapa Aub took to running about in little circles, grabbing at grasshoppers and beetles, while Ahlitah promptly lay down in the yellowed grass and rolled, immersing himself in the delicious convocation of aromas.

Looking back the way they had come, Simna could see only ground and growth, rock and soil. There was nothing to indicate to his eyes that they had just exited a corridor that tunneled between the color blue and the color green.

"It's really there?" he found himself asking his tall companion.

"Yes, Simna. It is really there."

The swordsman nodded somberly. "Wizardry. I've grown used to your denying it, Etjole, but that doesn't mean I accept it. We both know what you are."

"How can we both know what I am when I do not even know myself what I am?" Ehomba was not smiling. "I am a good tracker, friend Simna. Good at finding things."

"Things that no one else can find, or even suspect exist." Together, they resumed the trek westward. "If that's not sorcery, I don't know what is." Idly, the swordsman plucked a striking blue wildflower. He did not hold on to it for long, though, having had enough blue to last him for a while.

"Not true, Simna." Once again, Ehomba was using his spear as a walking stick. "Many of the Naumkib could have done what I just did." He grinned. "I am just a little better at such things than most of the villagers. I think it is because I am always questioning my surroundings that I have become good at seeing what others overlook." With his free hand he pointed slightly to their right. "For example, standing right there is a Gogloyyik, a fantastic animal with four eyes, purple wings, a tail three times the length of its body, and a head that is a mass of absurd-looking horns."

Following his friend's lead, Simna strained to locate this phantasmagoric creature. All he saw were insects whizzing back and forth above the tops of the grass, and something like a chartreuse bunny that scampered frantically out of sight on all fours.

"I don't see anything, Etjole. Is it only semi-invisible, like the tomuwog?"

"It's right there, right before your eyes, Simna! What's the matter with you?" The herdsman's irritation was palpable.

Simna's forehead was beginning to throb. Breaking away from the others, he jogged off in the direction Ehomba had indicated. Halting at what he thought was an excessive distance from his companions, the swordsman turned a slow circle.

"By Githwhent, bruther—there's nothing here! Where is this . . . ?" He stopped. Hunkapa Aub was chortling softly, his enormous chest heaving with muted laughter. Even the black litah was grinning, insofar as a cat is capable of such an expression. And the herdsman—Etjole Ehomba had a hand over his mouth and was shaking his head slowly as he strode along.

Simna's expression darkened. "Very funny, long bruther. Oh, vastly amusing, yes! Scare the insides out of a man one minute and make him the butt of jokes the next! How clever you are, how witty! How droll." Rejoining the group, he fell in step behind the herdsman, forswearing his company.

Padding up alongside him, Ahlitah was uncharacteristically sympathetic. "I understand, little man. Don't take it to heart. If it's any consolation, I don't agree with what your mentor just did."

Simna eyed the big cat warily. "You don't?"

"No. He can't make you the butt of jokes one minute, because to me you have been and will always be nothing more than a butt." With that the cat sauntered off, choosing to parallel rather than follow the herdsman's lead.

Will I ever figure him out? the swordsman mused as he gazed broodingly at the back of the tall southerner. "If you are a sorcerer, Etjole—and I still hold to that belief as strongly as ever—you will be the first one I ever met that had a sense of humor. Such as it is," he hastened to add.

Still grinning, the herdsman looked back at his friend. "I come from a simple village, friend Simna. You should expect my sense of humor to be simple as well."

"Hoy—that I won't argue." After a while he increased his pace to move back up alongside his companion. There followed an exchange of jokes that caused laughter to ring out across the plain. The guffawing was wholly human. It did not matter whether the jape was told by Ehomba or Simna. Strive as he might, Hunkapa Aub never got it, and the black litah did not want to.

As the resolute propounders of intermittent jocularity strode onward toward the beckoning sunset, accompanied by a hulking and perplexed mass of hair that lumbered after them on legs like hispid tree trunks, and one brooding black cat of striking size and grace, the Gogloyyik lifted its outlandish cranium and watched them go, not overlooking a chance to fenegrate the sookstrum that unexpectedly darted between its legs.

XIV

Peregriff wondered if he dared knock. The south castle aerie was but one of many that his master used for his regular rendezvous with the costly courtesans he imported from the city. Despite the many wild and scurrilous rumors that attended to his master, the chief of staff knew that Hymneth the Possessed was indeed a man, with all the needs and desires that implied. He was, however, glad that it was the job of others to select and escort the often reluctant women into his master's presence. What happened subsequently comprised scenarios he preferred not to speculate upon.

It had been some time since the last such visit to the castle, though. It might well be that the omnipotent ruler of fabled Ehl-Larimar simply decided to spend the afternoon in solitary, alone with thoughts only he could appreciate and assimilate. That only he would want to, Peregriff mused. Taking a deep breath, he rapped several times on the carved wooden door. A lesser man might have fled. But lesser men did not rise to the position of most valued aide to the Possessed.

At first there was no reply. Having done his duty by knocking, Peregriff was tempted to retire. If he had guessed wrongly and his master was otherwise occupied, persisting could draw the kind of reprimand that would reduce anyone else to a quivering sack of human jelly. His fist hovered before the door, hesitating.

A voice from within bade him enter. Neither irate nor expectant, it offered no clue to its owner's state of mind. Making certain his uniform was straight and correct in every detail, Peregriff lifted the heavy iron latch and pushed the door inward.

No suit of armor could really be called "playful," but the ruler's attire of the day was designed more to impress than intimidate. Dark blue leather banded with chased steel, it consisted of vest and lower skirt beneath which Hymneth wore mail of very fine links. His helmet was likewise fashioned from the finest, smoothest steel, engraved with scenes that were less than usually horrific. The eye slits were long and narrow, while the front of the helmet descended in a straight line from forehead to chin, hiding nose and mouth alike. It gave to the skull the look of a ship preparing to cleave the open waters.

Helmet and point turned away from the window out which they had been staring to face him. "What is it, Peregriff?"

The reverberant, commanding voice was tinged with indifference: a good sign, as far as the general was concerned. Yet still he hesitated to step into the room. Leaning imperceptibly forward, he managed a look to his right. The rack and bench were empty and showed no sign of having been subject to recent employment. As he bowed, he cut his eyes in the other direction. Likewise, the bed was undisturbed.

A pair of small, seemingly innocent dark clouds lolled above the richly embroidered spread. They grew active when he entered, only to become still as they recognized him. They knew that within the castle certain life lights were not for eating, and his was among them. When he straightened, it was with less concern and more confidence. Not that he ever really relaxed. Only fools and the deathly ignorant relaxed in the presence of Hymneth the Possessed, and Peregriff was neither.

"Don't you remember, Lord? This is the morning you wished to review the household guard." Turning slightly, he gestured at the open doorway. "I have come to escort you."

"Ah, yes. My mind was elsewhere, good Peregriff. On other matters."

The general hazarded a guess. "The one whose coming the Worm predicted?"

"Actually, no." Straightening, Hymneth rose to his full, towering height. "I have begun to believe no such person exists. If he did, and had power enough to inconvenience me even remotely, surely he would be here by now. I thought at the time that the Worm's words made no sense, and I've seen or heard nothing since to make me change that opinion."

"Still, Lord, it pays to be cautious."

From behind the burnished steel, unblinking eyes narrowed ever so slightly; the timbre of voice from beneath the helmet's projecting lip grew infinitesimally softer.

"Are you presuming to advise me on this matter, Peregriff?"

The general did not miss a beat in his reply. If there was one fault

Hymneth could not tolerate in his senior advisers, it was hesitancy. "No, Lord. It is only my abiding concern for your welfare that impels me to comment on the matter at all."

"Yes, well. Good intentions are always to be applauded." The voice returned to normal, and the slight tremor Peregriff had experienced was not repeated. He had lived and labored too long in the Possessed's service to frighten easily. It is hard to panic a man who has long since resigned himself to the possibility of perishing on the spur of the moment at the whim of another.

"It is not caution that eases my concern, Peregriff." Stepping away from window and wall, the autarchic ruler of Ehl-Larimar approached the doorway. "It is confidence." A mailed hand rose and gestured. The fingers were thicker and blunter than those of any normal individual. "Come, and let us review the troops before they grow bored."

Those servants who were not forewarned of the approach of the Possessed in time to scurry out of the way were compelled to stop whatever they happened to be doing at that moment and prostrate themselves before him. Hymneth considered himself a kind master, full of forbearance, a trait that he felt he displayed on numerous occasions. This morning was no exception.

When two serving maids engaged in animated conversation failed to notice his approach and continued to gab between themselves, the Possessed put a finger to the lower rim of his helmet and commanded Peregriff to silence. Advancing silently, he stole up behind the two before one of them noticed, or felt, a presence. Turning, she saw who it was and let out a heart-rending scream before fainting dead away. Instinctively, her friend caught her, or she too might have swooned with fear.

Hymneth found this vastly amusing. Reaching out and down, he tousled the hair of the unconscious servitor. "Get her some wine," he ordered the other woman. "When she awakes, tell her that I am not displeased. After all, fainting may be accounted a kind of bowing."

"Y-y-yes, Lord." Utterly terrified by her proximity to the looming, guttural figure, the other woman tried to curtsey and support her friend at the same time, with the result that both went down in a heap. This caused Hymneth to burst out laughing, a sound that many of his retainers found more dismaying than his explosive fits of anger.

"It's good when one's people can exalt and amuse you at the same time, eh, Peregriff?"

"Truly, Lord." Debating which expression would be suitable for the moment, the general settled on a slight smile.

There were no further interruptions, mirth-provoking or otherwise, as they descended the rest of the way to the main floor. Exiting the great hall, they emerged into another of the warm, spectacular days for which Ehl-Larimar was famed. Below the mountain to which the fortress clung, the city and harbor and ocean beyond spread out in three directions, a vision of consummate municipal harmony over which Hymneth the Possessed wielded unchallenged dominion.

Drawn up in three parallel lines before the castle entrance was his household guard, a small regiment of cavalry maintained by him and kept separate from the realm's regular army and police. As soon as his tall, overawing figure appeared in the arched portico of the castle's entrance, horns and drums struck up a welcoming tattoo.

With Peregriff hurrying to keep up, Hymneth strode forward to inspect the first line of fighters. Watching his master, the general could not help but feel that he was preoccupied.

Nevertheless, Hymneth moved down the first line of mounted soldiers with his eyes set left and not wandering. Peregriff noted that he scrutinized each and every individual fighter from boot to crested helmet. In any emergency or ultimate showdown, these were the men and women who had sworn to lay down their lives for him. There was no place in the household guard of the Possessed for slackers.

Leather boots pressed firmly into steel stirrups. Backs straight, armor shining, helmet visors up and locked, the men and women of Ehl-Larimar's most elite military force sat at attention in their saddles, eyes front and lances perfectly perpendicular to the ground. Even their mounts, a unique assortment of the finest steeds the country had to offer, remained motionless and poised in the presence of their commander in chief. A few heads bobbed and shook, an occasional leg lifted or twitched. These deviations Hymneth was willing to forgive—in a horse.

He could feel eyes flicking around to follow him as he and Peregriff came to the end of the first line, pivoted, and started down the second. Formal inspection of the ranks was a duty he could have delegated to the general, or even to one of lesser rank, but it had been some time since he had performed the task, and it was beneficial for the troops to see the individual to whom they had pledged their lives. Beneficial, and sometimes instructive.

Would Peregriff have noticed the way certain soldiers looked at him? Would he, sensitive and alert as he was, have remarked on the combination of fear and respect that dominated their expressions as he passed by? Despite their elevated equine seats, Hymneth the Possessed's great height allowed him to regard them almost eye-to-eye. None met his own. That was as it should be, he felt. Let them match stares with their officers, and not with him. A little terror was like soap: all-cleansing while leaving an almost imperceptible film in its wake. A remembrance of who stood above them.

Halfway through the third rank Hymneth stopped, his thoughts distracted. Behind the sloping helmet, penetrating eyes drew slightly together. Mailed hands clasped behind his back, he turned slightly in Peregriff's direction.

"Do you see that?"

The general, who had allowed himself to relax slightly, stiffened. "See what, Lord?"

High above him, the helmeted skull nodded slightly. "Sixth rider from the end."

Peregriff's gaze narrowed. He badly wanted to lie on behalf of the young man thus singled out, but did not for a moment seriously consider doing so. "Yes, Lord. I see it."

"What do you think we should do about it?" Behind Hymneth's back, steel-clad fingers tick-ticked against one another.

"I'm sure my Lord will think of something suitable."

Again the single, singular nod. "I dislike rendering precipitous judgments. Let's give him another minute or so to straighten himself out."

"Yes, Lord." As they resumed the inspection, the general betrayed no outward shift in expression or emotion. Inside, he found himself praying for the soul of the unfortunate young warrior.

Instead of improving, the soldier's condition continued to worsen. Already trembling badly, his shaking grew worse as Hymneth and Peregriff drew nearer. Halting beside the man's mount, the lord of Ehl-Larimar looked up at him speculatively. Quaking, the man looked down.

And dropped his lance.

Not knowing whether to dismount and recover it, flee, or remain as motionless as he could manage, the terrified soldier stayed where he was. Glancing down, Hymneth contemplated the fallen weapon. The ever-present pair of juvenile eromakadi circled it excitedly, inhaling of the potential darkness it represented.

After a moment or so, Hymneth looked up. "I'm afraid there's not much use in my household guard for a man who is spineless. It's one thing to fear me, something else to completely lose control in my presence." Extending a long arm, he indicated the lance lying in the short grass. "If you drop your weapon during an inspection, what would you do with it during a battle? Fling it aside and run?"

"No, Lord," the man stammered desperately. "I-I was nervous today, that's all. This is only my third full-dress inspection, and the first you have graced with your august presence." Risking all, he looked down and met the gaze of the Possessed. "Please, Lord. I have a wife, and a babe of six months. Give me another chance and I'll serve you well! My life is yours. It was—"

"Yes, yes, it was promised to me when you agreed to become a member of the guard. I know." Hymneth made a sweeping gesture that took in the rest of the mounted troop. Not a head had turned in the direction of the confrontation. The man and woman mounted on either side of the unfortunate one sat rock-steady and unmoving in their saddles, eyes front, backs stiff.

"But how can I rely on someone who shakes so badly he can't even keep control of his primary weapon during an inspection? I could give you another chance, but what if one wasn't enough? What if you needed a third chance, or a fourth?"

"Please, Lord, I beg you to—"

"And what sort of example does that set for your fellows? I don't see any of them asking for second chances when they make mistakes. Could it be that's because they don't make mistakes? Because I can't afford to tolerate mistakes in my household guard." Turning away, he looked back toward the sea that lay downslope and far away.

"You know, there are those in Ehl-Larimar who would give a great deal to see me dead." When Peregriff started to offer the requisite ritual objection, Hymneth waved him off. "No, it's true. For whatever reason, I am not universally loved by my people. I tolerate this because I must. A certain amount of dissension is valuable because it allows the discontented to let off steam, and to preserve the illusion that they enjoy a greater degree of personal freedom than is the case." With a resigned sigh he turned back to his general and to the heavily perspiring soldier.

"But I must strive for perfection in those who serve me, even as I aspire to perfection in myself. Especially among my personal bodyguard there can be no room for hesitation, or incertitude. The irresolute must live with the consequences of their own spinelessness." Having abandoned the fallen lance, the two eromakadi were now darting and dancing about his ankles. Clenching his fingers tightly, he lifted them up to the sweating soldier—and opened them.

Uttering an inarticulate cry, the young man wrenched on the reins of his mount, whirled, and bolted from the ranks.

Rotating slowly perhaps half an inch above Hymneth's open palm was a fist-sized sphere of dark green vapor shot through with black streaks. It was lit from within by a dull, miasmatic light. Miniature clouds roiled across its surface, evolving and vanishing after a few seconds of life. Lips tight, Peregriff held his ground. At Hymneth's feet, the eromakadi bounced and spun in a paroxysm of deviant delight.

With a gesture that reeked of bored indifference, he flicked his wrist in the direction of the deserting soldier. The fleeing fighter was already through the outer gate and racing down the road that led to the city, driving his mount hard with repeated blows of his ceremonial whip of gold braid. Seeing this, Hymneth frowned darkly behind his helmet. One thing he could not abide was unreasoning cruelty to animals—especially those that served him better than his people.

Trailing a long tail of ichorous green mist, the ball of vapor lifted from Hymneth's hand. It soared over the outer wall and down the mountainside. Having no need for road or trail, it made its own.

"Come, Peregriff. Let's finish this."

Together, lord and servant resumed the inspection. None of the assembled soldiers had moved during or subsequent to the unpleasant confrontation, and none of them moved now as Hymneth the Possessed strode past them, hands still busy behind his back. Only two mounted fighters remained to be scrutinized when an agonized, distant shriek wafted over the outer wall from somewhere on the road not far below. It carried with it all the horror of death without dying, of some finely conceived yet transitory torture. It expressed eloquently the shock of sudden realization of an exquisite torment artfully delivered. Pausing before the last soldier in line, Hymneth smiled, his revealed teeth concealed behind the protective steel.

"Good job, soldier." Reaching out, he patted the white-and-black gelding firmly on the side of its neck. The horse reacted with a slight shake of its head, ruffling its mane. At a terse nod from Peregriff, the individual thus singled out felt free to respond.

"Thank you, Lord."

"Think nothing of it. Good work is to be rewarded. Failure is—well, why don't you and this fine young gentleman here next to you ride out and bring back your hapless former associate?" At a gesture from their master, the two riders turned their mounts and galloped off in the direction of the outer gate.

Peregriff was uncertain. "Lord, he is not dead?"

"Of course not. What do you think of me, Peregriff? He had to be punished, and of course he is dismissed from the troop, but I would not kill someone simply because they proved unable to live up to the standards set for the guard. Besides, the man has a wife and infant. Having only the standards of the lower classes to aspire to, they have done nothing wrong. Therefore I will not deprive them of this man's company, however graceless it may be."

Walking back to the front of the troop, he eyed them from beneath his helmet for a long moment. Hands on hips, he addressed them prior to departing.

"You are a credit to your countrymen and to all of Ehl-Larimar! I am proud to call you members of my personal household, and am confident that should the time ever come that it is necessary to place my life in your hands, then it will be in the finest care available anywhere in the world. I salute you!" Raising one mailed hand, he held it, palm outward, toward them.

Lances rose, the small gold and blue pennants secured just below where blade met shaft dancing in the slight breeze that always blew from the mountain heights down toward the sea. Thus dismissed, they broke ranks and prepared to return to their barracks.

As Hymneth and his general were mounting the steps that led back into the inner castle, trailed by the snuffling, silent eromakadi, the two soldiers who had been dispatched to bring back the deserter returned, leading the man's mount between them. Across the saddle lay an oddly slack body. Its legs and arms were twitching, as was its neck, but it was as if they were no longer connected to one another. The man was beyond screaming now, reduced to a piteous sobbing that shook the spirits of all within and without the castle who happened to overhear it.

Dismounting, the pair of soldiers relieved the other horse of its burden. The man screamed anew when they pulled him off the saddle. He could no longer sit on his horse, or anywhere else. As he could not stand, he had to be carried off by his former comrades in arms. Since he had lost weight they were able to move him without much effort, though they had to be careful of his middle. It sagged flaccidly, chest and stomach sinking toward the ground as if that part of him were melting in the sun.

Hymneth paused long enough to watch the unfortunate being carried out of sight. "I suspected he was spineless when I first set eyes on him. Now he is for sure." Turning away, he led his second in command back into the castle. The inspection had made him hungry.

They ate together. Not in the formal dining room, but out on one of the second-floor terraces that overlooked the city and the sea. If there was anywhere else on earth that could boast of weather as serene and tranquil as that of Ehl-Larimar, Hymneth had not heard of it. Peregriff agreed; it was another fine day.

"You must be pleased, Lord, to know that you are so well protected. It must help you to sleep well at night." Before imbibing, the general considered the white wine in the superb fluted glass set before him, savoring the bouquet while admiring the color.

"The guard is a window dressing, Peregriff. Stalwart men and women in shiny uniforms to awe the people. I have never relied on them to protect me."

The general looked surprised. "But Lord, you said—"

"I said what I did for their benefit. It's hard to motivate those who serve if you tell them that ultimately even the potential sacrifice of their lives means nothing." Enjoying the sun that struck his face through the helmet, he gazed out across his realm, at ease if not content. "Oh, they are fine for making minor arrests and for dealing with undistinguished miscreants like that deserter or ordinary assassins. But anyone or anything powerful enough to seriously threaten me would toss them aside like straw." He sipped at his own drink. "Still, they look fine on parade."

The general considered carefully before commenting. "So you still feel that the Worm's warning was inaccurate, and that those whose coming he predicted will not reach Ehl-Larimar? Or is it that you do not believe the necromantic powers it spoke of are strong enough to pose a threat?"

"Pose a threat? There is no threat, Peregriff. It doesn't matter if the Worm's prophecy proves to be correct or not." He gestured diffidently. "You may pass the order to the navy to relax their alert. The household guard may stand down, and the instructions that were given to the border patrols to be on the alert for any unusual group of travelers seeking to enter the country are to be withdrawn."

Despite his master's mellow, even exuberant mood, the general was not reassured. "Is that wise, Lord? Maintaining a heightened military status does not require a great deal in the way of additional effort or expenditure. If it will ensure your safety . . ."

Hymneth waved him off. "I'm telling you, Peregriff: It doesn't matter. If these individuals exist, and if they manage to reach and cross the border, and if one of them happens to be a sorcerer of some small skill, it does not matter. Even if they succeed in reaching the castle there is no need for concern." Setting his wine aside and leaning across the small feast that had been provided for the midday meal, he lowered his voice in what the shocked general could only interpret as an intimate manner.

"There is no longer any reason to worry about such matters, Peregriff. Everything is well in hand. More so than you can imagine. Things have changed. Let them come to the castle. I am curious to meet those who would suffer such hardships and travel so far on behalf of the stiff and self-important aristocracy of far Laconda." Sounding as satisfied as the general had ever heard him, the lord of Ehl-Larimar sat back in his chair and did a most remarkable thing: He put his long legs up on the banister and crossed them contentedly. Rising from the porch, the eromakadi hovered above his feet, shading them from the sun.

To Peregriff's way of thinking, only one explanation seemed possible. "You have made some unique preparation in expectation of their possible arrival, Lord. Groundwork that you feel sure will counter anything they can do, no matter how unexpected or powerful."

"Something like that." More than anything, the ruler of Ehl-Larimar sounded amused. Peregriff was at a loss to know how to proceed.

"You want no special measures carried out, no extra guards posted either in the city, here at the fortress, nor even in your private quarters?"

"Peregriff, calm yourself. Should anything untoward occur, and it will not, no blame will accrue to you. I know perfectly well what I am doing. If the augury of the Worm turns out to be true, no harm can befall me. If it turns out to be false, no harm can befall anyone else. I await with anticipation the resolution of this conundrum that has so bedeviled my thoughts for far too long. You will see." He sipped from his glass. "Life will continue not as before, but better than ever. You have my word on it." He extended the chalice.

Automatically, the general picked up his and touched it to that of his master. In the placid light of midday their glasses clinked musically. Even as he swallowed the wood-tinged blood of the grape, Peregriff wondered what it was that he was toasting.

He was overlooking something, he knew. Priding himself as he did on his thorough knowledge of everything that went on both in the castle and in government, the omission was maddening. It was good that Hymneth seemed content, but the general knew all too well how rapidly and radically his master's moods could change. That insight had kept him alive and prospering far beyond the time of uncounted colleagues in the service of the Possessed who had long since fallen by the wayside.

But what could it be? As regularly as Hymneth consorted with the powers of darkness, it might involve some malevolent spell of unimaginable power. Peregriff knew that the baleful green vapor that had crippled the errant soldier was as nothing compared to the malign energies his master could muster if the circumstances demanded it. He had seen him do things in the privacy of his chambers that would have left lesser men huddled mewling on the floor, their eyes fastened to carpet or cold stone, their bodies curled into tight fetal positions.

He dared not probe. If and when the time came, Hymneth would reveal all to him. Peregriff knew the master did not trust him. That was to be expected. One in a position of absolute power could not afford to trust anyone. It was one way in which absolute power was maintained. But the ruler of Ehl-Larimar *would* occasionally confide in him. Their relationship was based on mutual respect for each other's abilities. That, and Peregriff's blood oath to support his master in everything he did.

It had been a good life and, if Hymneth was to be believed, one that the general could look forward to for many years to come. Had not the Possessed, through means of sorcery most profound, given him back the arm he had lost at the battle of Cercropai? He sat a little straighter in his chair. All was well in the kingdom, the nuncupative oozings of the Worm notwithstanding. Hymneth's confidence was reassuring.

Though he had not met and knew nothing of them, Peregriff found himself beginning to feel sorry for the unknown, unenlightened interlopers whose advent the Worm had foretold.

XV

Ehomba halted before the stark yet beautiful panorama. They had been walking for many days without a change of terrain, and it was unreasonable to think that it would not eventually give way to a different landscape. It was just that he had not expected the shift to be so abrupt, or so harsh.

"By Gowancare's jennies." A somber-voiced Simna stood next to him, contemplating the identical vista. "Surely we're not going to have to cross *that?*"

"I am afraid we must." As usual, the herdsman's voice betrayed no tightness, no unusual emotion. Raising an arm, he used the point of his spear to indicate the far horizon. "See those distant peaks? If all we have been told is true, those should be the outermost ramparts of the Curridgian Range. Beyond lies Ehl-Larimar. Once we cross over, we are near the end of my journey."

"First we have to reach them," Simna observed, noting the sunblasted desolation that lay between. His water bag was full, but already it felt perilously inadequate against his back.

Before them lay a land of weathered promontories devoid of vegetation. Predominantly beige and white, some of the hills were shot through with streaks of carmine and yellow. Where intermittent flash floods had carved more deeply into the eroded sandstone, layers of black and brown were visible. Stunted trees and battered brush huddled together in the deepest gullies, seeking protection from the unrelenting sun.

Beyond the hills and fronting the base of the mountains, the light gleamed brutally off a strip of perfectly flat whiteness. Ehomba recognized it from his deepest forays into the interior of Naumkib country.

"Salt pan," he informed his companions. "There was once a lake at the foot of those peaks, but the water all dried up long, long ago. Now there is nothing, and because of the salt not even a weed can grow there. They are terrible places." From his elevated vantage point on the edge of the grassy plateau he surveyed the land that had to be crossed. "So long as we have enough water, we should be able to cross the salt flat in two nights and a day." He indicated the beckoning, snow-capped peaks. "We should find springs at the base of the mountains."

"Should find." Simna's tone was flat. "And if we don't?"

The tall herdsman looked down at him. "Then we will get very thirsty. We will have to find water somewhere because we will not be able to carry enough to make a return crossing. I do not know what sources might lie between here and the pan. If we can find any it will be a great help."

Behind him, the black litah growled impatiently. "Naked veldt." Padding past the two humans, he started down the loose, scree-laden slope. "We waste water standing here."

As they descended from the ridge, the temperature rose perceptibly. Beneath their feet, the unstable surface made for poor walking. Except for the sure-footed cat, each of them slipped on more than one occasion. Conscious of the danger, however, no one suffered any injury. Everyone realized it would be an especially bad place to incur a twisted ankle or broken bone.

"This must remind you of home, Etjole." Pebbles sliding and bouncing away from beneath his sandals, Simna picked his way carefully down the slope.

"Not really." Ehomba used his spear to steady himself on the steeper portions of the descent. "It is true that the land of the Naumkib is dry, but there are many rivers that flow through it to the sea, and springs even along the beach that bring fresh water from distant mountains. The hills behind the village receive rain in the winter and heavy sea fog in the summer, so that there is almost always grass to be found somewhere. There are trees in the ravines and washes, and plenty of game." Sweat coursing down his face from the exertion of the descent, he paused and nodded at the terrain that lay before them.

"The country of the Naumkib is dry, but much cooler than here until and unless one travels far to the east. This is land that has been tortured."

They drank their fill and topped off their water bags from springs that bubbled from the base of the ridge. From there until they reached the mountains there was a real chance they would find no more water. The deepest gullies separating the low, rounded, multicolored hills held out the promise of moisture in their depths: The vegetation that grew there was proof enough of that. But it might well lie far below the surface, within reach of ancient roots but not desperate hands. They could not count on supplementing their supplies for many days.

"We'll need to watch what we eat as well," Simna commented as they headed off into the rolling, uneven terrain that lay ahead.

"Dry country often yields a surprising amount of food." Ehomba maintained a steady pace, his face a picture of determination. "Plants that look dead sometimes provide unexpected nourishment, and where there are plants there is at least some game." He nodded to his left. "We are lucky to have with us a game-catcher supreme."

"I can only kill what's there." The litah acknowledged the compliment with a terse grunt.

"Hunkapa hunt too," the hirsute hulk bringing up the rear added plaintively.

"Hoy, I'm sure you're well skilled at sneaking up on small burrowing creatures," Simna commented sarcastically. "No matter. We all need to be sharp of eye and alert of ear 'til we're through this hell, lest we overlook even one opportune meal."

Ehomba's dry-land lore and Ahlitah's hunting prowess notwithstanding, they could not eat what they could not find. In the days that followed, no game of any size showed itself, and the nearest thing they found to a water hole was a damp depression in the sand between two hills. Digging exposed only more sand; moist, but not drinkable.

The herdsman did locate a colony of honey ants. Digging out the bulbous bodies of the storage workers, he showed his companions how to make use of them.

"Hold them up by their heads, like this," he explained as he demonstrated, "and bite off the sugar-water-filled abdomen." This he proceeded to do, flicking the useless head and thorax aside when he was through.

Simna swallowed uncomfortably. But after trying one of the bloated insects, he found the sensation in his mouth surprisingly agreeable. The taste of the taut, thumbnail-sized golden sphere was sweet and refreshing.

It would have taken a dozen such colonies to slake their thirst, but the supplement to their dwindling reserve was welcome, and the sugar gave a boost to their energy and spirits.

Both had waned considerably when Ehomba, following a gully that led slightly northwestward, stepped around a sandstone column and ran into the demon.

Though understandably startled, the unflappable herdsman quickly regained his composure. Bunching up behind him, his companions were less sanguine. For its part, the demon regarded them warily but without fear. After all, there was very little reason for a true demon to dread the living. Protected as they were by all manner of spells and enchantments, there was not much a mortal could inflict on their person in the way of bodily harm.

Realizing this full well, Simna pressed close to his tall friend. Knowing that his own weapons would be useless against such a profoundly base creature, the herdsman's hand did not stray in the direction of his weapon. Swords and knives were no match for the hexes of the underworld. Fortunately, he was traveling in the company of one of the few people he had ever met who possessed the knowledge to ward off evil enchantments. Assuming, of course, that Ehomba had been lying to him all along about not being a wizard.

On the other hand, he decided as he edged out slightly from behind the herdsman's shadow, the appearance of this particular demon, though its ancestry and origins were never in doubt, was not of a kind to inspire immediate and unremitting terror. Above its slick bald forehead it wore a wide-brimmed hat, battered and notched, with two holes cut out to allow its horns room to protrude. The arrangement had the added benefit of helping to keep the hat on the apparition's head in a high wind. Needless to say, it was not perspiring.

In addition to the dusty hat, the creature wore long pants in the back of which a hole had been cut to allow the curling, pointed tail room to roam. Trouser legs were tucked into calf-high boots. Above the belt the hairy chest was partially covered by a checked vest of many pockets whose contents Simna decided he would prefer to remain in ignorance of. A red bandanna around its neck was decorated with an embroidered pattern of interlocked human figures writhing in torment. On its back it carried a huge pack secured with multiple straps of well-worn leather. Tied to the pack were a pick and two shovels, a shallow, broad-bottomed iron pan, and a tent and bedroll. The bloated, oversized load would have taxed the strength of Hunkapa Aub. Supernatural strength and stamina notwithstanding, it clearly taxed the endurance of the red-faced phantasm.

Herdsman and demon considered one another. Then the profane apparition clasped one clawed, long-fingered hand to its exposed scarlet chest and shivered.

"Sure is cold out today."

"We find it tolerable," Ehomba replied.

"You would." The demon began slapping its arms against its sides. It momentarily tripled their length so that it could also slap at its back and lower legs.

For once, Simna had nothing to say, preferring to let his lanky companion conduct the entire conversation. If he could at that moment have rendered himself wholly invisible, he would gladly have done so. While the physical appearance of the demon was no more abhorrent than that of certain bureaucrats the swordsman had known, its face was a mask of pure horror, a promise of all the torments and suffering the netherworld was heir to. One joked with such a hideous specter at the risk of one's life and limb.

Yet while his companions remained anxiously in the background, Ehomba took a step forward and calmly extended a hand. "We are strangers in this blasted country, and could do with some information."

"Information you want, is it?" Grinning to reveal a maw packed with jumbled, broken, sharp-pointed teeth, the bare-armed fiend accepted the proffered fingers, shaking but leaving them attached to Ehomba's hand. "I'll help if I can. I have to say, your ignorance does you proud. Like now, for instance." The clawed hand suddenly tightened around Ehomba's.

Instantly, steam began to rise from the virulent grip. Simna started to shout a warning that was already too late, then caught his breath. As the herdsman continued to sustain the handshake, the slitted yellow eyes of the demon began to widen. Eventually it released its hold.

To the amazement of fiend and friends alike, Ehomba's palm showed no evidence of damage from the searing handclasp. He smiled slightly. "It is also hot in my homeland. My skin is toughened from season after season of moving rocks that have lain in the sun for many years."

The demon nodded understandingly. Turning to one side, it spat out a soggy blob of brimstone. The impious spittle sizzled where it struck the sand. The chaw that bulged one of the creature's cheeks must have been composed of solid sulfur.

"I'd heard that some mortals could handle heat better than others. You must be one of them. What brings you to the Tortured Lands?"

Ehomba nodded in the direction of the demon's enormous pack. "I might ask you the same question."

"Fair enough." The back of a scaly red arm wiped thick, blubbery red lips. "I'm a prospector, plying my trade. It is by nature a solitary business, only rarely rewarding, but it suits me."

This was something Simna ibn Sind felt he could relate to. Stepping out from behind Ehomba, he essayed his most comradely smile. "What is it you're prospecting for out in this desolation? Gold, I would imagine.

Or silver, or another of the precious metals? Gems, perhaps, or the rare ingredients for arcane powders and potions?"

The horned skull shook slowly from side to side. "I am digging for lost souls." Once again extending an elastic arm farther than was natural, the demon fumbled at its pack. "Exhumations have been meager these past few weeks, but there's a little color in the pouch. Care to have a look?" From a small, tightly fastened, intricately inscribed leather bag there arose a faltering chorus of moans.

"That's all right." Making motions of demurral, the momentarily confident swordsman once more hastily took refuge alongside his lean companion.

With a shrug, the demon retracted his arm. "I understand. There's really not much to look at. Fair size, decent opacity. Impure, of course, or they wouldn't be here." Perking up, he smiled horribly. "I've been following traces for some time, hoping to hit a vein."

Not mine, Simna hoped feelingly. Despite the veneer of civility that overlay the ongoing exchange of pleasantries, he could not escape the feeling that if Etjole Ehomba were not standing between him and the eager phantasm, he and the others would already be staked out on the searing sand with their body cavities ripped open and their entrails exposed to the sun. Why this should be he could not have said. The herdsman had evinced no special protection, had thrown up no obvious defenses. But Simna was certain their continued salvation was due solely to the herdsman's presence among them. In this he believed as firmly as he believed in his own existence. Perhaps more so.

It was plain to see that even as they conversed amiably, the demon was sizing them up and paying particular attention to Ehomba. Either there was something about the herdsman's soul that rendered it unattractive, or else it was shielded by means and methods beyond the ken of a wandering swordsman. Whatever it was, Simna was exceedingly grateful for its existence, because it appeared to be protecting not only its owner, but his friends as well.

"I'm Hoarowb." The creature did not extend its hand again. "What do you want with the Blasted Lands? You don't look like soul miners to me."

"We are not," Ehomba admitted quietly as he leaned slightly on his spear for support.

"That's good. I don't much care for competition in my territory. Rich pockets of lost souls are few and far between, and it's the smart fiend who keeps their location a secret."

"Our business does not lie in this country." Raising his spear, the herdsman pointed to the distant, glistening crags of the Curridgians. "We travel through to the mountains, and beyond."

Sniffing like a pig snuffling for offal, the demon extended its head forward in the direction of the spearpoint. "Interesting poker you've got there. Positively rank with dead millennia." Again the hideous grin. "I don't suppose you'd consider trading for it? I have a couple of really quality souls, prime stuff. Fetch a good price on the nethermarket."

"Thank you, no." Ehomba smiled to show that he was not offended by the offer. "I need all my weapons, and I already have a soul."

The demon spat a gooey glob of yellowish brimstone to one side. It struck an ankle-high clump of green weed bursting with tiny purple flowers and promptly set it ablaze. "Everyone can use a spare soul or two. Comes in handy at the moment of Determination. But never mind. I can sense that you're not the trading type." Peering around the herdsman, the demonic countenance focused on Simna.

"You, on the other hand, smell like someone I could do business with."

"Maybe another time." The swordsman ventured a wan smile. "My soul's all tied up just now." He pointed to his companion. "With him."

"Pity." Straightening, the demon smiled affably at Ehomba. "I could split your sternum, tear out your heart, and leave you to bleed to death here in the sand." He shuddered slightly. "But I can tell that you'd spoil it all by resisting, and anyway it's too cold out this morning for sport. I've a ways to go before I dig a hole and make camp."

"Since you are not going to kill us," the herdsman replied good-naturedly, "could you tell us how far it is to the nearest water hole?"

"Water hole?" The demon eyed him in disbelief, then burst out roaring. It was laughter wild and withering enough to scald bare skin. Indeed, unprotected by fur or learning, Ehomba had to turn away from it to keep himself from being scorched.

"There's no water holes in this country. Hot springs, yes, and boiling mud pots, and steaming alkali lakes a being can take a proper bath in—but water holes?" One crimson, clawed finger elongated enough to reach up and over the specter's skull, pointing to the northwest.

"Only one place you might find running water, and that's Skawpane. They got everything in Skawpane. Another month or so and I'll be due for a visit there myself, depending on how well the prospecting goes." From the vicinity of the occulted leather bag, small screams bereft of all hope seeped futilely. Simna ibn Sind shuddered. The chill he felt had nothing whatsoever to do with the temperature, perceived or otherwise.

"What is this Skawpane?" Ehomba asked.

The demon sniggered at some private joke. "Only decent place in the Blasted Lands. There's other flyspecks claim to be, but Skawpane's the only real town." Oculi that reflected righteously hellish origins stared into the herdsman's. "Go there if you dare. If you seek water that's unboiled and nonpoisonous, that's the only place you might find it. I guarantee you one thing." It nodded knowingly. "You and your familiars will be a novelty. Don't get many mortals in Skawpane."

With that, the apparition tipped its hat politely, set it neatly back over the protruding horns, and ambled off down a side gully. In its wake the stink of masticated sulfur and burning brimstone corrupted the air, and bootprints fused the sand where they had trod into dungy glass.

Smiling pallidly, Simna was quick to offer a suggestion. "If we ration our remaining water carefully, we might well make it to the base of the mountains."

Ehomba considered. "That is what I wanted to believe. But I think now that I was allowing my common sense to be swept aside by optimism and hope. Hunkapa Aub in particular needs a lot of water." He sighed. "We must make our way to this Skawpane and refill our water bags there."

The swordsman was reluctant to concede the point. "How about we just let our common sense be swept, and hope that we find a spring as soon as we strike the foothills?"

Ehomba pursed his lips disapprovingly. "You are more afraid of what we may encounter in this town than you are of dying of thirst?"

Simna jerked a thumb toward the gully where the prospecting demon had disappeared. "If that thing was representative of the general citizenry of this particular metropolis, then my answer is yes."

It did not matter. He was outvoted. Having followed Etjole Ehomba this far, neither Hunkapa Aub nor the black litah was about to dispute his judgment. That was because both of them were dumb animals, Simna knew, though he was loath to point it out. Grumbling, he hoisted his pack and water bags and followed along.

Maybe he was worrying needlessly, he told himself. Maybe the demon had been having a little fun at their expense. Skawpane might prove to be a quaint, if isolated, little oasis of a community, its dusty streets shaded by palm trees, its inhabitants serene and content with their lot. Believing this, wanting to believe it, he marched along beside his tall companion with a renewed feeling of confidence. Even if he was wrong and his hopes were to prove unrealized, how bad could it be? A town was a town, with all the familiar urban baggage that implied.

When they finally reached the municipal outskirts, he saw that he was only partially correct. Skawpane was a community, all right.

But it was no oasis.

XVI

$\mathbf{D}$o we have to go in there?" Simna stood atop the smooth-surfaced, rounded boulder of yellow-white sandstone looking across the flat, hard-scrabble plain that separated the travelers from the first outlying structures.

Ehomba did not squint as he contemplated their imminent destination. He was used to the sun. "Unless you want to chance running out of water before we reach the mountains. I have seen men who tried to reach the coast of Naumkib from the interior but ran out of water before they found a stream or village. Even those who had not yet been located by scavengers were unpleasant to look upon."

"A fine choice," the swordsman grumbled. Resigned, he started down the gentle slope. "Hoy, maybe they'll have cold beer."

After a last, speculative glance, Ehomba followed and caught up to him. "Do you really believe that?"

"No," Simna confessed, "but here lately I find that I prefer refreshing delusions to the reality of our actual surroundings."

Skawpane turned out to be less appalling from a distance. From the disgusting state of the dirt streets that ran with dull green putrescence to the sewer grates designed to carry off flash floods of mucus, the act of merely walking quickly degenerated into a detestable activity. No edifice rose to a height of more than three stories, perhaps because of the lack of suitable building materials. Storefronts were fashioned of skin tanned to woody toughness by the repeated application of hot blood and salt water. The origin of these skins was a question the travelers by mutual unspoken consent decided not to ask.

Sidewalks rose a foot or more above the abominable streets. Instead of wooden slats, their planks were fashioned of split bones with the rounded side facing downward. Larger bones such as scapulae had been made into gleaming white shutters that flanked windows of thinly stretched corneas. Occasionally a poorly fashioned pane would blink desperately, reflecting its organic origin.

There were tall, narrow chimneys made of interlocking vertebrae, though what a home or shop would need with a chimney and fireplace in such a hellish climate Ehomba could not imagine. Troughs of liquid sulfur stood outside several of the establishments. Standing patiently at their hitching rails and nuzzling the noxious, toxic brew they contained were a diversity of infernal steeds. The herdsman saw desiccated horses whose pointed ribs protruded from their sides and whose lower incisors pierced their upper jaws like the tusks of bastard babirusas. All had prominent, protuberant eyes that shone with the madness that resided within.

Nor were they the only mounts secured or occasionally spiked to the railings. One storefront they passed had a pair of enormous, hirsute hogs roped to a trough at which they rooted ferociously. When these glanced up to espy the travelers, they strove hard to break their bonds. In so doing they exposed mouthfuls of long, sharp teeth that seemed to belong to some other animal. The saddles fastened to their backs were small and narrow, with disproportionately high pommels. What their riders looked like the visitors could only imagine.

Across the street three elephantine orange-green slugs lay melting in the sun. Their glutinous bodies renewed themselves as they liquefied and they emitted an odor so foul that it rose above all the other myriad stinks that afflicted the noisome concourse. In place of saddles they wore simple handgrips that were buried deep within the slimy flesh itself. Once more, their riders were thankfully conspicuous by their absence.

That did not mean that the streets were devoid of denizens. While Skawpane would never pass for a bustling metropolis, neither was it a ghost town—though ghosts shared the streets and fronting establishments with the rest of their fellow citizens. In addition to reddish demons who might have been related to the prospector they had encountered out in the layered hills, there were demonic folk of every stripe and color. Some were dressed in styles that would have been considered shocking in cities as far apart as Lybondai or Askaskos, but which in their current surroundings seemed perfectly appropriate. Others were content with plainer attire.

The population was a mélange of all that was disturbing and horrific, a veritable melting pot of the diabolical. Besides demons and ghosts there were less familiar phantasms, from towering, spindly brown creatures with bulging pop eyes to winged horrors boasting circular mouths that covered their entire black faces. The crows that haunted the tops of buildings and pecked at offal in the streets had membranous wings like bats, and sickly toothed beaks that looked fragile enough to crumble at a touch. A flower-crowned, tentacled horror lazing in a rocking chair made of human bones tracked their progress down this boulevard of horrors with organs that were not eyes. Next to where its feet would have been if it had had feet, a dog-sized lump of multilegged one-eyed phlegm lifted its rostrum and sniveled threateningly.

Wherever they went and whatever they passed, they attracted attention. Exactly as the prospector had predicted, the arrival of mortals in town was cause for comment. When a tubby yellow blob whose midsection was lined with gaping multiple mouths came bumbling off the sidewalk toward them with self-evident mayhem on whatever it possessed for a mind and both Ehomba and Simna drew swords and proceeded to cut it to pieces, none of the fiendish onlookers voiced a warning or raised an objection. In fact, several evinced what appeared to be evidence of macabre amusement. A few interested horrors that had been considering participating in the anticipated butchery changed their minds at this exhibition of formidable resistance on the part of the visiting quartet.

"I need to stop and clean myself." Repeatedly licking one forepaw, the black litah applied it to his eyes and snout. "I don't think I've ever felt so filthy."

"It is not the street here that makes one feel unclean." Striding along, the always curious Ehomba tried to identify the composition of the slimed, slaglike substance beneath his sandals. "It is the atmosphere."

"Hunkapa no like," declared the hairy mass that lumbered along in his wake.

"We agree on something." Holding his sword like a long gray flag of warning, Simna put all the confidence and cockiness he could muster into his stride. At the first sign of weakness here, he suspected, the four of them would go down beneath a horde of horrors, torn apart for a midday snack—and that was if they were lucky. It was vital to maintain an appearance of invincibility.

In this Ehomba was of no help. Ever since they had entered the town, the soft-voiced herdsman had altered nothing. His expression, his posture, the loose, casual manner in which he held his spear: all were unchanged. Whether this seeming indifference was perceived by the ghastly inhabitants of Skawpane as an invitation to feast or supreme confidence in powers they could not descry remained to be seen.

At least they were not immune to the effects of a well-honed blade, skillfully wielded, the swordsman reflected. He gripped his sword a little tighter.

"Hoy, bruther, where's the water you promised us?"

"Promised?" Ehomba glanced down at his friend. "If you would put food in my mouth with as much ease as you do words, I would never grow hungry again." Simna might think him detached, but his cool dark eyes missed nothing. "We need to ask someone."

"Don't you mean some*thing?*" The swordsman skipped agilely to one side as a crow soaring past overhead relieved itself. The dark red dropping sizzled where it struck the moist, mephitic street.

"I wonder why someone—or some*thing*—chose to put a town here, in the worst place imaginable?" Ehomba mused as they walked on. The buildings were moving slightly apart as the street widened. They were coming to some kind of central square or plaza.

Simna's retort was tense and edgy. "Maybe it's a summer resort, where the residents can come to escape the heat of their customary surroundings. Who knows what monstrosities like these consider attractive in the way of climate or countryside?"

"For one thing, we like it beautifully barren and destitute, visitor. To most of us this is splendid country."

Thus hailed, they halted. The figure that had spoken had paused in its stroll down the osseous promenade. It was a lizard, but while both Ehomba and Simna were familiar with the four-legged reptiles from their respective travels and homelands, neither man had ever encountered a lizard like the one they confronted now.

Standing on its severely bowed hind legs, the reptile was a good three feet tall. It wore a military-style cap, maroon vest with gold stripes, long, tattered brown pants, and no shoes. Stretching another three feet behind it, a brown-and-green tail whipped nervously back and forth as it spoke. Completing the unexpected costume were a pair of pince-nez glasses that rode comfortably halfway down its snout.

Inclining its head slightly downward so it could peer out over these at the visitors, the lizard tut-tutted softly. "I declare, you lot are the most peculiar collection I've seen in some time. If you don't like it here, I suggest you move on."

"That is exactly what we are planning to do," Ehomba responded politely. "Just as soon as we are able to top off our water supply."

"So it's water you want, is it? In Skawpane." The head bobbed rapidly up and down. "Interesting. We don't get many calls for water here. Sulfur now, or antimony, or cinnabar; those the general store stocks in bulk. But water—your options are mighty restricted." Slitted eyes blinked as they stared up the street. "So's your time."

"Why?" In the face of danger, it was typical for Simna's tone to turn belligerent. "Don't the locals like company? Who are you, anyway?"

"I'm the town monitor. As for my fellow citizens, they're an intemperate lot at best. Never know how the individual members of such a mixed bunch are likely to react in any given situation. There's folks here who'd like to talk to you, some who might invite you in for a game of cards or bowls, but most would probably prefer just to tear you limb from limb."

"Hungry?" Hunkapa Aub asked.

The lizard nodded. "Or just surly. Or wanting the exercise. Even established locals have to watch their step. The fiends among us are no respecters of residency. Skawpane's a popular place among the damned and doomed."

"Which are you?" Hunkapa inquired innocently.

"The downtrodden. In fact, things have been so bad hereabouts lately that I'm thinking of taking off for open country. You get tired of looking over your shoulder every minute. Trying to make a living in the midst of unrelenting demoniac anarchy takes a toll on one's health."

Holding firmly to his spear, Ehomba watched as a pair of blue demons with four legs and long, warty snouts crossed the street in front of them. They were trailed by three magnificently ugly but well-dressed miniature versions of themselves. Much to their parents' satisfaction, the young demons fought continuously among themselves. Darting in and among the impish offspring was a small, yapping bundle of thorns that had feet but no legs. Or head.

"You said that our options were restricted. That implies that options exist. What are ours?"

"For obtaining water?" The lizard turned, claws clattering on the bone sidewalk, and pointed. "The central plaza lies just ahead, on the other side of the memorial municipal ceremonial slaughterhouse. In the middle of the plaza is the town fountain. That's where you'll find your water."

"And no one will object to us filling our bags?"

The reptile shrugged. "Your very presence here is an insult to all that is profane and unredeemed. Mortals don't belong in Skawpane. Frankly, I'm surprised you're still alive. I would've thought by now that some enterprising perversion would have killed you, skinned you, and hung you out to cure in the sun. Or done so without killing you." Cold reptilian eyes regarded them speculatively. "As I said, you're an odd lot. You might get your water. Of course, after that you still have to make it safely out of town." A scaly thumb gestured.

"Remember: on past the slaughterhouse, middle of the central plaza. And good luck."

With that it resumed its stroll along the sidewalk and had not gone more than a couple of yards before something long, leprous, and scarlet shot out from within a shaded storefront to wrap snakelike several times around its middle. Hissing violently, the lizard was drawn back into the depths of the aperture. From within arose the sounds of violent and desperate conflict.

The travelers did not linger to witness the outcome. Ehomba led them onward, away from the noise of fighting. Not only was it the safe thing to do, it was the accepted reaction. None of the other locals out walking the streets paid the slightest attention to the shrouded life-and-death struggle taking place nearby. They went about their business as if nothing untoward were taking place—which for Skawpane was perfectly true.

Simna placed his feet carefully, doing his best to avoid stepping on the pale white maggots that infested the street slime and snapped hungrily at his ankles. They could not catch him, but there were certain places on the public avenue where it would clearly be unwise to loiter. Though everywhere awash in corruption and decay, some spots were perceptibly worse than others.

"Hoy, I've seen too many tentacles since joining your company, Etjole." The swordsman nodded back the way they had come. "That one was particularly long and vicious. Reminded me of our encounter with the Kraken, but at least in this case there was only one of them."

Ehomba kept his gaze alert as he unblinkingly scrutinized shadows and side passages. "Yes, but that was no tentacle, Simna. It was a tongue. And the storefront from which it emerged was not a place of business at all, but a mouth most carefully disguised. Little here is what it seems, and visitors such as ourselves can be sure of one thing only: the omnipresence of death."

"Hoy—thanks for that explanation, bruther. I feel so much better now." Behind them, the black litah paused repeatedly to flick slime from its paws.

"I am only pointing out what is true," Ehomba countered.

"Sometimes it's better to keep what's true to yourself." The swordsman nodded forward. "Looks like more of the friendly citizenry has come out to greet us."

From the ominous, looming double door that sealed the end of the slaughterhouse, more than a dozen of Skawpane's diverse inhabitants had emerged. They formed a line across the volcanic paving stones that marked the outskirts of the town plaza, blocking the only visible access to the center.

From their attire and accoutrements Ehomba decided that all or most of them must work in that dismal, odiferous structure. Several wore long aprons encrusted with revolting dark stains. Their expressions were frightful, their posture dire. It was clear that they had no intention of stepping aside to let the travelers pass.

Several stood more than ten feet tall and boasted multiple arms or boneless limbs. Others had three eyes, or no eyes at all. One of the creatures most nearly resembled the many-branched cacti that grew in isolated thickets back of the Naumkib's grazing lands. Toxic pus oozed from each quill, and the drool that ran in a steady trickle from a central orifice dissolved whatever it came in contact with.

All were armed. Not with weapons, but with the tools of their horrific, evil-smelling trade. Much in evidence were oversized skinning knives: long punctuation marks of metal, sharper than razors and blotchy with dried blood. The largest among the coterie of inhuman butchers fingered meat cleavers the size of small doors, weighty with malevolence. Standing in line, blocking progress, they watched the approach of the diverse quartet of advancing mortals. While most sported no expression at all (and indeed, some had nothing to express with), a few wore macabre grins that were crescent moons of pure evil.

Simna casually raised his sword. "Maybe we should go around; try entering the square from another part of town?"

"What makes you think these wicked corruptions of all that lives and breathes would not be waiting for us there as well?" Keeping his voice down, Ehomba slipped his spear into its sling on his back. "Besides, I have a strong feeling that if we were to turn our backs on any of the inhabitants of this place, they would take that as a sign of unqualified weakness and fall upon us in a body. From the moment we entered into the boundaries of Skawpane I sensed that sooner or later we would have to defend, and prove, ourselves." Reaching back over his shoulder, he drew forth the sword of etched sky metal. As always, it emitted an imperceptible hiss when drawn from its scabbard. "It seems it is to be sooner."

One of the biggest of the brutish butchers laughed hollowly at the sight of the two bright, slim weapons. Its impure tittering resonated through the soles of the travelers' feet.

"Puny mortal weapons will not serve here, little meat. We're going to carve you up, dress you down, and pick our teeth with your bones!"

Something that looked like it had been run over twenty times by a wagon laden with building stone weaved slowly back and forth on powerful, if unsteady, feet. It had one oversized, bloodshot eye and a second that seemed to float around the lower portion of its face like an iniquitous afterthought.

"Use your jugular for a straw and suck your blood. Nice 'n' salty."

"Eyes," declared something else that had no name, nor want of one. "I claim the eyes."

"Not all eight!" The cleaver-wielding hulk swaying next to it objected strenuously. "Half are mine." It raised the immense blade.

Holding his sword at the ready, with a tensed Hunkapa Aub guarding his left side, Simna ibn Sind brayed defiance. "Come on then, you piss-poor pack of putrescence! You motherless self-fornicators! We'll see who's skilled with a blade here, and who's ripe for butchering! I'm thirsty, and I mean to drink my fill at your town fountain. And if that means going through you instead of around, then by Gucoron, have at it!" He nodded to his right, where a tall figure stood silently holding a larger sword before him.

"This here is Etjole Ehomba, the most powerful wizard on either side of the Semordria Ocean! Press him, and he'll blow out your eyes and pickle your entrails!" He gestured with one hand. "Come on then, you long-winded flock of featherless foulness!"

"A wizard." One of the other butchers cackled. "Mortal magic doesn't work here, little meat. The atmosphere is all wrong. Too dry, or too hot, or too disrespectful. Skawpane is rife with impudence and contempt for anything that seeps in from the world outside. Your magic, if you command any, which by the looks of you I seriously doubt, will not save you here." Saclike, malignant eyes bored into those of the swordsman. "You're going to *die* here, little meat. But you won't be food for worms, because we leave no scraps for our pets."

"Had a pet once," mumbled the thing with one oversized eyeball and one too small, "but it made too much noise one day. So I ate it. It was greasy." Rubbery lips smacked. "I like grease."

With a roar that would have chilled the blood of less hardened pilgrims, two of the largest abominations lurched forward. Simna ducked a slice from a skinning knife that was easily big enough to decapitate a buffalo in a single swipe. Charging forward, Hunkapa Aub struck the creature beneath two of its four arms and knocked it off its feet. Ahlitah was an ebony blur, slashing and snapping anything that came near. Several of the rapacious monstrosities tried to surround the big cat, but it was much too quick for them.

Like a runaway guillotine, a gigantic meat cleaver descended in Ehomba's direction, aiming squarely for the herdsman's head. Bringing the sky-metal sword up and around, he parried the blow. Sparks flew as metal struck metal with a reverberant ring that echoed back and forth across the street. The attention of his own assailants momentarily diverted by Hunkapa Aub, Simna saw the two blades make contact—and his heart sank.

A chunk the size of a small plate had been taken out of the side of the sky-metal blade.

He wanted to shout at his friend, to hear an explanation for what had just happened. Sorcerer supreme Ehomba might be, or simple herder of cattle and sheep as he claimed, but there was no disputing the power of the singular sword. Simna had seen it in action too many times to doubt its alchemical provenance. Whatever happened to its owner, it was impossible for the weapon to fail. Impossible!

Yet, a second blow from the raging demon's cleaver took another piece out of the blade. Many more impacts like that and Ehomba would be left without anything to fight with. Somehow Simna knew that the herdsman's other weapon of choice would not save them here. The efficacy of the sea-bone sword this far from the ocean would be much in doubt. Butchers from the netherworld would probably greet the sharks the blade's teeth would bring forth as another welcome source of meat, be it solid or numinous.

As for the herdsman's spear, that was a last hope held in reserve, but the swordsman remembered his tall friend saying on more than one occasion that its startling effects were of brief duration, and therefore could not be counted upon for more than momentary salvation. As he looked on, the herdsman parried still another weighty swing. A third section of sword shattered violently.

The blighted butchers pressed their assault. Hunkapa was holding his own, and the black litah doing real damage. In a fair fight the visitors might well have prevailed. But they were outnumbered, and by creatures for whom Death itself was an old friend. Their assailants had relentless confidence and no fear.

Simna had to admire the way Ehomba fought on, stolid and expressionless, swinging his failing blade with steadfast determination as if nothing were wrong. By himself he was holding off the three biggest of their assailants, whose heavy cleavers were taking a terrible toll on the herdsman's weapon. The stocky mercenary was about to shout the suggestion that Ehomba throw away his deteriorating weapon and try the magic of the spear, when a glint out of the corner of his eye momentarily diverted his attention.

It was one of the many splinters the frenzied demons had struck from the surface of the sky-metal sword. The tiny bit of metal was glowing brightly, emitting a vaporous fragment of the deep azure light that

Simna had seen the whole sword give off when justly held in both Ehomba's long-fingered hands. As he stared, still vigorously defending himself but keeping an eye on the splinter, it rose from the slimed street, shining more brightly than ever. Beneath his disbelieving gaze it expanded until it was more than a foot long and pulsing with an intense blue light. He had seen that same fierce, cold, cobalt effulgence before— at moments that had preceded deliverance.

Something else put a claim on his attention. Three more of the shattered splinters were rising from the ground, elongating and glowing. Off to his left rose still another half dozen, burning with an angry, internal, azure radiance. Ahlitah gave ground as a handful of metal shavings beneath his feet lifted to luminous attention, and Hunkapa Aub paused in his exertions to stare mesmerized at the shards that were rising from the ooze beneath his very feet.

Everywhere splinters and fragments from the sky-metal sword had landed it was the same. Every flake and chip, no matter how small, no matter how seemingly insignificant, was rapidly regenerating itself as a smaller version of the matriarchal sword. At the sight the diabolic butchers slowed but did not halt their attack.

Then Ehomba took a step back from the conflict. Holding the sword hilt tightly in both hands, he raised the remnants of the primary blade over his head. In concert, a thousand smaller versions of the original weapon rose skyward and hung, glowing, parallel to the ground. The field of battle before the demonic slaughterhouse was engulfed in lambent blue.

When next the herdsman swung the peerless weapon aggressively, a thousand lustrous offspring mimicked the blow to glistening metallic perfection.

XVII

A cerulean wind moaned as the thousand blades struck at the loathsome assailants. When the demon-butchers attempted to rally and strike back, Ehomba dipped his sword and their blows were met by a thousand unyielding parries. At that moment more than the tide of battle turned: The dark heart, the evil essence of the enemy, evaporated like a palmful of water on the scorched approach to Skawpane.

Not that they ran. Flight was not in their nature. They fought on, continuing their efforts to slaughter the handful of obstreperous mortals. All that had changed was that one of their human opponents now wielded a thousand blades where moments ago there had been only one.

Come to think of it, everything had changed.

So elated by this unexpected turn of events was Simna ibn Sind that he forgot to taunt his lanky companion about his supposed lack of sorceral skills. The swordsman was too busy thrusting and hacking as he threw himself at their adversaries. One on one, he was convinced that nothing lived, of this Earth or anywhere else, that could stand against him. Part of this was due to actual skill, part to confidence, and part to pure bluster. Stirred together in the anima of the stocky swordsman, they made him a dangerously unpredictable opponent.

Bellowing defiance, Hunkapa Aub was breaking limbs and heaving opponents into nearby walls with unbridled gusto, his great strength and boundless energy giving even the most formidable of the fiends pause. The black litah was a dark streak of feline dynamism; blurred destruction. Fang and claw left their multiple marks on many assailants, who searched in vain for a tormentor who had already moved off to attack someone else.

A monstrous cleaver descended, only to have its path blocked by a hundred blades. Many splintered under the impact, but many did not. Bringing his weapon up and around, Ehomba visited a hundred deep cuts on his assailant. The towering brute gasped and clutched at its flank, unable to stop the flow of green blood from its side. And each of the metallic splinters from the dozens of smaller swords it had shattered arose afresh to give birth to a hundred new sharp points and edges.

Amputated arms and tentacles lay twitching in the street, some still futilely clutching their weapons. Green blood ran in rivers into animate sewers that sucked greedily at the flow. Blinded and crippled, sliced into smaller and smaller pieces, confronting a hostile and terrible magic where traditionally there should have been none, the would-be butchers fell back. Those that were still capable of movement retreated into the depths of the slaughterhouse and the unmentionable horrors that hung curing within. Others limped or crawled or dragged themselves into side alleys and away from the theater of battle.

They found neither safety nor surcease there, and certainly no compassion, the latter being an emotion as alien to Skawpane as love or understanding. From their places of concealment in dark byways and dank vents, fanged orifices and greedy claws shivered forth to drag the wounded away. Drifting faintly back to the main street, the sounds of this muted slaughter were dreadful in the extreme.

Only two of the foul crew of expectant butchers that had originally confronted the travelers were still capable of rapid movement. Without a word, they gave up at the same time, throwing their weapons and butchering tools aside as they hobbled for the safety of the slaughterhouse, slamming the great doors shut behind them and sealing themselves tightly inside.

Face alight with blood-lust, Simna was all for pursuing and finishing them off. Ehomba first restrained, then calmed, his friend.

"It is enough. I do not think they will trouble us for the duration of our stay in Skawpane."

"Gierot well right they won't!" Breathing hard, the swordsman employed his weapon to make several obscene gestures in the direction of the shut-up slaughterhouse. "What say you, shit-spawn? Not bad work for a few scraps of 'little meat,' hoy?"

Nearby, Hunkapa Aub was picking curiously through a pile of severed limbs, holding each one up for closer inspection, then tossing it aside as he moved on to the next. Ahlitah was sitting on the highest chunk of volcanic paving stone he had been able to find, one that was moderately free of slime, and was cleaning himself, licking his forepaws and using them to glean green gore, varicolored guts, and bits of torn flesh from his jaws and feet.

As Simna relaxed and his levels of excitement, energy, and adrenaline began to decline, he and his companions were treated to another piece of sorcery that, if asked, Etjole Ehomba would insist he had nothing to do with. Using a slightly different two-handed grip to hold the damaged sword out in front of him, the herdsman held himself steady and watched blue effulgence expand. Soon the chipped and scored blade was throbbing and vibrating like a live thing. The effort Ehomba was expending to hold it in place showed in the whitened knuckles of his fingers and the strained lines of his face.

Gradually, and then more swiftly, in ones and twos and small groups, the thousand-plus miniature swords that the conflict had given birth to returned to their metal of origin. Streaks of drifting, razor-edged silver-gray and blue bolted in the herdsman's direction, the combined rush of their mass returning generating a small blue typhoon that roared and howled above Ehomba's clenched hands. Steel swirled giddily about the parent blade. The etched span of sky metal drank them down, soaking up each and every sibling sword in an orgy of resplendent sapphire metalogenesis.

Then the last was gone; vanished, redigested and amalgamated by the original length of star steel. The cerulean glow faded, the complaining roar of displaced air fell to a whisper, and the sky-metal sword was once again whole.

Without a word of comment, its owner slid it back into its empty sheath. As was usually the case, Ehomba's expression could not be read, but it was clear that the effort had cost him. Perspiration poured in small vertical rivers down his face and body, staining his shirt and kilt and running off down his legs and between his toes. If he was not breathing as hard as Simna, he was certainly fatigued.

"I need something to eat," he informed his companions, "and a place to rest."

"Not rest here." As he delivered himself of the obvious, Hunkapa Aub kicked aside a mutilated, multimouthed length of tentacle as thick around as his thigh.

"No." Tired as he was, Ehomba was in complete agreement with his hirsute crony. "We will find a suitable place once we are well away from this blasphemous community." Straightening to his considerable, full height, he gestured ahead. "But first we will have the water that we have fought so hard to gain."

Eyes and photoreceptors that were not eyes and organs that did not even require the presence of light in order to see watched from the shadows as the four vanquishing mortals strode purposefully past the locked-down slaughterhouse and the remaining few buildings that barred them from the central square. Now and then, Simna ibn Sind would raise his sword and take a step sideways as if to confront one of the hidden watchers. In response, the concealed eyes always retreated—albeit some with greater reluctance than others.

When they finally reached the plaza that lay at Skawpane's heart, it was with a feeling of mutual relief. The unlucky lizard had not played them false: The fountain was there, exactly as it had told them it would be. Fenced off by blocks of volcanic scree, it bubbled and foamed to a height of more than fifteen feet. From all appearances, it was a natural spring. Fed from below, it could not be turned off. Hundreds of gallons of fresh water spouted into the sky, spilling down into cracks that carried it away, and all of it theirs for the taking. Except that it was perfectly useless to them.

Because Skawpane's fountain was a geyser.

It made sense, Ehomba mused. What more fitting as the centerpiece for a hellish town like this than a permanent font of boiling water? It was so hot that they could not get near it. Hunkapa Aub and the black litah had to keep well clear lest the sizzling droplets singe their bare feet and paws. Much of the water turned to steam before it could fall back to Earth. Even if they could figure out a way to approach close enough to catch the searing liquid, there was no way they could transport it: The heat would destroy their water bags.

As he considered the predicament, Ehomba felt a hand tapping urgently on his shoulder. Turning, he saw what Simna was pointing at.

Emboldened by the travelers' indecisiveness, a diverse collection of Skawpane's denizens began to emerge from their burrows, pits, sewers, and hiding places. Things with great glowing eyes and pincers in place of hands came crawling slowly toward the fountain. Tentacles writhed, and legs with joints in all the wrong places staggered stiffly out of dark recesses in the surrounding structures. They were not as well armed as the inhabitants of the slaughterhouse had been, but this time there were many more of them. It was as if the entire mephitic town had decided to creep forth to teach the interlopers a lesson.

Teeth clenched, Simna gripped his sword tightly. "Time for another fight, bruther. By Gowoar, there's a lot of them! I hope they don't realize how tired I am. Swinging a sword is heavy work."

"We are all tired," the herdsman observed. "Perhaps we will not have to fight."

"Not for this cursed 'water.' Useful for boiling a chicken or two, but we can't take it with us."

"Maybe we can." Ehomba was ignoring the swarming, slithering, advancing rabble to concentrate on the geyser. It hissed and sputtered angrily as it spewed from the earth. In his right hand he still held the sky-metal sword. Now he raised and aimed it—not at the salivating, noisome creatures that were humping their way toward him and his friends, but toward the geyser. This time the blue glow that emanated from the wondrous blade was so deep as to be almost purple.

"Hoy, long bruther," Simna exhorted him, "the enemy's over this way." Though fatigued, Hunkapa Aub and Ahlitah had lined up on either side of him.

Ehomba continued to point the radiant sword at the geyser. "Otjihanja told me that the sky metal can command more than the wind that rushes between worlds, and do more than send small ghosts of itself into battle. It also holds deep within its core the essence of the place where it was born."

Simna kept an uneasy eye on the advancing horrors. "So you're telling me it can spawn the heat of the fire in which it was forged? Somehow I don't think the ability to command heat is going to do us much good in Skawpane."

"Not where it was forged," the herdsman corrected his friend. "Where it was born."

Something leaped from the point of the sword to the geyser. A streak of impossibly dark blue, a flash of muted silver—Simna was looking the other way when it happened. There was a loud, violent cracking sound, like stone being shattered, only far more highly pitched.

One and all, the frightful denizens of Skawpane halted their advance. They stared out of eyes that bulged and eyes that were slitted, out of compound eyes and simple eyes that could detect only movement. They halted—and then turned and began to flee.

Simna gaped in disbelief. Then he began to whirl his sword above his head as he charged after them, yelling imprecations and insults. Less inclined to resume the slaughter, his companions heaved a joint sigh of relief and remained where they were. The black litah was more tired than he would have liked to admit, and Hunkapa Aub's oversized hairy feet hurt.

Having satisfied his desire for verbal if not corporeal retaliation, Simna turned and trotted back to rejoin his friends. As he did so he caught sight of what had frightened off their potential attackers, and found himself shivering as he approached. Many remarkable spectacles had been sighted in old Skawpane, the great majority of them horrific in nature. But never before had its infernal residents witnessed anything like this.

Ice. Calling forth the temperature in which it had been birthed, the sky-metal sword had turned the geyser instantly to ice.

The gleaming crystalline pillar radiated a cold that, even at a distance, raised bumps on Ehomba's skin. Carefully, he sheathed the extraordinary blade, feeling the lingering cold of it against his back through both his shirt and the heavy leather scabbard. Simna and the black litah kept their distance, but Hunkapa Aub, so far from his beloved mountains, all but embraced it.

The herdsman was quick to intercept him. "Do not touch it, my friend. I know you welcome the cold, but you have never experienced a cold like this. You may stand close, but make no contact, or your skin will freeze tight to it." Listening, the shaggy face nodded understandingly, but even Ehomba's warning could not mitigate the man-beast's delight. He had been uncomfortably warm for a long, long time.

As cold continued to spill in vaporous waves from the sides of the frozen obelisk, it drove the hideous heat-loving inhabitants of Skawpane ever deeper into their holes and hiding places, leaving the travelers with the run of the central plaza and allowing them to relax a little. Already, the unrelenting torridity of the Blasted Lands was beginning to affect the newly forged frigid monolith. Beneath the baleful, remorseless glare of the sun, it started to melt. Immediately, water bags were unlimbered and their spouts carefully positioned to catch the rapidly increasing drip, drip. Ehomba allowed Ahlitah to lap from his bag.

"How is it?"

A thick, fleshy black tongue emerged to lick upper and lower jaws and snout. The big cat did not quite sigh with pleasure. "It is cold and wet and deliriously delicious, man." Fierce yellow eyes regarded the weeping shaft longingly. "Are you sure it's not safe to lick?"

"Not unless you want your tongue frozen to the column," Ehomba warned him. "Be patient. It looks as if the cold is keeping away the horrid inhabitants of this dreadful town." He glanced up. Cold, fresh, mineral-rich water was pouring from the pillar's summit as the sun began to reduce it with a vengeance. What ran off onto the ground formed small puddles that evaporated before they could grow very large.

"Soon we will have more water than we can carry. Then we must make haste to leave before these detestable creatures have either their hot spring or their courage restored to them." As the litah lowered its head, Ehomba impulsively reached out to tousle the thick black mane.

"I understand what you are feeling. I could use a bath myself." Turning together, man and feline gazed longingly at the streams of cool water that cascaded off the frozen geyser, only to vanish as steam or disappear into cracks in the ground. The waste was painful to observe.

When the last of the water bags had been replenished to overflowing, they took turns drinking their fill. The liquid that was streaming down the icy monolith was already starting to grow warm. Soon the relentless, abiding pressure from below would overwhelm the temporary cold the sword had drawn down from the sky, and the frozen column would once more become a boiling, frothing tower of scalding liquid.

But the abominable inhabitants of Skawpane did not know that. They continued to huddle in their cavities and hiding places, away from the visitors and the terrible cold that had taken possession of the very center of their community. Frustrated and helpless to interfere, they watched as the quartet of edible travelers took their time repacking their gear before heading out of town. Not east, as would have been expected, but westward into country so barren and bleak even the lowliest of the town's denizens shunned it. To the west lay country where not even a renegade beetle could survive. Truly, these mysterious visitors commanded vast powers.

Or else, the more cynical among Skawpane's citizens mused, they were controlled by idiocy on a cosmic scale.

Shouldering his pack, grateful for the weight of cool water against his spine, Simna glanced often back the way they had come as they left the last of Skawpane's twisted, warped buildings and equally skewed inhabitants behind.

"What do you think, bruther? When they get over their fear of your chilling little demonstration, will they come after us?"

Ehomba turned to have a look. Already the ominous outlines of the town were receding, swallowed up by intervening boulders and cliffs. Soon it would recede permanently into memory and nightmare.

"I doubt it, Simna. Many who sprang from the slaughterhouse to beset us died. Those who merely suffered a touch of cold are probably counting themselves fortunate. Behind all those oozing fangs and sharp-edged suckers there must lie intelligence of a sort."

"Hoy," the swordsman agreed, "and they can probably imagine what you'd do to them if they tried to give chase." He clapped his rangy friend on the back.

"I do not know that I would, or could, do anything." The herdsman protested mildly. "Really, if any of them came after us I think I would have to try and run away. I am very tired, my friend. You cannot imagine how these exertions drain me. To use the swords or the gifts in my backpack is difficult. I am not trained in the ways of the necromantic arts as are old Likulu or Maumuno Kaudom."

"I know, I know." Hearing only what he wanted to hear, the swordsman grinned broadly. "You're just a rank amateur, a babe in the brush, a hopeless simpleton when it comes to matters of magic. So you've told me all along. Well, fine. Let it be that way, since you continue to insist it is so. I am satisfied with the consequences of your actions, if not the feeble explanations you offer for them."

Ehomba took umbrage as much at his companion's tone as his words. "I did not say that I was any of those things."

Despite the heat, Simna was enjoying himself. "But you still insist you are no sorcerer."

The herdsman drew himself up. "I am Naumkib. So I am neither a 'hopeless simpleton' nor a 'babe in the brush.' "

"Okay, okay." Simna chuckled softly. "Peace on you, bruther. You know, I wouldn't taunt you so much if you didn't take everything I said so literally."

The herdsman's gaze rose to fix on the high peaks of the Curridgian Range. They were markedly closer now. On the other side, he knew, lay Ehl-Larimar and the opportunity, at last, to fulfill his obligation. Those snowy crests held the promise of home.

Home, he thought. How much had Daki and Nelecha grown? Would they remember him as their father, or only as a distant, shimmering figure from their past? Many months had passed since he had made his farewells and set off northward up the coast. He fingered the cord from which had hung the carved figurine of old Fhastal, smiling to himself at the memory of her cackling laugh and coarse but encouraging comments.

He could turn for home even now, he mused. Forget this folly of abducted visionesses and possessed warlocks, of suspicious aristocrats and moribund noblemen. Put aside what, after all, were only words exchanged on a beach in a moment of compassion, and return to his beloved village and family.

Break a promise given to a dying man.

Lengthening his stride, Ehomba inhaled deeply. Other men might do such a thing, but he could not conceive of it. To do so would be to deny himself, to abjure what made him Naumkib. Even if his companions decided today, or tomorrow, or before the gates of this Hymneth's house, to turn about and return to their own homes, he knew that he would go on. Because he had to. Because it was all bound up inside him with what he was. Because he had given his word.

Mirhanja had understood. She hadn't liked it, but she had understood. That was understandable. She was Naumkib. He wondered if the children did, or if they even missed their father.

Immediately behind lay hesitant horror. Immediately ahead lay—

nothing. The ground was as flat as a bad argument, white with splotches of brown and pale red. Scorching heat caused distant objects to waver and ripple like the surface of a pond. Compared to the terrain that stretched out before them, the rocky gulches and boulder-strewn slopes they had crossed to reach Skawpane were a vision of rain-forest paradise.

Nothing broke the bleached, sterile surface in front of them: not a weed, not a bush, not a blade of errant grass. There was only flat, granular whiteness.

It was a dry lake, he was confident. A salt pan where nothing could live. There would be no game, no seeds or berries to gather, no moist and flavorful mushrooms crouched invitingly beneath shading logs. And most important of all, no water. At present they were well supplied, loaded down with the precious liquid. But the hulking Hunkapa Aub and the massive black litah needed far more water each day than any human. Despite their renewed supplies, he knew he would be able to relax only when they were safely across the blasted flats and in the foothills where springs or small streams might be found.

As for food, unless the mountains that towered skyward on the other side of the dry lake bed were closer than they appeared, both he and his companions could look forward in the coming days to dropping a considerable amount of weight. Hopefully, he reflected, that was all they would have to sacrifice.

XVIII

"What an awful place!" His stride measurably reduced, Simna ibn Sind struggled to keep pace with his long-legged companion. Nearby, the black litah padded silently onward, head drooping low, long black tongue lolling over the left side of its lower jaw like a piece of overlooked meat.

"Hunkapa not like." Though the big hulk was suffering visibly beneath his thick coat of silver-gray hair, he plodded along determinedly, his head hung down and his arms almost dragging the ground.

Ehomba was in better shape than any of them, but took no credit for it. He was used to spending long days standing out in the merciless sun, watching over the village herds. Now he squinted at the sky. They had awakened early from the day-sleep and had been marching for more than two hours westward into the advancing evening.

"Take heart. The sun will be down soon." He nodded toward the mountains. They loomed massively before the weary travelers, but the foothills still lay more than a day's hike distant. Or rather, a night's. To avoid the worst of the heat, they had opted to sleep during the day and trek after dark. "It will grow cooler, and walking will become easier."

"Hoy, you mean it will become less hot." The swordsman wiped perspiration from his brow and neck. "Not in any way, shape, or form does the word 'cool' apply to this place."

In the course of their travels they had encountered many strange life-forms surviving in equally strange environments. From the blizzard-cocooned crests of mountains to the high dunes of the desert, from swamps shallow and deep to the vast open reaches of the Semordria itself, there had always been life, be it nothing more than a limpet or a leaf. Until now, until this tormented, perfectly flat plain of desiccated salts. There was not even, a panting Ahlitah pointed out, a warm worm to tickle a cat's taste buds.

With the onset of evening the heat fell, but not as fast as the sun. Even after dark, parching temperatures persisted. Mentally, walking was easier without the brilliant bright bloodshot eye of the sun staring you ruthlessly in the face. Physically, it was only a little less difficult.

Their meals, such as they were, had been necessarily skewed by their topsy-turvy schedule. Supper became breakfast, lunch a midnight snack, and breakfast, supper. Not that it mattered. Their stores were limited in quantity and consequently offered little in the way of variety. What one ate was often the same, meal after meal. Such victuals kept them alive, but their bellies were not entertained.

At least the moon was on their side, Ehomba reflected as they trudged along. Nearly full, bright as stibnite crystals and almost as hard of aspect, it allowed them to stride forth with some idea not only of where they were going, but also of what lay in their immediate path. By its providential brightness obviating the need for torches, it allowed them to advance with a modicum of comfort.

By midnight the air had cooled sufficiently to raise their spirits. Water was still in plentiful supply. In light of the other hardships they were enduring, Ehomba had not had the heart to propose rationing. When he finally did venture to broach the subject, he was shouted down by all three of his companions. They might not have much else, but at least they could drink their fill. Furthermore, the more they drank, the less weight they had to carry. And as Ahlitah pointed out, he was confident he would be able to smell water as soon as they reached the mountains. It might not seem like much, but even the herdsman had to admit that a long, cool drink compensated for much of what they did not have.

Resuming the march rejuvenated and refreshed but acutely conscious of the ominous presence of the sun lurking just over the eastern horizon, they entered an area of the salt pan that was not flat. Merged as it was with its identically tinted surroundings, it was not surprising they had missed seeing it from a distance. Though equally devoid of food or water, it at least gave them something new to look at and comment upon.

Towers of salt rose around them, not numerous enough to impede their progress but sufficient to alter it from time to time. Worn by the wind and the occasional infrequent storm, they had been weathered into a fantastic array of shapes. Amusing themselves by assigning names to the formations, the travelers competed to see who could identify the most outrageous or exceptional.

Pointing sharply to a column of whitened, translucent halite that had been undercut by the wind, Hunkapa Aub conveyed childlike excitement in his voice. "See that, see there! An ape bowing to us, acknowledging our passage."

Simna cast a critical eye on the structure. "Looks more like a pile of rubbish to me."

"No, no!" Moving close and nearly knocking the swordsman down in the process, Hunkapa jabbed a thick, hirsute finger in the column's direction. "It an ape. See—the eye is there, those are the hands, down at the bottom are the—"

"Ask it if it can show us a shortcut out of here," Simna grunted. Nodding to his left, he singled out a ridge of distorted, eroded salt crystals. "Now that looks like something. The jade wall of the Grand Norin's palace, complete with open gates and war turrets." He gestured with a hand. "If you squint a little you can even see the floating gardens that front the palace over by . . ."

But Hunkapa Aub was not listening. Elated by one discovery of the imagination after another, he was prancing from the nearest formation to the next, gleefully assigning a name to each and every one as proudly as if his fanciful appellations were destined to appear on some future gilded traveler's map of the territory. Ehomba looked on tolerantly. Of them all, their hulking companion was suffering the most from the heat. Simna obviously thought the brute was making a fool of himself, but Ehomba knew that no one is a fool who can find humor in desolation.

He found himself playing the naming game. It was irresistible, the first harmless diversion they had enjoyed in many days. Not only was it gently amusing, especially when made-up names for the same formation were compared side by side, but it helped greatly to pass an otherwise disagreeable time. He and Simna wordlessly agreed to compete to find the most suitable cognomen for certain structures. The game was left to them in any case, since the black litah found it repetitive and Hunkapa Aub was quite lost, happily adrift on a sea of a thousand multitudinous namings of his own.

"That column there," the swordsman was saying, "see how it sparkles and dances in the moonlight?" He singled out a formation spotted with many small crystals of gypsum. "I once knew a dancer like that. She would glue pearls and precious gems all over herself. Then when at the end of her dance she removed the last of her veils it was revealed that the jewels were glued not to the fabric of her costume but to her naked skin, and that all along they had only been glistening through the sheer material she had been wearing." He turned to his companion. "What does it look like to you?"

"I would not think of disputing such a deeply felt description." The herdsman stepped over a series of inch-high rills that ran across the surface in a straight line. Deposited eons ago by water action, they looked fragile, but were in fact hard as rock and sharp enough to slice open a man's flesh where it lay exposed between the protective straps of his sandals.

"Over there I see a fisherman's hut by the ocean," he declared. "Not the ocean below my village, but another ocean."

"How can you see a difference?" Simna squinted in the indicated direction.

"Because this sea is calm. It is rarely calm beneath my village. There are always waves, even on clear, windless days. And no Naumkib would build a fishing hut so close to the water. Too much effort for too little reward, as the first storm would wash it away."

"I see the sea," the swordsman admitted, "and the hut, but what makes it a fishing hut?"

Ehomba pointed. "Those long blades of crystal salt there near the bottom. Those are the fisherman's poles, set aside while he rests within."

"I could use a rest myself, and something to eat that isn't dried and preserved." The swordsman turned slightly in the direction of the formation and wandered away for a moment before rejoining the others on their chosen course. In response to the herdsman's slightly stern, questioning look, he shrugged diffidently. "Hoy, I know it's made of salt—but it doesn't hurt to dream for a few seconds."

"That's a sentiment I'll confess to sharing." Ahlitah had come up behind them. As usual, so silent was his approach that even the reactive Ehomba was unaware of his presence until he spoke. With his head, the big cat nodded leftward. "For example, over that way I can see a large herd of saiga standing one behind the other, fat and plump and slow of foot, just waiting to be run down and disemboweled."

Peering in the indicated direction, Ehomba had to admit that the resemblance of the broken ridge of salt to a column of plodding antelope was remarkable.

Evidently Simna was of like mind. "Sure looks real. Like they could take off in all directions if somebody made a loud noise."

"You're already making a loud noise." Crouching low and making himself nearly invisible even in the bright moonlight, the big cat had begun to stalk the wind-sculpted ridge. Realistic they might be, but the salt formations did not move. Ehomba was about to say something when the swordsman put a constraining hand on his arm.

"Leave him alone. All cats need to play. Don't you think he's earned a few moments of amusement?"

"Yes, of course. But he is being so serious about it." Uncertainly,

Ehomba watched as Ahlitah continued to stalk the weathered parapet of halite crystals.

Simna shrugged it off. "I've never seen a cat that wasn't serious about its play. He'll catch up to us when he's through. Remember, he can cover a mile in the time it would take either one of us to run to that big ridge over there." He pointed. "See it? The one that looks like the entrance to a castle?"

Reluctantly, the herdsman allowed his attention to be diverted. Something did not feel right. Maybe, he thought, it was him. The heat was beginning to melt their thoughts. Behind them, the litah dropped even closer to the ground, maintaining its hunting posture as it stalked the salt. Try as he would, Ehomba could not see the harm in it.

Ahead and slightly to their right rose a massive hill of achromatic salts that had been eroded by the wind into a fantastic assortment of spires and steeples, turrets and minarets. The gleaming citadel boasted an arched entrance and dark recesses in the salt fortifications that during the day would not have commanded a second glance but which at night passed easily for windows. A breeze sprang up, advancing unimpeded across the dry lake bed. Whipping around the extravagant towers that had been precipitated ages ago out of a viscid solution of sodium chloride and other minerals, it imparted a carnival air to the formation, whistling and trilling through the hollows that had been worn in the salt. At a distance it almost sounded like people laughing and joking.

"Hoy, Etjole," the swordsman prompted him. "Come on now, don't let me win without a fight. I say it looks like a castle. What would you call it?" As they walked past, salt crystals crunching under their sandals, he studied the pale ramparts admiringly.

"I cannot argue with you this time, Simna. A castle or fortress of some kind. I could not imagine calling it anything else, because that is exactly what it looks like."

"Then we are agreed." Turning to his right, the swordsman started toward the silent formation. "Come on, bruther. Don't you want to see what it looks like up close?"

"I am certain it looks the same at close range, except that individual crystals of salt will begin to stand out."

Shaking his head, the swordsman continued toward the looming structure. "All this traveling in my company still hasn't made you a more jolly companion. Go on, pass up the chance to study up close a fascinating phenomenon you'll never see again."

As always, Ehomba's tone was unchanged, but his thoughts were churning fretfully. "Let me guess: You'll catch up to me in a few minutes."

"Depend on it, bruther." Turning away, Simna continued blithely toward the salt castle, moonlight reflecting off the hilt of the sword he wore against his back.

In front of Ehomba, nothing moved on the lake bed. No pennants of gleaming salt waved in the clear, stark light. No white-faced figures emerged from the weathered hill to greet him. Except for the barely perceptible breeze, all was silent, and still.

Frowning, he pivoted to look back the way they had come. It was with considerable relief that he saw the reassuring oversized shape of Hunkapa Aub standing and waiting patiently not more than a few yards behind him.

"Come on, Hunkapa. If these two want to amuse themselves with silly nighttime fancies, they will have to hurry to catch up with us." The massive, hirsute figure did not stir. Ehomba raised his voice slightly. "Hunkapa Aub? Come with me. There is no reason for us to wait here until these two finish their games."

When the hulking shape still did not move, a puzzled Ehomba walked back toward him, retracing his steps across the lake bed. He knew he was retracing his steps because he could see where his feet had sunk a quarter inch or more into the bleached, caked surface. He was on the verge of reaching out to grab his ungainly companion's shaggy wrist when something made him pause.

Despite Ehomba's proximity, Hunkapa Aub had yet to acknowledge the herdsman's presence. No, the tall southerner decided: It was worse than that. Hunkapa Aub was ignoring him completely, treating him as if he wasn't there. Now Ehomba did reach out to take his massive companion's hand. He pulled, none too gently. He might as well have been tugging on a tree growing from the side of a mountain. Hunkapa Aub did not budge, nor did he react in any way. Instead, he continued to stare straight ahead.

Turning uneasily to seek the source of the brute's fascination, Ehomba found his gaze settling on a tall, heavily eroded pillar of salt.

A pillar of salt that looked exactly like Hunkapa Aub.

The resemblance was more than a fortuitous coincidence, went deeper than something that looked vaguely like a shaggy head attached to a cumbersome body and limbs. The degree of detail was frightening, from the flattened nose to the wide, deep-set eyes. Edging closer, the herdsman found himself staring intently into hollow pits of fractured salt crystal. Should they shift, however slightly, to look back at him, he was afraid that he might cry out.

They did not. The image was composed wholly and unequivocally of salt; immobile, inanimate, and dead. Nothing more. But how then to explain the startling likeness? Not to mention Ahlitah's herd of sculpted prey and Simna's inviting castle. Reaching out, he took Hunkapa Aub's left wrist in both his hands and prepared to pull again, this time with all his strength. He did not. There was something odd about his hulking friend's hair. Usually it was soft and pliant, so much so that Simna often teased its wearer about its feminine feel. Now, suddenly, it felt granular and gritty. Releasing his grip, Ehomba put two fingers to his mouth and touched them cautiously with his tongue. The taste was all too familiar.

Salt.

Whirling, he raced back the way they had come. He found the black litah with his teeth sunk deeply into the side of a mound of slightly reddish salt. The big cat's burning yellow eyes were still open, still alert, but dimmed. As if slightly glazed over. With salt.

"Ahlitah, wake up, come out of it!" He pulled hard on one of the cat's front legs, then on its tail, all to no avail. Equally as heavy as Hunkapa Aub, the black litah was just as difficult to move. Stepping back, the herdsman saw to his horror that the sleek ebony flank was already beginning to show a crust of rapidly congealing halite crystals.

Uncertain what to do, he turned a slow circle. This part of the lake bed was a maze of mounds and pillars, knolls and motifs, configurations and oddly organic shapes. If he burrowed into some of the more recognizable forms, what might he find concealed in their brackish depths? How many of the formations were natural—and how many molded on unlucky travelers both human and otherwise who had preceded him and his companions to this occulted corner of reality? Did he dare dig within? High above, the blanched moon shone down and proffered no explanation.

His mouth set in a grim, determined line, he swung his backpack around in front of him and fumbled inside until he found the vial he was looking for. Little of the inordinately pungent liquid within remained. Hopefully, it would be enough. Since Ahlitah was the first and most seriously affected, Ehomba determined to try to emancipate the big cat first. But as he prepared to remove the stopper from the bottle, something off to his right caught his eye. He stared, then found himself staring harder, but it would not go away. Three pillars, streaked with brown and less so with red. One tall and two short, gazing back at him out of hollow, glistening eye sockets. Three pillars of accumulated, weathered, freshly precipitated mineral salts. Together, they formed a family of salt.

His family.

There was no mistaking the identify of the tallest figure. It was Mirhanja, complete to the smallest detail, her ashen arms extended pleadingly in his direction. He took an instinctive, automatic step toward her. Preparing to take another, he forced himself to halt. His right leg, his whole body trembled. A battle was taking place within, a war between himself as he was and himself as what he knew. It was a conflict that, if lost, would find him once more in the bosom of his family. Embraced by the ones he loved most in the entire world—and encased in patient, precipitating, all-embracing salt.

He would join his companions and their hapless predecessors not in crossing the surrounding sickly, bloodless terrain, but in becoming a part of it.

Always dispute what is happening around you, his father had told him. Never, ever, stop questioning everything and anything, even that which you perceive to be indisputably and undeniably real, for reality can play all manner of unpleasant tricks on the cocksure. Ehomba had grown up skeptical and politely suspicious of the world around him. As he was now.

Think! he screamed at himself. What has happened here? What *is* happening here? Ahlitah saw a herd of prey animals, and the salt became prey animals. Hunkapa Aub saw himself reflected in the salt, and the salt became his reflection. You see your family, the thing *you* most want to see.

But Simna ibn Sind had walked off toward a salt castle. Other travelers and animals could have wandered into this ghastly place and become embalmed by the salt, creating so many of the strange and now ominous formations surrounding him. But a castle couldn't just pick up and move. Therefore what they were seeing was being drawn, had to be drawn, from the hidden places of their own minds. Simna might dream a castle full of willing concubines, but he would want to take possession of the castle first. So the salt had, by inimical magicks unknown and unimaginable, risen up from the lake bed, precipitated out, and formed itself into a small castle for him to inspect. If he entered it fully, Ehomba sensed, his friend would never come out.

Reaching down to scratch an itch, his fingers came away with tiny white grains beneath the nails. Employing every ounce of energy and every iota of determination he could muster, he wrenched himself away from the heart-rendingly realistic figures of his family. As he did so, a cracking sounded beneath his sandals as he broke free of the encrusting salt that had already begun to crawl up his legs. He was free again, but for how long? And what of the fate of his friends?

No! he shouted silently. He had not brought them this far to lose them now, so near to their goal. Realizing that the nearly empty bottle of oris musk would not be enough to shatter the saline illusions the accursed landscape had precipitated around his friends, he fumbled anew with the contents of the backpack. But what could he possibly use? There was nothing, nothing he knew of that was stronger or had a more powerful effect on the living than oris musk.

No, he thought as he stopped digging through the jumble at the bottom of the pack. That wasn't true. There was something more powerful. Furthermore, he had plenty of it.

Slinging the pack around to where it rested comfortably against his shoulders once again, nestling against the twin scabbards, he unlimbered his water bag and tucked it firmly beneath his right arm. It was nearly full, brimming with the stuff of life hard-won in sinister Skawpane. Carefully he removed the stopper and let it dangle by its cord from the lip of the bag. The contents sloshed gently in response to his actions.

Turning his back on his imploring but inanimate family, he walked up to where the black litah stood frozen in the midst of suffocating halite. Taking careful aim with the mouth of the bag, he brought his right elbow and arm roughly against his side, squeezing the bag sharply. Water sprayed from the opening to drench the big cat. It struck his mane and shoulders, ribs and legs. It got in his eyes and nose.

For the first time in many long moments, Ahlitah blinked. Thanks to the water that had gone up his nostrils, this was followed by a sneeze of truly leonine proportions. Running down his flanks, the precious water dissolved away the salt. Even as the big cat was cleansed, fresh salt was trying to precipitate out around his feet, to make its way up his legs and trap him anew.

Shaking his head, the litah sent a shower of sparkling halite crystals flying in all directions. "What happened?" Wrinkling back his lips as only a big cat can do, he spat disgustedly to one side. "What have I been eating?"

Ehomba pointed out the places where the uncannily saiga-shaped lump of mineral salts showed claw and tooth marks. "Everyone likes a little salt with their meal, but there are limits. While you were trying to eat the salt, the salt was starting to eat you. It was not meat that was salted—it was your thoughts." Steeling himself, he turned and gestured in the direction of the three sculpted figures of his family. Now that he was fully conscious of the slow, terrible death they symbolized, he was able to look at them more clearly and see them for what they really were. This time they looked less like Mirhanja and his children than they did like three small pillars of accumulated whiteness.

Revelation proved sanguinary for Ahlitah as well. "I can't believe I was chewing so single-mindedly on that." His snarl of antipathy and contempt echoing across the lake bed, he brought one massive paw around in a great arc and decapitated the nearest formation. Lumps of shattered salt went skittering across the hard, crusty ground.

"Bring your water." Ehomba spun on one sandaled foot. "We have to free the others." He stamped down heavily as he walked. "And keep moving. Do not linger too long in one place. As swiftly as the salt distorts and affects your mind, it also clutches at your feet."

It took the contents of an entire water bag and part of another to free the hulking Hunkapa Aub from his saline entombment. When confronted with the reality of his mirrored self in salt, he could not be dissuaded from pushing it over. It smashed to bits, leaving a pile of salt rubble where moments before had stood a perfect likeness of the shag-covered man-beast.

Continuously brushing salt crystals from their arms and legs, they hurried on to the knoll of salts that had assumed the guise of a small castle. Breathing hard, Ehomba slowed before the sculpted entrance—but of his good friend and companion there was no sign.

Scratching ceaselessly as he fought off the persistent salt, Hunkapa Aub turned a slow circle. "Not see friend Simna."

"I don't smell him, either." Head back, the black litah was sniffing repeatedly at the air. "Between the new dampness and the old salt it's hard to scent anything else."

"Keep trying." Grateful for the moonlight, Ehomba strained to see through seams in the salt formations. They appeared to be taunting him, mocking his efforts to penetrate their encrusted secrets, laughing silently from origins he preferred not to contemplate.

His eyes widened slightly as he realized what must have happened. Whirling to face the blocky, crenellated formation once more, he aimed the water bag he was holding and directed Hunkapa Aub to do likewise with his. Bereft of hands, Ahlitah could only look on and watch.

Water gushed from the mouths of both bags to play over the flanks of the consolidated castle. Minarets dissolved into soggy lumps, and then the lumps themselves became components of thin briny rivers that flowed down the flanks of the formation. Turrets and spires sagged and crumbled, melding into the walls as they liquefied beneath the soaking assault.

It took more of their supply than the herdsman cared to think about, but halfway into the castle they finally caught a glimpse of Simna ibn Sind's backpack. Still riding high on the swordsman's shoulders, it gleamed dully in the moonlight. The surrounding, enclosing salt imparted a sickly blue cast to the exposed portions of his skin.

Moving closer and wielding the shrinking water bags like firearms, Ehomba and Hunkapa Aub dissolved the salt from around their friend's encrusted body. He had been completely entombed. Salt plugged his ears and formed a crust over his eyes. But his nostrils were still unblocked, though barely, the advancing salt having been held back by the moisture breathed out by his lungs.

Stiff and unbending, his body was dragged out into the open air and laid gently across Ahlitah's back. Lying him down on the ground was not contemplated, as it would just be returning him to the grip of the relentless, inimical salts. Water from still another bag was poured over him, drenching his body and clothing, soaking his face. When he finally revived, the herdsman did so sputtering violently and shaking his head.

Sitting up, he wiped animatedly at his face and took a long, deep breath. "What happened? I feel as if I've come back from the land of the dead." Rising to his feet, he suddenly pointed and yelled, "That cursed castle tried to kill me! It grabbed me and tried to suffocate me!"

"Salt you down is more like it." Careful to keep moving his feet and arms, Ehomba proceeded to explain. "I think that if we had been five minutes longer in melting you out, the salt would have filled your nose and stopped your breathing. And your heart."

Wiping at himself as if he had just emerged from hiding in the depths of a cesspool, the swordsman found himself prone to a momentary case of the shakes. He was prepared to face death, had been ever since he had taken up the sword, but suffocating alive was among the least pleasant ways imaginable for a man to expire.

"Away from this place," he declared with a sweep of his arm. "Let's get away from here."

His companions needed no urging. The matter of their suddenly and severely depleted water supply, which they had worked so hard to obtain in Skawpane, was not mentioned. Commentary was unnecessary. Having utilized the greater portion of it to free themselves from the grasp of the alkaline prison, it would now have to be rationed severely, and quickly replenished. In the waning moonlight, the silhouette of the Curridgian escarpment loomed before them more meaningful than ever.

There would be water there, Ehomba knew as he moved forward at the run. The snowy peaks promised as much. The only question was, how high up and how far back would they have to go to find it?

Behind them, fantastic contours and extravagant shapes stood silent sentinel over the salt plain. They did not move, and none uttered so much as a whisper. Rising from pools of rapidly dispersing and evaporating water, crystals of halite and gypsum sparkled like diamonds as they precipitated out of the chloride-heavy solution. In most places such a wealth of crystals would have been zealously guarded and protected, for salt was necessary to the perpetuation of life.

Only here, in this forsaken and barren place between mountain and misery, had it turned deadly.

XIX

The Drounge

It did not know how old it was. It did not know where it came from; whether mother and father, egg, spore, seed, or spontaneous generation. It could not remember when it had begun or how long it had been wandering. It did not know if there were others of its kind, but it had never seen another like itself. It knew only that it was in pain.

For as long as it could remember, which might very well be for as long as Time was, it had been so. Without any specific destination in mind it had wandered the world, its only purpose, its only motivation, to keep moving. It sought nothing, desired nothing, expected nothing—and that was what it got. On its singular plight it did not speculate. What was the use? It was what it was, and no amount of contemplation or conjecture was going to change that. To say that the Drounge was resigned to its condition would be to understate the situation grossly. Alternatives did not and had never existed.

There wasn't an antagonistic particle in its being. By the same token, it was too compassionate to be friendly. Where possible, it kept its distance. When contact with other living things was unavoidable, as was too often the case, it rendered neither judgment nor insensibility. It simply was, and then it moved on.

Most creatures could not see the Drounge so much as sense a disturbance in their surroundings when it was present. This was to the benefit of both, since the Drounge did not especially want to be seen and because it was not pleasant to look upon. Occasionally, the sharp-eyed and perceptive were able to separate it from its surroundings. Whenever that occurred, usually in times of stress or moments of panic, screaming frequently ensued. Followed by death, though this was not inevitable. Murder was the farthest thing from the Drounge's mind. When life departed in its presence, apathy was the strongest emotion it could muster. How could it feel for the demise of others when its own condition was so pitiable?

For the Drounge was a swab. It roved the world picking up the pain and misery and wounds and hurt of whatever it came in contact with. A vague amorphous shape the size of a hippopotamus, it humped and oozed along in the absence of legs or cilia, making slow but inevitable progress toward a nondestination. It had no arms, but could with difficulty extrude lengths of its own substance and utilize these to exert pressure on its surroundings. Other creatures, unseeing, often ran into it, giving rise to consequences that were disastrous for them but of no import to the Drounge.

Open, running sores bedecked its body the way spots adorn a leopard. Scabs formed continually and sloughed off, to be replaced by new ones ranging in size from small spots to others big as dinner plates. They were in constant lugubrious motion, traveling slowly like small continental plates across the viscous ocean of the Drounge's body. Foul pustules erupted like diminutive volcanoes, only to subside and reappear elsewhere. Cuts and bruises ran together to comprise what in any other living being would have been an outer epidermis.

None of this unstable, motile horror caused the Drounge any discomfort. It did not experience pain as others did, perhaps because it had never been allowed to distinguish pain from any other state of being. For it, it was the way things were, the circumstance to which existence had condemned it. It did not weep, because it had no eyes. It did not wail, because it had no mouth. Though capable of meditation and reflection, it did not bemoan its fate. It simply kept moving on.

Unable to alter its condition, it had long since become indifferent to the aftermath of its passing. As well to try to change the effect of the sun on the green Earth, or of the wind on small flying creatures. Incapable of change, it felt no culpability in the destruction of those it came in contact with. It was not a matter of caring or not caring. A force of one of the more benighted components of Nature, it simply was.

It did not matter what it encountered. Large or small, the consequences were similar, differing only in degree depending on the extent and length of time that contact was made. The Drounge acted as a sponge, soaking up the world's injuries and pain. And like a sponge, when something made contact with it, it leaked. Not water, but hurt, damage, wounds, and death. The process was involuntary and something over which the Drounge had no control.

Why it kept moving it did not know. Perhaps an instinctive feeling that so much pain should not long remain in any one place. Possibly some atavistic urge to seek a peace it had never known. Survival, reproduction, feeding—the normal components of life did not drive or affect it. Staring relentlessly forward out of oculi that were not eyes in the normal sense, but which were misshapen and damaged and bleeding, it existed in a state of perpetual migration.

Gliding over a field of grass, it would leave behind a spreading swath of brown. Fire would have had a similar effect, would have been cleaner, purer, but the Drounge was a collage, a mélange, a medley of murder, and not an elemental. In its wake the formerly healthy green blades would quickly break out in brown spots. These would expand to swallow up the entire blade, and then spread to its neighbors. It was not a disease but an entire panoply of diseases, a veritable deluge of afflictions not even the healthiest, most productive field could withstand. After a few days the formerly serene grassland or meadow would stand as devastated and barren as if it had been washed by lava.

Sensing solidity, a herd of wild goats brushed past the patient, persistent Drounge as it made its way northward. Tainted blood and other impure drippings promptly stained their flanks. Some hours later, their thick hair began to fall out in ragged clumps. One by one they grew dizzy and disoriented, dropping to their knees or keeling over on their sides. Tongues turned black and open lesions appeared on freshly exposed skin. Pregnant ewes spontaneously aborted deformed, stillborn fetuses, and the testicles of rams shrank and dried up.

Eyes bulging, black tongues lolling, the toughest and most resilient of them expired within a day. Vultures and foxes came to feast on the dead, only to shun the plethora of tempting carcasses. Something in the wind kept them away despite the presence of so much easy meat. It was a smell worse than death, more off-putting than disease. The fennecs twitched their astonishing ears as they paced uneasily back and forth, keeping their distance yet reluctant to abandon such a tempting supply of food. Vultures landed near the bodies, fanning the air with their dark, brooding wings. Accustomed as they were to the worst sort of decay, a couple took tentative bites out of the belly of a stinking ram.

Within minutes they were hopping unsteadily about. Feathers began to fall away. The hooked, yellow beak of one bird developed a spreading canker that rotted the face of its owner. Within an hour both hardened scavengers lay twitching and dying alongside the expired goats.

Enormous wings spread wide as the survivors took to the air. For the first time in their relentlessly efficient existence, they had encountered something not even they could digest. The foxes and hyenas slunk away as if pursued by invisible carnivores armed with immense claws and fangs. Only the insects, who could sustain the losses necessary to make a meal of the deceased, found the ruminant desolation to their benefit.

Field or forest, taiga or town, it was all the same to the Drounge as it proceeded on its never-ending march. What happened when it passed through a city was unpleasant to the point of becoming the stuff of nightmare legend. Some called it the judgment of the gods, others simply the plague. All agreed that the consequences were horrific beyond imagining.

People perished, not in ones and twos or even in family groups, but in droves. Symptoms varied depending on what afflicted part of the Drounge each encountered. Wounds refused to heal and bled unstoppably, until the unfortunate casualty shriveled like a grape left too long in the sun. Lesions blossomed like the flowers of death until they covered more of a sufferer's body than his skin. The daily clamor of the community; the give and take of commerce, the fluting arpeggios of gossip, the chatter of small children that was a constant, underlying giggling like a symphony of piccolos, was entirely subsumed in shrieks of pain and wails of despair.

So the city died, its inhabitants shunned by surrounding communities. Those who lived long enough to flee were denied sanctuary by their terrified neighbors. They wandered aimlessly, perishing in ditches that lined the sides of roads or beneath trees that could provide welcoming shade but were unable to mourn. Everyone who had come in contact with the Drounge died: the resigned elderly and the disbelieving young, the healthy laborers and the children who could not comprehend. They expired, and so did those who had been in contact with them. Those few who had seen the Drounge and remarked on its passage died differently, slaughtered by their panicked neighbors in a frenzy of ignorance and fear. Eventually, even the plague perished, exhausted by its own capacity for destruction.

And the Drounge moved on.

Nothing could stand in its way, and the perceptive got out of it. Those that were incapable of movement prepared themselves as best they were able, and expired as readily as those living things that could. The Drounge handed down no judgments, passed no resolutions, essayed no assessments.

Only solid rock barred its way or altered its course. Water it passed through as freely as it moved through air, sliding with damned grace into lake or pond and advancing by means of repeated humping motions. As on land, so it was beneath the surface of waves large and small.

Water plants withered and collapsed to the muddy bottom. The shells of unfortunate mollusks bled calcium until they deteriorated beyond usefulness. Abscesses appeared on the sensitive skin of amphibians, and the gills of passing fish swelled up until suffocation brought on a slow and painful death. Wading birds that ate the dead and dying fell from the sky as if shot, their eyes glazed, their intestines rotting. Emerging on the far shore, the Drounge left behind a body of water as devastated as any town or field. As always, in the aftermath of its passing, only the patient insects prospered.

The Drounge continued to move northward.

Eventually it reached a region it might have called home, had it possessed any thought of so removed a notion. For the first time in a long, long while it was able to advance without killing anything. Not because it had suddenly become any less lethal, the essence of itself any less virulent, but because there was so little life in its new surroundings to slaughter. It could not kill what did not live.

Dimly, through its persistent but restricted vision, it took note of rocks bare of bushes, of a soil so sterile it would not support the hardiest of weeds. An amazing place, as barren of life as the far side of the sky. But as if to ensure it could not relax, an occasional wandering or lost creature would materialize, only to make casual contact and die to remind the Drounge of the homicidal actuality that was itself.

Not many: just enough. A flowering grass that had somehow managed to establish itself in a shady crack in the blasted ground encountered the passing Drounge. Moments later its petals had dropped off, to skitter away in the detached grasp of a passing breeze. Then the stems bent, bowed by a sudden systemic affliction. The tiny stockade of glistening green blades yellowed and split. Within minutes the miniature oasis was no more, a flavescent smudge of decay against the sickly, pallid earth.

Where the snake had come from or how it had survived for as long as it had in that blasted land none could say. Heavy with eggs, it sought a place to lay. Searching for the shade of a boulder, it found instead the passing Drounge. Immediately, it began to cough, and to twist violently. The forked tongue flicked spasmodically. One long muscle, the snake writhed and coiled as if trying to choke itself. Eggs began to spew uncontrollably from the ventral orifice. Deposited exposed to the pitiless, blistering sunlight, they soon dried out, the desiccated life within never to see the light of day.

But for the most part the Drounge killed far less than usual, caused no havoc, induced no mass destruction. Apart from the few isolated encounters with weed and reptile, it lurched onward, enjoying an unusual period of grace and isolation. For a change, the only pain in its vicinity was its own.

It came eventually to a region of strange rock formations, peculiar spires and precipitates that contained the aspect but not the actuality of life. Composed entirely of inanimate minerals, they were immune and indifferent to the Drounge's presence. To its left rose a range of high mountains, their peaks ascending toward the clouds. Both would entail a detour, a delay in the march that knew no end, and to which the Drounge was wholly committed despite its lack of a purpose.

But between massif and hillocks lay an open plain, rising slightly as it approached the first foothills. It was almost perfectly flat, unadorned by plant life and devoid of rocky impediments. Offering an unobstructed route north, it was the path and direction the Drounge chose.

How long it had toiled forward over the arid plain before it once more encountered life it did not know. Time had no meaning for it, day being no different from night, summer accompanying the same suffering as winter. What life was doing in that place of desolation the Drounge could not imagine. It did not matter. It kept moving forward, always advancing, compelled to alter its chosen course to avoid solid stone but nothing else.

In some deep, buried, half-hidden part of itself it screamed at the creatures to change direction, to move out of the way, to do something to avoid contact. Having no lips, no palate, no tongue and no mouth, it could not shout a warning. It could only hope. But as had ever been the case with the Drounge, hope was a mostly forgotten component of its existence. What mattered, what was important, was that it keep moving, advancing, progressing. Why, it did not know. "Why" was a concept it could not afford.

At first it thought it would miss the creatures. They were highly active, agile, and traveling across the plain perpendicularly to the Drounge's course. If it had slowed down, if they had slowed down, contact could have been avoided. But they showed no inclination to accelerate or moderate their pace, and the Drounge could not. Catastrophe accompanied the Drounge the way remoras shadowed a shark.

Even so, a sliver of apathetic hope remained as it slid past first one, then another of the energetic vertebrates without making contact. They were an odd lot, the Drounge thought sluggishly. Paradoxical at best, mismatched at worst. A third member of the party trooped past without brushing against it or glancing in its lurching, pitching direction.

And then the fourth hesitated, reaching out as if feeling of the air in front of it, and grabbed a protruding wad of the Drounge's putrefying flesh just above one oculus.

Corruption spurted from the Drounge's fragile epidermis, surging forward to coagulate around the creature's fingers and wrist. Its eyes bugged and it gasped in agony as the relic residue of a thousand diseases and pestilences, of a million tumors and ulcerations, shot briefly through its flesh. Cinched by solidifying putridity to the left side of the Drounge, the luckless biped found itself dragged helplessly forward.

This was an unusual but not unprecedented occurrence. The Drounge knew exactly what would happen. Attached to its humping, gelatinous body, the trapped creature would find itself hauled along until the timeless poisons in the Drounge's system began to affect it the same way they affected every living thing. It would regain its freedom only when its pinioned limb rotted off at the wrist. Then the rest of the body would atrophy and die, most likely rotted away from within by the extreme contact it had made with the Drounge.

Instead of fleeing at the highest speed of which they were capable, the unfortunate's companions whirled and returned, rushing to catch up to him. Rushing to their own deaths, the Drounge reflected. No matter, no shame, no difference. It continued on its way, oblivious to their futile and soon-to-be-fatal efforts. Make contact with their friend or with it, and they too would die. Such had been the affliction of the Drounge's existence, and such would it always be.

Two of them stumbled and dodged about as if no longer in control of their own bodies. They were trying to react to something they could not see. Only the third now stared directly at the indefatigably advancing Drounge, peering into its seeping, pustulant optics, plainly sensible not only of its presence but of its bearing and appearance. Recognition, the Drounge knew, meant nothing. A minuscule part of it hoped the creature would keep its distance. The greater part of it was indifferent. After having induced tens of thousands of deaths, one or two more were of less significance to it than raindrops were to the sea.

At first it thought that the aware creature was digging into its own back, a pain the Drounge could have empathized with. Then it saw that the biped's own flesh remained inviolate. It was reaching into an artificial object that relied for motility on its organic host. Still avoiding contact with the advancing Drounge while making loud vocalizations to its companions, it withdrew from the sizable, lumpy object one that was smaller still.

Unlike the article that had given it birth, this small sac of treated and cured vacular material fit comfortably in its owner's palm. It had the shape of an onion, many thousands of which the Drounge had killed during its passage through formerly lush farmlands far, far to the south. Removing the tapered end of the sac, the vigorous biped proceeded to squeeze the bulb shape slightly. A small bit of thick, viscous paste oozed from the interior. Pale pink in color, it smelled sharply of rain-swept willow and other growing things.

Pacing the Drounge, the creature reached out and dabbed the bit of sticky mucilage on the spot where its companion's limb had become adhered. For a while nothing happened. The biped continued to trot alongside the lacerated flank of the Drounge, uttering comforting vocalizations to its entrapped friend, while the rest of its companions kept their distance.

Then something touched the Drounge.

This in itself was a most remarkable happenstance. Nothing touched the Drounge. It was the one that did all the touching; the imparting of death, the conveyance of misery, the transmission of suffering. So astonishing was the sensation that for the first time in living memory it reduced its habitual gait, slowing slightly the better to focus on what had occurred while simultaneously trying to analyze it.

It was not pain. Supreme among all living things on the subject of affliction, the Drounge was intimately familiar with agony in every conceivable, possible variance and permutation. This was something else. Something new and extraordinary. Unable to understand what had taken place, even in the abstract, it could only continue on its way, its direction and purpose temporarily muted but not swayed.

Instead of fading away, the phenomenon expanded its influence, until a portion of the Drounge the size of a pillow was fully involved. Within this segregated section of self, unprecedented processes were at work. Never having in its entire existence encountered or experienced anything like it before, the Drounge was at a loss to give a name to what was happening. It was not frightened. That which bears the burden of annihilation does not fear. But it was puzzled, if not a little confused.

Part of it, albeit a very small part, was changing. Metamorphosing in a most matchless and extreme fashion. It took place so rapidly that the Drounge was unable to react, nor did it quite know how to do so. Some sort of response seemed called for, but it could not begin to know exactly what.

The portion of itself that had engaged the creature foolish enough to initiate physical contact withdrew. Freed, the unfortunate dropped away from the Drounge's flank, falling to the ground while clutching its formerly impacted upper member. By now that limb should have been diseased beyond recognition, should be little more than a stick upon which a multitude of afflictions had worked their foul dissipation. Moreover, the general infection that was the Drounge ought to have spread to and throughout the creature's entire slight, vulnerable body, reducing it to a corrupted mass of dead and decaying tissue.

Nothing of the sort had happened. With the application of the soft paste, all that the Drounge had inflicted had been countered. The individual limb as well as the rest of its owner had been miraculously restored to health. Climbing to its feet, the smaller biped held its formerly impacted appendage and stared down its length as if examining an unexpected apparition. It manifested no evidence of damage and its expression was absent of anguish.

To the Drounge this amounted to nothing more than an incident. A striking incident, to be sure. One without precedent. But in the long lexicon of its existence merely a footnote, a quip of fate, a momentary interruption in its everlasting painful passage through reality. The quartet of creatures whose path it had ephemerally encountered fell behind; their identities unknown, their insignificant purposes in life restored. The spot on its side where the second biped had daubed the bit of odd ointment tingled, but that was all. No harm had come to the Drounge. How could anything injure that which carried upon and within itself all the world's hurt?

A small flurry of movement caused it to look back, a gesture that required an effort no less painful than simply moving forward. It could not believe what it was seeing. Apparently indifferent to the damage that had almost been done to its friend, the taller of the two bipeds with which the Drounge had experienced contact was running. Not away from the northward path as would have been sensible, but directly toward the methodically advancing, only intermittently visible organism. The absurd, demented creature was chasing *after* the Drounge instead of racing at maximum speed in the opposite direction!

Self-evidently it was deranged. What could unsettle a sentient being so, the Drounge could not imagine. It did not increase its pace, nor did it slow down. Whatever mad, lunatic purpose motivated the biped was beyond the Drounge's ability to affect or understand. It did not matter. In the scheme of things, it made no difference whether the crazed creature lived or died.

It halted abruptly before reaching the stoically retreating Drounge. That, at least, was a rational decision. Perhaps the creature, momentarily maddened, had suddenly come back to its senses. One of its upper, absurdly spindly limbs was upraised. As the Drounge ignored it, the creature brought this member forward. Propelled through the air by this slight physical action, something flew from the end of the appendage. Idly, the Drounge identified it as the onion-shaped object the creature had been carrying earlier.

The bulb-shape struck the Drounge in the middle of its back. Humping implacably forward, it treated the barely perceptible impact with the same indifference it treated all such contacts. Whenever something touched it, it was invariably the other that suffered.

On impact, the bulb burst, spilling its contents. The thick, pale unguent spread slowly across the curving bulk of the Drounge. Still its presence was ignored.

Until it started to sink in.

The tingling sensation the Drounge had heretofore experienced only at one small place on its left side started to penetrate deeply. It was not unpleasant. On the contrary, the Drounge would have found it pleasurable had it possessed a means for describing such a sensation. In the absence of applicable referents it could only struggle with physical feelings that were entirely new. As a novelty, the effects of the expanding emollient were exhilarating. They could not last, of course. Within moments they would be subsumed within and overwhelmed by the raging internal dissipation and disease that constituted the Drounge's customary state of existence.

Proceeding with its advance, the Drounge waited for this to happen. It did not. Instead, the effects of the free-flowing, penetrating balm continued to spread. A strange feeling came over the Drounge, quite unlike anything it had ever felt before. It was as if its whole body had been caught up in something as wonderful as it was unexpected, though it possessed no more referents for wonderful than it did for pleasurable. It was changing.

For the first time in millennia, the Drounge stopped.

The singular tingling sensation now dominated every corner of its being, penetrating to the farthest reaches of self, replacing eternal agony and perpetual discomfort with—something else. This was not a small thing; *not* an incident, *not* an insignificant transient episode. Its very shape was changing, twisting and buckling with neoteric forces it did not understand. Could not understand, because it had no experience of them.

With a last convulsive, wrenching sensation of dislocation, the unforeseen metamorphosis achieved final resolution. The Drounge stood as before, inviolate and untouched. Only, something was different. It took even the Drounge a moment to realize what that was.

It was no longer in pain.

The absence of agony was so extraordinary a sensation that the Drounge was momentarily paralyzed. It was all gone, all of it—all the suffering, all the disease and decay, all the everlasting affliction that had combined to comprise its physical and mental existence. In its place was something the Drounge could not put a name to: a calmness and tranquillity that were shocking in their unfamiliarity. And something else.

For not only had it changed internally, its appearance was radically altered as well. With a new inner individuality had come a new shell, a fresh and unspoiled outer self, courtesy of the tingling unguent that had affected a transformation far beyond what even its wielder could have envisioned.

Elation swept through the Drounge at its unexpected epiphany. Never having felt itself trapped, it hardly knew how to react to being free. Exhilaration was a sensation with which it had never before had to come to terms. Uncertain, tentative, it could only try.

As the tiny cluster of astonished, fragile creatures it had come close to killing looked on in wonder, the enormous butterfly that had materialized before their eyes spread six-foot wings of prismatic emerald and opalescent crimson and rose from the bleached desert floor, haltingly at first but with increasing confidence, into a cloudless and welcoming clear blue sky.

XX

Let me have another look at that hand."

Simna wordlessly raised the arm by which he had been attached to the lumbering horror. Rotting flesh had been miraculously renewed, nerves sutured, skin regrown, the bleeding stopped. With the impossible butterfly vanishing into the distance and his restored limb hanging healthy and normal from the end of his shoulder, his attention kept switching back and forth between wonders.

"By Gravulia, what—what was it?" he mumbled as his rangy companion critically inspected first palm and then individual fingers. "One minute I could see it clearly and the next, it wasn't there and something beautiful was."

Ehomba replied without looking up from his examination. "Disease is like that."

The swordsman blinked. The hallucinatory, spectacular butterfly was gone now, swallowed up by the sky and imagination, leaving him to contemplate his right hand. Moments ago it had been a putrefying, decaying ruin. Now it was restored. A small whitish scar, souvenir of a fight in a chieftain's hut on a distant steppe, had vanished from his index finger together with the more recent corruption.

"So it was a disease of some kind?"

"Not a disease. Disease itself, or some pitiful entity that it had become attached to. I am not really sure what it was, Simna. But there was no mistaking its effects. Even as I ran to help you I felt myself starting to grow weak and uneasy. If I had not been able to deal with it we might well all have died."

Feeling none too energetic himself after the mephitic encounter, the swordsman sat down on a rock. Nearby, Hunkapa Aub was studying the increasingly steep slopes that lay before them. The black litah was sunning itself on the brackish ground.

"The butterfly—" Simna looked up sharply. "Hoy, I remember you putting something on my hand! It set me free."

Ehomba nodded. "A salve prepared for me by Meruba. I was told that it was useful for dealing with cuts and scrapes, burns and punctures. When I saw what had caught ahold of you it was all I could think of to use." He gestured downward. "It cured your arm."

Holding his right hand in his left while gently rubbing it, Simna nodded gratefully. "My arm, yes, but that doesn't explain the butterfly." He shuddered once. "What I saw first, when it was visible to me, was no butterfly."

"No," the herdsman agreed solemnly. He smiled as he reminisced. "Meruba is known for her salves. It is said that, if applied in sufficient strength, they can cure anything. I used all that she gave me." Turning his head, his braids bouncing slightly against his neck, he gazed thoughtfully at the northern horizon. "Whatever it was that had hold of you, I think we healed it."

"Should've killed it," the swordsman grumbled. Releasing his hand, he started to shake it sharply.

"Hurt?" Ehomba looked suddenly concerned.

"Hoy, it throbs like my head the morning after a three-day binge! But it's nothing I can't handle, bruther." Rising from his seat, he straightened his pack on his back. Some of the straps had become loosened while he was being dragged along by the revolting apparition. "It's too damn hot here." He nodded briskly in the direction of the foothills and the rocky crags they fronted. "Let's find ourselves some cool shade and fresh water."

The ascent into the Curridgian Mountains proved arduous, but less so than their trek into the Hrugars. Deep gorges allowed them to avoid the need to scale the highest peaks, providing a natural approach to the towering escarpment. Where there was snow there was runoff, and the same canyons that guided them westward soon boasted of swiftly running streams and even small rivers. Ehomba was grateful they would not have to worry any longer about water. As they climbed higher the air grew cooler. The awful heat of the Tortured Lands receded until it was no more than a disagreeable memory.

Pines and redwoods, firs and kauris soon replaced weedy grasses and small-leaved brush, until they once again found themselves traipsing through forest. Ehomba and Simna were rejuvenated by the fresh air and increased humidity, while Ahlitah was largely indifferent. But Hunkapa

Aub was positively exhilarated. Of them all, he, with his heavy, shaggy coat, had suffered the most by far from the unrelenting heat they had left behind and below.

He even welcomed the mist that settled in around them as they climbed a slope luxuriant with wildflowers, their petals splashed with extravagant shades of scarlet and teal and lemon yellow. As the moist haze thickened, the blossoms took on an air of unreality, their variegated faces staring brazenly at the shrouded sun, kaleidoscopic denizens of a languid dream.

Soon the mist had congealed to the point where even the black litah was hard pressed to espy a route upward, and they were reduced to following the stream that had cut the canyon. Though the humid air was still temperate and the climbing not difficult, Ehomba found himself glancing around apprehensively. Noting his friend's unease, Simna edged close.

"Hoy, long bruther, something's troubling you." The swordsman strove, without much success, to penetrate the haze. "You see something?"

"No, it is not that, Simna." As the herdsman licked his lips he tried not to suck in any of the prevailing moisture. "I was—I am—trying to remember something." Raising a hand, he gestured imprecisely. "It is this fog."

Simna took a look around, then shrugged indifferently. "It's fog. Accursedly thick fog, but just fog. So what?"

"I remember it."

The swordsman couldn't help himself: He laughed without thinking. "Hoy, Etjole, a man remembers the deaths he escapes and the lovers he's had. He remembers long, restful mornings and nights awash in celebration. He *doesn't* remember fog."

Ehomba ignored his friend's good-natured chiding. There was something not in the air, but about it. A quality that stirred a particular memory. He struggled to recall it. Perhaps Simna was right. What was fog, after all, but droplets of moisture that hung in the air, too tired to rise as cloud, too lazy to fall as rain? How could anyone "remember" something so transient and ordinary?

Then he did. It was not just a fog, but *the* fog. The one that had tried to hold him back, the one that had attempted to enshroud and restrain him from ever beginning on this journey. It was the fog he had encountered not long after first leaving the village, so seemingly long ago. Failing to slow him then, it had come after him, abandoning its ocean home to confront him here, in these distant and foreign highlands.

Close by, the lumbering, mist-veiled mountain that was Hunkapa Aub called out uncertainly.

"Etjole, Hunkapa can't move. Hunkapa's legs not working."

A frustrated snarl sounded from just in front of the herdsman. Despite its great strength, the black litah too was finding progress suddenly difficult. Massive paws clawed at the sodden atmosphere in a futile attempt to advance.

The two humans were not immune to this sudden hindrance. Ignoring Simna's ensuing eruption of profanity, Ehomba concentrated on trying to take another step uphill. The sensation was akin to trying to walk through thin mud. It did not hold him back so much as slow him down to an unacceptable degree. At this rate they would be years getting through the mountains. Lifting his other leg, he struggled to take another stride. The result was the same. It was as if he had been wrapped in a waterlogged sheet not heavy enough to stop him, but sufficient to slow him dangerously.

Leaning forward, he put his weight into his next attempt. The gummy damp continued to cling to him, to drag him down and hold him back. Wanting to make certain that he had truly identified their adversary, he scanned every foot of the flower-laden meadow he could see, but with his range of vision reduced to a few feet, he was not able to make out any visible nemesis. For him to be able to see an enemy clearly in the fog, it would have to be right on top of him.

Which is when he was convinced once and for all that that was exactly the case.

"*Go baaaackk. . . .*" It was an auricular specter, a verbal shadow, a ghost of a voice, as though wind had momentarily been manipulated and palpitated to form a word in the same ponderous manner as a baker kneads heavy dough.

The unexpected voice induced him to take one last look around, but there was nothing else to see; nothing but flowers and field and fog. Determined, he tried to push on, only to experience the same sensation of being slowed down and held back. He was covering ground, but trying to force his legs forward through the persistent impediment would soon exhaust him completely.

"*Go . . . baaackk. . . .*" the sepulchral voice moaned. It seemed to come not from one particular place but from all around him. Which made sense, since that which was restraining him *was* all around him. But how to fight it? A man with a knife he would have known how to deal with immediately.

He searched in vain for a face, for eyes or a mouth, for something to focus on. There wasn't anything. There was only the fog, evanescent and everywhere present. "Why should I?" he asked guardedly, addressing his query to the damp, gently swirling mist.

The vaporous moan seemed to gather the slightest bit of additional strength from his reply. "Go back," it intoned in a dark whisper. "Go home." Airborne droplets of cool water eddied before his face. "It is all here, waiting for you. I have seen it. Disaster, complete and entire. You are doomed to unremitting misery, your quest to failure, the rest of your life to cold emptiness. Unless you end this now. Go home, back to your village and to your family. Before it is too late. Before you die."

This wouldn't do, he decided. Twice before, he had been compelled to listen to those exact same words—first from a seeress, then from a dog. Arms upraised in a gesture of defiance, he turned a slow circle and challenged the sky.

"A beauty gave me that augury, and then a witch. I did not heed *their* warnings, and I certainly will not heed this one!"

Nearby, his friend Simna ventured to comment hesitantly. "Etjole, you're arguing with the weather. That's a quarrel any man is bound to lose."

Ehomba begged to differ, but silently. Question he would, even the weather if need be, or he and his companions might never break free of the malicious atmosphere. They could not stay, and he would not turn back. Choosing, he reached back over his shoulder and drew the sky-metal sword Otjihanja had made for him. Crystallized iron caught the few isolated flashes of light that managed to penetrate the haze and broke them into sparks.

With his arm restrained by the cloying, clinging mist, he could not slash and cut with his usual ease, but he hacked away at the surrounding fog with as much strength and determination as he could muster. Results were immediate.

Bits and pieces of fog, cut off from the rest of the main body by the otherworldly blade, fell to the earth. Each squirmed glutinously across the ground as if seeking to rejoin the rest of the hovering gray mass, before finally falling motionless and evaporating. A louder moan surrounded him: a malign breeze off the mountain slopes wending its way among the rocks—or something else. He found himself wondering if fog could feel pain. It did not matter. There was work to be done, and he was the only one who could do it.

Patiently, wielding the sword with skill and care, he began to excavate a clear space for himself within the enveloping mist. As soon as it was large enough and his arms and legs were free, he cut his way over to Simna and liberated the swordsman. Hunkapa Aub and Ahlitah were next.

"Everyone all right?" he inquired. Looking at him, it was impossible to tell if the water pouring off his face and arms was perspiration or amputated mist. Assured that they had suffered nothing more than fatigue in their own efforts to free themselves, he turned and started work on chopping a path forward. Instead of wielding a machete against a wall of intervening jungle, or a shovel against a rampart of packed earth, he hacked away with something that was not of the Earth at that which was little more than nothing.

As he toiled, tendrils of fog strained to clutch at him afresh, reaching out with quivering slivers of damp gray for his arms and legs. He slashed away mercilessly, ignoring them as they fell among the flowers and grass, trampling the condensed moisture beneath his sandals. No more maybe-almost words teased his ears, but the moaning continued without pause. The fog did not bleed beneath his blade—it simply asserted its mastery of melancholy as it continued to do its utmost to detain him.

A man used to dealing daily with cattle and children was not about to have his progress denied by a recalcitrant mist. A tunnel appeared behind Ehomba and his friends as he pressed forward, a cylindrical tube in the fog into which the occasional grateful, sodden insect or arthropod found its way.

"Get off me!" he would shout from time to time. "Leave me be! I am near to my destination and will not be denied here. No mere weather, no matter how tenacious, is going to stop me!"

There was no reply. Only the continuous moaning, and the persistent, repetitious attempts to restrain his arms and legs. Occasionally he was forced to pause and hack clutching tentacles of moisture from the limbs of his friends. But for the most part, now that they once more had room in which to move, they were able to keep themselves relatively mist free.

He hewed his way forward for more than an hour. If the retentive, obstinate fog thought it could outwait him, or discourage him, it was more than wrong. It had never encountered anyone like Etjole Ehomba, whose arms rose and fell methodically, mechanically, as he cut his way forward, dead dew dripping like transparent blood from his blade of crystallized nickel-iron.

Then, realizing that all its efforts were doomed to failure, the fog began to dissipate. Vast quantities of it drew back, rising upward in the direction of the cold mountain peaks from which it drew sustenance, while isolated pockets fled downslope to evaporate. A few persistent tendrils continued to clutch at the arms and shoulders of the determined travelers, but these were soon cut away. As they ascended through the uppermost reaches of the fog bank, the sun returned, warming their damp bodies. The clinging fog had soaked Ehomba to the skin, but in the thin air the unobstructed sun made quick work of the lingering moisture.

A last gob of thick mist trailed him at a distance, darting and hiding behind one rocky outcropping after another. Used to watching for prowling predators while tending to the village herds, he kept track of it for a while, wondering at its intent. Perhaps it planned to drift down upon him when next he slept, covering his face, restraining not his arms and legs this time but his heart and lungs. He would not give it the chance.

Whirling, he rushed past a startled Simna to challenge the compacted cloud. Finding itself discovered, it immediately attempted to flee upward. The herdsman ran it down, catching up to it and dispatching it with his blade. Only the faintest hint of a moan rose from the wad of condensation as the meteoric sword-edge cut through its center, scattering droplets and inducing the rest of the gray blob to suicide beneath the unyielding rays of the morning sun.

Satisfied that he was no longer a source of interest to the vanished fog, or to any of its component parts, Ehomba sheathed the weapon and resumed his pace. Grass and soil in equal measure slid away beneath his sandals.

Free of the constraining, intemperate mist, they once again began to make good time. They had to. There was an obligation to fulfill, and a family and herd anxiously awaiting his return.

If anything else attempted to stop or slow them, Ehomba found himself musing, he hoped it would do so more openly and with some substance. He had not enjoyed fighting the fog. Instead of anger, or evil, there had been about it only an ineffable sadness, and he had found no satisfaction in slaying what was after all little more than a haunting melancholy.

After all, it had only, to its unfathomable, unknowable way of thinking, been trying to help him.

XXI

1t was not long after they had left the inimical fog behind that they encountered the procession of humans and apes. Trudging along a trail that crossed the river gorge from north to south, the procession was heavily laden with baggage, from household goods dangling from stout poles supported by two or more individuals, to blanket-wrapped infants riding on the backs of females.

They shied in terror at the sight of Ahlitah and Hunkapa Aub, and Ehomba had to hasten to reassure them. Their accent was thick and heavy, but with repetition and gestures each side managed to make itself understood. These were poor folk, the herdsman decided, simple and unsophisticated. Judging from the expressions they wore, their burdens were more than physical.

"Ehl-Larimar?" he asked of several individuals. After a number of inquiries a long-faced macaque clad in heavy overcoat and cap finally responded. Raising its long arm, it pointed westward up the canyon and nodded.

"Good. Thank you." As Ehomba started past him, the ape reached out and grabbed his arm. Simna's hand went immediately to the hilt of his sword, while among the column there was an anxious stirring. Primate hands fumbled for axes and clubs. Ahlitah growled low in his throat, his claws seeking purchase on the hard ground.

Ehomba hastened to calm his companions. "It is all right. He is not hurting me." Glancing down, he saw that the macaque's face was fraught with concern, not animosity. "What is wrong, my long-tailed friend?"

It was uncertain if the ape comprehended the herdsman's words, but he certainly understood his tone. Releasing his grasp, he raised a spindly arm and jabbed a finger violently upcanyon. "Khorixas, Khorixas!"

"Hoy, what's a Khorixas?" Simna's hand had slid away from his sword, but his fingers remained loose and easy in its vicinity. "Maybe an outlying town this side of Ehl-Larimar itself?"

"Possibly." Smiling reassuringly, Ehomba stepped away from the visibly agitated macaque and retreated slowly, taking one careful step at a time. "It is all right. My friends and I can take care of ourselves." Even as he tried to explain he wondered if the ape understood any of what he was saying: These people spoke a language different from that of old Gomo and the People of the Trees.

Arm rigid and still pointing westward, the aged macaque rumbled "Khorixas!" one more time before lowering his hand. With a sad-eyed shrug, he turned and rejoined his comrades. When he paused briefly for a last look back at the travelers, it was to shake his head dolefully from side to side.

"Grizzled old fella must not care much for this Khorixas, whatever it is." Striding confidently forward, Simna kept a careful watch on the steep slopes that walled them in. Nothing he saw or heard as they continued to hike upward led him to believe they might be walking into some kind of ambush, or a trap. Silhouetted against the scudding clouds, a few dragonets and condors soared on the updrafts. Marmosets and pacas scampered over the boulders and talus in search of nuts and berries. Thanks to the deep canyon, the travelers' line of march remained well below the tree line. The temperature dropped at night, but not precipitously so. When their blankets proved inadequate to the task of warding off the cold, Ehomba and Simna simply moved their bedding closer to the radiant bulks of Hunkapa Aub and the black litah.

They had just crossed the crest of the Curridgians, discernable by the fact that all streams now flowed westward instead of to the east, when they heard the first roll of thunder.

"Hunkapa no see clouds, no see storm." The hirsute hulk had his head tilted back while he squinted at the sky.

"It does not sound like that kind of thunder." Holding fast to his spear, Ehomba strode along in front, maintaining the same steady pace as always.

Simna ibn Sind cocked his head sideways as he regarded his tall companion. "There's more than one kind?"

The herdsman smiled down at him. "Many kinds. I myself have been trained to identify dozens of different varieties."

"Hoy then, if it's not a far-off storm clearing its throat that we're hearing, then what is it?"

"I do not know." A brilliant black-and-green spotted beetle landed on the herdsman's shirt, hitching a ride. Ehomba admired its glossy carapace and let it be.

"I thought you said you knew dozens of kinds of thunder?"

"I do." Ehomba's smile thinned. "But this one I do not recognize."

Whatever its source, it grew louder as they began to start downward. Its measured, treading rhythm was abnormal, suggesting an origin that was anything but natural. Yet the percussive volume was too loud to originate with anything man-made.

Only when they came around a cliff and entered a small alpine valley did they see that both of their assumptions were correct.

It had not been much of a village to begin with, and now it was in the process of being reduced to nothing at all. The stately thunder they had been hearing was caused by the concussion of hammer against stone. The stones ranged in size from small boulders to chinkers light enough for a child to move from place to place. The head of the hammer, on the very much larger other hand, was bigger than Ehomba.

It was being wielded by a giant—the first giant the herdsman had ever seen. The village elders knew many tales of giants, with which they often regaled their attentive, wide-eyed children. While growing up, Ehomba and his friends had listened to fanciful fables of one-eyed giants and hunchbacked giants, of giants with teeth like barracuda and giants lacking any teeth at all who sucked up their victims through straws made of hollow tree trunks. There were giants that swam in the deep green sea (but none that flew), and giants who lived in the densest jungles and never showed themselves (but some that were too big to hide).

There were ugly giants and uglier giants, giants who cooked their victims in a casserole of palm oil and sago pastry, and giants who simply swallowed them whole. Oura had once told of a vegetarian giant, and of another who was shunned by all others of his kind for washing his hair. Sometimes there seemed to be as many different kinds of giants as there were storytellers among the Naumkib, and that meant there were a great many varieties of giant indeed.

The one that stood before them using its great hammer to demolish the village was neither as horrific in appearance as he might have been nor as good-natured. Shoulder-length red hair tumbled in tangled tresses down his back and the sides of his head. Long hairs sprouted from pointed ears that stuck through the raggedy locks, and he had orange eyes. From his splotchety, crooked nose hung a booger the size of a boulder. His teeth were surprisingly white, glaring out from the rest of a baggy visage that as a face was mostly a failure. Dark and dirty treelike arms protruded from the sleeves of a vest comprised of many sewn-together skins, not all of them overtly animal. His furry lower garments were similarly fashioned, and his sandals with their knee-high laces bespoke the crudest attempts at cobblery.

He was three times the size of Hunkapa Aub, and when he swung the heavy hammer with its leather-clad head, the peal of disintegrating rock reverberated down every one of the surrounding canyons and gorges. Sweat poured from his coarse countenance in great rivulets, and even at a distance his stink was profound.

"Hoy, now we know what happened to the village of Khorixas." Simna's expression was grim. Another reverberant *boooom* echoed as the back wall of what had once been a fine two-story house came crashing down. "We also know why those hard-up folk we met a while back were migrating across the crest with their kids and all their possessions."

"We do not know anything." Ehomba was keeping one eye on the giant while assessing possible alternate routes with the other. The village lay directly athwart the most direct and easiest route westward and downslope. "We will go around," he announced resignedly. He started to turn away.

Hand on sword hilt, Simna all but jumped in front of him. "Hoy, long bruther, we have a chance to right a wrong here!" He nodded sharply in the direction of the crumbling village. "Whatever transpired between those poor wretches and this brute couldn't possibly justify the total ruination of their homes." He grinned knowingly. "Why, this great blundering ogre is *nothing* compared to the dangers you and I have dealt with these past months! Watch him work. See how slow he is, how ungainly his movements? We should teach him a lesson about picking on those smaller and weaker than himself and send him on his way. It will also earn us the undying gratitude of those simple mountain folk." His expression was eager. "What say you?"

Ehomba replied in his usual unshakable, even tone. "I do not need their gratitude, undying or otherwise." He nodded leftward, to where the giant was maintaining his steady rate of destruction. "Nor am I in the business of teaching lessons to rampaging giants or anyone else. My obligation draws me westward, to a destination that is, at long last, within reach if not sight." Supporting himself partially with his spear, he took a step to his right. "We will go around."

A disbelieving Simna's expression darkened. "I wouldn't have thought you a coward, Etjole."

The herdsman was not moved. "Or a fool either, I hope." Walking past the swordsman, Ehomba started up a narrow side canyon that led, if not due west, at only a modest inclination northward. Without a word between them, Hunkapa Aub and Ahlitah followed.

With his eyes Simna implored the others as they trooped past. When he found himself contemplating the last of the big cat's tail, he abruptly drew his sword. Waving it over his head and howling a defiant war cry, he spun and charged directly down toward the village and its ponderous, methodical enemy.

"Simna, no!" Ehomba's entreaties were ignored. Gritting his teeth, he started after his friend, hurdling grass and small rocks with long, lithe strides, holding his spear parallel to the ground beside him. Exchanging a glance, Hunkapa Aub and the black litah followed—at a sensible and leisurely pace.

Simna had already dashed in behind the giant to take a swipe at his ankles. The blow missed the main tendon but left a significant gash in the side of the left foot. Letting out a howl, the giant turned and brought his enormous hammer around in a sweeping, descending arc that would have smashed every bone in the swordsman's body—if he had remained standing where it was aimed. Quick as a jerboa, he'd darted out of its way. The wind of its passing ruffled his hair.

"Hoy, you great towheaded sack of pig piss! It's a little different when we fight back, isn't it? Come on, come on!" He proceeded to taunt the giant with gestures as well as words. "Surely you can handle one tiny fella like me!"

Grimacing, the giant brought an enormous foot up and stamped down, only to find that once again Simna ibn Sind had skipped nimbly out of the way. Not by the margin the swordsman had intended, however. The giant was clumsy, it was true, but he was not as slow as Simna had first supposed. His defiant smirk began to develop a nervous twitch.

Ehomba arrived with sword in hand. He was furious, but not at the giant.

"What do you think you are doing?" he snapped at his imprudently energetic friend.

"Saving what's left of a village for the good of its innocent inhabitants." Panting, Simna stood close to the herdsman. "You pick your noble causes, I'll pick mine."

"There is nothing noble in a senseless death." Ehomba noted that the giant was watching them warily, trying to determine the orientation of its next blow.

"I don't plan on dying."

"No one does, but it happens just the same." Taking a deep breath, Ehomba addressed the giant. No matter who, or what, his adversary, he firmly believed in trying reason before the sword. "Greetings, imposing one! Why are you destroying the village Khorixas?"

Red eyebrows dense and tangled as berry thickets drew together.

"What 'village' Khorixas? There is no village by that name." Callused and scored, a free hand indicated the ruins among which the oversized speaker was standing. "This miserable blot on the earth is Feo-Nottoa." The hand rose to smack sonorously against the broad chest. "*I* am the Berserker Khorixas!" The great hammer started to rise threateningly. "You should know the name of the one who is about to kill you."

"Why kill us?" Ehomba wondered aloud. "Why destroy this simple town?"

The head of the hammer lowered slightly, hovering. "I am a Berserker, and this is what Berserkers do." White teeth showed unpleasantly. "I am happy to be a Berserker. I like to destroy, and mangle, and exterminate. If I am fortunate, before I expire I will be able to eradicate every town and village in the southern part of the Curridgians." With his free hand he wiped his massive brow. "Annihilation, it is hard work."

"Hoy, it stops here!" Sneering, Simna gestured at his tall, laconic companion. "This is Etjole Ehomba of the Naumkib. Master of magic and all the necromantic arts, conjurer supreme, wizard of wizards, defender of the enfeebled and all who are preyed upon by bullies and ruffians!"

"I am not a bully," the Berserker Khorixas countered stiffly. "I am a professional." He squinted down at the two men. "And he doesn't look like much to me."

"Leave now." Simna took a challenging step forward. "Depart, flee, run away, before you are reduced to oblivion or slaughtered where you stand!"

"I'll take my chances," the Berserker Khorixas declared confidently, "but first I will make a paste of your bones to spread upon my bread for tomorrow morning's breakfast."

Simna stood his ground—making certain it was proximate to Ehomba's. As the stern-faced herdsman unsheathed the sky-metal sword and prepared to defend the two of them, the Berserker could be seen fumbling with the head of the majestic mallet. The coarse cord that secured the protective leather cover was untied and the tough brown casing removed. Exposed to the clear mountain air, the silver-gray hammerhead gleamed metallically. Extensive crystalline striations caught the sunlight and held it. The swordsman's jaw dropped.

The colossal hammer of the Berserker Khorixas was forged of the same sky metal as Etjole Ehomba's ensorcelled sword. And there was a lot more of it.

Without preamble or warning from its owner, it was promptly brought around in a vast, sweeping arc, its passage through the clear mountain air generating a deep, reverberant humming. Simna leaped one way and Ehomba the other. The hammerhead struck the ground between them, ringing all the way to the center of the Earth and setting up subtle vibrations in the lush mudcress fields of Pridon on the opposite side. It was a blow that would have crushed lesser men to a damp pulp—or men less attuned to the behavior of creatures such as giants.

Despite the fact that his heart had sunk somewhere to the vicinity of his ankles at the sight of the unveiled hammer, Simna did not flee. Having precipitated the confrontation, against Ehomba's wishes, he was honor-bound to stay and fight. But not to stand and fight. That way lay rapid demise. Instead, he darted and dodged, making sure first of the location and direction of that deadly maul before dashing in close to strike at the giant's legs with his own sword. His exceptional agility and skill allowed him to deliver several stabs and cuts, but the wounds were shallow and only succeeded in further enraging the already incensed Berserker.

From a nearby slope, the black litah and Hunkapa Aub observed the battle. "Hunkapa not want Etjole to die," the shaggy hulk commented mournfully. "Hunkapa go and help!"

"You'll only get in the way." Ahlitah moved to intercept his ineloquent companion. "Leave it to the herdsman. Many's the time I've seen him extract himself from desperate situations." Fiery yellow eyes surveyed the arena of conflict. "He'll do the same here."

"And if he not?" Hunkapa Aub observed the flow of battle dubiously.

"Then he will die, and that prattling monkey with him. And I will try to find my way back to the veldt, and you to your mountains, and the sun will set tonight and rise tomorrow and the world take not the slightest notice of his strivings or ours. That is how it has always been and that is how it will always be." A muted snarl sent every small rodent within hearing scurrying for their burrows.

"Ehomba will find a way to win, or he will not. If he cannot defeat the giant, it's certain you can't."

"You could help too," Hunkapa Aub pointed out guilelessly.

"I have sworn to support him." The majestic ebony cat hesitated. "But I'd be in the way as well. There is a time to stalk, a time to pounce—and a time to wait. I think this is a time to wait. If you're sensible, you'll do the same."

So Ahlitah and Hunkapa held back and watched. Hammer blow after hammer blow descended, cleaving the air with monstrous streaks of its etched metal head. Each time, its intended targets jumped or twisted out of the way. But avoidance, too, demands effort, and both men were growing tired.

"Do something, Etjole!" Breathing harder and faster than was reassuring, Simna ibn Sind wielded his sword as he yelled to his companion. "Blow him into a mountain, bring down a piece of sky on his head!" Even as he shouted this advice, the increasingly desperate swordsman knew he was suggesting the impractical. With he and Ehomba forced to dodge as often as they were, any wind the herdsman called up was as likely to blow them off the mountain as it was the giant, while anything falling from the heavens would smash into the ruins of the village with an unearthly indifference to whoever happened to be standing there.

Astoundingly, instead of striking at the Berserker, instead of cutting at his legs and feet and trying to bring him down, Ehomba was doing his utmost to taunt him further.

"Bruther, what are you doing?" Simna was badly confused. "The one thing we don't need to do is make him any madder!"

But the herdsman seemed not to hear his friend as again and again he darted dangerously close to the giant before skipping spryly out of his way.

"*Ai*, you doddering dolt, you clumsy buffoon! Is this the best you can do? I am smaller, but too quick for you. No wonder you beat up on houses. Buildings cannot run away, or they too would make you look silly and laugh at you!"

Infuriated, the Berserker swung the great hammer in swifter and swifter arcs, until the air howled and shrieked in the grip of the artificial storm created by its wake. Unlike the tiny humans who were tormenting him, he did not tire, but appeared to grow stronger and more determined with each swing. The hammerhead hummed, whistling through the air like the piece of burning sky Ehomba's sword had called down to annihilate the imperious Chlengguu. Soon it was a terrible silver-gray streak, a blur that obscured everything behind it. Not even a swordsman as skilled as the redoubtable Simna ibn Sind could avoid it forever.

There was nowhere to hide. The stone structures of doomed Feo-Nottoa were as cardboard beneath that irresistible chunk of sky metal. Even a cave, had one been close at hand, would have been an insufficient refuge, for in the hands of the Berserker Khorixas even a mountain could be pounded to rubble.

An exhausted, tiring Simna, lungs heaving and legs aching, was bemoaning his likely fate even as he cursed his rash impetuousness, when Ehomba suddenly darted forward at what appeared to be the absolutely worst possible moment. The swordsman screamed a hoarse warning, but his tall friend did not hear. Or he heard, and chose to ignore it. Simna froze as the hammer descended, describing an arc that looked certain to impact the charging herdsman fully.

At the last instant, Ehomba dodged. Not back, away from the falling hammerhead, nor forward as a wrestler might have done in an attempt to slip beneath his adversary's guard, but sideways. As he did so he ducked just enough, brought around his own weapon, and with both hands swung it as hard as he could, forward and up. To Simna's experienced eyes it looked like a futile gesture. The sword was bound to shatter against the much larger, infinitely heavier hammerhead.

It did not. Too fast even for the swordsman to see, the edge of the herdsman's blade struck the backside of the swooping hammer. In so doing it imparted to that tremendous swing all the additional momentum of which its master was capable. Impelled forward and upward by the force of its own rising on the backside of the swing and boosted by Ehomba's unexpected strike, instead of slowing down, the immense hammer continued to rise. Instinctively maintaining his grip, the startled Berserker Khorixas rose with it.

When he realized what was happening he contemplated letting go, even if it meant abandoning forever the incomparable tool. But by the time understanding penetrated that thick, unkempt skull, it was too late. The hammer had carried him too high. If he released his grip now he would fall long and far enough to break his neck, for even the spines of giants are made of flesh and bone.

So not only was he forced to maintain his grip, but he was compelled to strengthen it with the addition of his free hand. Berserker and hammer together, the one whistling and the other howling imprecations, rose into the cloud-free sky. Ehomba watched until giant and giant's weapon were a blot, then a dot, and finally a speck of indeterminate dust soaring over the southern horizon. Then he took a deep breath and started to shake.

"By Gowerben's footsteps, that's putting the arrogant assassin in his place!" A sweaty but elated Simna ibn Sind bounded down from the rock on which he had been standing and rushed to congratulate his companion. "Maybe it's as you say that you're no sorcerer, long bruther, but it's a master of unexpected gifts you are! I only wish that—"

The herdsman whirled on his friend with a fire in his eyes that for the barest, most intangible of instants exceeded that of the black litah. Rising and descending, his closed fist caught the swordsman flush on the side of the face. The report was loud enough to reach Hunkapa Aub and Ahlitah, who with the battle won were descending to rejoin their human companions.

Reflexively, Simna started to bring up his weapon even as he fell backward. Despite his shock, he caught himself halfway through the gesture. He landed hard on his thighs and backside. Not content with having delivered the blow, Ehomba strode forward until he was standing over the fallen swordsman. Glaring down, he shook a long finger in his friend's face. The hallucinatory blaze that had momentarily flared behind his eyes had vanished, but he was so furious that he trembled as he spoke.

"Never, ever, do anything like that again, Simna! Not in my presence or before my eyes, or I swear by all that the Naumkib respect and honor that I will abandon you to your infantile foolishness and let you perish!"

Stunned, Simna lay on the ground, gaping up at his enraged friend. From the first moment of their relationship there had been disagreements, debates, and disputations. But always words, words. Never blows. The only violence had been verbal. Clenching his teeth, he sprang to his feet, the bloodied sword dangling from his right hand. In an instant he was standing with head tilted slightly back, chest-to-chest with his companion, his unwavering gaze burning into that of the herdsman. Seeing this, Ahlitah growled and prepared to spring forward, but Hunkapa Aub reached down to put a massive hand on the big cat's rippling shoulder and restrain him.

The confrontation lasted only a moment, but to the tense pair of onlookers, one feline and the other only part human, it seemed the longest moment imaginable. Then Simna ibn Sind stepped back and, with slow deliberation, returned his reddened blade back to the scabbard on his back.

"You're a brave man, Etjole Ehomba. Brave and bold and maybe, just maybe, even wise. I've seen you do remarkable, astonishing things. But if you think that makes me afraid of you, you're wrong. Simna ibn Sind fears nothing living. Not soldiers, not giants, not even mystic and powerful sorcerers. And certainly not cattle farmers." Reaching up, he touched the place on his cheek where the herdsman's blow had landed. There would be a bruise there.

"I consider myself a fair and reasonable man, bruther. You don't want me to stand up for the evicted and downtrodden? Fine! I hereby relegate all my altruistic impulses to the bottom of my priorities for the duration of our partnership. In return, you'll keep your hands to yourself. I swear, I might allow one such blow to pass without redress, but I'll never let two."

Ehomba's voice had returned to normal. He looked away. "There is more at stake here, friend Simna, than your precious pride. Remember that I have a family I have not seen in far, far too long anxiously awaiting my return, and a home to go back to. You are burdened by no such responsibilities. You carry your home with you."

"Hoy, and after seeing these past many months how heavily such duties weigh on you, long bruther, I know for a certainty that it was I who made the right choice in deciding how best to contrive a journey through life. Homes!" His tone grew bitter and contemptuous. "They burn down or are pillaged, or storms and Earth-shakings destroy what a man takes years to build. Children die young, and wives grow bored and find excitement in unfaithfulness." He slapped himself on the chest. "I am a free man, Etjole! The whole world is my home, and everyone I choose to embrace is my family."

Ehomba's gaze was inclined westward, down the canyon that led to a no-longer-so-distant sea men called Aurreal. It stayed focused in that direction—as well as on other things. "The world may be your house, Simna. It is not your home. As for family, I wish you a real one some-day." With a casual wave of one hand as he sheathed the apparently undamaged sky-metal sword with the other, he beckoned for his companions to follow. Hunkapa Aub fell into step on his right while the black litah ranged farther afield off to his left.

Simna dropped into his usual place close by the herdsman's side. He was smiling once again, his mercurial nature having returned to the fore, the disagreeable incident of moments ago seemingly completely forgotten.

"Tell me, bruther: What would you have done if the Berserker had let loose of his hammer as soon as it started to fly away with him?"

Ehomba smiled reflectively. It took a little longer than usual for the slight upward curve of his mouth to manifest itself, but he smiled. "Why then, my friend, we would have had to slay him before he could recover from his fall. Beyond that I did not have time to think. What the wise men and women of the Naumkib have given me does not allow me to perform more than one miracle at a time."

Simna scratched at the slightly sore spot on his face where Ehomba had struck him. "For a man who spends his days shooing along sheep and cows, you pack a virtuous punch."

"It is harder to knock down a steer than a man." Ehomba declaimed this without so much as a smile. His attention remained concentrated on the path ahead.

The swordsman chuckled. "I only had a quick glimpse of his face before the Berserker sailed off into the sky. I wish I could be there when he finally comes down!"

Ehomba's tone was preoccupied, his gaze set. He strode rhythmically, easily, over the stony, pebble-strewn ground. *Not far now,* he told himself. It could not be much farther now. A part of him was aware that Simna had spoken, and was expecting a reply.

"Who said anything about him coming down?"

XXII

The view from the sun-swept ridge was breathtaking. Below, between the mountains and the sea, a lush plain dotted with small clumps of forest and the occasional gently rising hill ran from north to south as far as the eye could see. Homes and farms filled the land in between, forming neat patterns. Fronting a broad, sand-fringed bay was a denser concentration of streets and structures, of apartment blocks and businesses, warehouses and amphitheaters, schools and parks. Like the mandibles of a beetle, coralstone breakwaters enclosed the outer bay, creating shelter and a safe harbor for dozens of incoming and outgoing ships. Their sails spotted the water like the gulls that shadowed them.

Etjole Ehomba stood with one foot resting on a rock, leaning forward, his right arm resting on his thigh. From the semitropical plain and sea below, a warm, slightly moistened breeze rose upward into his face, making him blink and ruffling his braids. There were times these past many months, more times than he cared to remember, when he doubted whether he would ever stand in such a spot, inhaling such a view. Yet there it was, spread out below him, benignly welcoming his arrival.

Ehl-Larimar.

A voice, high-spirited and characteristically confident beyond reason, sounded next to him. "Hoy, long bruther—there it is." As the swordsman contemplated the breathtaking panorama, a flock of opalescent macaws flew past below them, cawing a raucous welcome, their wings glistening in the subdued sunlight as if coated with powdered gems. "Goyvank knows until now I was never really sure it existed."

"Hunkapa like." The largest member of their party grunted approvingly. "Pretty place."

"Too many people." When Ehomba glanced warningly at the big cat, Ahlitah growled irritably. "I know, I know: I can't eat anyone. At least not until after we've recovered this waylaid female."

"We are conspicuous," the herdsman reminded them unnecessarily, thinking out loud, "but this is another large and cosmopolitan city. A seaport as well. With luck our presence will go unremarked upon by the authorities until we have accomplished what we came for. Time is therefore most important."

"Hoy, since when wasn't it?" Simna commented dryly. "Myself, I'd like to take the time to linger and sample the delights a grand city like this surely has on offer, but after we've taken the treasure—and the lady, of course—I know how vital it'll be for us to depart posthaste." He winked at his lanky companion. "It was clever of you, bruther, to engage two such big and strong associates as the carpet and the cat. Either of them can haul more gold and jewels than the two of us put together."

"I am certain they have that capability." Ehomba's reply was devoid of sarcasm.

"And after we've made our escape, we'll head back through these same mountains." The swordsman was well satisfied with his imagined plan of action. "Outraged as they'll be, the authorities might pursue us for a while, if they manage to pick up our trail, but I've yet to meet the soldier who'd challenge all the country we've recently traversed, even on pain of lashing." He grinned at the herdsman. "Besides, they'll have no sorcerer along to help them deal with hypnotic, swallowing salts and the eager denizens of places like Skawpane."

Ehomba started down the mountain. The last mountain, he knew. "First there are questions we must ask of the natives. We need to find out where this Hymneth makes his home, what sort of defenses he keeps close around him. We need to see if anyone knows of the Visioness and where she is being held."

"And the treasure," Simna reminded him enthusiastically. "Don't forget to ask about the treasure."

Ehl-Larimar was as attractive within as it had been from a distance, with luxuriant, carefully tended parks, clean streets, and a healthy and attractive populace. Yet beneath the overt prosperity and occasional opulence there was an eerie sense of ill-being, as if everyone, rich and poor alike, were suffering from some nonfatal but persistent malady.

As Ehomba had hoped, while their presence was remarked upon, it caused no unusual stir among the locals. Once they succeeded in wending their way down to the harborfront, the travelers found themselves swept up in the usual swirl of commerce and industry, just another clutch of exotics in a sea of hardworking foreigners and industrious visitors. Other than the occasional curious glance, no one paid them the least heed.

Not only did the harborfront provide the anonymity Ehomba sought, it was also among the best places in any large city to obtain information. But whenever they mentioned Hymneth the Possessed, initially cordial locals shied away in quiet terror, and even wayfarers from distant lands found hasty excuses to take themselves elsewhere.

Eventually and by means of persistence (and the quiet, unspoken threat posed by Hunkapa Aub and Ahlitah's presence), they learned the location of their quarry's fortress home, as well as the knowledge that it was rumored he kept within its walls a woman of surpassing beauty who hailed from a far land. They now knew where they had to go. It was, as Ehomba put it in his pragmatically understated fashion, now simply a matter of going there.

They found temporary lodging in a waterfront hostel that catered to visitors from the far reaches of the Aurreal, and there they slept and rested all that night and through the following day, until their second night in Ehl-Larimar brought them the darkness they sought.

High, thin clouds obscured much of the light reflected by a quarter moon. The temperate climate of the coast allowed them to move quickly and effortlessly through the city. Once away from the harbor, urban activity began to decline. Those citizens who happened to chance upon the resolute travelers needed only to catch a glimpse of the mass of Hunkapa Aub, or the glowing yellow eyes of the black litah, to hurry on their way without pausing to ask questions.

Toward the high, somber castle they climbed: not by the winding, stone-paved road that provided access to conventional visitors, but up a hunters' trail that ascended from the city toward a broken peak lying between fortress and sea. This time Ehomba let the big cat lead the way, its sharper-than-human senses alert for signs of patrolling soldiers or armed citizens. Once, Ahlitah left the path between the brush and trees to pounce. His attention had been momentary diverted by an unlucky rabbit. Having never encountered at any time in its short life on the city's outskirts a predator of the size and aspect of the litah, it was too paralyzed with fear to scream. Swallowing his snack in two bites, the unapologetic big cat resumed the ascent.

Changing direction before the modest summit was reached, they turned slightly south and east to follow the ridgeline until they found themselves standing in the brush that grew thickly above and behind the castle. Looking down, it was easy to see that its master was the ruler of a rich and prosperous land. Turrets and battlements had been designed

with an eye toward appearance as well as efficacy. Only the finest building stone had been used in the construction of the fortress. From within
the keep as well as along the walls, flickering lights testified to the presence of oil lamps and torches.

They waited there, crouched down among the concealing chaparral,
grateful for the pleasant, balmy night. Owls hooted from within the dark
shadows of tall trees, to be answered by nocturnal dragonets whose occasional flights provided a diversion for the tarrying travelers. Moonlight
shining through their wings, they preyed on the bats that darted and
dove above the treetops in search of moths and other insects, homing in
on their victims with shrill, high-pitched squeaks. Between their oversized eyes and ears and long snouts lined with hundreds of thin, sharply
pointed teeth, there was not much room left for the rest of their efficient
but homely reptilian faces.

The moon had passed its zenith and was waning toward morning
when Ehomba shifted from the one-legged herdsman's stance in which
he had been resting. "It is time," he declared simply. Taking the point
from the black litah, he led the little company toward the castle.

Their initial impressions of its superior design and solid fortifications
were confirmed by close inspection as they sidled in single file along its
back wall. Nowhere could they find a loose stone to dig out, or a hole
through which to squeeze. High above, serene sentries paced their posts,
never thinking to look straight down. Why should they? Who would dare
to try to sneak uninvited into the fortress of Hymneth the Possessed,
and, more to the point, who would want to?

It was Simna ibn Sind, more familiar with castles and imposing stone
structures than his tall friend, who suggested they try the storm drain.
Large enough to allow all of them passage, even Hunkapa, it penetrated
the foot of the castle wall near its western edge. An iron grating blocked
ultimate ingress, but though well blacksmithed, it had not been designed
with an intruder the size of Hunkapa Aub in mind.

Lying sideways in the opening and bracing his feet against the interior wall, their shaggy companion gripped one of the bars of the grate in
both huge hands and pulled, intending to remove the bars one at a time.
Instead, there was a muted grinding noise as the entire grate came away
in his fingers. Hasty inspection revealed that, as might be expected of
iron that had spent much time standing in water, the footings of the
bottom bars were rusty. Not rusted through, but no longer possessed of
their original strength, either. That was important, because it had allowed Hunkapa Aub to remove the grate quietly as well as quickly.

With Ehomba still leading, they took turns crawling through. The
drain opened into a grooved, stone-faced flood-control channel that ran

the length of a spacious courtyard. Thus concealed below ground level, they were able to approach close to the back of the keep itself without being seen.

Approaching whistling forced them to halt, trapped with little more than the shadow of the building for cover. If they were discovered here, inside the main wall but outside the keep, they would have no choice but to retreat back the way they had come, knowing that the castle's defenders would subsequently be alert to any further encroachment and thereby making a renewed intrusion far more difficult. The whistling intensified and grew nearer. Simna silently removed his knife from his belt, only to have Ehomba put one hand on the swordsman's wrist and a long finger to his lips.

Around the corner sauntered a member of the household staff. Enjoying the windless, invigorating night air and oblivious to his immediate surroundings, he was on his way to work in the castle scullery when he blundered into the travelers. Stepping forward in a single stride, Ehomba put his right forearm around the man's neck and pulled, lifting and squeezing at the same time. In utter silence, the startled kitchen aide reached up with both hands to claw at his assailant's forearm. His eyes bulged and his lips worked, but, devoid of air from his lungs, no sound emerged.

Slowly, as if he were falling into a deep and gentle sleep, his eyes closed and his flailing hands and twitching body went limp. Without ever removing his forearm from the man's neck, Ehomba gently lowered him to the ground. Simna stepped forward to whisper admiringly.

"That's a fine move for a peaceful herdsman to know."

"Sometimes it is necessary to restrain a frolicsome calf from hurting itself." Almost invisible in the shadows, Ehomba moved forward, his sandals barely whispering across the courtyard flagstones. "There was no reason to kill him. He will sleep until morning and wake with nothing worse than a sore throat."

A grinning Simna silently sheathed his knife. "It's a kindly invader you are, long bruther. If all my adversaries were as considerate as you, I'd have fewer scars in embarrassing places."

"So you would if you had led a more restrained life." Finding a wooden door, the herdsman tried the iron latch. It opened at a touch, with an agreeable absence of noise.

They were in.

It was a storeroom of some kind, piled high with crates and containers of household goods. Though virtually pitch-black inside, there was among their company one for whom poor light and even the near absence thereof posed no obstacle. Following close behind Ahlitah, they made their way through the storeroom and into a hall beyond.

"Unless the interior layout of this pile is utterly different from every palace I've ever been in, there should be some kind of central chamber or meeting place." Simna gestured forward. Beyond the storeroom, feeble but adequate light filtered in through distant windows and ports, allowing them to advance with greater confidence. Once again Ehomba took the lead.

Sounds drifted down to them from the upper reaches of the fortress, but they were isolated and few. This late at night and this early in the morning, few denizens of the castle were stirring. Guards patrolled the main gates and outer wall, not the interior living quarters. Ehomba was concerned about the possibility of encountering free-roaming dogs but, oddly, none were about. Despite his interminable curiosity it was, however, a problem to which he could at the moment devote but little thought.

"Here, this way." Advancing, the herdsman gestured for the others to follow him to the left. Proceeding silently through a travertine-trimmed archway, they found themselves in the high-ceilinged, central chamber whose existence Simna had earlier propounded.

It was utterly silent. Moonlight entered through stained-glass windows of unsettling motif high above the floor. The swordsman was excited to discover that the floor was paved not with slabs of granite or even marble, but with semiprecious stone such as rhodochrosite and lapis, agate and onyx. There *was* treasure here; ample treasure. He could smell it.

"Now all we have to do is find the room where the Visioness is held," Ehomba whispered. "We will take a servant prisoner and seek the information from him." His voice was low and tight with expectancy. "Simna and I have dealt with guards before. With luck, we will be able to spirit her out of the castle and back along the route we used to enter. By daybreak we will be away from the city and safely in among the mountains."

"Hoy, that sounds grand, bruther. But what about the treasure?" Deeply concerned with other matters, Simna hovered close to his lanky companion.

"The Visioness first," Ehomba reminded him tautly. "When we have her, then we will discuss the matter of treasure. Better to worry now about guards, and whether this Hymneth the Possessed sleeps near at hand to the one called Themaryl."

"Tonight, he does not sleep!" The booming voice was shockingly loud and immediate.

Illumination flooded the audience chamber as the fifty fine lamps that lined the enclosing walls and hung from the high ceiling came simultaneously to life, filling the imposing room with light. Whirling as one, the four travelers found themselves staring at the far end of the chamber. There was a throne there, raised up on a high but modest dais. Seated on the throne was a towering, striking figure clad from head to foot in burnished armor of florid design and elegant execution. Bejeweled floor lamps of solid malachite blazed on either side of the chiseled seat of state, their light glimmering off the gold and azure armor.

From beneath a helmet of alloyed red and green gold, eyes blazed with no less intensity than the plethora of dazzling lamps. One mailed arm was upraised. As it lowered slightly, so did the light of the fifty lamps, reducing the blinding brilliance that flushed the chamber to a more tolerable level. Straight-backed and steely-eyed, white of hair and lean of muscle, a venerable soldier-sage stood to the left of the throne and slightly to its rear. Near the foot of the splendid dais fluttered two ominous, independently hovering puffs of malevolent black vapor.

The intruders scanned entrances and alcoves, but the rest of the chamber was deserted. There were no concealed guards, no approaching platoons of heavily armored soldiers, no murderous dogs snarling and snapping madly at the ends of handlers' chains. Only the imposing figure seated on the dais, and the single venerable attendant.

Simna's hand drifted away from his sword. The black litah rose slowly from his crouch. Around them, saturated wicks flickered and sputtered softly, fed by finely sieved and blended oils. Ehomba searched the helmet-shrouded eyes of the towering figure seated on the throne, and those same deep-set, intelligent eyes gazed unblinkingly back.

" 'A master of the necromantic arts,' the Worm said. 'A questioner of all that is unanswered.' " Leaning forward slightly on the dais, Hymneth the Possessed, Lord of Ehl-Larimar and Supreme Ruler of the central Aurreal coast all the way from the Wall of Motops to the frozen northlands, leaned his chin on his fist as he considered the taller of the two humans standing before him. "Have you really come from all the way across the Semordria, the eastern ocean?"

It took Simna a moment to find his voice. Swallowing hard but uncowed, he boldly took a step forward. "Not only from across the Semordria, but from far to the south as well."

The armored specter ignored the swordsman. For Hymneth, Simna ibn Sind did not exist. Nor, except as transitory curiosities, did Hunkapa Aub or the black litah. He had words only for the tall, slim, spear-wielding figure clad in simple shirt and kilt who met his gaze without flinching.

"I must say that you don't look the part." After holding the stare for another long, thoughtful moment, the Possessed sighed and sat back on his throne, dropping his arms to the sculpted dragon-headed rests. "After all this waiting, it's something of a disappointment. However, when it comes to reading tomorrows, even the Worm is not omnipotent."

"By Gosthenhark, we're due some respect here for what we've done!" Insults Simna could deal with, but he could not and would not be ignored. "This is my friend the Naumkib Etjole Ehomba, who comes from a land so far to the east and south you cannot conceive of the distance."

"Can't I?" Already, Hymneth was sounding bored.

"He is a wizard of inestimable wisdom and power, controlling forces you cannot hope to defeat." Straightening proudly, the swordsman touched a thumb to his chest. "*I* am Simna ibn Sind, virtuoso of blades and sixth-degree adept in the warrior arts of my homeland. We have not come all this way, defeating dangers and overcoming obstacles beyond your imagining, to be treated with contempt. We mean to have from you the Visioness Themaryl of Laconda, unwillingly abducted from her family and home, and return her to her people." He took a step back and then added hastily, "And whatever treasure of yours we can carry off with us as well."

Hymneth the Possessed nodded slowly, his posture and attitude indicative of a weary patience. The senior soldier at his side remained standing at attention, having moved not a muscle or, insofar as Ehomba could tell, an eye, during the entire confrontation. As for the amorphous blobs of black effluvium, Ehomba knew what they were.

"Well spoken," the Lord of Ehl-Larimar deigned to comment. "While I generally dislike volubility in my soldiers, you exhibit the kind of blind and dumb courage that can sometimes prove valuable. I might have use for you." Before a defiant Simna could reply, Hymneth returned his attention to the silently watching Ehomba.

"When first I was warned of your coming, I was concerned. Not afraid, mind, or worried, but concerned. It is a foolish man who is not concerned with the unknown. This consideration troubled my thoughts, and became so persistent as to unsettle my sleep. Then, things changed. Or rather, something of great importance changed. So much so that it no longer became a matter of interest to me whether you reached Ehl-Larimar or not." Behind the helmet there surfaced the suggestion of a smile.

"This came about because I became immune to anything you could do. Believe me, when the change took place it was a revelation as welcome as it was surprising." He leaned his head slightly to one side. "I look forward with complete indifference to whatever you may choose to do next."

Simna whispered tersely to his laconic friend. "He's bluffing. No matter how powerful he is, he knows nothing of our strengths or powers. Therefore he can't be as disinterested as he says." When Ehomba did not comment, the swordsman decided to go on the offensive. Raising his voice, he challenged the armored figure slumping on the throne.

"If you think you can intimidate us with words, then you've no idea of what we've gone through in the getting here." His fingers slid meaningfully to the hilt of his sword. "It doesn't matter if you're alone except for that old menial and a couple of black puffballs, or if your whole army is waiting just outside this room. We demand that the Visioness Themaryl be brought before us—and that's just for a start."

The helmeted skull nodded slowly. "As you will see, I can be quite an agreeable fellow." Turning slightly to his right, he gestured toward the shadows. "There is no need to send for her. She's right here."

From out of the darkness strode the abducted enchantress of far-distant Laconda. Trailing pale blue chiffon and silk, her flowing tresses bound up in a snood of gold wire set with sapphires and tourmalines, she seemed to glide across the floor toward the dais. Having been smitten with her aspect in a vision, Simna was no less overwhelmed by her loveliness in person. Though he had known many comely women, they were as thistles compared to the radiant rose that now stood before him.

Commanded to appear, he expected her to halt well short of the throne. She did not. As he searched for hidden chains or restraints, she mounted the dais until she was standing directly alongside the throne itself. Reaching out, she placed one hand on the metal-clad shoulder of Hymneth the Possessed. The swordsman hunted in vain for evidence of handcuffs or leg shackles.

And then she smiled.

Simna's lower jaw dropped. Beside him, Ehomba said nothing. Hunkapa Aub and Ahlitah waited behind the two men, confused and uncertain, not knowing how to react or what to do next.

To say that Hymneth was enjoying the effect the Visioness's actions had on his visitors was to understate the delight he hardly showed. "As I told you, something of a transformation has taken place here in Ehl-Larimar." Without taking his eyes from the stunned intruders, he murmured encouragingly to the woman standing by his side. "Tell them—my dear."

As it had been in the vision, her voice was molten gold, each syllable a chord in an infinite celestial cantata. "I am sorry if you have gone to much trouble. It is true that when I was abducted by Hymneth I was overflowing with hatred for him and all that he might stand for. Brave men and women died on my behalf, trying to liberate me. For that I am now and forever will be sorry. At the time and for many months thereafter I grieved for them even as I hoped another might come who would deliver me.

"Imprisoned here, a 'guest' who was not permitted to leave, I was well treated. I kept my own counsel, and nursed my anger and loathing, until eventually it became a thing separate and apart from me. Once that happened, I was able to stand back from it and consider more dispassionately my surroundings. Only then was I able to bring myself even to speak civilly with my captor. Only then did I come to appreciate his profound qualities."

"Profound qual—" Simna whirled on Ehomba. "Bruther, why don't you say something? Are you hearing this?"

Glancing down, the herdsman nodded. "I am hearing it, friend Simna."

Drawing herself up to her full height, the Visioness declaimed clearly. "I have chosen to remain here of my own free will. As his amenable consort, Hymneth has offered me the co-regency of Ehl-Larimar. I have accepted. I regret any personal inconvenience this may have caused you, but you may console yourselves with the knowledge that you are free to remain or depart, as you see fit. You will not be harmed."

Simna could not believe what he was hearing. "He's drugged her! Or she's been ensorcelled! She's not free to voice her own mind. Break the hex, Etjole! Free her from this corrupting stupor so that she can speak the truth!"

The herdsman leaned slightly on his spear. "No, Simna. I do not think she is suffering under a spell. I have been watching her posture, her lips, her eyes. She is herself and none other. The words she speaks are hers, and come from the heart as well as the mind. She truly means to remain here."

"Then—everything we've gone through; the battles we've fought, the dangers we've overcome, the lands and towns and armies and seas we've struggled to pass at the repeated risk of our very lives, it's all been for nothing? For nothing?" When again his friend did not reply, the swordsman sat down heavily on the exquisite, highly polished gemstone floor. And then he began to laugh.

His laughter grew louder, and wilder, echoing through the length and breadth of the great hall. He began to rock back and forth, both arms wrapped around his stomach as the laughter spilled out of him in long, rolling waves. Only when he had come close to laughing himself insensate did the calmly foreboding voice from the throne speak again.

"Unlike the beauteous Themaryl, I hardly ever feel sorry for anyone. People make the lives they live. I regret to admit that in certain quarters of my kingdom I am not considered a compassionate ruler. But tonight, though I would like to laugh with you, mercenary, I find that I cannot. I can only—feel sorry for you." He turned back to the silently staring Ehomba. "So you see, necromancer from across the Semordria, if such it is that you are, you are defeated before you can begin. That which you came to fight for no longer exists. Your reason and rationale have evaporated, like smoke." Steel-clad fingers reached out to cover the back of the Visioness Themaryl's perfect hand.

"Ordinarily, I would not be so generous to those who slink uninvited into my home, but my consort has spoken. You are free to leave, or stay, or do whatever you want. It is of no import to me. Enjoy the city if you like. Ehl-Larimar has much to offer the tired traveler." He nodded in the direction of the silent old soldier. "If you wish, Peregriff will find lodging for you tonight within the castle. Since I have no reason to deal with you as enemies, I suppose I might as well treat you as guests. Tomorrow you may dine with me. And with my incomparable, compliant consort." Turning his hand, he lifted hers up in his, bent forward, and kissed it. Seeing this was enough to set Simna ibn Sind to laughing uncontrollably all over again.

"No."

The seated swordsman's hysteria halted in mid-laugh. To the left of the throne, the impressive white eyebrows of General Peregriff narrowed ever so slightly. At the foot of the dais, tiny red eyes began to emerge and take shape within the cryptic depths of the cancerous black vapors.

Having started to rise from his throne, Hymneth the Possessed paused and peered across the reflective, lamplit floor. His voice was composed, even—but just the slightest bit perplexed.

"What did you say?"

"I said, no." For the first time since the lamps had burst to life in the regal audience chamber, it was Etjole Ehomba who stepped forward. "We cannot avail ourselves of your hospitality, or that of your kingdom." Lowering the tip of his spear, he pointed slightly to his left. "The Visioness Themaryl is coming with us."

Hymneth's voice grew quietly, dangerously frosty. "I am afraid I do not understand. She does not wish to go with you. She does not wish to return to Laconda or the life she knew there. She wishes to stay here with me. Of her own free will. You yourself acknowledged as much only moments ago."

The herdsman nodded. He had come a long way and was very tired, as if he had spent days chasing runaway animals through the hills and gullies back of the village. "When I first set out on this journey, not knowing how or when it would end or where it would take me, I did so because I had made a vow. A promise to a dying man who called himself Tarin Beckwith, of Laconda North. He made me swear not to rest until I returned the Visioness Themaryl to her home and family. This oath I reluctantly made. I have traveled far and at great expense of effort to fulfill that obligation. I intend to do so."

The wide, helmeted head was shaking slowly from side to side. "There is reason, and then there is insanity, but the likes of this I have never had to deal with before. Do you mean to tell me that in spite of her declared wishes to remain here you intend to take her back, by force if necessary?"

Ehomba nodded stoically. His voice never changed. "By force if necessary."

With the abruptness of a rogue wave shattering upon an unsuspecting shore, Hymneth the Possessed stood bolt upright before his throne and bellowed thunderously at the impious intruder.

"By Besune, this is worse than madness!" He was trembling with rage. "In spite of all the sleeplessness you have caused me, I offer you your life, and you demand death!" Reaching out toward the intolerable interloper, he made a cup of his extended fingers. "Since you so devoutly seek your doom, here it is, master of a doubtful magic. Here in this hand. Come and get it!"

Without a word, a grim-faced Ehomba let go of his spear. It had not yet struck the floor before he was running forward, reaching back over a shoulder to draw the sky-metal sword. A stunned Simna frantically began to scramble to his feet. Hunkapa Aub tensed, and the black litah let loose with a snarl that rattled the hanging banners high overhead. Rising to his full, dominating height before the throne, Hymneth the Possessed spread both arms wide to restrain the alerted Peregriff and shield the startled Themaryl. Then he let loose with an inarticulate howl of his own as he flung one arm forward at the tall, rangy herdsman racing toward him.

The dart that had been concealed within the sleeve of his armor struck the onrushing herdsman in his right shoulder. Without pausing, Ehomba reached up and pulled it free. Tossing it to one side, he showed no ill effects from the virulent poison it contained. Nor would he, thanks to the immunizing contents of his water bag, thoughtfully treated months ago by, as Simna was fond of saying, a long brother.

His gaze narrowing slightly, the ruler of Ehl-Larimar brought his other arm forward and uttered a word so loathsome and vile that the Visioness was compelled to clasp both hands to her ears to shut out the echo of it that lingered in the air. In response to his gesture, eyes now fully formed and ablaze, the two clouds of sooty vapor that had been hovering impatiently by his steel-booted feet ballooned to the size of black buffalo as they sped gleefully away from the dais to intercept the impudent, foolhardy human.

XXIII

Ehomba met the onrushing eromakadi head-on, without trying to dodge or step clear of their charge. In an instant he was enveloped in black cloud and completely obscured from view. Simna held his breath. Even so, he was less agitated than his companions, who unlike him had not had the benefit of seeing the herdsman deal with eromakadi. But as the minutes passed and nothing happened and Ehomba did not reappear, the swordsman found himself growing more and more uneasy.

Then a soft whistling became audible. It grew louder, until it dominated the room. The vaporous substance of the eromakadi began to twitch, then to jerk violently, and finally to shrink. Moments later everyone could see Ehomba, standing with sword in hand, inhaling and inhaling without seemingly pausing to breathe. Into his open mouth the eromakadi disappeared, sucked down like steam from a kettle traveling in reverse, until the last frantic, faintly mewling black tendril had been swallowed.

Without word or comment of any kind, an Ehomba none the apparent worse for the experience resumed his assault on the dais.

"An eromakasi!" Balling one hand into a fist, a surprised Hymneth raged at the onrushing herdsman. "What have you done with my pets, eromakasi?" Flinging his closed, armored hand forward, the Possessed opened his fingers the instant his arm was fully extended.

Ball lightning flew at Ehomba. It was olive green in hue and crackled with energy. Raising his blade, the herdsman parried the verdant globe. Deafening thunder rattled the reception hall. Simna and the others were momentarily blinded by the shower of green sparks that flew from the sky-metal sword.

Even as Ehomba was opposing this latest assault, the lofty figure seething before the throne of Ehl-Larimar was readying another. Hymneth continued to fling spheres of sickly green energy at his attacker as the herdsman persistently warded them off. In this manner Ehomba, though his approach was slowed by the need to fight off the tall sorcerer's successive attacks, sustained his advance on the throne. As he drew nearer, the ball lightning flew more often. Employing reflexes honed from years of fighting off predators intent on stealing from the Naumkib flocks, he struck down one blazing assault after another. The frenzy of emerald sparks that struck from his untiring blade outshone the far more subdued glow of the chamber's lamps.

Swinging the sword in short, deliberate arcs, he gained the first step, and then the second. If Hymneth the Possessed was growing anxious or uneasy, the evidence of such a condition remained his and his alone. His face remained hidden behind the magnificent helmet. His defense was as unremitting and incessant as Ehomba's advance, and he showed no sign of weakening or abandoning his position before the throne.

Surmounting the last step, Ehomba batted aside a lethal, crackling globe half his size and was swallowed up by the consequent deluge of rabid green sparks and shattered shafts of lightning. Emerging from this cataract of emerald energy, he brought his blade around in a low feint, then swung it up over his head and brought it straight down, edge on, with both hands. Hymneth the Possessed, Lord of Ehl-Larimar, was in the process of throwing another orb of lightning when he saw or sensed what his attacker intended. Quickly raising both mailed arms over his head, he crossed his wrists and caught the descending sword in the V they formed.

Green and white sparks erupted from the point of contact and the concussive wave thus generated knocked Peregriff, the Visioness Themaryl, and Simna ibn Sind off their feet. Only the larger and more powerful Ahlitah and Hunkapa Aub were able to remain standing, and even they were staggered by the force of the detonation.

When Simna's vision cleared and he could once again discern the drama being played out in front of the throne, a loss of feeling and belief gripped him the likes of which he had never experienced before, not even when as a child he had been cruelly assaulted by his peers. As receding thunderclaps rolled through the chamber and off into the distance, he saw the remnants of the shattered sky-metal sword lying scattered everywhere: on the steps leading up to the dais, on the floor, on the throne itself. Stare at them as he might, they did not slowly revive, did not become dozens or hundreds of new, smaller blades as they had in far

Skawpane. They had been smashed into ragged shards and strips of twisted steel, like the vulnerable metal of any common sword.

At the foot of the steps lay a crumpled, motionless figure.

"Etjole!" Heedless of whatever the domineering, armored figure commanding the dais might do, the swordsman rushed forward. Hunkapa Aub and the black litah were right behind him.

Throwing himself on the prone torso, Simna used both hands to wrench the valiant herdsman over onto his back. Ehomba's eyes were closed and his body limp. There hung about him a sharp, acrid smell, as if he had been singed by something as lethal as it was invisible. The swordsman shook the smooth, lean shoulders; gently at first, then more forcefully.

"Etjole! Bruther!" To his frantic entreaties there was no response. Pressing an ear to the herdsman's chest, Simna's eyes grew wide as he detected no sound from within. Hastily moistening a palm, he held it in front of the herdsman's unmoving lips. Nothing cooled his skin.

"It can't be." He drew back from the motionless body. *"It can't be."*

Dipping his maned head low over the prostrate form, Ahlitah listened and sniffed once, twice. Then yellow eyes rose, flicking first in the direction of Hymneth the Possessed, then meeting those of the stricken swordsman.

"It's over, Simna. He's dead. The herder of cattle is dead."

And he was.

Ehomba felt no pain. In fact, he did not "feel" at all. He knew instinctively, unarguably, that he was dead. Dead at the hands of another. Hymneth the Possessed had killed him. This knowledge caused him neither regret nor discomfort. Those were concerns that belonged to the world of the living, and he was no longer a part of that. He did not think of his condition as a failure, or lament for his lost family, or sorrow for anything left behind. After death, everything changed.

He was conscious that some time had passed, though whether seconds or years he could not have said. At first he had been aware of being above his body, utterly divorced from it and from everything of the living flesh. Very quickly thereafter and without any sense of transition or traveling he found himself in a void, an immeasurably vast space that would have been completely dark except for the presence of distant, unblinking stars. They were not the stars one saw in life. Somehow they seemed much closer, yet infinitely distant. There was no sense of ground, of up or down or direction, or of the presence of the Earth. Only the void, stars—and souls.

He thought of them as souls for lack of a better term. Present around him in the starry vastness was everyone who had ever lived. Though they were packed together in a single immense, amorphous mass, there was a feeling of adequate space between individuals. It was crowded, yet with no sense of crowding.

There was no movement of bodies. Everyone hung limp, drifting, eyes open and unblinking as they contemplated the star-washed heavens with a silent fusion of curiosity and wonderment. Ehomba was surprised to discover that he retained a sense of body, of the physical self. Gazing about, he was unable to identify or categorize individuals either as to sex or age. There was only the powerful, detached feeling of being surrounded by uncounted people.

He was able to sense more than this from only one nearby individual, whom he felt to be a foot soldier of young to middle age who hailed from an earlier eon. Only his eyes conveyed any familiar impressions at all. No one breathed, or smelled. It was possible that they, and he, could hear, but there was no noise, no sound in the accepted sense.

He was conscious of understanding words without actually hearing them as modulated waves pressing against his inner ear. The words were simply "there." Otherwise it was infinitely peaceful and quiet despite the drifting, floating mass of humanity. There was an inescapable feeling of equilibrium, of everything and everyone being held in silent, sensationless suspension. This despite a steady, unending flow of new arrivals who added wordlessly to the ever-increasing volume of individuals.

The only words he could comprehend seemed to be whispering "What time is it?" and "Does anyone here know the time?" Though conscious of, aware of, others around them, this was all that anyone could think of to say. Ehomba found it interesting that no one asked, or thought to ask, what day it was, or what month, or what year. Only, "What time?"

That, and endless self-reflective queries of "Didn't I just get here?" This gently querulous mantra was repeated over and over, yet without any feeling of repetition or tedium. There was never any sense of more than one minute passing before the question was heard again from another source, and then another, and another. "Didn't I just get here?" This even though an immense amount of time had obviously passed. How many millions, or billions of times the question had been ethereally posed Ehomba could not have said. It was the same for him as for everyone around him. The feeling, the certainty, that regardless of real time, no more than a minute had ever passed.

There was one other sensation. An inescapable, powerful, overriding sense of purpose to It All. What that might be, he never got a feel for. Catechist that he was, he was pleased to believe that there was a reason, a purpose behind It All, just as he was disappointed not to learn what that might be. It was frustrating, though he never felt frustrated in the familiar sense of the term.

There was no heat or cold, no feeling of weight. No pain or pleasure. Physicality without sensation. Just a sense of being—and the Purpose. No sense of a deity, either, or of anyone or anything watching or manipulating. Just souls, people, accumulating, wondering about the Purpose . . .

Standing tall and assured before the throne, Hymneth the Possessed straightened his helmet, which had in the course of the preceding clash been jolted slightly askew, and regarded the tableau of intruders below him.

"See to them, Peregriff."

"Yes, Lord," came the always prepared voice off to his left.

"As soon as they have recovered from their bathetic grieving, find out what they want to do. Offer the mercenary a position with the army—not my household staff. I'm not in the habit of recruiting the potentially vengeful. The cat is clearly intelligent beyond the level of his more modestly proportioned cousins. I suspect it will want to leave. Let it. As for the bloated rug-creature—I'm not sure what to do about it. Hopefully, it will depart in the company of the cat, and without soiling the floor on its way out." Turning to his right, he extended an arm.

"Come, my dear. I think this has been enough entertainment for one night."

Crouched alongside the motionless body of his tall friend, a disbelieving Simna cried unabashedly, the tears spilling copiously down his cheeks. "You crazy, single-minded fool! You gaunt, self-righteous bastard! Hoy, you weren't supposed to die! What am I going to tell your family?"

"Excuse me," murmured Hunkapa Aub as his huge frame inclined over the corpse, "would you please step back, Simna?"

"What difference will it make?" The swordsman sobbed angrily, consumed by passion and self-pity. "Why should I—" He broke off, sniffed long and hard, and gaped uncertainly at his oversized companion. "Wait a minute here. What did you say?"

Eyes of arctic blue gazed back at him. "I asked you to please step aside. I need room."

"You need . . . ?" The swordsman's expression narrowed. "All of a sudden it's not 'Hunkapa need' or 'Hunkapa want Simna move.' It's 'Would you please step back, Simna'—glib and polite as a thrice-bedamned court orator." He straightened and took a couple of steps backward, staring hard, hard, at the massive, looming figure. "By every goddamned god I've ever sworn by—what's going on here?"

"I need room in which to work." Having concluded his hasty but thorough examination of the herdsman's corpse, Hunkapa Aub rose to his full height, tilted his shaggy head back until he was gazing at the ceiling, closed his eyes, and stretched both arms up and out.

Opposite, Ahlitah was in stealthy retreat, muscles tensed, head held low. "I knew there was something about him. I knew it."

"What's that?" Simna shouted across Ehomba's prostrate body at the big cat. "What did you know?"

The black litah growled softly, its rending claws fully extended as they scraped backward across the floor. "He never *smelled* stupid."

"*Simbala!*" cried Hunkapa Aub, imploring forces that lay deeper than his words. "*Acenka sar vranutho!*"

A brilliant white glow appeared above his head, a fierce effulgence that pulsed with scarcely restrained energy. Descending on the far side of the dais, Hymneth the Possessed and his new consort paused and turned. Behind the helmet, the ruler of all Ehl-Larimar—blinked.

Eyes closed tight, chanting to himself, Hunkapa Aub lowered his arms until both hands were pointing at the floor—and at the prone figure of Etjole Ehomba. "*Haranath!*" he rumbled, and the pulsating, glittering orb responded. Drifting down from its location above the shaggy head, it impacted the body of the herdsman, and sank into it like milk into a sponge. A pale brilliance suffused the slender cadaver, over-flowing it with radiance from head to toe. Eyes still shut, Hunkapa sustained the incantation as an obviously agitated Hymneth released the Visioness Themaryl and started hurriedly back around the base of the dais.

" 'A master of all the necromantic arts' is coming, the Worm said—but it never described what he would look like!" Raising one hand, the sovereign warlock threw a crackling, virulent green sphere at the hulking hirsute figure. Lethal lightning darted straight for Hunkapa Aub's eyes.

Standing bolt upright, engulfed in a torrent of unadulterated white energy that was the shadow of the lingering breath of a billion unfinished, unfulfilled souls, Etjole Ehomba caught the sickly emerald globe square in the chest. It exploded on impact, shriveled green spikes flying off and spilling away in all directions like startled snakes. As Ehomba started toward him, Hymneth once more began throwing sphere after destructively lambent sphere. Those directed at himself the herdsman shattered with a simple wave of his hand, each finger armored with the massed white energy of a million souls. Any orbs aimed at Hunkapa Aub he merely deflected, sending them crashing destructively into the far corners of the quaking hall.

Crouched off to one side, Simna ibn Sind watched the clash of forces whose scope he could not judge and whose strength he could not imagine, and found himself struck most by something that was less than overwhelming but just as distinctive. Throughout all that had happened, his friend Ehomba had never lost his poise. His expression had been the same when first he had attacked Hymneth, when he had lain before the swordsman in death, and now when he was—what was he? Simna did not know. He was a man of the blade and not of the mind. As always, struggling with the latter caused him far more pain than any edge, no matter how sharp.

Ehomba's advance was deliberate and relentless. No matter what Hymneth threw at him, no matter how awesome the energy or irresistible the might, the herdsman continued to approach. Green and white lightning flooded the great chamber and obscured much of what was happening at its far end.

Until a burst of verdant ball lightning taller and wider than Hunkapa Aub smashed the shell of protective white energy that surrounded Ehomba. Exhausted but triumphant, perspiring heavily within his armor, Hymneth the Possessed prepared to raise his tired, trembling right hand one last time.

"Now, whatever you are become, we'll make an end to this, *and* to the secret master who has manipulated you all along!"

Like his expression, the herdsman's voice never changed. "I am Etjole Ehomba, of the Naumkib, and no one manipulates me." Parting his jaws and before Hymneth could bring his arm up and forward, he spat forcefully at the supreme sovereign of the central coast. Two dark, wet, black blobs flew from his lips, to strike the looming, armored figure right in the eye slit that creased the upper part of his helmet.

Hymneth's arm continued to rise—only to halt, quivering, halfway from the ground. The imposing figure stumbled once, shook itself, then staggered sideways. There came a metallic cracking sound as deep fissures appeared in his armor, running from magnificent helmet to mailed foot. The Visioness Themaryl screamed as the ruler of Ehl-Larimar collapsed sideways onto the floor. Struck by the half-digested essence of not one but two eromakadi, he lay in his useless armor, unmoving where he had fallen.

Reaching for his sword, Peregriff started forward, only to be intercepted by a still uncertain but increasingly confident Simna. Holding his blade out in front of him, the swordsman ventured a strained smile.

"No, my venerable friend! By Gequed, we'll see this thing done with by those who matter. You and I are insignificant components of any final rendering."

An awkward pause ensued while Hymneth's general glared down at the itinerant swordsman. Then he nodded, once, and dropped his hand from the hilt of his weapon. Together, both men turned to look.

Rushing forward, Themaryl had knelt beside the supine figure of her monarch. Concern wracked her countenance, but there were no tears. Fearful, she looked up at the rangy, solemn-visaged herdsman.

"Is—is he dead?"

"No." Ehomba studied the motionless figure somberly. Bits and pieces of fractured armor were starting to slough away from the body. "Only paralyzed, and that I think just from the shoulders down. Eventually, he should recover all movement."

She started to smile gratefully, then thought better of it, and instead turned her attention back to the recumbent torso.

Breathing hard, Simna ibn Sind joined his tall friend in gazing down at the motionless form. "Hoy, only paralyzed? Why leave the job half finished?" He aimed the point of his blade.

"No, my friend." Reaching out, Ehomba forestalled the swordsman's fatal intent. "That is not what I came for."

Simna eyed him imploringly. "By Gulvent, bruther, he tried to kill you! He *did* kill you! Speaking of which . . ." The swordsman turned to look at the indefatigable hulk that was Hunkapa Aub. Through his fur, the biggest member of their little party was smiling.

"I get it!" Simna blurted in sudden realization. "You weren't really dead! You were faking it all along."

Ehomba shook his head slowly. "No, my friend. I was dead. Well and truly dead. I know, because I spent time in the place where the dead go."

"Tell me," asked Hunkapa Aub seriously, "what is it like, the place where the dead go?"

"Slow," the herdsman told him. Reaching out, he put a firm hand on the swordsman's shoulder and smiled reassuringly. "I knew that I was going to die, Simna. It had been foretold. Not once, but three times. Once by a seductive seeress the memory of whose beauty and wisdom I will always treasure, once by a dog witch whose insight and affection I will always remember, and once even by a fog whose persistence I will never forget. 'Continue on and die,' they said—and so it had to be before we could triumph." Turning, he gazed gravely at the still unmoving body of Hymneth the Possessed: warlock, sorcerer, eminent ruler of illustrious Ehl-Larimar.

"But that was as far as their predictions went. Nothing was said about what might happen *after* I died." Raising his eyes, he smiled gratefully at the imposing, attentive, fraternal figure of Hunkapa Aub. "Nothing was said that would preclude my being resurrected."

Simna gaped at him, struggling to digest the import of his friend's serene words. Then—he grinned. The grin widened until it seemed to encompass the majority of his sweat-streaked face. And then he began to chuckle softly to himself. It never grew loud or boisterous like before, but it did not go away, either.

"Two sorcerers. All this time I've been traveling in the company of *two* sorcerers." Turning, he confronted Hunkapa Aub, whose eyes had become suddenly wise as well as blue. "As many days and nights as I have spent in your company, as many evils and dangers as we fought side by side, and I never suspected. I never *would* have suspected."

Hunkapa Aub's smile widened slightly. "Not all wizards look alike, good swordsman. Not everything in life appears as one imagines it to be. And it is not required that one be human to be a master of the thaumaturgic arts."

Simna could only stare and shake his head in lingering disbelief. "Why? Why the sham and the continuing charade? Why did you let the people of Netherbrae keep you in a cage and throw food at you and torment you with insults and curses?"

Clasping both immoderately hairy hands behind his back, the hulking wizard considered Simna's flurry of questions. "You would not understand, good swordsman. Even a sorcerer needs to learn by experience. I was traveling through that part of the world when I was accosted by the simple, shallow folk of that otherwise charming mountain town. I could easily have avoided capture, or freed myself at any time. But I was, and am always, curious as to what would motivate otherwise apparently intelligent and compassionate people to act in such a shameful fashion toward another of their fellow beings who had done them no harm. One can learn much about one's peers by spending time in a cage.

"Then you appeared in Netherbrae, and freed me. Finding you more interesting than anything else that tempted to engage me at that time, I chose to accompany you on your journey. It promised much of interest and elucidation. Suffice to say, I have not been disappointed."

"But why the pantomime?" An unsatisfied Simna persisted. "Why didn't you just tell us who and what you were from the beginning?"

Hunkapa Aub's smile was as sage as the look in his eyes. "Wizards have this 'effect' on people, good swordsman. In the presence of one they become muted things and no longer act themselves. I wanted to study you as you are, not as you would have become had you known my true identity."

Simna stammered angrily. "Study us? And what have you learned, maestro of a mumbling disguise, from the specimens you chose to keep so long in ignorance?"

"The best thing there is to learn about another. That you are good, all of you. Yea, even you, Simna ibn Sind, though you would argue long and hard to deny it. I know you well. You, and the great and noble cat." Raising his gaze, he considered the lanky figure of Etjole Ehomba. "Your friend and guide I am still not entirely sure about." Hirsute shoulders rose and fell in a prodigious shrug. "I think I will stay with you a while longer. I sense there is still more to learn from your company."

"Well, it's a good thing you turned out to be more than the untutored, shambling simpleton you seemed to be," Simna declared, adding hastily, "I mean nothing untoward by that, master. Who would have thought you the more powerful sorcerer than Hymneth the Possessed?"

"Who said I was more powerful?" Hunkapa Aub's smile faded. "I caught him unawares, after he had been tired and worn down by your friend Etjole. I did not defeat him. Ultimately, it demanded the combined efforts of both of us."

"Hoy, however it was done, the important thing is that you were able to overcome him." The swordsman glowered down at the recumbent, motionless figure from which ruined metal was sloughing like a second skin. As he did so, his eyes widened.

Exposed to the flicker of lamplight without his omnipresent armor, Hymneth the Possessed, lord of the central coast and absolute ruler of Ehl-Larimar the sublime, was after all had been said and done not all that he had appeared to be.

Curly black hair almost as thick as Hunkapa's covered the barrel chest as well as the long, massive forearms. But beneath the bulky upper body were tapered hips and shockingly short, stunted legs. These too were intermittently overlaid with still more of the thick body curls.

Formerly strapped to and now detached from the undersized lower limbs and feet were a pair of whitened, dying legs that had been taken from a much taller man. Amputated from an unknown owner, these fleshy prostheses were dying before the onlookers' eyes, the magic that had kept them attached to the warlock's feet having been shattered along with the rest of his protective spells. Nothing less than stilts made of meat, they had covertly provided a good portion of the lord of Ehl-Larimar's imposing height.

Atop a bull neck sat a massive head that seemed too large for the rest of the body. Thick, almost blubbery lips fronted a prognathic jawline. The ears were overlarge and set toward the rear of the skull. Most striking of all was the forehead, sloping well back from the thick, bony ridges that shaded the eyes. The raven hair atop the head had been trimmed short to eliminate the profusion of greasy curls to be found elsewhere on the squat body. It was a surpassingly ugly face, a visage that fluctuated uneasily between homely and repulsive. A face that was not quite human, though Ehomba knew what it was. Simna recalled a recent statement of Hunkapa Aub's.

"It is not necessary for one to be human to be a master of the thaumaturgic arts."

Hymneth the Possessed was a neander.

The partially paralyzed wizard was impotent to smash in the faces that were staring down at him or strike the pitying expressions from their countenances. Defeated, frustrated, revealed, naked, and exposed, he could only moan and howl helplessly.

"Go on; look, stare, gawk at me. My people wonder why I never appear among them unhelmeted or without armor. It's because if they saw me like this, as I *am*, they would repudiate me despite all my power and no matter what threats I rained down upon them. My forebears are from the far north, from the frozen wastes that cap the roof of the world. There they huddle, miserable and cold, dying young and struggling to eke out an existence I would not bequeath to a bird. Driven there by the 'healthy' ones. By people like yourselves." Unable to move more than his head, he glared defiantly up at a silently watching Ehomba.

"Only *I* was different. Only I devoured everything the wise ones muttered and mumbled, storing their knowledge within my heart as well as my head. I studied, and learned, and vowed to make a life different from theirs. A life of power and dominion over those who shunned and jeered the neanders.

"When I had learned enough, I found my way here, to Ehl-Larimar. The journey almost killed me, but I took the throne from the weakling who sat upon it and remade it in my own image. I extended my control to encompass all of the central coast. I could have done more, could have conquered farther to the north and south, but I did not. Power I'd wanted, and power I'd gained.

"Having attained so much, still I was not satisfied. Having acquired power over the real world, I sought the same over the supernatural. I immersed myself in whatever necromantic lore I could find. But nowhere did I encounter a spell that would render me human. That would make me 'normal.' On learning that there was nothing I could do to alter my ugliness in the sight of people, I resolved angrily to surround myself with beauty." Lifting his head, he nodded as well as he was able.

"The consequences of that obsession you see all around you. This castle, its furnishings, even the attendants and retainers who serve me within its walls; everything has been chosen as much for its attractiveness as for skill. It, and I, lacked only one thing: a consort. Someone to sit by my side, to be my queen. Feeling this great emptiness inside myself, I determined to seek out the most beautiful woman in the world. I found her, and took her from her lackeys and lickspittle suitors, and brought her here. A vain hope, perhaps, but I thought that given time and consideration and honor, she might come to at least tolerate, if not to love, me."

Kneeling beside him, the Visioness Themaryl took up the refrain. "He stole me away from my home and my family. My anger was boundless as the sea and the land I was carried across. I would neither converse, nor dine, nor sit with him.

"Then in the very late of one evening, when I thought the castle asleep, I stole downstairs in my endless search for a means or route of escape, and caught him slumped over his table, drunk—and unhelmeted. At first I was repulsed. But my constitution is not frail. I approached, and looked into his face that was half unconscious, and I saw the pain there." She sighed deeply, remembering.

"After that, it was different. I was cautious, and I believe that he was afraid to chance too much, but in time we came to know one another. All my life I have been courted, and promised, and drawn back from a chorus of suitors and swains that sometimes seemed to stretch from my home to the moon itself. I found them all much alike: vain, unambitious, conceited, too much in love with themselves to love another." She rested a hand on the exposed, thickly bearded chest. "Here I found something—different. If your journey homeward should take you back through Laconda, please assure my family that I am well, and content with my lot."

Simna finally stopped laughing. Shaking his head at the irony of it all, he gave his tall companion a friendly slap on the back. "Well, that's that, I suppose. All this way to rescue a princess who doesn't want to be rescued. Let's have a look around for the treasure and then I suppose we'll be off. There's nothing to hold us here any longer." He started past the herdsman, heading for the main entrance to the audience chamber.

For the second time that remarkable night, Etjole Ehomba said, quietly but firmly, "No."

"No?" A querulous Simna turned. "No what?" He gestured toward the toppled Hymneth and his angelic attendant. "You heard what she said. She wants to stay here."

"Nothing has changed, Simna. You heard what I told *him*. It does not matter." Walking over to where he had earlier dropped his spear, Ehomba recovered the weapon. Returning to the prone form of the Possessed, he brooded aloud over his lack of options.

"I vowed to Tarin Beckwith, a man of noble mien and honorable intention, on the occasion of his last breath, that I would return the Visioness Themaryl to her family. Though I have come a great distance and been too long away from home and friends, I intend to do this thing."

Her exquisite face upturned to him, Themaryl gaped in disbelief. "But I want to stay! It is as your friend says. I have cast my lot with this person. I will not go with you. Do not ask it of me."

"I will not," Ehomba replied. So saying, he bent down and slipped a slender but muscular arm around her waist. Lifting her up, he slung her over his shoulder, a position that found her stunned and outraged.

"Let me go! Put me down this instant! I, Themaryl, command you!"

"Only one woman commands me, and she is not here." Holding the kicking, flailing form firmly against his shoulder, he turned to the stupefied Simna. "Tie her hands before she thinks to try and draw my remaining sword, or to go fumbling in my pack. Quick now, Simna!"

"What? Yes, bruther. Hold her."

The swordsman was a master of blades, not knots, but he bound the wrists and legs of the Visioness securely enough with cord drawn from the richly brocaded curtains that framed one entryway. Unable to raise himself up or move more than his head and neck, Hymneth the Possessed raved and ranted at the meddling interlopers, vowing all manner of punishment and torture if they did not release her at once.

Seeing his master's distress, Peregriff was about to call out to the castle guard for assistance, only to find himself instantaneously confronted by a sleek black feline shape.

"I'd hold my tongue if I were you," Ahlitah warned the senior soldier. "Or I will." Prudent as always, Peregriff held his peace.

They left the general hovering over his master and calling not for armed soldiers but for medical assistance. No crawling along damp, filthy storm drains for them this time; they strode boldly out the main entrance to the fortress. The startled twilight guards scrambled to react, only to shy away from the presence of the long-striding Hunkapa Aub and the triumphantly snarling black litah.

Thus did the four visitors and one unwilling other depart the temperate and accommodating land of fabled Ehl-Larimar. As they did so it was hard to tell who was making the most noise: the enraged and disbelieving Visioness Themaryl, or the master of blades Simna ibn Sind, with his ceaseless grumbling about their failure to even look for, much less obtain, any treasure. Only Ehomba's promises of riches to come kept the seriously aggravated swordsman from remaining behind. The herdsman mollified his sorely disgruntled companion somewhat by placing him in charge of the Visioness and her security.

For the first time in recent memory, a determined Ehomba found himself heading deliberately and purposefully east.

XXIV

As if to confirm that their luck had changed, by dint of a hard march and fortuitous timing, they reached distant Doroune just as the *Grömsketter* was concluding the return leg of its tour of the trading towns and cities to the south. A joyous reunion there was, with Stanager Rose and all her crew astounded yet pleased to encounter their former passengers once again.

No one was disappointed that their eastward crossing of the Semordria was less eventful than before. Following Captain Rose's instructions, they allowed themselves to be put ashore well to the southwest of Hamacassar and its twitchy time guardians. By traveling south and then east from the point of disembarkation, they also avoided Laconda North, where because of the difficulties arising from their previous visit they would have been less than courteously received, and reentered Laconda itself from the west.

Simna was concerned that they might have difficulty approaching the capital quietly if the citizens of that prosperous province recognized their long-absent Visioness, but he needn't have concerned himself. After the long and tiring journey, her aspect was less than regal, and they arrived in the city without incident.

Disclosure of the Visioness's presence among them occasioned scenes of riotous joy among the populace, and the travelers were conveyed without delay into the presence of the Duke and his family.

All Themaryl's relations had gathered to salute her return: father and mother, doddering grandparents, gabby aunts and uncles and innumerable cousins. Haggard and drawn, she was forced to endure embrace upon embrace.

"Oh my delight," one uncle declared upon looking at her, "you do look like you've had a time of it!"

"I am not the same person I was when I was taken from here, Bennrik," she replied stiffly. "Things changed, and I changed with them."

"But you are home, back in the bosom of your family and your people, and that is all that matters." Duke Lewyth rose from his modest seat of power to gesture grandly at the outlandish quartet of foreigners who stood together and formed an exotic island in the midst of the rejoicing throng of aristocrats and courtiers. "And for that we have these stalwart, brave strangers to thank!" Smiling graciously, he nodded at Ehomba.

"Have you anything to say to the people of Laconda on this joyous occasion, sir? Any words you might care to speak will be received with gratitude and appreciation."

It was Simna who spoke up, raising his voice above the general clamor. "You have to understand, noble sir, that my friend here is no orator. It is more in his nature to . . ." He halted as, to his considerable surprise, Ehomba not only stepped forward but mounted the royal dais to stand opposite the Duke and next to the Visioness Themaryl. He did not bother to raise his hand to quiet the crowd, but instead simply began speaking in his usual calm, measured tone.

"I vowed to the dying Tarin Beckwith of Laconda North to return this woman to her home and family. This I have done." As he spoke, he ignored the Visioness's sullen, unyielding scowl. "My obligation to him is at last fulfilled." Turning to her he asked simply, directly, and utterly unexpectedly, "Now that I am free of any responsibility in this matter, I would like to know what it is that *you* want."

She gaped at him. For an instant she thought that the tall, singular southerner was taunting her, making fun of her condition. But in spite of herself she had come in the course of the long journey back to Laconda to know him at least as well as any of his odd clutch of companions. In all that time, she had never seen him taunt, or ridicule, or mock anyone. Was it possible that the query was an honest one?

She did not have to meditate on a reply. Nor did she hesitate. "I want to go back to Ehl-Larimar."

Ehomba nodded. Below, surrounded by celebrating, unwitting Lacondans, a dreadful realization was dawning on a profoundly confounded Simna ibn Sind. Hand on sword hilt, he began backing toward the nearest door.

To say that Themaryl's family was not pleased by her pronouncement was to understate the matter rather severely. Their vociferous objections to her announced departure manifested themselves in the form of clutching hands and the subsequent arrival of alarmed troops. Bearing in mind that these were her own people, Ehomba and his friends perpetrated as little violence as possible in the course of fleeing from her homeland. Despite the destruction of the sky-metal sword, the herdsman still had its oceanic counterpart and his walking spear to scatter the hostile. Where those uncommon weapons proved inappropriate to the task, he commanded the contents of his seemingly bottomless backpack.

The *Grömsketter* was unavailable to take them back, having embarked on an expedition up the Eynharrowk from Hamacassar, but they eventually managed to make contact with the crew of the legendary oceangoing three-master *Warebeth*. News and stories travel fast on a river, and her captain had heard of the exploits of Ehomba and his companions. For a few of the remaining pebbles in the herdsman's possession, he agreed to carry them westward back across the Semordria, a body of water with which Simna, at least, was becoming all too familiar.

The pall that had hung over the fortress of Ehl-Larimar's supreme ruler vanished at the announcement of her return. A downcast, disbelieving Hymneth greeted them in his private quarters. Unarmored, trembling so violently he could hardly rise, he embraced the woman he had never expected to see again. Smiling reassuringly, she rested her head against his and gently stroked the side of his misshapen, elongated face.

In the course of his difficult and less than exemplary life there had been much that had intrigued Hymneth the Possessed, and even more that had infuriated him, but he had rarely, if ever, been as bewildered as he was now.

"You brought her back. You crossed half a world to take her away from me, and then you brought her back." From beneath inhuman, bony ridges he stared at Ehomba, his confusion palpable. *"Why?"*

"I fulfilled my obligation to a dying man. Once I had done that, I was free." The herdsman nodded at Themaryl. "She has a good heart, and became less overbearing during the course of our return to her homeland. Though under no formal obligation, I felt obliged by circumstance to grant her one request. That request was to return here."

Hymneth pulled slightly away from his restored consort. "This will not change me, you know. I am still Hymneth the Possessed, lord of the central coast and of all Ehl-Larimar. Supreme ruler of this part of the world."

"I know." Ehomba smiled enigmatically. "I can only hope that you will now do a better job of it."

With that, Etjole Ehomba and his friends departed that naturally blessed but ill-governed province and once more made the difficult trek back to Doroune and the eastern coast. There they waited until they made contact with an especially bold captain and crew who agreed to attempt a crossing of the Semordria to the southeast, in hopes of landing their well-paying passengers not in the delta of the Eynharrowk, but somewhere nearer a certain small southern coastal village.

When Hunkapa Aub announced that he was remaining behind, regretful farewells were exchanged. While Simna delivered himself of effusive praise and a few obligatory coarse jokes, and the black litah growled diffidently and offered up a sociable paw, no words were exchanged between the shaggy sorcerer and his dark, lean counterpart. Simna knew that much passed between them, even if only by glance and gesture, that he was not a party to. Nor, frankly, did he want to be. As for himself, he chose to remain with Ehomba, reminding him yet again of his promise to reward a certain itinerant herdsman with wealth and fortune.

And so it was that after adventures too many and tortuous to mention, the three remaining travelers found themselves put ashore at the trading town of Askaskos, from which it was but a moderate and easy journey north to the last, small village on the southern coast. To Ehomba, the look on the face of his wife as he appeared outside their house was worth more than all the knowledge he had accumulated in the course of his travels, and all the riches he might have claimed. His children, grown since last he'd seen them, clustered close, Nelecha gripping his waist so tightly that it impacted his breathing.

Mirhanja and the other villagers extended a ready and grateful country welcome to the comrades of their wandering son. There followed several days of celebration and feasting, during which Simna ibn Sind in particular proved highly voluble on the subject of their many extraordinary exploits.

It was during one such evening feast, while Simna grandiosely held forth on the difficulties of crossing the wide and perilous Semordria, that Ehomba confronted the black litah. Belly full, half asleep, the big cat ignored the attentions of the young children who giggled into his mane and toyed with his tufted tail.

"What will you do now?" Ehomba asked him. "Compared to the distances we have covered together, it is not so very far to the veldt where first we met."

"Not so very far, no," Ahlitah responded. "But far enough. Haven't thought much about it. I have trouble thinking when my stomach is full."

Nodding, the herdsman sat down beside the noble head. "The domesticated herds of the Naumkib are extensive and require constant vigilance. This is because the hills where they graze are full of predators.

One such as yourself would be a welcome ally to those who must spend long hours watching over them."

The litah considered. "You saved my life, but I no longer owe you. The debt is repaid in full."

"More than in full," Ehomba admitted readily. They sat in silence for a while, listening to the sounds of happy feasting and tolerating the children's antics, until the litah spoke again.

"Among these predators that trouble you, are there cats? Cats like me?"

Ehomba's expression was grave. "Too many to count. Lionesses and she-cheetahs, leopards sleek of flank and smilodons long of tooth."

"It is a long way to the veldt." Ahlitah growled uncertainly. "You would trust me to guard your flocks and not devour them?"

His chin resting on folded hands as he watched the nearby celebration, the herdsman shrugged. "I have trusted you with more than a cow these past many months. Besides, those who stand watch over the herds also share in their bounty."

"And I would still be free to leave at any time, to run when the need overcame me?"

Ehomba glanced over at his massive, clawed companion. They had been through much together. "I would not ask of another that which I could never ask of myself."

The litah snorted. It was his way of saying little while saying much.

There came a morning when Simna ibn Sind confronted the other companion of his journeys well to the north of the last house. While admiring the supple play of cloth against the bodies of the young women who came to draw water for the day's activities, the swordsman hesitated at first to speak his mind.

"Come, my friend," Ehomba told him. "Something is troubling you."

"Hoy, I don't want to insult you, bruther, or the hospitality of your friends, which has been all that a man could ask for."

"And yet you are not content," Ehomba observed sagely.

"It's not that the food isn't good, or the accommodations unsuitable." The swordsman struggled to find the right words, then finally decided to plunge ahead. "It's just that I've spent my life trying to avoid places like this, Etjole." He made a sweeping gesture. "Maybe this is enough to satisfy a cat, but I don't belong here." He took a deep breath. "Also, there's the little matter of some treasure you've kept promising me. I knew when I first met you that you had access to some. I thought you were searching for it yourself. Then I believed you when you told me that it could be found in Ehl-Larimar. The only reason I'm here now is because I've kept on believing you." His tone and expression hardened.

"I've put myself in death's way for you more times than I care to count, bruther. Now I expect some reward."

Ehomba gestured at the sharp-edged mountains, the quiet village, the pristine air and peaceful surroundings. "Is this not reward enough for you? Were not the adventures we had treasure enough?"

The swordsman did not reply directly, but instead grinned while briskly rubbing the thumb and forefinger of his right hand against one another. Ehomba sighed. "There is no treasure here, Simna." He squinted up at the cloudless, impossibly blue sky. "Would you not like to go for a walk on the beach instead?"

"Listen to me, Etjole! You promised me that—" The shorter man halted his nascent tirade. A wide, sly grin spread across his weather-beaten, sun-scoured face. "A walk on the beach? By Goulouris, long bruther, I'd be happy to take a walk on the beach. I'd nearly forgotten about the beauty of the beaches above your village."

There were children playing at the water's edge when they arrived. Ehomba's daughter was among them, and he tried his best to explain to her the reason behind the comical antics of the funny man from the far north who threw himself on the shore and rolled about wildly, laughing at the top of his lungs while throwing fistfuls of pebbles up in the air and letting them land on his face and body. Eventually, the teary-eyed swordsman rose and began to gather some of those pebbles. Laughing Naumkib children helped him, delighting in his joy and praise when they handed him a particularly large or bright pebble.

Simna ibn Sind spent a pleasant and gratifying morning at the sea-shore, collecting pebbles until his backpack was half full.

"I'm not a greedy man," he told Ehomba when he was sated. He hefted his pack higher on his shoulders, and the weight of diamonds within clinked as they shifted and settled. "This little is enough for me. I'm going to go home and buy myself a small kingdom."

Ehomba regarded his friend gravely. "Are you sure that is what you really want, Simna? To own a small kingdom?"

The swordsman hesitated, his smile fading. For a long moment he stood there, listening to the waves roll in to rustle the beach of dia-monds, to the music of children playing, the chatter of merapes on the rocks offshore and the cries of seabirds and dragonets. Then he looked up at his tall friend and grinned anew.

"No, long bruther, I'm not sure that's what I want—but I am going to give it a try."

Ehomba nodded sadly. "Come into the village with me and we will arrange for the supplies you will need. I can give you some directions, and an introduction to a certain helpful monkey you may meet."

Simna left the following morning, the herdsman escorting him as far as the fifth beach north of the village, where the fog began.

"If you're ever in the far northeast," the swordsman told his friend, "seek out the khanate of Mizar-lohne. That's my homeland, and I'll settle myself somewhere nearby." He grinned one more time. "There are always kingdoms for sale thereabouts." He sighed ruefully. "Who knows? Perhaps I might make another journey to find Damura-sese."

"You have been a good friend, Simna ibn Sind, and a boon companion." One last time, Ehomba put a hand on his friend's shoulder. "Travel well, keep alert, and watch where you put your feet. Keep looking, keep searching, and perhaps one day, with luck, fortune might smile upon you and you might find Damura-sese."

The swordsman nodded, started to turn to go, and then paused. The sun was not yet high and it fell in his eyes, making him squint. "One last thing, Etjole. One thing I must ask." He moved closer so he would not have to squint as hard. "Are you, or are you not, a sorcerer?"

Turning away, the herdsman gazed off into the distance and smiled: that same familiar, enigmatic smile Simna had come to know so infuriatingly and so well in the course of their long journeying together.

"I have told you and told you, Simna. I am only a student, an asker of questions, who knows barely enough to make use of what the wise ones of the Naumkib provide me."

"By Gunkad, long bruther, answer the question!" Not to be denied or put off any longer by clever evasions, the swordsman fumed silently and stood his ground, both physical and forensic.

Ehomba looked down at him. "Simna, my friend, I swear to you by the blue of the sky and the green of the sea that I am no more a 'sorcerer' than any man or woman of my village, be they herder of cattle, hewer of wood, thresher of grain, or scraper of hides."

The swordsman met his gaze evenly and looked long and hard into the eyes of his friend. Then he nodded. "What will you do now?"

"Watch over the cattle and the sheep. Be with my wife and children. In the time I was gone, my son reached the age when all Naumkib are initiated into the lore of adults. That is a task I must begin tomorrow."

"Hoy, I wish I could stay, and I don't want to offend you, but I'm really not interested in sitting through some quaint ceremony where a boy learns how to castrate cattle or dock sheep or paint his face with vegetable dyes." With a last regretful grin, he spun on his sandals and headed north, pausing once at the top of a ridge to turn and wave. Then he vanished, welcomed and swallowed up by the sea fog that hung perpetually over the coast north of the village, and Ehomba saw him no more.

On the morning of the following day the herdsman took his son Daki out of the village, heading inland. Mirhanja packed them a lunch and bade them good-bye, but not after extracting from her husband a promise to be back well before nightfall.

The trail father and son trod was narrow and overgrown in many places with weeds and vines, so that it was difficult to see. It wound its obscure way into the grassy hills behind the village until it terminated next to a plain rock face at the end of a shallow canyon that looked exactly like a hundred other similar heavily eroded canyons. Clearing away some brush and dead twigs, Ehomba exposed a narrow, dark opening in the weathered granite. Preparing torches from the ample supply of dead wood that lay scattered about, the two men entered.

The downward-sloping floor of the tunnel had been worn smooth by centuries of running water and sandaled feet. They walked for an indeterminate time before their torches were no longer necessary. Daylight filtered in through cracks in a ceiling that was now high overhead. A little farther on, the tunnel widened and became a chamber. Very soon thereafter it widened a great deal more, and became something else entirely.

The slim but well-built Daki, wearing a solemn expression others would have immediately recognized as being derived from his sire, contemplated the sight before him with respectful reverence but without awe.

"What is this place, Father?"

"This is where the Naumkib come from, Daki." Raising an arm, Ehomba swept it before him in an expansive gesture to take in all that there was to be seen. "Too long ago to remember, our people settled here and built this place. They accumulated boundless knowledge and untold riches."

The youth looked up at him. "What happened to them?"

Ehomba patted his son on the shoulder. "When one feels one has no more to accomplish, the next thing one attains is boredom. The Naumkib abandoned this place. In ones and twos, in groups and in families, they scattered to the far corners of the world. Gradually they mingled with other peoples, and became one with them, and were content. Only a few remained behind."

"Us," the boy realized. "The people of the village."

"Yes. To not forget is a great responsibility. A legacy must be looked after, Daki. Not necessarily expanded upon, or exploited, but looked after." He started forward. "Now come, and I will show you more of yours."

They spent the remainder of the day exploring the deserted towers, and the great library, and the majestic arenas of knowledge. Daki marveled at the walls of solid gold, and the gemstone utensils the vanished inhabitants had left behind in their silent kitchens. Together, father and son turned the pages of ancient tomes bound in sheets of solid ruby, chosen not for its beauty but for its strength and ability to protect the far more valuable paper pages that lay between those crimson covers. They visited the observatory, with its telescopes still pointed at an especially large crack in the roof of the enormous cavern, and its congruent cupola with the ceiling that showed innumerable constellations fashioned from all manner of precious stones.

A captivated Daki did not want to leave, but Ehomba had to insist. "Your mother will be angry at us both if we are late," he reminded his son as they began the long hike back to the tunnel.

"Is this where you found the answers to all the questions you keep asking, Father?" the boy asked as they ascended wide stairs of marble and agate and sparkling goldenstone.

"No, Daki. This is where I find only more questions. I promise you: Someday, when you are a little older, we will come back here, as all men and women of Naumkib must, and you will find, whether you want to or not, many questions of your own."

The youth considered this reply as they ascended. Then he nodded slowly, hoping that he understood. "Does it have a name, this place? Or is it just called Naumkib?"

"We call ourselves the Naumkib," his father replied. "The ancient city and place of learning is, and always has been, known as Damurasese." He smiled as they neared the entrance to the tunnel. Mirhanja would have supper ready, and he was hungry. "The rest of the world knows it as a story, a rumor, hearsay. We keep it that way."

Daki picked up one of the torches they had left behind. "Part of our legacy?"

"Yes, son. Part of our legacy. A little secret of the Naumkib."

"But not the only one," the boy observed, displaying the wisdom for which his family was noted.

"No, Daki. Not the only one."

Etjole Ehomba, who was an honorable man, made his way with his son back out of the celebrated lost city, whose riches lay not in its fabulous trappings but in the learning it held, and back to the modest house by the sea, where as he had sworn to his friend Simna ibn Sind he was no more a renowned sorcerer than any man or woman of his village, be they herder of cattle, hewer of wood, thresher of grain or scraper of hides.